DARK CRIMES
2

DARK CRIMES
2

Modern Masters of Noir

*Edited with an introduction
by Ed Gorman*

Carroll & Graf Publishers, Inc.
New York

Introduction and collection copyright © 1993 by Ed Gorman

The acknowledgments listed on pages 9 to 10 constitute an extension of
this copyright page.

First Carroll & Graf edition 1993

Carroll & Graf Publishers, Inc.
260 Fifth Avenue
New York, NY 10001

ISBN for hardcover edition: 0-88184-865-4
ISBN for paperback edition: 0-88184-919-7

Manufactured in the United States of America

To Laura Langlie who does 95% of my work
and receives .00006% of the credit

Contents

Acknowledgments

For permission to reprint the stories and novels in this anthology, grateful acknowledgment is made to:

"The Dripping" copyright © 1972 by David Morrell. First published in *Ellery Queen's Mystery Magazine*.

"And Miles to Go Before I Sleep" copyright © 1965 by Lawrence Block.

Miranda was first published in *Fifteen Stories* in October 1950. Copyright © 1982 by John D. MacDonald Publishing, Inc. Reprinted by permission of the George Diskant Agency.

"Deceptions" copyright © 1987 by Marcia Muller. First published in *A Matter of Crime I*.

"The Long Silence After" copyright © 1991 by Ed Gorman. First published in *Dark at Heart* edited by Karen and Joe R. Lansdale.

"The Dead Past" copyright © 1989 by Nancy J. Pickard.

"All the Same" copyright © 1972 by H.S.D. Publications, Inc. Revised version copyright © 1992 by Bill Pronzini. First published in *Alfred Hitchcock's Mystery Magazine*. Reprinted by permission of the author.

"The View" copyright © 1983 by Brian Garfield. First published in *Ellery Queen's Mystery Magazine*, July 1983.

"Hector Gomez Provides" copyright © 1985 by Renown Publications, Inc. First published in *Mike Shayne Mystery Magazine*, August 1985.

"The Steel Valentine" copyright © 1989 by Joe R. Lansdale. First published in *Bizarre Hands Collection*.

Triangle copyright © 1982 by Teri White. First published by Ace Charter, New York.

Introduction

L
ike most forms of popular fiction, *noir* has evolved and changed over the past decade and a half.

No longer does Bogie stand at his lonely window, staring out at a world he frequently despises. Nor does the conventional private eye take us through his conventional private eye routines; and the conventional *femme fatale* . . . well, she doesn't invite us upstairs any more, either.

The new *noir* is as likely to be set in a trailer park as a gambling casino; in a small Texas town more often than New York; and feature not a slick mobster but a child molester as villain.

This isn't to disparage what has gone before. The other night I watched *Out of the Past* for perhaps the fiftieth time in my life . . . and I was struck again by how powerful and true a drama it is, especially in the almost reluctant way that Robert Mitchum reveals his true self to us. Many other films and books from that era also retain their power.

But new generations have led *noir* from the early pulp tradition to the mainstream realities of today. Loren Estleman's Amos Walker is a good example. Yes, he's a Chandleresque private eye superficially, but when you look carefully at his cases they encompass the same literary material that a Joyce Carol Oates, say, or Richard Ford or Raymond Carver have dealt with —the world of nightly news and morning newspapers. The real world. Drugs, random violence, heartbreak and an escalating sense of despair. Or try Nancy Pickard's elegant and elegaic "The Dead Past." Same thing.

Unlike volume one, DARK CRIMES 2 is a contemporary version of *noir*. Even John D. MacDonald's beautifully told tale from the forties, *Miranda,* has a decidedly contemporary feel.

Much as I like the material of the forties and fifties, today's *noir* fiction is just as good, just as exciting and is, I think, a little more ambitious in its purpose.

You've got some good stories awaiting you.

—Ed Gorman

The Dripping

by David Morrell

David Morrell is one of today's most compelling adventure writers. But his fame as the creator of Rambo overshadows his quieter work, the kind mistakenly called "horror" by too many people who should know better. This is a fine, dark tale.

First published in 1972.

That autumn we live in a house in the country, my mother's house, the house I was raised in. I have been to the village, struck more by how nothing in it has changed, yet everything has, because I am older now, seeing it differently. It is as though I am both here now and back then, at once with the mind of a boy and a man. It is so strange a doubling, so intense, so unsettling, that I am moved to work again, to try to paint it.

So I study the hardware store, the grain barrels in front, the twin square pillars holding up the drooping balcony onto which seared wax-faced men and women from the old people's hotel above come to sit and rock and watch. They look the same aging people I saw as a boy, the wood of the pillars and balcony looks as splintered.

Forgetful of time while I work, I do not begin the long walk home until late, at dusk. The day has been warm, but now in my shirt I am cold, and a half mile along I am caught in a sudden shower and forced to leave the gravel road for the shelter of a tree, its leaves already brown and yellow. The rain becomes a storm, streaking at me sideways, drenching me; I cinch the neck of my canvas bag to protect my painting and equipment, and decide to run, socks spongy in my shoes, when at last I reach the lane down to the house and barn.

The house and barn. They and my mother, they alone have changed, as if as one, warping, weathering, joints twisted and strained, their gray so unlike the white I recall as a boy. The place is weakening her. She is in tune with it, matches its decay. That is why we have come here to live. To revive. Once I thought to convince her to move away. But of her 65 years she has spent 40 here, and she insists she will spend the rest, what is left to her.

The rain falls stronger as I hurry past the side of the house, the light on in the kitchen, suppertime and I am late. The house is connected with the barn the way the small base of an L is connected to its stem. The entrance I always use is directly at the joining, and when I enter out of breath, clothes clinging to me cold and wet, the door to the barn to my left, the door to the kitchen straight ahead, I hear the dripping in the basement down the stairs to my right.

"Meg. Sorry I'm late," I call to my wife, setting down the water-beaded canvas sack, opening the kitchen door. There is no one. No settings on the table. Nothing on the stove. Only the yellow light from the sixty-watt bulb in the ceiling. The kind my mother prefers to the white of one hundred. It reminds her of candlelight, she says.

"Meg," I call again, and still no one answers. Asleep, I think. Dusk coming on, the dark clouds of the storm have lulled them, and they have lain down for a nap, expecting to wake before I return.

Still the dripping. Although the house is very old, the barn long disused, roofs crumbling, I have not thought it all so ill-maintained, the storm so strong that water can be seeping past the cellar windows, trickling, pattering on the old stone floor. I switch on the light to the basement, descend the wood stairs to the right, worn and squeaking, reach where the stairs turn to the left the rest of the way down to the floor, and see not water dripping. Milk. Milk everywhere. On the rafters, on the walls, dripping on the film of milk on the stones, gathering speckled with dirt in the channels between them. From side to side and everywhere.

Sarah, my child, has done this, I think. She has been fasci-nated by the big wood dollhouse that my father made for me when I was quite young, its blue paint chipped and peeling now. She has pulled it from the far corner to the middle of the basement. There are games and toy soldiers and blocks that have been taken from the wicker storage chest and played with on the floor, all covered with milk, the dollhouse, the chest, the scattered toys, milk dripping on them from the rafters, milk trickling on them.

Why has she done this, I think. Where can she have gotten so much milk? What was in her mind to do this thing?

"Sarah," I call. "Meg." Angry now, I mount the stairs into the quiet kitchen. "Sarah," I shout. She will clean the mess and stay indoors the remainder of the week.

I cross the kitchen, turn through the sitting room past the padded flower-patterned chairs and sofa that have faded since I knew them as a boy, past several of my paintings that my mother has hung up on the wall, bright-colored old ones of pastures and woods from when I was in grade school, brown-shaded new ones of the town, tinted as if old photographs. Two stairs at a time up to the bedrooms, wet shoes on the soft worn carpet on the stairs, hand streaking on the smooth polished maple bannister.

At the top I swing down the hall. The door to Sarah's room is open, it is dark in there. I switch on the light. She is not on the bed, nor has been; the satin spread is unrumpled, the rain pelting in through the open window, the wind fresh and cool. I have the feeling then and go uneasy into our bedroom; it is dark as well, empty too. My stomach has become hollow. Where are they? All in mother's room?

No. As I stand at the open door to mother's room I see from the yellow light I have turned on in the hall that only she is in there, her small torso stretched across the bed.

"Mother," I say, intending to add, "Where are Meg and Sarah?" But I stop before I do. One of my mother's shoes is off, the other askew on her foot. There is mud on the shoes. There is blood on her cotton dress. It is torn, her brittle hair disrupted, blood on her face, her bruised lips are swollen.

For several moments I am silent with shock. "My God, Mother," I finally manage to say, and as if the words are a spring releasing me to action I touch her to wake her. But I see that her eyes are open, staring ceilingward, unseeing though alive, and each breath is a sudden full gasp, then slow exhalation.

"Mother, what has happened? Who did this to you? Meg? Sarah?"

But she does not look at me, only constant toward the ceiling.

"For God's sake, Mother, answer me! Look at me! What has happened?"

Nothing. Eyes sightless. Between gasps she is like a statue.

What I think is hysterical. Disjointed, contradictory. I must find Meg and Sarah. They must be somewhere, beaten like my mother. Or worse. Find them. Where? But I cannot leave my mother. When she comes to consciousness, she too will be hysterical, frightened, in great pain. How did she end up on the bed?

In her room there is no sign of the struggle she must have put up against her attacker. It must have happened somewhere else. She crawled from there to here. Then I see the blood on the floor, the swath of blood down the hall from the stairs. Who did this? Where is he? Who would beat a gray, wrinkled, arthritic old woman? Why in God's name would he do it? I shudder. The pain of the arthritis as she struggled with him.

Perhaps he is still in the house, waiting for me.

To the hollow sickness in my stomach now comes fear, hot, pulsing, and I am frantic before I realize what I am doing— grabbing the spare cane my mother always keeps by her bed, flicking on the light in her room, throwing open the closet door and striking in with the cane. Viciously, sounds coming from my throat, the cane flailing among the faded dresses.

No one. Under the bed. No one. Behind the door. No one.

I search all the upstairs rooms that way, terrified, constantly checking behind me, clutching the cane and whacking into closets, under beds, behind doors, with a force that would certainly crack a skull. No one.

"Meg! Sarah!"

No answer, not even an echo in this sound-absorbing house.

There is no attic, just an overhead entry to a crawl space under the eaves, and that opening has long been sealed. No sign of tampering. No one has gone up.

I rush down the stairs, seeing the trail of blood my mother has left on the carpet, imagining her pain as she crawled, and search the rooms downstairs with the same desperate thoroughness. In the front closet. Behind the sofa and chairs. Behind the drapes.

No one.

I lock the front door, lest he be outside in the storm waiting to come in behind me. I remember to draw every blind, close every drape, lest he be out there peering at me. The rain pelts insistently against the windowpanes.

I cry out again and again for Meg and Sarah. The police. My mother. A doctor. I grab for the phone on the wall by the front stairs, fearful to listen to it, afraid he has cut the line outside. But it is droning. Droning. I ring for the police, working the handle at the side around and around and around.

They are coming, they say. A doctor with them. Stay where I am, they say. But I cannot. Meg and Sarah, I must find them. I know they are not in the basement where the milk is dripping— all the basement is open to view. Except for my childhood things, we have cleared out all the boxes and barrels and the shelves of jars the Saturday before.

But under the stairs. I have forgotten about under the stairs and now I race down and stand dreading in the milk; but there are only cobwebs there, already reformed from Saturday when we cleared them. I look up at the side door I first came through, and as if I am seeing through a telescope I focus largely on the handle. It seems to fidget. I have a panicked vision of the intruder bursting through, and I charge up to lock the door, and the door to the barn.

And then I think: if Meg and Sarah are not in the house they are likely in the barn. But I cannot bring myself to unlock the barn door and go through. *He* must be there as well. Not in the rain outside but in the shelter of the barn, and there are no lights to turn on there.

And why the milk? Did he do it and where did he get it? And why? Or did Sarah do it before? No, the milk is too freshly dripping. It has been put there too recently. By him. But why? And who is he? A tramp? An escapee from some prison? Or asylum? No, the nearest institution is far away, hundreds of miles. From the town then. Or a nearby farm.

I know my questions are for delay, to keep me from entering the barn. But I must. I take the flashlight from the kitchen drawer and unlock the door to the barn, force myself to go in quickly, cane ready, flashing my light. The stalls are still there, listing; and some of the equipment, churners, separators, dull and rusted, webbed and dirty. The must of decaying wood and crumbled hay, the fresh wet smell of the rain gusting through cracks in the walls. Once this was a dairy, as the other farms around still are.

Flicking my light toward the corners, edging toward the stalls, boards creaking, echoing, I try to control my fright, try to remember as a boy how the cows waited in the stalls for my father to milk them, how the barn was once board-tight and solid, warm to be in, how there was no connecting door from the barn to the house because my father did not want my mother to smell the animals in her kitchen.

I run my light down the walls, sweep it in arcs through the darkness before me as I draw nearer to the stalls, and in spite of myself I recall that other autumn when the snow came early, four feet deep by morning and still storming thickly, how my father went out to the barn to milk and never returned for lunch, nor supper. There was no phone then, no way to get help, and my mother and I waited all night, unable to make our way through the storm, listening to the slowly dying wind; and the next morning was clear and bright and blinding as we shoveled out to find the cows in agony in their stalls from not having been milked and my father dead, frozen rock-solid in the snow in the middle of the next field where he must have wandered when he lost his bearings in the storm.

There was a fox, risen earlier than us, nosing at him under the snow, and my father had to be sealed in his coffin before he could lie in state. Days after, the snow was melted, gone, the barnyard a sea of mud, and it was autumn again and my mother had the connecting door put in. My father should have tied a rope from the house to his waist to guide him back in case he lost his way. Certainly he knew enough. But then he was like that, always in a rush. When I was ten.

Thus I think as I light the shadows near the stalls, terrified of what I may find in any one of them, Meg and Sarah, or him, thinking of how my mother and I searched for my father and how I now search for my wife and child, trying to think of how it was once warm in here and pleasant, chatting with my father, helping him to milk, the sweet smell of new hay and grain, the different sweet smell of fresh droppings, something I always liked and neither my father nor my mother could understand. I know that if I do not think of these good times I will surely go mad in awful anticipation of what I may find. Pray God they have not died!

What can he have done to them? To assault a five-year-old girl? Split her. The hemorrhaging alone can have killed her.

And then, even in the barn, I hear my mother cry out for me. The relief I feel to leave and go to her unnerves me. I do want to find Meg and Sarah, to try to save them. Yet I am relieved to go. I think my mother will tell me what has happened, tell me where to find them. That is how I justify my leaving as I wave the light in circles around me, guarding my back, retreating through the door and locking it.

Upstairs she sits stiffly on her bed. I want to make her answer my questions, to shake her, to force her to help, but I know it will only frighten her more, maybe push her mind down to where I can never reach.

"Mother," I say to her softly, touching her gently. "What has happened?" My impatience can barely be contained. "Who did this? Where are Meg and Sarah?"

She smiles at me, reassured by the safety of my presence. Still she cannot answer.

"Mother. Please," I say. "I know how bad it must have been. But you must try to help. I must know where they are so I can help them."

She says, "Dolls."

It chills me. "What dolls, Mother? Did a man come here with dolls? What did he want? You mean he looked like a doll? Wearing a mask like one?"

Too many questions. All she can do is blink.

"Please, Mother. You must try your best to tell me. Where are Meg and Sarah?"

"Dolls," she says.

As I first had the foreboding of disaster at the sight of Sarah's unrumpled satin bedspread, now I am beginning to understand, rejecting it, fighting it.

"Yes, Mother, the dolls," I say, refusing to admit what I know. "Please, Mother. Where are Meg and Sarah?"

"You are a grown boy now. You must stop playing as a child. Your father. Without him you will have to be the man in the house. You must be brave."

"No, Mother." I can feel it swelling in my chest.

"There will be a great deal of work now, more than any child should know. But we have no choice. You must accept that God has chosen to take him from us, that you are all the man I have left to help me."

"No, Mother."

"Now you are a man and you must put away the things of a child."

Eyes streaming, I am barely able to straighten, leaning wearily against the door jamb, tears rippling from my face down to my shirt, wetting it cold where it had just begun to dry. I wipe my eyes and see her reaching for me, smiling, and I recoil down the hall, stumbling down the stairs, down, through the sitting room, the kitchen, down, down to the milk, splashing through it to the dollhouse, and in there, crammed and doubled, Sarah. And in the wicker chest, Meg. The toys not on the floor for Sarah to play with, but taken out so Meg could be put in. And both of them, their stomachs slashed, stuffed with sawdust, their eyes rolled up like dolls' eyes.

The police are knocking at the side door, pounding, calling out who they are, but I am powerless to let them in. They crash through the door, their rubber raincoats dripping as they stare down at me.

"The milk," I say.

They do not understand. Even as I wait, standing in the milk, listening to the rain pelting on the windows while they come over to see what is in the dollhouse and in the wicker chest, while they go upstairs to my mother and then return so I can tell them again, "The milk." But they still do not understand.

"She killed them of course," one man says. "But I don't see why the milk."

Only when they speak to the neighbors down the road and learn how she came to them, needing the cans of milk, insisting she carry them herself to the car, the agony she was in as she carried them, only when they find the empty cans and the knife in a stall in the barn, can I say, "The milk. The blood. There was so much blood, you know. She needed to deny it, so she washed it away with milk, purified it, started the dairy again. You see, there was so much blood."

That autumn we live in a house in the country, my mother's house, the house I was raised in. I have been to the village, struck even more by how nothing in it has changed, yet everything has, because I am older now, seeing it differently. It is as though I am both here now and back then, at once with the mind of a boy and a man . . .

And Miles to Go Before I Sleep

by Lawrence Block

After a long career trying to find his real voice and real audience, Lawrence Block has become one of the best American practitioners of the private eye form. His Matt Scudder novels are state-of-the-art. But the piece you're about to read will remind you that he's also written many fine short stories as well.

First published in 1965.

When the bullets struck, my first thought was that someone had raced up behind me to give me an abrupt shove. An instant later I registered the sound of the gunshots, and then there was fire in my side, burning pain, and the impact had lifted me off my feet and sent me sprawling at the edge of the lawn in front of my house.

I noticed the smell of the grass. Fresh, cut the night before and with the dew still on it.

I can recall fragments of the ambulance ride as if it took place in some dim dream. I worried at the impropriety of running the siren so early in the morning.

They'll wake half the town, I thought.

Another time, I heard one of the white-coated attendants say something about a red blanket. My mind leaped to recall the blanket that lay on my bed when I was a boy almost forty years ago. It was plaid, mostly red with some green in it. Was that what they were talking about?

These bits of awareness came one after another, like fast cuts in a film. There was no sensation of time passing between them.

I was in a hospital room. The operating room, I suppose. I was spread out on a long white table while a masked and green-gowned doctor probed a wound in the left side of my chest. I must have been under anesthetic—there was a mask on my face with a tube connected to it. And I believe my eyes were closed. Nevertheless, I was aware of what was happening, and I could see.

I don't know how to explain this.

There was a sensation I was able to identify as pain, although it didn't actually hurt me. Then I felt as though my side were a bottle and a cork were being drawn from it. It popped free. The doctor held up a misshapen bullet for examination. I watched it fall in slow motion from his forceps, landing with a plinking sound in a metal pan.

"Other's too close to the heart," I heard him say. "Can't get a grip on it. Don't dare touch it, way it's positioned. Kill him if it moves."

Cut.

Same place, an indefinite period of time later. A nurse saying, "Oh, God, he's going," and then all of them talking at once.

Then I was out of my body.

It just happened, just like that. One moment I was in my dying body on the table and a moment later I was floating somewhere beneath the ceiling. I could look down and see myself on the table and the doctors and nurses standing around me.

I'm dead, I thought.

I was very busy trying to decide how I felt about it. It didn't hurt. I had always thought it would hurt, that it would be awful. But it wasn't so terrible.

So this is death, I thought.

And it was odd seeing myself, my body, lying there. I thought, you were a good body. I'm all right, I don't need you, but you were a good body.

Then I was gone from that room. There was a rush of light that became brighter and brighter, and I was sucked through a long tunnel at a furious speed, and then I was in a world of light and in the presence of a Being of light.

This is hard to explain.

I don't know if the Being was a man or a woman. Maybe it was both, maybe it changed back and forth. I don't know. He was all in white, and He was light and was surrounded by light.

And in the distance behind Him were my father and my

mother and my grandparents. People who had gone before me, and they were holding out their hands to me and beaming at me with faces radiant with light and love.

I went to the Being, I was drawn to Him, and He held out His arm and said, "Behold your life."

And I looked, and I could behold my entire life. I don't know how to say what I saw. It was as if my whole life had happened at once and someone had taken a photograph of it and I was looking at that photograph. I could see in it everything that I remembered in my life and everything that I had forgotten, and it was all happening at once and I was seeing it happen. And I would see something bad that I'd done and think, I'm sorry about that. And I would see something good and be glad about it.

And at the end I woke and had breakfast and left the house to walk to work and a car passed by and a gun came out the window. There were two shots and I fell and the ambulance came and all the rest of it.

And I thought, Who killed me?

The Being said, "You must find out the answer."

I thought, I don't care, it doesn't matter.

He said, "You must go back and find the answer."

I thought, No, I don't want to go back.

All of the brilliant light began to fade. I reached out toward it because I didn't want to go back, I didn't want to be alive again. But it all continued to fade.

Then I was back in my body again.

"We almost lost you," the nurse said. Her smile was professional but the light in her eyes showed she meant it. "Your heart actually stopped on the operating table. You really had us scared there."

"I'm sorry," I said.

She thought that was funny. "The doctor was only able to remove one of the two bullets that were in you. So you've still got a chunk of lead in your chest. He sewed you up and put a drain in the wound, but obviously you won't be able to walk around like that. In fact it's important for you to lie absolutely still or the bullet might shift in position. It's right alongside your heart, you see."

It might shift even if I didn't move, I thought. But she knew better than to tell me that.

"In four or five days we'll have you scheduled for another

operation," she went on. "By then the bullet may move of its own accord to a more accessible position. If not, there are surgical techniques that can be employed." She told me some of the extraordinary things surgeons could do. I didn't pay attention.

After she left the room, I rolled back and forth on the bed, shifting my body as jerkily as I could. But the bullet did not change its position in my chest.

I was afraid of that.

I stayed in the hospital that night. No one came to see me during visiting hours, and I thought that was strange. I asked the nurse and was told I was in intensive care and could not have visitors.

I lost control of myself. I shouted that she was crazy. How could I learn who did it if I couldn't see anyone?

"The police will see you as soon as it's allowed," she said. She was terribly earnest. "Believe me," she said, "it's for your own protection. They want to ask you a million questions, naturally, but it would be bad for your health to let you get all excited."

Silly bitch, I thought. And almost put the thought into words.

Then I remembered the picture of my life and the pleasant and unpleasant things I had done and how they all had looked in the picture.

I smiled. "Sorry I lost control," I said. "But if they didn't want me to get excited they shouldn't have given me such a beautiful nurse."

She went out beaming.

I didn't sleep. It did not seem to be necessary.

I lay in bed wondering who had killed me.

My wife? We'd married young, then grown apart. Of course she hadn't shot at me because she'd been in bed asleep when I left the house that morning. But she might have a lover. Or she could have hired someone to pull the trigger for her.

My partner? Monty and I had turned a handful of borrowed capital into a million-dollar business. But I was better than Monty at holding onto money. He spent it, gambled it away, paid it out in divorce settlements. Profits were off lately. Had he been helping himself to funds and cooking the books? And did he then decide to cover his thefts the easy way?

My girl? Peg had a decent apartment, a closet full of clothes. Not a bad deal. But for awhile I'd let her think I'd divorce Julia when the kids were grown, and now she and I both knew better.

She'd seemed to adjust to the situation, but had the resentment festered inside her?

My children?

The thought was painful. Mark had gone to work for me after college. The arrangement didn't last long. He'd been too head-strong, while I'd been unwilling to give him the responsibility he wanted. Now he was talking about going into business for himself. But he lacked the capital.

If I died, he'd have all he needed.

Debbie was married and expecting a child. First she'd lived with another young man, one of whom I hadn't approved, and then she'd married Scott, who was hard-working and earnest and ambitious. Was the marriage bad for her, and did she blame me for costing her the other boy? Or did Scott's ambition prompt him to make Debbie an heiress?

These were painful thoughts.

Someone else? But who and why?

Some days ago I'd cut off another motorist at a traffic circle. I remembered the sound of his horn, his face glimpsed in my rearview mirror, red, ferocious. Had he copied down my license plate, determined my address, lain in ambush to gun me down?

It made no sense. But it did not make sense for anyone to kill me.

Julia? Monty? Peg? Mark? Debbie? Scott?

A stranger?

I lay there wondering and did not truly care. Someone had killed me and I was supposed to be dead. But I was not permitted to be dead until I knew the answer to the question.

Maybe the police would find it for me.

They didn't.

I saw two policemen the following day. I was still in intensive care, still denied visitors, but an exception was made for the police. They were very courteous and spoke in hushed voices. They had no leads whatsoever in their investigation and just wanted to know if I could suggest a single possible suspect.

I told them I couldn't.

My nurse turned white as paper.

"You're not supposed to be out of bed! You're not even sup-posed to move! What do you think you're doing?"

I was up and dressed. There was no pain. As an experiment, I'd been palming the pain pills they issued me every four hours, hiding them in the bedclothes instead of swallowing them. As I'd anticipated, I did not feel any pain.

The area of the wound was numb, as though that part of me had been excised altogether. But nothing hurt. I could feel the slug that was still in me and could tell that it remained in position. It did not hurt me, however.

She went on jabbering away at me. I remembered the picture of my life and avoided giving her a sharp answer.

"I'm going home," I said.

"Don't talk nonsense."

"You have no authority over me," I told her. "I'm legally entitled to take responsibility for my own life."

"For your own death, you mean."

"If it comes to that. You can't hold me here against my will. You can't operate on me without my consent."

"If you don't have that operation, you'll die."

"Everyone dies."

"I don't understand," she said, and her eyes were wide and filled with sorrow, and my heart went out to her.

"Don't worry about me," I said gently. "I know what I'm doing. And there's nothing anyone can do."

"They wouldn't even let me see you," Julia was saying. "And now you're home."

"It was a fast recovery."

"Shouldn't you be in bed?"

"The exercise is supposed to be good for me," I said. I looked at her, and for a moment I saw her as she'd appeared in parts of the picture of my life. As a bride. As a young mother.

"You know, you're a beautiful woman," I said.

She colored.

"I suppose we got married too young," I said. "We each had a lot of growing to do. And the business took too much of my time over the years. And I'm afraid I haven't been a very good husband."

"You weren't so bad."

"I'm glad we got married," I said. "And I'm glad we stayed together. And that you were here for me to come home to."

She started to cry. I held her until she stopped. Then, her face to my chest, she said, "At the hospital, waiting, I realized for the first time what it would mean for me to lose you. I thought we'd stopped loving each other a long time ago. I know you've had other women. For that matter, I've had lovers from time to time. I don't know if you knew that."

"It's not important."

"No," she said, "it's not important. I'm glad we got married, darling. And I'm glad you're going to be all right."

Monty said, "You had everybody worried there, kid. But what do you think you're doing down here? You're supposed to be home in bed."

"I'm supposed to get exercise. Besides, if I don't come down here how do I know you won't steal the firm into bankruptcy?"

My tone was light, but he flushed deeply. "You just hit a nerve," he said.

"What's the matter?"

"When they were busy cutting the bullet out of you, all I could think was you'd die thinking I was a thief."

"I don't know what you're talking about."

He lowered his eyes. "I was borrowing partnership funds," he said. "I was in a bind because of my own stupidity and I didn't want to admit it to you, so I dipped into the till. It was a temporary thing, a case of the shorts. I got everything straightened out before that clown took a shot at you. They know who it was yet?"

"Not yet."

"The night before you were shot, I stayed late and covered things. I wasn't going to say anything, and then I wondered if you'd been suspicious, and I decided I'd tell you about it first thing in the morning. Then it looked as though I wasn't going to get the chance. You didn't suspect anything?"

"I thought our cash position was light. But after all these years I certainly wasn't afraid of you stealing from me."

"All those years," he echoed, and I was seeing the picture of my life again. All the work Monty and I had put in side by side. The laughs we'd shared, the bad times we'd survived.

We looked at each other, and a great deal of feeling passed between us. Then he drew a breath and clapped me on the shoulder. "Well, that's enough about old times," he said gruffly. "Somebody's got to do a little work around here."

"I'm glad you're here," Peg said. "I couldn't even go to the hospital. All I could do was call every hour and ask anonymously for a report on your condition. Critical condition, that's what they said. Over and over."

"It must have been rough."

"It did something to me and for me," she said. "It made me realize that I've cheated myself out of a life. And I was the one who did it. You didn't do it to me."

"I told you I'd leave Julia."

"Oh, that was just a game we both played. I never really expected you to leave her. No, it's been my fault, dear. I settled into a nice secure life. But when you were on the critical list I decided my life was on the critical list, too, and that it was time I took some responsibility for it."

"Meaning?"

"Meaning it's good you came over tonight and not this afternoon, because you wouldn't have found me at home. I've got a job. It's not much, but it's enough to pay the rent. You see, I've decided it's time I started paying my own rent. In the fall I'll start night classes at the university."

"I see."

"You're not angry?"

"Angry? I'm happy for you."

"I don't regret what we've been to each other. I was a lost little girl with a screwed-up life and you made me feel loved and cared for. But I'm a big girl now. I'll still see you, if you want to see me, but from here on in I pay my own way."

"No more checks?"

"No more checks. I mean it."

I remembered some of our times together, seeing them as I had seen them in the picture of my life. I was filled with desire. I went and took her in my arms.

She said, "But is it safe? Won't it be dangerous for you?"

"The doctor said it'll do me good."

Her eyes sparkled. "Well, if it's just what the doctor ordered—" And she led me to the bedroom.

Afterward I wished I could have died in Peg's bed. Almost immediately I realized that would have been bad for her and bad for Julia.

Anyway, I hadn't yet done what I'd come back to do.

Later, while Julia slept, I lay awake in the darkness. I thought, This is crazy. I'm no detective. I'm a businessman. I died and You won't let me stay dead. Why can't I be dead?

I got out of bed, went downstairs and laid out the cards for a game of solitaire. I toasted a slice of bread and made myself a cup of tea.

I won the game of solitaire. It was a hard variety, one I could normally win once in fifty or a hundred times.

I thought, It's not Julia, it's not Monty, it's not Peg. All of them have love for me.

I felt good about that.

But who killed me? Who was left of my list?

I didn't feel good about that.

The following morning I was finishing my breakfast when Mark rang the bell. Julia went to the door and let him in. He came into the kitchen and got himself a cup of coffee from the pot on the stove.

"I was at the hospital," he said. "Night and day, but they wouldn't let any of us see you. I was there."

"Your mother told me."

"Then I had to leave town the day before yesterday and I just got back this morning. I had to meet with some men." A smile flickered on his face. He looked just like his mother when he smiled.

"I've got the financing," he said. "I'm in business."

"That's wonderful."

"I know you wanted me to follow in your footsteps, Dad. But I couldn't be happy having my future handed to me that way. I wanted to make it on my own."

"You're my son. I was the same myself."

"When I asked you for a loan—"

"I've been thinking about that," I said, remembering the scene as I'd witnessed it in the picture of my life. "I resented your independence and I envied your youth. I was wrong to turn you down."

"You were *right* to turn me down." That smile again, just like his mother. "I wanted to make it on my own, and then I turned around and asked for help from you. I'm just glad you knew better than to give me what I was weak enough to ask for. I realized that almost immediately, but I was too proud to say anything, and then some madman shot you and—well, I'm glad everything turned out all right, Dad."

"Yes," I said. "So am I."

Not Mark, then.

Not Debbie either. I always knew that, and knew it with utter certainty when she cried out "Oh, Daddy!" and rushed to me and threw herself into my arms. "I'm so glad," she kept saying. "I was so worried."

"Calm down," I told her. "I don't want my grandchild born with a nervous condition."

"Don't worry about your grandchild. You're grandchild's going to be just fine."

"And how about my daughter?"

"Your daughter's just fine. Do you want to know something? These past few days, wow, I've really learned a lot during these past few days."

"So have I."

"How close I am to you, for one thing. Waiting at the hospital, there was a time when I thought, God, he's gone. I just had this feeling. And then I shook my head and said, no, it was nonsense, you were all right. And you know what they told us afterward? Your heart stopped during the operation, and it must have happened right when I got that feeling. I *knew*, and then I knew again when it resumed beating."

When I looked at my son I saw his mother's smile. When I looked at Debbie I saw myself.

"And another thing I learned, and that's how much people need each other. People were so good to us! So many people called me, asked about you. Even Philip called, can you imagine? He just wanted to let me know that I should call on him if there was anything he could do."

"What could he possibly do?"

"I have no idea. It was funny hearing from him, though. I hadn't heard his voice since we were living together. But it was nice of him to call, wasn't it?"

I nodded. "It must have made you wonder what might have been."

"What it made me wonder was how I ever thought Philip and I were made for each other. Scott was with me every minute, you know, except when he went down to give blood for you—"

"He gave blood for me?"

"Didn't mother tell you? You and Scott are the same blood type. It's one of the rarer types and you both have it. Maybe that's why I fell in love with him."

"Not a bad reason."

"He was with me all the time, you know, and by the time you were out of danger I began to realize how close Scott and I have grown, how much I love him. And then when I heard Philip's voice I thought what kid stuff that relationship of ours had been. I know you never approved."

"It wasn't my business to approve or disapprove."

"Maybe not. But I know you approve of Scott, and that's important to me."

I went home.

I thought, What do You want from me? It's not my son-in-law. You don't try to kill a man and then donate blood for a transfusion. Nobody would do a thing like that.

The person I cut off at the traffic circle? But that was insane. And how would I know him anyway? I wouldn't know where to start looking for him.

Some other enemy? But I had no enemies.

Julia said, "The doctor called again. He still doesn't see how you could check yourself out of the hospital. But he called to say he wants to schedule you for surgery."

Not yet, I told her. Not until I'm ready.

"When will you be ready?"

When I feel right about it, I told her.

She called him back, relayed the message. "He's very nice," she reported. "He says any delay is hazardous, so you should let him schedule as soon as you possibly can. If you have something to attend to he says he can understand that, but try not to let it drag on too long."

I was glad he was a sympathetic and understanding man, and that she liked him. He might be a comfort to her later when she needed someone around to lean on.

Something clicked.

I called Debbie.

"Just the one telephone call," she said, puzzled. "He said he knew you never liked him but he always respected you and he knew what an influence you were in my life. And that I should feel free to call on him if I needed someone to turn to. It was nice of him, that's what I told myself at the time, but there was something creepy about the conversation."

And what had she told him?

"That it was nice to hear from him, and that, you know, my husband and I would be fine. Sort of stressing that I was married, but in a nice way. Why?"

* * *

The police were very dubious. Ancient history, they said. The boy had lived with my daughter a while ago, parted amicably, never made any trouble. Had he ever threatened me? Had we ever fought?

He's the one, I said. Watch him, I said. Keep an eye on him.

So they assigned men to watch Philip, and on the fourth day the surveillance paid off. They caught him tucking a bomb beneath the hood of a car. The car belonged to my son-in-law, Scott.

"He thought you were standing between them. When she said she was happily married, well, he shifted his sights to the husband."

There had always been something about Philip that I had not liked. Something creepy, as Debbie put it. Perhaps he'll get treatment now. In any event, he'll be unable to harm anyone.

Is that why I was permitted to return? So that I could prevent Philip from harming Scott?

Perhaps that was the purpose. The conversations with Julia, with Monty, with Peg, with Mark and Debbie, those were fringe benefits.

Or perhaps it was the other way around.

All right.

They've prepared me for surgery. The doctor, understanding as ever, called again. This time I let him schedule me, and I came here and let them prepare me. And I've prepared myself.

All right.

I'm ready now.

Miranda

by John D. MacDonald

John D. MacDonald was the best crime writer of his generation. While he ultimately got his due, many of his early paperback original novels got over-looked in the process. Look up April Evil *and* One Monday We Killed Them All *and* Soft Touch.

First published in 1950.

*T*hey put a plate in the back of my head and silver pins in the right thighbone. The arms were in traction longer than the legs. The eye, of course, was something they couldn't fix.

It was a big, busy place they had there. The way I had come in, I guess, was a sort of challenge to the doctors. A post-gradu-ate course. See, gentlemen, this thing is alive—indubitably alive. Watch, now. We will paste it back together the way God made it. Or almost as good.

My friends came—for a while. For a few months. I wasn't too cordial. I didn't need them. It was the same thing every time. How terrible to be all strung with wires and weights! Aren't you going mad from boredom, George?

I wasn't going mad from boredom. I learned how to keep my face from laughing, how to laugh on the inside. As if I was sitting back there in my mind, hugging myself, shrieking with laughter, rocking from side to side, laughing and laughing. But nothing but silence on the outside. The faraway dignity of the very sick.

They brought me in and I was dead. That is, for all practical purposes. The heart had no right to keep beating.

But you see, I knew. When you know a thing like that, you

can't die. When you know a thing like that, it is unfinished business.

Poor George. Poor old George.

And me all the time laughing away. It was a joke that I could understand, but nobody else would. The joke goes like this. I'll tell you and you can laugh with me too. We'll rock and giggle together. Once upon a time there was a good-natured, broad-shouldered slob named George A. Corliss who lived in an eleven-thousand-dollar frame house in an orderly little suburban community called Joanna Center. He lived at 88 April Lane. He made a hundred and thirty-eight fifty each and every week in a New York publishing house, carried a little more insurance than he should have, loved his dainty, fragile-boned, gray-eyed, silver-blond little wife named Connie very much indeed. In fact this slob had his happiest moments when Connie would give him a speculative look and tell him that he really did look a little like Van Johnson. This George Corliss, he made replicas of early American furniture in a basement workshop, bought a new Plymouth every time he had the old one about paid for, conscientiously read "good books" while commuting, and often brooded about the childlessness of the Corliss household, a thorn in his side.

He drove too fast, smoked too much, knocked off too many cocktails. In all respects a very average guy. But what George didn't know was that Connie, the little silver-blond wife, feeling the thirties coming on, had acquired an itch for a Latin-type twenty-two-year-old kid, a gas pumper at the local lubritorium, a pinch-waisted kid with melting eyes, muscles, and a fast line of chatter. Since the kid obviously could not support Connie in the style to which George had gradually accustomed her, nothing seemed simpler than to find some nice safe way of knocking George off and glomming onto the fifty-six thousand bucks his demise would bring in.

So one day when George had told Connie in advance that he had to take a run up to a mountain town called Crane, New York, to dicker with a recalcitrant author, Connie took the Plymouth to the garage and the kid, Louie Palmer by name, did a judicious job of diddling with the tie-rod ends with the idea of their parting when a turn was taken at high speed.

So I took a turn at high speed. Rather, I tried to take it. The steering wheel went loose and gummy in my hands. They killed me, all right. They killed George, the slob, all right.

Funny, how it was. Take the moment the car started rolling. I had maybe one second of consciousness left. And in that second a lot of little things added up. I'd had the steering checked in town that week. Connie always buying gas in one-dollar quantities. The funny way she'd said goodbye. At the last minute I wanted her to come along. She was emphatic about saying no. And there was the time I found the initialed cigarette case on the car floor. She took it and I forgot it until I saw that Louie Palmer using it. Then he got all red and bothered and said it had slipped out of his pocket while he was checking the car, maybe when he reached in to yank the gimmick that releases the hood.

And before things went out for me, in a blinding whiteness that reached across the world, I said to myself, almost calmly, "George, you're not going to let this kill you."

But it did kill the George I was talking to. The man who came out of the coma eight days later wasn't the old furniture builder, huckster, and loving husband.

No, he was the new George. The boy who could lie there and laugh inside at his joke. They tried to kill him and they did. And now he was going to kill them. Murder by a corpse. There's something you can get your teeth into and laugh at. But don't let it move the face muscles. It might pull out some of the deep stitches.

"You're the luckiest man in the world," the young doctor said. Young, with a nose like a bird's beak and no more hair than a stone.

"Sure," I said.

"I would have bet ten thousand to one against you."

"Good thing you didn't." I wanted him to go away. I wanted to think about Connie and Louie and just how I would do it to them.

He fingered the wasted arm muscles. "Doing those exercises?"

"Every day, Doc." I liked to see him wince when I called him Doc.

He clucked and muttered and prodded. "I warned you that you might not ever be able to walk again, the way those nerves were pinched. But the nurse told me you took a few steps today. I don't understand it."

I looked him in the eye, with the one I had left. "You see, Doc," I said, "I've got everything to live for."

The way I said it made him uneasy.

"Mr. Corliss, you're not going to be exactly as good as new.

We can improve that face for you by hooking a plastic eye in those muscles so that the eye will turn in its socket, but the two big scars will still show. You'll limp for a few years and you will have to be very careful for the rest of your life, protecting that plate in your head from any sudden jars. No sports, you understand. Bridge is going to be your speed."

"You've said this before, Doc."

"I want to impress it on you. A man can't go through what you went through and expect—"

"Doc, I don't expect a thing. I was thrown through a shatter-proof windshield and then the car rolled across me."

He didn't like me as a person. He loved me as a case. I made his mouth water. He had showed me to every doctor within a ten-mile radius. He was writing me up for some kind of medical journal. The before-and-after pictures were going to go in his scrapbook. But we always parted with him looking as though he wished I was healthy enough to hit in the mouth.

Pain to the average person is just that. Pain. Nothing else. A mashed finger or a bad headache. But when you have it a long time something else happens to it. It turns into something else. You live with it and get to know it. With me, it was a color. Green. Green is supposed to be restful. I would see it behind my eyes. Eye, I should say. I'd wake up in the night and look at the color. Dull dark green. That was good. That was above standard. That was more than you could expect. But there were the nights in the beginning when it was a hot, bright, harsh green, pulsating like a crazy living plant. That was when the night nurse was always there. During the first weeks she used the needle when it was bad, and later it was pills, which never worked as fast or as well.

One time it was that new green that they say you can see for two miles on a clear day. It stayed that way, they told me later, for four days. Something about those pinched nerves.

And one day I searched and searched and could find no green at all, even the dark, almost pleasant kind. I missed it. Believe me, I missed it.

I didn't want them coming, and they sensed it and didn't come any more. But I liked to have Connie come. I liked it when there was traction on the two arms and the leg and both legs felt dead and the bandages on my head covered all but my mouth and my right eye.

She came every day. She wept a little every time she came.

"Don't cry, Connie."

"I—I can't help it, George."

"I'm getting better, they keep telling me. So why are you crying?"

"It's so awful to see you there like this."

"Just think, Connie. I might be dead. Wouldn't that be worse, Connie? Wouldn't it? Or maybe you'd like that better."

"What do you mean? What do you mean?"

"Then there wouldn't be all this pain and suffering."

"Oh."

"What did you think I meant, Connie? What on earth could I have meant except that, dearest? I know that you love me very much. You've told me so often."

"It's hard to understand you, George, not seeing your face and all. Just your . . . eye. What you say just comes out . . . and it's hard to know what you mean sometimes." She always worked hard on that explanation. It meant a lot to her to get it right. Her knuckles always had a bone-white look while she talked to her loving husband.

Every time it was a lovely game. And I had all the time in between to plan the next visit.

"Connie, I hope you're taking good care of the car."

"But, George! It was a total loss."

"Sorry, dearest. I keep forgetting. We'll have to get a new one. But when we do you'll help me see that it's well taken care of."

"Of course, George."

There was a continuity about it. If I kept after her too hard she'd get suspicious. Then the fear would show in her eyes. I'd let her carry the fear around for a few visits and then I would drive it away.

"I'm so lucky to have a wife like you, Connie."

"Thank you, George."

"I know I've been acting strangely. But I haven't the courage to do what I planned. I wanted to estrange you, to drive you away, so that you could find a new life with a whole man, not some smashed item like me."

"Is that what you were doing?"

"Of course!"

"Oh, George! Darling, I thought—" A very abrupt stop.

"What did you think?"

"Well, that maybe the accident had . . . well, hurt your head in some way so that you were beginning to think I was to blame for the accident." Then she laughed to show how silly that idea was. She flushed, too. I imagine she was considering her boldness to be the best defense, in addition to being rather fun because of the risk.

"You? Hey, I was alone in the car, remember?"

"You've always driven too fast."

"Never again."

At the end of the visiting period she would kiss me and go. Before the bandages came off my face she would press her lips to mine very sweetly. Loving little silver-blond Connie with those enormous gray eyes and that dainty figure.

After the bandages came off and there was just the patch on the eye she kissed hard, but not in passion. As though it was something she had to do hard and quick in order to do it at all.

After her fears had gone away and after, I guessed, she had told Louie that she had been wrong about thinking that I might have guessed, I would slowly bring her suspicions back to a boil.

I was giving Connie and Louie some exciting dates. Giving them something to talk about.

A good thing about carrying too much life insurance is that you sometimes have too much accident insurance along with it. And I had a lot. Complete coverage of all medical expenses plus thirty-five hundred consolation prize for the loss of the eye plus six hundred a month for complete disability until I could get back to my job. They said a full year from the time of discharge from the hospital.

To go home would give me more time for the game I was playing with them. But it was good in the hospital, too. I could lie there at night, and it was as if I had them fastened to a string, two puppets. When I yanked the string they jumped.

The books talk about having to live with guilt and how it can subtly change the relationship of lovers. But I was no body, firmly and safely planted away. I was between them. I wondered if she could taste my lips when she kissed Louie, and if he looked deep into her eyes and saw a hospital bed. . . .

The nurse was something else. A tall, gawky girl, almost grotesquely angular and yet full of a strange grace. Miranda. She charged at the bed looking capable of tripping and falling over it, yet always her hands were light as moths. Her eyes were deep-set, smallish, a brilliant and Technicolor blue. She knew.

I saw it in the strange, wry amusement in her eyes.

Once she told me she knew. She cranked the bed up a little to rest tired muscles. She stood and folded her arms. I heard the starched rustle of the material. Her hair was a soft dusty black under the cap. Her mouth was wide and quite heavy.

"Delirium," she said in her abrupt voice, "is usually dull." She had a trick of starting a sentence boldly and then letting it fall away.

"I was delirious, I expect."

"But not dull, George." That was the tip. Up until that point it had been a most discreet and proper Mr. Corliss.

"Like living out a soap opera, Miranda?"

She shrugged. It was typical of her to shrug too hard, hiking her wide, thin shoulders almost up to her ears. "But no part in it for me, I would think."

I watched her. There was nothing awkward in our silence.

"Delirium isn't much to go on, Miranda. Not when there's been a brain injury."

"Perhaps the delirium is partly due to her. So sweet. She's all tinkle and ice and teensy little gestures. Oh, she's a one, that one. What mothers want their daughters to grow up to be—on the outside."

"And the inside. Will you hazard a guess on the inside, Dr. Miranda?"

No more banter. She looked hard at me, and up through the little blue eyes welled the fanatic light. "Rotten," she whispered. "Dead, soft rotten." She turned and walked out with her lunging stride, a whisper of starch.

It made the game better. A new piece on the board, allowing more permutations and combinations.

Later that day I had my arm around her as I walked. She looked as though her back and shoulders would feel hard, slatted. She was a softness and a warmth. I took five steps away from the bed and four back to the wheelchair. Her lip was caught under her teeth and her breath came hard as though it were she who was making the effort.

The next day, dozing on the sun porch, I felt someone staring at me. I looked over and saw Miranda in the doorway. We looked at each other for an impossible time, the white antiseptic walls and the neat floral arrangements tilting and spinning away until we looked across a bottomless void at each other and there was nothing alive in creation except the wild blue of her eyes. When she turned and left, without speaking, the time weave was ripped across with a sound I could almost hear.

The young doctor and the absentminded old one came in one morning and told me that this was the day I would go home, that an ambulance was being provided, that Connie had been informed, that arrangements had been made for Nurse Wysner to live in for a time until Connie became accustomed to the necessary work.

"In a couple of months you'll be ready for the eye work," the young doctor said.

"Yes, of course," I said. "We mustn't forget that."

He turned away, looking as though his mouth hurt him.

They didn't use the siren, and it awakened in me a childish disappointment. It would be fitting to arrive with siren, that sound which in our neat world has replaced the night cough of the unknown beast.

When they rolled me out onto the asphalt of the drive I lifted my head and looked at the house. This was where the big amiable clown who sometimes looked a little like V. Johnson had lived. All the details of it were sharp and it looked unreal, a house seen in a movie. I knew that all things would now look that way. Two eyes give depth perception. One eye gives everything a two-dimensional flatness.

Miranda Wysner, blinding white in the sun, stood tall and straight, with a tiny smile at the corner of her mouth. A smile no one else could see.

Connie trotted delicately back and forth between the wheeled cart and the side door, telling everybody to be careful, please, don't bump him on anything, and her voice was like the mirrored wind chimes in a lost lake house of long ago.

Connie had moved into the guest room across the hall from the bedroom we had shared—or rather the bedroom she had shared with George A. Corliss, who died in such an unfortunate accident. They put me in the big double bed, and the Hollywood frame creaked in a well-remembered way and I was very tired and went to sleep almost immediately.

I dreamed I was laid out in that room with candles at head and feet and the smell of flowers and soft chanting. I awoke in the purple-gray dusk and there were flowers and a distant chanting but no candles. The chanting was a muted newscaster, his Airedale voice tamed by a half twist of the dial. There were the sharp yelps of neighborhood children at play, and for a moment I was a guy who had taken a nap. Just a nap. Get up, go down, kiss Connie, mix the drinks, check the stove to see what dinner might be.

But Miranda came in with her starchy rustle and bent over

me and put her hand on my forehead. "Cool," she said. "Probably a little subnormal."

"We're living in a subnormal household. Where are you?"

"The next room. Beyond the bath. With both doors open, I'll hear you if you cry out in the night."

Connie smells sweet and dainty and feminine. Miranda had her special scent. Long illness makes the senses acute. Miranda smelled of medicinal alcohol, antiseptic, and, underneath, a deep perfume that throbbed. It was probably against regulations. It had a musky jungle beat.

"Maybe I'll just whimper."

"I'll hear that, too." There was just enough light so that I could see her teeth flash white. "I told her not to try to talk to you until tomorrow. Excitement, you know."

"Just like a county fair."

"I'll bring your tray."

When I awoke in the morning, a fat rain, oyster colored, viscid, was coming down in straight lines. I could see it bouncing off the roof peak across the street. The bedside clock said three minutes of six. Hospital habits. In three minutes Miranda came striding in with a basin of warm water, glass of cold, toothbrush, comb.

"I've put the coffee on," she said. I had finished breakfast and was shaving with an electric razor when Connie came in, her pink housecoat belted tightly around her child's waist, her face all cute and vacant with sleep.

"Goodness, you people get up early!"

Miranda turned from the window. "Good morning, Mrs. Corliss."

"Good morning, nurse. Welcome home, darling! Oh, welcome home!" She came over to the bed. Miranda watched stonily. Connie bent and gave me that quick, hard kiss. I got my hand around the back of her frail neck and prolonged it. When I released her she took a step backwards, her eyes wide, bringing her hand up as though to scrub her lips, not quite daring.

"Well!" she said unevenly.

At the end of the week, I made four full circuits of the room. At the end of two weeks I went downstairs, dressed for the first time. The clothes hung on me. The more independent I grew, the more coldness appeared in Connie's manner toward Miranda.

At the end of the second week she brought it to a head, in Miranda's presence.

"George, I think we can get along beautifully now without Nurse Wysner."

"I'll leave in the morning," Miranda said. "I'll pack tonight. That is, if you really feel you don't need me, Mr. Corliss."

I gave the words the proper emphasis. "I can handle everything myself," I said.

"You mustn't get too confident," Miranda said.

"I know my own limitations," I replied.

"You two talk as if I weren't here to help," Connie said with small-girl plaintiveness.

"I'm certain you'll be a great help, Mrs. Corliss," Miranda said, starting bluntly, sliding into her odd breathlessness at the end of the sentence.

"Then it's settled," Connie said brightly, clapping her hands once, a habit I had at one time found almost unbearably sweet. . . .

In the middle of the night Miranda's hand against my cheek awakened me. The bed stirred as she sat on it. The night was as black as a sealed coffin.

Her whisper had the same quality as her speaking voice. "You can't do it alone, you know."

"Do what?"

"Whatever it is that you've been planning, my darling."

"May I take this as a declaration of your great and undying passion?"

"See? You can't hurt me that way. You can't hurt me by trying to hurt me. That's a sort of secret we have. We've said more things with a look than we can ever say with words."

"I'm touched, deeply."

Her nearness was more vital than any caress. "You've got to let me help. You've got to let me share."

"Why?"

"Doing something and never having a sharing of it is bad. Then it's all on the inside. We can talk, you know. Afterward."

Nurse and patient, probing together a deep and desperate wound.

"But I have a way and you aren't in it."

"Then there must be a new way. Two can think better. You might forget something important."

"You're accepting the correctness of the decision, then?"

"Only because it's yours. I don't matter. I've never had any strong feelings about right and wrong."

"That's a lie, Miranda."

Hoarsely: "So it's a lie! When you've seen the evil I've seen—"

"I'll let you help on one condition, Miranda."

"Anything."

"We haven't used the words yet. I want you to say the words we've been skirting so carefully. I want you to say them slowly. All the words. Now, what are you going to do?"

Her hands found my wrist and the moth touch was gone. Her nails dug in with a surprising force. "I am going to help you kill your wife and her lover."

"Why?"

"Because they hurt you so badly, and it's something you want to do."

"But more than that. The other reason."

"Because after it is done it will be something so strong between us that we'll never be apart again."

"Love, then?"

"No. Something stronger than that. Something more exciting."

"You want half a man?"

"I'm strong enough for two. I knew it would be this way. Ever since that night I kept you from dying. You gave up that night. I sat and whispered in your ear why you had to live. Over and over. And you did."

"It's settled, then. Go in the morning. Be patient. I'll come to you when I can."

She left quickly, plunging towards the doorway, miraculously finding it in the blackness.

Strength slowly came back. My clothes began to fit again. Tone came back to the mended muscles. Connie stayed in the guest room. For a long time she seemed to be waiting, and when she saw that there would be no demands on her uxorial capacities, there seemed to be a relief in her. Once, when she was out, I went over her personal checks against the small income from her father. I checked back far enough to find out when it had started. They had been a little careless several months before my accident. Instead of cashing two of the checks, she had turned them over to her friend. The endorsements were a scrawled *L. Palmer,* with a self-conscious flowery squiggle under the name. I took those two checks. They were both for twenty-five.

I didn't hate either of them. I was cold—cold as any self-respecting corpse should be.

With the proceeds of the collision insurance I bought a good used car. I wasn't cold about that. It frightened me. That was unexpected. I sat behind the wheel, and when I shut my eyes I could feel the car rolling, first sideways and then end over end. I opened my eyes quickly and the world returned to sanity. The first time I drove to the city, the sweat ran down from my armpits, soaking my shirt. I had the checks photostated on that first trip, front and back. I returned them to her file.

That night, at dinner, I put the next brick in the foundation. I looked across at Connie. "You're mine, you know," I said.

Little puzzled wrinkles appeared above the bridge of her nose. "Of course, dear. What brought that on?"

"I just was thinking. You know how you imagine things. I was imagining how I would react if you ever wanted to leave me. The answer is very simple. I'd never, never let you go."

She smothered the quick alarm. "Why think of such a thing, George? Such an impossible thing!"

I shrugged. "I don't know. Say, the new car holds sixteen gallons of gas."

The fork trembled in her hand. "What's that got to do with—"

"Nothing, Connie. Don't be so silly. I saw the conversation disturbed you, so in my own feeble way I was changing the subject."

"Oh!"

"The steering seems pretty sound. I had it checked at the station. That Palmer boy seems to know his business."

Vacant stare. "Palmer? Oh, Louie, the dark one."

She was getting better at it. That was really a good effort. I thought it was too bad I couldn't tell her just how good an effort it was. Then she spoiled it by being unable to finish the dinner she was eating with such appetite. That's one thing about her that always amazed me. A tiny girl, yet almost rapacious about her food. Red lips eager and white teeth tearing and champing. Once upon a time it had been cute. Funny how little you can learn about a woman in seven years of marriage.

I had to make her see Louie. I had to give her a reason.

Over coffee I said, "I've been asking around."

"About what, darling?" A shade too much casualness and disinterest.

"We could make a good deal on this house right now."

The petulance showed immediately. "But, George! I love this house and this neighborhood. I don't want to move."

"I stopped in at the office. I told Mallory how the docs recommend I keep out in the air as much as possible. He hinted that they might be able to give me a traveling job, based in California. I'd cover eleven Western states, part promotion work, part digging up new talent for the list. I'd also do some coordination work with the movie agents. I'm to let him know."

She looked as if somebody had hit her in the stomach. "But isn't the job you had a better one? I mean, we could see that you got plenty of fresh air."

"I don't know if I'm too anxious to pick up this commuting treadmill again. I'm going to give it a lot of thought. We'd make a profit on the house. In the new job my trips would be so long that you would travel with me, naturally."

"I do get a little carsick," she said, the dread showing.

I laughed. "Say, remember in the hospital when I told you I was going to drive slow from then on?"

"Yes, I do."

"Found out today I've got my nerve back. I kicked it up to seventy-five on Route Twenty-eight. The old reflexes seem pretty good."

I watched and saw the speculative look dawn. She covered it by getting up to bring more coffee. But when she poured it into my cup, she spilled some in the saucer and didn't seem to notice.

At a quarter to nine she said she was going for a walk. I knew that the station closed at nine. I yawned and said I might go to bed. She left. I waited five minutes and backed the car out. The station was six blocks away. I was curious to see how it was done. I took the parallel road, then turned left after six blocks and parked in the tree shadows. I could see the station. Connie walked by it, very slowly, silhouetted against the station floodlights. She continued on down the street. I turned around in a driveway, went back to the parallel road, sped down three blocks, and parked as before. Soon Connie went by, walking quickly now, high heels twinkling. I eased out after her.

Thirteen blocks from our house on April Lane she turned left. It was a cheap neighborhood. Midway in the second block was a green neon sign against a pale brick front: UNICORN—BAR AND GRILL. Beyond it was another sign, *Ladies' Entrance*. She darted in there, reluctant to linger under the harsh green light.

I could remember the exact stage of pain that green light represented. Not the worst, but bad.

I went down the street, turned around, parked on the same side as the Unicorn, facing toward it. I was barely in time. A '40 Ford convertible parked across the street and Louie Palmer in jacket, open sports collar, hatless, walked across the street. He stopped in the full glare of green and lit a cigarette. He handled it in a thoroughly Bogart fashion, hand cupped completely around it, lowering it with calculated slowness after each drag. He looked up and down the street. He flipped it away, squared his shoulders, and went inside. After all, he was a desperate character. A real killer. The murder didn't quite pan out, but what the hell. The intent was there. Louie was a real sharp apple, all wound up in a capital A affair, just like out of James M. Cain.

It would be nice to tell him that he was a sniveling little grease monkey preening himself over a tramp wife, a hired banty rooster with grease in his hair. But that was a pleasure I would have to forego.

I was in bed when she got home an hour later. I heard her in the bathroom. I wondered how radiant she looked.

Miranda lived alone in an efficiency apartment crowded into what had apparently been one of the bedrooms of a vast old Victorian house. To the left of the house was the parking lot for a supermarket. The street had been widened until the bottom step of the porch was a yard from the sidewalk.

She came down the street from the bus stop, lean legs in the white cotton stockings scissoring below the hem of the cheap coat.

She watched the sidewalk ahead of her and suddenly looked across the street directly into my eyes and stopped. It did not seem strange that she should have that utter awareness.

She waited and I walked across to her. The small blue eyes narrowed just a bit. Her heavy lips were laid evenly together. She wore no lipstick, and the strange thinness of the skin of her lips made them look peeled, raw.

We did not speak to each other until she had shut the apartment door behind us. "You should take stairs more slowly," she said.

"Showing off, I guess."

"You look better, George. Give me your coat."

The apartment was absolutely characterless at first glance.

Then the signs of her presence intruded. An ashtray squared precisely to the edge of a table. Three birch logs, so perfect as to look artificial, stacked in the shallow, ashless fireplace. Shades all pulled to exactly the same level. She plunged back and forth through the room, physically threatening to derange all its neatness, but her touch on each object was light and precise. She pulled a glass-topped table closer to the armchair where I sat. From the kitchenette alcove she brought bottle, glass, small bowl of ice cubes, new bottle of soda. She set them down with evenly spaced clicks against the glass top. She made the drink deftly and said, "With you in a moment," and shut herself into the tiny bath.

She came out with her hair fluffed out of its rigid nurse's style, and she wore a turtle-necked gray sweater and a harsh tweed skirt in a discomfiting orange shade. No stockings. Ancient loafers. She fell toward a chair, sat lightly in it. The bones of her wrists and hips were sharp. She looked harsh, brittle, angular. I thought irrelevantly that she was a woman made for a blind man. To his touch she would have the remembered softness and warmth.

I put the drink down. "How do we start?"

"Tell me how we're going to do it." The sentence faded away. Each of her sentences brought silence after it, so that forever we spoke across silence more clearly than with words. Her eyes were dedicated blue flames.

"Not that fast. I want to know if you still insist on sharing this thing. Without knowing when or how we're to do it."

"I insist."

I studied her. "Have you ever wondered about your own sanity, Miranda?"

"Of course. Everyone does. They say that to wonder means that you are really quite all right."

"Odd that you're a nurse."

"Is it? People fighting, dying. I'm there. I can watch and decide about them. Oh, you don't have to do anything crude, like the wrong medicines. I like them caught between living and dying. Like you were. Then you can do it with words. You can decide, and it always comes out the way you say. It makes you strong to think about it."

I smiled, and my lips felt stiff. "Have you decided against anyone lately?"

"Oh, yes. This past week. An old man. They wanted him alive because, you see, he was a great-grandfather and in another month he'd be a great-great-grandfather and it was all a matter of pride with him and with them. To have all those generations living at once. He fought, that one, to keep living just for the sake of living, which is never any good. I whispered in his ear. 'Give up,' I said. 'Let it go. Stop fighting. Give up.' They say they can't hear you, but they can. They always can. He finally gave a great sigh and died. They couldn't understand why he died. But, of course, I couldn't tell them."

"You like doing that?"

"You kill the rotten ones and keep the good ones. Like sorting things. Like being neat about yourself."

"I'm one of the good ones?"

She shook her head, as though puzzled. "No, and yet I kept you. I keep wondering why."

My glass was empty. She sprang toward me, and had I not learned about her I would have flinched away. But she stopped in time and the new drink was made.

I caught her wrist and pulled her onto my lap. Oddly, she seemed lighter than Connie, though she was much heavier, I knew. The calm lips folded against mine. But there was nothing there. It was holding a senseless pose, like a charade that no one can guess. She went back to her chair.

"I expected anything but that," I said.

"Wait," she said. "Wait until afterwards. There isn't enough togetherness yet. Afterwards the thing shared will make it right."

"Maybe I died," I said. "Maybe this is a fancy-type hell, like the mythological one where the sinner is chained for eternity just out of reach of food and drink."

"Am I food and drink?" She showed, for the first time, a trace of coyness. Like a child's rattle placed atop a small white coffin.

"Maybe not that. But necessary. In an odd way. Essential."

"That's because I know more about these things. I'm like a guide. You're just learning."

"Is it a taste you can acquire?"

"That you can't help acquiring."

"But when there's no one left to kill?"

"Then we'll help each other find someone else. And do it in a better way than words."

I stood up. "I'll let you know."

"I'll be waiting."

On the way home I could feel the clear imprint of the plate

inlaid in my skull, the perfect outline of it, as though gentle fingers were pressing it against the jelly of my brain.

I went into the cellar and fitted a length of soft white pine into the lathe. I let my hands work the way they wanted to work, without direction. The cutting tool ate away the wood, turning angles into curves. I took it off the lathe and turned on the sander. I held it one way, then another way, rounding it the way my hands said. It turned into the crude elongated torso of a woman, a woman as thin as Miranda. Then I put it back into the lathe and cut it down to a round rod, shaving away the woman form.

The pressure against the plate had turned into an ache, the beginning of green behind my eyes. I broke the rod over my knee.

I went up to Connie and said, "Rub the back of my neck."

I stretched out on the couch. She was awkward about it, lacking the skill of Miranda. I turned and held her close, telling myself she was precious. I kissed her. I saw surprise in her eyes and then a most patient resignation. I sat beside her on the couch and took the patch off the empty socket. She shut her eyes hard. Her small fists were clenched. I tiptoed away from her and up the stairs and shut myself in my room. I heard her go out. I lay in the livid green and the world was green neon and the outline of the plate changed slowly, forming letters, pressing the word UNICORN deep into the gray-green brain, deep into the softness in which forever a car rolled and leaped and bounded like a child's toy thrown aside in petty rage.

"You won't be needing the car, will you?" I asked Connie.

She gave me her prettiest frown. "Gosh, I don't think so. How long will you have it?"

"Overnight."

"Where on earth are you going?"

"I went in and talked to Mallory yesterday. We decided I'd start to take on a few odd jobs, just to get my hand in. That splendid creative artist up in Crane is yammering at his agent to arrange a switch of publishers again."

"But that is where you were going when—"

"Correct. Sort of like a movie. This is when I came in."

"When are you leaving?"

"He keeps crazy hours. Starts writing after a midnight breakfast. It's a two-and-a-half-hour drive. I'll leave tonight after dark, and after I see him I'll hole up somewhere and come back down tomorrow. No point in getting too tired at this stage of the game."

The upper surfaces of her rounded arms had the faint tan that she never seems to lose, even in the dead of winter. I held her by the shoulders and looked into her eyes. She was facing the light. I saw then, and for the first time, the slight yellowness of the whites of her eyes. Once they had been that bluey white that only children seem to have. The pores of her snub nose and on her rounded cheeks were faintly enlarged, and everywhere, eye corners, around her mouth, across her forehead, I could see the spreading inevitable network of wrinkles, cobwebby against the skin. Enlarge those wrinkles to the maximum, and she would have the face of a withered monkey, out of which the gray eyes would still stare, acquiring through that contrast the knowledge of evil which had always been there but which I had never been able to see or understand.

She moved uncomfortably in my grasp. "What are you staring at?"

"My fine true wife, my loyal little Connie. Darling, what did I do to deserve you?"

She had the grace to blush. "Oh, come now."

"It's the truth, isn't it? Why, any other woman would be scheming and planning how to get rid of me. But not you, Connie. Not you. Love is bigger than expediency, isn't it?"

"If you say so, George."

"Read any good books lately?"

"George, right now you seem . . . more like yourself. You've been so odd, you know."

"I'll be my very own true self very soon now."

"Are we going to move away from here?"

"I think so."

Her voice became wheedling. "Darling, before you make up your mind for sure, let's go up to the cabin for a long week. Just the two of us. There won't be anybody around at this time of year. We can walk in the woods. Oh, we'll have a wonderful time."

"Just the two of us?"

Her eyes grew as opaque as gray glass. "Call it a second honeymoon," she breathed.

That would be ideal for them. Not difficult to arrange at all. So many ways to do it up there. I could almost see Louie Palmer pushing me off the high front porch onto the lake-front rocks and then lighting a cigarette in his Bogart way, saying, "I'll run along. You drive out and make the phone call. Remember, he complained about feeling dizzy and you told him not to go near the steps."

There would be a deep satisfaction in that for them. An end of tension. It had failed the first time. Their frozen world would begin to revolve again.

"A second honeymoon," I said. . . .

In the late afternoon I took the car down to the station. Conner, the owner, was there as well as Louie Palmer. Louie was in his coveralls, his sleeves rolled up over muscular forearms, a smear of grease on his chin near the corner of his mouth, a lank end of black hair curling down across his forehead to the black eyebrow. He avoided meeting my eye.

"Taking a little trip," I said heartily to Conner. "First one since my accident. Have Louie check the tires, steering arms, kingpin, front wheel bushings, please."

"Put it on the rack, kid," Conner said in his husky, domineering voice. I wondered how much Conner's constant scorn was a factor in Louie's bold play for big money. I watched the coveralls tighten across Louie's broad shoulders as he ducked under the car. How had it started? A few sidelong glances? The realization that the Corliss woman was coming around oftener than strictly necessary? Then, probably, "I guess we better road-test it, Mrs. Corliss. Just move over and I'll take the wheel."

How does it start?

"Change the oil, sir?" Louie asked.

"No thanks, kid," I said. I rasped that "kid" across him, saw the color creep up the back of his neck.

I waited, and when he was through I tipped him a quarter. He looked as if he might throw it in my face. "Buy yourself a beer," I said. "Try the Unicorn. I hear that's a good bar."

His mouth sagged a little, and the color left him. I grinned into his face and turned away. Louie was jumpy.

"Take it easy, Mr. Corliss," Conner advised.

"I'll do that," I said. "Made myself a promise that I'll never drive over forty-five again, and I'm sticking to it."

Beyond Conner I saw a puzzled look on Louie's lean white face.

I went over right after dinner. Miranda was waiting for me. Her eyes seemed deeper in her head, their glow strong and steady. The wide lips were parted a faint fraction of an inch. It added to the breathlessness of her words. The spring within her was wound as tightly as the key could be turned. A deb waiting for the grand march. A horse player waiting for the sixth race. An animal watching, from a limb, the trail beneath.

She shut the door and leaned against it. "Tonight?"

"Yes, tonight."

She shut her eyes for a moment. With her eyes shut she had a corpse face.

"How? Tell me how. Quickly!"

"They think I'll be gone. They think I'll be gone overnight. We'll come back."

"They'll be together?"

"Why not? They have planning to do."

"But how?"

"Electricity."

She looked disappointed. "Is—is that a good way?"

"The best. Clean and quick and final."

She nodded slowly. "Yes, I can see a lot of ways how it could be. But I won't just watch, will I? I'll be part of it." You there, little girl! Get into that game of musical chairs with the other children.

"You'll be part of it. I promised."

"Do they have a good chance of catching us, blaming us?"

"Not a chance in the world."

"Oh, good! And later . . . we'll go away."

"Far away."

"How much time is there?"

"Three hours. Four."

"Long hours to wait, George."

"We'll take a ride. That'll kill time. Come along."

She had not sat beside me in a car before. She was unexpectedly feline, a part of her that I had not noticed. She sat with her legs curled up under her, partly facing me, and I knew that she watched, not the road, but my face, the glow of the dash lights against it, the pendulum swing of the streetlamps.

"Scared?" I asked.

"No. Something else. Like when you're a child. You wake up in the morning. Another day. Then you see the snow on the windowsill and it all comes with a great rush. The day after tomorrow is Christmas, you say. One more day gone. Yesterday it was the day after the day after tomorrow. Now it's getting so close it closes your throat. That's how I feel. Getting one at last that isn't a sick one."

She inched closer so that the hard ball of her knee dug against my thigh. The musky perfume was thick in the car.

Without turning to see, I knew how her eyes would look. "We've never had to say much, have we?" she asked.

"Not very much. We knew without saying. A look can say everything."

"Later we can talk. We can say all the words that ever were. Good words and bad words. I've said bad words when I'm alone. I've never said them out loud to anybody. And we can say the other words too, and it won't be like after reading a story."

"How do you mean?"

"Oh, murder. Death. Kill. Blood. Bodies. I kill, you kill, we kill. The way you had to learn the Latin words in school."

"Conjugations, you mean."

"That's what I was trying to think of. Miranda Wysner, conjugate the verb to kill. I kill, I shall kill, I killed, I had killed, I should have killed."

She laughed. Her fingers shut on my arm above the elbow. "Think about it, George. Like swinging a big shining white sword. You swing it at evil and you tell yourself that's why you do it, but all the time way down inside your heart you know that it isn't the reason for it, it's the act itself."

I was on the road north out of town. She looked out the windows.

"Where are we going?"

"We'll just go north out of town up into the hills and then swing around and come back."

She was silent. I drove ever more rapidly. The road climbed and then began to gather unto itself a series of gentle curves that later would grow hard, the shoulders popping and crackling as the car threw itself at them.

I knew the landmarks. At the crest I slowed down, my arms tired from the strain. I started down the other side. The rising whine of the wind grew louder. The needle climbed. Sixty-five, seventy, seventy-five.

"We're killing the two of them, you see," I yelled above the wind. "We can't make the curve coming up. You wanted a part of it. You've got it, baby. You've got it. I left a letter with Mallory to open if I should die. It's all in there. They'll never worm out of this one. Electricity will kill them, all right. Courtesy of the State of New York, baby."

I saw the white posts of the curve in the farthest reach of the headlights.

Her scream filled the car, filled my ears, drilled into my soul.

"Faster, Georgie! Oh, faster!" Wild ecstasy, beyond the peak of human endurance.

I gave her one quick look. The dash lights hit the white-ridged bone structure of her face so that the shape of the skull was apparent. The mouth was wide-screaming, lip-spread. Her voice told me that she had known.

I came down hard on the brake. The car went into a long skid toward those posts. I let up on the brake, accelerated it straight, came down on the brake again. This time the skid was the other way so that the car headed toward the brink, still skidding sideways. I could hear only the scream of tortured rubber, then the jolting metallic scraping as tires were rolled right off the rims. I couldn't bring it out of the second skid. The front right wheel smacked the posts and the car spun so that I lost all sense of direction. For a moment it looked as though the car were spinning in one spot, like a top, completely ringed about with the white posts. Then it hit again and I was thrown toward Miranda. I tried to find her with my arms but I couldn't.

The crescendo of sound was fading. The car jolted, lurched, stood absolutely still in a world where there was no sound.

I got out. Other cars stopped. I looked for Miranda. I couldn't find her. The tow truck had a spotlight on it, and so did the trooper car. I made them shine the lights down and search down the slope. They looked and looked. After I told them a little more about her they stopped looking and they were most polite, and they took me to a doctor who gave me white powders.

I was in bed for ten days. I told Connie everything. She was very grave about it all and kept her eyes on my face as I answered every one of her questions.

By the time I was on my feet the car had been repaired. I didn't care what happened any more. I didn't protest when she took me to the gas station. Conner acted odd, and the questions seemed to embarrass him. He said, "Why, sure, a few times Mrs. Corliss cashed checks with me, and I guess I turned some of them over to Louie as part of his pay." Louie came over and shuffled his feet. He looked younger than I'd remembered. He was smoking a cigarette and he didn't hold it in his Bogart way.

"Louie," she said, "have you and I ever had a date?"

He stared at her. "What the hell! What the hell, Miz Corliss!"

"Have we?"

He manufactured a pretty good leer. "Well, now you bring the subject up, if you want a date, I'd—"

"Shut up!" Conner rasped.

"Get behind the wheel, George," Connie said, "and take me to the Unicorn."

I found the street. It wasn't there. I tried two other streets and then went back to the first one. I parked and went in a cigar store and asked what had happened to it. The man told me he'd been there twelve years and there'd never been a place of that name in the neighborhood.

We went home. I sat on the living-room couch. She pulled a small footstool over and sat directly in front of me.

"George, listen to me. I've been checking everything. That address you gave me. It's a parking lot. There aren't any old Victorian houses on that street made over into apartments. There's no local record of a nurse named Miranda Wysner. I brought you home from the hospital and took care of you myself. They told me I should put you in a psychiatric nursing home. They thought I was in danger from you. You said some pretty wild things about me in the hospital. I took the risk. For the first two weeks you were home you called me Miranda as often as you called me Connie. It was, I thought, the name of some girl you knew before we were married. Then you stopped doing that and you seemed better. That's why I thought it was safe to let you drive again. You were almost rational. No, you *were* rational. If it had been just almost rational, if I had thought that you were in danger, I wouldn't have permitted it. The steering did break when you had your accident. That's because the garage you took the car to installed a defective part."

I said haltingly, "But . . . you. The way you acted towards me. I know that I'm repulsive to you now. This eye and all—"

She left the room, came back quickly with a mirror. "Take off the patch, George." I did so. My two eyes, whole again, looked back at me. I touched the one that had been under the patch.

"I don't understand!" I cried out.

"You were convinced you had lost an eye. They gave up and decided to humor you when you demanded the patch. And as far as my turning away from you in disgust is concerned, that is precisely what you did, George. Not me."

I sat numbly. Her grave eyes watched me.

"I followed you that night," I said.

"I went for a walk. I didn't want you to see my cry again. I'd cried enough in front of you—until I thought that no more tears could come. But there are always more tears. Funny, isn't it? No matter how many already shed."

"Why have I done this to you?" I demanded.

"George, darling. You didn't do it. It wasn't you. It was the depressed fracture, the bone chips they pulled out of your brain, the plate they put in."

"Miranda," I whispered. "Who is Miranda? Who was Miranda?"

Connie tried to smile. Tears glistened in the gray eyes. "Miranda? Why, darling, she might have been an angel of death."

"When I nearly died, she was there. . . ."

"I was there," Connie said, with an upward lift of her chin. "I was there. And I held you and whispered to you how much you had to live for, how much I needed you."

"She said she whispered to all of them on that borderline."

"Maybe she does."

"Take me in your arms, George," Connie said.

I couldn't. I could only look at her. She waited a long time and then she went alone up the stairs. I heard her footsteps on the guest-room floor overhead.

We went to the cabin on the lake. I was sunk into the blackest depths of apathy. Once you have learned that no impression can be trusted, no obvious truth forever real, you know an isolation from the world too deep to be shattered.

I remembered the thin pink skin of her wide lips, the lurch of her walk, the unexpected competence of her hands.

I do not know how many days went by. I ate and slept and watched the lake.

And one day I looked up and there was Connie. She stood with the sun behind her and she looked down at me.

The smile came then. I felt it on my lips. I felt it dissolving all the old restraints. I reached for her and pulled her into my arms. The great shuddering sighs of thanksgiving came from her. She was my wife again, and she was in my arms, and everything between us was mended, as shining and new as in the earliest days of our marriage.

She wept and talked and laughed, all at once.

That night a wind was blowing off the lake.

When she slept I left her side and went to the windows. They look out onto the porch.

The old rocking chair creaked. Back and forth. Back and forth.

It was no surprise to me to see her sitting there. In the rocker. There was a wide path of reflected moonlight across the black water, and her underlip was moist enough to pick up the smallest of highlights from the lake.

We smiled at each other the way old friends smile who have at last learned to understand each other.

You see, Miranda knows about the drop from the top steps to the lakeshore rocks.

I turned back to gather up my small and dainty wife in my arms.

Deceptions

by Marcia Muller

Marcia Muller is one of the dominant voices on today's mystery scene. She gets better and more ambitious, each time out. She has a keen social eye and a gentle wit and a kind of wry tolerance for our sad little shortcomings as people. And she gets all this down in beautifully turned phrases and sentences.

First published in 1987.

San Francisco's Golden Gate Bridge is deceptively fragile-looking, especially when fog swirls across its high span. But from where I was standing, almost underneath it at the south end, even the mist couldn't disguise the massiveness of its concrete piers and the taut strength of its cables. I tipped my head back and looked up the tower to where it disappeared into the drifting grayness, thinking about the other ways the bridge is deceptive.

For one thing, its color isn't gold, but rust red, reminiscent of dried blood. And though the bridge is a marvel of engineering, it is also plagued by maintenance problems that keep the Bridge District in constant danger of financial collapse. For a reputedly romantic structure, it has seen more than its fair share of tragedy: Some eight hundred-odd lost souls have jumped to their deaths from its deck.

Today I was there to try to find out if that figure should be raised by one. So far I'd met with little success.

I was standing next to my car in the parking lot of Fort Point, a historic fortification at the mouth of San Francisco Bay. Where the pavement stopped, the land fell away to jagged black rocks; waves smashed against them, sending up geysers of salty spray.

Beyond the rocks the water was choppy, and Angel Island and Alcatraz were mere humpbacked shapes in the mist. I shivered, wishing I'd worn something heavier than my poplin jacket, and started toward the fort.

This was the last stop on a journey that had taken me from the toll booths and Bridge District offices to Vista Point at the Marin County end of the span, and back to the National Parks Services headquarters down the road from the fort. None of the Parks Service or bridge personnel—including a group of maintenance workers near the north tower—had seen the slender dark-haired woman in the picture I'd shown them, walking south on the pedestrian sidewalk at about four yesterday afternoon. None of them had seen her jump.

It was for that reason—plus the facts that her parents had revealed about twenty-two-year-old Vanessa DiCesare—that made me tend to doubt she actually had committed suicide, in spite of the note she'd left taped to the dashboard of the Honda she'd abandoned at Vista Point. Surely at four o'clock on a Monday afternoon *someone* would have noticed her. Still, I had to follow up every possibility, and the people at the Parks Service station had suggested I check with the rangers at Fort Point.

I entered the dark-brick structure through a long, low tunnel —called a sally port, the sign said—which was flanked at either end by massive wooden doors with iron studding. Years before I'd visited the fort, and now I recalled that it was more or less typical of harbor fortifications built in the Civil War era: a ground floor topped by two tiers of working and living quarters, encircling a central courtyard.

I emerged into the court and looked up at the west side; the tiers were a series of brick archways, their openings as black as empty eyesockets, each roped off by a narrow strip of yellow plastic strung across it at waist level. There was construction gear in the courtyard; the entire west side was under renovation and probably off limits to the public.

As I stood there trying to remember the layout of the place and wondering which way to go, I became aware of a hollow metallic clanking that echoed in the circular enclosure. The noise drew my eyes upward to the wooden watchtower atop the west tiers, and then to the red arch of the bridge's girders directly above it. The clanking seemed to have something to do with cars passing over the roadbed, and it was underlaid by a constant grumbling rush of tires on pavement. The sounds, coupled with the soaring height of the fog-laced girders, made me feel very small and insignificant. I shivered again and turned to my left, looking for one of the rangers.

The man who came out of a nearby doorway startled me, more because of his costume than the suddenness of his appearance. Instead of the Parks Service uniform I remembered the rangers wearing on my previous visit, he was clad in what looked like an old Union Army uniform: a dark blue frock coat, lighter blue trousers, and a wide-brimmed hat with a red plume. The long saber in a scabbard that was strapped to his waist made him look thoroughly authentic.

He smiled at my obvious surprise and came over to me, bushy eyebrows lifted inquiringly. "Can I help you, ma'am?"

I reached into my bag and took out my private investigator's license and showed it to him. "I'm Sharon McCone, from All Souls Legal Cooperative. Do you have a minute to answer some questions?"

He frowned, the way people often do when confronted by a private detective, probably trying to remember whether he'd done anything lately that would warrant investigation. Then he said, "Sure," and motioned for me to step into the shelter of the sally port.

"I'm investigating a disappearance, a possible suicide from the bridge," I said. "It would have happened about four yesterday afternoon. Were you on duty then?"

He shook his head. "Monday's my day off."

"Is there anyone else here who might have been working then?"

"You could check with Lee—Lee Gottschalk, the other ranger on this shift."

"Where can I find him?"

He moved back into the courtyard and looked around. "I saw him start taking a couple of tourists around just a few minutes ago. People are crazy; they'll come out in any kind of weather."

"Can you tell me which way he went?"

The ranger gestured to our right. "Along this side. When he's done down here, he'll take them up that iron stairway to the first tier, but I can't say how far he's gotten yet."

I thanked him and started off in the direction he'd indicated.

There were open doors in the cement wall between the sally port and the iron staircase. I glanced through the first and saw no one. The second led into a narrow dark hallway; when I was halfway down it, I saw that this was the fort's jail. One cell was set up as a display, complete with a mannequin prisoner; the other, beyond an archway that was not much taller than my own five-foot-six, was unrestored. Its waterstained walls were covered with graffiti, and a metal railing protected a two-foot-square iron grid on the floor in one corner. A sign said that it was a cistern with a forty-thousand-gallon capacity.

Well, I thought, that's interesting, but playing tourist isn't helping me catch up with Lee Gottschalk. Quickly I left the jail and hurried up the iron staircase the first ranger had indicated. At its top, I turned to my left and bumped into a chain link fence that blocked access to the area under renovation. Warning myself to watch where I was going, I went the other way, toward the east tier. The archways there were fenced off with similar chain link so no one could fall, and doors opened off the gallery into what I supposed had been the soldiers' living quarters. I pushed through the first one and stepped into a small museum.

The room was high-ceilinged, with tall, narrow windows in the outside wall. No ranger or tourists were in sight. I looked toward an interior door that led to the next room and saw a series of mirror images: one door within another leading off into the distance, each diminishing in size until the last seemed very tiny. I had the unpleasant sensation that if I walked along there, I would become progressively smaller and eventually disappear.

From somewhere down there came the sound of voices. I followed it, passing through more museum displays until I came to a room containing an old-fashioned bedstead and footlocker. A ranger, dressed the same as the man downstairs except that he was bearded and wore granny glasses, stood beyond the bedstead lecturing to a man and a woman who were bundled to their chins in bulky sweaters.

"You'll notice that the fireplaces are very small," he was saying, motioning to the one on the wall next to the bed, "and you can imagine how cold it could get for the soldiers garrisoned here. They didn't have a heated employees' lounge like we do." Smiling at his own little joke, he glanced at me. "Do you want to join the tour?"

I shook my head and stepped over by the footlocker. "Are you Lee Gottschalk?"

"Yes." He spoke the word a shade warily.

"I have a few questions I'd like to ask you. How long will the rest of the tour take?"

"At least half an hour. These folks want to see the unrestored rooms on the third floor."

I didn't want to wait around that long, so I said, "Could you take a couple of minutes and talk with me now?"

He moved his head so the light from the windows caught his granny glasses and I couldn't see the expression in his eyes, but his mouth tightened in a way that might have been annoyance. After a moment he said, "Well, the rest of the tour on this floor is pretty much self-guided." To the tourists, he added, "Why don't you go on ahead and I'll catch up after I talk with this lady."

They nodded agreeably and moved on into the next room. Lee Gottschalk folded his arms across his chest and leaned against the small fireplace. "Now what can I do for you?"

I introduced myself and showed him my license. His mouth twitched briefly in surprise, but he didn't comment. I said, "At about four yesterday afternoon, a young woman left her car at Vista Point with a suicide note in it. I'm trying to locate a witness who saw her jump." I took out the photograph I'd been showing to people and handed it to him. By now I had Vanessa DiCesare's features memorized: high forehead, straight nose, full lips, glossy wings of dark-brown hair curling inward at the jawbone. It was a strong face, not beautiful but striking—and a face I'd recognize anywhere.

Gottschalk studied the photo, then handed it back to me. "I read about her in the morning paper. Why are you trying to find a witness?"

"Her parents have hired me to look into it."

"The paper said her father is some big politician here in the city."

I didn't see any harm in discussing what had already appeared in print. "Yes, Ernest DiCesare—he's on the Board of Supes and likely to be our next mayor."

"And she was a law student, engaged to some hotshot lawyer who ran her father's last political campaign."

"Right again."

He shook his head, lips pushing out in bewilderment. "Sounds like she had a lot going for her. Why would she kill herself? Did that note taped inside her car explain it?"

I'd seen the note, but its contents were confidential. "No. Did you happen to see anything unusual yesterday afternoon?"

"No. But if I'd seen anyone jump, I'd have reported it to the Coast Guard station so they could try to recover the body before the current carried it out to sea."

"What about someone standing by the bridge railing, acting strangely, perhaps?"

"If I'd noticed anyone like that, I'd have reported it to the bridge offices so they could send out a suicide prevention team." He stared almost combatively at me, as if I'd accused him of some kind of wrongdoing, then seemed to relent a little. "Come outside," he said, "and I'll show you something."

We went through the door to the gallery, and he guided me to the chain link barrier in the archway and pointed up. "Look at the angle of the bridge, and the distance we are from it. You couldn't spot anyone standing at the rail from here, at least not well enough to tell if they were acting upset. And a jumper would have to hurl herself way out before she'd be noticeable."

"And there's nowhere else in the fort from where a jumper would be clearly visible?"

"Maybe from one of the watchtowers or the extreme west side. But they're off limits to the public, and we only give them one routine check at closing."

Satisfied now, I said, "Well, that about does it. I appreciate your taking the time."

He nodded and we started along the gallery. When we reached the other end, where an enclosed staircase spiraled up and down, I thanked him again and we parted company.

The way the facts looked to me now, Vanessa DiCesare had faked this suicide and just walked away—away from her wealthy old-line Italian family, from her up-and-coming liberal lawyer, from a life that either had become too much or just hadn't been enough. Vanessa was over twenty-one; she had a legal right to disappear if she wanted to. But her parents and her fiancé loved her, and they also had a right to know she was alive and well. If I could locate her and reassure them without ruining whatever new life she planned to create for herself, I would feel I'd performed the job I'd been hired to do. But right now I was weary, chilled to the bone, and out of leads. I decided to go back to All Souls and consider my next moves in warmth and comfort.

All Souls Legal Cooperative is housed in a ramshackle Victorian on one of the steeply sloping sidestreets of Bernal Heights, a working-class district in the southern part of the city. The co-op caters mainly to clients who live in the area: people with low to middle incomes who don't have much extra money for expensive lawyers. The sliding fee scale allows them to obtain quality legal assistance at reasonable prices—a concept that is probably outdated in the self-centered 1980s, but is kept alive by the people who staff All Souls. It's a place where the lawyers care about their clients, and a good place to work.

I left my MG at the curb and hurried up the front steps through the blowing fog. The warmth inside was almost a shock after the chilliness at Fort Point; I unbuttoned my jacket and went down the long deserted hallway to the big country kitchen at the rear. There I found my boss, Hank Zahn, stirring up a mug of the Navy grog he often concocts on cold November nights like this one.

He looked at me, pointed to the rum bottle, and said, "Shall I make you one?" When I nodded, he reached for another mug.

I went to the round oak table under the windows, moved a pile of newspapers from one of the chairs, and sat down. Hank added lemon juice, hot water, and sugar syrup to the rum; dusted it artistically with nutmeg; and set it in front of me with a flourish. I sampled it as he sat down across from me, then nodded my approval.

He said, "How's it going with the DiCesare investigation?"

Hank had a personal interest in the case; Vanessa's fiancé, Gary Stornetta, was a long-time friend of his, which was why I, rather than one of the large investigative firms her father normally favored, had been asked to look into it. I said, "Everything I've come up with points to it being a disappearance, not a suicide."

"Just as Gary and her parents suspected."

"Yes. I've covered the entire area around the bridge. There are absolutely no witnesses, except for the tour bus driver who saw her park her car at four and got suspicious when it was still there at seven and reported it. But even he didn't see her walk off toward the bridge." I drank some more grog, felt its warmth, and began to relax.

Behind his thick horn-rimmed glasses, Hank's eyes became concerned. "Did the DiCesares or Gary give you any idea why she would have done such a thing?"

"When I talked with Ernest and Sylvia this morning, they said Vanessa had changed her mind about marrying Gary. He's not admitting to that, but he doesn't speak of Vanessa the way a happy husband-to-be would. And it seems an unlikely match to me—he's close to twenty years older than she."

"More like fifteen," Hank said. "Gary's father was Ernest's best friend, and after Ron Stornetta died, Ernest more or less took him on as a protégé. Ernest was delighted that their families were finally going to be joined."

"Oh, he was delighted all right. He admitted to me that he'd practically arranged the marriage. 'Girl didn't know what was good for her,' he said. 'Needed a strong older man to guide her.' " I snorted.

Hank smiled faintly. He's a feminist, but over the years his sense of outrage has mellowed; mine still has a hair trigger.

"Anyway," I said, "when Vanessa first announced she was backing out of the engagement, Ernest told her he would cut off her funds for law school if she didn't go through with the wedding."

"Jesus, I had no idea he was capable of such . . . Neanderthal tactics."

"Well, he is. After that Vanessa went ahead and set the wedding date. But Sylvia said she suspected she wouldn't go through with it. Vanessa talked of quitting law school and moving out of their home. And she'd been seeing other men; she and her father had a bad quarrel about it just last week. Anyway, all of that, plus the fact that one of her suitcases and some clothing are missing, made them highly suspicious of the suicide."

Hank reached for my mug and went to get us more grog. I began thumbing through the copy of the morning paper that I'd moved off the chair, looking for the story on Vanessa. I found it on page three.

The daughter of Supervisor Ernest DiCesare apparently committed suicide by jumping from the Golden Gate Bridge late yesterday afternoon.

Vanessa DiCesare, 22, abandoned her 1985 Honda Civic at Vista Point at approximately four p.m., police said. There were no witnesses to her jump, and the body has not been recovered. The contents of a suicide note found in her car have not been disclosed.

Ms. DiCesare, a first-year student at Hastings College of Law, is the only child of the supervisor and his wife, Sylvia. She planned to be married next month to San Francisco attorney Gary R. Stornetta, a political associate of her father. . . .

Strange how routine it all sounded when reduced to journalistic language. And yet how mysterious—the "undisclosed contents" of the suicide note, for instance.

"You know," I said as Hank came back to the table and set
down the fresh mugs of grog, "that note is another factor that
makes me believe she staged this whole thing. It was so formal
and controlled. If they had samples of suicide notes in etiquette
books, I'd say she looked one up and copied it."

He ran his fingers through his wiry brown hair. "What I don't
understand is why she didn't just break off the engagement and
move out of the house. So what if her father cut off her money?
There are lots worse things than working your way through law
school."

"Oh, but this way she gets back at everyone, and has the
advantage of actually being alive to gloat over it. Imagine her
parents' and Gary's grief and guilt—it's the ultimate way of
getting even."

"She must be a very angry young woman."

"Yes. After I talked with Ernest and Sylvia and Gary, I spoke
briefly with Vanessa's best friend, a law student named Kathy
Graves. Kathy told me that Vanessa was furious with her father
for making her go through with the marriage. And she'd come
to hate Gary because she'd decided he was only marrying her
for her family's money and political power."

"Oh, come on. Gary's ambitious, sure. But you can't tell me
he doesn't genuinely care for Vanessa."

"I'm only giving you her side of the story."

"So now what do you plan to do?"

"Talk with Gary and the DiCesares again. See if I can't come
up with some bit of information that will help me find her."

"And then?"

"Then it's up to them to work it out."

The DiCesare home was mock-Tudor, brick and half-timber, set
on a corner knoll in the exclusive area of St. Francis Wood.
When I'd first come there that morning, I'd been slightly awed;
now the house had lost its power to impress me. After delving
into the lives of the family who lived there, I knew that it was
merely a pile of brick and mortar and wood that contained
more than the usual amount of misery.

The DiCesares and Gary Stornetta were waiting for me in the
living room, a strangely formal place with several groupings of
furniture and expensive-looking knickknacks laid out in precise

patterns on the tables. Vanessa's parents and fiancé—like the house—seemed diminished since my previous visit: Sylvia huddled in an armchair by the fireplace, her gray-blonde hair straggling from its elegant coiffure; Ernest stood behind her, haggard-faced, one hand protectively on her shoulder. Gary paced, smoking and clawing at his hair with his other hand. Occasionally he dropped ashes on the thick wall-to-wall carpeting, but no one called it to his attention.

They listened to what I had to report without interruption. When I finished, there was a long silence. Then Sylvia put a hand over her eyes and said, "How she must hate us to do a thing like this!"

Ernest tightened his grip on his wife's shoulder. His face was a conflict of anger, bewilderment, and sorrow.

There was no question of which emotion had hold of Gary; he smashed out his cigarette in an ashtray, lit another, and resumed pacing. But while his movements before had merely been nervous, now his tall, lean body was rigid with thinly controlled fury. "Damn her!" he said. "Damn her anyway!"

"Gary." There was a warning note in Ernest's voice.

Gary glanced at him, then at Sylvia. "Sorry."

I said, "The question now is, do you want me to continue looking for her?"

In shocked tones, Sylvia said, "Of course we do!" Then she tipped her head back and looked at her husband.

Ernest was silent, his fingers pressing hard against the black wool of her dress.

"Ernest?" Now Sylvia's voice held a note of panic.

"Of course we do," he said. But the words somehow lacked conviction.

I took out my notebook and pencil, glancing at Gary. He had stopped pacing and was watching the DiCesares. His craggy face was still mottled with anger, and I sensed he shared Ernest's uncertainty.

Opening the notebook, I said, "I need more details about Vanessa, what her life was like the past month or so. Perhaps something will occur to one of you that didn't this morning."

"Ms. McCone," Ernest said, "I don't think Sylvia's up to this right now. Why don't you and Gary talk, and then if there's anything else, I'll be glad to help you."

"Fine." Gary was the one I was primarily interested in questioning, anyway. I waited until Ernest and Sylvia had left the room, then turned to him.

When the door shut behind them, he hurled his cigarette into the empty fireplace. "Goddamn little bitch!" he said.

I said, "Why don't you sit down."

He looked at me for a few seconds, obviously wanting to keep on pacing, but then he flopped into the chair Sylvia had vacated. When I'd first met with Gary this morning, he'd been controlled and immaculately groomed, and he had seemed more solicitous of the DiCesares than concerned with his own feelings. Now his clothing was disheveled, his graying hair tousled, and he looked to be on the brink of a rage that would flatten anyone in its path.

Unfortunately, what I had to ask him would probably fan that rage. I braced myself and said, "Now tell me about Vanessa. And not all the stuff about her being a lovely young woman and a brilliant student. I heard all that this morning—but now we both know it isn't the whole truth, don't we?"

Surprisingly he reached for a cigarette and lit it slowly, using the time to calm himself. When he spoke, his voice was as level as my own. "All right, it's not the whole truth. Vanessa *is* lovely and brilliant. She'll make a top-notch lawyer. There's a hardness in her; she gets it from Ernest. It took guts to fake this suicide . . ."

"What do you think she hopes to gain from it?"

"Freedom. From me. From Ernest's domination. She's probably taken off somewhere for a good time. When she's ready she'll come back and make her demands."

"And what will they be?"

"Enough money to move into a place of her own and finish law school. And she'll get it, too. She's all her parents have."

"You don't think she's set out to make a new life for herself?"

"Hell, no. That would mean giving up all this." The sweep of his arm encompassed the house and all of the DiCesares's privileged world.

But there was one factor that made me doubt his assessment. I said, "What about the other men in her life?"

He tried to look surprised, but an angry muscle twitched in his jaw.

"Come on, Gary," I said, "you know there were other men. Even Ernest and Sylvia were aware of that."

"Ah, Christ!" He popped out of the chair and began pacing again. "All right, there were other men. It started a few months ago. I didn't understand it; things had been good with us; they still *were* good physically. But I thought, okay, she's young; this is only natural. So I decided to give her some rope, let her get it out of her system. She didn't throw it in my face, didn't embarrass me in front of my friends. Why shouldn't she have a last fling?"

"And then?"

"She began making noises about breaking off the engagement. And Ernest started that shit about not footing the bill for law school. Like a fool I went along with it, and she seemed to cave in from the pressure. But a few weeks later, it all started up again—only this time it was purposeful, cruel."

"In what way?"

"She'd know I was meeting political associates for lunch or dinner, and she'd show up at the restaurant with a date. Later she'd claim he was just a friend, but you couldn't prove it from the way they acted. We'd go to a party and she'd flirt with every man there. She got sly and secretive about where she'd been, what she'd been doing."

I had pictured Vanessa as a very angry young woman; now I realized she was not a particularly nice one, either.

Gary was saying, ". . . the last straw was on Halloween. We went to a costume party given by one of her friends from Hastings. I didn't want to go—costumes, a young crowd, not my kind of thing—and so she was angry with me to begin with. Anyway, she walked out with another man, some jerk in a soldier outfit. They were dancing . . ."

I sat up straighter. "Describe the costume."

"An old-fashioned soldier outfit. Wide-brimmed hat with a plume, frock coat, sword."

"What did the man look like?"

"Youngish. He had a full beard and wore granny glasses."

Lee Gottschalk.

The address I got from the phone directory for Lee Gottschalk was on California Street not far from Twenty-fifth Avenue and only a couple of miles from where I'd first met the ranger at Fort Point. When I arrived there and parked at the opposite curb, I didn't need to check the mailboxes to see which apartment was his; the corner windows on the second floor were ablaze with light, and inside I could see Gottschalk, sitting in an armchair in what appeared to be his living room. He seemed to be alone but expecting company, because frequently he looked up from the book he was reading and checked his watch.

In case the company was Vanessa DiCesare, I didn't want to

go barging in there. Gottschalk might find a way to warn her off, or simply not answer the door when she arrived. Besides, I didn't yet have a definite connection between the two of them; the "jerk in a soldier outfit" *could* have been someone else, someone in a rented costume that just happened to resemble the working uniform at the fort. But my suspicions were strong enough to keep me watching Gottschalk for well over an hour. The ranger *had* lied to me that afternoon.

The lies had been casual and convincing, except for two mistakes—such small mistakes that I hadn't caught them even when I'd read the newspaper account of Vanessa's purported suicide later. But now I recognized them for what they were: The paper had called Gary Stornetta a "political associate" of Vanessa's father, rather than his former campaign manager, as Lee had termed him. And while the paper mentioned the suicide note, it had not said it was *taped* inside the car. While Gottschalk conceivably could know about Gary managing Ernest's campaign for the Board of Supes from other newspaper accounts, there was no way he could have known how the note was secured— except from Vanessa herself.

Because of those mistakes, I continued watching Gottschalk, straining my eyes as the mist grew heavier, hoping Vanessa would show up or that he'd eventually lead me to her. The ranger appeared to be nervous: He got up a couple of times and turned on a TV, flipped through the channels, and turned it off again. For about ten minutes, he paced back and forth. Finally, around twelve-thirty, he checked his watch again, then got up and drew the draperies shut. The lights went out behind them.

I tensed, staring through the blowing mist at the door of the apartment building. Somehow Gottschalk hadn't looked like a man who was going to bed. And my impression was correct: In a few minutes he came through the door onto the sidewalk carrying a suitcase—pale leather like the one of Vanessa's Sylvia had described to me—and got into a dark-colored Mustang parked on his side of the street. The car started up and he made a U-turn, then went right on Twenty-fifth Avenue. I followed. After a few minutes, it became apparent that he was heading for Fort Point.

When Gottschalk turned into the road to the fort, I kept going until I could pull over on the shoulder. The brake lights of the Mustang flared, and then Gottschalk got out and unlocked the low iron bar that blocked the road from sunset to sunrise; after he'd driven through he closed it again, and the car's lights disappeared down the road.

Had Vanessa been hiding at drafty, cold Fort Point? It seemed a strange choice of place, since she could have used a motel or Gottschalk's apartment. But perhaps she'd been afraid someone would recognize her in a public place, or connect her with Gottschalk and come looking, as I had. And while the fort would be a miserable place to hide during the hours it was open to the public—she'd have had to keep to one of the off-limits areas, such as the west side—at night she could probably avail herself of the heated employees' lounge.

Now I could reconstruct most of the scenario of what had gone on: Vanessa meets Lee; they talk about his work; she decides he is the person to help her fake her suicide. Maybe there's a romantic entanglement, maybe not; but for whatever reason, he agrees to go along with the plan. She leaves her car at Vista Point, walks across the bridge, and later he drives over there and picks up the suitcase. . . .

But then why hadn't he delivered it to her at the fort? And to go after the suitcase after she'd abandoned the car was too much of a risk; he might have been seen, or the people at the fort might have noticed him leaving for too long a break. Also, if she'd walked across the bridge, surely at least one of the people I'd talked with would have seen her—the maintenance crew near the north tower, for instance.

There was no point in speculating on it now, I decided. The thing to do was to follow Gottschalk down there and confront Vanessa before she disappeared again. For a moment I debated taking my gun out of the glovebox, but then decided against it. I don't like to carry it unless I'm going into a dangerous situation, and neither Gottschalk nor Vanessa posed any particular threat to me. I was merely here to deliver a message from Vanessa's parents asking her to come home. If she didn't care to respond to it, that was not my business—or my problem.

I got out of my car and locked it, then hurried across the road and down the narrow lane to the gate, ducking under it and continuing along toward the ranger station. On either side of me were tall, thick groves of eucalyptus; I could smell their acrid fragrance and hear the fog-laden wind rustle their brittle leaves. Their shadows turned the lane into a black winding alley, and the only sound besides distant traffic noises was my tennis shoes slapping on the broken pavement. The ranger station was dark, but ahead I could see Gottschalk's car parked next to the fort.

The area was illuminated only by small security lights set at intervals on the walls of the structure. Above it the bridge arched, washed in fog-muted yellowish light; as I drew closer I became aware of the grumble and clank of traffic up there.

I ran across the parking area and checked Gottschalk's car. It was empty, but the suitcase rested on the passenger seat. I turned and started toward the sally port, noticing that its heavily studded door stood open a few inches. The low tunnel was completely dark. I felt my way along it toward the courtyard, one hand on its icy stone wall.

The doors to the courtyard also stood open. I peered through them into the gloom beyond. What light there was came from the bridge and more security beacons high up on the wooden watchtowers; I could barely make out the shapes of the construction equipment that stood near the west side. The clanking from the bridge was oppressive and eerie in the still night.

As I was about to step into the courtyard, there was a movement to my right. I drew back into the sally port as Lee Gottschalk came out of one of the ground-floor doorways. My first impulse was to confront him, but then I decided against it. He might shout, warn Vanessa, and she might escape before I could deliver her parents' message.

After a few seconds I looked out again, meaning to follow Gottschalk, but he was nowhere in sight. A faint shaft of light fell through the door from which he had emerged and rippled over the cobblestone floor. I went that way, through the door and along a narrow corridor to where an archway was illuminated. Then, realizing the archway led to the unrestored cell of the jail I'd seen earlier, I paused. Surely Vanessa wasn't hiding in there. . . .

I crept forward and looked through the arch. The light came from a heavy-duty flashlight that sat on the floor. It threw macabre shadows on the water-stained walls, showing their streaked paint and graffiti. My gaze followed its beams upward and then down, to where the grating of the cistern lay out of place on the floor beside the hole. Then I moved over to the railing, leaned across it, and trained the flashlight down into the well.

I saw, with a rush of shock and horror, the dark hair and once-handsome features of Vanessa DiCesare.

She had been hacked to death. Stabbed and slashed, as if in a frenzy. Her clothing was ripped; there were gashes on her face and hands; she was covered with dark smears of blood. Her eyes were open, staring with that horrible flatness of death.

I came back on my heels, clutching the railing for support. A wave of dizziness swept over me, followed by an icy coldness. I thought: He killed her. And then I pictured Gottschalk in his Union Army uniform, the saber hanging from his belt, and I knew what the weapon had been.

"God!" I said aloud.

Why had he murdered her? I had no way of knowing yet. But the answer to why he'd thrown her into the cistern, instead of just putting her into the bay, was clear: She was supposed to have committed suicide; and while bodies that fall from the Golden Gate Bridge sustain a great many injuries, slash and stab wounds aren't among them. Gottschalk could not count on the body being swept out to sea on the current; if she washed up somewhere along the coast, it would be obvious she had been murdered—and eventually an investigation might have led back to him. To him and his soldier's saber.

It also seemed clear that he'd come to the fort tonight to move the body. But why not last night, why leave her in the cistern all day? Probably he'd needed to plan, to secure keys to the gate and fort, to check the schedule of the night patrols for the best time to remove her. Whatever his reason, I realized now that I'd walked into a very dangerous situation. Walked right in without bringing my gun. I turned quickly to get out of there . . .

And came face-to-face with Lee Gottschalk.

His eyes were wide, his mouth drawn back in a snarl of surprise. In one hand he held a bundle of heavy canvas. "You!" he said. "What the hell are you doing here?"

I jerked back from him, bumped into the railing, and dropped the flashlight. It clattered on the floor and began rolling toward the mouth of the cistern. Gottschalk lunged toward me, and as I dodged, the light fell into the hole and the cell went dark. I managed to push past him and ran down the hallway to the courtyard.

Stumbling on the cobblestones, I ran blindly for the sally port. Its doors were shut now—he'd probably taken that precaution when he'd returned from getting the tarp to wrap her body in. I grabbed the iron hasp and tugged, but couldn't get it open. Gottschalk's footsteps were coming through the courtyard after me now. I let go of the hasp and ran again.

When I came to the enclosed staircase at the other end of the court, I started up. The steps were wide at the outside wall, narrow at the inside. My toes banged into the risers of the steps; a couple of times I teetered and almost fell backwards. At the first tier I paused, then kept going. Gottschalk had said something about unrestored rooms on the second tier; they'd be a better place to hide than in the museum.

Down below I could hear him climbing after me. The sound of his feet—clattering and stumbling—echoed in the close space. I could hear him grunt and mumble: low, ugly sounds that I knew were curses.

I had absolutely no doubt that if he caught me, he would kill me. Maybe do to me what he had done to Vanessa. . . .

I rounded the spiral once again and came out on the top floor gallery, my heart beating wildly, my breath coming in pants. To my left were archways, black outlines filled with dark-gray sky. To my right was blackness. I went that way, hands out, feeling my way.

My hands touched the rough wood of a door. I pushed, and it opened. As I passed through it, my shoulder bag caught on something; I yanked it loose and kept going. Beyond the door I heard Gottschalk curse loudly, the sound filled with surprise and pain; he must have fallen on the stairway. And that gave me a little more time.

The tug at my shoulder bag had reminded me of the small flashlight I keep there. Flattening myself against the wall next to the door, I rummaged through the bag and brought out the flash. Its beam showed high walls and arching ceilings, plaster and lath pulled away to expose dark brick. I saw cubicles and cubbyholes opening into dead ends, but to my right was an arch. I made a small involuntary sound of relief, then thought *Quiet!* Gottschalk's footsteps started up the stairway again as I moved through the archway.

The crumbling plaster walls beyond the archway were set at odd angles—an interlocking funhouse maze connected by small doors. I slipped through one and found an irregularly shaped room heaped with debris. There didn't seem to be an exit, so I ducked back into the first room and moved toward the outside wall, where gray outlines indicated small high-placed windows. I couldn't hear Gottschalk any more—couldn't hear anything but the roar and clank from the bridge directly overhead.

The front wall was brick and stone, and the windows had wide waist-high sills. I leaned across one, looked through the salt-caked glass, and saw the open sea. I was at the front of the fort, the part that faced beyond the Golden Gate; to my immediate right would be the unrestored portion. If I could slip over into that area, I might be able to hide until the other rangers came to work in the morning.

But Gottschalk could be anywhere. I couldn't hear his footsteps above the infernal noise from the bridge. He could be right here in the room with me, pinpointing me by the beam of my flashlight. . . .

Fighting down panic, I switched the light off and continued along the wall, my hands recoiling from its clammy stone surface. It was icy cold in the vast, echoing space, but my own flesh felt colder still. The air had a salt tang, underlaid by odors of rot and mildew. For a couple of minutes the darkness was unalleviated, but then I saw a lighter rectangular shape ahead of me.

When I reached it I found it was some sort of embrasure, about four feet tall, but only a little over a foot wide. Beyond it I could see the edge of the gallery where it curved and stopped at the chain link fence that barred entrance to the other side of the fort. The fence wasn't very high—only five feet or so. If I could get through this narrow opening, I could climb it and find refuge . . .

The sudden noise behind me was like a firecracker popping. I whirled, and saw a tall figure silhouetted against one of the seaward windows. He lurched forward, tripping over whatever he'd stepped on. Forcing back a cry, I hoisted myself up and began squeezing through the embrasure.

Its sides were rough brick. They scraped my flesh clear through my clothing. Behind me I heard the slap of Gottschalk's shoes on the wooden floor.

My hips wouldn't fit through the opening. I gasped, grunted, pulling with my arms on the outside wall. Then I turned on my side, sucking in my stomach. My bag caught again, and I let go of the wall long enough to rip its strap off my elbow. As my hips squeezed through the embrasure, I felt Gottschalk grab at my feet. I kicked out frantically, breaking his hold, and fell off the sill to the floor of the gallery.

Fighting for breath, I pushed off the floor, threw myself at the fence, and began climbing. The metal bit into my fingers, rattled and clashed with my weight. At the top, the leg of my jeans got hung up on the spiky wires. I tore it loose and jumped down the other side.

The door to the gallery burst open and Gottschalk came through it. I got up from a crouch and ran into the darkness ahead of me. The fence began to rattle as he started up it. I raced, half-stumbling, along the gallery, the open archways to my right. To my left was probably a warren of rooms similar to those on the east side. I could lose him in there . . .

Only I couldn't. The door I tried was locked. I ran to the next one and hurled my body against its wooden panels. It didn't give. I heard myself sob in fear and frustration.

Gottschalk was over the fence now, coming toward me, limping. His breath came in erratic gasps, loud enough to hear over the noise from the bridge. I twisted around, looking for shelter, and saw a pile of lumber lying across one of the open archways.

I dashed toward it and slipped behind, wedged between it and the pillar of the arch. The courtyard lay two dizzying stories below me. I grasped the end of the top two-by-four. It moved easily, as if on a fulcrum.

Gottschalk had seen me. He came on steadily, his right leg dragging behind him. When he reached the pile of lumber and started over it toward me, I yanked on the two-by-four. The other end moved and struck him on the knee.

He screamed and stumbled back. Then he came forward again, hands outstretched toward me. I pulled back further against the pillar. His clutching hands missed me, and when they did he lost his balance and toppled onto the pile of lumber. And then the boards began to slide toward the open archway.

He grabbed at the boards, yelling and flailing his arms. I tried to reach for him, but the lumber was moving like an avalanche now, pitching over the side and crashing down into the courtyard two stories below. It carried Gottschalk's thrashing body with it, and his screams echoed in its wake. For an awful few seconds the boards continued to crash down on him, and then everything was terribly still. Even the thrumming of the bridge traffic seemed muted.

I straightened slowly and looked down into the courtyard. Gottschalk lay unmoving among the scattered pieces of lumber. For a moment I breathed deeply to control my vertigo; then I ran back to the chain link fence, climbed it, and rushed down the spiral staircase to the courtyard.

When I got to the ranger's body, I could hear him moaning. I said, "Lie still. I'll call an ambulance."

He moaned louder as I ran across the courtyard and found a phone in the gift shop, but by the time I returned, he was silent. His breathing was so shallow that I thought he'd passed out, but then I heard mumbled words coming from his lips. I bent closer to listen.

"Vanessa," he said. "Wouldn't take me with her. . . ."

I said, "Take you where?"

"Going away together. Left my car . . . over there so she could drive across the bridge. But when she . . . brought it here she said she was going alone. . . ."

So you argued, I thought. And you lost your head and slashed her to death.

"Vanessa," he said again. "Never planned to take me . . . tricked me. . . ."

I started to put a hand on his arm, but found I couldn't touch him. "Don't talk any more. The ambulance'll be here soon."

"Vanessa," he said. "Oh God, what did you do to me?"

I looked up at the bridge, rust red through the darkness and the mist. In the distance, I could hear the wail of a siren.

Deceptions, I thought.

Deceptions. . . .

The Long Silence After

by Ed Gorman

First published in 1991.

The flight from Baltimore was bumpy. Not that Neely cared much. Not now.

At Hertz he asked for a city map. The counter woman, sweet in her chignon and early evening exhaustion, smiled sadly. As if she knew why he'd come here. She gave him the map and a brand new Buick that did not yet smell as if somebody had barfed in it and then covered up the stench with Air-Wick.

He had one more stop to make. The Fed-Ex office near O'Hare. A package waited there for him. He did not unwrap it until he got back to the car.

Inside the red white and blue wrapping, inside the well-lined box, he found what he'd sent himself here last night; a snub-nosed .38. From the adjacent small box he took the cartridges. He would never have gotten this stuff through airport security.

Finally now, he was ready.

He spent four hours driving. Street names meant nothing. Sometimes faces were white, sometimes black. He wanted a certain section. Three times he stopped at gas stations and described the area. How there was this drugstore on one corner and a Triple-XXX theater directly across the street and (cheap irony here) a big stone Catholic church a couple blocks down.

Finally, one guy said, Oh, yeah, and told him where he'd find it in relationship to Rogers Park (which was where he was now).

* * *

Around nine, just before he saw the drugstore and the XXX-theater, it started raining. Cold March rain. Beading on the windshield, giving all the neon the look of watercolors.

He found a parking garage. A black guy who had a big chaw of chewing tobacco kept spitting all the time he was taking the keys. And kind of glaring. Fucking suburban white dudes. Motherfuckers anyway.

In the front of the XXX-theater was a small shop where you could rent videos and buy various "appliances" (as they are called). He was never comfortable in such places. Probably his strict Lutheran upbringing. These are places of sin.

The man behind the counter had bad teeth and a wandering left eye. Somehow that was fitting in a place like this.

He described the woman he was looking for but the counter-man immediately shook his head. "Don't know her, pal."

He described the woman a little more but the man shook his head again. "Sorry," he said exhaling Pall Mall smoke through the brown stubs of his teeth.

He didn't expect to get lucky right off, and he sure didn't. He started at the west end of the street and worked down it: three bars, a massage parlor, a used clothing store, a tiny soup kitchen run by two old nuns, and a bar with a runway for strippers.

And nothing.

Sorry, my friend. Sorry, buddy. Sorry, Jack.

Never seen/heard of her. You know, pal?

And so then he started on the women themselves.

Because of the rain, which was steady and cold, they stood in doorways instead of along the curbsides. The thirty-four degree temperature kept them from any cute stuff. No whistling down drivers. No shaking their asses. No jumping into the streets.

Just huddling in doorways instead. And kind of shivering.

And it was the same with them: no help.

He'd describe her and they'd shrug or shake their heads or pretend they were thinking a long moment and go "Nope, 'fraid not, friend."

Only one of them got smart-mouth. She said, "She musta been somethin' really special, huh?" and all the time was rubbing her knuckles against his crotch.

Inside his nice respectable topcoat, the .38 was burning a fucking hole.

* * *

Around midnight he stopped in this small diner for coffee and a sandwich. He was tired, he already had sniffles from the cold steady rain, and he had a headache, too. He bought his food and a little aluminum deal of Bufferin and took them right down.

And then he asked the counter guy—having no hopes really, just asking the guy kind of automatically—and the guy looked at him and said, "Yeah. Betty."

"Yes. That's right. Her name was Betty."

Through the fog of four years, through the fog of a liquored-up night: yes, goddamit that's right, Betty was her name. Betty.

He asked, "Is she still around?"

The counter man, long hairy tattooed arms, leaned forward and gave him a kind of queer look. "Oh, yeah, she's still around."

The counter man sounded as if he expected the man to know what he was hinting at.

"You know where I can find her?"

The counter man shook his head. "I don't know if that'd be right, mister."

"How come?"

He shrugged. "Well, she's sort of a friend of mine."

"I see."

And from inside his respectable suburban topcoat, he took his long leather wallet and peeled off a twenty and laid it on the counter and felt like fucking Sam Spade. "I'd really like to talk to her tonight."

The counter man stared at the twenty. He licked dry lips with an obscene pink tongue. "I see what you mean."

"How about it?"

"She really is kind of a friend of mine."

So Sam Spade went back into action. He laid another crisp twenty on the original crisp twenty.

The tongue came out again. This time he couldn't watch the counter man. He pretended to be real interested in the coffee inside his cheap chipped cup.

So of course the counter man gave him her address and told him how to get there.

Fog. Rain. The sound of his footsteps. You could smell the rotting lumber of this ancient neighborhood now that it was soaked. Little shabby houses packed so close together you couldn't ride a bicycle between some of them. One-story brick jobs mostly that used to be packed with Slavs. But the Slavs have good factory jobs now so they had moved out and eager scared blacks had taken their place.

Hers was lime green stucco. Behind a heavy drape a faint light shone.

He gripped the gun.

On the sidewalk he stepped in two piles of dogshit. And now the next-door dog—as if to confirm his own existence—started barking.

He went up the narrow walk to her place.

He stood under the overhang. The concrete porch had long ago pulled away from the house and was wobbly. He felt as if he were trying to stand up on a capsizing row boat.

The door opened. A woman stood there. "Yes?"

His memory of her was that she'd been much heavier. Much.

He said, "Betty?"

"Right."

"Betty Malloy?"

"Right again." She sounded tired, even weak. "But not the old Betty Malloy."

"Beg pardon?"

"I ain't what I used to be."

Cryptic as her words were, he thought that they still made sense.

"I'd like to come in."

"Listen, I don't do that no more, all right?"

"I'd like to come in anyway."

"Why?"

He sighed. If he pulled the gun here, she might get the chance to slam the door and save herself.

He had to get inside.

He put his hand on the knob of the screen door.

It was latched.

Sonofabitch.

"I need to use your phone," he said.

"Who are you?"

In some naive way, he'd expected her to remember who he was. But of course she wouldn't.

"Could I use your phone?"

"For what?"

"To call Triple-A."

"Something's wrong with your car?"

"The battery went dead."

"Where's your car?"

"What?"

"I asked where your car was. I don't see no new car. And you definitely look like the kind of guy who'd be driving a new car."

So he decided screw it and pulled the gun.

He put it right up against the screen door.

She didn't cry out or slam the door or anything. She just stood there. The gun had mesmerized her.

"You gotta be crazy, mister."

"Unlatch the door."

And then he couldn't hit her anymore.

He heard in her tears the inevitable tears of his wife and children when they found out.

And he couldn't hit her at all any more.

She just sat there and sobbed, her whole body trembling, weaker with each moment.

He said, "I'm sorry."

She just kept crying.

He started pacing again.

"I can't believe this. I keep thinking that there's no way I could—"

He shook his head and looked over at her. She was daubing at her nose with an aqua piece of Kleenex.

"Do you get help?"

She nodded. She wouldn't look at him anymore. "The welfare folks. They send out people."

"I'm sorry I was so angry."

"I know."

"And I'm sorry I hit you."

"I know that too."

"I'm just so fucking scared and so fucking angry."

Now she looked at him again. "The anger goes after awhile. You get too tired to be angry anymore."

"I don't know how I'm going to tell my wife."

"You'll do it, mister. That's the only thing I figured out about this thing. You do what you've got to do. You really do."

He dumped the gun in the pocket of his respectable topcoat. And then he took out his wallet and flicked off a hundred dollars in twenties.

"You really must be crazy, mister," she said. "Leavin' me money like that."

"Yes," he said. "I really must be crazy."

She started crying again.

He closed the doors quietly behind him. Even halfway down the walk, even in the fog and even in the rain, he could still hear her crying.

There was a three o'clock flight to Baltimore. He wasn't sure he had nerve enough to tell her yet but he knew he would have to. He owed her so much; he certainly owed her the truth.

He walked faster now, and soon he disappeared completely inside the fog. He was just footsteps now; footsteps.

The Dead Past

by Nancy Pickard

Nancy Pickard's rise to the first rank of mystery writers has been relatively swift. While her books show a certain comedic fondness for small-town America, they're very serious, sometimes very dark, inquiries into the human condition of our particular era; a fact that the major critics are only now coming to understand.

First published in 1989.

At first, she was only a new name in the appointment book of the psychologist, Paul Laner, Ph.D.:
"March 3, Tues., 12:10 Ouvray, Elizabeth."

Then she was a lovely girl in the doorway of his office, young and slim, pale as a ghost, wearing grey trousers and sweater, and her platinum hair caught up at the sides of her scalp with translucent plastic barettes. Her beauty, Laner thought at the time, was the stunning natural kind that is formidable to look upon, and which instantly forms a wall that other people have to scale in order to reach the person behind it. According to the form she had filled out for his receptionist, Elizabeth Ouvray was nineteen years old. Laner, at forty-five, was old enough to be her father, and he felt at least that much more mature than she as he stared at the nervous, ghost-like girl in his doorway.

Indeed, like a ghost who was afraid to materialize, she hesitated, her head down, eyes averted. She looked to him as if she wished she were invisible. Her hair, parted in the middle, hung down from the barettes like curtains pulled over her face.

"Come in," he said.

She glanced up at him, and smiled stiffly, slightly, as if any facial expression was an effort. Instinctively, Laner wanted to put his hand under her elbow and lead her gently into his office, but he didn't. The doctor was careful not to touch her, not only because Elizabeth Ouvray looked as if she would flee at the slightest overture, but also because the hand of a male counselor on a female client could be so easily misinterpreted. A comforting pat on the shoulder, a gently intended squeeze of the hand could get even a well-respected psychologist like him into serious trouble.

She scooted past him without speaking, leaving in her wake a lemony scent that made his jaws ache. Saliva pooled on his tongue, and he swallowed. She was, easily, the best looking patient to walk through his doorway in his twenty-three years of professional counseling. He thought it poignant that a woman so blessed in her physical appearance should appear to feel so cursed. Following that thought, Laner experienced such an immediate and intense desire to find out *why* she felt cursed that he experienced a mild sexual arousal.

"Down boy," he commanded his libido. "Sublimate."

Behind her back, he smiled to himself. It pleased him that after all this time in his career he could still get excited about the human mysteries that awaited his unraveling.

"Sit anywhere you like," he suggested to her.

He observed her as she made the difficult and meaningful choice that faced every new client: whether to sit on the couch in the corner farthest away from him, or the Windsor chair midway between the couch and his desk, or in the rocking chair beside his desk. She finally chose the latter—not, he thought, because she was self-confident enough to sit that close to him or because she craved intimacy, or even because she had a bad back. Rather, he suspected, it was because she felt safer there than she would have felt all the way across the room by herself. The doctor couldn't help but make an instantaneous diagnosis in layman's terms: *fear*—stark, staring, trembling, not-quite-raving fear. This clearly neurotic young woman was afraid of her own shadow.

Laner smiled inwardly at his own Jungian pun.

He felt a warm surge of hope for this new patient and an even warmer surge of self confidence. Eagerly, almost buoyantly, he crossed the room and sat down at his desk, facing her. Sensing that small talk would not relax this patient who had yet to utter a word to him, he launched right in.

"How can I help you, Elizabeth?"

She didn't hesitate, but said in a soft voice, "I'm afraid."

Laner was surprised at her directness. But taking that as a

cue, he proceeded to be extremely direct and clear with her, himself.

"What are you afraid of, Elizabeth?"

"*Everything.*" She didn't smile when she said it.

"All right. Tell me one thing that frightens you."

"Coming here."

"Yes, everybody's nervous the first time."

Laner purposely cultivated a fatherly appearance in order to put his clients at ease. He knew that when she looked at him she perceived a nice, middle-aged man with frizzly grey hair, a bushy moustache and beard, bright, intense blue eyes and a tactful, sympathetic smile.

He presented that smile to her. "What else?"

"I'm not *just* nervous," she protested, as if he had belittled her complaint. Her near-whisper had a defensive, annoyed edge to it. *What was this?* he wondered. Was she proud of her neurosis (many patients secretly were) or did she already have resources of courage and independence with which to defend herself? That would be a hopeful sign for her prognosis, he thought.

"I believe you," he said quickly. "What else scares you, Elizabeth?"

"People," she said, and he was inwardly amused to see her look suspiciously, even furtively at him. "Strangers."

"I see. What else scares you?"

"Oh God, you name it!" she burst out. "I think I'm really crazy. I must be crazy to be so frightened all the time."

"Nobody is afraid for no reason, Elizabeth," he told her. "My experience tells me that we will discover that your fears are the natural, if perhaps rather exaggerated, effects of certain causes. Our job will be to uncover those causes, so that we may eliminate the effects of them. You understand what I'm saying?"

"Yes, but it sounds too . . . easy."

"Would it make you feel better if I assure you that it probably won't be easy?" He smiled at her. "We often find that the greater the fear, the more deeply buried the cause. I will help you, Elizabeth, but I can almost guarantee that it will not be in one easy lesson."

"You'll help me?"

"I will," he said firmly, and was delighted to see the relieved expression in her eyes, and the slight relaxation of her tense body. "Tell me, Elizabeth, do you feel scared all of the time?"

"Yes! Every minute. All the time."

"Right now?"

"Yes!"

"How does that affect your life?"

There was anguish in her eyes. "It ruins it."

"How does it ruin it?"

"I don't want to be around anybody. I don't want to go out, I don't want to go anyplace. I don't date. I've never had many friends. I was in college, but I quit, and now I just get up in the morning, I go to work, I go home, and I stay at home until it's time to go to work in the morning."

"Not much of a life," Laner commented, gently.

She began to cry. "No, it's not much of a life."

He encouraged her to weep the sadness out. In truth, at that point, he foresaw a long and difficult therapy, but he was not for a minute afraid of failing her.

First, the psychologist attempted conventional therapy, fully expecting it to work.

He began by administering psychological tests, which served to confirm his original hypothesis that Elizabeth was deeply neurotic due to abnormally deep-seated fears of undetermined origin. Or, as he commented privately to his wife, "The poor girl's scared shitless."

Twice weekly, he asked probing questions and Elizabeth reacted, sometimes calmly, sometimes decidedly not. But none of them was the *right* question; none of her answers was *the* answer. Sometimes Laner felt she was telling him the truth; other times, not.

"Tell me about your mother, Elizabeth," he said.

"She raised me by herself."

"Where was your father?"

"Pretending I didn't exist."

"Tell me how you felt about school, Elizabeth," he suggested. ". . . about God, Elizabeth . . . about men . . . tell me about your dreams, Elizabeth . . . your daydreams, your fantasies. Tell me, Elizabeth . . ."

Over time, it became clear that she was not getting better. Instead, to his dismay, she grew progressively worse. Her appearance disintegrated. Laner grieved at the loss of her remarkable beauty, at her frightening weight loss, at the acne that ruined her beautiful skin, at her humped, defensive posture, and the sad, grey cast to her eyes.

"I've quit my job," she announced one day.

She lost her insurance, and couldn't pay his fee.

Laner adjusted his sliding scale to compensate, until finally he was treating her for free, something he had always sworn he would never do for clients because it would increase their dependency on him and destroy one of their main motivations to change.

"You're taking this case awfully hard," his wife finally said. What she really meant, he knew, was that he was taking it too personally. "Watch it, Paul," his colleagues warned, "you're becoming obsessed by this case." Their comments infuriated him, although he couldn't deny them. But he couldn't quite believe them, either.

It was not conceivable that Dr. Paul Laner could so miserably and completely fail to help one of his patients. No one, he thought, would be able to comprehend it, least of all him. "I'm a *good* psychologist," he kept telling himself; in fact, the peer recognition he had achieved over a long career suggested that many considered him to be a great one. But the doctor began to sleep less well, and to be aware of vague, unpleasant stirrings in his chest and abdomen. He did not need a psychiatrist to diagnose: anxiety.

He was not yet ready to call it fear.

But that's what he was: afraid, terrified that Elizabeth Ouvray was dying before his eyes, a little more every week, incrementally every session. He could not even be sure that his "treatment," his reknowned methods of analysis, were helping to keep her alive. It was even possible that he was—mistakenly, unintentionally, horribly—speeding the painful process of her death.

At the beginning of the final month of his treatment of Elizabeth Ouvray, Dr. Paul Laner tried hypnosis for the first time. It was not a mode of treatment he particularly condoned, believing as he did in the more conventional forms of therapy. Indeed, he had to cram a quick refresher course on hypnosis with a younger, more holistically-inclined psychologist of his acquaintance.

"Let your scalp relax," he began the first time, using his deepest, most soothing and mellifluous voice, and feeling faintly ridiculous even saying the words. Elizabeth lay on her back on the couch in the corner of his office, her skeletal hands folded over her stomach, her eyes closed.

He was seated beside her right shoulder.

"Allow even your hair to relax . . . relax your forehead, feel your forehead grow smooth, smooth . . . relax your eyebrows, eyelids, let your eyes fall back in your head, feel your eyes relax, feel them relax . . . relax your cheekbones . . . your lips, relax your tongue, let your jaw relax . . . relax the back of your neck, and now your throat . . . feel how relaxed your whole head is, your whole neck and throat . . . now let that feeling of complete relaxation slide down into your shoulders . . ."

When Elizabeth was visibly relaxed and breathing easily, he led her through a series of non-threatening questions and answers. Then he said, "Let's go further back now, Elizabeth, to a time when you were just a little girl. Now, while you are absolutely safe and secure in the present, I will ask you to go back to a time in your childhood when you were afraid. Remember, Elizabeth, that whatever it was that frightened you then, cannot hurt you now. The past is over. It is safe for you to remember what frightened you. When I count to three, you will remember something that frightened you when you were a little girl. One, two, three . . ."

"I'm in my bedroom," she said immediately.

Laner stared, surprised. This had the sound of something new, something previously uncovered.

"How old are you in this bedroom?"

"I don't know. Young. I'm really young."

"Look around the room, Elizabeth. What do you see?"

"Oh!" Suddenly, her voice was like a child's. "It's our first little apartment! I'm two."

Good grief, Laner thought, can this be true?

"Are you two years old?"

"Yes."

"Is it night time?"

"Yes."

"Your mother has put you to bed?"

"Yes."

"Are you alone in the bed?"

"No."

"No, Elizabeth?"

"Tubby."

"Your teddy bear is with you."

"Yes."

"And you feel . . . how do you feel?"

"Scared! I'm awake. I don't know why I'm awake. It's dark! Where's Mommy? Mommy? There's a noise! Mommy!"

Laner's own heart was beating rapidly, but he leaned forward to calm her.

"You are safe from the noise, Elizabeth, it cannot hurt you, I will not let it hurt you. Are you calling out for your mother?"

"Yes. No! I thought I was! But I'm not, I'm too scared, oh, what is that, who is that? *Mommy!*"

The last word burst from Elizabeth's throat as if it had broken loose from paralyzed vocal chords. She remained lying on the couch, but her head and shoulders strained upward, her eyes bulged beneath their lids, and she breathed in ragged gasps.

"It cannot hurt you, Elizabeth," Laner said, hoping he did not sound as unnerved as he felt. "Tell me what you see, tell me what it is that frightens you so."

"A face!" Elizabeth began sobbing, quick, keening sobs that sounded like a frightened child's. She was trembling all over, and his own hands were shaking. "He's got a flashlight. He's got curly hair. He's got a mean face, oh, it's the meanest face I ever saw! He's looking down at me, he's angry at me, he's going to hurt me!"

"Does he hurt you, Elizabeth?"

"Oh!" Her sobs caught in her throat, as if she were startled. "He's gone! Mommy's here and she's holding me . . . a burglar," she said next, in a wondering voice. "I can hear Mommy saying that. Shhh, Mommy says to me, it's all right, baby girl, it was just a dream, it was only a bad dream, that's all it was, forget all about it now, go back to sleep, it didn't happen, it never happened, it was only a bad dream . . ."

Soon after that, Laner brought Elizabeth up out of the hypnotic trance. She remembered nothing of what had transpired, so he told her.

"A *burglar?*" She was still as wide-eyed as a child. "That's where my nightmares came from? But my mother only meant to protect me."

"I'm sure that's true, Elizabeth."

"She told me it was only a dream . . ."

"And it became a recurring nightmare."

"Is that why I'm frightened of strangers, too?"

"What do you think, Elizabeth?"

She smiled tentatively. "I think maybe it is."

He thought maybe it was, too. In fact, he was positive of it. And he felt sure that now that Elizabeth had at last delved far enough into her subconscious to uncover the source of her fears, she would begin to recover.

But she did not.

She began to report horrifying nightmares.

At their next session, she reported a continued terror of strangers, along with her many other fears. Indeed, she looked as if she had slept even less that week than before. She reported that the headaches and muscle cramps that Laner suspected were a consequence of malnutrition had increased in frequency and intensity. He had been on the verge of hospitalizing her before; now he felt he surely must. But what an admission of failure on his part that would be! Still, how much worse it would be if she died when simple medical procedures like an IV might keep her alive.

The psychologist's own sleep was not much better than hers.

"She looks awful," he thought, "and what am I going to do now?"

He decided to hypnotize her again.

"All right," she said, dully.

Again, he relaxed her, although it took a long time, as he was anything but relaxed himself. Again, he led her through safe and easy memories, then back through the traumatic memory of the burglar, and then . . .

"Go further back now, Elizabeth, back as far as you can go to the first, the very first frightening thing that ever happened to you . . ."

"Please, I won't tell anyone!" she cried.

"What?" Laner was confused at the sudden and dramatic change in her voice and tone. "Where are you?"

"In my bedroom. Oh my God, please don't do that. I swear to you that I never told anyone, I won't tell anyone, I swear it."

"Elizabeth, how old are you?"

"Twenty-two."

What? Laner thought—twenty-two? But she was only nineteen in the present, in the here and now. What was going on?

"Where are you?" he asked again, trying to orient himself as much as to orient her.

"I'm sitting here on the edge of my bed, and I'm begging him, begging him . . ."

She began to sob convulsively.

"Begging him to do what, Elizabeth?"

"Begging him not to kill me. I won't tell anyone. I swear I won't. Please, please . . ."

She screamed, and Laner jumped back in his chair.

"Elizabeth," he said slowly, "who are you?"

"Susan Naylor," she whispered, "I am dying . . ."

Oh my God, he thought, my God, my God, what is this, what is this that is happening here?

This time when he brought her out of hypnosis, he did not tell her what she had said and done. He could hardly credit it himself. How could a 19-year-old patient suddenly "become" a different, even an older woman entirely? Could this possibly be an example of past-life regression such as he had read about (and disbelieved) in some medical journals? Could it be a form of ESP? If he wrote it up as such, he'd be laughed out of his practice. The psychologist sent her home, canceled all of his appointments for the rest of that day and secreted himself in a secluded recess of the medical library at a nearby hospital. For the rest of that afternoon, he read every case study he could locate that even slightly resembled the strange events that had transpired in his office.

He found no reassuring answers.

Near dinnertime, he called his wife.

"I'll be late," he told her. "I have to see a patient."

Elizabeth Ouvray lived in the second-floor rear apartment of a brick fourplex in a shabby neighborhood. It was twilight and getting cool outside by the time he rang her doorbell.

"Dr. Laner?" she said, when she saw him.

She was pale, exhausted-looking, shaking, and so was he.

"May I please come in, Elizabeth?"

"I'm . . ." She looked as if she were trying to come up with some good reason to turn him away. He suspected he was the first person to enter her apartment in a very long time. "I . . . all right . . . yes."

The doctor followed her into her living room, which was starkly decorated with furniture so nondescript it could have been rented. He sat down in the middle of her couch, but Elizabeth remained standing, propping herself against a wall as if it alone gave her the strength to remain upright.

"Elizabeth, today . . ."

"I don't want to know!"

"You're aware then, that something happened . . . something unusual . . . during hypnosis?"

"I think so . . . yes."

"Elizabeth, who is . . . was . . . Susan Naylor?"

The doctor held his breath, hoping she'd come up with some explanation, some conscious recognition of the name that would explain how a 22-year-old dead woman's memories got into Elizabeth Ouvray's brain.

She looked blank. "Who?"

He felt like crying. It wasn't only her life that was at stake here. His reputation, his 23-year counseling career, was about to go down the tubes because this insane young woman had memories she had no logical reason for having!

"I'm sorry," she whispered.

Laner was appalled to realize he had actually spoken his thoughts aloud to her. He felt desperate enough to suggest, "I want to hypnotize you again, Elizabeth."

"Right here, Dr. Laner? You mean now?"

"Please," he said softly, gently. "Please."

She said she'd be most comfortable seated at the table in the kitchen, and so she led him there. She faced the chrome door of the refrigerator as he attempted one more time to relax her into a deep trance state. The contorted reflection he saw over her shoulders was of an old man who looked as if he had just been told that his favorite grandchild had been run over on her tricycle. The haggard woman reflected in the chrome bore little resemblance to the blonde beauty who'd walked through his office door at a time that now seemed so long ago.

When she appeared to be deep in trance, he made the hypnotic suggestion: "You are now Susan Naylor," and then he stood back to see what might happen next.

It was instantaneous.

"No!" she screamed, loud enough for the neighbors to hear. *"Please, no! Get away from me! Don't hurt me, I won't tell anyone! Please, don't hurt me, don't hurt me!"* She lurched to her feet, knocking the stool over, still screaming, *"No, no, no!"* When she turned toward the doctor, she was holding a butcher knife. *"Please don't kill me!"* she screamed—over and over, as she stabbed him in his throat.

When the police arrived at the urgent summons of several of the neighbors, they found Elizabeth, weeping and bloody, still holding the knife with which she had killed Dr. Paul Laner. Her blouse was torn, revealing her ripped bra, and the zipper of her jeans was broken so that she had to hold it together with one hand.

"Tell us what happened," a detective, a woman, urged her. "Your neighbors reported hearing your scream for help."

"He was my psychologist," Elizabeth whispered. "I trusted him. And he came here tonight, and he tried to rape me. I'm so afraid all the time, of everything, that's what he was treating me for, he knew how horribly afraid I am of men, and when he attacked me, I . . . I . . . killed him."

On the way to the hospital, she whispered to the police-woman, "Somebody told me that Dr. Laner got into trouble years ago with another female patient, but he was so good to me that I didn't believe it. Do you think it could be true?"

"It's true," the policewoman called her at the hospital to say. "At least I think it's true, although it was only a rumor at the time. It makes sense though, considering how obsessed even his wife and his colleagues admit that he was about you. What I've learned is that when he was just starting out, twenty-three years ago, there were rumors that he had an affair with a patient, supposedly as a part of her treatment, and that she had a child by him. Lousy bastard, abusing his power like that. They said she was blonde, like you, only 22 years old, and very beautiful."

"I'd like to hear her name," Elizabeth whispered.

"Naylor, Susan Naylor," the policewoman said, and then, be-cause she heard Elizabeth moan, she added sharply, "What's the matter?"

"Nothing."

"There was a rumor that she was going to file a paternity suit," the policewoman continued, "but before that could hap-pen she was murdered. Susan Naylor was stabbed one night by someone who broke into her apartment."

"Oh God," Elizabeth breathed. "They didn't catch him."

"Nope. They interrogated Laner, because of the rumors. But their only witness was the baby, Susan Naylor's two-year-old little girl. And the only word they got out of her was 'burglar.' Poor little thing. After her mother's murder, she was taken by her grandparents. Do you think Laner was her father? I'll bet you the bastard was, and I'll bet you he killed her mother to keep his precious reputation intact." The cop laughed. "At least, that's my wild theory, what do you think of it?"

"I think you're right," Elizabeth whispered.

"Well, you get to feeling better, okay?"

"I will now."

"What?"

"Bye."

"Bye."

The policewoman's hand lingered on the receiver after she hung up the phone. On her desk lay the old homicide file from which she'd been quoting to Elizabeth.

Elizabeth.

The child's name was Elizabeth.

"I think you're right," the policewoman whispered to herself. When no one was looking, she slid a few pages out of the file and slipped them into her morning newspaper, which she folded in half and dropped into her wastebasket.

All the Same

by Bill Pronzini

Bill Pronzini's "Nameless" detective grows in popularity and critical stature every year. The reason is simple. Pronzini has set for himself the difficult task of writing a man's autobiography in installments, disguised as private-eye novels. Pronzini is not Nameless but certainly there are many similarities—middle-aged, blue collar, decent, intelligent, grumpy and very, very funny. Dell will soon reissue all of them. Keep checking your newsstand.

First published in 1972.

J effords lay on the bed, smoking and thinking about Penny. Outside the open window, the night was choked with heat. The air smelled of mesquite; there was no moon. He listened to the night sounds. An animal screamed somewhere in the desert, and in the motel courtyard, a car engine idled roughly. Voices rose from the room next door, shrill, plaintive.

The cigarette was raw in Jeffords' throat. He stubbed it out in the glass ashtray resting on his bare chest. He wore only a pair of shorts, and sweat coated his skin, glistening in the darkness. The sheets were wet beneath him.

"You fool!" somebody said clearly in the next room, and then it was silent again.

Jeffords reached across to the night stand for another cigarette; the pack was empty. He tried to remember if there was a machine in the motel office. Potted plant and wrought iron furniture and a long, flat Formica counter; rack with magazines . . . Was there a damned machine in that office?

His temples had begun to throb. Jeffords swung his legs off the bed and sat with his head in his hands. After a time he got to his feet, located a towel under his clothes on the chair, and wiped his chest dry. Then he put on his trousers and a soiled white shirt, not buttoning the shirt, and opened the door and stepped outside.

The motel was set in the shape of a horseshoe, with the open end facing out toward the highway. The office was the first one on the right as you came in. His room was at the closed end of the horseshoe.

Jeffords stood there breathing the thick air through his mouth. There was a white stone patio in the center of the courtyard, with an oval-shaped swimming pool, a strobe light mounted behind it, at one end. The light flashed red and blue and green, and the glare hurt Jeffords' eyes after the darkness of the room.

The drive that circled the patio was graveled; his steps crunched loudly in the stillness as he walked toward the office. A small white light burned over the door. As he approached, Jeffords could see a sleek white sports car parked in the driveway beside the office; its engine was idling, and Jeffords thought that it must be the one he had heard from his room. Someone was behind the wheel, a black, still shadow.

Jeffords passed the car and came up to the office. Just as he did, the door opened and a girl came out. He stopped. She was blonde, with her hair pulled into a ponytail at the back, fastened with a wide blue band. She wore a pair of white shorts and a yellow bolero-type shirt with little bobbing tassels on the bottom.

She cocked her head to one side, holding the office door open with one hand, looking at him. A quizzical smile played at the corners of her mouth. Jeffords wanted to say something to her, but he could not think of anything. He wet his lips and nodded meaninglessly. She was still holding the door; he reached out and took it, and she gave him a wide smile and then went to where the car stood idling.

Jeffords watched her get inside. The black shadow at the wheel let out the clutch. The rear tires spun, spewing gravel. The car went to the closed end of the horseshoe and stopped before a room two away from Jeffords'. He realized he was still holding the door open. He turned and went inside.

The fat woman in the shapeless sundress who had given him the room that afternoon was still behind the counter. She was looking at Jeffords as he came in. "Yeah?" she said.

"Do you have a cigarette machine?" he asked.

"Right there against the wall."

Jeffords turned and saw the machine. He went to it, seeing himself in the mirrored front. His black hair was tangled and damp and beard stubble flecked his gaunt cheeks. His deep-set eyes were rimmed in red. He fished in his pocket for change; all he had was a quarter. He took out his wallet and went to the counter again.

"Change for a dollar?"

"No change," the woman said.

"What do you mean, no change?"

"Just that. Safe's locked for the night."

"Then open it," Jeffords said irritably. "I want to get some cigarettes."

"Can't."

"Well, why the hell not?"

"Watch your mouth, sonny."

"Listen," Jeffords said, "how can you run a damned business? Suppose somebody comes in for a room?"

"I said to watch your mouth," the woman told him. She had little pig eyes, and they were staring a hole through Jeffords.

"You fat old biddy," he said.

The woman's face grew bright red. She stood up, pointed a finger; fat jiggled on her bare arm like gelatin. "I'll have you thrown out, you bum!" she shouted. "You get out of here or I'll have my husband throw you out!"

Jeffords stared at her. "You're all the same," he said. "Every one of you."

"What? What?"

He turned and went outside and slammed the door.

Back in his room, he lay once more on the bed. Immediately, he began to think about Penny—his wife Penny. Damn her, why had she run out on him the way she had? What had made her take up with that big, ugly salesman? He'd given her everything, bought her fine clothes, and still she'd run off with that salesman after just three months of marriage. She'd taken all the money with her, too—almost two thousand dollars from their joint checking and savings accounts; all she'd left him was the six hundred dollars in his special account, the six hundred which had dwindled to the four hundred and eighty he now had in his wallet.

Six hundred dollars and the furnished apartment and his car, that was all.

When he'd discovered that she was gone, he'd been half-crazy. He hadn't known what to do. Finally, he had quit his job

and packed his few belongings in his car and gone looking for
her. That had been ten days ago, and now here he was, in the
middle of the desert, with no idea where to go next. Where was
there to go? A hundred places, a thousand places, and all of
them empty . . .

Jeffords lay looking up at the ceiling. He had slept very little
in the past week, and it was beginning to tell on him; he dozed,
lying there. The sharp knocking on the door snapped him off
the bed and onto his feet, his heart pounding wildly, the inside
of his head spinning with the fog of sleep.

The knocking grew more insistent.

Jeffords put on his trousers and went to the door, shaking his
head and wiping sweat and sleep from his eyes. It was the girl
from the sports car, the blonde girl with the ponytail. Her eyes
were wide and dark and flashing, and the front of her bolero
shirt was torn.

"Let me in, will you?" she said.

Jeffords did not know what to think. "What is it?"

"Just let me in," the girl said. "Please let me in."

"All right." He stood aside and she came in and he shut the
door behind her.

"He tried to attack me," she said, turning to look at him.

"Who did?"

"Van."

"Who's Van?"

"The fellow I was with," the girl said. "I had to hit him. I hit
him with a lamp."

Jeffords felt a sudden panic. "Listen, I don't want to get involved in anything."

"I knocked him out," the girl said. "He's lying in my room,
knocked out."

"Why did you come to me? What do you want me to do?"

"I don't know. I remembered you from the office."

"How did you know which room was mine?"

"I saw you through the window when you came back."

Jeffords sat down on the bed. "Why did you come here with
this Van? Didn't you know he'd try something?"

"No, he was nice and very polite when he gave me the ride,"
the girl said. "When he suggested we stop for the night, he said
we'd take separate rooms and he even let me go in to register. I
said good night to him but a little while later he forced his way
into my room and went kind of wild." She paused, studying

Jeffords. "Look, are you waiting here or something? For some-body to come?"

"No," he said.

"When are you leaving?"

"In the morning."

"Can't you go now?"

"What for?"

"I want to get away from here. Can you take me with you?"

"You're nuts," Jeffords said. "I can't take you."

"Have you got a wife somewhere?"

"No," Jeffords said bitterly. "I don't have any wife."

"Where are you going?"

"I don't know. Los Angeles, maybe."

"Take me along."

"I can't do that."

"I don't want to be here when Van wakes up," the girl said. "I don't know what he might do."

"I can't help you."

"And I don't like the police. We don't get along too well, the police and me."

"I'm sorry."

"Come on," she said. "Please."

Jeffords stared at her, at her pleading eyes, and he felt himself softening inside. Girls like her—like Penny—always affected him that way. He wanted to believe in them, in their basic good-ness, and he always ended up getting involved in one way or another.

He moistened his lips. *You're crazy if you do it,* he told himself. *She's trouble. Can't you see it? She's just like Penny; she's another one of the same. Don't do it, don't get involved with her.*

Even as he thought this, he heard himself saying, "All right, come on," as if his vocal chords and his brain were separate entities, as if he were two people instead of one.

"Thanks," she said breathlessly. "Thanks."

Jeffords had just one suitcase, and he threw his clothes into it and put on his shirt. The girl took his arm and they went out-side.

He said, "Do you have any luggage?"

"Just one small bag."

"You'd better get it."

"I don't want to go back over there."

"I'll go with you. You don't want to leave your stuff here."

"What if Van's conscious by now? I didn't hit him very hard."

"If he is, I'll take care of him."

They went across to the girl's unit and inside. Van was a pudgy man in his late forties, lying face down with his arms spread. There was blood on his right temple, but he was breathing. The porcelain lamp the girl had hit him with was shattered on the floor beside him.

"Is he still out?" she asked.

"Yeah."

She gathered up her bag and they went outside again. She said, "Where's your car?"

"Over there."

"Let's go then, before he wakes up."

Jeffords felt the hot desert wind on his face, blowing in through the open window. He stared out at the long, straight black ribbon of the highway. The desert was a half-world of shadows on either side.

The girl—her name was Marci, she told him—leaned against the passenger door, watching him. After a while she said, "You're kind of quiet, aren't you?"

"Sometimes."

She laughed. "You have to watch out for the quiet ones."

Jeffords was silent for a moment. Then he said, "What are you doing out here? All by yourself?"

"Just drifting with the wind," Marci said. "Hitchhiking. Seeing some of this big wide country."

"You're kind of young for that."

"Oh, hell."

"You can get into a lot of trouble."

"Like with Van, you mean?"

"Like with him."

"There aren't many like him."

"How old are you, anyway?"

"Twenty-one."

"You ought to be married or something," Jeffords said, and wondered why he had said it.

Marci laughed. "Sure, someday. Right now, my bag is grins. That's what makes the world go round."

Like Penny, he thought. *Just like Penny. Why did I have to take her with me, why did I have to feel sorry for her?*

"Hey," Marci said, "have you ever been to Los Angeles?"

"Yes," Jeffords answered.

"It must be some place. Everybody I ever knew who went to Los Angeles said it was some place."

"It's some place, all right."

Marci yawned and turned on the seat, moving close to Jeffords. She put her head on his shoulder. "I'm getting sleepy," she said.

"Go to sleep then."

"Okay. You don't mind?"

"No, I don't mind."

They drove through the night and, subtly, Jeffords felt his mood change. He could smell the soft, sweet fragrance of the girl's hair, and her body was warm resting against his. *She's just a kid,* he thought. *Kind of wild, but nice—a good kid. Maybe she's different from the rest, maybe she's one of the good ones . . .*

It was past dawn when Marci awoke. They were coming out of the desert now, into Barstow. The morning sun was hot, bright, in the eastern sky; the reflection of it off the shining metal of the hood was blinding, but it didn't bother Jeffords, not at all.

Marci stretched. "Where are we?"

"Barstow. How did you sleep?"

"Like the proverbial log."

"Are you hungry?"

"Am I!"

"We'll stop for breakfast."

They ate bacon and eggs at a small cafe, and Jeffords found himself in a light, carefree mood. It was the girl who made him feel that way. He couldn't explain it; it was almost as if he were coming alive again, as if things mattered again. *Marci,* he thought, savoring the name. *Marci.*

They lingered over coffee, bought sandwiches for the remainder of the trip. They drove through to the coast, stopping once to eat a picnic lunch. They laughed a lot, talked a lot, and Jeffords' buoyant mood increased. By the time they reached Los Angeles, shortly after dark, he felt as he had on his honeymoon with Penny: right with everything, happy with everything.

"Well," he said, "we made it."

"We made it, all right."

"Do you want to stop somewhere?"

"Okay. You must be tired."

"I am."

They took a motel—two rooms with a connecting door between. Marci kissed him good night with feeling and promise, and he went to bed and slept deeply, dreaming good dreams.

He awoke at ten in the morning, rested. He got up and

dressed and opened the connecting door, peered into the ad-
joining room.

Marci wasn't there.

Jeffords went outside and looked around and didn't see her.
He walked down to the motel office. The same man who had
given them the rooms the night before was still there.

"Have you seen the girl I came here with?" Jeffords asked.

"Oh, I saw her, sure," the man said.

"Where is she?"

"Gone."

"Gone? Gone where?"

The man shrugged. "She got on the San Diego bus."

"What? She got on the what?"

"The bus for San Diego," the man said. "It stops right out
front. She got on about an hour ago. I figured the two of you—"

Jeffords did not hear the rest of it. He ran outside and back to
his room. His temples were pounding as he opened his suitcase;
he had put his wallet in there the night before, when he had
gone to bed. The wallet was still there, spread open on top of his
shirts. He picked it up.

It was empty.

Jeffords stood remembering the pudgy man, Van, lying on
the floor of the motel unit in the desert. Marci had said he'd
tried to attack her, but maybe the truth was, he had caught her
going through his things, looking for money or valuables. Or
maybe the truth was, she hadn't wanted to wait for him to go to
sleep, and she had hit him with the lamp when his back was
turned. Well, it didn't matter. Nothing mattered now.

Jeffords put his wallet back into the suitcase. He took the car
keys from his pocket, went outside to where his car was parked
and opened the trunk. There was a small brown box inside,
behind the spare tire, and he took that out and returned to the
motel room.

He put the case on the writing desk, unfastened the catches,
and took out the gun.

He stood looking at it for a time. Then he put it into his belt,
under his shirt, took the suitcase and the small box out to his
car, and left the motel. He drove onto the freeway, south toward
San Diego.

They're all the same, he thought. *All the same, every one of them in
the world.*

He knew what he had to do—what he would have to do again
and again and again.

When he found Marci, he would put the muzzle of the gun against her heart and he would pull the trigger—just like he had done with Penny when he'd found her alone in the Las Vegas motel three days before . . .

The View

by Brian Garfield

Brian Garfield has never gotten his due as a writer of prose. His sentences sparkle. There's never an excess word. And he's equally good at human psychology, his novel Necessity *being a good example. He took the woman-in-jeopardy genre, stood it on its head, and created something brand new. He is, in all respects, an intelligent and gifted writer and if you're trying to learn how to write, study him carefully.*

First published in 1983.

The day before the murder I made the usual rounds.

Tom Todhunter's house on the hilltop was my next-to-last stop on Mondays and Thursdays. Normally I tried to arrive early because the old man was one of my favorite clients and I enjoyed provoking his stories about the early days. Today I was a bit late because I had other things on my mind—Marilynn and the problem of Stanley Orcutt.

Steep and sinuous, the narrow road was a low-gear climb to its cul-de-sac end. I crimped the wheels into the curb and set the brake and glanced through the wrought-iron archway with its embroidered *T. X. T.* centered in filigree. Sometimes old Tom would await me there on the flagstone walk: he had exceptional hearing and could identify the particular grind of my van.

He wasn't in sight. I unloaded my gear from the van and lugged it to the door. I was preoccupied with my dilemma—mine and Marilynn's—and it must have been several minutes before I realized no one had answered the door. I rang the bell again and listened to the silence and felt a jolt of adrenalin: it was true he was in remarkable condition but Tom was just a month short of eighty-seven and I was alerted by the actuarial knowledge that any visit to him might be my last.

I left my things at the door and went around to the side, past the garage that housed Tom's huge old Packard and around a stand of bamboo and out along the red-tile walkway that led to the back of the property. I ducked under an arched trellis of purple bougainvillea and emerged onto the apron of the swimming pool. The vista was stunning: past the pool the hill plummeted into a brush-studded crumple of canyons and you could see a panorama that looked like the view from an airplane: mountain serrates along half the skyline and the Pacific Ocean along the rest—Catalina Island dark on the horizon. Today even the blue haze was gone; the hot Santa Anas were blowing out of the east and the air was glass-sharp for forty miles.

Tom was sitting in a high canvas director's chair, MR. TODHUNTER painted across the back. He scowled out at the vista, so lost in thought he didn't hear me behind him until I spoke:

"Are you all right?"

It startled him. "No." Then his back stiffened. He twisted to look at me. "Who? —It's you, Christopher. 'Time's it?"

"Ten after three. Sorry I'm late, sir. Are you all—"

He squinted at me the way he'd squinted at rustlers, land-grabbers, and other "B"-picture varmints. His rasping deep voice had a younger man's timbre. "Of course I'm all right."

"You didn't answer the doorbell . . ."

"I see," he said. "Listen: just because I don't answer every damn bell that rings doesn't mean you need to call the undertakers just yet."

I watched him brace both gnarled hands on the arms of the chair and heave himself to his feet. He kept looking out at the canyon but his attention was elsewhere: somewhere inside him.

After a moment he glanced at me. "Thank you for your concern. I guess you want to get started."

I smiled assent and began to turn away but his voice arrested me: "Look down there."

I tried to figure out what he was looking at. Below the escarpment the scrub-oak hills tumbled toward the canyon bottom. Sunlight dappled mica particles in the rocks; once in a while you could get a glimpse of deer down there—occasionally a coyote. The gorge curled to the left; out of sight beyond those massive shoulders of rock and brush lurked the blighted plastic sprawl of Santa Monica and Los Angeles.

He said, "They used to set the camera tripod right up here

and I used to climb up on that big white horse and chase bad guys all through those trees. Real good angle from right here, looking north so you never got the sun in the lens. My dad was a director, you know."

"I know."

"We made forty-eight pictures together. Way back—silent-movie days. Before your time. I used to know every rock and every bush. See that clump of juniper? We used to have a soft bed of sand right below there. I'd ride up alongside of old Fred Kohler or Charlie King and jump him from my horse onto his horse and we'd both take a tumble right on the sand there. I always won those hand-to-hands, of course. The good guy. I like happy endings, you know . . . Did our own stunts in those days, mainly."

Usually he enjoyed reminiscing but he seemed sour today. He said: "Enjoy the view while you can."

"What do you mean?"

At first he didn't answer.

From here only five or six houses were visible, strewn haphazardly about, each one trailing an umbilical driveway that depended circuitously to the paved two-lane highway by the river. The biggest of those houses was Marilynn Orcutt's and I'd be going there directly after finishing up with Tom.

Even from here it was imposing: a Spanish grandee had built the hacienda with its adobe outbuildings, its corrals and its red-tile roofs around the open courtyard. You could have held scrimmages in that courtyard.

Tom's place was fifty or sixty years old; the hacienda down there dated back to the Eighteenth Century. Stanley Orcutt had modernized it. Even from up here, nearly a mile above it, I could hear the slap and pound of the diesel generator that provided electricity for the hacienda. Sound carried far in these mountains.

The hacienda was tucked into a steep canyon and it commanded only a narrow wedge of a view. Like the grandees, Marilynn's husband didn't care about views unless you could measure them monetarily.

Tom's voice startled me with its bitterness: he spat the words as if they were bitter-tasting insects that had flown into his mouth:

"Resort complex. *Condominiums.*"

Then he went into the house.

I brought my gear into the spare bedroom and set up the

folding massage table and laid out the oils and conditioners. There was an oil portrait of Tom's late wife as she'd been in her thirties: a pert redhead with a huge smile. She'd died five or six years ago but still whenever he mentioned her his voice went soft with love.

Wrapped in a big towel he came into the room carrying a rolled-up newspaper. He set it aside and climbed aboard the table face-down. He was smaller than he'd been as a young man; a bit gaunt now, nothing left of the robust beer belly he'd carried during his last few paunchy years in the saddle on the Monogram Pictures back lot, and his face was crosshatched with cracks but it was still recognizably the face I'd seen in all those black-and-white programmers: the same slant of the pale eyes, the familiar heavy thrust of the big jaw.

I began to knead his left foot. "Something interesting in the newspaper?"

"There is." He didn't explain.

After a bit I said, "You're remarkably fit. You still contend you haven't got a portrait hidden away in the attic someplace?"

"You can't take personal credit for longevity. It's just blind luck." Then the ghost of the familiar big grin: "But if you push me into a corner with a microphone in my face I'll attribute it to booze, broads, and 'bacco."

He lapsed silent for a while. Occasionally he'd grunt when I probed a knotted muscle too hard. The old man was a hedonist; he vocalized his pleasure with sighs and groans.

I'd met him two years ago in the hospital: I did two days a week of physiotherapy there and he'd just had surgery for prostate cancer and they'd sent me in to make him more comfortable. After a few days they'd sent him home but he'd asked me to continue working on him as a private client. Eighty-four and he'd only just discovered the benefits of massage.

The first few months he'd been fragile and tentative, scared by looming mortality. But then the doctors had told him it looked as if they'd caught it in time and he was in remission. After that he'd perked right up and found a young writer who was eager to ghost-write The Thomas X. Todhunter Story, and what with that and his glorious view and his numerous friends and his sippin' whisky and his twice-weekly massage he was a happy man.

One Thursday afternoon Tom had confided in me: "Some of those old boys likely to get real uncomfortable—the ones that ain't dead yet. The rest, I expect they'll be rolling cartwheels in their graves. Listen: I could've been dead in the operating room. I'm way past the allotted threescore and ten. Borrowed time, Christopher. What've I got to lose? I'm telling it plain and true, boy. I'm letting the buffalo chips fall wherever they want to." His laughter was loud and wild.

I did the legs and arms and then got down to serious business on his back. He liked to hear the joints crack when I manipulated them.

Finally I worked his face and head and neck. That was his favorite; I could always count on his ritual approval: "I swear if you could bottle that you could sell it for millions."

But he didn't say it today. He just got off the table and held the towel around him, stared a while at his wife's portrait— brooding, as if he needed her counsel about something. A sudden suspicion grenaded into me and I said, "Did you get the results from that check-up you had last week?"

"Sure." He dismissed the question casually. "Everything's negative—everything's fine. I'll live to be at least a hundred and five." He nodded his head emphatically to confirm it. "I'm not going to fall down, boy. They're going to have to *knock* me down."

Then he picked up the rolled newspaper and looked at it and the sudden disgust in his voice was profound:

"Seems my neighbor Mr. Stanley Orcutt has been buying up parcels of land. Seems he owns the better part of what you can see from here, excepting perhaps the Pacific Ocean. Seems he's put in for county permission to develop the land."

He flung the newspaper down on the massage table and poked an accusing finger toward the photograph. "Look at it."

It was Sunday's real-estate section. The headline was DEVEL-OPER PLANS TOPANGA CONDOS. The photo showed an architect's conception of hilltops tiered and flattened, each one supporting a random jumble of squat apartments that looked rather like children's toy blocks that might have been glued together at odd corners and then strewn askew.

Tom said: "Brings a whole new meaning to the word 'ugly,' doesn't it."

"Yes sir, I guess it does."

"Arrogant fool wants to turn these mountains into a slum."

"Maybe it won't happen," I said.

The old man said, "Aagh," dismissing it with disbelief; and then he said: "Even his own wife hates what he's doing. You know the woman, don't you?"

I was packing the oils away in my doctor-style bag. "I know them both. I give them massages."

"Beautiful woman. She's got a sweet disposition."

"Yes sir, she does."

Tom gave me a speculative look. He was a man of the world. But he was gentleman enough to keep his suspicions to himself.

I gave the newspaper back to him so I could fold up the table. A few minutes later I said goodbye.

It was less than a mile as the crow might fly; but the road made it just two-tenths short of four miles and it was an eleven-minute journey in the van.

Just beyond the turn-off to Tom's house there was a lookout point at the side of the road—room for two or three parked cars —and from that curve you could see Orcutt's hacienda; beyond that point you couldn't see it any more because the hills got in the way.

I went on along to the Orcutt mailbox and drove up the gravel drive. The doors to the triple garage were open. The steel-grey Seville and Marilynn's white Mercedes convertible were in their stalls. The third stall was empty—from which I concluded that Stanley Orcutt was out somewhere in the Rolls, doing business—bringing more new meanings to the word "ugly."

A dented pickup was parked in the circular driveway. I saw lawn-mowers and spreading machines in its stretch bed. *Gutierrez Gardening Service.* One of the gardeners was making a loud racket with one of those putt-putting backpack blowers, spraying high-pressure air along the entranceway to clear it of twigs and dead leaves. He nodded to me and smiled when I carried my gear past him.

The cleaning lady admitted me to the house and then left me on my own; I was hired help, not deserving of an escort, and I knew the way. I went on back to the exercise room.

Marilynn was in the sauna. I announced myself and heard her voice through the wooden door: "I'll be right out." Then— mischievously: "Go ahead and start without me."

I set up the table and laid out the oils and cremes. She said: "Did your agent have any news about your script?"

"They're still thinking about it at the network. 'Taking' meetings."

"Don't be too crestfallen if they don't buy it, Christopher. Everyone knows they're idiots. The script's probably too good for them." Her voice hadn't revealed anxiety but when she came out of the sauna I could see it in her eyes.

She was in a green terrycloth robe that matched the color of her eyes. A few wisps of disobedient yellow hair protruded from the towel she'd turbaned around her head. Despite the dressing-room garb she carried herself with glamourous languid grace. She went to the door and looked out into the corridor. When she was satisfied, she pushed it shut and locked it and came back to the table. Soft and hot from the sauna, she came right into my arms.

Despite the heat she was trembling.

After a long while she went away from me, crossing the room. There was anger in her and she was too jangly to lie in my embrace. From the far side of the room she watched me for the longest time and then said, "What would you say—would you think I was insane if I told you I am seriously thinking about committing murder?"

"It's come down to that, has it?"

She took a deep breath as if to calm herself. "He's gone public. Did you see the monstrosity in yesterday's paper?"

"Tom Todhunter showed it to me."

"Tom phoned here yesterday. I could have heard him without a telephone. Stanley wasn't here. He was in Malibu or someplace, playing games with balance sheets or whatever that crowd does. I think he's involved in cocaine deals—I can't prove it, it's just a feeling. Anyway—what was I talking about? Oh. Old Tom Todhunter—he called yesterday. I already said that, didn't I—you can see how upset I am . . . When Tom calmed down I told him I'm just as furious about it as he is. I'm really fond of him. He's such a dear old thing." She composed herself and came back to the subject at hand. "I've been sorting out murder methods. Poison—a gun—a knife—holding his head under the swimming pool . . ."

I said, "You don't have to kill anybody. Just divorce him."

She released a tiny laugh into the room. "I'm going to. But I won't get a penny from him, you know. I signed that damned pre-nuptial agreement. He *owes* me . . ."

I took her in my arms. "Forget it. We'll get by. Why, when I'm a famous screenwriter we'll be able to buy and sell guys like Stanley."

"I know a couple of successful writers," she said. "You've got an exaggerated idea of how much money they make."

"Is money that important to you?"

"I honestly don't know, Christopher. I've never been without it."

Her father had inherited the family business and Marilynn had grown up on the wealthy coast of Rhode Island—*old* money country, where families were aged in wood like good whisky—but her father had gambled it all away, everything including the button factory. By that time she'd already married Stanley Orcutt.

Astonishing how unpredictably people could change. When Marilynn married Orcutt she'd been just out of Vassar and he'd been young, vigorous, blond, and handsome, a Yale man with lineage as impeccable as her own. They both came from the sort of families that guarded their riches jealously: that was why the pre-nuptial agreements had been signed—contracts by which neither of them could lay hands on the other's fortune. As things had turned out, Marilynn's fortune evaporated while Stanley's multiplied.

She was one of those fair-skinned ice princesses and he was the rich son of an ambitious father and he'd inherited both the wealth and the ambition: he was determined to keep getting richer, and in the process he grew a belly and lost his charm and humanity along with the hair on his scalp. Now he was just another middle-aged overweight hustler—only richer and more powerful than most; and a lot more dangerous: he'd developed the instincts and the personality of a boa constrictor.

He had the remains of a healthy constitution but the muscles were layered over with flab and he depended on massages rather than exercise to keep him from falling apart completely. Providing his semi-weekly rubdowns was no pleasure for me and I wouldn't have kept him as a client if it hadn't been for Marilynn. I hadn't planned on falling in love with her—or on her falling in love with me.

She said: "He doesn't want to hear the word divorce. I'm his property, bought and paid for. That's how he sees it. I'm decorative and decorous. The proper hostess. You have to read between the lines with Stanley because he's too clever to say anything outright that you might hold against him later—but his meaning is clear enough. If I try to divorce him he'll make life a holy hell for me and anybody connected with me."

"Come on, darling. Aren't you dramatizing just a little? He's not a gangster."

"I'm not talking about breaking your arms and legs. He's more subtle than that. You'd never sell a script in this town, I suspect. You'd get fired by the hospital. Your clients would begin to phone you—so sorry, but we're going to have to dispense with your services. And then maybe the state would find some irregularity in your license to practice physiotherapy . . ." She was looking at the floor, in a dismal frame of mind. "You and I —we'd end up on food stamps."

"Better that than Death Row," I said gently. "You weren't serious, were you?"

"About murdering him?" She looked up at last: she met my eyes. "Honestly, I don't know whether I'm serious or not. God knows he's made me hate him enough—"

"Hey," I said quietly. "Murder isn't a solution. Murder's a problem."

With a wan attempt at a smile she folded herself against me. "What are we going to do, then?"

"I wish I knew."

It was just after five Tuesday when the phone in my apartment rang. I'd only been home half an hour or so; I was sucking beer from a can and wrestling at the typewriter with a clumsy transition in the new script. The strident demand of the telephone annoyed me and I was inclined not to answer but after the fourth ring I knew my concentration was broken so I picked it up, stifling anger. "Hello?"

"Christopher—I need help . . ."

Her voice brought me bolt upright in the chair. "Marilynn— what is it?"

"Stanley . . . He's dead . . . Two shots; two bullets . . . Can you come—right away?"

"I don't believe it," I said lamely. "What happened?"

"Please—can you just come up? *Now?* I need you, darling . . ."

She sounded forlorn, waiflike—an urchin begging for solace. I flung the van up the Pacific Coast Highway toward Topanga Canyon, cursing the clots of traffic that slowed me. I was filled with alarm and fear. Not for Stanley but for Marilynn: the implications of what she'd said were enough to put the coppery taste of fear on my tongue.

Going up the corkscrew road I heard a police siren somewhere ahead of me. I went caroming past the turnoff to Tom Todhunter's place and a moment later was slithering through the sharp bend where the lookout point gave me a glimpse of the hacienda. I could see the three-car garage from there—the doors open as they always were, all three cars parked abreast in the stalls. There were no vehicles parked in the driveway.

As I sped away from the viewpoint I heard a crack of sound that could have been a gunshot; it was half obscured by the wailing sirens up-canyon and I couldn't be sure.

The police would get there ahead of me. Still, she must have telephoned me quite some time before she'd called them; they'd be from the Malibu sheriff's station and I'd had farther to come. If it hadn't been for the evening traffic I'd have been there ahead of them.

When I made the turn onto the gravel driveway I was hoping she'd have the sense to say nothing at all: nothing except, "I want to see my lawyer." I wondered if she had one. Surely with all Stanley's shady dealings and high-powered contacts she must know a good lawyer . . .

The two black-and-white sheriff's cars were parked just behind Tom Todhunter's distinctive old Packard. I left the van in the driveway, not bothering to move it out of anyone's way, and went at a run up to the house. I didn't ring the bell; the door was half open and I just walked inside. I could hear voices just along the corridor and went that way to the open door of Orcutt's study.

I heard an unfamiliar male voice: "There's three empties in the cylinder here. I only see two wounds. Anybody see a bullet hole in the furniture or anyplace?"

As I arrived at the door I heard Tom Todhunter say, "It could have gone out that window there."

They all were in that room: three men in deputy uniforms; one official-looking man with iron-grey hair in a khaki-colored suit and tie; Marilynn slumped in a chair looking faint; Tom Todhunter on his feet with his back flat against the bookcase, looking down at Stanley Orcutt—at least I assumed it was Orcutt. The dead man was lying on the floor with his back to me and there were two darkening stains on the back of his shirt. The smell in the room was acrid and not pleasant. I noticed the window beyond the desk was wide open; a bit of a breeze tickled my face.

One of the cops discovered me in the doorway and went rigid. "Who's this—who's this?"

It made Marilynn look up. She said: "Oh, thank God." I went toward her as she rose to her feet; I embraced her.

The one in plainclothes with the steel-colored hair said, "What's your name?"

"Christopher Ainsworth," I answered. "What's yours?"

"McKittrick." Then he added, with emphasis, "Sergeant McKittrick." He had a pencil in his hand. From it a revolver dangled by its trigger guard. He turned to one of the uniformed cops and said, "Bag this," and the cop produced a folded transparent plastic bag from his pocket. McKittrick dropped the revolver into it and the cop sealed the bag shut with a twist-tie and wrote something on its tag.

Old Tom Todhunter said to me, "You see that, boy? Even dead he's still ugly." He looked down at the dead man again.

During all this Marilynn clung to me, squeezing me with great violence as if by pressing herself close enough she could draw strength directly from me. She was breathing very fast. Weeping now; drawing in great sucking gasps. I held her in a tender grip and stroked her hair: "Okay, all right, take it easy now, just try to relax, it's okay, you'll be all right, go ahead and let it out"—talking to her as you'd talk to a skittish animal, just letting the words flow, trying to make the voice soothing.

Over her head I could see Tom Todhunter's cracked-leather face. He was gazing at us—at me or at Marilynn, I couldn't tell which—and he looked preternaturally sad: compassion and concern flowed from his eyes. Then he turned to McKittrick and held his gnarled hands out, wrists together. "You got handcuffs or something?"

McKittrick said, "I guess we won't need them."

"You think I couldn't make a run for it? You think I'm too old?"

I didn't understand. "What's going on? What are you talking about?"

Marilynn blurted out a sobbing cry. She turned in the circle of my arms and tried to focus through her tears. In a half strangled voice she said: "For God's sake, don't let him—"

"Never mind!" old Tom roared. "I'll confess any damn time I please. I've done us all a favor here. This world's better off without that ugly man and his ugly condominiums. I ain't sorry. I'd do it again."

She struggled to break free of my grasp. "Tom—you can't—"

"Honey love," the old man said, "I can and I did. Now just hush up and let your young man take care of you there. There's nothing you can do now. Nothing that happens now is going to change the way things are—this man can't get any deader." He prodded the corpse with his toe; it prompted one of the cops to grip his arm and pull him away; and Tom said in a dust-dry voice, "Sorry—I didn't mean to disturb the evidence."

Then he turned to Marilynn. "I expect you stand to inherit from him. You're not going to go ahead building those ugly things, are you? You won't ugly up this landscape—I know you won't. That's what counts. The view."

By then I had it figured out and when Marilynn opened her mouth to speak another objection, I squeezed her arms very hard. It was surreptitious and the cops couldn't possibly notice it, but she felt it all right and she didn't speak again.

After a while they took Tom away.

I parked the van in front of the archway and walked in below his initials, carried my gear into the house and started to work. He took a long swallow of bourbon and grunted with pleasure. "First rubdown in nearly two weeks. Only things I've been missing—rubdowns and good whisky. Hadn't been for that I wouldn't have minded staying in jail. Nice comfortable private cell and the food's not too bad. But now you're here I'm glad they made bail for me. By the way—I didn't get your bill for last month."

"It's on the house."

"Come on. I may be under indictment but I'm not broke."

I said, "We owe you more than anybody can ever pay."

"Well, somebody had to stop him before he ruined this whole countryside."

"That's not what I mean. And you know it."

"She told you, did she?"

"No. I figured it out for myself. I haven't said a word to her."

"Nor she to you? I wonder how long she can keep it bottled up." Then he twisted his head to squint up at me. "How'd you figure it out?"

"I came up the road just behind the police. When I looked across the canyon there weren't any cars parked in Orcutt's driveway. And I heard a gunshot. I could hear it; the police couldn't—not with those sirens right above their heads. A few minutes later I came up the driveway and your Packard was parked there, in front of the police cars. You got there just a couple minutes ahead of the cops. You took the gun away from her and you fired a shot out the window—so that they'd find powder burns on your hand. How'd you know about it? Did she telephone you?"

"No. I heard the two shots—you know how sound carries in

these hills. I went out by the pool to have a look around and I saw her come running out of the house over there and then run back inside. Too far to see much but I could tell she was distraught all right. Put that together with the noise of the shots I'd heard—I guessed something was wrong. I decided to go over and see if I could help. But the Packard wouldn't start up right away and I had to hook up the quick-charger on the battery for fifteen, twenty minutes. Then I heard the sirens coming up from the bottom and I knew I'd need to hurry."

I said, "You gave her back her life."

"Well, she's a sweet thing. She was going to tell you about it but I told her to hold off—I thought you might take it better coming from me. Look, he goaded her into it, he provoked it, he drove her to it the same way the picador drives the bull to it in the ring. Mr. Stanley Orcutt might as well have pulled the trigger himself. He'd found out about you. He was going to have you—*punished*. That's how he put it. He flaunted that in front of her. He was going to run you out of business and then he made some talk about breaking your hands real good so you'd never massage anybody again. And of course naturally she was never to see you again. So forth, etcetera, so on."

I said, "Your check-up last week—"

"Well, they found cancer. I guess it's metastasized. I won't be alive to go to trial." The side of his face that I could see was smiling. "I kind of like happy endings," he said.

Hector Gomez Provides

by John Lutz

John Lutz has written so many good novels and short stories that he gets taken for granted. Yes, he's won the Edgar; yes, one, perhaps two major movies have been made from his books (I say "perhaps" because at press time he's got a deal pending); and yes, he's generally regarded as one of the genre's best stylists. Now it's up to you to make him a household name. He deserves it.

First published in 1985.

Here, a hundred and fifty feet high on the ancient stone Tower of Saint Marcos, Hector Gomez felt free. The wind whipped about his lithe body, threatening to snatch him and hurl him out into high, cool space above the sea. A pelican flew past, lower than Hector, and gazed obliquely at him between wingbeats then soared in an ascending arc toward the sun. Below Hector the waves rolled in and became graceful ribbons of white surf, then boiling white water, against the rocks.

To Hector's right was the Avenue Del Mar, where three *turista* buses were parked in a line at the side of the road. Along the top of the stone wall above the sea, Mexican vendors had their glittering handmade wares displayed on blankets for sale to the Americans.

Directly below Hector was a tiny, semi-isolated portion of the sea. Saint Marcos Cove. The swells roared into the miniature cove regularly and smashed in white foam over jagged rock along the shore. The sides of the cove, less than a hundred feet apart, were also lined with sharp rock. Only in its center, for brief moments, was the water relatively calm.

Three times a day, Hector Gomez dived from atop the Tower of Saint Marcos into the center of the tiny cove. He had to time each dive perfectly with an oncoming swell, hitting the water just as the wave rolled into the cove. Otherwise the water in the cove was only about four feet deep, and the bottom was lined with hard pebbles rolled smooth by the waves. It was indeed a matter of delicate timing, Hector's dive. And a matter of courage. Everyone, tourist and native alike, knew that the dive was extremely dangerous.

And Hector knew the danger. With the detachment and freedom he felt before each dive came the accompanying price of fear.

Below him the *turistas* were all out of the buses, staring up at him, pointing, focusing their cameras. Sunlight glinted off Mexican silver spread along the sea wall, off the windows of the buses and off upturned camera lenses.

Hector's feeling of freedom passed. It was time for business; he had Maria and their two children to feed and shelter. And the bus driver-guides below had by now finished telling the *turistas* the manufactured legend of Spanish gold hidden somewhere at the bottom of the cove. Perhaps someday the brave diver would emerge with a handful of doubloons and no longer have to risk his life; the prospect, said the guides, was what compelled him to face death daily, even though the gold was cursed.

Hector let the first two swells roll into the cove and break; they were too small and the water in the cove wouldn't be deep enough for the dive.

The third wave appeared large enough. Fear tried to crawl up Hector's throat again as he raised his right arm in a signal to the *turista* that he was about to dive, that they should ready their cameras. Now there was no turning back and still living a man's life with self-respect.

When the glittering emerald swell was at just the right point, almost ready to roll into the cove, Hector swallowed his near-panic, flexed his knees, and hurled himself off the tower.

The freedom again. The fear. He had to leap far enough out to clear the outcropping of cliff below. Had to keep his back tightly arched before going into the vertical position, or he might flip over too far backward and land wrong, on his back, breaking himself on the water even before he struck the cove's bottom. Yet if he didn't straighten his body in time, there was the cliff.

He timed it, *uno, dos, tres* . . . and he aimed his outstretched arms forward and down and brought his feet up, legs strained straight and rigid. He willed his body out away from the cliff, clenching his teeth so hard that a sharp pain shot through his jaws.

The tops of his tucked-in toes brushed the outcropping of rock seventy feet above the water, and he knew it would be a good dive.

Barely had he realized this when his fists broke the rushing surface of the wave rolling into the cove. There was a crash of water that he heard only for an instant. He arched his back again, flattening out quickly beneath the surface to slow his descent. Still he struck bottom hard, scraping his chest and thighs even though he pushed away from the smooth pebbles with his palms. His breath rushed out from between his lips in a graceful swirl of pearl-like bubbles, his blood pulsed in his ears, and he forced himself to stay calm as he rose to the surface.

The *turistas* were applauding. Even in the sun's heat, Hector felt the warm glow of their appreciation; they had been entertained. The Americans didn't know that this part of his act, reaching shore without being smashed against the rocks, was almost as dangerous as the dive.

Hector stroked cautiously toward where the surf broke over the rocks, watching warily behind him for the next wave to come crashing in through the mouth of the cove. When it came, he prudently ducked beneath it and let it roll over him, feeling its force pass him by, rather than let it carry him tumbling out of control toward the jagged rocks. As the wave receded and the water again became momentarily calm, he raised his head and stroked again for shore.

He had to deal with three waves this way before he finally was safe on the rocks. Smiling, he climbed up to the road and walked wet and triumphant among the *turistas,* gratefully accepting their compliments, pesos, and the admiring glances of the young women. The *turistas* voiced appreciation of his great courage. He smiled and told them he hoped they had gotten good photographs to take home from their Mexican vacations.

When the *turistas* had left, Vicente Escobar, one of the silver vendors, walked over to Hector and stood with him watching the exhaust-darkened square backs of the departing buses. A few of the *turistas*waved from open windows, then quickly closed the glass to conserve air conditioning.

"You're going to kill yourself," Vicente Escobar said. "Why do you continue to dive?" Even as he asked, he knew it was a question for which there was a universal answer.

"I do it for this," Hector said, holding up the fistful of pesos he had collected for his dive. He had in his hand over eleven hundred pesos. Almost seven American dollars.

At the end of the day, Hector changed from his low-cut black trunks into worn jeans and a sleeveless red tee-shirt. Then, with his day's profits locked in a steel box in the car's trunk, he climbed into his ten-year-old gray Plymouth and drove south twenty miles to the village of Barbilla, where he lived with Maria, their five-year-old son Eugenio, and their six-year-old daughter Ramona.

The Gomezes' lifestyle was much like everyone else's in Barbilla. Their home was small, simple, with a dirt floor, and a sheet metal roof held down by nails driven through bottle caps whose cork linings kept out the seasonal rains. In the Gomez home was running water, and a bathroom. Because Hector dived rather than eke out a living as a fisherman, the Gomezes were only occasionally hungry.

Maria Gomez watched her husband walk up the path to their home. To her right, where the land overlooked the ocean, she knew that the American Martin still stood before his canvas and easel, painting another of his seascapes. She had gone up the trail to the rocks and talked to the American again today. Why not? She was lonely, with Hector always gone. To be alone with two small children was enough to drive any twenty-five-year-old woman *loco,* especially a woman as energetic and pretty as Maria. Probably, she thought, lowering her hands to wipe grease from tortillas onto her print skirt, Hector wouldn't object to her talking with the American Martin. But it would be just as well if Hector never found out. He had a man's foolish pride.

Eugenio saw Hector and ran out to embrace his father. Young Ramona followed. Hector hugged his children to him, smiling whitely, his lean muscles dancing and cording as he lifted a child in each arm.

"It was a profitable day," he said, as he lowered the children and bent to kiss Maria. "Almost four thousand pesos." He was beaming proudly, this man who risked death to provide for his family, so she smiled at him. "Soon we might have enough saved to move away from here, into Mazatlan."

Into a house almost like this only larger, Maria thought, though she said, "Supper is almost ready."

He walked past her. She could feel the weariness emanating from his body. Herself weary, she followed him into the house and tended to the rice and shrimp on the propane gas stove. If Hector moved them to Mazatlan Maria might have an electric stove; she'd heard they were better. But she wanted more than that, really. She wanted her meals cooked for her like the rich in the cities. She wanted not just better clothes, but fine clothes. For herself. For her children. For the foolishly daring Hector.

What she did not want was for Hector to time one of his dives wrong and die. Or worse, become a cripple she would have to support for the rest of their marriage. Maria, living in poverty, remembered abject poverty, and was afraid of it. When she passed a beggar in the square, pleading respectfully with the *turistas* for money for herself and the children, Maria felt something cold crawl about inside her. She could be that woman, she knew. The difference between what she was and what she might become was only a fraction of a second, an insane risk taken three times a day every day twenty miles down the coast at the Tower of Saint Marcos.

Hector ate greedily, gratefully, complimenting Maria on her cooking. After supper he played with the children, laughing and making promises he couldn't keep. Though he was a man, and a good one, there was something childlike in Hector's dark, lithe handsomeness. His was a youthful, whipcord body that moved with a matador's grace and strength. Yet now he was thirty-four, and above his black diving trunks was the beginning of a stomach paunch. Maria knew that Hector was at the time of life when men's reflexes and timing were beginning to deteriorate without them even suspecting it. This was a time of danger, especially in Hector's line of work.

In bed, he placed his lean, strong arms about her, and immediately fell asleep.

The next morning, the American Martin was again at his easel on the rocks overlooking the sea and a view of the coast, and was working on the painting he'd begun yesterday. Before speaking to him, Maria stood silently at the bend in the steep path, watching him work. His huge hands were gentle and sure with the brush, lending the canvas life. He was a tall, muscular man with pale blue eyes and a full red beard. Always beside his easel was a gray foam cooler containing ice and beer. Maria had heard that he painted dozens of pictures, then drove them into the Arts and Crafts Center in Mazatlan and sold them to *turistas*. She didn't know where Martin lived; no one seemed to know that.

He must have heard her, or sensed her presence on the path. "Good morning, Maria," he said, not looking away from his canvas. He was dabbing clouds in a blue sky.

She said nothing but moved nearer.

"What do you think?" he asked, nodding his shaggy head toward the canvas.

It amazed her that anyone could create a likeness so accurately. *"Bonito,"* she said. Pretty. Not beautiful. Not majestic. Only *Bonito.*

The American Martin smiled bitterly. "Here," he said, moving away from before the easel. He gripped her elbow and positioned her to stand where he had stood, placed a brush in her hand and moved behind her. His thick arms, pale and dusted with reddish hair, slipped around her waist.

For the next two weeks, Maria went almost every day to the rocks above the ocean. The American Martin's gentle, thick hands did things to her that she had never dreamed possible, that Hector could never imagine. In Martin's loving clasp she poured out all of her fears, and he gladly accepted them and kept them safely where they no longer haunted her and foretold a bleak future.

During the third week, while Hector was at the Tower of Saint Marcos, Martin said, "Drive into Mazatlan with me. We can bring your children. There's a man I want you to meet. His name is Anderson."

"Hector will be home soon."

"It doesn't matter," Martin told her. "We'll be back within a few hours; Hector won't know you've been gone, unless the kids mention it."

"They won't if I tell them not to," Maria said. "And Hector will be tired and go to sleep soon after he eats supper."

"Then come with me," Martin coaxed. He kissed her. When his lips had barely left hers, he said, "Anderson can make us rich, you and me."

Maria knew that, like Hector, she was poised above a steep, exhilarating plunge. It would take courage to leap free.

She nodded silently, walked down the path and got the chil-

dren, and they drove with Martin in his dusty Jeep into Mazatlan.

That Saturday, high above half a dozen tour buses and scores of
American *turistas,* Hector stood poised on the Tower of Saint
Marcos and felt the freedom, but not the fear.

That puzzled him. He studied the incoming swells, waiting
for the right one to time for his dive. The ribbons of white surf
along the coast beyond the cove seemed to undulate and move
in unfamiliar rhythms and patterns. The sea was behaving
strangely today. Perhaps that was why he wasn't afraid; the
strangeness had something to do with his own new fearlessness.

At last Hector saw an oncoming swell that would provide
deep enough water when it entered the cove. He watched it
approach, a rolling, glittering vast hill of water, shot with sunlight as if it contained thousands of diamonds.

It seemed to take forever to reach the point Hector had chosen, where he knew it would begin to curl into a green, sloping
wall for its assault on the cove. The point from where it would
enter the cove only a moment before the plummeting Hector
sliced into its cool depths.

In that last few seconds, Hector realized there was something
wrong. The oncoming swell wasn't approaching smoothly; it
was pausing, then rushing forward, wavering like liquid rippling in a drunkard's unsteady glass. Hector didn't want to dive.

But his right arm was already raised, signaling to the *turistas,*
all watching from below through admiring, apprehensive eyes.
Many were peering through camera lenses, hastily setting F-
stops and shutter speeds, not admitting to the secret desire to
record on film a brave man's death. It was too late for Hector to
turn away with self-respect.

As soon as he launched himself into the air, Hector felt his
confidence return. Only when he had safely passed the outcropping of rock and his body was out of its arch and vertical, did he
glimpse for an instant below him the backwash of blue-green
water.

The wave was receding!

Terror clutched at his throat and contorted his body. There
was no time to scream. He struck the water with a dark thunder
that he knew was death.

"That's that," Martin said to Anderson, the next day in Anderson's cluttered office in Mexico City. Anderson was a gangly

giraffe of a man who breathed through his mouth and per-
spired a lot. "Maria slipped him some *peyote*. It's a drug that
distorts time sense just enough. Will there be any trouble col-
lecting from the company?"

Anderson shook his long, pale head and said, "No problem at
all; no clouds on the horizon. Why should there be? A wife uses
her husband's earnings to buy life insurance on him. And why
not? He was in a dangerous occupation and she had two children to think about. Remember, I'm Great Intercontinental Insurance's Mexico claims agent; I can verify Hector's signature
on the policy. I'll recommend to the company that they pay his
widow the settlement. There's no way for Great Intercontinental, or anyone else, to know you and I are soon going to split
that settlement fifty-fifty. And what they don't know can't hurt
us. By the way, where's the wealthy widow?"

"She and the kids are getting into Mexico City tomorrow,"
Martin said. "After the funeral. I've already rented them a nice
furnished apartment on the Reforma, where we'll live happily if
not ever after."

"Can you get her to sign a policy with you as the beneficiary?"
Anderson asked. "A genuine signature is always best. You can't
beat the real McCoy."

"I'll tell her it's a form she needs to sign to collect the settlement. She'll believe it. She can barely read and write." Martin
paced to the dirty window, gazed out at the traffic on Avenue
Morelos, then bit the end off a cigar. He plucked the tobacco
crumbs and leaf from his tongue and rolled them between his
thumb and forefinger into a tight little ball, which he tossed on
the floor. Anderson's litany of smug little platitudes irritated
him. Yet he didn't want to do even one more canvas and sell it to
oafs for an insultingly small sum. "I'm not so confident about
this one, Anderson. Are you sure the company won't suspect?"

Anderson tilted back his narrow, balding head and laughed
through his nose. "Do you know how many Maria Gomezes
there are in Mexico? They're like Smiths and Joneses in the
United States. Like pebbles on the beach. The company will
pay; they'll never even know that this Mexico City Gomez was
related to Hector Gomez of Barbilla. And your name as beneficiary won't ring any bells at the home office. Believe me, Martin,
we're touching all the bases. We'll soon be home free."

"Okay," Martin said, lighting the cigar. He blew smoke off to
the side. "Get the policy written up and I'll get Maria to sign

tomorrow night, while she's still disoriented from the funeral and the trip here. There's no point in wasting time."

"You're a man after my own heart," Anderson said, smiling and sliding open a desk drawer. "Time is money."

"For both of us," Martin said.

Or one of us, Anderson thought behind his smile. He was a man who planned ahead even as he tied loose ends.

So the Spanish gold in Saint Marcos Cove was not entirely a legend concocted for *turistas*. After his last and deepest dive, Hector Gomez did indeed produce a treasure. Complete with a curse.

The Steel Valentine

by Joe R. Lansdale

Joe R. Lansdale writes and thinks like nobody else. While he's frequently called dark, what makes his work both different and masterful is its humor. There's a great exasperated cosmic laugh in virtually all of Lansdale's best work. He knows how pitiful we are, and he's eager to tell us about it.

First published in 1989.

For Jeff Banks

Even before Morley told him, Dennis knew things were about to get ugly.

A man did not club you unconscious, bring you to his estate and tie you to a chair in an empty storage shed out back of the place if he merely intended to give you a valentine.

Morley had found out about him and Julie.

Dennis blinked his eyes several times as he came to, and each time he did, more of the dimly lit room came into view. It was the room where he and Julie had first made love. It was the only building on the estate that looked out of place; it was old, worn, and not even used for storage; it was a collector of dust, cobwebs, spiders and desiccated flies.

There was a table in front of Dennis, a kerosine lantern on it, and beyond, partially hidden in shadow, a man sitting in a chair smoking a cigarette. Dennis could see the red tip glowing in the dark and the smoke from it drifted against the lantern light and hung in the air like thin, suspended wads of cotton.

The man leaned out of shadow, and as Dennis expected, it

was Morley. His shaved, bullet-shaped head was sweaty and reflected the light. He was smiling with his fine, white teeth, and the high cheekbones were round, flushed circles that looked like clown rouge. The tightness of his skin, the few wrinkles, made him look younger than his fifty-one years.

And in most ways he was younger than his age. He was a man who took care of himself. Jogged eight miles every morning before breakfast, lifted weights three times a week and had only one bad habit—cigarettes. He smoked three packs a day. Dennis knew all that and he had only met the man twice. He had learned it from Julie, Morley's wife. She told him about Morley while they lay in bed. She liked to talk and she often talked about Morley; about how much she hated him.

"Good to see you," Morley said, and blew smoke across the table into Dennis's face. "Happy Valentine's Day, my good man. I was beginning to think I hit you too hard, put you in a coma."

"What is this, Morley?" Dennis found that the mere act of speaking sent nails of pain through his skull. Morley really had lowered the boom on him.

"Spare me the innocent act, lover boy. You've been laying the pipe to Julie, and I don't like it."

"This is silly, Morley. Let me loose."

"God, they do say stupid things like that in real life. It isn't just the movies . . . You think I brought you here just to let you go, lover boy?"

Dennis didn't answer. He tried to silently work the ropes loose that held his hands to the back of the chair. If he could get free, maybe he could grab the lantern, toss it in Morley's face. There would still be the strand holding his ankles to the chair, but maybe it wouldn't take too long to undo that. And even if it did, it was at least some kind of plan.

If he got the chance to go one on one with Morley, he might take him. He was twenty-five years younger and in good shape himself. Not as good as when he was playing pro basketball, but good shape nonetheless. He had height, reach, and he still had wind. He kept the latter with plenty of jogging and tossing the special-made, sixty-five pound medicine ball around with Raul at the gym.

Still, Morley was strong. Plenty strong. Dennis could testify to that. The pulsating knot on the side of his head was there to remind him.

He remembered the voice in the parking lot, turning toward

it and seeing a fist. Nothing more, just a fist hurtling toward him like a comet. Next thing he knew, he was here, the outbuilding.

Last time he was here, circumstances were different, and better. He was with Julie. He met her for the first time at the club where he worked out, and they had spoken, and ended up playing racquetball together. Eventually she brought him here and they made love on an old mattress in the corner; lay there afterward in the June heat of a Mexican summer, holding each other in a warm, sweaty embrace.

After that, there had been many other times. In the great house; in cars; hotels. Always careful to arrange a tryst when Morley was out of town. Or so they thought. But somehow he had found out.

"This is where you first had her," Morley said suddenly. "And don't look so wide-eyed. I'm not a mind reader. She told me all the other times and places too. She spat at me when I told her I knew, but I made her tell me every little detail, even when I knew them. I wanted it to come from her lips. She got so she couldn't wait to tell me. She was begging to tell me. She asked me to forgive her and take her back. She no longer wanted to leave Mexico and go back to the States with you. She just wanted to live."

"You bastard. If you've hurt her—"

"You'll what? Shit your pants? That's the best you can do, Dennis. You see, it's me that has *you* tied to the chair. Not the other way around."

Morley leaned back into the shadows again, and his hands came to rest on the table, the perfectly manicured fingertips steepling together, twitching ever so gently.

"I think it would have been inconsiderate of her to have gone back to the States with you, Dennis. Very inconsiderate. She knows I'm a wanted man there, that I can't go back. She thought she'd be rid of me. Start a new life with her ex-basketball player. That hurt my feelings, Dennis. Right to the bone." Morley smiled. "But she wouldn't have been rid of me, lover boy. Not by a long shot. I've got connections in my business. I could have followed her anywhere . . . In fact, the idea that she thought I couldn't offended my sense of pride."

"Where is she? What have you done with her, you bald-headed bastard?"

After a moment of silence, during which Morley examined Dennis's face, he said, "Let me put it this way. Do you remember her dogs?"

Of course he remembered the dogs. Seven Dobermans. Attack dogs. They always frightened him. They were big mothers, too. Except for her favorite, a reddish, undersized Doberman named Chum. He was about sixty pounds, and vicious. "Light, but quick," Julie used to say. "Light, but quick."

Oh yeah, he remembered those goddamn dogs. Sometimes when they made love in an estate bedroom, the dogs would wander in, sit down around the bed and watch. Dennis felt they were considering the soft, rolling meat of his testicles, savoring the possibility. It made him feel like a mean kid teasing them with a treat he never intended to give. The idea of them taking that treat by force made his erection soften, and he finally convinced Julie, who found his nervousness hysterically funny, that the dogs should be banned from the bedroom, the door closed.

Except for Julie, those dogs hated everyone. Morley included. They obeyed him, but they did not like him. Julie felt that under the right circumstances, they might go nuts and tear him apart. Something she hoped for, but never happened.

"Sure," Morley continued. "You remember her little pets. Especially Chum, her favorite. He'd growl at me when I tried to touch her. Can you imagine that? All I had to do was touch her, and that damn beast would growl. He was crazy about his mistress, just crazy about her."

Dennis couldn't figure what Morley was leading up to, but he knew in some way he was being baited. And it was working. He was starting to sweat.

"Been what," Morley asked, "a week since you've seen your precious sweetheart? Am I right?"

Dennis did not answer, but Morley was right. A week. He had gone back to the States for a while to settle some matters, get part of his inheritance out of legal bondage so he could come back, get Julie, and take her to the States for good. He was tired of the Mexican heat and tired of Morley owning the woman he loved.

It was Julie who had arranged for him to meet Morley in the first place, and probably even then the old bastard had suspected. She told Morley a partial truth. That she had met Dennis at the club, that they had played racquetball together, and that since he was an American, and supposedly a mean hand at chess, she thought Morley might enjoy the company. This way Julie had a chance to be with her lover, and let Dennis see exactly what kind of man Morley was.

And from the first moment Dennis met him, he knew he had

to get Julie away from him. Even if he hadn't loved her and wanted her, he would have helped her leave Morley.

It wasn't that Morley was openly abusive—in fact, he was the perfect host all the while Dennis was there—but there was an obvious undercurrent of connubial dominance and menace that revealed itself like a shark fin everytime he looked at Julie.

Still, in a strange way, Dennis found Morley interesting, if not likeable. He was a bright and intriguing talker, and a wizard at chess. But when they played and Morley took a piece, he smirked over it in such a way as to make you feel he had actually vanquished an opponent.

The second and last time Dennis visited the house was the night before he left for the States. Morley had wiped him out in chess, and when finally Julie walked him to the door and called the dogs in from the yard so he could leave without being eaten, she whispered, "I can't take him much longer."

"I know," he whispered back. "See you in about a week. And it'll be all over."

Dennis looked over his shoulder, back into the house, and there was Morley leaning against the fireplace mantle drinking a martini. He lifted the glass to Dennis as if in salute and smiled. Dennis smiled back, called goodbye to Morley and went out to his car feeling uneasy. The smile Morley had given him was exactly the same one he used when he took a chess piece from the board.

"Tonight. Valentine's Day," Morley sad, "that's when you two planned to meet again, wasn't it? In the parking lot of your hotel. That's sweet. Really. Lovers planning to elope on Valentine's Day. It has a sort of poetry, don't you think?"

Morley held up a huge fist. "But what you met instead of your sweetheart was this . . . I beat a man to death with this once, lover boy. Enjoyed every second of it."

Morley moved swiftly around the table, came to stand behind Dennis. He put his hands on the sides of Dennis's face. "I could twist your head until your neck broke, lover boy. You believe that, don't you? Don't you? . . . Goddamnit, answer me."

"Yes," Dennis said, and the word was soft because his mouth was so dry.

"Good. That's good. Let me show you something. Dennis."

Morley picked up the chair from behind, carried Dennis effortlessly to the center of the room, then went back for the lantern and the other chair. He sat down across from Dennis and turned the wick of the lantern up. And even before Dennis saw the dog, he heard the growl.

The dog was straining at a large leather strap attached to the wall. He was muzzled and ragged looking. At his feet lay something red and white. "Chum," Morley said. "The light bothers him. You remember ole Chum, don't you? Julie's favorite pet . . . Ah, but I see you're wondering what that is at his feet. That sort of surprises me, Dennis. Really. As intimate as you and Julie were, I'd think you'd know her. Even without her makeup."

Now that Dennis knew what he was looking at, he could make out the white bone of her skull, a dark patch of matted hair still clinging to it. He also recognized what was left of the dress she had been wearing. It was a red and white tennis dress, the one she wore when they played racquetball. It was mostly red now. Her entire body had been gnawed savagely.

"Murderer!" Dennis rocked savagely in the chair, tried to pull free of his bonds. After a moment of useless struggle and useless epithets, he leaned forward and let the lava hot gorge in his stomach pour out.

"Oh, Dennis," Morley said. "That's going to be stinky. Just awful. Will you look at your shoes? And calling me a murderer. Now, I ask you, Dennis, is that nice? I didn't murder anyone. Chum did the dirty work. After four days without food and water he was ravenous and thirsty. Wouldn't you be? And he was a little crazy too. I burned his feet some. Not as bad as I burned Julie's, but enough to really piss him off. And I sprayed him with this."

Morley reached into his coat pocket, produced an aerosol canister and waved it at Dennis.

"This was invented by some business associate of mine. It came out of some chemical warfare research I'm conducting. I'm in, shall we say . . . espionage? I work for the highest bidder. I have plans here for arms and chemical warfare . . . If it's profitable and ugly, I'm involved. I'm a real stinker sometimes. I certainly am."

Morley was still waving the canister, as if trying to hypnotize Dennis with it. "We came up with this to train attack dogs. We found we could spray a padded up man with this and the dogs would go bonkers. Rip the pads right off of him. Sometimes the only way to stop the beggers was to shoot them. It was a failure actually. It activated the dogs, but it drove them out of their minds and they couldn't be controlled at all. And after a short time the odor faded, and the spray became quite the reverse. It made it so the dogs couldn't smell the spray at all. It made whoever was wearing it odorless. Still, I found a use for it. A very personal use.

"I let Chum go a few days without food and water while I worked on Julie . . . And she wasn't tough at all, Dennis. Not even a little bit. Spilled her guts. Now that isn't entirely correct. She didn't spill her guts until later, when Chum got hold of her . . . Anyway, she told me what I wanted to know about you two, then I sprayed that delicate thirty-six, twenty-four, thirty-six figure of hers with this. And with Chum so hungry, and me having burned his feet and done some mean things to him, he was not in the best of humor when I gave him Julie.

"It was disgusting, Dennis. Really. I had to come back when it was over and shoot Chum with a tranquilizer dart, get him tied and muzzled for your arrival."

Morley leaned forward, sprayed Dennis from head to foot with the canister. Dennis turned his head and closed his eyes, tried not to breathe the foul-smelling mist.

"He's probably not all that hungry now," Morley said, "but this will still drive him wild."

Already Chum had gotten a whiff and was leaping at his leash. Foam burst from between his lips and frothed on the leather bands of the muzzle.

"I suppose it isn't polite to lecture a captive audience, Dennis, but I thought you might like to know a few things about dogs. No need to take notes. You won't be around for a quiz later.

"But here's some things to tuck in the back of your mind while you and Chum are alone. Dogs are very strong, Dennis. Very. They look small compared to a man, even a big dog like a Doberman, but they can exert a lot of pressure with their bite. I've seen dogs like Chum here, especially when they're exposed to my little spray, bite through the thicker end of a baseball bat. And they're quick. You'd have a better chance against a black belt in karate than an attack dog."

"Morley," Dennis said softly, "you can't do this."

"I can't?" Morley seemed to consider. "No, Dennis, I believe I can. I give myself permission. But hey, Dennis, I'm going to give you a chance. This is the good part now, so listen up. You're a sporting man. Basketball. Racquetball. Chess. Another man's woman. So you'll like this. This will appeal to your sense of competition.

"Julie didn't give Chum a fight at all. She just couldn't believe her Chummy-whummy wanted to eat her . . . Just wouldn't.

She held out her hand, trying to soothe the old boy, and he just bit it right off. Right off. Got half the palm and the fingers in one bite. That's when I left them alone. I had a feeling her Chummy-whummy might start on me next, and I wouldn't have wanted that. Oooohhh, those sharp teeth. Like nails being driven into you."

"Morley, listen—"

"Shut up! You, Mr. Cock Dog and Basketball Star, just might have a chance. Not much of one, but I know you'll fight. You're not a quitter. I can tell by the way you play chess. You still lose, but you're not a quitter. You hang in there to the bitter end."

Morley took a deep breath, stood in the chair and hung the lantern on a low rafter. There was something else up there too. A coiled chain. Morley pulled it down and it clattered to the floor. At the sound of it Chum leaped against his leash and flecks of saliva flew from his mouth and Dennis felt them fall lightly on his hands and face.

Morley lifted one end of the chain toward Dennis. There was a thin, open collar attached to it.

"Once this closes it locks and can only be opened with this." Morley reached into his coat pocket and produced a key, held it up briefly and returned it. "There's a collar for Chum on the other end. Both are made out of good leather over strong, steel chain. See what I'm getting at here, Dennis?"

Morley leaned forward and snapped the collar around Dennis's neck.

"Oh, Dennis," Morley said, standing back to observe his handiwork. "It's you. Really. Great fit. And considering the day, just call this my valentine to you."

"You bastard."

"The biggest."

Morley walked over to Chum. Chum lunged at him, but with the muzzle on he was relatively harmless. Still, his weight hit Morley's legs, almost knocked him down.

Turning to smile at Dennis, Morley said, "See how strong he is? Add teeth to this little engine, some maneuverability . . . it's going to be awesome, lover boy. Awesome."

Morley slipped the collar under Chum's leash and snapped it into place even as the dog rushed against him, nearly knocking him down. But it wasn't Morley he wanted. He was trying to get at the smell. At Dennis. Dennis felt as if the fluids in his body were running out of drains at the bottoms of his feet.

"Was a little poontang worth this, Dennis? I certainly hope

you think so. I hope it was the best goddamn piece you ever got. Sincerely, I do. Because death by dog is slow and ugly, lover boy. They like the throat and balls. So, you watch those spots, hear?"

"Morley, for God's sake, don't do this!"

Morley pulled a revolver from his coat pocket and walked over to Dennis. "I'm going to untie you now, stud. I want you to be real good, or I'll shoot you. If I shoot you, I'll gut shoot you, then let the dog loose. You got no chance that way. At least my way you've got a sporting chance—slim to none."

He untied Dennis. "Now stand."

Dennis stood in front of the chair, his knees quivering. He was looking at Chum and Chum was looking at him, tugging wildly at the leash, which looked ready to snap. Saliva was thick as shaving cream over the front of Chum's muzzle.

Morley held the revolver on Dennis with one hand, and with the other he reproduced the aerosol can, sprayed Dennis once more. The stench made Dennis's head float.

"Last word of advice," Morley said. "He'll go straight for you."

"Morley . . ." Dennis started, but one look at the man and he knew he was better off saving the breath. He was going to need it.

Still holding the gun on Dennis, Morley eased behind the frantic dog, took hold of the muzzle with his free hand, and with a quick ripping motion, pulled it and the leash loose.

Chum sprang.

Dennis stepped back, caught the chair between his legs, lost his balance. Chum's leap carried him into Dennis's chest, and they both went flipping over the chair.

Chum kept rolling and the chain pulled across Dennis's face as the dog tumbled to its full length; the jerk of the sixty pound weight against Dennis's neck was like a blow.

The chain went slack, and Dennis knew Chum was coming. In that same instant he heard the door open, glimpsed a wedge of moonlight that came and went, heard the door lock and Morley laugh. Then he was rolling, coming to his knees, grabbing the chair, pointing it with the legs out.

And Chum hit him.

The chair took most of the impact, but it was like trying to block a cannonball. The chair's bottom cracked and a leg broke off, went skidding across the floor.

The truncated triangle of the Doberman's head appeared over the top of the chair, straining for Dennis's face. Dennis rammed the chair forward.

Chum dipped under it, grabbed Dennis's ankle. It was like stepping into a bear trap. The agony wasn't just in the ankle, it was a sizzling web of electricity that surged through his entire body.

The dog's teeth grated bone and Dennis let forth with a noise that was too wicked to be called a scream.

Blackness waved in and out, but the thought of Julie lying there in ragged display gave him new determination.

He brought the chair down on the dog's head with all his might.

Chum let out a yelp, and the dark head darted away.

Dennis stayed low, pulled his wounded leg back, attempted to keep the chair in front of him. But Chum was a black bullet. He shot under again, hit Dennis in the same leg, higher up this time. The impact slid Dennis back a foot. Still, he felt a certain relief. The dog's teeth had missed his balls by an inch.

Oddly there was little pain this time. It was as if he were being encased in dark amber; floating in limbo. Must be like this when a shark hits, he thought. So hard and fast and clean you don't really feel it at first. Just go numb. Look down for your leg and it's gone.

The dark amber was penetrated by a bright stab of pain. But Dennis was grateful for it. It meant that his brain was working again. He swiped at Chum with the chair, broke him loose.

Swiveling on one knee, Dennis again used the chair as a shield. Chum launched forward, trying to go under it, but Dennis was ready this time and brought it down hard against the floor.

Chum hit the bottom of the chair with such an impact, his head broke through the thin slats. Teeth snapped in Dennis's face, but the dog couldn't squirm its shoulders completely through the hole and reach him.

Dennis let go of the chair with one hand, slugged the dog in the side of the head with the other. Chum twisted and the chair came loose from Dennis. The dog bounded away, leaping and whipping its body left and right, finally tossing off the wooden collar.

Grabbing the slack of the chain, Dennis used both hands to whip it into the dog's head, then swung it back and caught Chum's feet, knocking him on his side with a loud splat.

Even as Chum was scrambling to his feet, out of the corner of his eye Dennis spotted the leg that had broken off the chair. It was lying less than three feet away.

Chum rushed and Dennis dove for the leg, grabbed it, twisted and swatted at the Doberman. On the floor as he was, he couldn't get full power into the blow, but still it was a good one.

The dog skidded sideways on its belly and forelegs. When it came to a halt, it tried to raise its head, but didn't completely make it.

Dennis scrambled forward on his hands and knees, chopped the chair leg down on the Doberman's head with every ounce of muscle he could muster. The strike was solid, caught the dog right between the pointed ears and drove his head to the floor.

The dog whimpered. Dennis hit him again. And again.

Chum lay still.

Dennis took a deep breath, watched the dog and held his club cocked.

Chum did not move. He lay on the floor with his legs spread wide, his tongue sticking out of his foam-wet mouth.

Dennis was breathing heavily, and his wounded leg felt as if it were melting. He tried to stretch it out, alleviate some of the pain, but nothing helped.

He checked the dog again.

Still not moving.

He took hold of the chain and jerked it. Chum's head came up and smacked back down against the floor.

The dog was dead. He could see that.

He relaxed, closed his eyes and tried to make the spinning stop. He knew he had to bandage his leg somehow, stop the flow of blood. But at the moment he could hardly think.

And Chum, who was not dead, but stunned, lifted his head, and at the same moment, Dennis opened his eyes.

The Doberman's recovery was remarkable. It came off the floor with only the slightest wobble and jumped.

Dennis couldn't get the chair leg around in time and it deflected off of the animal's smooth back and slipped from his grasp.

He got Chum around the throat and tried to strangle him, but the collar was in the way and the dog's neck was too damn big.

Trying to get better traction, Dennis got his bad leg under him and made an effort to stand, lifting the dog with him. He used his good leg to knee Chum sharply in the chest, but the injured leg wasn't good for holding him up for another move like that. He kept trying to ease his thumbs beneath the collar and lock them behind the dog's windpipe.

Chum's hind legs were off the floor and scrambling, the toenails tearing at Dennis's lower abdomen and crotch.

Dennis couldn't believe how strong the dog was. Sixty pounds of pure muscle and energy, made more deadly by Morley's spray and tortures.

Sixty pounds of muscle.

The thought went through Dennis's head again.

Sixty pounds.

The medicine ball he tossed at the gym weighed more. It didn't have teeth, muscle and determination, but it did weigh more.

And as the realization soaked in, as his grip weakened and Chum's rancid breath coated his face, Dennis lifted his eyes to a rafter just two feet above his head; considered there was another two feet of space between the rafter and the ceiling.

He quit trying to choke Chum, eased his left hand into the dog's collar, and grabbed a hind leg with his other. Slowly, he lifted Chum over his head. Teeth snapped at Dennis's hair, pulled loose a few tufts.

Dennis spread his legs slightly. The wounded leg wobbled like an old pipe cleaner, but held. The dog seemed to weigh a hundred pounds. Even the sweat on his face and the dense, hot air in the room seemed heavy.

Sixty pounds.

A basketball weighed little to nothing, and the dog weighed less than the huge medicine ball in the gym. Somewhere between the two was a happy medium; he had the strength to lift the dog, the skill to make the shot—the most important of his life.

Grunting, cocking the wiggling dog into position, he prepared to shoot. Chum nearly twisted free, but Dennis gritted his teeth, and with a wild scream, launched the dog into space.

Chum didn't go up straight, but he did go up. He hit the top of the rafter with his back, tried to twist in the direction he had come, couldn't, and went over the other side.

Dennis grabbed the chain as high up as possible, bracing as Chum's weight came down on the other side so violently it pulled him onto his toes.

The dog made a gurgling sound, spun on the end of the chain, legs thrashing.

It took a long fifteen minutes for Chum to strangle.

When Chum was dead, Dennis tried to pull him over the rafter. The dog's weight, Dennis's bad leg, and his now aching arms and back, made it a greater chore than he had anticipated. Chum's head kept slamming against the rafter. Dennis got hold of the unbroken chair, and used it as a stepladder. He managed the Doberman over, and Chum fell to the floor, his neck flopping loosely.

Dennis sat down on the floor beside the dog and patted it on the head. "Sorry," he said.

He took off his shirt, tore it into rags and bound his bad leg with it. It was still bleeding steadily, but not gushing; no major artery had been torn. His ankle wasn't bleeding as much, but in the dim lantern light he could see that Chum had bitten him to the bone. He used most of the shirt to wrap and strengthen the ankle.

When he finished, he managed to stand. The shirt binding had stopped the bleeding and the short rest had slightly rejuvenated him.

He found his eyes drawn to the mess in the corner that was Julie, and his first thought was to cover her, but there wasn't anything in the room sufficient for the job.

He closed his eyes and tried to remember how it had been before. When she was whole and the room had a mattress and they had made love all the long, sweet, Mexican afternoon. But the right images would not come. Even with his eyes closed, he could see her mauled body on the floor.

Ducking his head made some of the dizziness go away, and he was able to get Julie out of his mind by thinking of Morley. He wondered when he would come back. If he was waiting outside.

But no, that wouldn't be Morley's way. He wouldn't be anxious. He was cocksure of himself, he would go back to the estate for a drink and maybe play a game of chess against himself, gloat a long, sweet while before coming back to check on his handiwork. It would never occur to Morley to think he had survived. That would not cross his mind. Morley saw himself as Life's best chess master, and he did not make wrong moves; things went according to plan. Most likely, he wouldn't even check until morning.

The more Dennis thought about it, the madder he got and the stronger he felt. He moved the chair beneath the rafter where the lantern was hung, climbed up and got it down. He inspected the windows and doors. The door had a sound lock, but the windows were merely boarded. Barrier enough when he was busy with the dog, but not now.

He put the lantern on the floor, turned it up, found the chair leg he had used against Chum, and substituted it for a pry bar. It was hard work and by the time he had worked the boards off the window his hands were bleeding and full of splinters. His face looked demonic.

Pulling Chum to him, he tossed him out the window, climbed after him clutching the chair leg. He took up the chain's slack and hitched it around his forearm. He wondered about the other Dobermans. Wondered if Morley had killed them too, or if he was keeping them around. As he recalled, the Dobermans were usually loose on the yard at night. The rest of the time they had free run of the house, except Morley's study, his sanctuary. And hadn't Morley said that later on the spray killed a man's scent? That was worth something; it could be the edge he needed.

But it didn't really matter. Nothing mattered anymore. Six dogs. Six war elephants. He was going after Morley.

He began dragging the floppy-necked Chum toward the estate.

Morley was sitting at his desk playing a game of chess with himself, and both sides were doing quite well, he thought. He had a glass of brandy at his elbow, and from time to time he would drink from it, cock his head and consider his next move.

Outside the study door, in the hall, he could hear Julie's dogs padding nervously. They wanted out, and in the past they would have been on the yard long before now. But tonight he hadn't bothered. He hated those bastards, and just maybe he'd get rid of them. Shoot them and install a burglar alarm. Alarms didn't have to eat or be let out to shit, and they wouldn't turn on you. And he wouldn't have to listen to the sound of dog toenails clicking on the tile outside of his study door.

He considered letting the Dobermans out, but hesitated. Instead, he opened a box of special Cuban cigars, took one, rolled it between his fingers near his ear so he could hear the fresh crackle of good tobacco. He clipped the end off the cigar with a silver clipper, put it in his mouth and lit it with a desk lighter without actually putting the flame to it. He drew in a deep lungfull of smoke and relished it, let it out with a soft, contented sigh.

At the same moment he heard a sound, like something being

dragged across the gravel drive. He sat motionless a moment, not batting an eye. It couldn't be lover boy, he thought. No way.

He walked across the room, pulled the curtain back from the huge glass door, unlocked it and slid it open.

A cool wind had come along and it was shaking the trees in the yard, but nothing else was moving. Morley searched the tree shadows for some tell-tale sign, but saw nothing.

Still, he was not one for imagination. He *had* heard something. He went back to the desk chair where his coat hung, reached the revolver from his pocket, turned.

And there was Dennis. Shirtless, one pants leg mostly ripped away. There were blood-stained bandages on his thigh and ankle. He had the chain partially coiled around one arm, and Chum, quite dead, was lying on the floor beside him. In his right hand Dennis held a chair leg, and at the same moment Morley noted this and raised the revolver, Dennis threw it.

The leg hit Morley squarely between the eyes, knocked him against his desk, and as he tried to right himself, Dennis took hold of the chain and used it to swing the dead dog. Chum struck Morley on the ankles and took him down like a scythe cutting fresh wheat. Morley's head slammed into the edge of the desk and blood dribbled into his eyes; everything seemed to be in a mixmaster, whirling so fast nothing was identifiable.

When the world came to rest, he saw Dennis standing over him with the revolver. Morley could not believe the man's appearance. His lips were split in a thin grin that barely showed his teeth. His face was drawn and his eyes were strange and savage. It was apparent he had found the key in the coat, because the collar was gone.

Out in the hall, bouncing against the door, Morley could hear Julie's dogs. They sensed the intruder and wanted at him. He wished now he had left the study door open, or put them out on the yard.

"I've got money," Morley said.

"Fuck your money," Dennis screamed. "I'm not selling anything here. Get up and get over here."

Morley followed the wave of the revolver to the front of his desk. Dennis swept the chess set and stuff aside with a swipe of his arm and bent Morley backwards over the desk. He put one of the collars around Morley's neck, pulled the chain around the desk a few times, pushed it under and fastened the other collar over Morley's ankles.

Tucking the revolver into the waistband of his pants, Dennis picked up Chum and tenderly placed him on the desk chair, half-curled. He tried to poke the dog's tongue back into his mouth, but that didn't work. He patted Chum on the head, said, "There, now."

Dennis went around and stood in front of Morley and looked at him, as if memorizing the moment.

At his back the Dobermans rattled the door.

"We can make a deal," Morley said. "I can give you a lot of money, and you can go away. We'll call it even."

Dennis unfastened Morley's pants, pulled them down to his knees. He pulled the underwear down. He went around and got the spray can out of Morley's coat and came back.

"This isn't sporting, Dennis. At least I gave you a fighting chance."

"I'm not a sport," Dennis said.

He sprayed Morley's testicles with the chemical. When he finished he tossed the canister aside, walked over to the door and listened to the Dobermans scuttling on the other side.

"Dennis!"

Dennis took hold of the doorknob.

"Screw you then," Morley said. "I'm not afraid. I won't scream. I won't give you the pleasure."

"You didn't even love her," Dennis said, and opened the door.

The Dobermans went straight for the stench of the spray, straight for Morley's testicles.

Dennis walked calmly out the back way, closed the glass door. And as he limped down the drive, making for the gate, he began to laugh.

Morley had lied. He did too scream. In fact, he was still screaming.

Triangle

by Teri White

Triangle *not only won the Edgar in its year, it is generally considered to be one of the best novels of its decade. It certainly foreshadows what White would do in future years—offer us a very Graham Greene-like sense of America's mean streets . . . a spicy admixture of sass and sorrow. Soon enough her work will be recognized for its own very special attributes.*

First published in 1982.

PROLOGUE

The baby blue BMW glided almost silently through the alley, stopping finally behind a modest brick apartment building. A moment later the car door opened and Johnny slid out of the passenger seat. He pushed the door gently and it closed with a muffled thud. The man behind the wheel lit a cigarette and slid down in the seat a little.

Johnny walked with long strides toward the building, his soft-soled shoes making no sound against the brick surface. The morning felt clean, somehow filled with newness after last night's rain. It was Johnny's favorite kind of day, and he took a couple of deep, satisfying breaths, smiling with quiet pleasure as he moved.

When he reached the back door of the apartment building, he paused, taking a narrow length of steel from his pocket. It took exactly five point six seconds for the lock to click open beneath his slender fingers. Without turning, he lifted one hand in a V-for-Victory gesture over his shoulder.

The door opened at his touch and he slipped into the dim coolness of the hallway. As expected, it was quiet. Sunday was the best time to work. Somehow, no one ever seemed to anticipate anything unpleasant happening as he digested his eggs and comic papers.

Johnny knew exactly where he was going. Nothing was ever left to chance during these operations, and he had complete faith in the plan as it had been explained to him. Apartment eleven was at the far end of the hallway and Johnny didn't even pause until he was standing directly in front of the door. He knocked firmly with his left hand, at the same time reaching his right inside the worn corduroy sport coat to grasp the gun that hung at his side. The eight-inch barreled piece of blue steel rested easily in his grip as he waited patiently for a response to his knock.

The door opened finally and Papagallos stood there smiling, a plump grey-haired man wearing a red silk robe and black patent slippers. The smile lost a little of its brightness as he realized that this visitor was not whom he had expected to find on his threshold this particular Sabbath morning. His expression, however, remained genial. Johnny often noticed that same reaction on other faces. People just seemed to trust him on sight, even people like Papagallos, who had reason to fear every stranger at the door.

One day, after Johnny had given a great deal of thought to the whole matter, but was still unable to figure out why everyone seemed to trust him so implicitly, he went to Mac for an explanation. Mac, who usually had all the answers, only shrugged. "You just have a nice face," he said absently. That wasn't much of an answer, but Mac seemed satisfied, so Johnny accepted it.

Papagallos obviously felt no fear, no sudden pang of apprehension. No premonition. His apparently somewhat near-sighted gaze swept over the tall blond man in the doorway, seeing the battered running shoes, the much-faded, too-tight Levis, the bright yellow T-shirt topped by the brown cord jacket. And then he noticed the gun, but by then it was too late, because the bullet was already on its way toward him.

The jacketed hollow point slug collided with Papagallos' forehead. Blood, fragments of bone, and lumpy pieces of grey brain matter splattered against the seagreen brocaded wallpaper of the foyer as Papagallos, still smiling, slid to the floor.

It was not until then that Johnny saw the other man inside the room and the sight momentarily confused him. Papagallos was supposed to have been alone for at least another hour. The confusion didn't last long, however. His instructions had been drilled into him time after time. No witnesses. A finger pressed against the trigger once more, the silenced gun popped, and the gangly redhead flew back against the chair, blood gushing from his chest.

Carefully avoiding Papagallos' body, Johnny reached in to pull the door closed, wiping the polished brass knob with the sleeve of his jacket. He tucked the gun back into his holster before walking swiftly, but calmly, back down the hall.

Emerging into the sunshine and fresh air again, he paused, giving a sigh as light as the gentle spring breeze, then moved briskly back to the car. Mac already had the engine purring softly. "Everything go okay?" he asked, as always.

Johnny ignored the question, resting back against the seat, his eyes closed. The car pulled out of the alley, slipping neatly into the flow of traffic. For nearly five minutes, the two men rode in silence. Finally Johnny straightened. He took off his tinted aviator glasses and began to clean them with a crumpled tissue. "Do you know what I'd like?" he asked dreamily.

Mac's grip on the steering wheel relaxed. "What?"

"A strawberry ice cream cone." Johnny put the glasses back on, settling them precisely on his nose, and peered at Mac. "Could I get one, please?"

"Sure, if we can find a place open this early."

Johnny smiled.

It took a little searching, but they managed finally to locate a small dairy store with an OPEN sign stuck in the front window. Mac pulled the car into the parking lot and stopped. "Strawberry, you said, right?"

"Yeah. Two scoops."

"Coming right up." Mac got out of the car and walked into the grimy little store, his hand-tooled western boots making sharp clicking noises on the linoleum floor.

There was no one in the place except a pimple-faced teenage clerk, who gave Mac a look of complete boredom. "Yeah?" he said around a wad of gum.

"Double dip of strawberry."

"Cup cone or sugar?"

"Ah, sugar," Mac said absently, never able to remember which kind Johnny preferred. He turned around to stare through the dirt-streaked window. Sunlight reflected off the hand-polished finish of the BMW. Johnny sat slumped in the seat, his glasses catching rays of the golden light, making it look as if he had a bright halo around his head. The sight bemused

Mac and the clerk spoke twice before he really heard him. "Huh?"

"Sixty cents, mister," the kid repeated wearily.

He tossed some coins down onto the sticky counter and took the cone carefully, grabbing a couple of napkins from the dispenser at the same time.

Johnny greeted his return with another smile, reaching out to take the cone. "Thank you," he said.

Mac only grunted a reply as he got behind the wheel again and headed the car back toward the motel. Johnny was quiet during the ride, eating the ice cream with studied concentration.

It took only fifteen minutes for them to reach the Welcome Inn. Their room was undoubtedly a depressing place to inhabit, with walls that were painted an indeterminate color somewhere between brown and grey, and painfully utilitarian furnishings, but the type was so familiar that neither one of them even noticed the quality of their surroundings anymore.

Mac stood at the window, watching the traffic on the busy street just beyond, and listening to the crescendo of the shower running in the bathroom. Behind him, the fuzzy black-and-white TV flickered soundlessly as a white-haired video preacher exhorted the masses to spiritual awakening. Mac smoked three cigarettes in a row as he waited for the shower to go off.

Johnny came out finally, barefooted and shirtless, his Levis sporting damp patches, his face flushed. "Someday you're going to boil yourself alive," Mac said sourly. Johnny only shrugged, turning up the volume on the TV.

". . . and Jesus Christ wants you to accept His offer of eternal life."

Mac turned to stare at the screen. "Why do you listen to that crap?"

"'Bonanza' comes on after," Johnny replied. "Little Joe might get hung." He sat down on the edge of the bed and moved his shoulders slightly. Mac crushed out his just-lit fourth cigarette and came over. Using both hands, he began to massage the tense muscles in Johnny's neck and shoulders. "So?" he said shortly. "What's the matter?"

"There was somebody with him," Johnny said after a moment.

Mac's hands paused briefly in their movements, then resumed the massage. "Yeah?"

Johnny nodded. "A skinny redheaded guy. You told me Papagallos would be by himself." It was an accusation.

"Sorry." Mac never wasted much time regretting what couldn't be helped. "So?"

"I shot him."

Mac's fingers moved efficiently through still-damp blond curls clinging to the back of Johnny's neck. "Well, you had to."

"Yeah, I know. I know." Johnny's voice sounded old and very tired. He moved away from the massage abruptly and stretched out on the chenille bedspread, covering his eyes with one arm.

Mac watched him for a moment, then picked up a faded green windbreaker and pulled it on. "I'm going out," he said. "I probably won't be gone long." He waited for a response, but when there was none, he left the room, shutting the door carefully behind himself.

BOOK

I

Chapter 1

They had been humping through the bush for three days now, and nobody really knew why. In fact, no one was even sure just where the hell they were. Mac just kept them moving, following a map that must have been drawn by an idiot with one thumb up his ass. He figured that the simple momentum of their journey would sooner or later provide a motive for the trip.

Needing to piss, Mac stepped off the path and let the line of men continue to move past him. As he sprayed the nearby plants, his mind was trying to dredge up the title of an old song made famous by Nat King Cole. Something he used to play all the time on the jukebox in the Hi-Time Cafe back in Okie City. Years ago. Must have played that damned song two thousand times, he thought, zipping his trousers. Why can't I remember the fucking title? He wiped his hand on the seat of his trousers. Wonder if maybe I'm losing my mind?

It wasn't the first time that question had presented itself.

The last man had gone by him. What would happen, he mused, if he just started walking the other way? Maybe it was time he just checked out of this whole fucking mess. Nobody told him there was going to be a war when he joined the goddamned army. It wasn't fair. Somebody had changed the rules on him.

He stepped back onto the trail and found himself walking next to Crazy George. George was an old man of nineteen. His eyes looked at least a hundred years old, though he hadn't yet been able to raise a moustache. The soft line of down across his upper lip just made him look as if he'd been drinking chocolate milk. "Hey, Lieutenant," he said, "where we going anyway?"

"Beats the hell out of me, George," he said lightly.

"Shit. Well, I hope we get there soon."

"Why?"

"'Cause I like to know where the hell I'm at."

Crazy George made him nervous, ever since the night they'd

caught him trying to rig a grenade to the door of the officers' latrine. Mac nodded and smiled, moving a little faster until he caught up with Washington, his sergeant. Washington was a good man, and he even seemed almost sane.

The smell hit them first.

The acrid, too-familiar odor of gunfire and smoke floated across the heavy humid air, making their noses itch. Everybody tensed. Mac rubbed his burning eyes with the back of one hand, trying to ignore the creepy, crawly sensation beginning to flicker across his groin.

There was a small rise edging the city of Tan Pret, and they moved over it cautiously, staring down into what had to be a corner of hell. "Jee-sus," someone said aloud.

Even from where they stood, the bodies were clearly visible— women, children, old men, the fallen figures making little patches of color against the smoldering brown earth.

The only signs of life in the devastated village came from the American troops walking through the remains. As Mac and his men moved down the rise toward them, one of the soldiers looked up. His face was red; his eyes glittered. "Spies," he said loudly enough for them to hear. "All of them were spies. Had to root them out . . . had to. . . ." His voice trailed off.

Mac could only stare.

It came to him suddenly. *Mona Lisa.* That was the name of the goddamned song.

He didn't know what the hell he was supposed to do, so he decided not to do anything at all, at least for the moment. Leaving Wash to deploy some men around the perimeter of the village, Mac just walked away from it all. He walked as far as a large boulder that rested on the eastern edge of Tan Pret. Resting his automatic on the ground, he perched on the rock and closed his eyes.

. . . *Mona Lisa, Mona Lisa, men have named you.* . . .

Now he couldn't get the damned song out of his mind. Made him think about the apple pie they used to serve at the old Hi-Time. With homemade vanilla ice cream plunked on top. Crust real crisp, with cinnamon sprinkled on.

But that was before he joined the army and how was he to know that fifteen years later he'd be sitting in the middle of a frigging jungle gagging from the stink of death. The recruiter promised him he could become an auto mechanic.

. . . *or is this the way you hide a broken heart.* . . .

This was a helluva fucked-up mess. How come it all had to fall into his lap anyway? And what the devil should he do now?

"What a helluva fucked-up mess." He said the words aloud that time. It was then that he opened his eyes and realized that he wasn't alone. He turned wearily, not ready yet to give an order, to take charge.

The unwelcome intruder was a stranger. Tall and slender, he had shaggy blond hair that stuck out from beneath his helmet and blue eyes that were as dead as Tan Pret itself. "Yeah?" Mac grunted, thinking that the kid looked like a choirboy in search of a congregation. Except for the empty eyes. "What?"

There was no answer. The man kept staring at him.

"What's your name, Sergeant?" When there was still no reply, Mac reached out and took hold of the guy's dogtags. The stranger flinched away, as if he expected to be struck. "Take it easy, buddy. I only want to find out who you are. Griffith, John Paul." He released the tags.

Griffith suddenly opened his hands, letting the M-16 fall to the ground. He stared at the weapon for a long time, as if he'd never seen it before, as if it had nothing at all to do with him.

"Griffith?" Belatedly, Mac realized that the man was suffering from some kind of shock. Shit, it was no wonder. He slid from the boulder and stood in front of the blank gaze. "Hey, man, can you hear me?" There wasn't even a flicker of response. Mac sighed. Great. A real whacko. Just what they needed at a time like this. Maybe he should go find Crazy George; the two of them could probably have a great conversation.

He turned away, looking back across the village. There must be something to be done here, although only God knew what it was. He felt a light but urgent tugging at his sleeve and glanced around. Griffith was holding on to him. "It's all right," Mac said absently. "I'm not going anywhere." There was no change in Griffith's expression, but his hand slipped away from Mac's arm.

Washington appeared. "Some bitchin' thing, massa."

"Yeah. And I don't know what the hell I'm supposed to do about it."

"Better you than me." Washington gestured. "Who's the zombie?"

Mac shrugged. "One of them, I guess. A real spaceman." He sighed, rubbing a hand across his face. "Well, we better get something going here, right? See if you can find the bastard in charge."

Washington gave a mock salute and walked away.

Mac sat on the rock again. "You a Nat King Cole fan, by any chance?" he asked. "No, guess not. Probably too young, right? Hell, when I joined this man's army you were—" He did a little mental calculation from the birthdate on the dogtags. "—twelve. Christ, this is a frigging children's crusade." Griffith wasn't a child, of course. He was twenty-seven. Mac shrugged. "I could listen to that man sing for hours." He leaned forward a little. "Hey, John? Anything getting through to you? Are you in there?"

Nothing.

"Hell. Sit down, dummy." Surprisingly, Griffith sank down onto the rock. Mac figured that was a step in the right direction. "Hi. Welcome to my rock. You may not talk much, but you take orders real fine, don't you? That's an outstanding quality in a soldier." Mac had the fleeting thought that it didn't say much for his own mental state that he would sit and talk to a zombie, but what the hell. "How do you feel about apple pie, John?"

The lieutenant in charge, a hard-faced man named Delgado, managed to be both belligerent and non-communicative when he finally appeared. They talked about what had happened, or what Delgado claimed had happened, or maybe what he'd dreamed had happened, but it all added up to nothing. Finally, in disgust, he sent Delgado off to organize his men to dig some trenches into which the late citizens of Tan Pret could be dumped. Mustn't litter up the country, Mac thought.

He turned back to Griffith, who sat very still, both hands folded neatly in his lap, his young face guileless. "I have to go talk to Wash," Mac said slowly and distinctly, as if he were speaking to a backward child. "You just sit tight, okay? I'll be right back." Griffith didn't acknowledge his words, but neither did he try to keep him from going.

Washington was supervising the digging of a shallow trench. "Tote that barge, lift that bale," he murmured as Mac joined him.

"How long is this gonna take?"

"Couple hours, I guess." They watched the digging for several moments. "What happens after that?"

"I don't know." Mac rubbed the bridge of his nose. "Shit." He kicked at a lump of brown earth, sending it flying through the air.

A moment later, almost as if in perverse response to his action, the world began to explode around them. From somewhere beyond the trees an artillery barrage descended upon the already dead village. The grave diggers scattered, some heading for the trees and the rest leaping into the unfinished trench in a desperate search for cover.

Mac turned quickly and peered through the smoke and mass confusion. Griffith was sitting where he'd left him, his hands still folded, his apparently unseeing eyes fixed on Mac. He seemed unaware of the flaming apocalypse around him. "Jesus H. Christ," Mac whispered, beginning a broken field run across the space between them.

The shelling ended as suddenly as it had begun.

He reached the boulder, aware that dark figures were entering the village. The Americans were still scattering in all directions. He knew that he should have done something, given an order, taken charge, but all he wanted to do was run. He grabbed his rifle with one hand and Griffith's arm with the other. "Move it, dummy!" he shouted.

Mac didn't know or care what was happening behind them. He only knew that they had to get away. It wasn't only the enemy he was scared of; it was the village of Tan Pret and all its horrifying implications.

So they ran.

Chapter 2

For years after, Mac would dream about the days following Tan Pret. He would never be able to forget wandering through that damned jungle, sweating, stinking, tired to the point of tears, his every step through that purgatory dogged by a mute shadow.

He didn't know where they were, didn't know which way they should go; he didn't know a goddamned thing, except that he was going to lose whatever little bit of his sanity remained unless something happened soon. He was heartily sick of the sound of his own voice and sick of playing nursemaid to Griffith.

As night approached on the third day of their odyssey, they both collapsed beneath the vines and branches of a fallen tree. "Looks like home for the night, John. Okay with you?"

Griffith smiled. It was the same smile he used when Mac grunted a morning greeting, or when they shared a melted chocolate bar from Mac's pack. He smiled and he smiled, but he never said a word.

Mac dug into his pack and found the last can of fruit cocktail.
He opened it and wiped the spoon on the edge of his shirt.
"Better enjoy, buddy-boy," he said. "Might be the last food we
see for a while. Maybe you'd like to feed yourself this time?"

But Griffith just sat there. Mac sighed and lifted some fruit
onto the spoon. "Open your mouth," he said flatly. "Or I'll stick
the fucking garbage in your ear."

The blond's mouth opened obediently, and the spoon slipped
in. They alternated bites until nothing was left in the can except
the sweet syrup, which he irritably fed to Griffith. After only
three days, his already slender face was etched into sharp lines.
Beneath the foggy blue eyes, his cheekbones were painfully
prominent.

Mac reached into the pack again and took out the bottle of
cheap scotch. It was almost empty. He dumped the rest of the
pale amber liquid into his canteen and pressed it into Griffith's
hand. "Drink some," he ordered absently. Griffith drank and,
without prompting, handed the cup back. Mac rewarded that
unexpected burst of initiative with the weary imitation of a
smile. "Good boy. Maybe I can teach you some more tricks. You
could probably roll over and play dead real good."

Mac downed the rest of the scotch in one gulp. "So who do
you like in the World Series, kid?" he said.

Griffith smiled.

It was like being trapped with a recalcitrant child, and Mac
often felt like a parent driven to the end of his patience, wanting
to slap the cheerfully blank face into some kind of realization.
But he fought for self-control. "We better get some sleep," he
said.

Mac spent some time trying to figure out how many new
insect bites his body had acquired, but then realized that he
didn't give a damn anymore. He finally fell asleep listening to
the soft sound of Griffith's breathing.

It was very dark when he woke up. The pale moonlight seemed
much too fragile to penetrate the blackness in which they were
enveloped. Griffith slept like a child, curled on one side, his
hand stretched toward Mac, almost touching him.

Mac needed to piss. He got up slowly and moved out of their
hiding place, trying to stretch his cramped muscles. His flesh
stank of sweat and Tan Pret. Of death.

He peed, then lit a cigarette and walked a few more feet away,
not ready yet to try sleeping again. The situation they had here

was going to get critical before much longer. At least, by the time he got back he'd have some money waiting. This time, he wasn't going to blow it all in one of Wash's damned poker games. Hell, no, he'd go into Saigon and treat himself to a steak, some booze, a good screw. Yeah.

"Mac!"

A cry of naked, nearly animalistic terror rang through the heavy humid night, and Mac jumped, burning his cupped hand against the glowing cigarette. "Shit," he swore in startled reaction to both the cry and the burn.

"Mac!"

It was Griffith, of course, but the sudden sound of another human voice was as frightening as the previous silence had been. Mac dropped the rest of the cigarette, crushing it under his heel, then stumbled back through the tall grass to the place where Griffith had been sleeping peacefully a few minutes earlier.

He was unmistakably awake now, crouching like a caged animal, both arms wrapped around his legs. Even in the washed-out moonlight the terror on his face was clearly visible. His head jerked around as Mac crashed into their refuge. "Mac," he said again, this time the word a hoarse sob. He scrabbled across the distance between them, grabbing Mac's legs. "I thought you were gone. You said if I couldn't keep up, you'd leave me and I thought you did; I thought you left me." The words came in a rush, as if he'd had them bottled up for a long time and somebody had just pulled out the cork. He stopped finally, taking deep gulps of air.

Mac sank down, gripping the trembling man by both arms. "Hey, you're talking. That's good, kid, real good."

"I woke up and you weren't here, Mac."

"I just went to taking a fucking leak, Johnny, that's all. Hell, you think I'd just *go?*"

Johnny seemed to be calming a little, but his hands still clutched convulsively at Mac, shaking fingers seeking a firm hold. "I'm sorry," he said. "I'm sorry. I didn't mean to be bad. Please, don't be mad."

Mac didn't know what to do. He wrapped both arms around Griffith and just held on. "It's okay, Johnny," he said. "Don't worry."

"Something terrible happened, but I don't remember what it was. I can't remember, Mac. I just remember you and me running."

"It doesn't matter. Go to sleep, kid."

"Okay." Johnny twisted his fingers in Mac's shirt. "But you won't go away, will you?" The eyes were intense, unrelenting.

"No, I'm not going anywhere," Mac promised.

They didn't talk anymore. Mac just sat there, rocking back and forth, humming 'Mona Lisa.' After a long time, the tense body relaxed against him and the ragged breathing steadied. Mac shifted slightly, untangling the slender fingers from their death grip, and rested the sleeping man on the ground. Stretching out next to him, Mac spent the rest of the night staring through the branches at the sky.

Chapter 3

It was two days later when they stumbled across the Marine patrol. Mac was so worn out by then, so exhausted physically and mentally, that he just let someone else take over. Johnny, who'd spent the time since he'd started talking rambling on in great detail about his life, seemed to creep back into a shell of silence with others around.

With no time lost, they were shuffled from the Marine camp onto a truck for Saigon. It was a long, hot, bumpy ride. Johnny spent most of the time huddled in one corner, staring with disconcerting intensity at Mac.

"Hey," he said at last.

Mac lowered the beer he was drinking and looked at him.

"What's going to happen when we get to Saigon?" Johnny's words echoed hollowly in the truck.

"Nothing. What the hell do you think is going to happen?" Mac felt angry, without knowing why, and he saw Johnny flinch away at the sharp tone. He took a deep breath. "Don't worry," he said more quietly, not even sure what the hell he meant. "Just don't worry about it, okay?"

Empty as the words were, they seemed to be accepted at face value. Johnny closed his eyes and in a few minutes was asleep.

Mac sighed and lit another cigarette.

What happened when they got to Saigon was a fast shuffle. Everyone wanted to keep Tan Pret and what had happened there quiet. *In the interest of national security.* Mac swallowed the bad taste it was leaving in his mouth, and agreed to abide by the official line. Johnny took no interest at all in the proceedings, apparently content to just sit back and let Mac handle it.

He managed to talk headquarters into a three-day pass for each of them, trying not to think of it as a payoff for his silence. At last, they escaped the major's office and relaxed in the hall.

Johnny wiped both palms on the front of his shirt. "Thanks," he said, the first word he'd uttered in several hours.

"What?"

"For the pass."

"Oh, hell. I just figured we could both use a little time to get our heads on straight." There was a moment of silence. Mac stared down the hall and out through the glass door, watching the people walking by in the sunshine. "Well," he said finally, "guess I better see about finding someplace to crash. Until I can collect my pay, I'm flat. Why don't we have a drink or something later, huh?"

Johnny didn't say anything.

Mac grinned and held out his hand, taking care not to meet the other man's eyes. "Quite a time we had, huh, kid?"

They shook. Johnny's hand felt cold to the touch, but he returned the pressure of Mac's grip firmly. Mac broke the contact and turned, walking swiftly toward the door. Behind him there was silence.

He reached the door and put both hands on it to push. He paused. Damn, he thought, I'm not responsible for him. I saved his fucking ass out there and got him a pass on top of it. What the hell more can I do? It's not my business. I don't want it to be. The guy's a nutcase. Besides, I have enough trouble just looking out for myself.

Alexander McCarthy had spent thirty-five years avoiding involvement. If he'd learned nothing else growing up at Our Lady of Mercy Orphanage, he had learned that it didn't pay to get close to other people. If you made a friend, he'd get adopted and leave. The couple who took you home and offered the chance of a real family decided after three months that what they wanted was a baby, not a gangly eleven-year-old who swore like a sailor and played cards with deadly intensity. After things like that happened too often, he learned. Even with women he didn't like to take chances. Maybe that was why he never found the right girl to marry and make all his fantasies of a home and family real. If he paid for what he got, there was no chance of being disappointed. Of being hurt.

He had the army and he had his poker. That was all he

needed. Goddamn, he especially didn't need this. Didn't want it.

He pushed the door open with a vicious shove, then let it swing closed again. Oh, hell. A couple days. What could it hurt? "Johnny?" he said without turning around.

"Yes, Mac?"

He turned then. John Paul Griffith was still standing where he'd left him, arms at his sides, his expression reminding Mac of the look he'd seen on the faces of gook refugees leaving bombed-out villages. "You want to come with me? We could hang around together for a day or two, I guess. If you want."

Johnny took a deep breath. "I-I—" He shrugged helplessly. "Yes. I'd like that."

"You have any money?" Mac asked, wondering glumly just what the hell he was getting into.

Johnny moved toward him, making Mac think of a kid on his way into a circus tent. "Yeah, sure, I have money," he said eagerly. "Plenty of money."

Somehow that figured.

They stepped out onto the sun-dappled sidewalk. Johnny was grinning now and there was something infectious about his mood. "Shit," Mac said generously. "Who the hell knows? We might even have a good time."

Chapter 4

The apartment was stifling hot. A small ceiling fan managed only to stir the heavy air around a little. The only sounds were the soft slap of card against card and the low murmur of an occasional comment by one of the players.

The game itself was a total mystery to Johnny—even Old Maid and Authors had been frowned upon in the strict fundamentalist household where he'd grown up. In the years since, it had not been the supposed evils of cards he had avoided, but the enforced society of others entailed in the games. He sat in one corner of the couch, drinking the cold beer someone had handed him, and watched as Mac played poker. The six men had been playing for hours, but Johnny wasn't bored. He was watching Mac, bemused and a little frightened by the changes that had come over him when he sat down to play. The differences were visible in the way Mac handled the deck, with quick, familiar fingers, and even more so in the eager, intense expression on his face. The jade eyes seemed to glow.

Johnny was glad he'd given Mac the stake money to get into the game. Mac had been reluctant, at first, to accept, but Johnny had convinced him. It made Mac happy to be here and that pleased Johnny.

If he was also a little frightened by the intensity on Mac's face, the almost ferocious determination with which he seemed to approach each hand, Johnny chose to ignore the fear.

As if aware of the scrutiny, Mac looked up from his deal and met Johnny's gaze. Nothing in his face changed, no hint of emotion that might be intercepted by the other players. Despite that, Johnny felt sure that Mac was glad to have him there. He shoved away his own apprehensions and took a gulp of beer as he watched Mac finish the deal.

Mac came out of the game a winner. Not a big winner, but at least not a loser, and that put him in a good mood. He grinned at Johnny as they walked back onto the street. "Let's celebrate my luck," he suggested, shoving the small wad of bills away.

Johnny forgot to ask for his stake money back.

They went into a bar, where Mac ordered a bottle of cheap wine so they could toast his win. Johnny wasn't used to drinking and he didn't much like the taste, but he didn't want to disappoint Mac, so he drank whatever was poured. As the level of wine in the bottle began to drop, the evening started to grow fuzzy around the edges for Johnny. He was never quite sure just when the two women joined their party, or why. All he really knew was that a small redhead had slipped into the booth next to him, and that the conversation was all too hazy for him to understand. He talked very little, never quite sure what he was saying, and listened without knowing what he was hearing.

Sometime later, he found himself walking along the sidewalk with the redhead. Mac and the other girl were several feet ahead of them, and Johnny could see that they were talking, but the words were too soft for him to hear. The redhead had her hand in his and she was telling him about her job at the embassy. None of it made any sense.

When they reached the girls' apartment, someone opened more wine and someone else turned on the stereo. Mathis began to sing in soft, intimate tones. Johnny felt as if he were on a runaway roller coaster, speeding toward some dangerous place he didn't want to go.

Before very long Mac and the other girl disappeared through a door, and he was alone with Kathi. "With an 'i'," she'd said, giggling. Johnny wondered what the joke was. She brought her glass of wine and curled on the couch next to him. Beneath the thin cotton blouse she wore, he could see the dark circles of her nipples. When he moved away slightly, she laughed. "You're very shy, aren't you? Well, that's okay, because so am I. It's just that over here things seem to move so much faster. I guess we sort of live for today, because who knows about tomorrow?"

He thought her words sounded familiar, like lines out of The Late Show. Her hand undid the buttons on his shirt, then slid in across his chest. He shivered at the cool touch and her breath quickened in response. Without any conscious thought on his part, they were both suddenly stretched out on the sofa. He kissed her tentatively, without opening his mouth. She poked and probed with her tongue, until his lips parted. He could taste salt and wine and raspberry-flavored lip gloss.

"Oh, boy," she sighed. Her hand slipped down to the zipper on his fly, and a moment later he could feel her fingers twisting in the soft hairs on his groin. "You wanna do it, John?" she breathed into his ear.

His hand was on her thigh; he felt the slender body turn, shifting, so that his fingers nestled in warm dampness. He started to shake, a black terror beginning deep inside, rushing headlong toward the surface, threatening to drown him in its waves. She was suddenly all over him, her mouth and her hands trying to devour him. She whispered as she moved, but the words were swallowed up by another voice, the echo of his father's words coming down the years to attack him again. Condemning him. Damning him. The heat that had built up inside him turned icy, and he was afraid. He looked toward the bedroom, praying for help, but the door stayed closed.

Her lips touched him again, possessing him. His arms stiffened abruptly and he pushed her away. She fell to the floor with a thud. "Hey," she said, shocked, "what the hell—?"

Without answering, he lurched up from the sofa and tried to find the door. He knocked over a table, sending a lamp crashing against the wall as he tried desperately to escape, fighting back the nausea rising in his throat.

"What's the matter with you? Are you crazy?" She was screaming at him.

He ignored her. Finally, blindly, his fingers found the knob and he plunged out into the hallway. The door slammed shut behind him and he felt safe at last. Wearily, he leaned against the wall, sliding to the floor.

He had no idea how much time passed before he heard the door open again. Heavy footsteps came toward him, then Mac crouched down. "Johnny?"

He couldn't look up, afraid of what he might see in the other man's face.

"Hey, Johnny, you okay?"

He nodded.

"What's wrong?"

"Nothing," he said, his voice muffled against his arm.

"Kid, if nothing's wrong, why'd you run out like that? You scared Kathi half to death."

"I'm sorry." He lifted his head finally, looking up at the other man. Mac's shirt was on, but unbuttoned, and his craggy face was bewildered. "Tell her . . . I'm sorry."

Mac relaxed on the floor next to him. He lit two cigarettes and handed one to Johnny. "Can I ask you something, kid?" he said, a hand resting on Johnny's leg.

"Sure."

"Haven't you ever made it with a broad?"

He shook his head.

"You a fag?" There was no change in the voice, or in the grip of Mac's hand on his leg. "'Cause if you are, Johnny, that's okay. I mean, to each his own, you know?"

"No," Johnny said wearily, "I'm not a fag, either. I just never did. Not with anybody."

"Hell." Mac glanced at the closed apartment door. "She was hot to trot, that's for damned sure. Probably all over you, huh?"

Johnny nodded again. "She was on top of me and I felt like . . . like I was suffocating. Like I was gonna disappear." He could feel himself trembling. "One time I knew this girl, can't remember her name, but she and I were kissing, that's all, I swear, just kissing, and my father caught us. He made me stand up in front of the whole church and tell everybody what I'd been doing. He was the minister. I had to tell them all." He gagged slightly. "My father said I could go to hell for that." He fought to hold back the tears that threatened to spill out. "I don't want to go to hell, Mac."

"You won't. That was a long time ago, Johnny. Your father can't do anything to you now. They're long dead and gone, right?" Mac grinned a little. "Hell, boy, I've been screwing around for years. You think I'm going to hell?"

"No."

"Well, then?" Mac sobered. "Hey, look, I know the first time is a little scary, but it'll be okay."

"You don't understand." Johnny wiped his sweaty face against one sleeve.

"So explain it to me."

Johnny stared into the green eyes, wanting to gauge the reaction to his words. "I don't want to do it. Why do I have to?"

Mac blinked twice. "Hey," he said finally, "you *don't* have to. It doesn't matter."

Johnny took a long drag on the unaccustomed cigarette, then coughed. "I must be some kind of freak." It was not quite a question.

"Hell, no, you're not. Some people just aren't interested. It's your business." Mac smiled again. "Shit, half the time fucking's overrated anyhow."

Johnny kept looking at him. "Can we still be friends?" He'd never called anybody friend before. The word felt a little strange on his lips.

But Mac didn't laugh. He just gave Johnny's leg a squeeze. "Of course. Whether or not you screw that broad has nothing to do with us."

Johnny sighed in relief. He lowered his eyes. "I would have tried, Mac, if you wanted me to," he said very, very softly.

Mac didn't say anything.

Johnny rested his head back against the wall. "My father always used to tell me that I was a burden," he said almost dreamily. "Like the Lord sent me just to test them, and see if their faith could carry them through. They were stuck with me because they were my parents." He rubbed at the floor with the heel of his hand.

"Yeah?" Mac crushed out his cigarette.

"You ever wonder why you were born, Mac?"

He snorted. "Hell, kid, I know why I was born."

Johnny stared at him. "Really? Why?"

"Because, asshole, otherwise you'd be sitting in this hallway talking to yourself."

Johnny laughed aloud. It didn't last long, though. "I just meant . . . well, you don't have to feel responsible for me or anything."

"I know that."

Johnny felt a sudden chill course through him. He wrapped

both arms around himself, trying to get warm. "I didn't mean to screw up your pass, Mac."

"Why do you keep apologizing all the time? It doesn't matter."

The tears wouldn't stay back any longer; they flowed down Johnny's face. "I'm scared, Mac. I just get so scared."

"I know." Mac put one hand on his shoulder and gripped. "It's gonna be okay, kid," he said. "Stop crying, huh?"

Johnny nodded and rubbed at his face with both hands.

Mac looked at him for a long moment; his face seemed almost angry, but when he spoke, his voice was soft. "Tomorrow I'm going into Major Henderson's office and have you transferred to my unit," he said.

Johnny swallowed hard, trying to understand. "What?"

"I said, you're coming with me. You're not going back to your old unit."

"Thank you," Johnny whispered. "I . . . just, thank you."

They were quiet for awhile, then Mac stood. "I'm gonna go finish what I started in there," he said. "You zip your pants and get the hell out of here."

"Okay, Mac, whatever you say. I'll wait for you back at the hotel, huh?"

"Sure, fine."

Johnny sat on the floor and watched until Mac had disappeared inside. Then he stood, zipped his fly, and left. He went back to the hotel and waited for Mac to come home.

Chapter 5

For the first time in weeks it wasn't raining as Mac made his way through the knee-deep mud that covered the compound. It was too bad, he thought, that the breakfast waiting for him in the mess tent wasn't worth all the trouble it took to get there.

Crazy George was standing outside the tent.

"Morning, George," Mac said, stopping to scrape his boots on the large rock set by the door for that purpose.

George only scowled at him.

Mac shrugged and went inside. He paused long enough to roll his trouser legs down again, then went to pick up eggs, toast, and coffee, which he carried to a table. "Morning," he said, unloading the tray.

"Good morning," Johnny said cheerfully.

Mac, the lifelong loner, still couldn't quite get used to the idea that someone was actually glad to see him every morning, but for whatever reasons existed inside his poor befuddled head, John Griffith apparently was. He made an effort at returning Johnny's smile, then bent his head over the eggs. They were cold, of course.

"How was the game last night?"

Mac grimaced. "Don't ask." He looked up, chewing diligently. "I haven't held a decent hand since that night in Saigon. Maybe you should come kibbitz again."

"No." The finality of the word allowed for no discussion.

Mac shrugged. "I was only kidding." He didn't understand Johnny's firm refusal to come watch him play cards, but he accepted it as just one more quirk in a personality loaded with them. Maybe poker bored him.

"How much did you lose?"

"All of it." He didn't bother mentioning the several I.O.U.s.

"All?" Johnny shook his head, a bewildered expression on his face. "Maybe you shouldn't play so much."

Mac stopped with the tin mug of coffee halfway to his lips and stared at Johnny. "Get the fuck off my back," he said coldly. "You're not my wife or my mother, so lay off. Butt out of my life."

Johnny flinched back from the words as if they were physical blows. "I . . . I'm sorry. I didn't mean to make you mad. I'm sorry." He fumbled for his wallet. "I have fifty left. Take it for your stake tonight."

Mac stared at the bills, then shook his head. "Keep your goddamned money," he mumbled. "I don't want it."

"Please." Johnny's voice cracked, and for one terrible minute Mac thought the other man was going to cry. "Don't be mad at me. I shouldn't have said that. It's none of my business what you do with the money."

"Half of what I lost last night was yours," Mac said bitterly. "I guess you're entitled to bellyache."

"No, no, I'm not. I don't care. The money doesn't matter. Please, Mac."

After another long moment, Mac's fingers closed around the bills. "Hey," he said, "I shouldn't have blown up like I did." When Johnny didn't look up, Mac reached across the table and lightly punched him on the shoulder. "Hey, Johnny-boy, you in there?" He hated it when Johnny wouldn't talk.

Johnny sighed finally and raised his eyes. "Are we okay again?"

"Sure." Mac tucked the money into his shirt pocket. "We're okay, Johnny, of course we are."

Griffith smiled.

Mac could feel a knot of tension forming in his neck. That seemed to happen a lot lately. "I gotta go," he said, gulping the last of the cold coffee. "Staff briefing in a couple of minutes."

"Okay," Johnny said. "Have a nice day."

Mac stopped in mid-stride and turned back to Johnny, a helpless smile playing around the corners of his mouth. Jesus. Griffith sometimes said the damnedest things; there was just no way to figure the guy out. "You have a nice day, too," Mac said after a moment. Johnny nodded and Mac walked out of the tent.

Crazy George was still standing there. "Hey, Lieutenant," he said softly.

Mac paused. "Yeah, George?"

George stepped closer and lowered his voice. "I know the secret," he said.

"What?" Mac looked into George's eyes and saw the madness there. Entranced by that, he didn't even see the knife until the blade was already moving through the air. "Hey, don't—" he started to say.

The knife sliced through his upper arm and blood spurted out over them both. George lifted his hand again, and Mac fell away, crashing through the side of the tent. George kept coming, yelling something about God and Lyndon Johnson. Mac tried to get away, but his legs were tangled in the heavy, muddy canvas. "Oh, hell," he said aloud, thinking that this was a fucking stupid way to die. "Damn."

The air was suddenly filled with a noise that sounded like it came from an animal in mortal pain. Through the mud and confusion, Mac was aware of a blur flying past him and colliding with George. The two tangled figures sprawled in the mud and standing puddles.

Mac struggled to sit up, watching Johnny and George roll around, the knife blade flashing between them. A crowd had gathered by this time, and a couple of the men made a half-hearted attempt to stop the battle, but most just stood there watching. George's arm jerked and the knife slashed across Johnny's cheek. Johnny swung a hand wildly in response, sending the weapon skidding away. Mac finally got himself untan-

gled from the tent and sat up, trying to stop the flow of blood
from his arm. "Johnny!" he yelled.

Johnny, if he even heard him, ignored the shout. He was on
top of George now, clutching the larger man by the hair. In the
sudden silence of the crowd, Mac could hear the terrible dull
thuds of George's head against the rock upon which he'd
cleaned his boots earlier. Again and again flesh and bone
crashed against the rock. Two men tried to pull Johnny away,
but he shrugged them off almost nonchalantly. It was hard to
believe that there was so much strength in the slender body.

Mac half-ran, half-crawled across the distance between them
and plowed into Johnny with the full force of his body, sending
them both into a puddle. Somebody immediately dragged
George away. Mac lay heavily on top of Johnny, who still
writhed and jerked from the emotional frenzy of the fight.
"Johnny, Johnny," he crooned, like a man trying to calm a
distraught animal. "Take it easy, babe, take it easy."

Slowly Johnny relaxed and his breathing returned to normal.
"Did he hurt you, Mac?" he asked in a hoarse voice.

"No, kid, I'm okay. Just cut my arm a little." Mac rolled off
Johnny. A short distance away, a medic was bent over George.
"Sit up," Mac ordered.

Johnny struggled up. Both his eyes were already starting to
discolor and the cut on his cheek was bleeding. "You really okay,
Mac?" he persisted.

"Yeah, yeah," he said, although his arm was throbbing like
hell.

"He was trying to kill you."

"Well, I guess. George is crazy."

"Is he dead?"

"No, of course not," he said reassuringly, although he didn't
know.

"I wish he was." Mac looked up in surprise. The expression
that he could see in Johnny's eyes was scary, a little too much
like the look he'd seen in George's eyes just before the attack.
"He was going to kill you, Mac," Johnny said by way of apparent
explanation. "He deserves to die."

Mac sat speechless for a moment, then jerked his head
around. "We need a goddamned medic over here!" he yelled.
"Can't you see we're bleeding to death?"

He felt dizzy suddenly and leaned against Johnny to keep
from falling into the puddle again.

Chapter 6

He walked across the compound to the supply tent, knowing that Johnny would be there taking inventory. That was all Johnny did, by Mac's order. It was a good job for him, because he could work alone, and by the time he finished counting all the bandages and cases of corned beef hash and the bullets, it was time to start over again. Everyone knew, of course, why Dumb Johnny had been assigned the task. Everyone except Johnny.

He was there, bent over the omnipresent clipboard. All that remained of the fight with George was the healing scar on his cheek. Mac leaned against a case of powdered eggs. "How's it going, kid?"

Johnny looked up, startled, until he saw who it was, then he smiled. "Okay. Except I think I need glasses. The numbers keep getting smaller."

Mac cleared his throat. "I got my orders."

"Your orders?"

"Shipping home. Next Wednesday."

Johnny lowered the clipboard. The scar suddenly stood out, vivid red against his pale skin. "Wednesday?"

"Yeah."

He shook his head, the eyes even more bewildered than before. "But, Mac, I—"

"Hey, you'll be okay, kid," Mac said quickly, trying to sound a hell of a lot more sure than he felt. "You've only got eight weeks left, right?"

"I won't make it."

The words should have sounded melodramatic, but they didn't. Instead there was the simple starkness of truth. Mac didn't say anything and after a moment, Johnny sighed and raised the clipboard. "Johnny, hey—"

"It doesn't matter," he said quietly. "Fifty-two, fifty-three—"

"What the hell is that supposed to mean, it doesn't matter?"

"Nothing. I'm glad you're getting out of this mess. Sixty-four, sixty-five—"

"Johnny . . ."

"I'm trying to count this stuff, Mac. It's my job. Seventy-three, seventy—"

Mac suddenly moved toward him, grabbed the clipboard, and

threw it across the tent. "Forget the fucking inventory," he said. "Nobody cares if you stand in here counting things."

Johnny's hands dropped to his sides, and he stared at the floor.

"Johnny?"

The silence rang loudly in the tent.

"Johnny, say something to me."

But he didn't.

Mac clenched his fingers around the edge of a packing case. "Don't do this, Johnny. It's stupid."

Instead of answering, Johnny relaxed his legs and slid down the pile of boxes, huddling on the floor. Mac could feel a seething white anger well up inside him. "You stop it," he said raspingly. "Stop it now, or I'll . . . I'll. . . ." Words wouldn't come; he didn't even know what the hell he wanted to say. He crashed a fist against the top of the box. "Damn you. I don't care what happens. I don't care if you sit there until hell freezes over. You bastard. You crazy son of a bitch."

He turned around and walked out of the tent, not looking back.

Johnny didn't show up for supper. Mac sat alone, for the first time in months, but he didn't eat much. He pushed the food around on the plate for awhile, then left. Bumming a bottle of cheap wine from Wash, he crawled into his cot, resolving to drink until he passed out.

He almost made it.

But he couldn't stop thinking about Griffith sitting in the supply tent, huddled on the floor like a scared kid. The image finally propelled him off the cot. Gingerly walking what he hoped was a reasonably straight line, he made his way across the compound. Just to cover all his bases, he checked the mess tent and Johnny's quarters, but then he went back to the supply tent.

Johnny was still there, sitting on the floor, with his legs crossed Indian-style, and a .45 in his hand. Mac stumbled into the circle of pale yellow light. "What the hell are you doing?" he demanded, wishing that his tongue didn't feel quite so thick.

Johnny looked up at him. "I don't want to stay here by myself," he said quietly.

"Shit, man, everybody ain't leaving, just me. You'll still have lots of company."

Johnny's glance at him was filled with scorn. "You know what I mean," he said. "I don't want to stay here by myself."

Mac nodded. "Okay. I know what you mean. But what the hell are you gonna do about it?"

"Go away, Mac."

He didn't go away; he sat down facing Johnny. "This is great, you know, really great."

"What?"

"We have a problem here, kid, and what happens? Do you give me a chance to handle it, to figure out what to do? No, sir, all you want to do is blow your fucking brains out. Assuming you have any brains in there, which I doubt very much. Some buddy you are. Christ."

Johnny stared at the gun for a moment, then lifted his gaze to Mac. "I'm sorry," he said. "I just thought—"

"You thought? When the hell did you start thinking?"

"I didn't know it mattered what I did."

"Well, it matters." Mac was quiet for a moment, trying to clear his fuzzy brain. "It matters, you stupid son of a bitch."

Carefully Johnny set the gun down onto the floor. "You said you didn't care."

"Oh, shut up. Nobody else around this place pays a goddamned bit of attention to anything I say; why the hell should you?"

They were quiet for a couple of minutes as Johnny chewed thoughtfully on a fingernail. "What are we gonna do?" he asked finally.

"I don't know yet."

"I could just go AWOL," Johnny suggested.

"Oh, sure, that's a terrific idea. Then they could stick you in Leavenworth or in front of a firing squad." Mac rubbed his temples. "Look, will you just let me handle it? Leave the thinking to me. I promise I'll get you out of here, okay?"

"Okay."

Mac sighed. "But right now I have to get some sleep." He pushed himself to his feet wearily and started out. "Good night," he mumbled.

"Sleep tight," Johnny returned cheerfully.

Mac didn't know whether to laugh or cry. He did neither, just shook his head and kept moving.

Chapter 7

Mac was drunk. But it was his bon voyage party, so he figured he was entitled. They were drinking some punch Washington had created. It seemed to be nothing more than an uneasy mingling of all the booze in camp, with a can of fruit cocktail dumped in to give it an air of festivity.

Mac sat in one corner, trying to dig a green grape from the bottom of his glass. He looked up blearily as Wash dropped next to him. "Great party," he said.

Washington surveyed the roomful of drunk men glumly. "I guess."

Mac almost captured the grape, but at the last minute it slithered away. "Damn. Slippery little fucker."

"I got a question for you, Lieutenant-buddy."

Mac looked at him.

"What are you gonna do with the zombie when you get back?"

They both glanced across the tent to where Johnny sat alone, watching the proceedings with a faint smile. Mac shrugged. "I'm not gonna do anything. He wanted out and I got him out. That's all."

Washington wiped his sweating brow. "You know the guy is a real screwball, don't you?"

"Ahh, he's okay. A little weird, but okay."

"Mac, John Griffith is sick." The black man's voice was flat.

Mac took a gulp of the punch, wishing they weren't having this conversation. "Hell, Wash, so is everybody else around here."

"Whenever you ain't around, he don't talk, man."

There was a by-now-familiar knot of tension in Mac's neck, and despite the punch he felt sober again. "He gets scared, is all."

"That's not all." A hand rested firmly on Mac's shoulder. "Take my advice and get him into a hospital."

"You mean turn him over to the shrinks?"

"He needs help."

"No," Mac said flatly. "I can't do that." He was quiet for a moment, letting the memories wash over him. "My old lady bought it in one of those places. I can't do that to Johnny."

"Fine," Washington replied. "What will you do? Dump him on the street in Frisco and walk away?"

Mac finally captured the elusive grape and pulled it out of the glass. He studied it, then threw it across the table, watching as it bounced and rolled to the ground. "Once we're out of here, he's on his own. He knows that."

Washington snorted. "Shit, he don't know what his own name is unless you tell him every so often."

The hammer was pounding in the back of Mac's skull. "He'll be okay."

"Yeah, sure, Mac. Zombies probably make out real good on their own."

Johnny had seen Mac staring at him. He grinned and started to make his way through the crowd toward them. Washington got to his feet. "But I guess that's not your problem, is it? It will be though, unless you get out from under, and soon." He smiled, suddenly and without humor. "Or else adopt the bastard." He walked away.

Mac watched Johnny approach. Get out from under . . . out from under. Damn it, maybe Wash was right. If he didn't set this thing straight right now, he was liable to have Griffith around his neck for a long time. "We have to talk," he said abruptly when the blond reached him. "Let's go outside."

"Sure, Mac," Johnny agreed, as usual.

Mac led the way across the room and outside. They wandered across the compound aimlessly as he lit a cigarette. Back at the party somebody's eight-track was blasting Beatles music. "What are your plans, Johnny?"

"Plans?"

"What are you gonna do when we get back home?"

Johnny shook his head. "I don't know, Mac."

"Well, you better start to think about it."

The younger man looked genuinely bewildered. "I thought you were going to do all the thinking, Mac. That's what you said. Leave the thinking to me, you said."

Mac took a long drag on the cigarette. "I only meant while we were here, Johnny, not forever. When we get Stateside, you're on your own. You understand that, don't you?"

"Oh." The word was soft.

Mac kept his eyes on the ground. "I mean, we have to get on with our own lives, right? I have things to do, you know?" He wondered as he spoke just what the hell he had to do. He was finished in the army; his own promise not to re-up was part of the deal he'd struck for Johnny's early-out. This wasn't the time to think about that, though. "There must be people you want to see and stuff to do, right?"

"No."

"Well, you'll think of something." The words were sharp.

"Sure, Mac," Johnny whispered.

He tried to ignore the tightness in his gut. Shit, he was only getting out from under. It was the smart thing to do. He sure as hell didn't need to have John Paul Griffith hanging around his neck like some kind of goddamned millstone. He was going to have a hard enough time keeping himself afloat. Given a burden like that, they'd probably both go under. So it was best to dump him now, like Wash had said.

So what if the guy was glad to see him every morning?

Suddenly, irrationally, he knew, Mac was angry at Wash. Where the hell did that black bastard get off butting in to say that Johnny was crazy and that Mac would be better off without him? Sure, the kid had some problems, but who the hell didn't? Given a little time, they could work it out.

He glanced sidewise at Johnny walking next to him.

Wash was a good guy, and a good friend, but this time he was wrong. Griffith was okay. He liked the kid, damn it, and to hell with what anybody else thought. When the rest of the fucking world kept out of it, he and Johnny got along just fine. Where the hell was it written that Alexander McCarthy couldn't have a friend?

He stopped walking and turned to face Johnny.

"Hey."

Johnny raised his head, looking like a puppy dog that couldn't understand why its beloved master has suddenly kicked him. "What, Mac?"

"We could sort of stick together for awhile. Until we get our bearings. I have some connections in New York, so we might head east and see what happens. If you want." He was surprised to realize how much he wanted Johnny to say yes.

Johnny was staring at the ground again. "What do *you* want?" he asked very softly.

"I think it sounds okay."

"I think so, too. I don't get so scared when I'm with you." Johnny's face was suddenly anxious, as if he'd said too much. "Is that okay?"

Mac smiled. "Yeah, sure." He was quiet for a moment, then shrugged. "You want to know something, Johnny?"

"What?"

He dropped the cigarette and crushed it under his heel. "I
don't get so scared when I'm with you, either." He heard his
own words with bemusement, figuring he wasn't as sober as
he'd thought, and hoping to hell he wasn't going to regret this
in the morning.

Johnny laughed, as if he'd said something very funny.
"You're never scared," he said complacently.

Mac opened his mouth to set the kid straight on that, but then
he only shook his head helplessly. "Let's go back to the party,"
he said instead.

"Sure, Mac, whatever you say."

They turned and walked back across the compound.

Chapter 8

It was a good night for Johnny. His Bowie knife style of throwing the darts was right on target time after time, and he won
three straight games, raking in a total of thirty dollars. Prudently, he decided to go out a winner, despite the mild protests
of his defeated opponents, who wanted a chance to get even.
They didn't press him too hard, however, because they realized
that there would be other nights.

Johnny was a familiar figure in the Pirate's Cove Bar, although nobody really knew any more about him than his name.
He came in several nights a week with a grim-faced poker
player. The card game took place in the back room, but Johnny
never went in there. He stayed in the front, perfecting his dart
throwing skills to a deadly degree of accuracy. Although he was
always willing for a game if asked, the other players soon discovered that it wasn't easy to carry on a conversation with him.
When a few words were pulled out of him, they were said in
tones so soft as to be almost impossible to hear.

Mostly he just sat in the rear booth, drinking a beer or two—
never more—and waiting until the poker player came out.
Then the two of them would leave.

Johnny fingered the three tens as he sat drinking a beer. This
was the most he'd ever won at darts and it gave him a good
feeling. Maybe, he hoped, the money would make Mac feel better, too.

A frown creased Johnny's brow as he thought of his friend.
Mac's luck hadn't been too good lately. The first few months in

New York were okay, although Mac's "connections" never came through as he'd hoped they would. They both still had some army money left, though, and for a while the cards seemed to run his way more often than not. Life was turning out okay.

But then things started to go wrong and for the past three months it had all grown steadily worse. Johnny didn't mind getting along on a diet of cheap hamburgers, or moving from one grimy, depressing room to the next. None of that mattered much to him. But he did mind a whole lot seeing what it was doing to Mac.

He took a thoughtful sip of beer. At least the angry outbursts didn't scare him so much anymore. He'd learned finally that Mac's rages were not directed at him, but at the circumstances, and that though he might smash a glass or put his fist through the plasterboard wall of whatever cheap room they were in at any given moment, he would never turn the anger toward Johnny.

Johnny frowned again. It was true that Mac said things sometimes, things that hurt more than a blow might have. Especially when he threatened to just take off and leave all of his problems behind. They both knew that he meant Johnny himself was the biggest problem. But Johnny also knew that Mac didn't mean those things when he said them. And he always apologized when the outburst was over, not in words, maybe, but with a candy bar or just by hanging around the room a little longer than usual to keep Johnny company.

The door to the back room opened suddenly and Mac came out. Johnny bit his lower lip, knowing from the expression on the tall man's face that tonight's luck hadn't been any better than all the others lately. Mac stopped at the bar for a drink, paying for it with a handful of change, then came and slumped down across from Johnny.

Neither of them spoke for several minutes.

Johnny finally broke the silence. "Guess what?" he said softly.
"What?"

"I won thirty dollars." He pushed the crumpled bills across the table. "Here."

Mac looked at the money for a moment. "Where'd you get this?" he asked, picking it up.

"Playing darts. I won three games. Thirty dollars." Johnny smiled, feeling proud.

"Shit," Mac said. "I just dropped two hundred dollars in there." It was the last of the money from the pawn shop. The cassette player. Johnny's gold watch. The cheap portable TV. Their possessions endured a nomadic existence, bouncing back and forth between them and the hock shop with regularity. "I just lost everything we had, kid. What good is thirty fucking dollars?" He threw the money back across the table at Johnny. The bills hit him in the face and fell, landing in a puddle of spilled beer. Mac downed the rest of his drink and got to his feet. "You coming?" He stalked toward the door, not waiting for an answer.

Johnny carefully picked up the bills and put them into his shirt pocket, before hurrying to catch up.

It was a fifteen minute walk to their fourth floor furnished room, a journey that passed in complete silence. Once inside, Mac took a lukewarm beer out of the haphazardly operative refrigerator, and sat down in front of the only window, apparently hoping for a breeze. He propped his feet on the sill and stared glumly out at the flashing neon sign across the street. ANCI G IRLS.

Johnny stripped to his shorts in an effort to feel cooler and stretched out on the couch which doubled as his bed. He could hear the faint sound of a TV next door and listened until he could identify the show. "Mannix." He couldn't make out much of the action, but in a couple of minutes he'd heard enough to know that he'd already seen that episode. Taking off his glasses, he rubbed his eyes wearily.

Mac cleared his throat finally. "You must be getting pretty good at throwing those darts."

Johnny shrugged.

"Thirty dollars, huh?"

"Uh-huh. I probably could've won more, but I was afraid of losing the thirty, so I quit."

Mac sighed. "That's why you're always gonna be a loser, Johnny. You're too damned scared to take a chance. You have to live dangerously if you want to be a big winner."

"I guess you're right, Mac."

"Sure as hell am, kid." He was quiet for several moments. "Still, thirty dollars is pretty good."

"You think so?" Johnny got up from the couch, picking up his shirt from the floor. He pulled the money out and handed it to Mac. "Here."

Mac held the beer-damp bills tentatively. "You don't have to give me this, you know."

Johnny was bewildered. "But you need a stake. I don't need it for anything."

"You could get the TV out of hock."

Johnny thought about that for a moment; he sure missed having the small set around for company. Then he shrugged. "Ahh, hell," he said. "Nothing on now but reruns anyway."

After a second, Mac grinned. "Yeah. Hey, you know what?"

Johnny was smiling now, too, feeling good again. "What?"

"This dough might just change my luck. And if it does, we could get a brand new set. A color one. Maybe before the new season starts. Wouldn't that be great?"

"Yeah, sure, Mac. I'd like a color set."

"Terrific. So we'll just let that crummy little black-and-white stay where it is, and I'll use this to get going again. I feel really lucky now, Johnny."

"Good." It was terrific when Mac was up like this. Johnny went to the refrigerator and took out a Coke. He'd join Mac at the window and they could talk.

But Mac had a familiar expression on his face, a sort of hungry look that Johnny knew well. "In fact, why wait until tomorrow, huh? If I'm feeling hot right now?" He shoved the money away and got to his feet. "You want to come back to the Cove with me?"

Johnny shook his head. "Think I'll just go to bed."

"Okay, kid." Mac drained the beer can on the way to the door, then tossed it into the wastebasket, where it landed with a thud. "See? That's a sign that my luck is changing." He paused by the door. "Hey, that's really great, you winning all this money, Johnny. Really great. I'm gonna have to watch you play sometime, okay?"

Johnny felt his face grow hot with pride over the unexpected praise. "Sure, Mac," he said shyly. "Anytime."

"Terrific." Mac was keyed up, ready to go. "Good night," he said.

"'Night, Mac."

The door closed. Alone, Johnny went to stand by the window and looked down at the sidewalk. He leaned against the wall, sipping soda, and listening to the end of "Mannix" from the next room, and watching until Mac disappeared around the corner.

Chapter 9

By the time fall arrived, they weren't going to the Pirate's Cove anymore. Mac explained it by saying that in his line of work "fluidity" was very important. A new game, new money, it was all crucial. Mac didn't bother to explain that his line of credit at the Cove had been cut off and that a couple of people were beginning to get uptight about late payments. He figured that Johnny wouldn't understand all that financial stuff anyway, so why bother him with it? All the kid really cared about was having his TV to watch and plenty of Coke to drink.

So they moved to Brooklyn, to a small room over a pizzeria, and Mac found new games. Each beginning brought the same hopes of a break in his streak of bad luck, and in fact, there were enough wins to keep his hopes alive, though never quite enough to get him out of the hole. Johnny surprised the very hell out of him by getting a job washing dishes for the old dago downstairs. Mac didn't like the idea very much, because Johnny was too smart to have to put up with a chickenshit job like that. But, of course, there wasn't any way the rest of the world could know how smart he was when he was also too damned scared to open his mouth. Down there, he didn't have to talk; all he had to do was wash the dishes and haul the garbage and keep the floor swept. He was invisible, as the people who do that kind of work always are, and he was content. Once a week he brought his pay envelope upstairs and gave it to Mac. The money, once they paid rent on the room, was hardly enough to keep Mac in cigarettes, but it was something, and it seemed very important to Johnny.

And at least he had a job. Mac tried. He worked for three days in a shoe store, but he figured a week of that and he'd be as spaced-out as Johnny, so he quit. For awhile after that he read the classifieds every morning over breakfast, solemnly discussing the offerings with Johnny, but they never found anything that seemed suited to his particular talents. So he played cards and Johnny washed dishes for the dago and they got by.

Chinese Eddie raked the chips across the table with both his tiny hands. "Sorry about this, Mac," he said cheerfully. "You been going through a cold streak lately, ain't you?"

Mac threw his cards down in disgust. "All my fucking life," he mumbled. "Well, that finishes me. Unless you'll take my marker?"

But Eddie shook his head woefully, causing his several chins to jiggle. "No can do, man. I'm already getting static from upstairs."

"I'm good for it."

The other players had suddenly become very interested in their drinks; he and Eddie might have been alone in the dimly lit room. Eddie was slowly shuffling a new deck. "Have you totaled your markers lately?" he asked casually.

"No, but—"

"They come to almost four thousand dollars, Mac, between here and the Cove. That's a lot of money."

The amount stunned Mac a little, and he reached for a cigarette, trying not to let his fingers tremble as he lit it. "Well, yeah, I know it sounds like a lot. Hell, it *is* a lot, but—"

Eddie carefully cut the deck, not even looking at him. "There are no 'buts,' Mac. The boys would like you to arrange some settlement for this account."

The atmosphere in the room had turned vaguely ominous. Mac took a couple of quick drags on the cigarette, then smiled. "Sure, look, I know how it is. But, see, I've got a couple of very hot prospects that ought to start paying off real soon."

Eddie smiled, beaming as if his fondest dreams had been realized. "I'm very glad about that, Mac, because I like you." A faint, a very faint hint of worry crossed the vast expanse of his face. "I can only hope that these prospects start paying off within the next twenty-four hours."

Mac's mouth was dry, but there wasn't any whiskey left in his glass. "But that's not enough time. . . ." His voice dwindled off as he realized the futility of protest.

Eddie spread his fingers helplessly. "I don't make the rules, Mac."

"Sure, Eddie," he said bitterly. He jerked his coat on and left the room.

It was almost two A.M., time for Johnny to get off work, so instead of going up to the room, Mac pushed open the door of the pizzeria. The old dago was sitting bent over the racing form and he barely glanced up. "He's in the alley taking the garbage," he said, already studying the sheet again.

Mac nodded and walked past him to the rear of the place.

"Hi," he began, pushing the back door open. He stopped. Johnny wasn't alone.

Two gorillas had him against the fence that lined the alley. One of the apes had both hands on Johnny's shoulders. The glow from the streetlamp reflected off the lenses of Johnny's glasses, hiding his eyes from view, but Mac knew what expression he would have seen there. "What the hell is going on here?" he asked quietly, recognizing both men from the Cove game.

Frank, one of the tough guys, turned. "Why nothing's going on, Mr. McCarthy," he said. "We was only leaving a message with your friend here." The massive fingers dug into Johnny's shoulders and he winced visibly. The men were built like bull elephants stuffed into polyester suits. Johnny was six-one and Mac six-four, and while the other two may not have been any taller, they were considerably heavier. Not to mention the fact that beneath each shiny jacket could be seen the obvious outline of a holster. The fingers squeezed again. "You get that message straight, dummy?"

Johnny nodded jerkily.

"Good." The hands released him, and Johnny slumped against the fence. Frank and his buddy Al grinned at Mac and disappeared down the alley.

Mac moved, grabbing Johnny by one arm. "You okay?"

"Yeah."

"You sure, kid?"

"Yeah, Mac, I'm okay."

He nodded, releasing his breath in a long sigh, then turned to look off into the darkness as they heard a car start up and drive away. "Bastards. They don't have any business coming around here bothering you."

Johnny took several deep breaths. "They said to tell you twenty-four hours. What's that mean?"

"Nothing." He realized that Johnny, in his shirt sleeves, was shivering as the sharp November wind hit him. "Get your coat and let's go home."

Some home, he thought bitterly as they climbed the stairs. A room about four feet square, stinking all the time of tomato sauce and olive oil. Johnny stood in front of the space heater and tried to get rid of the chills that still wracked his body. Or maybe it was fear. Mac poured two slugs of dago red and handed one to him. "Drink it," he ordered when Johnny made a face.

"Mac, what's happening?"

"Nothing."

"But those guys—"

"Shut up, Johnny," Mac said sharply. "Drink your wine and shut up about it."

Johnny shut up and drank the wine.

Mac sat down on his bed. "Ahh, Johnny," he said after a long time. "I've really screwed things up."

Johnny shook his head. "It wasn't your fault."

"Goddamnit, Johnny, listen to me for once, willya? I owe these people a lot of money. Four fucking thousand dollars." He stared at the empty glass in his hand, then suddenly threw it across the room. It shattered against the wall. The room was quiet for a moment. "Oh, Christ, Johnny, I'm scared. I'm really scared."

Johnny came over and sat beside him. He patted Mac's arm. "It'll be okay."

"These people aren't playing games, you idiot. They had guns."

Johnny's face was pale, but his voice was steady. "You'll take care of it."

Mac sneered. "Oh, yeah, sure. I'll take care of it. Superman lives, right? You gotta stop watching so goddamned much TV; it's rotting away what few brains you have left." He felt so tired. All he wanted to do was get out of this lousy room, away from the hassles, away from those damned blue eyes that were always watching him. Trusting him. God, he didn't want to be trusted anymore, not anymore. The walls were closing in, suffocating him. Almost desperately he reached for his jacket and pulled it on again. "I gotta go out for awhile," he mumbled.

"But, Mac . . ."

"Don't worry." He opened the door, then paused. "I'll be back, Johnny. I'll be back, but I just have to get out for a while, okay?" He left before Johnny could speak again.

He walked for a long time, rode the subway for awhile, and ended up in the New Amsterdam Theater on Forty-second Street. His was the only white face in the crowd. He made his way up the aisle, which was sticky with spilled soda, cigarette butts, and discarded hot dogs, and found a seat in the last row of the balcony. Lighting a cigarette, he propped both feet on the back of the seat in front of him and stared at the screen.

He had no idea what movie was playing, but it didn't matter.

Half-asleep, he watched the flickering images on the screen un-til his eyes grew tired of staring at the garish pictures, then tipped his head back to gaze at the vast, vaulted ceiling over-head.

He dozed, waking once to find a hand on his thigh, edging upwards toward his crotch. Without opening his eyes, he spoke. "Get away from me, you mother-fucking fag bastard," he said very softly, "or I'll ram this chair up your ass."

The hand vanished. Mac scrunched further down in the seat and watched the movie.

Chapter 10

Johnny sat in the room for a long time after Mac left. He was trying to think about what to do. Mac needed help and Johnny wanted desperately to help him. Finally, he got up and left the room.

He knew all about the faulty lock on the back door of the pizzeria. It took him only a couple of minutes to snap it free and push the door open. As he stepped inside, his father's voice rang clearly in his mind, sounding as if the old man were standing there next to him. "Thou shalt not steal," the harsh voice said.

Johnny brushed the words away impatiently. This wasn't stealing. The old man had money. Mac needed money. It was as simple as that, really. You didn't need a whole religion and lots of rules to know right from wrong, he decided. Things just were what they were, and the only thing to do was make the best of it.

Carefully he made his way through the kitchen, into the small cubicle that served as an office. A narrow sliver of light leaked in from outside. He started opening desk drawers at random, until he reached the bottom drawer, which was locked. He pulled out his pocket knife again and started to work. This one took a little longer than the lock on the door had, but finally it, too, snapped open. A small steel box sat there. Now he had to get that open. He knew that it would have been easier to just take the box along, but that wouldn't be fair. He didn't want all the dago's money, just four thousand dollars, the amount that Mac needed. So he began a studied attack on the padlock securing the box. His breathing was quick and raspy as he worked, but his fingers were steady.

Blinding white light suddenly exploded in the room. Johnny looked up, surprised, blinking against the sudden invasion of brightness. A massive black cop stood in the doorway, his gun leveled at Johnny. "Freeze."

Johnny froze. "Don't shoot," he whispered. "Please, don't shoot me."

"I'm not going to shoot, if you do what you're told. Just put the knife down on the desk and stand up slowly."

He dropped the penknife and stood.

Another cop slipped into the room, coming forward to frisk him quickly and efficiently. "What's your name?"

Johnny's head turned toward him. "Huh?"

"Your name, buddy, what is it?"

Johnny's hands were still in the air. "John Paul Griffith," he said hoarsely.

"Okay, Griffith, you're under arrest." The cop pulled a worn card out of his pocket and glanced at it. "You have the right to remain silent. If you give up that right, everything you say can and will be used against you in a court of law. You have the right—"

The voice faded away slowly until, although he could still see the man's lips moving, Johnny couldn't hear any of the words. He stared dumbly at the moving lips as the terror filled him, consumed him.

The black cop said something and then Johnny's arms were jerked around behind his back and cuffed there. Johnny wanted to tell them that he hadn't been doing anything wrong, that he'd only wanted to get the money for Mac. But the words wouldn't come. The cops took him out through the front, past the other tenants from upstairs, and past Giancarlo, who pointed a finger, like a parent scolding a small child. "Thief, thief," he said.

Johnny was pushed into the backseat of the radio car. He huddled against the door, staring at the mesh screen that separated him from the cops in front. A taste of hot bile rose in his throat, but he swallowed the bitter fluid back down, afraid of what might happen if he threw up all over the police car.

Mac is going to be so mad, he thought dimly. Oh God, where *was* Mac? Even if he was going to be mad and yell, Johnny wanted him there. "Mac?" His lips formed the word, but no sound came out. Mac, please, I need you.

They took him to the precinct house four blocks away, turning him over to a heavyset man in a rumpled brown suit. The man shoved a paper into the typewriter. "Name?" he snapped around an unlit cigar.

Johnny's hands, freed from the cuffs, were clasped together in his lap. Someone, he thought, was talking to him, but the words were muffled and he had to strain to understand them.

"What's your name, pal?"

A familiar face, the black cop who'd busted him, appeared briefly, a papercup of coffee in one hand. "He told us it was Griffith. John Paul. Then he just clammed up. Acts like he's stoned."

The detective typed the name. "Address?"

The room was filled with a strange empty darkness, but the void didn't scare him. It was safe where he was. He slid down in the seat, smiling a little.

"Hey, Griffith, where do you live?"

With Mac, he thought, but he didn't tell them that. He just kept smiling and waiting for Mac to show up and take care of this.

They gave up finally, and took him away for booking, prints, and pictures. When all that was done, Johnny was taken to a holding cell. He curled up on the cot there, watching and waiting.

Chapter 11

Driven almost equally by weariness and the need for company, Mac finally went home. It was almost noon by the time he got back to the empty room. He sat down on his bed, a little bewildered. The pizzeria didn't open until two, and Johnny rarely went anywhere else alone. Except to the movies. Then he remembered that there was a spaghetti western playing down the street. Johnny loved the noisy shoot 'em ups. Mac was a little disgruntled, wishing Johnny were there. They needed to talk.

The soft tapping at the door startled him.

He got up to answer it; the old woman from across the hall was there, looking even more fluttery than usual. Mac knew her only slightly. Johnny would sometimes help her carry groceries or something. "Yes?" he said, trying to sound polite.

"I thought you ought to know," she stage-whispered.

"Know what?"

"They took him away."

Mac's eyes felt gritty after his long night, and he shook his head a little, hoping to clear away the fog in his brain. "Excuse me, Mrs. Jakubjansky, but what are you talking about?"

She sighed, as if impatient with his stupidity. "The police took him away. In the handcuffs. They said he stole money from Mr. Giancarlo." She shook her head sorrowfully. "John is a good boy. I don't think he would take money."

Mac managed to thank the woman and get rid of her, although he felt like someone had just delivered a quick punch to his mid-section. When she was gone, he rested his forehead against the door and closed his eyes. Johnny? Busted? Hauled off in cuffs?

He felt sick, like he might throw up. Oh goddamn, he thought, the kid did it for me, because I need money. That idiot. That goddamned stupid fucking idiot.

Christ, he must be scared to death.

Mac left the room, clattering noisily down the stairs, and running all the way to the police station. By the time he reached the front desk, he was gasping hoarsely for air. The desk sergeant looked up without much interest. "Yeah?"

He stood still for a moment, trying to catch his breath. "Uh, Griffith," he finally managed to say. "You have John Griffith here?"

The sergeant started pawing through some papers. "Griffith?"

Another cop looked up from his magazine. "That's the flake up on three," he said helpfully.

"Oh, yeah, right. Go to the third floor and ask for Lieutenant Mazzeretti."

When he asked, Mac was directed to a small office at one end of the squadroom. Mazzeretti, a dark-skinned, slender man in a grey sharkskin suit, frowned at the rumpled, unshaven figure before him. "Alex McCarthy? What's your interest in Griffith? You're not a lawyer? Or a relative?"

Mac shook his head. "No, I'm just a friend. He doesn't have a family or anything. Can I see John?"

Mazzeretti was toying with a gold ballpoint pen. "He's in the holding cell around the corner, but I don't know about seeing him." He clicked the pen open, studied the point for a moment, then clicked it closed again. "I have a transfer order pending."

"Transfer to where?"

"Bellevue."

Mac kept his face poker blank, although an icy hand seemed to be squeezing at his gut. "No, don't do that." The cop seemed startled by his tone and Mac forced himself to speak more quietly. "I mean, he's okay. He doesn't need Bellevue. Just let me talk to him for a minute."

Mazzeretti frowned. "That's the problem, man. He won't talk. Hasn't said word one since they brought him in."

The icy hand gripped more tightly. "He'll talk to me," Mac mumbled, hoping to hell it was the truth.

After a moment, Mazzeretti shrugged and stood. "Come on."

They left the office and walked around to the holding cell. Johnny was curled on the cot, staring blankly at the activity swirling around him. Mac stopped, gripping the bars with both hands, wanting to rip them aside and get Johnny out of this cage. "Hey, John," he said quietly.

Mazzeretti was standing next to him. "See what I mean? Nothing."

"Can I go in?"

The dapper cop hesitated. "He might be dangerous."

Mac gave him a look. "Him?"

The lieutenant had the grace to look fleetingly sheepish, then he unlocked the door. He closed it behind Mac, but didn't secure the lock.

Mac crouched on the floor next to the cot. "Johnny?" he whispered. "Listen up, kid. It's me, Johnny."

Slowly the foggy eyes cleared; the lips lifted in a tentative smile.

Casting a triumphant look toward Mazzeretti, Mac spoke again, more softly so only Johnny could hear. "What the hell are you doing?" he asked fiercely. "You stupid dumb jackass."

The hesitant smile faded and Johnny squeezed back against the wall.

"See?" Mazzeretti said. "That's why the order for Bellevue. The guy obviously has problems."

Mac ignored him, reaching out to take one of Johnny's hands between both of his. "Johnny?" he said, softening his tone. "Please. Don't do this. They're gonna take you away and lock you up in a padded cell someplace. Is that what you want?" His hold tightened helplessly. "Please, kid, snap out of it."

The inert hand moved a little and the smile slowly returned. "Hi, Mac," Johnny said. "I was waiting for you. I knew you'd come."

"Well, of course I came," Mac said, relief making his voice hoarse. "So you just knock off this zombie stuff, willya?" He squeezed the hand once more, then released it.

Johnny bit his lower lip. "What are they gonna do to me?"

"Nothing, kid, I promise. Everything is going to be okay. You just cooperate with them and I'll take care of it."

Johnny's face was anxious, and his eyes stared into Mac's. "Are you mad at me? I'm really sorry, Mac. I didn't mean to get into trouble."

"Shh, it's okay, never mind that." He was quiet for a moment. "No, I'm not mad. I know why you did it. Shit, Johnny," he said, "nobody ever cared enough before to . . . well, never mind. But thanks." He got up from his position by the bed. "Can I talk to you?" he asked Mazzeretti.

The lieutenant nodded and Mac started out. Johnny's hand around his wrist stopped him. "Mac?"

"I gotta go now, kid. But I'll be back in a little while. You just take it easy, okay?"

Johnny nodded, letting his fingers slip slowly from their grip.

Mac followed Mazzeretti back to his office, where the lieutenant paused long enough to light a thin black cigar with a gold lighter that matched the pen. "Griffith is a head case," he said succinctly.

Mac drew a level breath. "The guy has some problems," he admitted. "He was in Nam."

Mazzeretti nodded. "Doesn't surprise me much."

"But he doesn't need to be locked up. The help he needs, he's already getting." Was it really a lie? Mac didn't think so. Johnny needed help, yeah, needed to be . . . taken care of. But not by a bunch of shrinks. He helped Johnny just by being his friend, and when everybody else left them alone, it was just fine.

"He's never been busted before." It wasn't a question; apparently they'd checked.

"No, John is a good kid."

Mazzeretti raised his brows. "Kid? How old is he anyway?"

Mac had to stop and think. "Twenty-nine," he said after a moment. The figure surprised him a little; somehow, he always thought of Johnny as being so much younger.

"Hardly a kid," Mazzeretti murmured almost to himself.

"He wouldn't hurt anybody, Lieutenant, really. What happened last night was a . . . a mistake. He honestly thought he was doing the right thing." Like a child, Mac thought. Yeah, he was only trying to help. To help me.

Mazzeretti watched the lengthening ash on the tip of his cigar. "Well, McCarthy, I sympathize, but as long as Mr. Giancarlo insists on pressing charges, there's absolutely nothing I can do."

Mac nodded. Maybe there was nothing the cop could do, but he had no intention of letting them haul Johnny off to some nuthouse. "Thank you," he said, getting to his feet. Perhaps Mazzeretti knew that he intended to go see Giancarlo, but neither man said anything about it as Mac left.

He skirted the area of the holding cell, not wanting Johnny to see him again right then. Outside, the day had turned grey and overcast, and the gloom fit his mood perfectly.

Was Johnny crazy?

Mac had wondered about that before, of course. Ever since their first meeting amid the horror of Tan Pret, the issue of Johnny's sanity had plagued Mac. He seemed to be the only one with any doubts on the matter. Everybody else was so damned sure that they knew better than he about Griffith.

Well, Johnny *was* different, that much was true enough. He had a lot of weird habits. Like clamming up whenever things got tough. That wasn't normal, for sure. And his hang-ups about sex. And his dependency on Mac. He was just like a kid sometimes, no matter how old he really was in years.

So? They were friends, and shouldn't friends depend on each other? Hell, he depended on Johnny, too.

Yeah, I do.

What would happen to Johnny if they sent him away? Mac remembered the hospital where his mother had died. He could still smell the gagging odor of disinfectant that mingled with rather than hid the other smells of the place. He could still hear the screams, the animal cries, the low anguished moans that echoed in the hallways. Most of all, though, he remembered the people themselves, like his mother, with their various madnesses written on their faces. Bony hands reached out toward him as he walked past, swaggering a little so the nun wouldn't know how scared he was. Even now the horror of it all filled him whenever he thought about it.

Johnny, quiet, sweet-natured, childlike Johnny, wouldn't last ten minutes in a place like that.

Another question came to Mac. What'll happen to *me* if they send him away? He stopped abruptly on the sidewalk. A fat man dressed in filthy work clothes bumped into him and snarled an obscenity, but Mac ignored him. He stared into the window of a dress shop, seeing only his face reflected among the swirl of colors there. His own eyes stared back at him as if they were seeing a stranger.

Does it make a fucking bit of difference to me if Johnny is as crazy as everybody else says he is?

The answer came back in almost the same moment.

No.

Giancarlo was behind the counter of the restaurant, scribbling figures into a worn black ledger, and he looked up sullenly as Mac entered. "You come to make trouble," he said, "I gonna call the cops again."

"No trouble," Mac replied quickly. "I just want to talk."

"About John?"

"About John, yes."

"I got nothing to say. He's a thief."

Mac hadn't seen old lady Jakubjansky come in just behind him, but she spoke up now. "Antonio, you old fool, John is a good boy."

"He was trying to rob from my store. A crook, that's what he is."

Mac leaned across the counter and Giancarlo scooted back a little. "I think we all know that John has problems," Mac said softly, feeling a twinge of disloyalty, but dismissing it impatiently.

Giancarlo tapped his forehead. "Yeah, I always know he is a little funny in the head, but I never think he also be a thief."

"He's not, not really."

"We caught him right here."

Mac picked up a paper napkin and twisted it in his fingers. "John was doing that for me. I told him I needed money and he . . . he just didn't think. He was only trying to do what he thought was right."

"Why should he take my money? He belongs in jail."

Mac glanced around at Mrs. Jakubjansky and she seemed to see the despair he was feeling reflected in his face. She came closer to the counter. "Antonio, you always been a big talker about how wonderful is this country. Well, John was a soldier fighting for you. Is it his fault the war made him a little sick in the head? He's a good boy now, but if they put him in jail with all the killers and crooks, who knows what will happen to him? Mr. McCarthy takes good care of John, better than a jail."

Giancarlo seemed to waver just a little. "But he was stealing. . . ."

Mac crumpled the napkin and tossed it onto the counter. "Look, if you'll drop the charges, they'll let him go. We'll leave;

I'll take him away right now, today, and we'll never bother you again. I swear to God, all we want to do is get away from here."

It took about ten more minutes for the two of them to convince Giancarlo, but he finally put up his hands and surrendered. As the disgruntled man went off to the precinct house, Mac ran upstairs to pack. He also shaved and changed, before piling their meager belongings just inside the door for easy pick-up. As he was finishing, old lady Jakubjansky appeared at the door again, a foil-wrapped package in one hand. "My sugar cookies," she said. "John likes them."

Mac took the package. "Thank you," he said awkwardly.

"He is like a little boy sometimes."

"Yeah."

Her face grew stern and she pointed a skinny finger at him. "He is your responsibility. Take better care for him."

Mac nodded and she left. He stared at the package of cookies for a moment, then set it on top of the luggage and left.

By the time he got to the station, Johnny was already out of the holding cell, sitting in the squad room, drinking a Coke and listening to Mazzeretti. Johnny didn't seem to be saying much, but he nodded occasionally in response to something the cop was saying. As Mac got closer, Johnny looked up and saw him coming across the room. His face broke into a broad grin. Mac grinned in response and walked a little faster. He felt good now, and ignored Mazzeretti's troubled dark gaze that rested on them as he and Johnny greeted each other. "How you doing, kid?" he asked, giving Johnny a light punch on the arm.

"I'm okay, Mac," he replied softly.

Mazzeretti stepped forward. "McCarthy, I want to talk to you."

"What about?" Mac asked, only wanting to take Johnny and go.

"In my office."

Mac glanced at Johnny, who was watching the conversation.

"John can wait here," Mazzeretti said.

Giving the suddenly frightened blue eyes a quick A-OK sign, Mac followed the detective. They sat facing one another across the desk. Mazzeretti lit another cigar, and Mac took out a cigarette.

"Tell me about John."

Mac shifted in the seat. "I thought you said he could go, if the charges were dropped."

"He can go. As soon as we've talked."

"I don't know what you want me to say." Mac took a deep drag on his cigarette.

"I want to know what his problems are."

"I already told you; he was in Nam."

"So were a lot of people."

The small office was quiet for several moments. Mac finally sighed. "Some people can hack war," he said. "Some can't. Johnny didn't belong there." He looked at the cop. "But that was all a long time ago. Johnny's okay now."

"Except when he gets scared, like tonight, right?"

"He's okay," Mac repeated stubbornly.

"You said he's getting help?"

"Sure," Mac lied.

"What's his doctor's name?"

He frowned, glancing out to the other room. "He goes to the VA hospital," he improvised. "Look, can we go now?"

After a moment, Mazzeretti nodded. "All right," he said. "But I suggest you keep an eye on him. Next time he might get into more serious trouble."

Mac was already at the door. "Sure," he said quickly. "I'll take care of him."

Johnny looked up from his intent contemplation of the floor and smiled as Mac approached. "Can we go now?" he asked softly.

"Sure, kid, come on." He took Johnny by one arm and guided him through the squadroom, feeling Mazzeretti's eyes on them all the while.

Chapter 12

Mac spent the next two days running all over the city, trying to parlay his pitifully small stake into four thousand dollars before the people he owed could catch up with him. He hustled like he never had before, chasing down guys he hadn't seen in months, scrounging every cent he could.

They had a new home, a cockroach-ridden room behind a second-hand furniture store, and Johnny stayed there. He was restless and a little bewildered, but as always, he obeyed Mac's orders unquestioningly. The last thing Mac needed was to have Johnny wandering the streets, easy prey for Frank and Al, the two gorillas.

At the end of forty-eight hours, he'd managed to turn his

pittance into three-hundred and seventy-five dollars. A tidy sum, yeah, but still a helluva long way from what he needed. It was nearly ten P.M. when he finally gave up and started home. He was very tired, a little drunk, feeling the almost unbearable loneliness of the deserted side street. The chilling wind cut through the heavy denim jacket he wore as if it were made of paper. He walked a little faster, wanting to be home, not wanting to be alone anymore.

He was three blocks from the room when Frank and Al stepped out of an alley and stopped in front of him. Mac pulled his hands out of his pockets, tensing. "Hi," he said.

"Hi, there, Mr. McCarthy. We've been looking for you."

"I've been around."

"So we hear."

Mac ran the tip of his tongue across his lips. "You want something?"

"Yeah, sir, we want something. In fact, we want four thousand somethings. And we want them now."

"Oh, yeah." He reached toward his pocket. "I have three-hundred and seventy-five dollars," he said. "You take it. Well, look, on second thought, take only three, why don't you, and leave me the seventy-five for a stake, so I can—"

He never finished the sentence. A fist, augmented by brass knuckles and backed by Frank's well-over two-hundred pounds, crashed into his stomach. Grunting, Mac bent over. The same fist collided with his jaw, sending him reeling backwards. He collided with a brick wall.

"See," Al said kindly, "you don't owe three-hundred. You owe four thousand. And on top of that, see, you ran out so we had to chase you all over the city."

"I . . . wasn't trying . . . to run out," Mac gasped. "I was only . . . trying to raise the cash."

"Yes, well, that's fine and good. But you didn't get it, did you? So now we have to collect the interest." Al stepped aside.

Mac tried to avoid the next blow from Frank. He sidestepped, shoving both arms into Frank's mid-section. The fat man grunted a little. Before Mac could take advantage of that momentary victory, Al crashed what felt like the butt of a gun into the back of his head.

Colored lights exploded in his skull. Mac sprawled onto the gritty concrete, tasting the hot blood that gushed from his nose, feeling the surface of his palms scraped raw. He rolled onto his back, hoping to be able to kick upwards and make his escape.

Before he could move and put his plan, such as it was, into operation, a steel-tipped shoe was propelled into his side once, then again and again. The heel of another shoe was pressed slowly, deliberately, into his outstretched palm. All of this took place in an eerie silence, broken only by the sound of his own raspy breaths.

Absently Mac kept a tally of the bruising kicks to his body. He could feel the bile rising up, threatening to choke him, and he turned his head, letting the hot liquid roll out the side of his mouth. It made him mad to realize that he might die here, amid the over-turned garbage cans, finished off by a couple of shitheads like these two. It also made him sad, although he didn't know why. Life hadn't been such a barrel of laughs that he should mind very much checking out a little early.

The beating had stopped without Mac's really being aware of it, and someone was pawing through his pockets. The hard-earned money was removed. "We'll be around for the rest," a voice said. "Understand?" Another kick. "Understand?"

He managed to nod. They walked away, leaving him alone in the alley to die.

A long time passed, and he didn't move at all. It was kind of peaceful there, actually, just him and a couple of roving tomcats. Or maybe they were rats; he really couldn't see too well. The flow of blood from his nose had slowed to a trickle. He wondered how long it took to die.

"Oh, shit," he mumbled suddenly. "I forgot about him."

So much for a nice quiet death here in the alley. Johnny was waiting for him in that terrible little room above the furniture store, and if he didn't come back, that idiot would probably just sit there until he died of starvation or something.

Mac tried to roll over, and on his third attempt, he made it. The effort brought tears to his eyes, but he didn't take time to catch his breath before pushing himself to his knees. *"Ohjesus,"* he said. *"Ohchrist."* Putting his hands against the side of the building, he managed slowly and excruciatingly to push himself to a standing position. He leaned his face against the cold surface of the bricks. It felt so good that he just wanted to stand there forever, but after a while he knew that it was time to move on.

The first step nearly finished him. He shuffled about six inches and then stopped, doubled over in pain, throwing up again. "Help me," he whispered to the emptiness. "Help me, Johnny." Oh great, he thought, things were so bad that he needed help from the dumbass kid. His breath came in sharp, gravelly gasps that whistled every once in a while. With shaking fingers, he poked and probed until he came to the conclusion that no matter how much they hurt, all of his ribs were still somehow intact.

Finally, by sliding his feet along the pavement, he managed to move. He kept both arms wrapped around his stomach, stopping every once in a while to catch his breath. Think about something else, he ordered himself. Shit, it was so damned cold. Almost Christmas. Yeah, think about Christmas.

When he was ten, he spent the holiday with some minister's family. What the hell was their name? Loomis, that was it. The Loomises were Episcopalians, but the nuns were so anxious to find a home for the gangly, solitary boy that they decided to forget liturgical differences and let him go. The minister was a nice man. Dumb, but nice. His wife baked cookies all the time. While the minister wrote his Christmas Eve sermon and the wife turned out seemingly endless pans of cookies, Mac spent time with their son. The boy was fifteen. Mac hadn't thought about Brian Loomis in a long time. The minister's son and the orphan boy hid in the cellar, where they smoked illicit cigarettes and looked at dirty pictures. Whenever Brian got a hard-on, he would make Mac jerk him off. That happened a couple times every day during his one-week stay.

He wondered what had happened to Brian Loomis.

Mac looked up and realized that he still had a block to go. Think some more. Christmas. Last year he and Johnny had humped down to the Salvation Army for a free meal. His luck had been on a bad streak then.

He tried to laugh, but it hurt too much.

Still, the meal hadn't been so bad. Turkey and everything, and they even let Johnny have seconds on the pumpkin pie. Afterward, he treated Johnny to a double feature, both westerns. Johnny, shyness making him even more tongue-tied than usual, presented him with a carton of cigarettes.

Hell, when he stopped to think about it, last Christmas had been pretty good. Better than most. Maybe even the best.

He reached the corner. Just a little further, he thought, and I'll be home. Then everything will be okay. That thought kept him moving, when all he really wanted to do was fall into the gutter and let blessed oblivion wash over him. But finally, finally, he dragged his weary body up the stairs and reached the door to their room. Without even enough strength left to knock, he lifted one hand and scratched feebly at the chipped painted surface. He waited a century or two, then scratched again.

"Who's there?" said a soft voice from within.

"John," he gasped out. "It's me, Johnny."

The door flew open. He got one look at Johnny's scared face before everything started to spin around, the blackness taking over at last, and he pitched forward into Johnny's arms.

His next awareness was of a dull, throbbing ache in his side, and then of a soft insistent whisper very close to his ear. "Mac? Hey, buddy? Please, Mac, don't die."

He couldn't even open his eyes yet. Instead, he lay very still and took a groggy inventory. The bloody clothes were gone, his body had been cleaned, and he was lying in bed, feeling warm and almost comfortable. It was nice and he was tempted to just drift away again.

But there was that whisper. "Mac, please, wake up."

Allowing himself to be dragged back from the edge, he managed to move his hand a little, searching, until his fingers closed around Johnny's wrist. He squeezed lightly. "S'okay," he mumbled through swollen lips.

"Mac?"

Finally he opened his eyes. Johnny, pale and wearing a T-shirt that was caked with blood, sat on the edge of the bed. His eyes, wide blue pools behind the glasses, were panic-stricken. "Hey," Mac said, "s'okay, really."

"Should I get a doctor or something?"

"Uh-uh. Hurts like hell, but I don't think anything's broken."

Johnny released his breath in a long sigh.

"Thanks for patching me up."

"Yeah, sure." Johnny grinned. "Maybe I should've been a doctor, right?" The smile vanished as suddenly as it had appeared. He stood and walked a few steps away from the bed, not looking at Mac. "I was so damned scared," he said hoarsely. "I thought you were—" He broke off.

"I must've looked like death warmed over," Mac said, trying to speak lightly.

Johnny whirled around to face him. "I was so scared, Mac. I'm sorry to be so scared all the time. I don't like being a coward."

Mac tried to lift his head, but immediately gave it up as a bad idea. "That's a stupid thing to say. You're not a coward."

Johnny shivered a little. "Yeah, Mac, I am, and that's no good. I hate myself sometimes and you must hate me, too."

"Stop it," Mac said wearily. "Just knock off the crap, willya? I'm really not up to it right now. I don't hate you."

"I'm sorry."

"Yeah, kid, I know." Every inch of his body hurt. "Shit. We have any booze?"

Johnny got an almost empty bottle of whiskey from the cupboard and brought it to him. "Who did this to you?"

"Al and Frank, of course. That shouldn't surprise you."

"Because of the money?"

"Yeah, because of the money." In one long drink, Mac drained the bottle. "Took my fucking three-seventy-five, too."

Johnny kept wiping his hands on his blue jeans, as if he were still trying to get rid of the blood. "They almost killed you."

He handed the empty bottle back. "Yeah, well, that was an oversight I'm sure they'll correct the next time." He leaned back and closed his eyes as the alcohol began to work on his system. "Gotta sleep, babe," he mumbled. "Ev'rythin' be okay, ya'know."

"I know."

Johnny's voice sounded faint and far away as Mac finally let the warm darkness wash over him and sweep him away.

Chapter 13

He watched Mac sleep for a long time.

When at last he was convinced that the reassuring up-and-down movements of the other man's chest would continue, Johnny stood, stretching his cramped muscles. The bloody T-shirt stuck to his body unpleasantly, and he grimaced a little, pulling the offending garment over his head and tossing it into the trash.

He washed away the last traces of Mac's blood and put on an old khaki shirt that was a little too large. After checking on Mac again, Johnny went to the battered dresser and quietly slid the top drawer open. Inside the drawer there was a jumble of Mac's things, all dumped there indiscriminately. It was the way they lived, from one cheap room to another, an existence that made objects more of an annoyance than anything else. A thing that had no value at the pawnshop meant nothing. The drawer held socks and underwear, mostly G.I. Discharge papers for both men. Lieutenant's bars. Old matchbooks. A couple back issues of *Playboy*. Johnny scooted all the junk aside, reaching beneath the clutter until his fingers closed around the grip of the Army issue .45. The one item of value that never went to the pawnshop.

Johnny pulled the gun out, frowning a little. The feel of the cold metal in his hand reminded him fleetingly of something, but the memory was lost in that void he had in his past. Fragments came back once in a while, mostly at night, causing him to wake up trembling and drenched in sweat. At times like that, he would wake Mac, and Mac would talk to him, quietly and calmly, not about the dreams or what caused them, but about other things. Like the trip to Hollywood they were going to take soon. Or he told stories about some of the funny things that had happened to him back at the orphanage. It didn't matter what he said anyway; it was just the sound of the deep voice that drove away the demons.

Johnny shook off the thoughts and went back to the chair, holding the gun easily in one hand. Just as he sat down, Mac stirred restlessly, mumbling something Johnny couldn't understand. He reached out with his free hand and pulled the blanket up, tucking it more tightly around the sleeping man. "S'okay," he soothed. "I'm not scared now."

He checked the gun, saw that there was a full clip inside, and tucked the weapon into his waistband. Like Steve McGarrett, he thought. Or Matt Dillon. Leaning forward a little, he spoke again, his fingers resting lightly on Mac's arm. "I'll be back as soon as I can, buddy," he said softly.

Shrugging into his dark blue ski jacket, he turned off the overhead light, leaving a small lamp on, and went out of the room. The air outside smelled of approaching snow. Johnny shoved both hands into his pockets, ducking his head against the bite of the wind as he walked quickly toward the subway.

There was only one other person waiting for the train, a middle-aged black woman carrying a brown paper shopping bag. They eyed one another with mutual suspicion, before Johnny smiled blankly and moved several yards away.

It was nearly five minutes before the train roared to a stop. The car was crowded with a noisy bunch of teenagers, all of whom seemed to be high. They pushed and shoved up and down the aisle, singing, laughing, exuding an excitement that hovered on the near edge of violence. Johnny huddled in a seat by the door, careful not to look at any of the kids, afraid, terrified that they would notice him and . . . and what? He didn't really know what they might do, but the fear was so strong that he could taste it, metallic and bitter in his mouth. Only the thought that Mac was counting on him kept Johnny from fleeing the train at the next stop.

The fifteen minutes it took to reach his stop seemed endless, but at last Johnny could scurry out of the car and up the steps, emerging onto a crowded sidewalk. Despite the late hour and the cold, there were still plenty of people out and about. Hustlers, night wanderers, funseekers, moving in and out of the bars, massage parlors, and bookstores that lined the street. Surrounded by a universe of threatening strangers, Johnny drew further into himself, edging cautiously through the crowd, one hand resting on the gun. The lump of steel dug into his belly, but rather than being an annoyance, the presence of the weapon, Mac's gun, was reassuring. Almost like having Mac himself there.

Johnny's feelings were as jumbled as had been the contents of the drawer earlier. Fear, certainly. But not of the moment, itself, or even of what he intended to do. Only fear, as always, of the people swirling around him, watching him. Two hookers, one female and one male, approached him in the space of half a block. He ignored their graphic invitations.

Even the fear, though, was over-shadowed by his sense of purpose. It was the first time that he could ever remember feeling really important. Except maybe for the time he made the speech at graduation. The whole auditorium listened to him that night. He could still remember the speech. "As we the class of 1960 embark upon the great adventure of life," he whispered into the knife-edged wind, "we are strengthened and emboldened by the lessons learned here. The road we are about to set foot upon will not be easy. The dangers are many, but we face them unafraid. No one knows what the future may hold, but I am confident. I look into the next decade with all its promises and all its problems, and I feel a great sense of exhilaration."

They all applauded and cheered when he finished. Of course, it was maybe a little bit because they felt sorry for him, his parents being just dead and all. But still it was a good speech.

So now here he was, finally *doing* something, finally taking action. This was almost like those holy missions his parents used to go on. They went to save souls from the Devil. Well, Al and Frank were like devils. They were evil and cruel, and it was his duty to save Mac's soul from them, to save Mac. The wages of sin is death, and they had sinned by the terrible thing they had done to Mac. And they might do worse unless he stopped them. Their evil could not be allowed to triumph over Mac's goodness.

When he reached the Pirate's Cove, Johnny didn't go in. Instead, he ducked into the alley and walked to the rear of the building. Loud rock music from bars on either side of the Cove filled the air. He hunched down behind some empty packing crates and leaned against the side of the building to wait.

It was getting colder. He blew on his fingers every couple of minutes to warm them a little. Hope this doesn't take too long, he fretted. Mac shouldn't be by himself, in case he needs me.

And, the thought came, what will Mac say about this?

Johnny chewed on his chapped lower lip. I gotta do everything just right, or he'll get mad at me. I hate it worse than anything when Mac is mad at me.

He sighed and gripped the gun more tightly. Where the hell were Al and Frank? They always turned up sooner or later at the Cove; it was a part of their routine. Johnny's knowledge of what went on around him would have startled even Mac, who was fully aware that he wasn't nearly as spaced out as everybody else thought. But even Mac had no idea how completely Johnny assimilated his surroundings. The vague blue eyes missed nothing. No one knew Johnny; he knew everyone.

His legs were beginning to cramp. Without standing, he straightened first one and then the other, trying to ease the kinks.

It wasn't that he really hated Al and Frank. Hatred implied feeling and he felt nothing at all for them. They existed only insofar as they posed a threat to Mac. They wanted to kill him. The very thought made Johnny shake deep inside, and he pushed it away quickly.

After what seemed like a very long time, the back door of the Cove creaked open. Johnny tensed, then leaned forward a little, until he could see two dark profiles standing just a few feet away. They talked together in muffled tones as Al struggled to light a cigar in the wind.

Johnny rested his arm across the top of a crate, sighting carefully as if he were throwing a dart at a target, and squeezed the trigger of the .45. The first bullet struck Frank in the back of the head and the big man toppled over, already dead. Al lifted his head in startled reaction. Johnny fired again, the sound of the shot nearly swallowed up by the wind and the music, and this bullet hit Al in the chest. He fumbled inside of his coat desperately. Johnny fired again, and this time the bullet smashed into Al's forehead.

Johnny waited a moment, the gun still poised, but neither of the men moved. He slipped out of his hiding place and knelt next to Al, rummaging through the dead man's pockets until he found a fat money belt. Quickly he counted out exactly $375, then shoved the rest back.

An instant later he stepped out of the alley, mingling once again with the crowd on the sidewalk. Inside the jacket pocket, one hand still clutched the gun.

Now that it was over, he felt numb. Two men were dead and he was the one who'd killed them. It wasn't the first time he'd killed, of course. But, no, he wouldn't think about that, wouldn't try to focus on the grey memory that haunted him. Mac said it didn't matter.

He stopped to buy an Orange Julius and carried it down to the subway to wait for the train that would take him home. That was all he wanted. To get home, back to the small room that meant safety, back to Mac.

Chapter 14

He woke once and stirred restlessly, feeling strangely alone. But that was stupid, because he knew that Johnny was there, sound asleep probably, just across the small room. It was senseless to wake him. Mac wanted to turn his head for a quick look, just to be sure that everything was okay, but the effort involved in such a maneuver seemed beyond his meager resources at that moment. With the thought still half-formed, he fell asleep again.

The next time he woke, Johnny was there, sitting next to the bed. Mac grunted a greeting, trying to focus his fuzzy gaze. Johnny, he noted, idly, was fully dressed and holding the gun in his hand.

The gun?

Now Mac was wide awake. "Hey," he managed to say through a dry throat.

After a beat, Johnny glanced up. "Hi," he said dully.

"I could use . . . some water, babe."

Johnny nodded, but otherwise didn't move.

Mac was bewildered, as if the beating had scrambled his

brains and maybe it had. "Johnny? What's wrong? What're you doing with the gun?"

Johnny looked at the gun in surprise, as if he'd forgotten that it was clenched in his fingers. "Don't be mad," he whispered. "Promise you won't get mad at me, Mac." Before Mac could respond, Johnny set the gun carefully on the floor and went over to the sink. He let the water run for a minute to get cold, then filled a glass, and brought it back to the bed. "Here."

Mac raised himself a little and sipped tentatively. Everything seemed to be working okay, and he relaxed slightly. "Why should I get mad?" he asked when his throat felt better. "Johnny, what's going on?"

Johnny sat on the edge of the bed. He ducked his head, staring at the blanket, fingering a small hole in the cheap material. "Please, Mac. Promise."

"I promise," Mac said after a moment, suddenly afraid without knowing why.

Johnny sighed, watching his fingers enlarge the tear in the blanket. "I killed them."

"What? Who?" Mac realized that the poor guy was having another nightmare about Tan Pret. There hadn't been so many lately, but they still upset the kid a lot. "Hey, we've talked about this before, right?"

"No. This is something else. I killed Al and Frank."

Mac heard the words and even understood them, but the meaning didn't register. "What?"

"I killed Al and Frank a little while ago. I shot them both."

"*Ohmygod*," Mac breathed, drawing back a little. "You did what?" He gripped Johnny's arm with a strength he didn't think his battered body still had. "Is this a dream, John? That's it, right? Some kind of a crazy dream?"

But Johnny shook his head. "No," he said, still whispering. "It's not a dream. It really happened."

"*What* happened?" Mac realized that his voice was cracking. He finished the water in a gulp and took a deep breath. "Tell me all about it, Johnny. From the beginning." Something in Johnny's face made him add, "I'm not mad, kid. I just want to know."

Johnny relaxed a little. "After you fell asleep, I took your gun and caught the subway over to the Cove, 'cause that's where they hang out. I waited in the alley for a long time. It was really cold, too," he added. "Finally they came out, Al and Frank. I shot Frank first, because he was the closest. I shot him in the head. Then I shot Al, but the first bullet didn't kill him, so I had to do it again. They were both dead." He fumbled in his pocket. "I got your money back. Three hundred and seventy-five, right? He had a lot more, but I only took yours." When Mac didn't reach for the bills, Johnny dropped them onto the floor next to the gun. "Then I bought an Orange Julius and caught the subway home." He made the entire recitation flatly, without the slightest trace of emotion, sounding like a TV anchorman delivering the evening news on a dull day. Finished, he raised his eyes and met Mac's gaze. Now his voice was strained. "I had to do it, Mac. They hurt you and they were going to kill you next time; you said so."

Mac suddenly remembered the expression in Johnny's eyes the day he tried to grease Crazy George; that same look was there now. The water he'd just finished threatened to come right back up. "Oh, Johnny," he said helplessly. He shook his head. "Ohchrist, kid."

Johnny's brow wrinkled anxiously. "You're not mad, are you? Please, don't be. You promised."

Mac released his hold on Johnny's arm. "No," he said absently, his mind on other things. "I'm not mad."

Johnny smiled a little. "Okay, then, it's all right."

"All right?" Mac leaned back and closed his eyes, trying to think. There was no way that the weapon used could be traced to him. He'd won the gun in a poker game in Nam, won it from a guy who'd bought it on the black market in Da Nang. At least they were safe on that front. "Nobody saw what happened?" he asked, opening his eyes. "You're sure?"

"Nobody saw, Mac. It was dark. The music was so loud that they couldn't even hear the shots."

"Well, thank god for that, anyway. Maybe we can pull this off."

"You understand why I had to do it, don't you?"

Mac stared into the guileless blue eyes that begged for approval like a child would, or a pet dog seeking the loving attention of its master. "Yeah, Johnny," he said finally, "I know why you did it." That was a lie, of course, because he didn't understand, not really, not completely anyway. But the blue eyes needed reassurance and so he lied. "Don't think about it anymore right now, okay? It's over and done with, so now things will be better. Understand?"

"Sure, Mac, just as long as you're not mad at me." Johnny stood and began to undress.

Mac watched him absently, rubbing the bridge of his sore nose gently. Well, it wasn't as if those two bastards would ever be missed by anyone. And, hell, they really might have killed him. Probably would have, if he hadn't come up with the rest of the cash. He sighed.

Johnny, stripped to his shorts, stood in the center of the room, looking around helplessly, as if he couldn't remember what the hell he'd been doing. Then a frown crossed his face. "Mac?"

"Huh?" Mac replied vaguely, still finding it hard to believe that this bewildered man-child had just finished blowing away two of the toughest collectors in the city. "What, kid?"

"Could I . . . could I stay over here with you for a while? I don't want to be by myself."

Mac hesitated, then attempted a shrug. "Okay, come on." He scooted over to make room, grimacing a little as his body protested.

Johnny turned off the lamp and stretched out next to him, giving a long sigh. "Thank you."

"What for?"

"Everything. For not being mad, and for letting me stay here with you."

Mac wanted to smash somebody's head against the wall, but whether it should be his own or Johnny's, he didn't know. "Ah, shit, Johnny," he said finally. "Go to sleep."

"Okay. Things are gonna be better now, huh?"

Mac closed his eyes. "Yeah, kid, sure," he said. "Things are gonna pick up."

"Good."

"But for now go to sleep, willya?"

Johnny didn't answer, but in only a few minutes, his breathing had taken on the regular pattern of sleep. Mac finally turned his face to the wall and slept as well.

Chapter 15

Despite the morning chill that touched the room, the two bodies lying together in the narrow bed created a damp heat of their own, and it was that warmth which woke Mac finally. He shifted uncomfortably, trying to ease out from under the weight of Johnny's arm across his chest. The pressure and the heat combined until he felt as if he would suffocate. He moved again and

Johnny moaned a soft, wordless protest, but didn't awaken. Mac finally managed to plant both feet on the floor and get up from the bed.

The cold air hit like an electric shock against his hot, flushed skin, and he stood still for a moment, feeling strangely breathless. At last he began to move, albeit slowly. His body ached all over, and the brief glimpse he took in the mirror revealed a face that would take two weeks to heal. But despite all that, Al and Frank were—had been—pros, and they hadn't really intended to do him any serious damage last night. This first time was only meant to serve as a warning. Well, there wouldn't be a second time. He glanced at Johnny, still curled in the bed, sleeping as deeply as a child. It was still almost impossible to believe what he'd done.

Moving carefully, Mac got dressed. When he'd donned cords and a sweater, and finished a can of flat soda pop he found on the table, he went back to crouch by the bed. "John?" he whispered.

Two bleary eyes snapped open. "Huh?"

"I have to go someplace. You stay inside today, understand?"

Fear flickered through the sleepy blue gaze. "Where are you going?"

"Just out. I want to see if there's anything going down about what happened."

"About what I did, you mean?"

"Yeah." Mac picked up the money from the floor where Johnny had dropped it the night before. "You okay?"

"I guess so."

Mac patted his shoulder absently. "Sure you are. See you in a little while." Grabbing his coat, Mac left the room quickly. Outside, he paused, taking deep gulps of the icy air. He felt like a drowning man being given oxygen. The cold seemed to steady him a little, and he was able to walk almost briskly to the Coffee Cup Cafe three blocks away.

Taking a seat at the counter, he ordered coffee and a Danish, and reached for the communal copy of the morning paper. Of course, he realized that it was too soon for there to be anything on the shooting, but he read each headline anyway, just in case.

When that task was complete, he gestured for another cup of coffee and glanced down the length of the counter, spotting a familiar face. "Working so early in the morning, Shirl?" he asked lightly.

The scrawny blonde grinned. "Rent's due, Alex. A girl's gotta keep a roof over her head."

"Yeah, I guess." He watched Shirley sip Coke through a straw. She was young, about Johnny's age, but she looked older. Not bad, though.

"You walk into a door or something?" she asked.

"Huh?"

"Your face. Looks like a meat grinder worked you over."

"Close." He grimaced. "You know how it is."

She nodded glumly. "Sure do. How's John?"

"Okay," he replied, feeling the familiar tightening of tension in his gut. "Why?"

She shrugged. "Just wondering. I like John. He's funny."

"Funny?"

"Uh-huh. He makes me laugh sometimes."

Mac didn't particularly like the idea of people laughing at the kid. He was weird, yeah, but he had feelings like everybody else.

Shirley must have seen the disapproval on his face, because she suddenly spit the piece of ice she'd been sucking on back into the glass. "Hey, I didn't mean anything bad, you know? I don't laugh at John because of . . . well, because of the way he's kinda slow and all. I just meant that he makes jokes sometimes."

"Yeah, sure," he said. "Johnny's a regular Bob Hope once he gets going." Shit, if the kid ever made a joke, it must have been an accident. He probably wondered why the hell everybody was laughing. "He's not really slow, you know," he said. "Johnny was the valedictorian of his high school class."

"Yeah? That's good, huh?"

"Means he was the smartest one there." Mac glumly crumpled the last of his Danish. It wasn't even noon yet, and the rest of the day stretched out endlessly in front of him. He could spend the time walking the streets trying to find out what anybody might know about the killings. Or he could go back to the room, that damned room that threatened sometimes to suffocate him, and try to carry on a conversation with Johnny. Right at the moment, though, he didn't feel up to that challenge.

"You feeling down, Alex?" she asked.

"Yeah, I guess so."

"Why?"

He sipped the cooling coffee and wondered what she would do if he actually told her all his problems. Fall asleep, probably. "Why not?" was all he said.

"I got a couple of joints, if you're interested."

"No. Thanks anyway." Not about to mess up my mind like that, he thought. Booze is one thing, but I don't need any of that other shit. Hell, one spaceman in the family was enough.

Maybe there was something else he could do to kill some time until the late editions hit the street. "Fifty bucks pay your rent?"

"And then some."

He shoved the empty cup away. "How about I pick up a bottle and we go to your place?"

She pushed blonde strands out of her eyes. "Sounds good. Beats the hell out of standing on a street corner in this weather." She grinned. "Besides, sometimes it's nice making it with a friend, you know?"

It was already dark when he finally left Shirley's place, still a little drunk, groggy with too much sleep and sex and alcohol. He walked home slowly, stopping at a candy store for a paper; as an afterthought to appease his guilt over having left Johnny sitting alone in the room for so long, he also bought a candy bar.

Johnny was slumped in the chair, half-asleep, a copy of *TV Guide* open in his lap. Crazy kid read the guide every week, even though they didn't have the set anymore. He woke with a start when the door opened, then smiled. "Hi."

"Hi, buddy." He tossed the candy into his lap. "I got that for you."

"Thanks."

Mac grunted and sat down on the bed, opening the newspaper. The story was on page three. "Two men found shot," he read aloud. "You want to hear this?"

"I don't care." Johnny was carefully unwrapping the chocolate.

" 'Police are investigating the shooting deaths of two men reputed to have ties to local gambling interests. The bodies of Francis Muldair and Albert Nueman were found behind the Pirate's Cove Bar in Manhattan. According to a police spokesman, there are no leads thus far in the double slaying. The two men reportedly worked for Daniel Tedesco, local gambling kingpin.' " He looked up. "That's all it says."

Johnny nodded. "They don't know I did it."

Mac threw the paper aside and began unlacing his shoes. "Everything go okay today?"

"Yes. I stayed here, just like you said to."

"Good boy." Mac grinned. "To tell the truth, babe, I'm a little drunk."

"I know."

"You can tell, huh? How?" Mac pulled off his sweater and pants.

"Because whenever you're drunk, you have this stupid-looking smile on your face," Johnny said mildly.

"Thanks a lot." He flopped back onto his bed. "Tomorrow, Johnny, we really gotta talk."

"Sure, Mac, whenever you want."

He lay there for a long time in a sort of fuzzy glow, all the tension of the morning gone, watching Johnny finish the candy bar and then undress for the night. It was a pleasant moment, and he wished it could be like this all the time. Johnny pushed the chair and footstool together and spread out the blanket, as Mac still watched. "'Night, Johnny," he mumbled as the light went out.

"Good night, Mac. Thanks for the candy."

He nodded, although Johnny couldn't see him in the dark, and fell asleep.

Chapter 16

They didn't talk the next day after all. Somehow the right moment never seemed to arrive, and as several more days went by, they both seemed more than willing to simply forget what had happened. Although deep inside himself Mac knew that a day of reckoning would have to come sooner or later, he decided to just go with the flow as old Wash used to say. Go with the flow. Mac's luck was on an upswing suddenly and he was winning regularly, winning big. He got the TV out of hock and even blew a wad on a pair of genuine leather gloves for Johnny. The kid, meanwhile, was overdosing on soda and television.

All this good fortune lasted exactly one week. On Wednesday afternoon, they went to see the new western playing up the street. Afterward, they parted company amiably, Johnny going over to the Coffee Cup for a hamburger, and Mac eager to get an early start on the night's game.

He should've gone to eat instead.

His luck was suddenly as sour as it had been good, and in only a few hours, he was down seven hundred dollars. At that point, he quit. The cards were just running cold for him, and there wasn't much sense in blowing his last hundred and fifty bucks. Tomorrow night would be better.

He left the store front where the game was currently operating and started home, his mood gloomy. Why the hell couldn't they ever get far enough ahead to relax? One lousy week of feeling good, of spending money, of having some frigging fun, for chrissake, and now things had to turn rotten again. Shit. Just when he'd gotten John all keyed up about maybe taking a trip to California. Shit. Well, the trip would just have to wait. And Johnny wouldn't care, of course. He wouldn't even utter a word of complaint, but only smile that same idiotic smile and say, "That's okay, Mac."

Yeah, sure, that's okay, Mac.

Just once, he wished that Johnny would haul off and hit him. Then he could hit back, and everybody would be a whole lot happier. He kicked at an empty beer can and swore, but whether the anger was directed at John Griffith or himself wasn't really clear.

Lost in somewhat weary contemplation of his life, he wasn't aware that a car had pulled up behind him, or that two men had gotten out, until one of them touched his elbow. "McCarthy?" The tone was polite, but steely.

He spun around. "Huh?"

"Please get into the car."

He tried to pull away from the abruptly vise-like grip on his arm. "Why the hell should I?"

"Because I asked you to. Besides, you have an appointment and we wouldn't want you to be late."

"I don't understand," Mac said doubtfully.

"Please, Mr. McCarthy, into the car."

A gun barrel pressed lightly into his spine, and he decided not to argue anymore. Discretion and all that. He climbed into the back seat of the limo. One of the men joined him and the other got in front with the driver. The situation was absurd, of course. Like something out of one of those really bad gangster flicks Johnny loved so much. He opened his mouth to ask just where the hell they were going, but after a glance at the man sitting next to him, changed his mind and kept quiet. Go with the flow, Alex, go with the flow.

It was only a few minutes before they pulled into an alley behind a large warehouse and stopped. "Get out," the watchdog ordered. "Don't try anything funny, or I'll blow your guts all over the sidewalk."

"I wouldn't think of it," Mac replied sincerely. Christ, even the dialogue was right out of a B feature. He had a feeling, though, that the bullets in the gun weren't props.

The four of them entered the warehouse and walked across a vast empty area. Mac wondered if maybe they were taking him someplace secluded just for the purpose of killing him. That didn't seem unlikely, and he suppressed a sigh. Talk about your fucking losing streaks.

The office they went into was filled with oak and leather. Class stuff. Mac was pushed gently but firmly into a chair. He rested two sweaty palms on his knees and looked at the man sitting behind the desk.

He was stocky, grey-haired, and he cleared his throat elegantly. "My name is Daniel Tedesco," he said in a soft, musical voice.

Surprise, surprise. Mr. Big himself. Mac just nodded.

"We have a little business to discuss."

Mac tried for a grin. "Hey, yeah, the money. Well, look, I haven't forgotten that, ya'know."

Tedesco almost smiled. "I wasn't speaking of the money. We can deal with that matter later. At the moment, I have something else on my mind."

Mac slumped in the chair. "Yeah? What's that?"

"There is the question of my two employees. Or more correctly, my two late employees. The two men you killed."

Mac straightened quickly. "Me? I didn't—"

Tedesco held up a hand. "Denials are a waste of time. I am quite sure that you killed Al and Frank."

"But I—"

"Please," Tedesco said gently. "Either you killed my boys, or you know who did. If it wasn't you, then give me a name." He waited patiently.

Mac tried desperately to moisten his dry mouth. He lowered his eyes and stared at his fingers. Hell, he thought. Goddamnit to hell anyway. "Okay," he said after a few moments of rapidly considered and summarily rejected alternatives. "I did it." His voice was flat.

"Very good. Now we can begin to talk. Honesty is very important to me." Tedesco paused. One of the lackeys held out an intricately carved humidor, and with great deliberation, the old man made a selection. "You know," he said parenthetically as he prepared to light the cigar, "it wasn't very bright on your part to take only the three seventy-five. Since that was exactly the amount recorded in their book as having been collected from you earlier in the evening, it aided our investigation immensely."

"Yeah, I'm sure it did," Mac agreed bitterly. That dumb bastard Johnny. *If there was a way to screw things up, you could always count on him to do it. I oughtta just turn the son of a bitch over to Tedesco and solve all my problems at one time.* "So what now? You going to burn me, too?"

"Well, that's certainly an option," Tedesco said a little too quickly to suit Mac.

He wondered how they'd do it. *A quick bullet to the head? Or maybe a trip over to the Hudson. Concrete and chains? Hell, I've been seeing too many of those damned movies with Johnny. And thinking of Johnny . . . well, that was a line of thought best left alone. There wasn't a damned thing he could do for the kid now, except keep his name out of it. John would cope. Somehow.* He realized belatedly that Tedesco was talking to him. "Sorry, sir?"

"Please give me your complete attention. I dislike having to repeat myself."

"Yeah, okay."

"I find myself in the need of a new collector to replace the late and much-lamented Mr. Nueman. Would you be interested in the job?"

"Me?" Mac laughed sharply, until he realized that there was no hint of humor in Tedesco's flat, grey eyes. He leaned back in the chair. "You're serious, aren't you?"

"I'm always serious, Mr. McCarthy. Correct me if I'm wrong, but you're in a rather precarious position at the moment, are you not? Shall I enumerate? You owe this organization four thousand dollars. Plus interest. On top of that, you admit to killing two of my best boys." He paused and studied the glowing tip of the cigar. "Of course, perhaps you've already managed to devise some way to extricate yourself from these various complications?"

Mac shook his head. "No," he said softly.

"I thought not. So perhaps you should give my offer serious consideration."

"Just exactly what is your 'offer'?"

"You will handle my collections. A percentage of your cut will be applied toward liquidating your debt. In no time at all, you'll be free and clear once again."

"Uh-huh," Mac said noncommittally.

"Additionally, I am prepared to forgive and forget the matter of my boys being killed like they were. It would become a family matter and go no further."

Mac sighed, looking around the plush office. What chance did he and Johnny have against somebody like Tedesco? They were just a couple of losers in way over their frigging heads. If it was just him. . . . He sighed again, realizing that it wasn't just him and hadn't been for a long time, maybe even since that first day in Tan Pret. At that moment, more clearly than ever before, he was aware that it would never be just him again. Somehow, without really understanding why or how, he seemed to have made a commitment to John Griffith. There would always be someone else to consider. He rubbed his hands along the sides of the chair. Felt like real leather. "Can I have some time?"

"Of course. Take twenty-four hours."

He stood. "Thanks. How can I reach you?"

"Don't bother."

"Can I go now?" He wanted to be home very much.

"Certainly. Can my boys drop you someplace?"

He didn't want any of them near the place. "No. Thanks." He walked to the door, then paused. "This job. It's just making collections, right? Nothing else? No rough stuff like Al and Frank pulled on me?"

Tedesco spread his hands, looking for the moment like a genial uncle. "The job is yours. Handle it anyway you wish. Just bring me my money, and I'll be happy." He smiled. "We'll be in touch."

"Yeah," Mac muttered as he left the office. "I'm sure you will." As he walked across the empty warehouse again, the only sound was the eerie echo of his own footsteps. He resisted the urge to run.

After nearly a week of clouds, the next day brought a bright sun and clear sky. The weather, unfortunately, didn't do much to improve Mac's mood. He toyed unenthusiastically with his scrambled eggs, and watched Johnny across the table at the Coffee Cup. "Hey, I just got an idea," he said finally, dropping his fork.

Johnny was ladling strawberry jam onto toast, his face a study in the same intensity he devoted to every task, no matter how mundane. He finished the job and carefully replaced the spoon in the jelly dish before looking up. "What idea?"

"Why don't we take a ferry boat ride?"

"Today, you mean?"

"Sure. Now. Right after breakfast."

A smile crossed Johnny's face; he dearly loved the boat rides. Then he sobered and chewed the toast thoughtfully, before asking the primary question. "Can we afford it?"

The question irritated Mac. "Of course we can, damn it. Would I suggest it if we couldn't?"

Diplomatically, Johnny refrained from answering. "Okay," he said, smiling again. "That would be fun."

Mac felt dragged out, wondering if he'd gotten even twenty minutes' sleep the night before. He gulped coffee impatiently as Johnny took his own sweet time finishing breakfast. At first, he had considered accepting Tedesco's "offer" and simply not tell Johnny anything about it. But that could lead to all sorts of complications he wasn't really sure he was ready for.

And besides. Yeah, besides. It wouldn't be fair to Johnny to get him mixed up in something like this totally ignorant of what was going on. Even Johnny—spaced-out, screwed-up John— deserved the chance to make a decision like this for himself. Mac wondered if maybe he had a small streak of honor somewhere inside himself. He liked to think so.

On the other hand, there was one more thing, something Mac had admitted to himself only after hours of tossing and turning the night before. He was scared. Just plain scared. If he was going to do what Tedesco had said—and what real choice did he have?—he didn't want to be doing it alone. He wanted Johnny there, too. After all, he admitted in a burst of brutal honesty, Johnny wasn't the only one who needed somebody.

Last night it had all seemed fairly simple. But now, in the sharp glare of the winter morning, with Johnny watching him, it wasn't quite so simple. In fact, it was damned hard.

He didn't say much of anything else until they were actually on the return trip, heading from the Statue of Liberty back to the city. Johnny leaned over the railing, the sharp wind off the water making his face red and tousling his hair. Mac stood back a few feet, watching, both hands wrapped around a cup of hot chocolate from the snack bar. At last, he took a deep breath and walked over to stand beside Johnny. "Want some?" he asked, holding out the cup.

"Thanks." Johnny took a couple of sips, then handed it back. "What's wrong?" he asked suddenly.

Mac took a gulp of chocolate. "Wrong?" He stared back at the Statue of Liberty, before looking at Johnny.

Johnny smiled. This wasn't one of his usual bland grins, but a much rarer expression, one filled with a kind of wry self-awareness. It was an expression Mac had come to enjoy, hoping perhaps it signified that the kid was sort of snapping out of it a little. "Hey, Mac, I know you pretty good by this time."

Mac returned the smile. "Yeah, kid, I guess you do."

The moment passed, and the blue eyes clouded again. "Did I do something wrong, Mac? 'Cause if I did, I'm sorry."

Mac crumpled the empty cup and dropped it into the water. "No, you didn't do anything." He was quiet for a moment and Johnny waited patiently. "I won't bother to apologize to you for screwing things up again. I could spend a whole lot of time doing that."

Johnny's eyes flickered over Mac's face. "You don't have to."

"I know. I know, and that makes it worse, because I *don't* have to apologize. Makes it too easy for me to be a bastard."

Johnny shook his head. "You're not."

Mac shrugged. "Well, anyway. You ever hear of a guy called Daniel Tedesco?"

He thought for a moment. "Uh-huh. He's the guy who runs the gambling stuff. Like your card games."

"Right. He's also the guy Al and Frank worked for, remember?"

The color faded from Johnny's chilled face. "Yeah," he whispered.

Mac shoved both hands into the pockets of his cords. "A couple of his apes snatched me last night, and I had a personal meeting with Mr. Big himself."

Johnny's teeth were chattering, but whether it was from the cold or from fear, Mac couldn't tell. He lifted a hand, as if to touch Mac, then lowered it again. "Did they hurt you?"

Mac shook his head impatiently. "No, no, of course not. Tedesco just wanted to talk. About Al and Frank."

"Ohmygod." Johnny clutched at the railing, his fear-blanked eyes staring at Mac. "Do they know what I did?"

"No." Mac grinned. "They think I did it. And I just let them go right on thinking that." He pulled his hands out and ducked his head to light a cigarette.

"But, Mac . . ." Now Johnny grabbed him by one arm. "You didn't kill them. I did and it isn't fair for you to take the blame."

"Shut up, willya, dummy?" Mac shook off Johnny's hand, aware of the other passengers standing nearby. "You did it because of me. That makes me responsible, too."

Johnny moved away from the railing and huddled against the wall. Mac swore to himself and tossed the cigarette away. People were beginning to look at Johnny, and Mac moved over very close to him. "Johnny, it's okay, kid, everything's gonna be okay."

Johnny just shook his head.

"Come over here," Mac muttered through clenched teeth, dragging him around the corner to where they could be alone, at least for the moment. He stared into Johnny's vacant face. "Man, don't fold up on me now. I need you."

A new, unfamiliar look came into Johnny's eyes. "Yeah?"

"Yeah. Goddamned right."

The idea of being needed seemed to amuse Johnny fleetingly. Mac shook him by the shoulder. "Are you listening to me?"

"I'm listening."

"Good. Now look, Tedesco isn't going to do anything to me at all. At least, not if I go along with what he wants."

"What's that?"

Mac shrugged. "He wants me to take over Al's job. To become his collector."

"Are you going to?"

"I don't know. That's why I'm talking to you about it. So we can decide together."

In a couple more minutes, the ferry docked. They disembarked, not talking much again until they were on the subway platform, waiting for a train to take them home. Johnny broke the silence finally. "What's going to happen, Mac, if you say yes?"

"Tedesco told me that I could just do the job anyway I want. Part of what I make goes to pay off the money I owe. I figure when that's taken care of, we could save most of the money, and then get out of this town. Go to L.A. and make a fresh start."

Johnny nodded thoughtfully. "And what happens if you say no?"

Mac gave a sharp laugh. "Then I think that my future will pretty much take care of itself." He bit his tongue, tasting blood. Shit. That was just the kind of thing he hadn't wanted to say. "Oh, hell, we could figure out something," he said quickly, but the look in Johnny's eyes told him that the damage was already done. He averted his gaze, studying the graffiti on the wall beyond. One extremely ambitious spray-canner had scrawled his message in large red letters that seemed to go on forever, like splashes of blood against the concrete. I'VE GIVEN UP

SEARCHING FOR THE TRUTH, it read, AND NOW I'M LOOKING FOR A REALLY GOOD FANTASY. "I thought maybe we could handle the job together," he said at last.

"Yeah?" Johnny replied.

"Yeah. It might be a way out of this hole. But only if you want to, John. Otherwise, I'll just tell Tedesco no deal, and we'll think of something else." Sure we will, he thought hopelessly.

It was several minutes before Johnny spoke again, and by then they had boarded the express. "There is something else I could do," he said.

"What?"

His voice was very soft and Mac had to lean close to hear him. "I could go to the police and tell them what I did. Then nobody would bother you."

Mac could only look at him, stunned by the unexpected suggestion. "Don't you know what they'd do to you?"

"Put me in jail, like that other time."

Mac snorted. "Shit, man, they'd shove you into a padded cell so fast that your head would be spinning."

"But it would help you."

"Oh, yeah, sure, John, sure," Mac said in disgust. "How long have you had this Jesus Christ complex? Well, you might as well climb down off your fuckin' cross, 'cause I'm not gonna play that game. If we go down in flames, we go together. We're not heroes, either one of us."

Johnny relaxed. "Thanks," he said. "I didn't really want to do that."

"No kidding?"

Johnny's fingers twisted around the edge of the seat. "If we work for Tedesco, I wouldn't have to do anything by myself, would I?"

"No," Mac said firmly. "And neither would I."

He sighed. "Okay, Mac. If you think we should do it, that's okay with me. Whatever you say."

Mac couldn't look at Johnny. Instead, he watched the tunnel lights flash by. God, he thought, God, what am I doing? Whatever I say is okay? I don't know what to say, you poor dumb bastard, except that I'm scared. And that's the one thing I can't say, not to you, because I'm supposed to be strong enough for both of us. Christ, how did I ever get myself into such a fucked-up place? "Oh, hell, Johnny," he said suddenly, "sometimes I get so tired."

"I know," Johnny replied unexpectedly.

Mac rested his head against the window behind him and closed his eyes. Johnny began a soft, rhythmic patting of his shoulder, a childlike gesture apparently intended to reassure or comfort him. Mac appreciated the effort, although he didn't say so.

Chapter 17

Her name was Toni and her picture had once been in *Playboy*. She told Mac all about it when they were finished and he was getting dressed. Her body, covered only by a thin sheet, stretched languidly. "Maybe you saw it?" she suggested hopefully.

He shook his head as he leaned over to tie his shoes. "No, I don't think so."

"Yeah, well, it was there. Page eighty-two." She tossed her head in a well-practiced gesture that sent amber curls tumbling over her shoulders. "You know, man, that was sort of a quickie. Sure you have to take off so soon?"

"Yeah. Well, I gotta go to work. See ya around."

"Sure," she replied, reaching one bare hand out to touch his arm, and then snuggling back under the sheet again.

Mac left the room and hurried down two flights of steps to the street, emerging into the soft darkness of the spring night. An almost warm breeze blew against him, lightly ruffling his hair. He glanced at his watch and grimaced. Damn. Nearly thirty minutes late.

Luckily, it was only three blocks to the restaurant. Arriving a little out of breath, he paused just inside the door to search the dimly lit room. The place really wasn't classy enough to justify the lack of lighting, but at least they were trying. After a moment, Mac grinned and moved to a corner table. "Hi," he said.

Johnny glanced up from his plate of spaghetti. "About time you showed up." The complaint was half-hearted at best, but he smiled anyway, as if to take any possible sting from his words.

"Yeah, sorry about that," Mac replied, dropping into a chair.

"Hungry?"

"Uh-uh. Maybe later." He picked up the salad fork and absently began wrapping strands of pasta around the tines. "You know, Johnny, we really have to do something tonight about this guy Karlin."

Johnny frowned. "Do we?"

"Yeah." Mac started on his second forkful of spaghetti. "Tedesco got on my ass about him this afternoon."

"Karlin told us last month—" Johnny began softly.

"Hell," Mac broke in, "he's been *telling* us everytime we see him, but he never *does* anything. Tedesco wants results."

"Or else?" Johnny asked, giving up finally and shoving the plate across the table toward Mac.

Mac gave him a sheepish grin and kept eating. "With Tedesco, kid, it's always 'or else.' You should know that by this time."

"I do know it."

Mac's lips tightened at the bitterness he could hear in Johnny's usually mild voice. "It doesn't do any good to worry about it," he said. "We just have to do what we have to do."

"I know that, too, Mac."

"Good." He smiled again. "Look, babe, this shit isn't going to last forever. Pretty soon now we'll be living it up in Los Angeles."

"Uh-huh."

Mac shoved a piece of meatball around the plate and frowned. "If I hadn't dropped so much in that damned game last week, of course, we'd be in better shape."

Johnny looked at him sharply. "That was just bad luck, Mac. It wasn't your fault."

"Yeah, sure, kid, I know." He pushed the plate away. "We better go."

They left the restaurant, hailing a cab for the twenty-minute ride to Karlin's. The whole operation had become routine in the last six months, and they were very good at it. They knew it—or, at least, Mac did—and Tedesco also knew it, which was probably why he gave them a little more leeway than was usual before cracking down, as he had that afternoon about Karlin. Mac and Johnny showed a high rate of return and managed to do so with a minimum of fuss. Tedesco had no reason to regret the addition of John Griffith to his organization. In fact, it was quite likely that it was Griffith, more than McCarthy, who accounted for the success of the team. Mac talked a good tough line, and looked dangerous, but he had never yet laid a hand on anybody. It must have startled more than a few people when the tough guy smiled pleasantly, then stepped aside to watch as his blond and gentle-looking companion moved in to take over. Tedesco knew that he was onto a good thing here and he was pleased. Just so long as he didn't have to actually *see* Griffith.

Something in the pale blue eyes caused a chill inside the old man, and so he met only with Mac.

Karlin lived in a small wooden frame house tucked between two factories. They left the cab waiting at the curb and walked around the house to the back porch. Karlin, a balding, paunchy man with a penchant for also-rans at the track, answered Mac's sharp knock and stepped outside, pulling the door closed carefully. "My wife," he explained. "She gets upset."

Mac leaned against the porch railing, lighting a cigarette and tucking the cheap lighter back into his pocket before speaking. "I think maybe she has good reason to get upset, sir," he said politely. "Our employer, he's a little upset, too."

"I know I've missed a couple of payments, but—"

"Four," Mac interrupted gently. "You've missed four payments." He took a long drag on the cigarette, and with off-hand deliberation, blew smoke into Karlin's face. "We want the money, you bastard," he said, his voice suddenly harsh. "Or else."

"But I don't have . . . give me more time . . . please."

"Everybody runs out of time, man, and you just did." He nodded toward Johnny. "You remember my associate?"

Karlin glanced toward the shadows. "Yeah, sure."

Johnny stepped into the circle of brightness cast by the porch light. Two blue chips of ice glittered in his pale face. He reached out and gave Karlin three quick open-handed slaps in succession. "You have to pay the money, sir," he said. Another slap, this one hard enough to knock Karlin backwards. "Please," Johnny added coldly. He took Karlin's face in one hand and pushed hard, crashing his head against the house. "Do you understand that this is your last chance?"

Karlin tried to nod. "Yeah, yeah."

Johnny nodded, satisfied, and released him, stepping back immediately into the shadows. Mac tossed the cigarette into the bushes. "Twenty-four hours, Karlin. Then it's out of our hands." He almost smiled. "And we're the nice guys. Good night."

He led the way back to the waiting cab. Johnny got in first, scooting over to the far door, and sat there, both hands folded neatly in his lap. Mac leaned toward him. "You okay?" he asked in a low voice.

Johnny only nodded.

"*Are* you?" Mac insisted.

"Yes."

It was only one word, muttered through clenched teeth, but it was enough for Mac. He relaxed. This was a helluva way to make a living, yeah, but they didn't have much of a choice right now. Someday, someday damn it, they'd get out from under. Out from under. The words had a familiar ring. Yeah, that's what Wash had told him a long time ago. He'd been talking about getting rid of Johnny, of course. But Mac had ignored that advice.

And look at me now, he thought glumly.

As if he were somehow aware of Mac's thought, Johnny lifted his gaze and looked at him. "Hey, Mac," he said.

"Yeah, kiddo?"

"There's a new movie at the Variety. Will you come with me?"

Mac glanced at his watch. "I have a game," he began, but then he looked into Johnny's hopeful eyes, and shrugged. "What the hell; the game will be there later. Sure, let's go."

Johnny smiled.

Chapter 18

Mac was disgusted. The game hadn't gone very well, at least as far as he was concerned, and it didn't help his mood much to emerge onto the street close to midnight and find out that the temperature was still hovering somewhere around the ninety degree mark. By the time he'd walked half a block, he was already drenched in sweat. Summer in this city really sucked. Even Johnny seemed dragged out by the heat and humidity that blanketed New York day after day. He spent most of his time parked in front of the TV, swilling down gallons of soda.

When the car horn beeped lightly behind Mac, he closed his eyes in weariness for a moment, before turning to see, as he'd expected, Tedesco's limo sitting by the curb. It was something of a surprise, however, to see that the old man himself was in the back seat. He waved Mac over. At least it's cool in here, he thought as he climbed in and eyed Tedesco. "Yeah?"

Tedesco smiled, looking cool and unruffled in a white suit and Panama hat. "How is it going for you, Alexander?"

"Okay," he grunted. "But I'm sure you already know how it's going for me. Right down to the last nickle. You probably already know how I came out of tonight's game."

It wasn't denied. "Every life has its little ups and downs, right?"

"Right."

"When you get as old as me, you'll know how to take these things in stride."

"Probably."

"And how is John?"

Mac knew that there would be no business discussed until all of these preliminaries were out of the way. "John is fine," he said, enjoying the feel of the sweat chilling on his body.

"Good, good, I like all my boys to be happy." Tedesco paused before continuing in a saddened tone. "We have a little problem, Alexander."

His mind moved quickly over the past couple of weeks to see if there were something he had done—or Johnny—to get them into trouble, but nothing came back to him. "What problem?"

"You are perhaps familiar with the name Mike Danata?"

He thought some more, then shook his head. "No. Should I be?"

"Probably not. He hasn't been in town very long. Out of Chicago, Mr. Danata is."

Mac just looked at him, wondering where the hell all this was leading. There had to be a point to it; the old man never talked just to make conversation.

Tedesco sighed. "Like so many young men, Danata is ambitious. That in itself is not bad, because without ambitious young men, where would this country be? Am I right?"

"Yes, sir, you're right."

"Unfortunately, in Mr. Danata's case, his ambition has led him to make some foolish mistakes. Such as intruding into areas that are my concern. We have warned him about this, but he has chosen to ignore us." The musical voice turned hard. "I want Danata taken out. For good. And I want you to do it."

Mac straightened slowly in the seat. "Me?" he said hoarsely. "You must be kidding." The chill he felt now was not pleasant.

"I told you once before that I'm always quite serious about what I say."

"Then you must be smoking something funny in those damned Havanas of yours. Hey, man, I'm a collector. Period. Not some two-bit hitman."

"You're my employee, Alexander."

"That doesn't mean I'm a killer."

"Come now," Tedesco said, smiling. "It wouldn't be the first time you've killed."

"I never, except for the war, I never—" He broke off. Shit, he thought.

Tedesco's black eyes glittered in the dim light. "Well, we mustn't forget Al and Frank, right?"

"Yeah, right," Mac mumbled, slumping in the seat again. "Those two."

"Except for one minor point."

"Which is?"

Tedesco discovered a small spot of dirt on his right trouser leg. He frowned and brushed at it. "You didn't kill them, did you?"

"Sure. Of course I did."

"No," Tedesco said gently. "You just said that Alexander McCarthy is not a killer. I believe that."

Mac's face was stony. "Look, this whole conversation is a lot of shit. Cut it out, huh?"

"All right. To the point. John Griffith killed Al and Frank, didn't he?"

"No. It was me," Mac said.

"Your sense of loyalty is admirable, but totally unnecessary. At any rate, it's quite irrelevant. I want Danata eliminated. You will do it. Or John will do it for you. He does whatever you tell him, doesn't he? I don't care very much either way, just so long as the job gets done. Otherwise . . . well, we won't discuss the various unpleasant alternatives right now, will we?"

Mac realized suddenly that the car had stopped in front of their apartment building. "I don't want to talk about this," he said.

"Fine. It's late. Go upstairs. Sleep on it, as they say. Perhaps discuss it with John. If you can talk to him about such things," Tedesco added, tapping his forehead significantly.

Mac opened the car door. "John isn't crazy," he said, wondering why the hell it mattered now.

"Whatever. We'll be in touch."

Mac got out of the car and hurried into the building, not waiting to watch Tedesco leave.

His gut hurt.

This was the nicest place they'd ever lived in. It wasn't luxury, by a long shot, but at least the hallways didn't smell of piss, and the apartment itself had two beds and a small kitchen. Life had been sort of okay lately. Until now.

Johnny was sitting in the middle of his bed, watching TV, the small fan aimed right at his body, a can of Coke in one hand. He looked up and grinned when Mac came in. "Hi, buddy."

Mac tried to smile and went to get a beer. He flopped down onto his bed. "Things okay with you, John?"

"Oh, sure, fine." Johnny reached over and turned the fan slightly, so part of the air flow hit Mac, too. "Things okay with you?"

Mac took a long drink of beer. "Yeah, babe, fine."

Johnny looked at him for a moment, then turned back to the TV. "This is a good movie. *Paleface,* with Bob Hope."

"Yeah? Well, you watch it, huh? I'm tired." Standing, he pulled off his clothes, gulped down the rest of the beer, and then stretched out on the bed again. Maybe they should just get out of town. Yeah, like that other guy. What was his name? Bright? Something like that. He'd crossed Tedesco. Mac didn't know any of the details, but he knew that Bright had left town, figuring that would solve his problems. All it did was to get him wasted in Cleveland, instead of New York. Big fucking deal.

Mac turned to face the wall and closed his eyes. Maybe Tedesco would just let it drop. The meeting tonight might have been just a feeler, and now that he knew exactly how Mac felt, the matter might be forgotten.

He stopped thinking about it and finally fell asleep, listening to Johnny's soft laughter as he watched the movie.

It seemed like only moments, but it must have been a couple of hours later when Mac was jerked abruptly back into wakefulness. The room was suddenly filled with light and noise. He rolled over and found himself staring into the twin barrels of a sawed-off shotgun. "Oh, shit," he said.

The man with the gun smiled humorlessly. "Sorry to wake you up."

Mac slowly turned his head. Two more men stood by Johnny's bed, one of them holding a .357 Magnum, the barrel of which was tangled in blond hair. Without his glasses, Johnny peered myopically around the room, his face bewildered.

"What the hell's going on here?" Mac asked.

"Nothing to get excited about, Mr. McCarthy," said the man without a gun. He was slowly pulling on a pair of black leather gloves.

"Mac?" Johnny's voice was a hoarse whisper.

"It's okay, kid," Mac said quietly, realizing suddenly just what was going down. "I think they're just here to deliver a message."

"You got it, man."

"Well, I'm the one the message is for, not him."

The man flexed his fingers inside the gloves. "Oh, the message is for you, all right." He looked at Johnny. "You right-handed or left-handed, dummy?"

Johnny only blinked, obviously incapable of answering.

"He's right-handed," Mac said wearily. "Why?"

"We don't want to put him out of commission."

Mac swallowed. "Don't hurt him. I'm the one who's supposed to get the message and, believe me, I got it."

"But we're supposed to impress upon you the importance of the message. Just so there's no mistake." The man lifted Johnny's left arm.

Mac licked his upper lip. "I'm as impressed as hell. Listen, you son of a bitch, he doesn't even know what's going on."

The man shrugged. "It's nothing personal. We're just following orders."

Mac tensed and leaned forward to push himself up from the bed. "Don't do it, sweetheart," his keeper murmured, pressing the shotgun against his chest. "Unless you want to have yourself spread all over the walls."

He relaxed again.

Johnny tried to pull away from the hands gripping him. "No," he whispered. "Don't hurt me, please." The fingers closed around his wrist. "Mac? Help me. . . ."

Mac closed his eyes.

He had to. There wasn't anything he could have done for Johnny, except witness his ordeal, and that he wouldn't do. In the quiet of the room, the sound of bone snapping echoed like a gunshot. A faint gasp of pain was Johnny's only reaction. Mac felt hot bile rising in his throat; he leaned sideways and threw up. "Nonono," he whispered to the floor, one long, almost soundless, word.

The gloved hands released Johnny, who slumped back against the wall. The three men walked to the door. "He'll be in touch," the spokesman said.

Mac nodded, wiping his mouth with the back of one hand. When the three men were gone, he sat very still, staring at the closed door.

"Mac, it hurts," Johnny said quietly.

"I'm sorry." He got up from the bed, carefully avoiding the pool of vomit on the floor, and went to sit next to Johnny. "God, kid, I'm sorry."

"You didn't do it."

At last, he forced himself to look into Johnny's eyes, seeing the unshed tears gathered there helplessly. "But it's my fault."

Johnny just shook his head. He drew a deep, shuddering breath. "Damn, Mac, it hurts."

Mac tried to look at the arm without moving it, almost retching when he saw the swelling, discolored wrist. "Ohjesus, baby, this needs a doctor."

"Yeah."

Mac tried to remember his first aid training. Immobilize it, he thought, until we can get to the hospital. He stood, looking around the room for something to use as a splint.

"Mac, why'd they do this? We don't even know those guys."

He didn't answer immediately. He picked up a copy of *TV Guide,* and yanked a tie out of the closet, then sat down again. His hand moved restlessly across Johnny's shoulders, touching sweat-damp curls that clung to his neck. "Later, kid, I'll explain. Later, okay? Right now, we have to get you to the hospital," he whispered. What magic words he could say later that would make this all okay, he didn't know, but there was no time now to wonder. He tucked the magazine around the wrist and secured it with the tie. Johnny didn't make a sound during the procedure, although Mac knew it had to hurt like hell. "Think we can get some clothes on you?" He tried for a smile. "Don't want you running around in your skivvies."

"Yeah, I think so."

Mac pulled his own clothes on, then helped Johnny into blue jeans and sandals. He draped his windbreaker over Johnny's bare shoulders. By this time, Johnny was a sick white color. Sweat poured down his face as he watched everything Mac did with two glazed eyes. "It hurts," he kept saying. "It hurts, Mac."

"I know, I know," Mac muttered, urging him out the door and down to the sidewalk. He managed to get a cab almost immediately and eased Johnny into the back seat carefully.

By the time they walked into the emergency room, Johnny was trembling continuously, his flesh felt cold and clammy, and his eyes seemed unable to focus. But he wasn't bleeding and his breathing, though shallow, showed no signs of stopping immediately. A skinny Spanish nurse waved them to the waiting room, which was already jammed. Mac managed to find some space on a plastic couch in one corner, and he lowered Johnny onto it, then sat next to him. He lit a cigarette and draped one arm lightly around Johnny's shoulders. "How you doing, kiddo?"

" 'Kay," Johnny said thickly. "Killed my dog."

"What?"

"He killed my dog."

Mac hunched closer to him. "I don't know what you're talking about, babe."

"Had a dog. Raffles. Nice dog. Mine. Dog loved me."

"Yeah, dogs'll do that," Mac agreed, massaging the back of Johnny's neck.

"I stole money from my mother's purse. Five dollars." He shivered. "Cold." It must have been eighty-five degrees in the room. Mac gently tugged the windbreaker more closely around Johnny. "Took the money, you know, so I could buy candy. Thought the kids would like me, but it didn't work. They took the candy and then they ran off. Then my father found out. He hit me. That was okay . . . deserved it." Johnny turned his head and looked blindly at Mac. "But he didn't have to kill my dog, did he?"

"No, man. He shouldn't have done that. It was mean."

"Yeah. He was mean."

Mac reached toward the ash tray and crushed out the cigarette. "But that was a long time ago, kid. Forget it, huh?"

"Yeah, forget it. You're my friend now, so everything is okay. You're a good friend, Mac."

"Oh, sure thing," he replied bitterly. "I'm a blue ribbon buddy, I am."

They didn't talk anymore. Finally a door opened and a tired-looking black nurse stuck her head out. "Mr. Griffith?" she called out.

Mac pulled Johnny to his feet and walked him over. The nurse nodded and took hold of Johnny's good arm. "Wait here, please," she said to Mac.

"But can't I just—"

"Please, sir, we're busy, and it's very crowded back here. Just have a seat."

He wanted to protest further, but the nurse gave him no chance. She closed the door. He went back to the couch and lit another cigarette. Anger and pain and guilt were tearing up his insides, causing him to ache. He pressed a hand to his side. Goddamn, the world was a rotten place. People. Motherfucking people, anyway. Why the hell did they have to hurt somebody like Johnny? It wasn't fair. He stared across the aisle, watching distantly as an old black woman pressed a bloody towel to a young boy's shoulder.

"Sir?"

The voice sounded impatient, as if it had been speaking to him for some time. He turned. "Yeah?"

Another nurse. "We need some information for the records. Please come to the desk."

"You know how long it's gonna take back there?" he asked, as they both sat at the desk.

"No, sir. What is the patient's full name?"

"John Paul Griffith."

"Age?"

"Thirty."

"Address?"

The door to the treatment rooms opened and Mac answered absently, his eyes on the people coming out, but Johnny wasn't among them.

"Is the patient covered by Blue Cross?"

Mac managed not to laugh. "No. He doesn't have any insurance."

She frowned. "How will the bill be taken care of?"

Send it to Tedesco, he wanted to say. Better yet, I'll take it personally and shove it up his ass. "I'll pay it," was what he said aloud.

"Your name?"

"Alex McCarthy. Same address. Look, could you maybe just check and make sure he's okay? He gets kind of upset sometimes and—"

"How did the injury occur?"

Mac slid down in the chair. Bitch. Cold-hearted cunt. Thought nurses were supposed to be nice, to care about people. All she cares about are the frigging forms. "He fell on the steps."

"Name of his next of kin?"

"He doesn't have any family." Just one fucked-up friend. Poor John Paul Griffith. No family. No Blue Cross. Just me.

"Will you make a preliminary payment now?"

"How much?"

"Fifty dollars."

He sighed, but handed her the money. After a couple more questions that seemed to have very little to do with a broken wrist, she sent him back to the couch to wait some more.

He had time to smoke three more cigarettes, read three very old issues of *Time,* and count the other people waiting several times before Johnny appeared in the doorway, a short cast gleaming on his forearm. He stood still, his eyes darting wildly around the room, until he spotted Mac and hurried toward him.

Mac stood, carefully gripping Johnny by both shoulders. "You okay?" he asked softly.

Johnny nodded.

They stood in the awkward half-embrace a moment longer, then Mac led Johnny out of the place. "They gave me a shot, Mac, so it doesn't hurt so much," he said, keeping a tight grip on Mac's arm, just as he used to do when they were walking through the jungles of Nam.

"I'm glad, kid." They walked for a couple more minutes, then Mac spotted an all-night coffeeshop. "You want to get something?" he asked.

"Yeah, I guess."

Once they were sitting in a booth and Johnny had ordered a Coke and a jelly doughnut, and Mac coffee, they sat in silence for a long time. Mac still found it hard to meet Johnny's eyes. He stared, instead, at the cast. "It seems like I just keep getting us in deeper and deeper," he said finally.

Johnny was examining the doughnut. "I don't understand."

"What happened tonight—Tedesco did it."

"I sort of figured that," Johnny said thoughtfully. "But why? Did I do something wrong, Mac?"

"No, of course not." Mac took a quick gulp of coffee. "It's me. He wants me to do something and I told him no. This is his way of getting me to change my mind." He set the cup down with a crash. "That bastard. That goddamned motherfucking bastard. He could have come after me."

"Hey, Mac, it's okay. Don't get mad, please."

Mac didn't say anything.

Johnny licked sugar from his fingers. "What's he want you to do?"

"Kill a man," Mac said flatly.

"Oh." Johnny's face didn't change. He shook his head. "I wish that we had never got mixed up with Tedesco."

"Yeah, well, you can thank me for that piece of luck, too, can't you?" Mac said. He pushed himself out of the booth suddenly. "Man, I've been screwing things up for a long time. You'd have been better off never meeting me. You think I'm a friend? Well, the joke's on you, dummy. I'm just a fucked-up loser, so why don't I do us both a favor and get lost for good?" He turned and walked out, his back stiff.

Mac walked around the block slowly, smoking a cigarette. He passed a dancehall and paused awhile to watch the crowd milling restlessly on the sidewalk. Couples shared cigarettes and necked in the shadows. Everybody seemed to be having a good time. Nobody else was alone.

He didn't like being alone. Finally he sighed and walked back to the coffeeshop. He sat down in the booth, once again avoiding Johnny's eyes.

"Don't do that," Johnny said very quietly. "Don't you ever run out on me like that."

Mac reached for the Coke and took a swallow. "You knew damned well I'd be back," he muttered.

"Yeah?" Johnny thought about that for a moment. "Well, maybe I did, but that doesn't matter. It isn't fair for you to do that to me."

"All right, all right, I'm sorry." He was. "I won't do it again."

"Promise?"

The blue eyes gleamed. Shit, what a preacher the kid woulda made if he'd followed in the footsteps of his folks. "I promise."

Johnny nodded then, forgiving with the ease of a child.

"Come on," Mac said, leaving a quarter tip, "let's go home."

They left the coffeeshop and started walking slowly, half-heartedly looking for a taxi, but really content just to walk. "Who are we supposed to kill?" Johnny asked after a couple of minutes.

"Some guy named Danata. He's trying to muscle in on Tedesco's territory." Mac kicked at an empty beer can. "But let's not fool ourselves. This would only be the beginning."

"Tedesco still has an 'or else,' right?"

"Oh, yeah. Breaking a bone or two is just for openers."

Johnny stopped walking and fumbled in his pocket, pulling out a white envelope. He put two tiny yellow pills on his tongue. "It's starting to hurt again," he explained as they walked some more. "We have to do it, don't we?"

Mac took a deep breath. "Unless we want to risk Tedesco's 'or else.' And I don't know if we're ready for that." He reached out and touched the cast with a fleeting fingertip. "I'm not ready, at least. I don't have that much strength."

Johnny was frowning. "He might hurt you."

"I guess."

Johnny shrugged. "Then we don't have any choice, do we?"

"I guess not." They were quiet for awhile. Mac finally cleared his throat. "It's a helluva thing for a fifteen-year Army man to admit, but I'm not much of a shot." Self-hatred filled him, waves of it washing over him. At that moment, he hated himself more than he had ever hated anyone in his life, even Tedesco. Instead of looking at Johnny, Mac stared at the empty beer cans, cigarette butts, fast food wrappers, and other less identifiable pieces of litter that filled the sidewalk. People were such slobs.

"That's all right," Johnny said wearily. "I'll do it."

They looked at one another. "Thank you," Mac said softly.

Johnny shrugged. "You'll come with me, won't you?" he asked suddenly.

"Sure."

"That'll be okay, then. There's a cab. I'm tired."

Mac nodded and raised his arm to summon the taxi.

Chapter 19

The messenger, a skinny kid in an ill-fitting suit, handed a box to Mac and then was gone again immediately. Mac brought the package in and set it on the table. Involuntarily, he wiped both hands on the front of his dark green T-shirt.

Johnny was awkwardly trying to manipulate a shirt on over his cast. He looked up curiously. "What's that?"

"Tedesco sent it over," Mac replied shortly. "Must be the gun."

"We have a gun already."

"No good. He wants us to use this one. It's new. Clean. No way to trace it to anyone."

"Oh." Johnny finally got the shirt on and began to button it with one hand. "Open it," he ordered suddenly. "I want to see the gun."

"Why?"

"It's mine, isn't it?"

Mac looked at him, a little bewildered by the edge in his voice. "Yeah, it's yours," he muttered. With a quick jerk, he snapped the string and then ripped away the brown paper. He took off the lid and pulled aside the cotton wadding. A shiver ran the length of his spine as he stared at the blue-steel monster, with its eight-inch barrel. He shoved the box across the table toward Johnny. "There. Your toy."

Apparently oblivious to the sarcasm in the words, Johnny

lifted the gun out with his right hand, hefting its weight thoughtfully. Some emotion Mac couldn't quite read flickered through the blue eyes. "Mac?" he said faintly.

"What?"

"I killed a lot of people in the war, didn't I?"

Mac began crumpling the brown paper. "What difference does it make now? That was a long time ago."

"I was just wondering. I did, didn't I?"

"You did the same as everybody else." Mac wondered, not for the first time, just what had happened at Tan Pret. What had turned John Griffith, high school valedictorian, into the shattered child he'd met? The child he was apparently stuck with for good. Well, he'd probably never know. Not that it mattered much now.

Johnny was squinting down the barrel of the gun.

"Be careful, willya? That fucker might be loaded."

"I know. When you're in a war, it's okay to kill, I guess."

Mac was clearing away the breakfast dishes. "I guess it is."

Johnny put the gun down and tried to scratch inside the cast. His face was thoughtful. A danger sign. When Johnny starting thinking, things usually started to get weird. "That's because you have to get them before they get you," he announced seriously.

"Yeah," Mac said heavily. "That's right, but why talk about it now?"

Johnny picked up the gun again. "Because that's what we're doing here, too, isn't it?"

Mac nodded.

Johnny thought for another moment. "I understand now."

He ran hot water into the sink. "You understand what, kid?"

"That you don't have to be brave to be a good soldier. You just have to be scared enough." He sighed and bent his attention to the gun once again.

Mac crashed the silverware into the sink.

Mac was enjoying the feel of the car beneath his hands as he guided the rented Camero over the Jersey roads. "We oughta get us a car," he said enthusiastically. "I had an old Dodge once that was great."

"Yeah," Johnny agreed. "This is fun." He had the radio blaring and the window rolled down so that the sun-drenched wind blew across his face. "When I was a kid, we never had a car."

"Well, we're gonna get one," Mac decided.

"Could you teach me how to drive?"

"Don't you know? Shit, I didn't think there was anyone who couldn't drive."

"I'm sorry," Johnny said.

"What for? If you don't know, you don't know. I'll teach you. Then we won't be so tied to the frigging city."

Johnny grinned. "Could we get a blue car?"

"Sure, whatever kind you want."

He finally found what he was looking for, a wooded area isolated from the main road. He parked the car behind some trees, and they got out, Johnny carrying the gun box with his good arm. They walked until the trees thinned out a little. Mac used a thumbtack to attach the centerfold from an old *Playboy* to a tree, then paced off about fifty feet. "Come here," he ordered.

Johnny walked over, eyeing the picture curiously. "You want me to hit that?"

"Yeah, boy, that's the general idea. Hit it."

He took the gun out of the box. "Who is she?"

"What the hell difference does that make? Miss April or something."

Johnny smiled faintly as he took position. "It's almost like throwing darts, huh?"

Mac nodded. "Something like that, yeah."

He lined up the shot, squinting a little, hesitated for a moment, then squeezed the trigger. The powerful gun exploded, startling him with its force, knocking him off balance. He straightened and watched eagerly as Mac walked back to the tree. "How'd I do?"

"You did good," Mac said after a moment. "Right through the middle. Damn good, kid."

Johnny beamed with pleasure at the praise. "It was easy, Mac."

Mac ripped that page down and put up another target, this one a magazine cover displaying the face of Richard Nixon. "Come closer this time," he ordered. "Pretend like you just knocked on the door, and this guy opened it. Be fast, because he probably has a gun, too. Understand?"

"Uh-huh." Johnny's face was a study in concentration as he acted out the scene as Mac had directed. He walked closer to the tree, raised his hand as if to knock, waited a moment, then lifted the gun and, without seeming to aim at all, fired again. The top of Nixon's head vanished. Johnny looked around, his face anxious. "Was it okay, Mac?"

Mac looked away for a moment, trying to swallow the bitter bile that threatened to gag him, then he managed to smile at Johnny. "That's good, kiddo. You're a damned good shot."

Johnny's grin threatened to split his face in two. "Want me to do it again?"

"No, that's enough." He pulled the page down and crumpled it savagely.

They were both reluctant to have the day end, so on the way back to the city they stopped for dinner. The place Johnny picked was an old country inn, all stone and wood, with an enormous fireplace that burned cheerfully at the same time the air conditioner worked overtime to keep the room bearable in the summer heat. Mac, feeling out of place in his T-shirt and blue jeans, wasn't even very hungry. Still, it was so nice being away from the city, just the two of them having a good time, that he managed to eat a little, as Johnny devoured prime rib. They shared a carafe of house wine and talked about everything except guns or Daniel Tedesco.

Mac pushed apple pie around on the plate for awhile and finally gave up. "Hey, Johnny," he said.

Johnny looked up, a slight flush from the unaccustomed wine touching his face. "Huh?"

"Did you ever get another dog after your old man killed Raffles?"

He looked puzzled for a moment, then nodded. "Yeah. My folks gave me another one. But it wasn't the same. I just kept him because I had to. I mean, he needed to be taken care of. And I guess having him around was better than being all by myself. I never cared about him like I did about Raffles, though. Raffles really *belonged* to me, you know?" He licked ice cream from the spoon thoughtfully. "He finally ran away one day, but I didn't care very much."

He shrugged and bent to finish the pie a la mode.

At home later, Mac cleaned and reloaded the gun, while Johnny watched "Ironside" on TV. Mac picked up his beer and took a gulp, frowning at the snowy picture on the set. "You want a color TV for your birthday, kid?"

"Yeah, that'd be nice," Johnny said, not looking away from the screen.

"Well, Tedesco should pay us plenty for this job, so I'll get you one."

"Thanks."

Mac finished with the gun and replaced it in the box. He tipped his chair back on two legs, whistling softly to himself, wondering if he should go over to the game. Supposed to be some big uptown money in there tonight. Of course, after renting the car and paying for dinner, he was a little low on cash, but he had enough to buy his way in.

A commercial came on. "You know something," Johnny said as he went for a Coke.

"What?"

"I saw Chief Ironside on a talk show the other day, and he wasn't in a wheel chair at all."

"Of course not, dummy. That's just part of the story."

Johnny sat down again. "Yeah, well, I guess I knew that, but still, it was sort of strange to see him walking around like everybody else."

Mac's mind wandered a little as he stared at Johnny, once again engrossed in the story. Hey, guy, he wanted to ask, what do you really think about this whole fucking mess? Do you think about it at all? Don't you *care*? Why don't you hate me? Or maybe you do. What the hell makes you tick, John Paul?

The same old questions and never any answers.

Johnny must have become aware of the scrutiny, because he turned around suddenly, the familiar smile on his lips. The flickering lights and shadows from the television were reflected in his glasses.

Mac crashed his chair to the floor. "Going out," he said abruptly. "Probably be late." He was gone before Johnny could respond.

Chapter 20

"Will you for chrissake quit playing with that goddamned thing?" Mac spoke more harshly than he had intended, tension and a hangover making him short-tempered.

Johnny looked up in surprise, then he carefully put the gun back into the box. "I'm sorry," he said.

"Yeah, I know." Mac swallowed some more aspirin and gulped cold coffee. "I have a headache." The remark served as an apology.

Without replying, Johnny walked over and stood by the window, watching the traffic on the street below. Finally, hearing

mumbling, he turned back into the room. Mac was thumbing
through an old address book, the pages long loosened.

"What did you say, Mac?"

"I was just saying that I can't remember exactly where the
bastard lived. Probably moved halfway across the country by
this time anyway."

Johnny sat down, watching him curiously. "You gonna call
somebody, Mac?"

"I'm going to try." Mac was flipping through pages quickly,
an idea that had been forming in his brain all day finally taking
shape. "If we can just get out of the country for a while, babe, we
might be able to dodge Tedesco."

Johnny frowned. "I don't understand. I thought we were
going to do what Tedesco wants."

"I can't." Mac looked up. "You don't know how sick it made
me to see you shooting that gun yesterday."

"Didn't I do it right? You said I was a good shot." Johnny
leaned forward and spoke earnestly. "I could practice, Mac."

Mac tried to swallow down his sense of despair and speak
quietly. "You did fine, Johnny. Really. I just don't want . . .
goddamnit, kid, you have to know what a terrible thing this is,
don't you? I don't want us to turn into a couple of killers."

"But Tedesco will hurt you." Johnny walked back over and sat
on the arm of Mac's chair. He reached out to touch Mac's hand
lightly, stroking absently.

Mac had long since learned to accept the touching that
Johnny seemed to need so much. When the kid got scared or
upset or just seemed to be feeling lonely, he turned to Mac,
seeming to crave the physical contact of a strong hand or maybe
a hug. When Mac bothered to think about this at all, he decided
that it all had something to do with Johnny's childhood. Probably nobody ever hugged him much. Mac returned the stroking
for a moment, until he felt Johnny relax a little. "He can't hurt
me if we're not here," he said, returning his attention to the
phone book.

"Where will we go?"

"I don't know," Mac mumbled, running his finger down the
page. "Mexico, maybe. Whaddaya think?"

"I guess. Whatever you say."

"I don't think even Tedesco can get us in Mexico. Yeah, here
it is," he said, looking up. "Robert L. Washington."

Johnny was rubbing the cast on his wrist nervously. "Who,
Mac?"

"Wash. You remember Sergeant Washington from Nam, don't you?"

After a moment, Johnny nodded. "Yeah. He didn't like me."

"He lives way the hell out on the Island, if he's still around, anyway," he said. "That's stupid. Why do you say he didn't like you?"

"He just didn't. Why are you going to call him?"

Mac stood, searching in his pockets for a dime. "To see if he can let me have some money. It's gonna cost a bundle to get us to Mexico." He went out to the hall phone and pulled some change out of his jeans. It took only a few moments before he had Washington on the line. "How the hell are you, Wash?" he said cheerfully.

"Fine, fine. Didn't know you were in the city."

"Yeah, sure. Look, man, I'd like to see you. Got sort of a problem and I need a friendly ear."

Washington seemed a little hesitant, but they finally set up a meeting for later that day, at the bowling alley in his neighborhood. He gave Mac directions on train and bus connections and they hung up.

Johnny was standing in the doorway, watching. "Can I go, too?" he asked.

"If you want to."

Johnny wanted to, so a short time later they caught a bus over to Penn Station and picked up the train out to Long Island. Mac read a *Times* that someone had left on the seat and listened to Johnny hum tunelessly.

"He said I was crazy," Johnny said suddenly.

"What?"

"Washington. He told me I was crazy and should be in a hospital."

Mac folded the paper carefully. "Yeah? Well, everybody's entitled to their opinion, I guess."

Johnny was quiet for several minutes. "Mac?"

"Huh?" He didn't look up from the sports page.

"Am I?"

"Are you what, kid?"

"Crazy."

He patted Johnny's knee. "No, of course not. You act a little weird sometimes, but that's okay."

Johnny gave a sigh and looked out the window again.

*   *   *

They found seats in the snack bar of the bowling alley and waited. Johnny finished off a Coke and an order of french fries doused in catsup, then he looked up. "They have some pinball machines back there, Mac," he said.

Mac pulled some change from his pocket. "Okay, go ahead."

Johnny smiled and took off in the direction of the noisy games.

Mac ordered another cup of coffee and settled back. In another moment, he saw a vaguely familiar figure enter and look around. "Wash," he said, half-standing.

The black man saw him and came over. "Mac, you son of a bitch, how're you doing?"

They shook hands and Wash sat down, ordering some coffee. Mac glanced toward the pinball machines, but Johnny seemed totally absorbed in his game. "So what're you up to these days, Wash?" he asked.

"Working in the Post Office, man. We just had another kid. That makes three."

Mac expressed the proper enthusiasm, and the talk shifted to Nam briefly, and the various fates of people they had known. Wash slowly stirred his coffee. "What ever happened to the zombie?" he asked suddenly. "Griffith?"

Mac hunched over the table a little. "Nothing," he said.

"He's probably living very happily in a padded cell someplace. You take my advice and dump him when the two of you got Stateside?"

Mac shook his head. He didn't realize that Johnny had approached the table, until he spoke. "I used up all that money, Mac," he said softly. "Can I have some more?"

Not looking at Washington, Mac hauled out some more change and handed it over. "But that's all," he mumbled, "so don't come back looking for more."

"Okay, Mac." Johnny hurried away.

Washington released his breath in a long sigh. "No, I guess you didn't take my advice."

"I couldn't. He needed somebody to take care of him."

"Yeah, right. But why you?"

Mac didn't answer right away, as they both watched Johnny. "Maybe I just needed somebody, too, Wash," he said finally, quietly. "Maybe I was just tired of being by myself. Johnny likes me. I like him. We get along okay when the rest of the frigging world leaves us alone." He took a gulp of coffee. "I tried, Wash. I tried to dump him, a couple of times."

He looked across the room to where Johnny was bent over some damned game, his whole body tense with concentration. "He just couldn't make it on his own."

"So you adopted him." Washington took a roll of mints out of his pocket. "Trying to quit smoking," he explained with a grimace. He popped candy into his mouth. "Why couldn't you let the Army handle it, Mac?"

"Hell. I know what they would've done to him." He smiled a little. "Henderson thought we were queer for each other." He shot Washington a look. "We're not."

"I didn't ask."

"Yeah, well."

"So what's the problem you mentioned on the phone?" Washington asked abruptly.

"I owe some guys money, Wash. They're starting to get nasty about it."

Washington didn't look surprised. "You never got smart enough to give up poker either, huh?"

"No. And things were going okay for a while. But then I had a run of bad luck and got in over my head."

The black man sighed. "Hell, man, you were always over your head."

Mac tapped the tabletop. "I know, but that's all over now. What I want, see, is for the kid and me to get out of town and make a new start someplace else." He wanted it so much that it hurt, deep inside his chest.

"Sure. Find a new game, you mean, right?"

"No, Wash, really."

They were quiet for a moment. "You ever think that maybe if you stopped treating him like a kid, he might grow up?" Washington asked mildly.

"Johnny's okay. I take care of him, you know?"

"What's with the cast on his wrist? He talk back to you or something?"

"What the hell is that supposed to mean?"

Washington ate another mint. "Buddy, I've seen you smash your fist through a door because you couldn't draw a good hand. I wouldn't want you mad at me."

"You think I . . . ?" Mac glanced toward the games. Johnny had apparently spent all the money, because he was walking back toward them. "Jesus, Wash, what kind of a creep do you think I am? I wouldn't do anything like that to him." Then he lowered his gaze. "I told you these guys I owe the money to are starting to get nasty."

Washington's glance was filled with scorn. "Oh, yeah, you take good care of him."

Johnny slid into the booth next to Mac. "I scored 70,000 points."

"Good, Johnny."

"How're you, Griffith?" Washington asked.

"Fine." Johnny kept his eyes down.

"Wash, we need some money," Mac said urgently. "Johnny and I have to get to Mexico for a while."

"Mexico?" Washington gave a soft laugh. "Man, you don't want much, do you? I deliver the *mail*, buddy; it's nice, steady work, but it don't pay much. Especially when you've got a wife and three kids and a mortgage. You know how much all that costs?"

Mac shook his head wearily. "No, I don't know anything about that stuff."

"Right." Washington searched his pockets. "Damn," he muttered. "I forgot. If I eat another one of those damned mints, I'll throw up." He looked at Mac. "Why don't you stop being such a goddamned asshole and try earning a real living for a change? Lay off the cards, man. If you've gone and appointed yourself babysitter, then you damned well ought to do a better job of it. Shape up, Mac, and quit expecting other people to bail you out all the time."

Johnny leaned forward suddenly. "Stop it," he said in a shakey voice. "Mac does the best he can. It's not his fault if the luck just ran bad."

The three men were silent for a long moment. Mac spoke finally, his voice low. "Please, buddy. I'm begging you. We need the money and there's no one else I can ask. Please."

Washington sighed. "I just don't have it, Mac. I'm sorry."

Mac nodded, his fragile hope turning to ashes. He spread his hands helplessly. "Okay," he said flatly. "I understand. Thanks anyway."

"You want some advice?"

"What?"

"Turn Griffith over to the V.A. and hop the first train out of town." He tossed a dollar bill down onto the table and was gone.

They sat there a few minutes, not talking. Mac rubbed the back of his neck. "Let's go home, babe," he said finally.

"Okay. I guess we're not going to Mexico, huh?"

"No, I guess not. I'm sorry, Johnny."

"That's all right. I don't mind so much."

Mac pushed himself to his feet. "You don't mind much of anything, do you?"

"I guess not. Except this cast," Johnny said with a slight smile. "I'm kinda tired of it."

Mac dug into his pocket and came up with a quarter. "Here," he said, "get a candy bar to eat on the train."

Johnny took the money with another smile and disappeared in the direction of the counter. Mac started toward the door. He wasn't even scared anymore; like Johnny, he was just tired. So damned tired.

Chapter 21

Mike Danata looked more like a TV star than a two-bit hood angling for bigger things. Or maybe he only looked like TV's notion of a hood. One of those actors who seemed to work steadily, always playing the bad guy, so that whenever he came onto the screen, you immediately knew that before the hour was up, the hero would have exposed the guy as the villain. Anyway, what Danata looked like or what he aspired to didn't matter much at this point.

Mac slid the eight by ten color glossy back into the manila envelope. "So that's him," he said. "According to what Tedesco said, he'll be alone after midnight."

Johnny was slouched opposite him in the booth, a sullen expression on his face as he ate a cheeseburger. "Yeah, yeah, I know, you told me all that before."

Mac leaned across the table and spoke in an icy voice. "John, this isn't a game. It all has to be planned; the odds have to be figured perfectly. I don't especially want to be cleaning your insides up from all over Danata's hallway."

Johnny ate a catsup-drenched french fry, pouting. "Okay, okay. You don't have to get so mad."

"I'm not mad, goddamnit, it's just—" Mac broke off and took a deep breath. Christ. They were both on edge, in danger of becoming a couple of basket cases. "I'm sorry, Johnny."

"Me, too." Johnny took a long slurping drink of his chocolate shake and frowned. "Listen, won't this guy get suspicious if somebody comes knocking on his door so late?"

"No, because he'll be expecting his broad. She's a dancer at some strip joint downtown, and she comes over every night after the show. But tonight a couple of Tedesco's creeps are making sure she's late." Mac finished his coffee and crumpled the styrofoam cup. "You done?"

"Uh-huh."

They left the fast food joint and walked three blocks to the outdoor lot where Mac had parked the rented car. There didn't seem to be anything else to say and so it was a quiet drive over to Danata's apartment building. When they got there, it was exactly twelve-fifteen. "Right on time," Mac said, pulling into the alley and shutting off the engine. He turned in the seat. "You okay?" he asked quietly.

"Yeah." Johnny picked up the gun from the seat between them and shoved it into his jacket pocket, keeping one hand on the grip. "Need a holster for the damned thing," he muttered. "How can I carry a gun without a holster?"

"You remember the apartment number?"

Johnny, his face patient, looked at Mac. "I remember everything you told me," he said softly. "I'm not stupid, buddy."

"I know that, Johnny, it's just—" Mac stared out into the dark alley, gripping the steering wheel so tightly that his knuckles turned white. "Be careful, huh?"

"I will. Promise." Johnny opened the car door. "It's like a movie," he said, whether to himself or Mac wasn't quite clear. "It's just a movie, that's all." He got out and walked without hesitation into the apartment building.

Mac started the car again. He lit a cigarette and began to watch the clock. This was crazy. Really crazy. Johnny and him carrying on like a couple of creeps from a late movie. Did they really expect to get away with this? Johnny would probably get blown away, was probably getting his guts splattered all over the hallway as he sat here, blowing smoke rings and watching the lighted clock face.

And if that happened, what should his own next move be? Well, he might make a run for it.

Run where?

Home and hide under the bed, I guess.

Except that home wouldn't be there anymore, not really. It would be just an empty room. It had been too damned long since he'd lived in an empty room, and he wasn't sure he could hack it again. You got used to having somebody around. Maybe Johnny wasn't the greatest company in the world, but then again maybe he was. They got along just fine.

Mac touched the .45 tucked into his belt. So he better stay here and shoot it out. Shoot the bad guys and shoot the good guys; shoot any damned bastard that got in his way.

Oh, yeah, tough guy. You're so frigging tough, so goddamned hot to start blowing the bums away, how come he's in there and you're out here?

It seemed like hours, but was really only four minutes ticking away on the clock before the door to the apartment building opened, and Johnny appeared. One hand was shoved into his pocket and the dirty cast caught the dim moonlight. He kept his head bent as he walked swiftly to the car and slid inside.

Mac pulled out of the alley immediately. "You all right?"

There was no answer from Johnny. He bent forward, resting against the dashboard, his face hidden, his breath sounding harsh and raspy.

"Johnny? Did you do it? You okay?" When there was still no answer, Mac pulled the car off the street, into another dark alley, turning off the engine. He switched on the interior light and stared at Johnny in the pale white glow. "Hey, man?" He reached over, putting a hesitant hand on Johnny's shoulder and pulling the unresisting form up. "Babe? Hey, say something, please."

Johnny took a deep breath and then bit his lip. "I did it," he said finally. "I knocked and he opened the door and I shot him in the face." He gagged a little, then recovered. "I closed the door. Nobody saw me." His eyes behind the glasses were bright as he looked beseechingly at Mac. "Was it right, Mac? Did I do what you wanted?"

"Oh, shit, Johnny," Mac said, pulling the other man closer. For a long time, he just held on, feeling Johnny's heart race. "Yeah," he whispered at last, the word muffled in blond hair. "You did fine, kid, real good."

It was Johnny who pulled away finally, straightening in the seat. His face looked confused and a little flushed. "Next time it'll be easier," he said; his voice sounded husky.

"Don't worry about that right now. Let's just take this one step at a time." He started the car and they rode silently back to the parking lot, leaving the car there to be picked up by one of Tedesco's lackeys.

One of Tedesco's *other* lackeys, Mac thought as they walked home.

When they reached the apartment, Johnny put the gun away in the bottom of a drawer, covering it carefully with an old sweatshirt. They stood awkwardly in the middle of the room, not looking at one another. "You mind if I go out?" Mac said at last.

Johnny shook his head. "Can I have some money?" he asked. "Maybe I'll go to a movie or something."

"Good idea," Mac said, handing him a couple of bills. "Be careful. Don't get mugged or anything."

"I won't."

Mac patted his shoulder. "See you later."

"Yeah." Johnny smiled a little. "Have fun."

Mac hesitated another second, feeling as if he should say something more, but not knowing what. "You have fun, too," he finally mumbled, then left.

He picked her up in a bar called Eddie's. The place was filled with people trying to make connections quickly, because the night was disappearing much too soon. Her name was Sherry. Or Carrie. Something like that. The music was very loud, and he wasn't really listening anyway.

They had a couple of drinks and then went to her place, which was located, conveniently, just around the corner from the bar. Once there, she disappeared into the bathroom. Mac took off his clothes and stretched out on the bed, lighting a cigarette. He stared at the cracks in the ceiling, trying to find some recognizable object in the criss-crossed lines.

He knew that the hit had come down too late to make the morning papers, but the later editions should have something. Tedesco had said that as soon as he knew for sure that Danata was dead, they'd be paid.

Shit, Johnny had been pretty cool about the whole thing. Blowing off a guy's head, after all, was a damned hard thing to do. But the kid did it. Of course, it wasn't the first time for him. He'd killed Al and Frank. And the people in Tan Pret. Almost iced Crazy George that time, too.

Always because of me.

That was an uncomfortable thought and one he wished he could deny. But it was true. Except for Tan Pret, which didn't really count, because it was war and all, every time Johnny killed or came close to killing, it was for him. Weird. Really weird.

Mac frowned at the cracks on the ceiling, deciding that they looked like the state of Oklahoma. Of course, Johnny was a little shook afterward, but who the hell wouldn't be? Hell, he thought, I was shook, too, and I didn't even do anything.

Could that be used in court? I didn't do anything, your honor. Except plan it all and drive him over and tell him the apartment number. Little things like that.

Mac ran through the whole evening again, replaying it like a movie in his mind. Pulling into the alley behind Danata's place. Watching Johnny go in. The waiting, watching the seconds tick away so damned slowly. Johnny coming back at last, all pale and spaced-out. The moments later in the car and the terrible crashing of Johnny's heart against his own.

The girl, whatever her name was, slipped into bed next to him and put a hand between his legs. She giggled. "All ready for me, huh? You don't leave a girl much to do except lay back and enjoy it, do you?"

Slowly, he crushed out the cigarette and then rolled over on top of her. Ignoring the preliminaries, he pushed himself into her, moving back and forth silently, still thinking about the kill. Remembering it all in excruciating detail. He clutched at the pillow beneath her head, closed his eyes, and remembered.

He opened the door and I shot him in the face.

Mac pictured the eight by ten glossy looking like the magazine cover of Nixon's face after Johnny shot it.

Was it right, Mac? Did I do what you wanted?

The eyes, pleading, needing.

Oh, shit, Johnny.

Johnny's heart beating so fast, too fast.

Mac came much too quickly. He rolled off her body and stared at the ceiling again. "Shit," he said aloud.

She said something he didn't hear. A moment later, she began to kiss his neck and chest, working her hips against his. He sighed, then tangled his fingers in her tawny hair, pushing her head down between his legs.

A part of his mind was very aware of her presence, of her mouth on him, sucking, nibbling, urging, and the heat began to rise in his groin again. Another piece of his consciousness, though, was apart from what was happening, hovering somewhere up above it all, lingering up there by the absurdist rendering of Oklahoma, watching with weary bemusement.

They were murderers, he and Johnny, and that truth bound them together in a reality that was much more interesting than the fact that a girl whose name he didn't even know was sucking him off in a cheap room around the corner from a bar called Eddie's.

* * *

He could hear the television as he walked up the stairs and unlocked the door. Johnny was sitting on his bed. "Hi, Johnny," Mac mumbled wearily.

"Hi."

"What's on?" Mac asked, getting a beer from the refrigerator and starting to undress.

"Bogart. The one about the truck drivers."

"Oh, yeah, you like that one." He turned out all the lights but one, then sat on the edge of Johnny's bed. "Did you go out?"

"Uh-huh. I saw a movie. A western."

"Terrific."

"And I had a giant Chunky and some popcorn and a lemonade."

"Quite an evening."

They watched the movie until the next commercial. "You okay?" Mac asked, staring at the ad for toothpaste.

Johnny nodded.

"You were great tonight."

"Thanks." He shrugged. "It wasn't so hard, I guess."

"Sooner or later, kid, we're going to figure a way out of this. Sooner or later, life is gonna turn around for us."

"Life is okay." Johnny shifted the weight of the cast with a weary sigh.

"Bet you're sick of that damned thing."

"Yeah."

"Three more weeks, the doctor said."

"I know." Johnny stood, pulling off his jeans. "Mac?"

"Yeah?"

"Stay here with me awhile, would you, please?"

Mac nodded. He reached over to switch off the lamp and turned the volume all the way down on the TV, leaving the image of Bogart flickering on in silence. He stretched out next to Johnny on the bed.

"Danata knew," Johnny said softly. "He saw the gun, and for just a second, he knew what was going to happen."

"Yeah?"

"His eyes got all sort of scared. He didn't want to die."

"Nobody does, kid."

Johnny sighed, his breath warm and damp against Mac's skin. "I wanted to explain it to him, you know? Tell him *why* it had to be this way."

"He knew why. Because he crossed Tedesco."

Johnny shook his head and blond strands brushed against Mac's chest. "No, not that. I wanted to tell him that he had to die so that Tedesco would leave us alone. Because if I didn't kill him, you might get hurt."

Mac stroked Johnny's hair gently. "Don't think about it anymore. Just forget it. Go to sleep, boy."

After a few more minutes, Johnny relaxed against him and his breathing softened into the steady pattern of sleep.

Mac was alone then in the dark, except for the tiny figures on the silenced TV screen. He sighed deeply. The tears were unexpected, but he didn't try to hold them back. He made no sound that might disturb Johnny, but let the tears roll down his cheeks unheeded, dampening the pillow and the blond strands that touched his face.

The movie ended, but Mac was still awake, still stroking Johnny's hair with a kind of quiet desperation, waiting hopelessly for the morning.

Chapter 22

Mac kept running. The knife of pain stabbed against his left side every time his shoes hit the pavement, and he was starting to get dizzy, but he kept running. Finally, just before he collapsed completely, he reached his goal.

Johnny looked up, grinning. " 'Bout time you got here."

Mac gave him a dirty look and dropped onto the bench next to him. "Don't . . . forget," he panted, "you've got . . . some years on . . . me, you bastard."

"Hah," Johnny sneered. "Eight years. Big deal."

Mac managed to catch his breath and smiled, shakily. "Well, from where you're sitting, eight years may not seem like much, but it's a helluva lot from where I'm sitting."

"Not easy being over forty, is it?" Johnny asked, even at thirty-three managing to look about twelve.

"Remind me to ask you that in a few years." Mac became aware that the grey November wind was getting colder. He blew on his fingers. "I need some coffee."

Johnny jumped to his feet, jogging in place. "Let's go then, old man." He smiled again and took off across the park. "See you at the drugstore!" he called back over one shoulder.

"Son of a bitch," Mac mumbled. He pushed himself up and

started after Johnny, trying to remember whose bright idea it had been that they should start jogging. Probably his own. It sounded like the kind of suggestion he might make, especially if he was drunk at the time. And, of course, that idiot Johnny would agree. Hell, Johnny would agree to walking across a bed of hot coals in his bare feet if Mac suggested it.

Mac shrugged. After six years, he was used to Johnny.

"Mr. McCarthy?"

The quiet voice came from behind him. He tensed, as always half-expecting to feel a bullet crash into his body. When none did, he turned slowly. "Yeah?"

A husky man nearly his own height stood there. He obviously wasn't a jogger, because he wore a long leather coat and carried a briefcase. Automatically, Mac surveyed the immediate area. He wasn't surprised to see two gorillas hovering nearby. "Yeah?" he said again.

"Could we talk, please?"

Mac glanced around, but Johnny had already vanished. "What about? I'm supposed to—"

"Mr. Griffith will wait, I'm sure."

Mac gave the man a sharp look. A lot of people knew his name; not many knew Johnny's, and it didn't especially make him feel good that this guy did. He tucked both hands under the jogging jacket. Out of the corner of his eye, he could see the two apes straighten. "I'm cold," he said loudly enough for them to hear. They relaxed again. "Who are you anyway?"

"My name is Hagen."

The name sounded vaguely familiar, and Mac thought for a moment. "From Philly, aren't you?"

Now it was Hagen's turn to be surprised. "Yes, as a matter of fact, I am."

"So? What do you want with me?"

"I have a business proposition to offer."

"We don't deal that way," Mac said shortly. "You're in the company; you must know how it works. All our deals come down through—a higher authority." He turned to walk away.

"I'm offering you a chance to get out from under Daniel Tedesco's thumb." Hagen spoke softly, but his words reached Mac clearly.

He stopped. "What?"

"Can we talk?"

Mac looked around the park again, wondering what the hell

was going on. This wasn't part of the routine. Shit, he thought. "It's too cold here. Come on."

They walked out of the park and across the street to the drugstore. The two apes trailed behind, taking up position just inside the door. Johnny was already in a booth, two cups of coffee in front of him. He was spooning sugar liberally into one cup. "At last. Thought you were crawling on your—" He saw Hagen and broke off, looking at Mac, puzzled.

Mac slid into the booth next to him. "Mr. Hagen here wants to talk some business," he explained, wrapping his chilled fingers around the coffee mug.

"Oh." Johnny took a gulp of his over-sweetened coffee and added one more load of sugar to the cup. "Maybe I'll go look at the magazines," he mumbled.

"Okay." Mac moved to let him out, then waved Hagen into the booth.

Hagen sat down across from him, his eyes on Johnny, who was already engrossed in the magazine display. "He doesn't seem very interested in what I have to say."

"He's not."

"It concerns his future, too."

Mac lifted the coffee mug. "I'll take care of his future. You said you wanted to talk. I'm waiting to listen."

"You two make a good team."

"Uh-huh. I already know that, Hagen."

"Over the past couple of years you've handled some very tough jobs for Tedesco."

The coffee was as bad as usual, worse than the stuff Johnny made, and that was the pits, but at least it was hot. "Have we?" he asked after taking several sips.

Hagen smiled. "Thirteen, to be precise. Beginning with Mike Danata and then, last week, Karl Schmidt."

Mac shrugged. "I heard he was shot."

"Right. You two never miss. A lot of people are very impressed."

Mac smiled blandly. "I'm not sure I understand what you're talking about. And even if I did, like I said before, we don't take on outside jobs."

Hagen was searching his pockets. "This isn't really that kind of thing. It's very much within the company."

"Yeah? Then how come Tedesco isn't telling me about it himself?"

Hagen didn't answer.

Mac drank coffee and watched Johnny snicker over something he was reading. Suddenly, he looked at Hagen, realization dawning. "Hey, you mean . . . *him?*"

Hagen took time to light a cigarette. "Want one?" he asked, holding out a gold case.

Mac shook his head. "Trying to quit."

"Smart man. These things will probably get all of us sooner or later." He tucked the case away. "Tedesco owns you, McCarthy. He owns both you and your programmed killing machine over there."

They both glanced toward Johnny, who was oblivious. "You seem to know a lot about it," Mac said.

"I know everything about it."

Mac sighed. "I still don't know exactly what it is you're saying here, man."

"It's very simple, and very much a matter of company politics, which I'm sure don't interest you at all."

"You got that right. You guys can screw each other around all you want, as long as you leave us alone to do our job."

"Fair enough." Hagen folded his neatly manicured hands on top of the formica table. "Let me just say this much. Tedesco has fallen out of favor in recent months, and it's been decided by the board of directors that his territory should be redistributed."

"And Tedesco himself?"

Hagen sighed and looked unhappy. "Well, the old man was offered a very generous retirement plan. Which he, unfortunately, has chosen to reject."

"Uh-huh."

"So we have naturally decided that a more permanent solution is called for."

"Naturally." Mac waved the waitress over and waited while she poured him another cup of coffee. When she was gone, he leaned across the table. "What's in this for us? *If* we decide to go along?"

"Twenty-five thousand dollars."

The figure stunned Mac a little. He sat back. Shit. With that much cash, he could pay off every fucking I.O.U. he had, and still have plenty left. Enough for a car. A color TV. Maybe even enough to get out of this city. Go to L.A. Or Vegas. He glanced toward the magazine rack again. Johnny would love to get out of New York. "And then what happens?" he asked Hagen almost absently, still lost in thought over what they could do with that much money.

"You and Griffith could do whatever you like."

He smiled bitterly. "Within reason, you mean?"

Hagen shrugged. "Well, of course, we would still have, let's say, an option on your services. But at least Tedesco wouldn't be giving all the orders." The man smiled. "You could freelance. Does that sound good?"

"We'll think it over."

"Fair enough." Hagen stood. "But don't take too long, Mc-Carthy. The bandwagon is rolling, and you're either on or off. I'll be in touch." He turned and walked out, both apes at his heels.

Johnny came back and slid into the booth next to Mac. "Everything okay?"

"Huh? Oh, yeah, fine, kiddo," he said absently.

"Who was that guy?"

"Hagen." He looked at Johnny. "He wants us to do a job." He smiled humorlessly. "He wants us to ice Tedesco."

Johnny's eyes gleamed for just a moment behind the glasses, then he lowered his gaze. "Good," was all he said.

"I don't know what it might mean in the long run. But at least we'll get our hands on some cash. A lot of cash."

"Enough for a car?"

"Sure. Yeah, we'll get a car this time. I promise."

"Okay." Johnny was quiet for a moment, then he looked up and smiled. "Think you can make it home, old man?"

Mac shoved him out of the booth. "Fuck off, punk," he said cheerfully. Zipping the jogging jacket again, he followed Johnny out of the drugstore.

Chapter 23

Johnny woke abruptly, sitting straight up in the seat. He usually woke that way, as if something had startled him. He groped for his glasses. "Where are we?" he mumbled, his voice still thick with sleep.

"Just coming into Frisco," Mac replied, rubbing his eyes with the heel of one hand. He was tired after the trip from Vegas. Not for the first time, he wished that Johnny had been able to get a license so that he could share the driving. But although he'd passed the written tests with perfect scores in New York, Chicago, Vegas, and Los Angeles, he just couldn't hack the be-hind-the-wheel part of the test. Not that he couldn't drive—he could, as well as anybody. It was just that the pressure of having to perform with a complete stranger sitting next to him, watching and evaluating his every move, wiped him out whenever he tried. The first couple of times it happened, the kid nearly cried. Finally, he just gave up, and never mentioned driving again.

Several times over the last couple of years, Mac had been sorely tempted to just sell the car. The cash would have come in very handy on more than one occasion. But Johnny was so crazy about it. Spent hours polishing it whenever he could. He really loved the blue BMW, so Mac was stuck with it. He sighed. "Hey, guy, what was the name of the motel we stayed at the last time we were here?"

Johnny frowned thoughtfully. "Something stupid . . . Welcome Inn, that's it."

"Yeah, right. Was it cheap?"

Two blue eyes peered at him. "Of course it was cheap," Johnny said drily. "Didn't I just say we stayed there?"

Mac shot him a glance. "Don't try to be funny so fucking early, willya?"

Johnny snickered. "Sorry."

They found the Welcome Inn and got a room. Johnny, as usual, was hungry and wanted breakfast, but Mac just wanted to sleep. He peeled off his clothes and crawled into one of the beds, barely aware of Johnny's departure.

It was early afternoon before Mac woke, feeling groggy and joint-stiff from being in the car so long. He staggered into the bathroom and got under a hot shower. When he'd finished that, and shaved and dressed, he felt halfway human again. Shoving his wallet into the back pocket of his jeans, he stepped out onto the motel balcony.

Johnny was in the parking lot below, his shirt off, carefully buffing the car. He wasn't alone, however. A young man in tight swimming trunks had evidently wandered over from the pool, and they were talking as Johnny worked. Mac stood watching for a moment. It was obvious to him that the conversation— probably about the car—was of less interest to the young man than was Johnny himself. He could scarcely take his eyes off Johnny's bare torso and sunlit golden hair. The kid was oblivious to the attention as he enthusiastically pointed out the advantages of his car.

Mac frowned and leaned over the balcony rail. "Hi," he said.

Johnny looked up, shading his eyes against the sun. "Hi, yourself," he replied, grinning.

The young man looked up as well, and it was his turn to frown when he saw Mac staring at him. "Friend of yours?" he asked Johnny.

"Yeah," Johnny said cheerfully.

Mac just kept his icy gaze on the intruder, until he shrugged. "I gotta get my laps done," he muttered.

"Fucking faggot," Mac mumbled, watching him go.

"What'd you say?" Johnny asked.

He looked down at him and grinned. "I said you're gonna rub the frigging paint off that damned thing one of these days."

"You think so?" Johnny gave one more swipe at the hood. "Okay, I'm done anyway."

"Look, I have to meet a guy in Golden Gate Park later. Want to get something to eat and then go on over? We could throw the frisbee around for a while."

Johnny reacted with his usual enthusiasm, grabbing his shirt and pulling it on hurriedly. "That sounds great."

Mac walked down the steps. "Who was that guy, anyway?"

Johnny paused by the car door, looking toward the pool vaguely. "Oh, I don't know. Rick or Rich. Something like that. He was asking me questions about the car. Said he thought it was very nice."

"I'm sure," Mac muttered, getting behind the wheel.

"Huh?"

Mac glanced at him. "Be careful who you talk to, willya?"

"I am." Johnny looked dismayed. "I wouldn't ever say anything about . . . anything I shouldn't, Mac."

Mac patted his knee. "I know that, kiddo. It's just . . . well, never mind. What do we want for lunch?"

"Pizza?" Johnny suggested.

Mac groaned. "Only you could be three blocks from Fisherman's Wharf and want pizza. You're hopeless."

He started looking for a pizza place.

The park was crowded, but they managed to find a patch of unoccupied grass, and tossed the bright orange frisbee back and forth for nearly an hour. Finally, begrudgingly, Mac glanced at his watch. "I gotta meet that guy, babe. See you at the car in a little while, okay?"

Johnny jumped into the air to catch Mac's final toss of the frisbee. "Yeah, sure."

Mac waved a half-hearted farewell and started across the park.

The man in the brown suit was waiting when Mac arrived. He eyed Mac's T-shirt and blue jeans with some surprise. "You McCarthy?"

Mac lit a cigarette, coughed, then nodded. "Yep."

The man handed him a large envelope. "A picture and all the particulars are inside." He studied Mac again and frowned. "I hope you know what you're doing. Papagallos is no fool."

"Neither are we," Mac said coldly. He hefted the envelope. "The money is in here, too, right?"

"Yeah. Just like you said."

"Fine. That's it, then." He turned to walk away.

"Hey!"

"What?"

"Aren't you going to tell me about how you're planning to do this? I just gave you a lot of money. I know you come highly recommended, but—"

Mac stared at the man. "What we do, and how we do it, is our business." He nodded sharply and walked across the grass, back to where the car was parked.

Johnny was sitting on the front bumper, idly spinning the frisbee between his hands as he watched a softball game. He turned and smiled as Mac sat down next to him. "All done?"

"Yeah." Mac lit a cigarette and they settled back to watch the rest of the game.

They went down to Fisherman's Wharf for dinner, and then back to the Welcome Inn. Mac spread the material on Papagallos out onto the bed and began to figure the angles of the job. "I have a headache," Johnny complained.

Mac reached for the aspirin bottle and tossed it to him without looking up. Johnny dropped four of the pills into a can of Coke and stretched out to watch *Beau Geste* on television.

"I'm gonna need two days, I think," Mac said. "The hit comes down on Sunday."

"Okay," Johnny replied, his eyes glued to the screen.

Mac folded all the papers again, and shoved them back into the envelope. He stretched out, propping his head against the wall, and watched the movie.

Mac woke up first on Sunday morning. He showered and shaved and dressed quietly, making a cup of instant coffee out of tap water. He sipped the disgusting brew as he moved around the room in the early morning half-light. When he'd tucked his shirt in and zipped his jeans, and pulled on his cowboy boots, he walked over and jerked the blanket off Johnny's bed. "Wake up," he said.

Johnny sat up quickly. "Huh?"

"Time to go to work."

"Oh." Johnny swung his legs over the side of the bed and rubbed his eyes. "I forgot." He stretched. "What's the guy's name?"

"Papagallos."

"Oh, yeah." He got up and walked into the bathroom, emerging fifteen minutes later, toweling his hair dry.

Mac shoved a can of Coke into his hand. "You awake?"

Johnny took a long gulp of the soda, then nodded. "Yeah." He dressed quickly.

"You want breakfast?"

"Huh-uh." He pulled the holster on, settling its familiar weight against his body. "I saw a good movie last night."

"Yeah?" Mac shoved the omnipresent .45 into his belt.

"Yeah. It was all about this cowboy that was maybe a ghost and maybe not. He came riding into this town and he painted it all red and got revenge on the people who killed him, sort of."

"Sounds good." Mac was used to Johnny's rather unique synopses of the movies he saw. He tried to remember what he'd done the night before. He could recall the card game. Then drinking at some dive. A broad. It all added up to nothing. So what else was new? "Let's go," he said shortly.

They never talked much on the way to a job. Johnny propped his knees against the dashboard and whistled softly to himself. Mac pulled into the alley behind the apartment building. "Be careful," he said ritualistically.

Johnny nodded and got out of the car. Mac watched him go, watched as he worked on the door; then, as the slender figure slipped inside, Mac lit a cigarette and bent over the steering wheel to wait.

BOOK

II

Chapter 1

His Christian wife refused to get up early on Sunday mornings in order to make his breakfast. Since it was the one concession to her faith that she held onto with any degree of seriousness, Simon Hirsch did not argue the matter. As the son of a rabbi, he felt obligated to indulge such religious fervor.

He stopped at the Dunkin' Donut shop on his way over to the stakeout and bought three glazed and a cup of coffee, black. The girl behind the counter was painfully ugly, with a voice like sandpaper and a grating, loud personality. She had only one saving grace, that being the fact that she dearly loved cops, so he flirted with her as she got his order together. He even let his denim jacket flop open, so she could see his holster. Why not. It was Sunday; give the broad a thrill. Cops, after all, had to take their friends where they could find them.

It was nearly twenty after eight by the time he reached the stakeout. He parked just behind the innocuous brown sedan and got out, bringing the doughnut bag. Delaney, red-eyed and bewhiskered, greeted him with a yawn. "You're late."

Simon leaned against the car. "Yeah? Anything happen?"

"Sure," Delaney said, taking the doughnut Simon offered. "Papagallos peed. Took a shower. Gargled." The last word was muffled around a bite of pastry.

"Gee, I'm sorry I missed all that. How's Mike sound?"

Delaney snorted. "How does Mike always sound before his morning coffee?"

"Mean?"

"You got it."

Simon grinned. "Poor Papagallos. The man may be a no-good rotten bastard, but what's he ever done to deserve Mike first thing in the morning?"

Delaney wiped crumbs from his face and started the car. "It's all yours, Hirsch."

Simon stepped back. "Thanks for nothing," he muttered. He

walked back to his own car and got behind the wheel again, switching on his receiver with one hand as he snapped the plastic lid off the coffee cup with the other. Every noise made in the apartment nearly three blocks away came to him clearly.

The first voice he heard was not that of Papagallos, but of his own partner, one Wild Mike Conroy. "Coffee's ready, Mr. Papagallos. You want some?"

"No, but help yourself," came the reply from the gravel-voiced racketeer. "Me, I'm gonna wait until my guest arrives, and we'll have breakfast together."

There was silence then, except for the sound of someone turning the pages of a newspaper, and the soft clink of a spoon against a cup. Simon smiled a little, imagining the almost orgasmic expression that would cross Mike's face as he finally got his first gulp of coffee. The hyper redhead was worthless until that morning fix.

"When she gets here," Papagallos said, "you make yourself scarce."

"Yes, sir."

The servile tone of Conroy's voice was so totally out of character that it brought a soft chuckle from Simon. The guy shoulda been a goddamned actor, he thought admiringly. Over the past month the wily undercover cop had insinuated himself so well into the Papagallos organization that odds were being given around the squad room of just how long it would be before the aging gangster gifted Michael Francis Conroy with control of his empire.

Simon wasn't betting, holding out, insisting that the old fart would probably adopt Conroy inside of another month. Wild Mike thought that sounded pretty damned good. He'd always wanted to be an heir, and the only thing his own father had left him were ten younger siblings to support and a sizable bar tab.

Simon finished the coffee and crumpled the cup. He really hated this part of the job. The waiting. The subtle feeling of helplessness. It was much better when the situation was reversed. He liked being on the inside. Working undercover, the edge of excitement kept him on his toes every minute. It was partly fear, of course, never knowing exactly what was going down from one minute to the next. The fear, however, was balanced by the security of knowing that Mike was someplace close, waiting to back him up.

Mike, he knew, was feeling the same way now. It was amazing and a little scary the way they balanced one another so perfectly.

The odd couple, as they were called around the squad room. The tough Irish street kid and the Jew from Boston.

Simon rolled down the car window, letting the fresh air from last night's rain blow gently against his face. Papagallos must be expecting his newest broad. Idly, he thumbed through the pages of his notebook. Karen Hope, that was her name. A looker, too, from what Mike had said. Well, that figured. Lookers always went for guys with money.

Of course, Kimberly was a looker. Blonde. Regal. The original ice princess. But that wasn't a very good example, because when they'd gotten married, she'd figured that she was hooking up with the future partner in some big deal Boston law firm. It had never occurred to her that she would end up married to a cop and living in a tract house in San Francisco. Hell, she could have married a WASP, if that was the kind of life she'd wanted.

Simon frowned a little, scratching at an earlobe.

The fight last night still rankled. It was so absurd. He didn't even give a damn about the anniversary party, but suddenly the celebration of their fifteen years of wedded bliss seemed to have assumed painful importance to Kimberly. He'd given her carte blanche to do whatever the hell she wanted. Except for one thing.

Kimberly was flatly refusing to invite Mike and his wife.

"I will not have that drunken Irishman ruin another party," she said, sounding regal. "Remember New Year's Eve?"

He remembered. The memory brought a faint smile to his lips. Wild Mike had been in top form that night. It wasn't even as if the vase he broke was an antique or anything. It was just a vase. And Mike had paid for it, a fact that didn't seem to mollify Kimberly at all.

When the fight ended, long after midnight, the issue wasn't really resolved. She just kept insisting that Mike wasn't going to be invited, and he simply said that, in that case, she shouldn't expect him to show up either. Hell.

Simon stopped thinking about it, focusing his full attention on what was happening in the apartment. It was a little after nine when he heard the knock at the door. "Aha," Papagallos said, sounding pleased. "She's a little early. Couldn't wait, I guess."

"I guess," Mike agreed.

Simon could hear the sound of footsteps crossing the tiled foyer and of the door opening. The muffled crack of the silenced gunshot seemed to roar through the car, startling Simon so that his head jerked around. A muscle pulled in his neck. "What the shit," he mumbled. A second shot followed almost immediately. Before its echo died completely, he had the car started. He turned the volume on the receiver all the way up. The door to the apartment closed softly, but he heard it. "Mike?" he said aloud.

Almost as if in response, a faint moan came over the radio.

Simon grabbed for the microphone and with a mouth that was suddenly dry, requested back-up and an ambulance. He careened around the corner, pounding the accelerator to the floor, just missing a fire hydrant and two pedestrians.

He was out of the car before it came to a complete stop, running across the lawn, and into the building as if demons from hell were on his heels. He pulled out his gun as he moved, clutching it in his left hand and pushing the door open with his right shoulder.

His running footsteps echoed hollowly in the corridor. The door to Papagallos' apartment was closed. Not wanting to touch the knob, Simon raised one foot and kicked until the wood cracked and the door flew open. He fell through the entrance, almost tripping over Papagallos' body sprawled there in a bloody pool. "Mike?" he gasped out frantically.

His partner was huddled in a chair. There was blood everywhere. Simon crossed the room in three leaps, bending over the chair, wrapping both arms around Conroy. "Oh, shit," he sighed. "Mikey?"

Conroy's eyes fluttered open. He wanted to smile. "Hey, partner." A trail of blood ran out the corner of his mouth and down his chin.

Simon tried to wipe the blood away with the sleeve of his jacket. "There's help coming, babe, so you just hang tough. Hang tough, okay?"

Conroy coughed. "Hell." His fingers scrabbled weakly for a hold on Simon. "Knew you'd get here, buddy." His soft brown eyes squinted as he tried to think. "Saw the guy."

"Was it somebody we know?"

"Uh-uh. Hurts, Simon. Simon?"

"It's okay, Mike," he said. "I'm here."

"Blond guy," Mike mumbled. "Tall."

"Yeah, okay, I'll get him. Don't worry, buddy, I'll get the son of a bitch who did this." Mike began to shake violently. Simon bent over him, pressing his face to Conroy's. "Mike? Oh, god, Mike, I'm sorry. I'm so fuckin' sorry."

His partner stilled, tried to smile again, and died.

Simon listened desperately for a heartbeat, then shook the body a little. "Mike? Oh, damnit, man, why'd you have to go and die?" His voice was angry. "Why'd you do this to me?" Bloody, trembling fingers pushed a limp auburn curl off Mike's forehead. "Why?"

Simon heard the other cops come in, but he didn't say anything to them. He just slumped next to the bloody chair, holding onto Wild Mike Conroy's body and crying.

The wheels of officialdom began to move quickly, in their roughshod, uncaring way. The room was soon filled with blue uniforms, with snapping cameras, with men in grey suits, all talking in low, urgent voices. Simon ignored them, not caring either. He only spoke once, to tell them that he was going in the ambulance with Conroy's body. A white-clad intern started to object, but Simon pushed by him, climbing in next to the stretcher. Michael Francis Conroy wouldn't take this ride alone.

Simon held his partner's hand, until the nurses at the hospital gently, but firmly, pried him loose. Lieutenant Troy was there, dressed in golfing clothes, his lined face grim. "What the hell happened, Simon?" he snapped at once.

Simon shrugged. "I don't know."

"You don't know? What the hell does that mean? You were supposed to be covering him."

Simon raised his head slowly and stared at Troy, his dark blue eyes cold. "I was covering him," he said very softly. "God-damnit, I *was*. It was you who put the fucking stakeout three blocks away."

"That was necessary; we couldn't afford to tip Papagallos off." Troy wasn't looking at Simon.

"Yeah. Right." Simon returned his gaze to the swinging doors through which they'd taken the bodies. "It just happened so fast. Someone knocked at the door, Papagallos went to answer it, and then I heard the shots. By the time I could get there, nothing."

"Did he say anything before he . . . before?"

Simon nodded. "Yeah. Said the guy was tall. And blond."

"That's it?" Troy sounded disappointed.

"The man had a bullet in his chest. He was hurting." Simon stretched out his arms, bracing himself against the wall.

"Go home, Simon," Troy said quietly.

He shook his head. "No, can't. Too much to do."

"You can't do anything like that."

Simon lowered his arms and looked at his hands. They trembled. "I'll be okay."

"You're covered in blood," Troy said flatly.

He noticed the blood for the first time and his stomach lurched. "Christ," he said. "He was bleeding so much." His voice cracked a little. "All right. I'll see you back at headquarters."

Troy nodded.

Simon hitched a ride back to the apartment building with a patrol car. The sidewalk was still jammed with sightseers and the press. A couple of reporters spotted him as he crossed the street toward his car. "Hey, Hirsch," one called.

"Yeah?"

"What happened here?"

Someone shoved a tape recorder in front of his face; he stared at it dumbly. "What?"

"Can you give us the details of today's double murder?"

He shook his head. "No. I don't have anything to say." Quickly he got into the car and started the engine, barely giving the press time to scatter before he squealed away from the curb.

Details. They wanted details.

He shook his head again, trying to clear away the fog. The only detail he could remember was the sight of Conroy's face as he died. He had a horrible feeling that he'd never be able to forget that.

Without being aware of the journey at all, he soon turned onto his block. The neighborhood was Sunday afternoon quiet. The only noise came from some kids playing ball in the middle of the street. They interrupted the game briefly to let him go by. He parked in the driveway and hurried to the house, hoping no one would see his bloody clothes. The door was locked. He fumbled for the key, found it finally, and shoved the door open, stumbling across the threshold.

Kimberly was stretched out on the chaise, reading. She looked up in surprise that turned to shock as he burst into the living room. Her face paled. "My god, Simon! What happened? Are you hurt?"

He stared at her.

The book she'd been reading slipped from her fingers as she got to her feet. "Simon?"

He walked past her, across the room to the mantel. Stupid, fucking mantel, he thought distantly. Why have a mantel when

there wasn't any fireplace? A large cut-glass vase sat on one end
of the useless appendage.

"Say something," Kimberly pleaded.

Without even looking at her, he picked up the vase and deliberately smashed it against the wall. The glass shattered and a
hairline crack appeared in the plaster.

"Simon!"

Their daughter appeared in the doorway, her just-painted,
blood-red nails fluttering. "What's going on? Daddy?"

Kimberly waved her out, then walked over to Simon. "Have
you gone crazy?"

He stared at the shattered vase, then leaned wearily against
the wall. "Mike is dead," he said in a muffled voice. "Somebody
killed Mike."

Kimberly took a step backwards. Death, he knew, didn't belong in her world, at least not this way. Dying should be quiet
and filled with dignity; it should be neat. There shouldn't be a
madman covered with blood running into her all-white living
room, smashing things and talking about death. "Oh, no," she
said at last.

Simon gave a rattling laugh, still not looking at his wife. "You
don't have to worry about him ruining your goddamned party
now," he said.

Her porcelain skin flushed. "That isn't fair, Simon. I never
wanted anything like this to happen."

He sighed. "Yeah, I know. I'm sorry I said that. It's just . . .
damn it, Kim, I heard the shots. I heard it all happen, but by the
time I got there, he was dying. There wasn't anything I could
do."

"It must have been terrible."

"Yeah." Simon ran a hand down the front of his blood-en-
crusted T-shirt, denim jacket, jeans. "He just . . . died."

Kimberly was recovering. He admired that quality in her.
Probably it came from her Methodist past. Solid American stock,
people who never let any adversity keep them down long. "I
always told you something like this could happen. Thank good-
ness it wasn't you."

"Yeah," Simon said. "Thank God for that, huh? My partner is
dead, but, boy, I'm just fine and dandy. I was backing him up.
Great job I did." He crashed a fist against the wall. "Goddamn
motherfucking bastards."

"Shh, Tammy will hear you."

He only looked at her, his wife, and the neat white living

room. Sometimes, he got the feeling that he didn't belong here at all. It was as if he lived two lives. One was out on the street with Mike, where they saw the blood and pain and shit that went down with monotonous sameness year after year; and his other life was here, surrounded by nice clean things, with a woman who didn't like some words because they scared her. Because they reminded her that beyond the wall-to-wall carpeting and the patch of green lawn that surrounded this mortgaged haven, there was a universe that was dangerous and dirty.

Simon wondered which life was his real one. Or maybe his real life hadn't started yet. If there was such a thing as real life.

He shrugged. "I gotta clean up and get downtown."

"Maybe you shouldn't go. You look terrible. They can't expect you to work after what you just went through."

"I don't know what 'they' expect, Kim. I know what I have to do. Somebody killed my partner, and I'm going to find the son of a bitch."

She shivered. "It scares me to hear you talk like that," she whispered.

He grimaced and started out.

Kimberly knelt on the carpet and began carefully to pick up the pieces of jagged-edged glass.

Simon stopped. "Don't do that," he said sharply.

"What?"

"Leave it there."

She picked up another piece of glass. "Don't be silly, honey. I can't leave this—"

He took a step toward her. "Leave the fucking thing there!" he shouted.

Her hand dropped the shards. They stared at one another for a long moment, then Simon spun around and went into the bedroom.

Just about an hour later, he walked into the squad room. Although he had showered in the hottest water his body could stand, scrubbing until his skin was raw, and dressed in clean clothes, he still felt as if he were covered in blood. The too-starched white shirt and neat sport coat seemed to chafe his flesh.

He sat down, propping both feet on his desk. A couple of other homicide dicks were in the room, and they looked at him without saying anything. There wasn't anything to say. He lit a cigarette and tried to ignore the desk opposite his, with its familiar clutter.

Troy, clad now in a suit, came in. "You okay?"

Simon nodded shortly. "Anything turn up?"

"No. We're still waiting to get the bullets. None of the neighbors saw or heard anything."

"Yeah, that figures."

"Probably they really didn't. This was a smooth job, Hirsch, pro all the way."

"Except for one little thing," Simon replied, flicking ashes toward the already over-flowing ashtray, and missing.

"What?"

"I think Mike being there was a surprise. There was just the slightest hesitation between the two shots, as if whoever was pulling the trigger had to . . . readjust his plan. Mike's death was an afterthought." Simon smiled bitterly. "Hell. An afterthought."

"You may be right." Troy gestured impatiently. "Which gets us absolutely nowhere."

"This is my case, of course," Simon said.

"Is that a good idea, Hirsch? You might be too close to things."

"I promised Conroy. It's my case."

Troy looked at him for a moment before answering. "All right. As long as I think you can handle it. When I decide you can't, that's it."

Simon shrugged. "I'll have the bastard before then."

Troy moved closer. "I know how you must be feeling right now, Simon."

"Yeah?"

"I lost a partner once."

Simon crushed out the cigarette. Yeah, he wanted to say, but you didn't lose Mike Conroy. Instead, he crashed his feet to the floor. "I gotta clean out his desk."

"Somebody else can do that, man."

He shook his head. "My job."

"At least wait awhile."

Simon sighed. "I have to sit here and work. I can't be looking at that mess."

Troy nodded and left the room.

Simon moved around and sat in Conroy's chair. He pulled open a drawer and made a face. "God, that guy was a slob," he said hoarsely.

The other men in the room took pity on him and turned away.

Simon started piling old magazines, wrinkled report forms, and discarded candy wrappers on top of the desk. "A goddamned slob," he said, this time to himself.

Chapter 2

Simon stood hunched over the snack bar, chewing on the rubbery hot dog and waiting. Sometimes it seemed like they spent half their lives just waiting. Just over sixty hours had passed since the shooting, and he'd spent a lot of that time in a sort of limbo. He hadn't been home since that trip on Sunday to get rid of the bloody clothes. Hadn't changed since then, or shaved, or slept. He took a gulp of too-sweet Coke. Thank God for caffeine.

Where the hell was Danny anyway? That was the trouble with a junkie snitch; they were too damned unreliable. Danny, of course, might not show at all, since the creep really wasn't his snitch at all, but Mike's.

At the thought of his partner, Simon glanced at his watch and frowned. It was getting late. Now there wouldn't be time for him to go home and change before stopping at the funeral parlor. Hell, if Danny didn't get here soon, he'd miss the visitation entirely. Not that he was looking forward to it, but it had to be done. Some things just had to be gotten through and then, hopefully, gotten over. Like the report that he still had to write on the shooting. And like the funeral tomorrow.

He looked up again impatiently and saw the gimpy little junkie crossing the street toward him. The two of them made a nice pair at the end of the counter as Danny arrived and sidled up next to him. "About time you got here," Simon complained.

"Couldn't help it." Danny sniffled. "Very busy."

Simon nodded glumly.

Danny shuffled his feet. "Damned shame about Mike. Damned shame. I was real sorry to hear it."

"Yeah, I'll bet."

"I mean, he was a good guy, y'know? Ain't that always the way? The good ones always get it."

"Yeah, Danny, that's the way it is. The good guys get it, and the garbage like you keeps right on walking around."

Danny could no longer afford the luxury of being insulted by anything Simon said to him. "Mike, he understood how it is, y'know? Always had a few bucks to slip a guy," the junkie reminisced.

Simon pushed a folded bill down the counter toward him, but kept a finger on it. "Mike was always a sucker for a sob story," he said coldly. "But not me. I'm different. When I pay, I want something in return."

"I always try and give good value," Danny said.

Simon released the bill. "So I'm waiting."

Danny pocketed the money quickly and wiped his nose on his sleeve. "Ahh, well, that's the thing about this case. The streets is real dead, Inspector."

"Yeah, well, Mike Conroy is real dead, too, you prick."

"Damned shame."

"You said that already. Come on, Danny, you must have heard something. Christ, man, you spend all your time in the gutter."

Danny picked up the remains of Simon's hot dog and shoved it into his mouth. He mumbled something, spraying drops of saliva and crumbs over the counter.

"Swallow first, asshole."

He swallowed. "Well, word has it that the job was done by imported talent."

"Imported from where?"

"Don't know." He belched. "Back east somewheres, I guess."

"I need a name, Danny."

Danny washed the rest of the hot dog down with the last gulp of Simon's Coke. "No names, man. There ain't no name. It was big time stuff, though. Big time." He began to edge away. "Sorry about Mike," he mumbled. "Damned shame. He was a good guy." Danny slipped out the door, melting quickly into the crowd on the sidewalk.

Simon slumped against the counter, burying his face in his hands. Nearly four hours it took just to track Danny down and set up this meet. And all for what? A big fat zilch.

"You okay, Inspector?" asked a quiet voice at his elbow.

He raised his head and saw the young patrolman. Aginisto, he recalled after a moment. The cop had a worried expression on his boyish face. Boyish? I'm only thirty-five, Simon thought bitterly. I'm not old. "Huh?" he said.

"I just wondered if you were okay," Aginisto said hesitantly.

Simon nodded. "Yeah," he said wearily. "I'm fine. Thanks for asking."

Aginisto studied the wall. "Sorry about Inspector Conroy."

"Right." Simon gave him a smile and started toward the door. He stopped abruptly, staring across the room. A tall, slender man with shaggy blond hair stood at the far end of the counter, concentrating intently on a slice of pizza. After a few moments, he apparently became aware of the scrutiny. He turned curiously, peering around until his gaze rested on Simon.

Simon broke the uneasy eye contact first and walked out the door, mentally kicking himself. Hell, he couldn't start suspecting every tall blond man he saw. A guy could get real paranoid that way.

The parking lot of the O'Boyle Funeral Home was crowded, and he had to drive around twice before finding a spot to pull his car into. He locked the battered VW and went up the steps leading into the imposing brick building.

His first stop was the men's room. He splashed cold water on his face, then straightened to look into the mirror. Rather hopelessly, he tried to pull his comb through his tangled mop of dark curls. He gave that up quickly and simply tried to smooth the mess a little. His clothes were fairly hopeless, as well, but he stuffed the shirttail in where it belonged, and gave a quick polish to each shoe on the legs of his trousers.

Well, he thought, that was as good as it was going to get, and to hell with it anyway.

A discreet sign directed him to the right room. He pushed open a heavy oak door and slipped in. The young man standing just inside looked so much like Mike had when they were first teamed eight years ago, that it sent a stab of pain through him. The kid turned and looked questioningly at Simon. "Uh . . . I'm Hirsch," he mumbled, trying to smooth his hair again.

A familiar smile flickered across the young man's face. "You're Mike's partner."

"Yeah, I am. Was." Simon looked around the crowded room. "I just wanted to come by and . . . just to come by. I hope it's okay?"

"Sure. You belong here. I feel like I know you already, Mike talked about you so much. I'm his brother, Kevin."

"Yes."

"Siobahn's been expecting you."

Simon could see Mike's wife—widow—sitting in the front row. She looked pale, but composed. Turning, she saw him and smiled a little. He nodded.

Kevin leaned closer. "You can go up front if you like."

He didn't want to. He'd already seen Conroy dead once and that seemed like quite enough, but apparently it was expected, so he walked down the aisle toward the casket. A man and a young girl stood there. They each made the sign of the cross, then the girl leaned over and brushed her lips against Mike's cheek. Then she turned and followed the man up the aisle past Simon.

Walking more slowly, Simon approached the coffin. It was strange to see Mike in his dress blues, instead of jeans and a T-shirt. His face was waxen. He didn't look asleep, like people sometimes said about corpses. He just looked dead.

Simon dropped to his knees, touching the side of the polished wood box. Ahh, Mikey, he thought wearily, was it worth it? Was any of it worth this? A guy like you, your life should've come to something more than just an afterthought of some bastard with a gun.

His thoughts drifted fuzzily.

He realized suddenly that he was about to fall asleep right there against the casket, and he got to his feet quickly, hoping no one had noticed. For one more minute he stood there, staring down at what was left of Wild Mike Conroy, then he bent and kissed his partner's forehead. "Thanks, buddy," he whispered.

Siobahn was waiting for him in the hallway. "Thank you for coming, Simon," she said. "Have you met Mike's brother, Kevin?"

"Yes." Simon was staring at a large crucifix over the door. "Siobahn, I don't know what to say. If I could've got there sooner—"

She put a finger to his lips. "Hush. Don't say that."

"Well, I'm just so damned sorry."

"I know that. We're all sorry, everyone who loved him."

"Yeah," Simon said.

"I have a favor to ask of you."

He brought his gaze back to her face. "Sure, anything."

"Will you speak at the funeral?"

"Me?" he said, surprised. "But I'm not family or . . . I'm not even Catholic."

She smiled. "Mike thought of you as family. In some ways, you were closer to him than anybody else, including me. He loved you, and I think it would please him." Her eyes darkened. "If you would like to."

Simon nodded slowly. "All right. I . . . I hope I can say the right things."

She kissed his cheek. "You will." She gave him a gentle push toward the door. "Go home and get some sleep. You look terrible."

He shook hands again with Mike's brother, whose name he couldn't remember, and left the two of them standing in the hall.

By the time he got home, all the lights were off. He let himself in quietly and switched on a small lamp in the living room. The pieces of broken glass were still there on the rug. Simon knelt and began to pick them up. A shadow fell across the room. "Simon?"

He didn't look up. "Sorry I woke you."

"That's okay. Don't cut yourself."

"I won't."

"Are you all right?"

He picked up the last piece of glass and got to his feet. "Uh-huh. The funeral is at two tomorrow."

"I know. I'll be ready."

"Thank you. Go back to bed, Kim."

"Aren't you coming?"

"Yeah, sure. Soon as I dump this into the trash."

She stood there a moment longer, then vanished. Simon walked through the house to the back door. The plastic trash can sat beside the porch. He lifted the lid and dropped all the pieces of glass but one in. He held that single jagged sliver thoughtfully. After a moment, he took it between the fingers of his left hand, and carefully ran the sharp edge across his right palm. A thin trail of blood appeared in the wake of the moving glass. It hurt. He stared at the cut for a moment, then dropped the glass in with the rest, and went back into the house.

Chapter 3

Joey Belmondo was a punk.

It wasn't the first time Belmondo had faced Simon across the table in the interrogation room. If anything, they knew one another too well. That had the advantage, at least, of cutting down on the preliminaries. Simon, dressed in his best (only) black suit, a new white shirt, and a black tie, came into the room and sat down. He lit a cigarette. "I don't have a whole lot of time, Joey," he said flatly. "So let's just skip the foreplay and get right down to business."

Joey stared at him, grinning. "You look like a fucking preacher or something."

"Maybe I finally got religion."

That seemed to strike Joey's funny bone and he laughed. "Hey," he said, "I got it—they must be planting your late deceased partner today."

Simon took a long drag on the cigarette. "As a matter of fact, they are." He flicked ashes onto the floor, keeping his gaze on Joey. "So maybe you'll understand that I'm not in the best of moods this morning."

Joey shrugged. "Nobody ever did accuse you of being Mr. Nice Guy, far as I know."

"You got it. I've always been irritable. Now I'm mean." It had been at their first interrogation together that the roles were set. He was the bad cop and Mike was the good, buddy-buddy cop. Now he couldn't remember if the choice had been an accident, maybe decided by flipping a coin, or whether it had actually been an astute case of type-casting. Anyway, by this time, it came easier being hostile than being nice. Especially today. "Talk to me, Joey. Who wanted Papagallos dead?"

"Gee, I don't know," Joey said, scratching his head in mock thoughtfulness. "Who wanted your partner dead?" He brightened. "You know, that's an idea. Did'ja stop to think that maybe somebody was really after Conroy and got Papa by mistake?"

Simon just looked at him.

Joey shifted in the chair a little. "I got a question."

"Yeah?"

"I'd like to know how Conroy got so close to Papa. Hell, I worked for that bastard three years, and I only saw him once. Never talked to him at all. How'd he do it?"

Simon slowly crushed out the cigarette. "Conroy was smart," he said.

"Yeah?" Joey laughed again. "So how come he's dead, and I'm still here?"

There was a long silence in the room. Simon put two fingers inside his collar and tugged at the tie that was strangling him. "Joey," he said finally, gently, "I got a ten-year-old boy waiting in the wings. A kid named Teddy Newhouse. You remember Teddy?"

Some of the bravado seemed to drain from Belmondo. "Never heard of him," he mumbled.

"Gee, that's funny, Joey, because he remembers you real

good. He especially remembers the night you took him behind the garage to play games."

Joey sank further into the chair, his face pushed into a fatuous pout. "Ah, shit," he said sullenly.

"I've been keeping Teddy on ice, because he's just a kid and I sort of hated to make him get on the stand and go over the whole thing again." He paused, checking his watch. "But, see, that won't wash anymore. Ask me why, Joey."

"Why?"

"Because I want to find out who killed Conroy. No, wait a minute, scratch that. I *will* find out who did it." He stood, carefully shaking down the crease in his trousers. "And I'll tell you something else, Joey. I don't much care who gets run over in the process." He smiled pleasantly. "I gotta go now, but we'll talk again. Count on that."

He walked out and found Troy, wearing his dress uniform for the funeral, standing in the hall. The lieutenant had been listening to the interrogation on the intercom. He turned and looked at Simon. "Did you mean that?"

Simon didn't glance up as he busied himself brushing some ashes from the sleeve of his jacket. "What?"

"About not caring who gets run over."

Now Simon looked at him. "I meant it."

Troy's face was suddenly older. "You're a cop, Hirsch, not a vigilante."

"I know that."

The other man nodded grimly. "Make sure you don't forget it."

Simon pulled at his shirt cuffs. The vivid gash across his palm made his hand feel stiff and awkward. "I won't."

"What happened to your hand?"

He shrugged. "Cut it, I guess. Hey, I gotta go. Kim's waiting. See you later."

The building was beginning to look strangely empty as all but the most essential office personnel left to attend the funeral. Simon hurried through the quiet hallways to the parking garage.

The traffic jam began four blocks from St. David's. Their car inched forward slowly, as Simon hunched over the wheel, his face closed and expressionless. Kimberly sat next to him, tugging at the hem of her black dress nervously.

"She should've come," he muttered finally.

"Why? It would only upset her."

"Maybe it's time she got a little upset over something. I don't think it shows much respect for her not to be here."

Kimberly sighed. "Honey, we've been all through this. Tammy didn't want to come, and I don't think it would have been a very good idea to force her." She glanced at him. "Besides, she has cheerleading tryouts today."

"Oh, yeah, sure." He shut up about it, but the fact that his own daughter wasn't there left a bad taste in his mouth.

He managed to get the car to within a block of the church. At that point, he waved to a traffic cop he knew slightly. "Hey, Jeff, I gotta get in there. Take care of this thing for me, willya?"

The cop nodded. "Sure thing, Inspector."

They got out of the car and Kimberly held his arm as they walked to the church and up the wide steps. Just before going in, Simon paused. He pulled a black yarmulke from his pocket and settled it on his head.

The large church was already packed. They stood for a moment, looking around for a place to sit, before Mike's brother came up the aisle toward them. "Hi, Inspector," he said softly.

Simon nodded, still not remembering the kid's name.

"Your places are down front." He led them to the second row, just behind Siobahn and the two kids, boys, aged five and seven. Siobahn turned her head and smiled. Simon sat straight-backed, both hands resting on his knees.

"So many people," Kimberly whispered.

"Mike had a lot of friends."

"I even saw a TV camera outside."

Simon's fingers moved a little against the material of the black suit. "He was a hero," he said softly. "The media loves a hero."

"Will they put you on the news, do you think?"

"Me? Why the hell should they? I'm just the guy who got there too late." He couldn't take his eyes off the coffin, draped in the flag, that sat in front of the altar. Outside, an airplane roared over, drowning out the soft hum of conversation, and the noise of people settling in.

It was nearly twenty minutes before the service began. The priest, a tall, gaunt man with steel-grey hair led the proceedings. Simon scarcely listened. He followed the lead of those around him in when to stand and sit. He couldn't kneel, though.

When the priest nodded at him, he took a deep breath and walked to the front, pausing only a split second as he passed the coffin. Standing behind the pulpit, he stared out over the sea of faces. He cleared his throat, wishing that he'd thought to write down what he wanted to say. Except that he didn't know. His first words were in Aramaic, then he translated. "Magnified and sanctified is the name of the Lord." He tried to focus on the faces below. "Those are the opening words of the Kaddish, the Jewish prayer for the dead. My father is a rabbi, and I know all the right things to say when someone dies."

His glance went to the coffin.

He sighed. "Yeah, I know the words, all right, but I don't think I can say them. Not for Mike. Because once the words are said, it all becomes very real." His voice was growing stronger. "Mike was a cop, and I guess every officer on the force knows that someday this could happen to him. We all think about it." He shook his head, smiling faintly. "Yeah, I figured it might happen to me. But I never once thought about it happening to Mike. That's kinda funny, isn't it? Guess I was tempting the fates."

He bit his lip, deciding that was probably the wrong thing to say in church.

"Being a cop is not a very nice job sometimes, but having Mike for a partner made it easier. Made it bearable. A lot of times when I wanted to cry over some of the shit we have to deal with, he would make me laugh instead." As he spoke, Simon absently rubbed one finger over the cut on his palm. "I guess I'll probably still laugh. I mean, life goes on, right? Yeah, right. It's gonna be a whole lot harder now, though." He was quiet for a moment, staring out over the crowd. "I said before that my father is a rabbi. There have been a lot of rabbis in my family. There had never been a cop before. Doctors, lawyers, yeah. But no cops. Until me." The cut began to bleed. "My father thinks I have chosen a degrading way of life. A dirty job. He's right. But it's also an important job. I guess."

He could see Kimberly watching him, and Siobahn, and Mike's brother, and other men from the department. And a lot of strangers—people, he realized suddenly, that had been a part of Mike's other life, the part that he didn't know.

Abruptly, he felt very tired. "But there is something I want to say. If being a cop brought me nothing but pain, if my father never speaks to me again, if the rest of my life goes to hell because of the job, if it all adds up to nothing more than a bullet for me, too . . . if all this is true, it still will have been worth it, because once I had a partner and a friend like Mike Conroy."

He looked down and saw the blood on his hand. He closed the fingers into a fist. "None of this is probably what I should have said up here. I don't know. Probably I should have talked about God, or faith, or how Mike is in heaven now. But I'm not a very religious person. If there is a heaven, I know Mike is there, but, see, that doesn't make me feel any better. I don't want him in heaven. I want him here." He stopped to take a breath. "Or maybe I should have talked about some of the things Mike and I did together. But those memories belong to me. I'm just not very good at talking in public. I only know about doing my job."

He leaned forward a little. "The Bible says 'an eye for an eye.' That's my job. Exacting justice." He raised both hands, palms upwards, in a gesture of total hopelessness. "But what kind of justice can there be for Mike?" He looked around and stared at the priest, almost expecting—hoping—that there would be an answer. But the man was silent, so Simon turned back to the front. "Michael Francis Conroy was a good cop. A good man. And the best damned partner in the world. I'm sorry he's dead." He took two steps backwards and ducked his head a little. "I guess that's all I have to say," he mumbled.

He left the altar, this time stopping to rest his hand on top of the coffin briefly. A little of his blood stained the fabric of the flag.

The rest of the service was a blur for Simon, and without really knowing how, he found himself standing on the front steps of the church again. Siobahn was there, too, and she embraced him. "Thank you, Simon."

He shoved both hands into his pockets. "I didn't know what to say."

"You said what was in your heart. It was fine."

He tried to smile, then followed Kimberly to where the car was parked. They fell into place behind the winding motorcade making its slow way to the cemetery. Kimberly twisted her handkerchief. "I hate funerals," she said.

"Yeah, they're not much fun," he agreed.

She looked at him. "That was kind of a funny eulogy you gave."

"Was it?" He had no idea what he'd said. "I'm sorry."

"Well," she said, obviously trying to put the best light on it, "they probably just assumed it's because you're Jewish."

"Probably."

The graveside ceremony was mercifully brief, almost military.

Simon spent most of the time watching the birds overhead. When the rifle salute shattered the stillness, he flinched visibly, hearing all too clearly the echo of the shots that had come over his radio on Sunday. The flag was folded and presented to Siobahn. Simon joined the line of people walking slowly by the grave. He bent and picked up a handful of dirt, held it tightly for a moment, then sprinkled the soil on top of the coffin.

Back in the car, finally, Kimberly relaxed with a long sigh. "Oh, God, I'll be glad to get home."

"We have to go by Mike's . . . Siobahn's first," he said shortly, pulling the car out of the cemetery drive sharply.

"Why?"

"It's expected."

She didn't argue.

There was a table of food set up in the dining room, and a lot of people stood around eating and drinking and talking, mostly about Mike. Siobahn sat in a rocking chair in the living room, accepting the condolences with a kind of weary grace. Simon poured himself a shot of whiskey from the bar on the sideboard, and walked around the room, sipping the drink slowly. He stopped finally in front of a large framed photo of Mike and himself, taken some four years earlier, after an intra-departmental softball game. They were both sweaty and filthy, grinning like idiots.

He stood there for a long time, letting the crowd flow around him unnoticed. When he turned away finally, it was with the feeling that those moments, not the funeral, had been his own farewell to Mike.

They left soon.

When they got home, he pulled up in front of the house, but didn't turn the car's engine off. He jerked the tie from around his neck. "Take this inside for me," he said, handing it to Kimberly.

"Aren't you coming?"

He shook his head. "Gotta get downtown."

"You're going back to work?"

"Yeah. Don't know when I'll get home."

She looked at him in silence, then shrugged and got out of the car. Simon drove away immediately, his mind already centered on the case.

Chapter 4

Some cops are plodders. They accomplish their jobs not with muscle or with quixotic undercover escapades, but instead through the patient gathering of facts, the tedious linking up of disparate bits of information, the slow and careful drawing of a conclusion from the collage thus assembled.

Douglas Campbell was that kind of cop. The stocky, beginning-to-bald inspector spent a lot of time poring over written reports, comparing statements, checking and rechecking old crime records. He usually ate lunch at his desk, chewing thoughtfully on a tuna fish sandwich packed by his wife, his eyes sharp behind the old-fashioned bifocals.

Campbell was Simon's new partner.

When Troy first broke the news, two days after the funeral, Simon just stared at him, his caffeine and tobacco-numbed brain unable to fully assimilate the crisply worded order. "A new partner?" he mumbled thickly, wishing that his mouth didn't taste like last week's coffee. "What the hell are you talking about?"

Troy was in the middle of lighting a cigar; he paused and looked up. "What the devil do you mean, what am I talking about? Nobody in this squad is the Lone Ranger. Everybody has a partner. Campbell is yours. As of today."

Simon felt a lurching in his stomach; he pressed a hand to his gut to help ease the pain. "God, you could at least wait until the body gets cold," he said.

Troy squinted. "That's uncalled for, Hirsch. And unfair. I'm not asking you to fall in love with Campbell, just to work with him. He's a good cop."

"This is *my* case."

"This is everybody's case, Inspector." Troy finally got the cigar lit. "You do want to break this thing, don't you?"

Of course he did. So he didn't argue anymore; he just sighed and got up to leave Troy's office.

"And, Hirsch—"

"Yeah?"

"Would you for chrissake go home and change out of that damned mourning suit? You're beginning to smell like an old tennis shoe."

Since then, every couple of days, Troy or someone would remind him to go home and change. Sometimes he even slept a little, before showering, shaving, eating a meal served by a silent

Kimberly, and coming back. In between those trips home, he grabbed catnaps on a cot at headquarters, and lived on coffee and candy bars.

It was almost time for another pit stop.

He sat at his desk, feet propped up, glumly watching Campbell. "We should be out on the street," he said for the hundredth or so time in the last two weeks.

Campbell didn't even bother to look up. "We already talked to everybody, Hirsch," he said patiently. "There isn't any sense in going over the same territory again and again."

"It beats the hell out of sitting around here like some kind of fucking file clerk, reading old reports. We never once made a big bust sitting on our asses."

Campbell closed the file he was working on and sighed. "Simon, can I say something to you?"

Simon shrugged.

"I know you were partnered with Conroy a long time—"

"Eight years."

"Fine. Eight years. And I know that you were a terrific team. Highest arrest and conviction record in the city. The dynamic duo. That was great." He toyed with the folder. "But I'm not Mike Conroy. I don't operate the way he did."

"I noticed," Simon muttered.

"Probably we won't ever be friends, but I think we *can* work together. If we both try. Why not ease up a little? Compromise isn't a dirty word."

Simon was quiet for a time, rubbing his stubbled chin. "Doug," he said finally, "let me try to explain something to you. I'm not really interested in how you operate versus how Wild Mike used to do the job. I'm not at all interested in cementing our relationship, or in pulling together to win this one for the Gipper. I don't give a frigging damn about compromising. I only care about one thing. I only want to find out who killed my partner."

"Your former partner," Campbell said mildly. "I'm your partner now."

Simon sat very still. Then, slowly, he lowered his feet to the floor and stood. "I'm checking out for a while," he said quietly. "Going home to change and get a meal. Later, I'm going out on the street. See what I can pick up from some snitches. Rattle a few garbage cans. Break this case." He walked to the door. "What are you going to do?"

Campbell looked at him, studied him, and finally seemed to

come to a decision. "I'll be here," he said wearily. "Still waiting on that follow-up ballistics check from Washington. They're so damned slow."

Simon met the other man's eyes. Deciding that they now understood one another, he allowed himself a small smile. "Okay, Doug. I'll be in touch."

Campbell nodded, reaching for his tuna fish sandwich with one hand and another file with the other.

Kimberly fixed him bacon and eggs, then sat at the table with him as he ate. They didn't talk much. Simon kept his eyes on his plate, concentrating on the meal. Kimberly clasped her hands on top of the table and stared at the wall. "You look like a zombie," she said finally.

"I'm okay," he said around a mouthful of food.

"You're never home. Tammy and I almost forget what you look like."

"I'm busy. As soon as this case is over. . . ."

"This case." She sighed, toying absently with an errant blonde strand. "Tammy won the election."

He looked blank. "Election?"

"For the cheerleading squad."

"Oh, yeah." He poured more milk into his glass and gulped it. "That was why she wouldn't go to the funeral."

"She thought you'd be proud."

"I am. If that's what she wants."

"She's thirteen years old, Simon; of course it's what she wants. Why shouldn't it be?"

He ran a piece of toast around the plate, wiping up egg and bacon grease, then swallowed it with the last gulp of milk. "I don't know. No reason, I guess."

She leaned forward suddenly. "When are you going to stop this?"

Simon shoved the plate away and lit a cigarette. "Stop what?"

"Working all the time. Not sleeping. Eating once every two days. Ignoring your family." She flattened her hands against the table.

He relaxed in the chair, closing his eyes. "I'm just doing what I have to do."

"That sounds like a line out of some old movie. You're not some kind of superhero."

"I know that. I'm just a dumb Jew cop, trying to do my job."

"Are you? I don't think you care about the job so much. I think this is some kind of private war you're waging."

He shut out the sound of her voice. Instead of listening, he ran through the killing in his mind again, watching it happen as if the whole thing were a technicolor movie. He could see it all— Papagallos going to answer the door, Mike sitting in the chair drinking coffee, the killer appearing in the doorway. And that was where his dream image always stopped, at the faceless man with the gun. Over the past two weeks, he'd replayed the scene countless times. At first, all he saw was Mike—the bullet smashing into him, the blood, the expression on his face as he died. But the vision expanded until now he felt as if he'd actually been there for the whole thing. He could even see the killer approach the door, see the tall, blond, faceless man pull the gun.

"Simon!"

The voice cut through his groggy thoughts. He jerked awake, straightening with a grunt. "What?"

"Why don't you go to bed?"

He rubbed a hand over his just-shaved skin. "Can't."

Kimberly stood and began to clear the dishes. "I think you should see a doctor. Or maybe talk to Manny."

He pushed himself to his feet, searching in his pockets for the car keys. "I'm not sick, just a little tired. And why the hell should I talk to my brother?"

She was rinsing the plates. "I just think it might help. You seem so . . . sad all the time." She glanced toward him, then away. "I called him last night."

Simon stared at her. "What the hell gives you two the right to talk about me behind my back?"

"It wasn't like that. I was just worried about you. Manny said it was the right thing for me to do."

"Yeah? My fucking bigshot psychiatrist brother. Who the hell cares?"

Her hands sloshed through soapy water. "He said you're probably suffering from unresolved guilt feelings, because Mike is dead and you're still alive." She was obviously quoting a long-distance diagnosis.

He took his windbreaker from the back of the chair and pulled it on. "Manny is an ass. If you make any more calls to Boston to talk about my private life, I'll pull the fucking phone out of the wall." He walked to the door, opened it, then stopped. "I know this isn't easy, honey. But it's so important.

I'm going to see this thing through. I have to find that man. He killed someone. He killed Mike. It's my duty to find him. You can understand that, can't you?"

She shook her head, banging dishes in the sink. "No, not really. I mean, I know you feel bad about Mike. I know he was your friend. But there are other people working on it, too. I don't know why you have to do it all."

Simon opened his mouth to answer her, then realized that he didn't know what to say. He simply shrugged and left the house, shutting the door carefully.

Chapter 5

The wind blowing through Golden Gate Park was unseasonably chilly, and the clouds skittering overhead looked ominous. Simon huddled on a bench, hands shoved into his jacket pockets, watching as a couple of hardy joggers chased one another in a seemingly endless circle.

At last, he saw Doug Campbell approaching. The stolid figure, clad in a black raincoat, sat down next to him. They were quiet for a moment. "Lieutenant Troy would like to see you," Campbell said finally.

Simon gave a hoarse chuckle. "Yeah, I bet he would."

Campbell reached into the pocket of his raincoat and pulled out a bag of unshelled peanuts. He began to crack and eat them. "It finally dawned on him that I've been at my desk almost every day for the past two weeks, and he hasn't seen you at all. He asked some rather pointed questions about our working relationship."

"And what did you tell him?"

"That things were going along fine."

"Good."

They were quiet again, watching as a well-developed redhead jogged and bounced by. Campbell sighed and cracked another peanut between his teeth. "Simon, he just dumped two new cases on us."

Simon straightened. "How the hell can he do that? We've got to keep right on top of this thing with Mike. Let him give this other stuff to somebody else."

Campbell spread his fingers helplessly. "Life goes on, man. The squad is only so big. Murders keep happening. It's been over a month now, and we haven't been able to give him one solid lead. He said we've just been spinning our wheels, and it's time to put Papagallos on the back burner."

"I don't give a fucking damn about Papagallos, but it's not fair for him to pull us off Mike."

"What can I tell you? Besides, he's not pulling us off; he's just spreading us out a little. And he has a point, Simon. You know that it's almost impossible to crack one of these inside pro jobs. How often can we do it? Face it, man, we haven't come up with shit." He offered the bag of peanuts to Simon. "So now we've got the hooker strangling and the stabbing on the cable car."

Simon took a nut, but instead of eating it, began tossing it back and forth in his hands. "I don't believe this, Doug. A cop got killed. One of our own buys it, and everybody is in such a goddamned hurry to forget it."

"Nobody wants to forget it, Simon. It's just that there are other things that matter, too."

"Not to me."

"Well, they better start mattering." Campbell shoved the bag back into his pocket. "Come on, Hirsch. Maybe it's time you stop feeling so sorry for yourself, and remember that you're supposed to be a cop. All these other dead people deserve some attention, too. Even the hooker. I located her pimp. Let's go ask the gentleman a few questions."

Simon got to his feet, swearing softly and savagely. He threw the peanut out over the grass as he followed Campbell to the car.

It wasn't until they were riding along Geary Street en route to the pimp's apartment that Campbell spoke again. "Oh, by the way, I found something that might relate to Conroy's case."

Simon blew out the match in his fingers and looked at Campbell through a curtain of smoke. "What?"

"Three days ago, there was a hit in Denver. Somebody eliminated a smalltime hood named Willy Simpson."

"Yeah? So?"

"It was the same M.O. He opened the front door early one morning and took a slug through the head. I haven't been able to get a ballistics report yet, but it might be worth checking on." Campbell negotiated a turn carefully. "And about eighteen months ago, there was a killing right here. Remember Lefty Bergen?"

"Yeah. Numbers, right?"

"Right. Well, he was the same thing. The bullet there was too damned messed up for a firm check, though. Same caliber."

Simon sat back, nodding. "You might have something, Doug. That case in Denver—you have any more on it?"

"No, but I figured you might want to talk to them."

"I sure as hell do. Now."

"After we see the man," Campbell said firmly.

"Shit." Simon glanced at him. "Thanks, Doug."

"Just part of the job. I don't have any intention of giving up on this either, Simon."

They finished the ride in silence.

The forty minutes they spent talking to the sullen black man were forty minutes wasted. He told them nothing, and there wasn't anything they could pull him in on. So they warned him not to leave town—as if he would, with a stable of six women still working the streets for him—and went over to headquarters.

Troy passed them in the hallway and stopped, looking surprised. "Well, Inspector Hirsch. Nice of you to drop in on us."

"Yeah, sure, Lieutenant," Simon replied hurriedly. "I gotta make a phone call." But as he began to dial, Simon suddenly changed his mind and replaced the receiver. "Doug?"

Campbell didn't glance up from the report he was typing on their talk with the pimp. "Huh?"

"I'm going to Denver."

Now the other man swiveled his chair around to look at him. "What?"

"I think I should go to Denver myself and see just what the story is. I have a feeling that this is my boy."

"You have a feeling, huh? Troy will love that."

Simon stood. "Well, whether he does or not, I'm going." He turned toward Troy's office, giving Campbell a quick thumbs-up gesture. Campbell shook his head and bent over the typewriter again.

Campbell was right. Troy loved it. He slammed a desk drawer shut with a bang. "Oh, I love this, Hirsch. We have corpses popping up all over the frigging town and now you want to fly off to Denver to check out some two-bit stiff there. Because it might—*might*—have something to do with a case here. A case, by the way, that's supposed to be in pending. You have a *feeling*?"

Simon nodded. "This is my boy."

"This is your boy. Great. Do you really expect me to authorize travel vouchers because you're getting psychic vibes halfway across the goddamned country?"

"This is him, Troy, the same guy who wasted Mike."

"You think. You 'feel.' " Troy shook his head. "Sorry, Simon, but I can't sanction an official trip with no more than that to go on."

Simon took a deep breath. "I'm going anyway. Sir. I have some sick days coming. I'll use that time and pay for the trip myself."

Troy looked at him curiously. "You're kidding. Aren't you?"

"Are you refusing to grant me the days?" Simon asked flatly.

After a moment, Troy shook his head. "No, I'm not refusing. Take the days."

"Thank you." Simon got to his feet.

"Hirsch."

"Yes?"

"I can understand what you're doing." He seemed to read skepticism in Simon's face. "Damn it, man, no one ever gave you a monopoly on caring."

"I know that."

"Good. But you can't let this thing screw up your perspective. Make this trip to Denver, and I hope to hell something turns up for you. But if it doesn't, then you have to be able to live with that. To come back and shape up your life again."

"Yeah," Simon replied. "Sure."

The two men looked at one another in strained silence. Neither pair of eyes gave way, until finally Simon simply turned on his heel and walked out of the office.

Kimberly watched him throw shaving gear, clean underwear and socks, and an extra shirt into the overnight bag. She had both arms wrapped around her body, as if the bedroom were chilly. "I don't know why you're doing this, Simon."

"Because it might help."

"Lieutenant Troy doesn't think so, you admit that."

"I don't care very much what Troy thinks."

She moved around the room restlessly. "Do you care what I think?"

He was surprised by the question. "Well, of course," he mumbled. "You know that. But this is my job, and you can't tell me how to do it."

"How much does it cost to fly to Denver and back?"

He snapped the bag closed. "Don't worry about it."

"I have to worry about it," she said, her voice sharp. They were almost circling one another, tentative, like boxers during the first round of a match. She took a deep breath, then spoke more softly. "I'm worried about *you*, Simon."

He shrugged it off. "I'm all right, except that I'm running late. I don't want to miss the plane."

She grabbed his arm. "Simon, just stop for a minute and *think*. Look at yourself."

His gaze flickered past her, to the mirror on the wall. He saw himself. The jeans and shirt hung a little more loosely on his body than they had, and he needed a haircut. But that was all. "I'm all right," he repeated.

Her eyes flashed. "Shit." There was no passion in the word, only weariness. "Mike Conroy is dead. Are you trying to crawl into the grave with him?"

He froze for a moment, then jerked his arm away. "Shut up. That's a crazy thing to say."

"I'm not the one who's acting crazy; you are. I'm sick and tired of having Mike Conroy in the middle of our lives. It was bad enough when he was alive, but now it's ghoulish."

He shook his head and stepped around her, avoiding her hand, avoiding her words. "I'll call from Denver," he mumbled.

She didn't answer.

He hurried through the house and out to the car. Why couldn't she understand? Why the hell couldn't anyone understand? Mike understood. Until a bullet ended it all. Until that tall blond stranger raised his gun and blew Mike away.

Simon banged the heel of his hand against the steering wheel. Shit. Damn them all. Well, just wait. Just wait. When he had the guy, they'd all be sorry then.

Chapter 6

Simon stared glumly out the small window of the plane, looking down at the early morning fog that enshrouded the city. His two days in Denver had been disappointing. To say the least. All he had been able to do was study the ballistics report on the Denver hit, and compare it to the slugs taken out of Mike and Papagallos. Even that was only a qualified success. Although he was absolutely convinced that the killings were all done with the same weapon, the Denver police would only say that it was a "probable" match.

Still, as important as that piece of information seemed to him, he had a feeling that some others would scarcely feel as though it justified the trip.

He retrieved his car from the airport parking lot and drove

directly to headquarters. The first thing he did when he reached his desk was to call Kimberly. "I'm back," he said by way of greeting. "Everything okay at home?"

"Do you care?"

He leaned back in the chair, rubbing one hand over his face. "Come on, Kim. I had a long flight, and I'm tired. Could you maybe just not bitch at me quite yet?"

There was silence on the other end. "Well," she said finally, "you haven't forgotten about tomorrow, have you?"

"Tomorrow?" he said, stalling as he reached toward the desk calendar, then tried to remember why the hell the next day was circled in red. It came to him. "Of course I haven't forgotten. The anniversary party. Eight o'clock, right?"

"It would be nice if you could get home before then."

"I'll try." He hung up before she could say anymore, and saw Troy approaching.

"Hirsch, glad to see you back. What happened in Denver?"

Simon leaned forward onto the desk. "Well, it's definitely the same gun, sir. If I can keep right on top of this, I can—"

"There's been another hooker strangled," Troy broke in. "Campbell is on his way to the scene. You meet him there." He dropped a slip of paper onto the desk. "That's the address."

"But I wanted to start going through these records," Simon said. "Maybe Campbell's fucking file clerk methods might work here. If I can—"

Troy slammed one hand down. "Inspector Hirsch, that wasn't a suggestion. It was a direct order. Get your butt out of here and find out who's killing off the hookers. Before the Chamber of Commerce gets upset."

Simon stared at him for a moment, then grabbed the paper with the address, and stalked out.

Campbell seemed surprised to see him get out of the car and walk across the street. "How was Denver?" he asked, scribbling something down in his notebook.

"High," Simon muttered. He looked grimly at the body still huddled in the alley. She looked about seventeen. "Nice to see that things are still the same around here."

"Oh, yeah. Constancy is the one thing we can count on in our line of work."

They moved a few steps away, so that the photographer could snap his grisly pictures. Simon coughed and lit a cigarette. "So what the hell is going on here?" he asked, gesturing toward the body.

Campbell shrugged, putting the notebook away. "I hate to say it, but we might have a real nut on our hands. Two dead hookers in one week begins to look suspiciously like a pattern."

"Shit. That's all I need now."

Two men from the meat wagon moved in with a plastic body bag. "So?" Campbell asked. "What happened in Denver?"

They started toward their cars. "Not much. All they had was the ballistics report. And the word on the local hotline was saying that the job was done by out-of-town talent."

"Like here."

"Yeah, like here. That boy of mine gets around." He stopped by his car and opened the door. "See you back at the office. Or should I go over to the morgue and try for an I.D.?"

"No, head in. I'll see you there."

Simon nodded and slid behind the wheel. He sat there until all the official vehicles and most of the sightseers were gone. His eyes felt gritty and tired. He stared out at the empty street, absently scratching at the slowly healing cut on his palm. San Francisco. Denver. He wondered where the guy was now. Wondered what he did when he wasn't killing people.

This damned hooker thing. It was just the kind of case that used to excite him. Something he and Mike could really go to town on. But now it was only an annoyance, because it kept him from thinking about the blond guy. Damn the bitches anyway, for getting killed.

At last, he started the car and headed back toward the office.

The rest of the day was spent trying to trace the dead hooker's movements during her last hours, and also catching up on the inevitable paperwork that had accumulated in his absence. Troy wandered through the squad room frequently, giving Simon the feeling that he was operating under a none-too-subtle surveillance. It irritated him, much like Kimberly irritated him by her watchful gaze when he was home. What the hell did they expect to see?

The shift ended finally. As the office slowly emptied of daymen and the nightshift trickled in, Simon took a pot of coffee and secreted himself in an empty cubicle with a stack of files. Campbell had offered to stay for a while, but Simon waved him out. He didn't need any interlopers poking into his investigation. Screw the department. They wanted to just forget the whole thing, so he'd do it alone.

By the time he finished reading the last report, and drank the final cup of bitter coffee, it was much too late to bother driving home, so he just crawled wearily into the by-now-familiar cot, hoping to grab at least a little sleep before his next shift began.

He lit a cigarette, watching the orange glow in the darkness, and listening to the nearby sounds of phones and voices. The past hours had been fruitless, but Simon wasn't discouraged. Relaxing in the lumpy cot, he felt confident and even a little cheerful. This reminded him a little of when he was a boy back in Boston, and the steamy summer nights when every kid on the block would be out playing hide and seek. He'd always been very good at that game, not at hiding as much as at finding the others. The same kind of adrenalin was pumping through him now.

And there was something more. It was strange, but he almost felt like they were connected, he and the killer, by some kind of weird cosmic bond. Mike would have laughed at that, of course, but then Mike had been a true believer. Simon really didn't believe in anything anymore. If he ever had, beyond himself and his friendship with Mike. Cosmic bonds and shit like that might not make much sense to anybody else, but he understood the feeling, and he knew that the other guy did, too. It was as if he could reach out in the night and if he just knew *where* exactly to reach, he could touch the man.

He wondered if the blond guy could feel that psychic hand.

At last, Simon leaned over and crushed out the cigarette. Time to sleep.

Nobody killed a hooker in San Francisco that night.

That was good news not only for the ladies plying their trade on the streets and their respective gentlemen (not to mention the Chamber of Commerce), but for one cop named Simon Hirsch, because it gave him more time to think about his case, the only case that mattered.

Campbell came in from Records, juggling a couple of files. His thoughtful face was creased in a frown. "You ever stop to think about how many crazy people are walking around out there?" he asked, sitting down opposite Simon.

"No."

"Too damned many. I don't even mean the ones we bust, but just the real ordinary-looking people, walking right out there with the rest of us. You could sit right next to one in the movies, or talk to him on the cable car, and never know that inside he's completely bonkers."

Simon was only half-listening.

Campbell tossed one of the files across the desk toward him. "The world is one big asylum," he said flatly. "And we're the keepers."

Simon stretched a little. "You sure we're not as crazy as the rest of them?" he mumbled.

Before Campbell could respond to that bit of wisdom, they both saw the old wino enter the squadroom and look around vaguely. Simon began to slide down in his chair. "Shit. Wanta bet he's on his way here?"

"Why?"

"Because all the freaks end up at my desk sooner or later. It's a legacy. Wild Mike attracted them like flies." It was easier talking about Mike now; the pain was a little less every day. The loneliness, though, was still a sharp-edged blade. He was glad that in his wallet there was a picture of his partner, because sometimes it was hard to remember exactly what he'd looked like.

Sure enough, the filthy creature in the ratty brown suit was shuffling in their direction. He cleared his throat loudly, before realizing that there was no place to spit. He swallowed. When he reached the perimeter of their territory, he paused. "One of youse named Hershey?"

"No," Hirsch said. "You've got the wrong guys."

The drunk looked even more bewildered. "The guy at the desk told me it was one of youse." He scratched his ass thoughtfully. "I'm looking for the guy what was old Mike Conroy's partner."

Simon surrendered to his fate. "Yeah, that's me. The name is Hirsch."

"Whatever," the man said. "I heared you been looking for whoever done it to Mike."

They already had several hundred "tips" shoved into the file, none of which came to a damned thing, so Simon didn't get very excited over this opportunity. "You know something, do you?" he asked, reaching with one hand for his notebook. "And, by the way, what's your name?"

"Most folks call me Red. On account of my hair."

Simon stared pointedly at the man's bald head, but the look went unnoticed. "Okay, Red, what's on your mind?"

He settled back comfortably, as if they were best buddies getting ready to have a long chat. The sour odors emanating from his body wafted across the desk, and Simon tried to listen without breathing. "I was in the Emerald Palace last night. My favorite place. You know the old Emerald?"

Simon nodded. It was a rundown bar near the wharf. Hardly a night went by without at least one squad car being forced to make a run over there.

"Well, I was sitting there minding my own business, like always, and I heard these two guys talking. Not that I was snooping or nothing, you understand?"

"Yeah, yeah, I understand," Simon said impatiently. Handling crumbs like this guy took a certain knack, and he just didn't have it. Mike used to. He glanced toward Campbell, who seemed content just to listen, not like Wild Mike, who could deal with every piece of shit that came in off the street. "Can you get to the point, Red?"

"These two guys was saying something about wasting a cop."

Simon pulled himself up in the chair a little. "Yeah?"

Red nodded solemnly. "I always liked Mr. Conroy," he said, his voice displaying an unexpected degree of sincerity. "I think whoever done him in oughta get caught."

Simon stared at the old man, feeling a sudden tightness in his chest. After a moment, he cleared his throat. "What can you tell me about the guys, Red?"

Red rubbed his bald head. "One of them was a big guy, real big. Brown hair, I think. The other guy was blond. Don't know their names, but I seen 'em in there a lot." Red got to his feet. "That's all I know. They was talking about doing in some cop."

Simon reached across the desk to shake his hand. "Thanks, Red." A thought struck him, and he pulled his wallet out.

Red shrugged. "This weren't no money tip," he said. "I done it for Mr. Conroy."

Campbell and Simon watched the old man shuffle out. "People," Campbell said finally.

Simon nodded.

The rest of the day seemed to drag endlessly, although they kept busy trying to find some link between the two hookers who'd been killed. By the end of the shift, though, it appeared that the only thing the two women had in common was the occupation. And their deaths, of course.

After checking out, Simon headed straight for the Emerald

Palace. It was not a trip he took with much hope; after all, how could his boy have been in this bar, when he had just recently been in Denver? But maybe this city was his home base. Anyway, no tip was too small to follow up on.

It was still early when he arrived, and the bar was nearly empty. He took a seat in the rear booth, ordering a beer. No one paid him very much attention; it was his knack of being able to blend into the furnishings that made him a good undercover operative. They'd always done the job differently. Mike could charm the pants off an up-tight virgin—or worm his way into the affections of a bitter old hood like Papagallos. He conned people, pure and simple. But with Simon, charm wouldn't work. He did the job by watching, waiting, making people forget he was there. Or by being tough. Now was a time for waiting.

So he waited. He nursed the beer grudgingly as the bar began to fill. By shortly after nine, a goodly collection of the usual creeps and jerks had gathered. Simon checked out everybody who came through the door, but it wasn't until nine-thirty that two men entered who seemed to fit what Red had told him. The first man was large, sloppy, dressed in grimy work clothes, and had a fleshy, sullen face. The other was younger, gangly, with light-colored hair that wasn't quite blond. Simon watched as they perched at the bar. Already he knew that this wasn't his guy. There was no way these two idiots could plan and execute hits like his boy did. But he had to be sure. He picked up his beer mug and wandered over.

They ignored him, and he realized suddenly that he must look like all the other patrons. Time to change clothes and shave again, he thought, easing onto a stool next to the younger man. They were talking about baseball. He listened to their conversation for nearly thirty minutes, hearing about the big man's fat wife, the kid's hot girlfriend, the foreman on the dock, about the supposed sex habits of several women in the bar.

"What about the pig?" the kid asked finally.

The big man snorted.

Simon tensed over his beer.

"That pig," the slob snorted. "He gimme another fuckin' parkin' ticket last night."

The kid giggled. "How many that make, anyway?"

"Twelve. Someday, man, I'm gonna get that nigger pig."

"Yeah, sure."

"Gonna run the son of a bitch down with my car."

"He'll give you another ticket."

They both seemed to find that line unbearably funny, and as they dissolved in laughter, Simon gave a sigh and slid from the barstool. He walked out without a second glance. Of course that prick couldn't have been his boy. The guy he was looking for had style. Class. Brains.

He decided to go home.

The block was filled with parked cars, and he swore under his breath as he edged his way down the street toward his own driveway. It wasn't until he had actually parked and was pulling the key from the ignition that he remembered.

The anniversary party.

"Oh, shit," he said aloud, resting his head against the steering wheel. All the lights in the house were on, and he could hear the faint strain of music from his stereo. Well, it wasn't going to get any better, so he might as well face up to it now. Sliding out of the car, he tried to smooth some of the worst wrinkles from his clothes. It didn't help much.

Everyone turned as he opened the door and walked into the living room. They were all dressed up, holding glasses of champagne. Kimberly stood in the center of the room, looking beautiful. She looked at him, and he ached because she was so damned beautiful. "Hi," he said, painfully aware of his slept-in clothes and two-day growth of beard. "Sorry I'm late, but I had a tip, and . . ." His voice dwindled off.

"No one cares, Simon," Kimberly said in her most regal voice. "We're having a party."

"Yeah, yeah," he said, rubbing both hands against the front of his windbreaker. "I wanted to get here on time, really, but there was this tip, you know?" He looked around the room at the faces all watching him. "It might have been him, you know? It wasn't, but it might have been."

Kimberly walked over to the stereo and turned the volume up.

Simon stood there a moment longer, then turned around and went into the bedroom. He undressed and got into bed. The noise of the party only kept him awake for about five minutes.

Chapter 7

Campbell came into the squad room and dropped a teletyped message onto Simon's desk. "You might be interested in that," he said, sitting down.

Simon picked up the sheet and read it quickly. "I'll be damned. That boy of mine never misses, does he?" There was more than a trace of admiration in his voice.

Campbell gave him a sharp glance. "Doesn't seem to."

The details of the hit were sketchy, but Simon was sure that it was the same killer. He read and reread the terse message, before folding the paper and slipping it thoughtfully into his pocket.

Campbell was still watching him. "I hope you're not getting any dumb ideas," he said.

"Such as?"

"Such as taking off on another wild goose chase. Like a trip to Phoenix."

Simon ran a hand through his already unruly hair. "Why is that so dumb? Hell, man, this murder is fresh. Could be my boy is still hanging around."

"Your boy, huh?" Campbell was quiet for a moment. "Troy would take your star and shove it up your ass," he said mildly. "And I don't think your wife would be too thrilled, either."

Simon shrugged. "I don't give a damn what Troy does. He cares more about finding out who's wasting these damned whores than about busting this killer of mine." His face twisted in a wry grin. "And my wife hasn't spoken to me in three weeks anyway."

Campbell picked up a pencil and twisted it in his fingers. "Simon, you ever stop to think that maybe everybody else is right about this and you're wrong?"

The smile disappeared. "What do you mean?"

"I mean, maybe you've gone a little overboard on this case."

Simon's face closed. "I don't think so."

"Can I ask you a question?"

"Yeah, why not?"

Campbell hesitated. "What do you think about at night, just before you go to sleep?"

Simon was bewildered by the question. "What the hell are you talking about?"

"Do you think about Wild Mike? About the old days?"

"Sometimes," Simon mumbled.

"Do you think about your family?"

"Yeah, I guess. I don't understand what you're getting at."

"Do you sometimes think about him?"

Simon studied the surface of his desk. "Him?"

"Your mysterious blond killer. Your 'boy.' I'll bet you spend a lot of time thinking about him, don't you?"

Simon decided that he didn't like the questions, didn't like the searching expression he could see in Campbell's face, didn't like the fact that the man was nosing around in his private business. "Cut it out, Campbell," he said coldly.

"I'm only trying to help you, man."

Simon rubbed at the thin white line that zigzagged across his palm. "When I decide that I want or need your help, I'll ask for it. All right?"

Campbell sighed. "All right, Hirsch. Forget it. Come on, we're supposed to be cruising the dock area anyway, not sitting around here."

"Go on down to the car. I gotta take a leak first."

When Campbell was gone, Simon reached for the yellow pages and then the phone. He waited on hold, listening to the canned music, until the almost mechanical voice came back on the line. "Yes, sir?"

"When's the next flight to Phoenix?"

A pause. "One hour from now."

"Can I get a seat?"

He could, and with the reservation made, he left the squadroom. Avoiding the garage where Campbell waited, he went out the front door and walked around the corner to his own car.

He went directly from the airport to the Phoenix police. A couple of questions got him to Homicide, and to the detective in charge of the Tidmore investigation. Red Wing, a massive Indian wearing a lavishly embroidered Western shirt and a string tie, eyed Simon curiously, no doubt wondering if all the inspectors on the S.F.P.D. habitually ran around the country in faded Levis and sweat-patched teeshirts. "So you're from Frisco," he drawled, sounding more like John Wayne than Cochise.

"San Francisco, yeah." Simon shoved his I.D. across the desk.

Red Wing barely glanced at it before pushing it back. "I was there once. Still got that bridge?"

"Last time I looked."

"Nice place. What's your interest in Tidmore?" he asked abruptly.

Simon closed his I.D. case and tucked it away. "I don't have any interest in Tidmore at all. I'm only interested in who iced him."

"Why?"

"Because I think the same guy blew away a couple of people in my town. Including a cop."

"Yeah?" Red Wing was studying his fingers, twisting and turning a large turquoise ring. "That surprises me a little. The company usually doesn't kill outsiders. Unless the cop was on the pad and crossed them."

"This cop wasn't on the pad," Simon said sharply. "He just got in their way. He died because he was in the wrong place at the wrong time."

"Oh. Tough luck."

"Yeah, tough. About Tidmore?"

The Indian leaned back in his swivel chair precariously. "Smalltime operator. Numbers, mostly. Maybe a little pushing. Nobody around here will miss him much. A punk. The only question being asked is what on earth this insignificant being could have done to get himself killed."

Simon looked for a cigarette. "Any leads?"

"Out-of-town talent."

The same old line. "That's it?"

"Essentially. It's not easy to get hard info on what happens inside the company."

He found a cigarette and lit it. "Can I see the ballistics report?"

Red Wing shuffled through the papers on his desk, then tossed a manila envelope toward him. "Be my guest. One bullet, right through the forehead."

The office was quiet as Simon read the brief report. He compared the photos included with his pictures of the bullet taken from Mike. Finally he looked up. "Same gun."

Red Wing looked. "Could be," he agreed.

"It is." Simon carefully replaced his pictures. "You have any idea who might have wanted Tidmore on ice?"

Red Wing leaned forward again, pushing the telephone directory toward him. "Start at 'A'," he said.

"That's not very helpful," Simon said wearily. "I really hoped . . ." His words dwindled off.

Red Wing swiveled his chair back and forth slowly. "You really came here just on the chance of finding something?"

"Yeah. Guess it was a waste of time and money." He sighed. "Shit."

The detective shoved aside the pile of folders. "Sorry." He stood, his massive body seeming to fill the room. "You a believer in gossip?"

"Man, at the moment, I'd put my faith in a frigging Ouija board, if I had one."

"Come on, then. I need lunch. We can talk."

They walked across the street, stopping at an outdoor snackbar. Red Wing inhaled four onion and cheese-laden chili dogs, washing them down with two large orange sodas. Simon toyed with a plain hot dog and gulped a cup of bitter coffee. With the edge apparently taken off his appetite, Red Wing seemed inclined to talk. "I think everyone ought to have a hobby, don't you?" he commented, apropos of nothing, as far as Simon could tell.

"I guess." Simon was hot, feeling sweat prickling his armpits and running down the backs of his legs beneath the sticky Levis.

"You have a hobby?"

"No."

"That's bad. Especially for a cop, buddy. This job'll drive you crazy real fast."

"That's the truth. I used to play softball," he offered.

"Yeah. Want to know what my hobby is?"

"What?" Simon asked without much interest.

"I keep myself informed on the local company, if you follow my drift. I like to be up on all the gossip. In fact, I have a scrapbook at home that could send about half a dozen people to prison for a very long time. If I could prove any of it." He grinned. " 'Course it could also get me very dead." He reached one large hand into his pocket and extracted a chocolate bar, which he began to eat slowly. "Unofficially, I'd be willing to bet the mortgage on my teepee that the hit on Tidmore was bought and paid for by a guy named Graven. He runs a car leasing agency in town. And he's connected."

"Why would he want Tidmore hit?"

"My guess is that it was something personal, not company business. I think Tidmore probably crossed him on some deal. Don't know any specifics, of course."

Simon could feel a stirring of excitement, like the kind he

used to have when they were closing in on a case. "Have you talked to Graven?"

"No."

"Why not?"

Red Wing shrugged. "No reason to. I don't have a single piece of hard evidence linking him to Tidmore." He tapped his forehead. "But I just know he did it. Unfortunately, his lawyer would raise holy hell if I approached his client."

"Any objection to me having a few words with the gentleman?"

"No objections. But watch your step. He doesn't like people snooping around in his business. Especially cops."

"Me, a cop? Do I look like a cop?" Simon grinned. "Man, you never saw Wild Mike in action. When it comes to conning crooks, I had the best damned teacher in the world."

"Wild Mike?"

The smile faded. "My partner." He looked away. "He's dead now."

"That's why you're here?"

"Uh-huh." Simon kicked at the wall softly. "Nobody else seems to care, you know?"

Red Wing took a scrap of paper from his pocket and scribbled an address. "You can find Graven here. But be careful. I'd hate to have to ship you home on your shield, instead of with it."

Simon took the paper. "Thanks. One question—who's El Supremo in these parts?"

"Old man Antonelli. He's been in charge of things for thirty years. A real old time resident."

"How close is this Graven crumb to him?"

"Does the king talk to the peon?" Red Wing smiled. "You know where to reach me."

"Yep." Simon watched the huge Indian move with surprising lightness back across the street. With a sigh, he leaned forward onto the counter and picked up the rest of his hot dog. He began to eat thoughtfully.

Thank God for credit cards, Simon thought, studying his image in the mirror. Gone was the gritty teeshirt-clad cop with the perpetual five o'clock shadow. Simon Hirsch was now another man. The Italian-made white suit, French cut midnight blue shirt, and glossy black shoes all proclaimed his new persona. A pimp, maybe. A numbers man on the way up. He grinned at himself.

He studied a city map briefly, before going out to his rented Caddy. When Kimberly saw the bills at the end of the month, she'd hit the roof, but it was too late to worry about that now. And too soon to worry about dealing with Troy and the repercussions of taking off like he had.

Anyway, none of that mattered. He was getting close, so close that he could almost see the face of the man he was hunting.

Graven's office was in a small, discreet building on the fringe of the downtown area. The receptionist, an auburn-haired broad who looked like she belonged in a strip show instead of behind a desk, surveyed Simon carefully and apparently approved of what she saw, favoring him with a smile.

A few moments later, she ushered him into Graven's office, leaving him with a cup of coffee and a lingering glance. He settled back in the chair and fixed Graven with what Mike used to call his Al Caponestein stare. "So, Mr. Graven," he said mildly.

The plump, greying man nodded, his face looking a little worried. "Yes, uh, Mr. Hirsch, is it?"

"Right."

Graven occupied himself with selecting and lighting a thin black cigar. "What can I do for you?"

"Nothing. This is more or less in the nature of a follow-up visit."

"Follow-up?"

"Yes. Mr. Antonelli sent me."

Some of the color faded from Graven's face. "Yes, sir?" he said, straightening a little, perhaps unconsciously. "Always a pleasure to meet one of Mr. Antonelli's representatives."

Simon reached for his cigarettes and shook one into his hand. "Oh, we've met before."

"Have we?"

His brows lifted. "You don't remember?"

Graven thought hard. "Oh," he said finally, hopefully. "At the, uh, Olympic Club, wasn't it?"

Simon allowed himself to smile. "Right. The Olympic Club."

"Sure, I remember now. Nice to see you again, uh, Hirsch."

"Uh-hmmm." He lit the cigarette, then looked for an ashtray. Graven shoved one toward him. Simon tossed the match in negligently and then sat back. "In the matter of the late Mr. Tidmore," he began.

Graven's pigmentation lost several more degrees of color. "I, uh, don't know . . ."

Simon raised a hand. "No problem. Mr. Antonelli understands perfectly. He just wanted you to know that."

"Oh, yeah?" Graven relaxed a little.

"In fact, as you know, Mr. Antonelli admires initiative. And Tidmore . . . well, frankly, Mr. Tidmore had become something of an annoyance." They were quiet for a moment, each apparently reflecting on the short-comings of the late Mr. Tidmore. Simon grinned, buddy-style, deciding it was time to plunge right in. He sent a little prayer for help. You listening, Mike? "That blond son of a bitch can really do a job, huh?" Crooks, he told himself, were usually stupid.

Graven looked puzzled. "Blond guy? Oh, you must be talking about the trigger man."

"Right."

"Yeah, he did a good job."

Simon hitched forward a little. Time for a little confidentiality. "Can I ask you something? Just between you and me?"

"Sure."

"What'd you think of the guy? Personally? Mr. Antonelli would maybe like to engage his services, but he wants to sound out some people first, people whose opinion he respects, and get a reading on him first."

Graven looked appropriately flattered, then disappointed. "Well, to tell the truth, Hirsch, I never actually talked to him."

Simon frowned. "What?"

Graven shrugged. "I never even saw the triggerman. Just this other guy, the contact. Mac."

A name. Simon kept his face blank and took a long drag on the cigarette. "So all your dealings were with Mac?"

Graven nodded.

"Good man. Haven't seen him in a couple of years. How is he?"

"Fine, I guess. Only saw him once. We met in the park for about five minutes, and that was it. A real pro."

"He always was. Mac still fat?"

Graven looked at him curiously. "No. As a matter of fact, he was real thin. Not skinny, but lean."

"Yeah? Well, good. He used to be too damned fat." Simon crushed out the cigarette. Time to move. Never overstay your welcome was a rule they always followed carefully. At least he wasn't leaving empty-handed.

The good-byes were brief and business-like as they promised to get together for lunch at the Olympic Club real soon, and a few minutes later he was back in the Caddy. So, he thought as he fiddled with the controls of the air conditioner. It was a team, huh? The mechanic, his mysterious blond, and the other guy, the business manager. Mac.

It wasn't much, but it was something. More than anyone else had. "I'm gonna get you, boy," he said aloud, pulling into traffic. "I'm gonna get you good, kid."

Now, however, it was time to get himself out of town, before Antonelli discovered that someone was dropping his name rather freely. Simon was grinning as he drove toward the motel.

Kimberly was sitting at the kitchen table with a Bloody Mary and the new *Redbook* magazine when he came in. He dropped the car keys onto the counter and went to the refrigerator for the milk. "Hi," he said. When she didn't answer, he shrugged and took a long gulp straight from the carton.

"I've asked you a million times not to do that," Kimberly said without looking up. "It's disgusting for the rest of us who have to drink the milk."

"Sorry." He snapped the carton closed and replaced it, then came to sit at the table with her. "I guess you know I went to Phoenix."

"Doug Campbell told me. He assumed that's where you were anyway."

"I tried to call you last night, but there wasn't any answer."

"I heard the phone."

"Why didn't you answer it?"

She closed the magazine carefully. "Because I didn't want to talk to you."

He looked at her. "Well, that's clear enough."

"Good."

His hands moved restlessly on top of the table, rearranging salt and pepper shakers, sugar bowl, napkin holder. "Okay, you're pissed. I can understand that. I should've let you know I was going, but it just all happened so damned fast. But, Kim, I found something. A name. Not the actual killer, but his upfront man. Mac." He slapped the table. "A real name. It's just a matter of time now, honey."

"Lieutenant Troy called."

Simon grimaced. "Did he sound upset?"

"He sounded as angry as he has a right to be." She lifted the drink and took a sip.

"Well, it'll be okay when I give him my news. It was beautiful, Kim. What a job I did on that damned son of a bitch."

Something like pity moved fleetingly across Kim's face. "You really don't understand what's going on here, do you?"

He was puzzled. "What?"

She shook her head in obvious weariness. "Never mind, Simon."

He stood, trying to smooth some of the wrinkles out of the white suit. "I better get down to the office." He pulled the blue tie out of his pocket and draped it around his neck, planning to knot it later.

"Yes, you better."

He bent toward her for a kiss, but she opened the magazine again and leaned over the page. "Kim?"

"Hmm?"

"Everything's going to be okay."

"Is it?"

"Sure, soon as I—"

"Don't," she broke in. "Don't say one damned word about finding that killer. I'm tired of hearing you talk about it." She laughed harshly. "That man, whoever he is, will never know that he really killed two cops that day."

"What are you talking about?"

Her hand gave a small wave. "Nothing, Simon. Go to work. Just . . . go."

So he picked up the car keys and left.

Campbell was the only one in the squadroom when Simon arrived. The other man's mild face was creased in a frown. "You look like a pimp on a downhill run," he said sourly.

"Thanks," Simon muttered as he dropped into his chair, realizing only then that the ends of the tie still flopped freely. "What's up?"

"Troy, mostly."

"Yeah," Simon acknowledged ruefully, "I'll just bet. Well, it won't matter. This trip was really worth it, Doug. I got a name."

"Really? I got another dead hooker."

Simon kicked the desk. "Shit. Sorry about that."

"Yeah, well, it's not your problem, is it?"

Before Simon could ask him what the hell he meant by that, Dembroski, an eager young hustler just up from uniform, stuck his head into the room. "Ready, Doug?"

Not looking at Simon, Campbell got to his feet and gathered

some papers. "Yeah, Ed, on my way." He walked to the door, then stopped and turned to face Simon. "Better go see Troy," he said, his voice suddenly kind.

Simon nodded.

Alone in the room, he picked up an empty report form and slowly bent it into a paper airplane. With a sigh, he tossed it into the air and watched it nosedive into a file cabinet. He got up and went into Troy's office.

The Lieutenant was bent over a pile of papers. When he noticed Simon standing there, he took off his glasses and pinched the bridge of his nose. "Inspector," he said.

"Lieutenant."

They looked at one another for a long time, when Troy sighed. "Maybe it's my fault. I should've taken you off the case a long time ago. Or never given it to you in the first place."

"I don't understand."

"I know you don't. Sit down, please."

Simon sat, but didn't relax. "Let me tell you what I found," he said.

"What?"

"A name, sir. Mac. He's the upfront man."

"Mac?" Troy pyramided his fingers on the desk. "That isn't much to go on, Simon."

He would not—could not—allow his enthusiasm to be quenched. "Well, I know it may not sound like much, but—"

"Inspector Hirsch," Troy said abruptly.

"Huh?"

"You're on departmental suspension, pending a hearing to determine your fitness to remain on the force."

Simon frowned, not quite understanding. "What?"

"You've disobeyed direct orders, Hirsch. Took off without telling anyone. Man, I've been breaking my ass to cooperate with you ever since Conroy was killed and . . ." Troy broke off. "I'm sorry, but this can't go on."

"I see." Simon brushed at a scattering of ashes on the front of his jacket. "When is the hearing?"

"Two weeks from today." Troy hesitated. "I'll need your star and gun, Simon."

He nodded wordlessly, setting the requested items on the desk.

"Simon, use these two weeks to get yourself together, will you? Think about this whole mess, and then come before the board ready to return to work. If you make the effort, you'll have no problem being reinstated."

"Okay." He felt numb, like when the dentist used novocaine on his mouth, except that this was his whole body. The conversation with Troy seemed over, so Simon left, stopping only long enough to pick up a couple of things from his desk, then walking out of the building to his car.

The first thing he had to do was get another gun.

Chapter 8

The screened-in back porch, long a neglected cubbyhole for disposing of those items with no immediate purpose apparent, but which seemed too good to just throw away, became his office. He spent the next day cleaning it, clearing out the old rake and ancient grass seed, a battered wicker picnic basket, a torn plastic swimming pool. When the room was empty, he swept the indoor-outdoor carpet thoroughly and pulled a discarded dinette table back out to use as a desk. All his notes on the case, his (unauthorized Xerox) copies of every report, he piled neatly on the table. Index cards charting the course of his investigation were taped neatly to the screen over the desk, so that he could refer to them at a glance.

Kimberly watched his activity in silence.

At last, he hooked up the electric coffee pot and set it on a corner of the desk, standing back to survey the scene with satisfaction. "Screw the department," he said to himself.

She was standing in the doorway. "What about money?"

"Huh?"

"Money, Simon."

He waved aside her words. "Oh, hell, we've got enough to get along on for a while. Don't worry so much. Now that I don't have to waste time on all that shit for Troy, I can get the case wrapped up a lot faster." He indicated the piles of folders and the index cards. "The answer is someplace there, honey. I know it is."

She waited a moment longer, then disappeared back into the house.

The day after that, he hit the streets again, wearing the new .45 strapped under his arm. He started right back at square one. Papagallos' apartment. An old man was trimming the bushes that lined the front of the building. Simon mentally shuffled through his hundreds of notecards until he hit on the right one. Ralph Ortega, handyman. Was in his basement apartment on the morning of the shooting, and didn't see or hear anything. Was probably drunk, but didn't want anyone to know it.

The grizzled figure turned, shading his eyes against the sun as Simon approached. "Help you?"

"Mr. Ortega? Remember me? Inspector Hirsch? I spoke to you after Papagallos and the police officer were killed here."

"Oh, yeah." He snipped away a couple more branches. "Didn't catch the guy yet, huh?"

"No, not yet, but we're still looking. I just came by to ask if maybe there wasn't something you might have remembered since the last time we talked."

Ortega wrinkled his face, apparently to show that he was thinking seriously about the question. Then he shook his head. "Nope, like I told you before, I was sleeping. It was Sunday, man. Who gets up early on Sunday?"

"Nobody but cops and killers, I guess," Simon muttered to himself. He twisted the worn black notebook in his hands and stared down the block. "Well," he said with a sigh, "what about the day before? Any strangers around then?"

"You asked me that before, too," Ortega grumbled.

"So I'm asking you again. Humor me."

Ortega resumed his work. "I didn't see no strangers. This is a quiet street." Another twig fell to the ground.

"There was a stranger."

The high voice came from across the lawn. Simon turned around. "What?"

The being sitting in the shadows of the porch was surely a joke perpetrated by nature upon unsuspecting humans. The boy—he might have been ten or twenty years old, there was no way of telling—had a face that was nearly classic in its beauty, but the body beneath it was an offense. The huge mound of flesh was clothed in a shapeless garment that did nothing to disguise the form beneath it.

Ortega snorted softly. "That's Billy," he said. A dirty finger tapped his forehead. "You don't want to pay him no mind. He's got nothing to tell you."

"Neither do you, apparently," Simon said. He walked over to the porch. "Hi. I'm Inspector Hirsch."

"Billy D'Angelo. You really a cop?"

"Sure."

Simon perched on the steps. "I didn't talk to you before, did I?" he asked, knowing he could not have forgotten it if he had.

"Uh-uh. I was in the hospital. The old ticker gave out."

"Yeah?"

"Fourth time," Billy said with a strange ring of pride.

"So you weren't here when the killings took place?"

"No." The mound of flesh jiggled. "Kinda funny. I hang around here year in and year out, waiting for something exciting to happen, and the first time it does, I miss it."

Simon, who had his notebook open again, slapped it shut. "So I guess there's nothing you can tell me?"

"Not about the murder itself, no. But I saw the stranger."

"Yeah? When?"

"The day before. Saturday. Before I got sick." He hesitated. "Let me tell you a fact of life, Inspector, can I?"

"Sure."

"Nobody pays much attention to freaks." There was no emotion in the voice, only naked objectivity.

Simon looked at the ground instead of the boy.

"Don't be embarrassed. I believe in calling a spade a spade. No offense intended to anyone. But when people see someone like me, they think I must be mentally deficient—like old man Ortega there thinks. Or else they pretend not to notice me at all. Quite a feat that, I would say. They just want to get away as quickly as possible." He chuckled again. "Maybe they think it's catching."

"And the stranger? Which category did he fall into?"

Billy lifted one hand in a surprisingly elegant gesture. "Now that, sir, is an amusing irony."

"Yeah?"

"He was an exception. Like you."

"What do you mean?"

"The man spoke to me as if he were talking to an ordinary person." There was a wistful note in the thin voice. "In fact, he was nice. A very kind man, I think. Maybe he didn't have anything to do with the killings."

"Maybe." Simon tried to keep his hands from shaking with excitement. "Tell me about the man, please, Billy."

"He said he was from the fire department. Inspecting for smoke alarms." A smile crossed the face. "It was a rather transparent cover, now that I think about it. I guess that even if he was nice, he didn't see me as any danger to what he was doing."

"What did you talk about?"

"Cards."

"What?"

"I was playing solitaire. An avocation of mine."

"Where were you?"

"Right here. He came around the corner. On foot. He went inside, stayed for about ten minutes, and came out. I had the cards spread on a lap board, and he stopped to look. 'Put your black eight on the red nine,' he said."

"Did he mention his name?"

"No. We just talked about cards. I explained my system of solitaire, and he told me that his game was poker." Billy shrugged. "That was all."

"Can you describe him? Was he blond?"

"No. He was tall, six three or four, I'd say. Slender. With brown hair and green eyes."

"You sound very sure."

"My memory is exceptional," Billy said simply.

"How old was he?"

"Forty or so, I guess. Good-looking."

Simon jotted down a couple of words. "Billy, if I sent a police artist over, would you work with him? Maybe we could get a sketch of the guy."

"Okay, Inspector, sure." Billy frowned. "He was a really nice guy. You think he's a killer?"

Simon shook his head. "No, Billy, not him. But I think he's involved."

The boy shrugged philosophically. "Well, he was still nice."

"Yeah?" Simon grimaced. "That's the way it goes, Billy." That old adrenalin was pumping through his body. It wasn't his boy, but it was a connection. Find Mac and he'd find the blond. He realized that Billy was watching him curiously, and he pushed himself to his feet. "I'll be in touch," he said.

As he drove away, he could see the strange figure on the porch, hovering there like an Occidental Buddha.

Chapter 9

Kimberly watched him dress for the hearing before the board.

He took care with his appearance, putting on a conservative grey suit and tie. He'd even gotten a haircut the day before. "Well?" he asked, turning from the mirror. "How do I look?"

"Fine. Very handsome."

It was the first nice thing she'd said in a long time, and he grinned. "Gonna bowl 'em over, honey, don't worry. Hell, they'll probably end up offering me a promotion."

She nodded.

He walked past her, out of the bedroom, to the porch. She followed. His old briefcase, from his time in law school, lay open on the desk, and Simon began to shove stacks of index cards and folders into it. Kimberly frowned. "What are you doing?"

He took the folder with the sketch of Mac in it and tucked it in carefully. "What?" He glanced at her in surprise. "Getting ready for the hearing, of course."

She stepped out onto the porch, twisting the gold ring around her finger. "But you can't take all that stuff with you. You're not, are you, Simon?"

He was confused. "Well, of course, honey. How else can I show them what I've been doing? Once they see how my investigation is going—"

Kimberly leaned against the desk suddenly. "They'll lock you up in a rubber room someplace," she broke in. "Simon, if you want your job back, don't do this. Please, for God's sake, leave it alone!"

He smiled. "Don't worry." He snapped the bulging briefcase closed. "See you later."

She didn't look at him.

He left.

They kept him waiting a little while before he was ushered into the hearing room. The Chief was there, Captain Janoski, and two civilians. Simon smiled at them all pleasantly and took his place.

"You understand the reason for this hearing, Inspector?" the Chief asked.

"Yes, sir."

"Lieutenant Troy has already spoken to us. He wants you to come back to work. How do you feel?"

"Fine, just fine. Eager to get back, sir, believe me." As Simon spoke, he began to pull things from the briefcase. The pile of cards and files grew rapidly.

The Chief glanced at the others. "Hirsch, the Lieutenant seemed to feel that the difficulties you were having stemmed from your problems accepting the death of your partner. What's your reaction to that?"

Simon paused thoughtfully for a moment, then nodded.

"Yeah, that's right, I guess. Losing Mike kinda blew my mind for awhile. We were pretty close, you know?"

"I think we can all understand that." The Chief sighed suddenly. "Inspector, what *is* all of that stuff?"

Simon put the last pile of cards onto the table. "This? My records on the case, of course."

"The case?"

"Yes. I think you'll be really pleased to hear how far I've moved in the last two weeks. For example . . ." He fumbled for the right folder. "I have here a sketch of one of the two men involved—"

"Simon," one of the civilians broke in gently.

"Sir?"

"I'm Doctor Friedkin."

"Doctor?"

"I'm a psychiatrist employed by the department. Could we hold off on all that for a moment while I ask you some questions?"

"Well, if you think it's necessary," Simon said reluctantly.

"I think it might help."

He shrugged.

"Do you have any trouble sleeping, Simon?"

"No. Not much."

Two bushy brows raised. "Not much?"

Simon rested his hands on the edge of the table, feeling a thin line of sweat beginning across his upper lip. He hadn't expected this; he had figured that they'd want to talk about the case. This was almost like getting him here under false pretenses. "Not trouble, really," he said. "It's just that sometimes there's so much to think about, that it's kind of hard to settle down."

"What do you think about?"

The guy was beginning to sound like Campbell. "Everything."

"The case, mostly?"

"Yes." Sweat was running down inside his collar.

"How's your appetite?"

"Okay." Simon shifted in the chair restlessly. "Look, I want to cooperate, but this is really a waste of time."

"Why?"

"What the hell does my appetite have to do with anything? Or how well I sleep? Or my sex life?"

Friedkin smiled faintly. "I didn't ask you about your sex life, did I?"

"Not yet." Now Simon smiled, too. "But my brother is a shrink, and I know how you guys operate. It always comes down to sex sooner or later." His fingers snapped the rubber band around one pile of cards. "If you want to know—and I'm sure you do—my wife and I aren't sleeping together."

"Why not?"

"Beats the hell out of me. Maybe she just has a lot of headaches. I've been busy. A lot of reasons."

"Do you want to sleep with her?"

He snapped the rubber band again. "I don't think I have to answer these personal questions." He looked at the Chief. "Do I, sir?"

"No, Inspector, not if you don't want to."

"I don't."

"Can I ask you something else, then?" Captain Janoski said.

"Sure."

"Do you want to come back to work?"

"Yes, of course."

"Why?"

"Because I'm a cop," he said simply. "That's who I am."

The Chief leaned forward. "Are you ready to perform your duties?"

He straightened. "I have always done that, sir."

"What I mean is, are you prepared to drop this private investigation of yours? Will you leave it to the others?"

Simon frowned. "This is my case. Look, can't I just show you . . ." He shuffled through the papers. "I have a sketch here . . ."

"The unauthorized drawing done by the police artist?"

He found the picture. "Unauthorized?"

"As a suspended officer, you had no right to order the work done."

"Yeah, well, I needed it. This is one of the killers. His name is Mac." He held up the sketch.

"You have proof of this?"

"I *know* it." He replaced the drawing and pulled the rubber band off one pile of cards. "These are notes on other hits I believe have been committed by the same—"

"Simon," Friedkin broke in quietly, "have you considered getting professional help?"

Simon was puzzled again. "Sir?"

"I think you need some psychiatric help, Simon."

He looked at the Chief. "Sir, I want to come back. Please. I need the job. My family. . . ."

"Give up the case, Simon."

His hands pulled the pile of papers closer. "I can't. I have to find him."

"He'll be caught, Simon, sooner or later. If not by us, then by some other department."

"He belongs to me!" Simon wasn't aware that he was shouting, until he heard his own words echoing back. "He belongs to me," he repeated in a whisper.

The room was quiet for a long time. Finally, the Chief sighed. "Would you wait outside, please, Inspector? We'll try not to be too long."

"But . . . ?" Didn't they want to hear? Didn't they care? He stared at the four men as he gathered together all the papers and shoved everything back into the briefcase.

He stopped by the door and looked at them once more. "I don't understand this," he said quietly. "I'm only trying to do what's right. If this was a movie or a TV show, I'd be the god-damned hero, don't you know that?"

He closed the door very quietly.

Kimberly was sitting on the couch, a drink in her hand. "Well?" she said.

He dropped the briefcase and sat down. "They said I couldn't come back. They said I'm not . . . emotionally stable enough to be on the force."

She didn't look surprised as she took another slow sip of the Bloody Mary. "What now, Simon?"

"I don't know." He yanked off the tie. "I don't know." He shook his head, trying to clear away some of the fog. "I just don't understand what's going on here, Kim. None of it makes any sense." He stood again, picking up the briefcase, and clutched it tightly. "I don't understand."

She only looked at him. He couldn't read anything in the flat grey eyes, and after a moment, he turned and walked out to the porch.

It was late. Simon didn't really know what time it was, but he knew that it was very late. He was stretched out on the cot he'd set up in one corner of the porch. Although he was tired as hell, he couldn't seem to fall asleep. So he smoked one cigarette after another and stared at the ceiling.

Kimberly came out to the porch, her slipper-clad feet making no sound on the carpet. "Simon," she said, "we have to talk."

He shrugged.

She pulled the chair closer and sat down, her hands clasped tightly together in her lap. "I'm going to give you a choice, Simon," she said firmly.

He rolled onto his side and looked at her. "What choice?"

"Either you give all this up and get help, or . . . or I want you to leave."

He smoked in silence for a moment. "Give what up, Kim?"

Her eyes moved around the office. "This insanity. This . . . obsession. Give it up, Simon. Talk to Manny. Get help."

"I can't do that, honey," he said gently.

"You're ruining our lives. Your daughter is ashamed to bring her friends here anymore, do you know that?"

He was genuinely bewildered. "Why?"

"Because she's afraid they'll see you out here talking to yourself, piling up some more of those damned cards."

"It's my job," he said with dignity.

"It's madness."

"You don't understand."

She gestured hopelessly. "You're right. I *don't* understand. But, Simon, I don't *want* to understand anymore. I just don't care."

"What should I do?" His voice was soft.

"That's your decision to make."

"If you don't want me here, I'll go."

"Thank you." She stood.

He grabbed the edge of the robe. "Don't you love me anymore?"

It was a long time before she answered. "I feel very sorry for you," she said, staring down into his face.

Nodding, he released her. "I'll leave tomorrow."

Without responding, she went back inside.

Simon lit another cigarette. It wouldn't be forever. This whole thing would work out sooner or later. In the meantime, it was probably all for the best. Now he didn't have to worry about the job or his family. It was as if his universe were getting smaller, more manageable. All he had to think about now was finding him. When that was done, when he had the blond guy, then he would worry about how to straighten out these things.

* * *

He took his daughter to lunch the next day. They bought hamburgers at McDonald's and took them to Golden Gate Park to eat, sitting on the grass and watching the frisbee throwers. He unwrapped his cheeseburger. "I'm going away for a while," he said, not looking at her.

"Are you and Mom getting a divorce?" she asked.

"No, what makes you ask that?"

"It's the usual next step."

He chewed thoughtfully. "Well, I don't know what's going to happen. Whatever she wants, I guess. Do you understand why this is happening?"

She swept blonde hair from in front of her eyes, looking just like her mother. "Sort of."

"Yeah?"

"You lost your job. You and Mom stopped sleeping together." She ate a french fry. "It's because you don't seem to care about anything but this stupid case."

"It's not stupid to me, Tammy. It means a lot."

She suddenly looked older than her years. "More than Mom and me?"

"No, but—"

"But what, Dad? If we mean more to you than the case, then why are you leaving?"

"Because I have to," he said softly, gathering the food wrappers and shoving them into the sack. "I have to do this, because I don't know what else to do. Can't you try to understand that?"

"And so what are Mom and I supposed to do while you're off playing knight-in-shining-armor?"

He plucked at the grass. "Is that how you see it? You make it sound like I'm just playing some kind of game."

She shook her head, sending golden curls tumbling. "No, Dad, it's not a game. You want to know what I think it is?"

"What, honey?"

"It's a sick joke." She jumped up. "I hate this so much. Maybe I even hate you. I'll catch a bus home." She was gone before he could speak.

Slowly he gathered the remains of their lunch and got up to throw it all into a trash bin. He walked back across the park to his car.

He went to the bank and took exactly half the money from their joint checking account. He also cashed some bonds given to him by his grandfather. Kimberly had a little money from her family and she could probably get more. Besides, that wasn't his problem anymore; she was kicking him out, so she could just handle life on her own.

From the bank, he went back to the house. Neither Kimberly nor Tammy was there, probably by design. He packed everything from the porch into a couple of cardboard boxes, and loaded them into the car. His clothes and other things fit into two suitcases. When he stopped to think about it, there wasn't much in the house that meant a whole lot to him. The house was Kimberly's and everything in it reflected her image, not his. He wondered why he'd ever thought he belonged here anyway.

The street was strangely deserted as he packed the car, as if no one wanted to witness his departure. He went back inside for a six-pack of beer from the refrigerator and paused long enough to take a drink out of the milk carton.

He tossed the six-pack into the front seat and got behind the wheel. One small boy stood at the curb, aiming a toy six-shooter at him. "Bang, bang, you're dead," the kid said.

Simon grinned and clutched at his chest. The kid stuck out his tongue and ran off.

He started the car and drove away without looking back.

Chapter 10

He lived like a gypsy, sleeping in the car to save money, eating at fast food joints, moving, always moving, either in the car or on foot. Most of his movement had no real destination; it was the motion itself that mattered.

After nearly a month of this restless existence, he called Campbell. "Doug, can we meet someplace?"

The cop hesitated. "Okay," he said finally. "Chico's for lunch?"

"Thanks, man." He hung up and walked back to the cooling Egg McMuffin that was his breakfast. The newspaper article absorbed his attention again. SUSPECTED MOBSTER SLAIN was the headline, and the article was datelined Kansas City.

Reputed gangland boss Sam Lancinelli was shot and killed early yesterday. Lancinelli, long a powerful figure in local union dealings, was slain as he was preparing to give testimony before a grand jury investigating charges of the misuse of union funds. According to Artie Day, an aide to

Lancinelli, he was in the next room preparing a breakfast tray when there was a knock at the door of the penthouse apartment. Lancinelli himself went to answer it, and Day heard a single shot. By the time he reached the living room, the killer had vanished. Police are questioning Day further.

The story ended there.

Simon grinned to himself. Day was that close and didn't even get a glimpse of him? Hell, my boy is good, but he's not a goddamned wizard. Five'll get you ten that the son of a bitch was in on what was coming down, and that was why he just happened to be in the next room. He could only hope that the dumb cops in Kansas City knew the right questions to ask.

When breakfast was over, he drove out to Mike's house. It was a visit he'd been intending to make for a long time, but which he'd kept putting off. Today, though, he needed to go.

One of Mike's sons was playing in the front yard and he looked up curiously at Simon's approach. "Hi, kid," Simon said. "Remember me?"

After a moment, he nodded. "Yeah, sure. You're my Daddy's friend."

"Right. Is your mother home?"

"Uh-huh. In the backyard."

Simon stood there a minute longer, feeling as if there were more to be said to Mike's son, but not knowing what. Then he only smiled vaguely and walked around the corner of the house. Siobahn was bent over a small flower garden. "Hi," he said.

She jumped a little, then turned. "Oh, Simon, you startled me."

"I'm sorry. The kid said you were back here."

She stood, wiping both hands on the front of her jeans. "It's nice to see you."

He stepped forward and they embraced fleetingly. The human contact felt good, and Simon realized that he didn't touch people anymore. He wondered when he'd stopped being touched. And why. They pulled apart. "How are you, Siobahn?"

"Fine." She looked tanned and relaxed. "We're getting along. Sit down, and I'll get some iced tea."

He perched uneasily on a lawn chair and she vanished inside, returning a moment later with two glasses and a pitcher. He watched as she poured. "Thanks," he said, taking a glass.

She sipped the tea, eyeing him. "I'm glad you came by, Simon. I've been wanting to talk to you."

"Have you?" He grinned suddenly. "This old patio looks pretty good, doesn't it?"

"What?"

"Hell, how long ago did we put this in? Six years, it must be, right?"

"Yes." She was still watching him.

"Neither one of us knew what the hell we were doing, but it looks pretty damned good. Had a lot of fun that day, didn't we?"

"Uh-huh," she replied absently. "I heard about your problems with the department, Simon."

He glanced at her quickly, then away. "Yeah, well . . ."

"And about you and Kimberly. I'm really sorry."

He played with the sprig of mint floating in the glass. "The problem," he said slowly, "is that nobody understands what I'm doing. I kept trying to explain, but I couldn't get anybody to listen."

"Explain it to me, Simon," she said gently. "I'll listen."

He looked up in surprise. "I didn't think I'd have to explain it to you. You must know already."

Siobahn poured them each more tea. "I'd like to hear what you have to say. If you'd like to tell me."

He shrugged. "All I want to do is find out who killed my partner. That isn't so damned remarkable, is it? I thought that's what I was supposed to do. Why does that make me so peculiar? Sometimes they all treated me like I was crazy or something."

Siobahn's finger moved up and down the side of the glass. "I know you think that you're doing the best thing, Simon, but at what cost? Your job? Your wife and child? Mike wouldn't want that sacrifice from you."

"Yes, he would," Simon said sharply. "He'd do the same for me, if it was the other way around."

Siobahn sighed and shook her head. "I don't think so."

Simon looked at her. "Yes, he would. Mike was my partner."

"I know. And he loved you, Simon, truly he did." She was silent for a moment, watching the drops of moisture run slowly down the side of the pitcher. "He used to worry about you, did you know?"

He hadn't known. "Why?"

"Because you were always so . . . intense about everything. Sometimes he practically had to force you to let go for a little while, and remember that there was a life beyond the job. Sometimes you just wore him out, Simon."

He could feel something beginning to crumble deep inside and he wished that he hadn't come here at all. "You make it sound bad. Mike and I, we worked so hard because we liked it."

"Yes. But Mike also cared about other things." She was frowning, as if the effort of trying to say what she wanted to in just the right way was very difficult. "You could be just overwhelming sometimes, but he cared so much that he never wanted to hurt you by saying anything."

Simon couldn't quite understand what she was telling him. The words seemed like little shafts of ice cutting into him, and he wanted to tell her not to say anymore. Instead, he gulped tea and stared at the patio he and Mike had built. "Say, you remember how we—" He stopped suddenly, realizing that she didn't want to listen to any more of his memories.

"Mike always said that a good partnership was like a marriage. He could handle that, Simon. Mike had so much caring in him that he could give me and the children everything we needed, and still have enough left to offer you. Not everyone can do that." She stopped and carefully set her glass on the small table. "It hurts me to see you like this, Simon."

"I'm not any different," he mumbled.

She stared at him, then nodded slowly. "I guess that's true, really. You're too skinny, and your hair is getting too darned long. Your clothes look like you slept in them, and you need a shave. But that's all superficial, isn't it? Basically, you're still the same man. That's why Mike worried about you. He thought you ran on the edge too much. He was afraid that someday you were going to fall over."

Simon put his glass down next to hers and stood. "Don't tell me any more, okay?"

She got to her feet, putting a hand on his arm. "I'm not saying any of this to hurt you. Just please stop and think about what you're doing. For your own sake."

He stared at her coldly. "I guess you're getting along just fine, aren't you? That's nice. You don't think about him at all, I guess."

She released his arm, stung. "That's not true. I think about him every day. Every night. But I have to live, Simon. My children have to go on. Mike is dead, but we're alive. You're alive, too, Simon. Don't let your life end because his did."

Simon walked to the end of the patio, then stopped, crouching down to look at the rocks set in concrete, rubbing a hand over the edge. "We did a damned good job on this." He sighed. "I always thought that he cared the same way I did."

"He *did* care, Simon."

"Yeah? Not as much, though, I guess."

She held out a hand as if to touch him, but stopped in midair. "No two people can care in exactly the same way."

Simon straightened, kicking lightly at the crumbling border of the patio. "We screwed this part up. It's falling apart. It's all falling apart." He looked at her. "I feel like he just died all over again. All I had left was the memory, and now you're taking that away from me."

"No," she whispered, "I didn't mean to. . . ."

"I gotta go. I gotta get out of here." He walked away quickly, his head ducked.

"Simon!"

He stopped by the corner of the house, one hand resting on the weathered wood. "Needs painting again," he said. "We did it two years ago, right?"

"Let go, Simon," she said softly. "Let go so that you can both find some peace."

He glanced around at her, smiling with half his mouth. "I can't let go, Siobahn. Because if I let go of Mike, then I won't have anything left to hold on to. And then I'll go over that edge."

He ran back to his car, not stopping even when Mike's son called out to him.

It was no good anymore. Siobahn had taken what was left and shattered it beyond repair. He could feel himself falling, slipping away, and he tried desperately to find something he could hold on to.

He started to think about the killer. Mr. X. The missing character in this fucked-up Greek tragedy. It was a strangely comforting thought that somewhere out there the deadly blond stranger was waiting for him.

He was almost smiling as he started the car.

Campbell was already waiting when Simon walked into Chico's. They both ordered tacos and beer, then carried the food to a rear booth. "Anything break on the hooker killings?" Simon asked as he sprinkled hot sauce on his order.

Campbell glanced at him in obvious surprise. "We caught the guy, Simon, three days ago. Didn't you see it in the paper?"

"No, guess I must have missed it. I was reading about the Lancinelli hit, though."

"Lancinelli? Who's that?"

"In Kansas City."

Campbell took a bite of taco and chewed. "Kansas City, huh? Missouri or Kansas?"

Simon frowned. "Gee . . . I don't know. Better find out, I guess."

Campbell sighed. "It doesn't matter. I have enough trouble keeping track of the murders here, buddy. I don't spend a whole lot of time worrying about what happened halfway across the country."

"But this was my boy again, I'm sure of it. Same M.O."

"I suppose you're going to Kansas City now?"

Simon nodded, taking a swipe at his chin with a wadded paper napkin. "That's why I wanted to see you. I don't know a damned soul in that part of the country. Aren't you from someplace around there?"

"Nebraska."

"You know anybody in Kansas City?"

"My second cousin."

Simon looked up hopefully. "He a cop?"

Campbell shook his head. "No, not a cop. He runs a flower shop. But he's a real nice guy."

Simon frowned his disappointment. "Nobody else?"

"Nope."

"Damn. Well, guess I'll just have to go in cold."

Campbell looked at his food, then shoved it away abruptly. "You're taking this all the way, aren't you?"

"I don't have any choice." Simon wadded another napkin. "And no lecture, please. I've had enough good advice for one day." It still hurt to think about what Siobahn had said. "You probably think I'm crazy, don't you?" He laughed softly, bitterly. "Well, join the club. I just found out that even Mike thought I was a little flaky."

"But you're still going after his killer?"

A little smile flickered around the corners of Simon's lips. "Of course."

"Why?"

Simon picked up a taco. "Because the killer and I, we're the only ones who still care." He took a big bite of the taco. Campbell watched him for a moment, then returned to his own lunch.

Chapter 11

Life quickly fell into a pattern. He went to Kansas City, as he'd told Campbell he would, arriving just in time to be there when they pulled Day's body from the river. Beyond his disappointment at being cheated out of talking to the man, Simon wasn't the slightest bit interested in that murder. His boy didn't go around blasting people with shotguns and then dumping their bodies.

He left Kansas City and went to Memphis. Then to Atlanta. Milwaukee. Cleveland. One tip led to another, and although some of the hits were several years old, he followed them all up. He sometimes wondered how many people the blond had killed.

Nearly six months after he'd left San Francisco, a hit went down in Boston that sounded good. He drove straight through from Philadelphia to follow up on it. He found a cheap motel and was all checked in, settled down to a dinner of cooling hamburgers, before he realized that he was home. He dumped the cheap meal into the wastebasket and headed for the car.

His parents still lived in the same house where he'd grown up, and the lights in the dining room told him that the old rituals were still observed. Sabbath dinner was at seven.

The black woman who answered his knock looked at him blankly. "Yessir?"

"I'm Simon Hirsch. Can I come in?"

She moved aside. "Of course. Dinner is about to be served."

He paused in the curved doorway of the oaklined dining room. The table was covered with a pristine white cloth. Tall ivory candles gave off tiny glows of light that danced off the polished silver and china. His parents were there, of course. Manny and his wife. A couple of teenagers who must have been Manny's. Everyone was dressed up and he realized belatedly that he probably should have changed from his jeans and windbreaker. "Hi," he said after a moment.

Everyone looked up. "Simon!" his mother said. "I don't believe it."

"Yeah, it's me." He walked into the room, his tennis shoes silent against the thick rug. "Hi, Manny. Papa." He thought for a moment. "Esther." He nodded at the kids, not even trying to remember their names.

Manny, fleshy and successful-looking, came around the table

and clasped Simon by both arms. "Kid, it's good to see you. Damn, we've been worried about you, wondering where the hell you were. Kim didn't seem to have any idea."

Simon shrugged. "I move around a lot."

The maid reappeared. "Shall I set another place, sir?"

Everyone looked at the rabbi, who nodded. "My son will join us."

"Thank you, Papa."

He took the empty chair at one end of the table. His mother was watching him. "You look bad, son."

"I'm fine, Mama, really."

"Too thin."

He made no response, and the ritual of the meal began. Simon concentrated on the food, both because he was hungry and because he hoped that would forestall any conversation.

At the end of the formalized meal, the two teenagers hurriedly excused themselves. A few moments later, the two women left. The Rabbi and his two sons stayed at the table, not talking until the dishes were cleared and each had a glass of wine in front of him.

"So," Manny said. "What's going on with you anyway?"

"Not much."

The rabbi leaned forward. "You leave your home, your family, your job, to run all over the country, and that's not much?"

"Papa, you never liked my job anyway, remember? And you weren't all that crazy about my *shiksa* wife, either."

"I should like you better as a bum?"

Simon's shoulders hunched forward. "I'm just doing what I have to do." His fingers twisted around the slender stem of the wine glass.

His father snorted. "So now you sound like John Wayne."

"With this nose?" Simon mumbled.

Manny held up a conciliatory hand, and Simon suddenly realized that his brother had spent a lot of time over the years trying to negotiate peace. "Let's just talk, shall we?" he said quietly. "Simon, we've been very worried about you. Even before you left home, Kim had called me several times. She was afraid for your emotional health."

"She thought I was crazy," Simon said flatly. "So did a lot of people."

"She was only worried because she cared. A lot of people care."

"Right, Manny, right." He sighed and took a slow sip of wine.

"Why are you in town?" his father asked.

"The Flynn hit."

"What?"

"Robert Flynn was gunned down three days ago. He was a prime pusher, controlled almost half the city. I think my boy did the job. By this time, I can recognize his work a mile off." He gave a grin of helpless admiration. "Damn, he's good."

The rabbi shook his head. "How long will this go on?"

"Until I find him, Papa."

Manny was staring at Simon's face. "And then what?"

"Huh?"

"What happens after you catch this killer? What will you do then?"

Simon took another drink, then licked wine from his lips. "Hell, you know," he mumbled.

"You don't have any plans, do you?"

They were quiet for a moment. "Your wife is suing for divorce," his father said.

"Is she?" He thought about that for a moment. "Well, okay, if that's what she wants."

The old man stood. "I must go. Will I see you again, Simon?"

He shrugged. "Don't know, Papa. Depends."

He and Manny watched as their father slowly left the room. "He does care, kid, you know."

"Does he?" Simon smiled a little. "I upset people, Manny. I make them uncomfortable. They don't want me around."

"Even the Lone Ranger had Tonto, right?" Manny said.

"Yeah."

Manny studied him. "Don't you ever get lonely, Simon?"

He lifted a shoulder helplessly. "Sure. Don't you?"

Manny looked a little startled, then nodded. "But I have my family. My work."

"I have my work, too." He could have told Manny more. That he never really felt alone, because the guy was always with him. Funny, although he still didn't know what the killer looked like, he felt like he knew him very well. Better than he'd ever known anyone. Sometimes now if he opened his wallet and saw the picture of Mike, it took him just a moment to place the face in his memory. The blond guy . . . he was always there. But Manny wouldn't understand that. "My work is finding the man," was all he said aloud.

"An eye for an eye?"

"I guess."

"Will you kill him, Simon? Or turn him over to the authorities?"

Again he shrugged.

Manny poured them each more wine. "So much hatred hurts you far more than it hurts him."

Simon was surprised. "I don't hate him, Manny," he said. "I don't hate him at all. I just . . . want to find him." He drained the glass and got to his feet. "I gotta go. Tomorrow is going to be a busy day."

"Let us know before you leave town."

"I will," Simon said.

Manny handed him a roll of bills, which Simon shoved into his pocket.

But he forgot to let them know. He spent two days in Boston and then drove to New York. Pete Rossi, a high school classmate, was on the D.A.'s staff, and Simon went to see him. It took about twenty minutes for him to lay out what he wanted. When he was finished, Rossi frowned thoughtfully. "Look," he said finally, "I know a cop, one of the best. You go talk to him, okay?"

"Sure, Pete, I appreciate this."

The cop's name was Mazzeretti and he looked more like a successful pimp than a homicide dick. His suit was obviously tailor-made and his hairstyle probably cost more than all the clothes Simon was wearing. He tapped a gold ballpoint against the desk and listened as Simon talked. When Simon pulled out the pencil sketch of Mac, Mazzeretti leaned forward and stared at it for a long time. He finally glanced up and Simon caught something flickering through the black eyes. "You know the guy?" he asked eagerly.

"Not sure. Hell, I see so many punks. He got a name?"

"Mac."

"That's it?"

"Yeah. He works with the blond guy. No name on him yet."

Mazzeretti leaned back in the chair and closed his eyes. The room was quiet for a long time, before he sat up and nodded. "Yeah, that's the guy, all right."

Simon felt a lurching in his gut. "You know him?"

"Yeah. Hell, must be eight years ago. At least. Had a guy in here on an attempted burglary rap."

"Him?"

"No, no. A blond guy." Mazzeretti dropped the pen and fumbled for a gold lighter. "You know how some cases just stick in your mind? A face, something that has hold of your memory, and won't let go?"

"Yeah." He knew.

"That's the way it is with this. The blond guy was a real nutcase. A Viet vet. I wanted to send him over to Bellevue, but this guy, this Mac, asked me not to. Then the owner of the store or whatever the hell it was showed up, and dropped the charges." He shrugged elegantly. "So we let the kid go."

"Kid?"

Mazzeretti frowned. "Well, he wasn't that young, really, but he was weird. Very spacey. Wouldn't even talk until this Mac showed up." He shook his head. "I knew he was strange. Didn't seem like a killer, though."

"You have a name?"

"Hold on." He made a couple of phone calls, and in a surprisingly short time, a policewoman came in and dropped a file on the desk. Mazzeretti opened it and grinned. "John Paul Griffith." He shoved the file toward Simon. "That's him."

Simon stared at the mug shot. He gripped the edge of the desk to keep his hands from shaking. The face in the picture looked scared. "John Paul Griffith," he whispered. It was almost like a greeting.

Mazzeretti was still shuffling through some handwritten notes from the file. "I did a follow-up on the other guy, too," he said. "Just to satisfy my own curiosity. One Alexander McCarthy. A known gambler, and not a very lucky one, either. Also served in Nam."

Simon was still staring at John Griffith and only half-listening, but he nodded. "Could I have a copy of this picture?"

"Well, it's not really kosher, but okay. Give me a few minutes." He left, taking the file with him.

Simon leaned back, releasing his breath in a long sigh. He didn't really need a copy of the photo. The image of that scared, childlike face was burned into his memory. Closing his eyes now, he could still see it clearly. "John Paul Griffith," he whispered again. "John." He smiled. "I'm getting close, Johnny. It's just a matter of time now. Do you know that, Johnny? Can you feel me getting close?"

Yeah, he thought, Johnny knew.

He went to the address in the police report. There had once been a pizza place on the first floor, but it was boarded up and empty now. Simon climbed to the second floor and tapped at a door.

A very tiny old lady opened the door. "Yes?" she chirped.

"Sorry to bother you, ma'm," he said, "but could I ask you a couple of questions?"

"Oh, is this one of those surveys? I'm all the time reading about them, but nobody ever asked me anything before."

Simon smiled. "Well, this isn't exactly like that. How long have you lived here?"

"Close to twenty years now."

"You wouldn't happen to remember a man who used to live here by the name of John Griffith?"

"John? Of course I remember him. A nice boy." Her face turned anxious. "I hope he's not in trouble?"

"I hope not. He lived here with another man, right?"

"Yes, that would be Mr. McCarthy. I didn't know him so well, but I think he must have been a good man."

Simon was leaning against the wall. He lit a cigarette. "Why do you think so?"

"Because John thought so highly of him. Every other word from that boy was 'Mac says this' or 'Mac says that.'" She frowned a little. "I hope John is all right. He was such a sweet boy."

Sweet?

The old lady didn't know any more than that. He thanked her and walked back down to the sidewalk.

Simon was feeling very good. He whistled a little as he got into his car. Won't be long now, Johnny, he thought cheerfully. I can almost touch you now.

Do you feel me getting close, babe?

Book
III

Chapter 1

Waking up.

There was, as always, that first terrifying moment, that initial instant of consciousness during which the fear still held him captive. Slowly the scene and its comfortable familiarity penetrated the sleep-fogged edges of his mind. The car was barreling down the highway into the darkness; Mac was driving; everything was okay. Johnny relaxed against the seat.

"Welcome back, Sleeping Beauty," Mac said. "Christ, I thought you'd died."

"Was I sleeping a long time?"

"Couple hours."

"I'm sorry." He felt guilty, knowing that Mac liked company as he drove. "I won't sleep anymore." Reaching for a cigarette with one hand, he punched the lighter in with the other.

Mac glanced over. "Thought you were gonna quit that," he said sourly.

Johnny pulled the lighter out and touched the glowing orange filament to the end of his cigarette. "You're a fine one to talk. You smoke like a chimney."

"I have a lot of bad habits, but that doesn't mean you should have them, too."

"I don't want the rest of them," Johnny said mildly. "Just this one."

Mac swung the car out of the lane to pass a slow-moving eighteen-wheeler. "Well, it's your life."

"Right." They smiled at one another. The next few minutes passed in silence as Mac watched the traffic and Johnny concentrated on the smoke curling up toward the roof of the car. "Where are we going anyway?" he asked after a moment of thought.

"L.A." There was a sharp edge of irritation in Mac's voice. "You know that, Johnny. I already told you twice that we're going to Los Angeles."

Johnny flinched away from the tone. "I forgot," he said in a whisper.

"Well, for chrissake try to remember things like that, will you?"

"Okay, I'm sorry. Don't be mad." Johnny felt the familiar chill begin inside. His hand reached out, but stopped before it touched Mac, resting instead on the back of the seat.

Mac rubbed the bridge of his nose. "I'm not mad, Johnny. I just wish. . . ." He broke off. "Light one of those for me, willya?"

"Sure." Pleased to be of some use, Johnny devoted his full attention to the task, and not until the cigarette was stuck between Mac's lips did he speak again. "What do you wish, Mac?"

"I don't know." Now his voice just sounded tired. "I need some coffee," he said abruptly. "There's a truck stop."

It was late and there were only a few customers in the diner. The interior was all white formica and the waitress looked like she'd been on her feet since early morning. After they'd ordered, Johnny dug some coins out of his pocket and went over to the jukebox. He punched up several selections, then came back to the booth, sliding in across from Mac. They didn't talk much until the waitress had delivered Mac's coffee and Johnny's lemon meringue pie and Coke. "I'm really sorry that I forgot where we're going," Johnny finally said, watching as his fork penetrated the stiff white meringue.

A Billy Joel song was playing in the background. "It doesn't matter, kid," Mac replied.

But Johnny wanted to explain. "I try to remember things, but they just seem to get lost in my head sometimes."

"I know, Johnny. Don't worry about it."

He ate the pie slowly, aware that Mac was watching him. After a few more moments, a new song began on the jukebox. Delighted with his surprise, Johnny grinned. "There."

"What?"

He waved the fork in the direction of the music. "I played that song for you."

Mac looked puzzled. "What is it?"

"Nat King Cole. You told me that you liked Nat King Cole."

"I did? When?"

He licked lemon pudding from the fork. "A long time ago."

Mac shrugged.

Anxiety replaced Johnny's pleasure. "That's right, isn't it? You do like him, don't you?"

"Sure," Mac said quickly. "He's one of my favorites."

Johnny relaxed again.

In a few more minutes they left the diner, but instead of pulling back onto the highway, Mac drove around behind the building and parked again. "I want to try and get some sleep," he explained, leaning back against the seat. "Just an hour or so."

"Okay," Johnny said agreeably. He lit another cigarette.

Mac's eyes were closed. "Johnny?"

"Huh?"

"Thanks for playing the song."

A warm feeling rushed through him. "Sure, Mac. And I'll try not to forget so many things."

"Hell, you remembered about me liking Nat King Cole. Don't worry about it." He smiled, his eyes still closed, and in a minute he was asleep.

It was quiet then, except for the faint and reassuring sound of Mac's snoring. White-silver waves of light from the moon washed over the scene, enveloping them in an aura of unreality that Johnny could feel, if not define. He watched Mac, noticing with solemn wonder how sleep eased the worry lines from the craggy, familiar face.

Los Angeles. Los Angeles, California. He wouldn't forget again. Mac would be proud of how well he could remember things when he tried. Johnny wanted Mac to be proud of him. Or at least not to be mad at him. Mac's anger was an earthquake that shook the foundations of Johnny's world. He sighed, resolving yet again to be better, to do nothing that would disappoint Mac, or make the green eyes flash with lightning. Resting one hand lightly on the other man's lean arm, Johnny solemnized the promise. Mac stirred a little in his sleep, almost seeming to turn toward the touch.

Sometimes Johnny tried to remember what his life had been like before, but it was all just a barren landscape inhabited by grey, indifferent figures hovering always just beyond his reach. No one ever touched him. His father, one of the indistinct memories, used to talk about Jesus a lot. That much Johnny remembered, and in the old man's words Christ was an incandescent being, a brightness that cut through the darkness of human existence. Johnny had never seen the Lord, though, never felt the pull, never understood what his father had been talking about.

But now he knew.

Mac was the golden light, the savior, the epicenter of Johnny's being, and his benign approval was like a long swallow of cool spring water to a parched man. Johnny sometimes yearned inside, without knowing what it was he craved, desired without knowing why. But for now he was content to sit in the bathing calm of the moonglow, watching as Mac slept, letting the night wrap around them like a blanket.

He moved a little closer and rested against Mac. The other man stirred restlessly, patting Johnny's shoulder. "S'okay, kid," Mac mumbled sleepily.

Johnny sighed. He dared a little more, draping one arm across Mac's chest. The sleeping man moved into the embrace, murmuring something that Johnny couldn't quite hear. It didn't matter. He smiled and closed his eyes.

Chapter 2

He sat in the motel room, watching M*A*S*H, and waiting for Mac to come back with the hamburgers. It seemed to be taking a very long time. Johnny got up from the bed a couple of times and walked over to peer out the window. Sometimes, he knew, Mac got sort of distracted and ended up playing cards or something when he was supposed to be running an errand. Usually, Johnny didn't mind, but tonight he was awfully hungry. And a little lonely.

At last, Johnny heard the sound of the key in the lock and the familiar lanky figure came into the room. His relief was reflected in a wide smile. "Hi."

Mac grunted a reply and dropped a paper bag of food and a six-pack onto Johnny's bed. "Goddamned place was busy," he muttered, pulling off his windbreaker.

Johnny's smile slowly faded. "What's the matter?"

"Nothing."

"You act like there is," he insisted.

Mac finally sat down, too. "I have a headache, that's all. Don't worry about it."

Johnny nodded, accepting that, and opened the sack. "Eat something," he ordered. "You'll feel better."

"Yeah? You sure about that?"

"That's what you always tell me." Johnny smiled again and this time Mac returned it.

"Guess I'm just tense," Mac said, chewing the rubbery hamburger thoughtfully. "We've been sitting in this damned room for three days, and the contact hasn't been made. Shit, I hope this job didn't fall through."

"If it did, there'll be something else." Johnny was carefully squeezing catsup on his french fries.

"Better be. We're almost broke."

Johnny turned the volume up on the TV. "Don't worry so much," he mumbled. "You'll get an ulcer."

Mac popped open a can of beer and took a long drink. "If I don't worry, who will?"

"Want me to for a while?"

"Hah, you're too dumb to worry," Mac said, shoving the rest of the hamburger back into the sack.

Johnny shrugged and finished the meal in silence. When they were done, he gathered all the trash and shoved it into the wastebasket. "Feel better?"

"No."

Johnny frowned. "You mad at me, Mac?"

Mac shook his head.

"You sure? Because if I did something wrong, I'm sorry, really, I—"

Mac stood abruptly. "Johnny, I'm not mad." He sighed, running a hand through his hair. "I keep saying the same things, don't I?" The words seemed to be directed more at himself than at Johnny. "Year in and fucking year out. Are you as tired of it all as I am?" He stared at Johnny, who only looked back at him, having no idea what Mac wanted him to say, and long ago having learned that in such a case, it was best to keep his mouth shut. "Shit," Mac said finally.

"Yeah," Johnny agreed, not really understanding what was going on, but knowing instinctively that the worst of Mac's mood had passed. He opened a can of beer for himself and another for Mac. It was quiet again as they sat watching TV.

At last, Mac crushed out his cigarette and drained the last of the beer. "I've got a game," he said.

"Okay. Good luck."

"Oh, sure." Mac smiled a good-bye. "See you later."

"Uh-huh."

He left and the room seemed too quiet. Johnny tried to concentrate on a cop show, but the silence seemed to press in on him unbearably. After a few minutes, he grabbed his jacket and fled, leaving the loneliness behind.

The harsh vibrations of downtown Los Angeles closed around

him as he moved through the crowd of night people that cluttered the sidewalks around the bars and discos. The noise and
movement of the scene surrounded him, and he relaxed a little,
losing himself in the safety of anonymity.

What he really wanted to do was see a movie, but he stopped
in front of several rundown theatres, and they were all showing
the same kind of film. The posters were of fierce-looking black
men towering over frightened white men, or of Oriental martial
arts experts practicing their skills on still more hapless whites.
Johnny wished he could find one of the westerns he liked, the
kind with lots of loud music and heroes that talked through
clenched teeth.

He finally gave up on the idea of a movie, and went into a
drugstore for a candy bar and a copy of *TV Guide*. As he left the
store, already eating the chocolate, he got the feeling that someone was following him. It wasn't the first time lately he'd felt
that way, but when he turned around, no one seemed to be
paying any special attention to him, so he shrugged and walked
on.

A young black kid approached him. "Hey, man."

They were standing on the corner, waiting for the light to
change. "Hey," Johnny replied, wishing that the boy didn't look
quite so much like one of those movie posters.

"You looking for some action?"

"What?" Johnny was staring at the pavement.

"I got what you need."

"I don't . . . uh, no. Thanks." The words were a painful
whisper.

"Come on, man, everybody needs something. Girls? Boys?
Uppers? Downers?"

The light changed at last, and Johnny plunged out into the
street, trying to escape. He kept moving, not looking back, until
finally he could duck into the safety of a coffeeshop. The booths
were all filled, so he sat at the counter, giving his order in a
breathless voice, trying to stop the helpless trembling of his
hands.

When the waitress brought his dish of ice cream, he opened
the *TV Guide* and bent over its familiar pages gratefully.

"What flavor is that?" a voice asked suddenly.

Johnny, still edgy, jumped a little. "Huh?"

"That ice cream looks good. I was just wondering what kind it
is."

The man had a friendly grin, and Johnny managed a faint

smile in return. "Oh. It's boysenberry ripple. It *is* good," he added.

"I'll take your word for it." The guy summoned the waitress and ordered.

Johnny glanced down at his magazine, wondering if it would be rude to start reading again. "There's a Humphrey Bogart movie on tonight," he said finally.

"Yeah? He's great. They don't make movies like that anymore."

He sounded really interested and Johnny gained a little courage. "I like westerns best, though," he said eagerly.

"Me, too." The man sampled the ice cream. "Hey, this is good." He looked at Johnny. "You live around here?"

Some of the panic returned. That was the worst part about talking to people; sooner or later, they always asked questions, and he never knew what to say. If he said the wrong thing, Mac would get very mad, so it was best not to talk at all. "I gotta go," he mumbled, slipping from the stool. "Bye."

Not waiting for an answer, he jammed the *TV Guide* into his jacket pocket and hurried away, feeling the man's eyes boring into his back as he went.

He watched the Bogart movie until Mac came in. The evening had left Johnny feeling vaguely unsettled and nervous. He watched by the glow of the TV as Mac undressed and got into bed. "How was the game?"

"Okay. I broke even."

"That's good." He sighed and turned off the television.

"Don't you want to watch the rest of the movie?"

"No." He pulled off his jeans. "I'm tired. Can I sleep with you tonight?"

As always, Mac just nodded, scooting over to make room. Johnny slipped in next to him, feeling some of the tension drain from his body at the familiar warmth of the shared bed. "You okay, kid?" Mac sounded worried.

"Uh-huh."

"Sure?"

Johnny nodded. "Yeah." He pulled the sheet up a little. "There were sure a lot of people walking around tonight."

"Did somebody bother you, babe?"

"No." He sighed. "Good night, Mac."

Mac muttered a reply. He lit a cigarette, and Johnny fell asleep watching the orange glow in the darkness.

Chapter 3

His first big break came in Vegas. A rumor was circulating about a hit about to come down in Los Angeles. An intra-company squabble had been going on for months, and it was about to come to a halt. Somebody was going to play the role of sacrificial lamb.

Simon couldn't get a line on who was supposed to carry out the hit, but it sounded like the kind of thing Johnny might be involved in, so he headed for L.A.

It was the Sunset Strip hooker who put the final piece of the puzzle into place. Her name was Chrissie. Or Kristy. Something like that. The bar was filled with noise and smoke, and he wasn't really listening anyway. The meeting might have been accidental, just another of the quick encounters that took place every night in the bar. But it wasn't.

Someone pointed her out to Simon, remembering having seen her with a gambler named Mac on at least one occasion. So he picked her up, bought her a couple of drinks, left with her. They walked to her place. Once they were sitting on the couch, drinks in hand, Simon pulled out the police drawing of Mac. It was creased and bent from the months in his wallet. "You know this guy?"

She studied it, then shrugged. "Yeah, I've seen him a couple times. Alec. Or Alex. Something like that." As she spoke, she began to undress.

"When'd you see him last?" Simon unbuttoned his shirt.

"Couple days ago." She stood and pulled off the rest of her clothes. Wearing only bra and panties, she padded into the bedroom.

Simon followed. "You know where he's living?" he asked, piling his clothes on a chair.

"Nope." She climbed into bed. "He was playing cards with Tony DePalma, though."

He stretched out next to her, trying to remember when he'd last had sex. Not since his wife. Kimberly. A long time ago. But even so, he moved against the naked body almost absently. His hands kneaded her breasts slowly. "What was he like?" he whispered past blonde strands.

"Who?"

"Alex McCarthy."

"He was okay. Good." She squirmed. "At least he didn't talk about some other guy while we were screwing."

Simon ignored that. "He tell you anything about himself?"

"No," she said through clenched teeth.

His body continued to move against hers. If Mac was in town, Johnny had to be as well. It began to look as if the rumors he'd heard in Vegas were true.

She was wriggling beneath him, making urgent little sounds.

Simon was thinking about Johnny. Who did he screw in Los Angeles? He thought about that as his body drove with increased urgency into Chrissie/Kristy, the girl Mac had screwed. Ahh, Johnny, he thought, it's almost over now. Pretty soon, kid, pretty soon.

Johnny was somewhere in the city and Simon wondered if he knew how close the end was.

It wasn't at all what he'd expected. His first sight of John Paul Griffith caused a surge of bewildering emotions inside him.

The final steps had been so simple, really. It took only a couple of hours to track down DePalma. A few questions and a few dollars persuaded him to reveal the make and color of Mac's car; a few more dollars pried loose the name of a motel where Mac might possibly be staying.

He waited outside the motel that night, waited until the door opened and John Paul Griffith came out. Simon lit a cigarette, his hands trembling, and got out of his car.

He followed the tall thin blond for almost two hours, watching him move through the city like a phantom. The encounter with the young black pimp was curious, because Johnny seemed scared by the boy. It seemed out of character for a seasoned hitman to be afraid of an under-age street hustler.

Simon's confusion grew when he sat down at the coffeeshop counter next to Johnny. Their conversation was so brief and so totally absurd—ice cream and Humphrey Bogart—yet there was something beyond the brevity and absurdity of the confrontation that stayed with him. He knew fear when he saw it, and there was a lot of it in the pale blue eyes.

After following Johnny back to the motel and picking up his car, Simon went to his own cheap room and sat glumly over a six-pack, trying to wash away the taste of that damned ice cream, staring at the old mugshot. Johnny was a cold-blooded killer and no one knew that better than Simon, but he looked more like a scared kid who needed . . . needed what?

Simon Hirsch didn't know.

Shit, he thought, I don't even know what *I* need.

It occurred to him that he should have been celebrating. For such a long time he'd been hunting this man. He'd lost track of the times he'd crisscrossed the country. No more job. No more family. No more anything, except the mugshot and his need to find John Griffith. And so this evening they met over boysenberry ice cream and talked about Bogart.

He threw an empty beer can across the room. It hit the wall and fell with a clatter to the uncarpeted floor. He opened another can. What was it his brother Manny the Wise had said? "And what then?"

"Yeah," Simon said to the mugshot. "What now, Johnny?"

He was waiting outside the motel again the next night. He saw Alex McCarthy come out first. The lean figure in the dark windbreaker paused long enough to light a cigarette, and in the sudden flare of the match, Simon could see the sharp-featured face and thin, ascetic lips. That, he thought, was the face of a killer. McCarthy tossed the match aside and got into the pale blue BMW. Simon stepped back into the shadows as the headlights swept the lot and then vanished.

It was only a few minutes later when Johnny came out. Ducking his head and shoving both hands into the pockets of his jeans, he walked toward the nearby bright lights and noise, apparently unaware that he was being followed.

The routine was much the same as it had been the night before. Johnny walked slowly along the main drags, window shopping, pausing in front of every movie theater to check out the attraction, then moving on. They might have been the only two people in the city. Simon sensed an almost unbearable loneliness in the slumped shoulders and impassive face he caught glimpses of in the windows they passed.

Loneliness, after all, was something he was sort of an expert on.

When at last Johnny went into a penny arcade, Simon followed. The blond paused in front of a U-Drive-It machine, not noticing as Simon approached. "Hi, there," he said, grinning.

Johnny spun around. "Huh?"

Christ is he strung tight, Simon thought. "Remember me? We met last night. Boysenberry ice cream?"

Johnny seemed to relax a little. "Uh, yeah, I remember. Hi."

"We seem to cover the same territory."

"I guess." He glanced around, obviously looking for an escape route.

Simon moved a little closer. "Don't take off again, man," he
said.

Johnny blushed. "I only . . . I . . ." He shrugged.

"You any good at that?" Simon asked, gesturing toward the
game.

"Yeah, I am." Seeming relieved at the chance to do something
besides talk, Johnny slipped a quarter into the machine and
began to manipulate the toy car skillfully through the treacher-
ous path. He completed the game with a perfect score.

Simon grinned approvingly. "Hell, man, you're a frigging
expert."

"It's easy. You try."

Simon dug for a coin and took his turn, but he sent the vehicle skidding off a mountain road and fell to a fiery death. "Oh,
well," he said with a shrug. "Guess I better stay out of the mountains."

Johnny gave him an uneasy half-smile, then started edging
toward the door.

Simon almost grabbed him by the arm; instead, he spoke
quickly. "I'm hungry. You wanna split a pizza? Oh, by the way,
my name is Simon."

After a pause, Johnny took the proferred hand and shook
tentatively. "John," he whispered.

"So? How about a pizza?"

Johnny checked the time. "Well, I guess it'd be okay."

They walked about half-a-block to a small beer and pizza
joint. It was crowded, but they managed to find a table near the
back. Simon kept getting the feeling that Johnny was about to
vanish, take off like a frightened deer might disappear into the
woods, so he kept his voice calm and made no sudden moves.

Once the beers and pizza were on the table in front of them,
Johnny relaxed a little. Simon pulled a slice of pizza off the tray.
"This is a lonely city, isn't it?" he said. The words surprised him;
he hadn't intended to say that.

Johnny looked blank.

"I mean, if you don't have any friends," Simon added lamely.
The cheese burned his tongue and he took a quick gulp of beer.

Johnny was bent over the table, concentrating on the food. "I
have a friend," he said after taking a bite and swallowing. Then
an anxious look appeared in his eyes, as if he'd said something
wrong, and he took another bite.

"Yeah? That's nice." Simon lifted a piece of pepperoni and ate it slowly, remembering the dangerous face he'd seen in the match glow earlier. Some friend, kid, who keeps you so scared all the time. "I haven't been in L.A. very long," he offered in a moment. "I'm from back east."

Johnny looked up. "New York?"

"I've been there, yeah."

"We used to live in New York." There was an edge of nostalgia in the words.

"Too crowded." Simon poured them each more beer from the pitcher.

"I didn't mind so much," Johnny said thoughtfully. "I liked the ferry boat. We used to ride out to Staten Island and back sometimes. That was fun." He looked even younger suddenly, and Simon wondered, fleetingly, if maybe this was all a mistake. Johnny Griffith was no killer. He was just a nice, shy kid. Then the blond frowned, as if some of his memories weren't so pleasant. "There were some really terrible people there, though."

"What'd they do?"

Johnny only shrugged. He checked the time again. "I better go."

"It's early yet. Want to take in a movie or something?"

But he shook his head. "No, I hafta be there when . . . well, I better go."

They split the check evenly and walked outside. "Maybe we'll run into each other again, John."

"Maybe so," he said, not sounding like he gave a damn. He nodded, shoved both hands into his pockets and walked off quickly.

Simon waited a moment, then followed, keeping out of sight all the way back to the motel. Once there, he sat in the shadows and waited. It was nearly two hours before the BMW pulled into the lot and McCarthy got out.

Simon could tell from the studied care in the man's walk that he was drunk. He dropped the key trying to insert it into the lock, then just pounded on the door instead.

Simon could see Johnny in the doorway, helping McCarthy across the threshold, then bending to pick up the fallen key. The door closed. All he could see then were two dark shadows behind the curtains. After a few more minutes, the light went out.

Simon waited a little longer, then he crept to the window, and tried to see into the room. The only thing visible was the tiny

orange glow of a cigarette. There was some soft-voiced conversation, but he couldn't make out any of the words. What could
they talk about, the hawk-faced assassin and Johnny?

After a few more minutes, he got into his car and left. Instead
of going back to his motel, he drove all the way down to the
beach and parked. Staring out over the moon-washed water, he
thought about the evening. It had been so damned long since
he'd just sat and had a few beers and rapped with somebody.

He pulled his wallet out and flipped it open to the picture of
Mike Conroy. None of the old feelings were left; sometimes he'd
almost forgotten why he was looking for John Paul Griffith.

Now he had Griffith.

"Then what?" said Manny the Wise.

Now what.

He reached into the glove compartment and took out the
envelope with the mugshot in it. What, he wondered again, did
Johnny and McCarthy talk about?

Poor Johnny. How could somebody who was really just an
over-grown kid defend himself against a killer like McCarthy?

Simon stayed on the beach until dawn.

Chapter 4

The shrill, impatient ringing of the phone pulled Mac up from
the heavy, hung-over sleep. He rolled over, reaching for the
offending instrument, and saw Johnny sitting across the room,
fully dressed. "Why'nt you answer the fuckin' thing?" he mumbled, lifting the receiver. "Yeah?"

"Mac?"

"Yeah? So?"

"Be out at the beach. Usual place. One o'clock." The man
hung up.

Mac dropped the phone and closed his eyes again.

"I figured it was business," Johnny said softly. "I don't know
anything about that."

"You know how to say hello, don'tcha?"

"I'm sorry."

"Yeah, yeah, can it. Shit, my head is splitting."

Johnny got up and went into the bathroom, coming back a
moment later with the aspirin bottle and a glass of water.
"Here," he said.

Mac took six of the aspirin and gulped them down at one

time. "Thanks." He lay back to give the pills time to work. "Good thing that bastard called," he said. "I dropped it all last night."

"Run of bad luck, huh?" Johnny asked sympathetically.

Mac laughed, then grimaced as his head pounded in reaction. "Yeah, you could say that. A run of bad luck. That's what they're going to carve on my headstone. Here lies Alexander McCarthy. He had a run of fucking bad luck." He rubbed at his forehead. "Hell, the way I feel, they might be carving it today."

Johnny sat down again. "You shouldn't make jokes about dying," he said sternly.

"I wasn't joking." He sat up suddenly, staring at Johnny. "You ever think about dying, kiddo?"

"No. Not very much."

Mac hated philosophical discussions, especially with Johnny, most particularly when his head was being ripped apart from the inside. Still, maybe it was important that Johnny be forced to look cold, hard reality in the face every once in a while. Besides, he felt so goddamned rotten that it only seemed fair that Johnny should suffer a little, too. "Well, you better think about it," he muttered. "'Cause someday we're gonna get blown away. Or else we'll get busted and sentenced to about seventeen life terms apiece."

Johnny seemed to think about that for a while. He frowned, wiping both palms on his jeans. "They won't put us in different places, will they?" he asked very quietly.

Mac sighed, already regretting that he'd ever gotten into this whole conversation. "No, Johnny," he said with bitter weariness. "I'm sure they'll give us one cozy cell."

"Well, that's okay then." Johnny's voice was placid.

The scary part was that Mac knew Johnny really meant that. After a moment, he rolled off the bed and staggered toward the bathroom. "I gotta go to the beach," he said before closing the door. "If you want, you can come."

"Okay."

Mac showered and shaved, managing to come alive a little in the process. Johnny was staring at some game show on TV, but he turned his head to watch as Mac got dressed. "Mac?" he said in a dreamy voice.

He pulled his jeans up and snapped them. "Huh?"

"If I get blown away, will you be okay?"

Mac pulled his teeshirt on with a sudden jerk and stared at Johnny's reflection in the mirror. "What?"

"I said, if I get—"

"I *heard* what you said," Mac broke in. "I'm just trying to figure out what the hell you're talking about."

Johnny's face was solemn. "I was just thinking, is all."

Mac swore under his breath and started combing his hair. "Look, man, I told you years ago to leave the thinking to me. By any chance do you remember that?"

Johnny nodded. "Yeah, I remember."

"All right then. Do it. Okay?"

In a minute, he nodded again. "Okay, Mac." A grin split his face. "Could I swim while we're at the beach?"

"Sure. Let's go now, so you'll have plenty of time."

Johnny pulled his swimming trunks on, then donned his jeans again, and they were ready to go. On the way out of town, Mac stopped at a drive-in for some coffee to drink en route. Johnny had a large orangeade.

His head felt slightly more normal by the time they'd reached the beach, parked, and walked down to the water's edge. He sat cross-legged on the sand, watching idly as Johnny went to swim. What they had to do, he decided, was just get a fucking little ahead, and clear out. Maybe go to Mexico and forget all this ever happened. This life was rotten. Just a goddamned little ahead, that was all.

Johnny was a good swimmer, and he especially liked it when the breakers crashed over him, submerging him completely. Everytime it happened, Mac—who disliked water in large bodies—watched apprehensively, not even aware that he was holding his breath, until the drenched blond head appeared again, glistening golden under the sun.

At last Johnny apparently had enough. He jogged across the sand and dropped down next to Mac. "Have fun?" Mac asked, lifting his sunglasses to look at him.

"Yeah, felt good." He shook his head vigorously and drops of water hit against Mac. "I'm hungry."

"You're always hungry." Mac glanced at his watch. "I gotta meet a guy. I'll bring you back an ice cream."

"Okay. Chocolate, please." Johnny stretched out on the sand, using one arm to shade his face.

Mac got to his feet, then stood still for a moment, staring down at Johnny. "See you."

Johnny smiled, but didn't say anything.

The man was standing by the boardwalk rail, reading a newspaper, which he folded when Mac appeared. "Hello, Mac. It's been a long time."

"A year," Mac replied.

"You're looking good."

Mac leaned against the rail and stared out across the crowded beach, trying to spot Johnny. He couldn't. "You have the envelope?"

"I have it, I have it. You're always in such a hurry."

"Time is money," he said absently.

"A man should never be too busy for the amenities. How is John?"

"John is fine."

"Good, good." The man took a manila envelope from his pocket. "All the usual information is in here."

Mac put the envelope away without looking at it. "And the usual money, of course?"

"Of course."

"All right." He turned to go.

"What's the rush?"

Mac paused. "John wants an ice cream."

He smiled. "Oh, well, by all means, you must go. Immediately. We want to keep John happy, don't we?"

Without answering, Mac walked away.

They both stayed in that night. Johnny stretched out on his bed watching "Charlie's Angels" and "Vegas", as Mac studied the data on their target. It was late by the time he finished. The "Tonight Show" was on, with one guest host or another, but Johnny, his face a little red from the sun at the beach, had fallen asleep. Mac undressed slowly, turned off the TV, and got into bed.

He smoked two cigarettes, but still couldn't fall asleep. At last, he got up and crawled into bed with Johnny. Sometimes, when his own demons seemed a little too close for comfort, sharing the night helped.

Tonight, though, some vague thought kept nagging at his mind. He tossed and turned until Johnny finally stirred. "What's wrong?" he mumbled.

"Nothing. Sorry I woke you." He wasn't really sorry; he was glad for the company.

"That's okay."

Mac rolled over so that he could look into the face shadowed in the half-light. "Johnny?"

The blue eyes fluttered open again. "Hmm?"

"We're gonna get out of this. Soon. Before anything bad happens. Okay?"

"Okay, Mac."

"Don't be scared."

Johnny looked at him for a long moment, then smiled a little. "Don't you be scared either, Mac."

"Okay."

Johnny rested against the pillow. "Good night," he said.

"Night, babe," Mac replied.

The blond was asleep in moments. Mac sighed, resisting the urge to light another cigarette. Instead, he closed his eyes and tried to force himself to sleep. One hand absently stroked Johnny's bare arm.

Johnny made a soft sound and sighed in his sleep.

"Shh," Mac said, his lips pressed against soft blond strands.

It was a long time before he fell asleep.

Chapter 5

The next night he followed Johnny again, approaching him outside a theatre. Johnny returned his greeting with a hesitant smile. "Hi, Simon," he said, speaking in that soft voice that was so difficult to hear over the city noises.

Simon gestured toward the marquee. "Gonna see the movie?"

Johnny shook his head. "I thought they'd be changing the bill today, but it's still the same old thing."

"Well, then, how about grabbing a beer?"

After the usual hesitation, Johnny agreed.

The bar they chose wasn't too crowded this early in the evening, so they got a booth near the front. Simon waited until the beers were served. "How much longer you gonna be around town?" he asked suddenly.

The tactic worked. Caught off-guard by the abrupt question, Johnny shrugged. "Couple days, I guess. Depends."

Simon realized that the hit must be getting close; his nights were spent following Johnny, but his days were spent on McCarthy's trail. He knew who was going to be hit and he had a pretty good idea of when. "You travel a lot, huh?"

"Uh-huh." Johnny began to doodle in the wet patches on the

table. "How come they don't have very many westerns anymore, I wonder," he said.

Simon took a sip of beer. "Guess not enough people like them." He glanced around, trying to come up with another line of conversation. "You play pool?" he asked, spotting a table in the back.

"No." Johnny looked up, brightening. "I like darts, though. One time I won thirty dollars playing darts."

"Well, I'm not that good, but how about a game?"

Carrying their beers along, they went into the back room. Johnny took first turn, aiming and throwing with a concentration that was total. Each shot was better than the last. Simon shrugged, grinning. "Hell, I might as well quit now."

"No, it's easy," Johnny urged. "Just pretend like you're aiming a gun."

Simon looked at him sharply, but the blue eyes were guileless as a child's.

They played for nearly an hour, betting pennies, until Johnny had accumulated almost two dollars' worth. He gathered his winnings with the air of a man who watched his money carefully. Simon wondered about that. Hell, he and his pal were damned good, and they made damned good money for what they did. How come they lived like paupers? Of course, Mac was a gambler, and not too lucky. He also drove around in a fancy car. But what the hell did Johnny do with his share of their earnings? He had no car, no bad habits as far as Simon could see, and he dressed in old blue jeans and tennis shoes. Where did his money go?

That, of course, was a question Simon couldn't ask.

They ordered a couple more beers and found seats again. Simon was trying to sort out and understand his confused emotions. The man sitting across from him was a killer. A cold-blooded assassin in a T-shirt which read "Niagara Falls." Conroy was dead because of him. Simon tried to remember Mike's face, but the image was too blurry. The only face he saw was John Griffith's. With the hesitant, soft voice; the blue eyes, foggy and unfocused even behind the glasses; his painful shyness, Griffith was not at all what Simon had expected to find. Had wanted to find.

"What then?" Manny had asked.

Simon still didn't know. He resisted the urge to run to the nearest telephone and call Manny.

Johnny seemed to realize that he was being watched, and he

raised his eyes. Their gazes met, locked, held for a full minute, before Simon looked away. The blue gaze was empty.

Mac spent about twenty minutes talking to her in the bar, then they left there and went to her place. Her name was Joanie, and she worked as a file clerk in a downtown office, and she was from Kansas originally. He drank a can of beer from her meager stock, watching as she undressed and released the aureate hair from its rubber band, to fall in soft locks over her shoulders. Her clothes were carefully folded and stacked on a chair. No wonder she was a file clerk. Her glasses were set to one side and her blue eyes studied him thoughtfully.

He got up, setting the beer can aside, and undressed.

"You don't say much, do you?"

He shrugged.

She gave up then, waiting silently as he finished the beer before getting into bed. He began to stroke her body, her face, tangling his fingers in her hair. She was moving beneath his touch, making soft gasping sounds as the fervor of his stroking increased.

His mind left her, left the crummy room, left even the more fevered movements of his own body. He began to think about the hit. Sunday morning, best time. Early, before seven. Then he and Johnny could be out of town early. Maybe they would go to Frisco. Or Vegas. If he could take the cash from this job and run it up a ways, they could quit. Say good-bye to the whole fucking world. Find a beach in Mexico and drink margaritas in the sun. The image filled his mind like a picture postcard. The sun, the peace. Johnny could swim all he wanted to in the perfect blue of the water.

Blue. Her blue eyes stared up at him, into his own gaze, and she probably thought they were communicating on some deep level.

Johnny's eyes were blue.

He loved swimming and he was good at it, his slender form cutting gracefully through the water, golden under the sun.

Mac was in her now, thrusting, bracing himself against the bed. He began to build, gasping a little with each forward push, building, building. Sweat poured down his face, and he closed his eyes against it.

She arched upwards toward him, her soft sounds growing louder.

As he exploded inside her writhing body, he opened his eyes, staring down into her face, with its two vague pools and tousled blonde hair. A chill stabbed through him, because all at once it wasn't her, this nameless broad, he was screwing.

It was Johnny.

His body finished its convulsive spasms, and he threw himself from her, huddling on the far side of the bed, staring blindly at the ceiling.

"Jesus," she sighed. "That was good."

Caught up in his own swirling thoughts, he didn't answer. Johnny. No. It was just some crazy dream. Christ, he didn't want to . . . to do that with Johnny. Not *Johnny.*

She rolled toward him, giving his still-heaving chest little kisses.

He ignored her.

Think, he ordered himself. It's just nerves. The hit coming down. Johnny's dumb conversation the day before about getting iced. Yeah, that was it. Nerves. Shit, that had to be it. *Johnny,* for chrissake. Hell, the guy had never been to bed with anybody. He was like a kid when it came to sex.

And I never wanted to do that with a guy, Mac thought. Never.

She was talking to him, but he couldn't seem to understand what she was saying. Hell, he decided, enough of this bitch. I gotta get home. A pizza, he thought as, still silent, he got out of bed and started dressing. I'll find Johnny, he never wanders too far, and we'll get a pizza. Take it home and watch one of those damned old movies on TV. Johnny would like that. And once he saw the kid, the dream image would vanish. Everything would be all right again.

"Maybe we'll see each other again," she—what the hell was her name?—said hopefully.

He looked at her blankly, already unsure of what role she had played in his life. "Yeah," he mumbled.

He drove back to the motel first, but Johnny wasn't there. That didn't surprise him much; he knew Johnny's habits well. Leaving the car, he began to walk. Johnny would be surprised to see him. It would be enough to make him grin, probably. Poor dumb Johnny. Offer him a frigging pizza and some company and, Christ, you'd think the guy had just drawn a royal flush.

Mac shook his head, smiling a little. Never would be able to understand that kid.

He read the posters outside a couple of movies, but knew that

Johnny wouldn't be interested in seeing the pictures advertised. Continuing his search, he tried the penny arcade and a couple of fast food joints. It was in a small, crowded bar that he finally saw Johnny. The blond head was like a beacon in the dimly lighted room, and Mac started over, figuring to have a beer here before getting the pizza.

It was then that he spotted the other guy, a slender, sharp-eyed man with a mass of dark curls falling into his face. The man was talking, smiling, gesturing. Johnny was listening, nodding. Almost smiling.

Mac felt a stabbing pain go through him. Johnny didn't see him standing there and he turned and walked out quickly. As he walked back to the motel, he shoved the pain aside, not understanding the hurt he felt, letting anger creep in to take its place. What the hell did that stupid son of a bitch think he was doing? He was so damned stupid that if he started talking, he might say something that could get them both busted or killed. Well, that was fine if he wanted to screw up his own life, that was fine, but the son of a bitch wasn't going to do it to him. No way.

Talking to some bastard in a bar. Jesus. The guy might be a cop, for all Johnny knew. Or a pervert of some kind. Serve Johnny right if something happened to him.

By the time he got back to the motel, Mac could feel the knot of tension in his gut. It hurt like hell. He dug a bottle of whiskey from his suitcase and sat in the dark room, smoking, drinking, staring at the door.

Chapter 6

Johnny saw the car in the parking lot and quickened his step. Mac was home. His mood lifted; the loneliness vanished instantly. He opened the door and turned on the light, feeling his happiness become a smile. "Hi, Mac," he said.

Mac lifted an almost empty bottle and took a long drink, flicking a cigarette butt into the wastebasket. He didn't say anything at all. He only looked at Johnny with eyes that were two chips of green ice.

Johnny's smile lost a little of its brightness. "You came back so early. I'm really glad. There's a Cagney movie on. Will you watch it with me?"

Mac stared at him. Stared through him. "What the hell do

you think you're doing?" His voice was like ice water rolling over Johnny.

Johnny took off his jacket and tossed it aside. "I don't understand, Mac," he said very softly.

"Don't you? Don't you understand?" Mac's voice rose.

Johnny sank down onto the bed in front of Mac. "Are you mad at me? Did I do something wrong, Mac? Because if I did, I'm sorry—"

Mac hit him. The open-handed slap across the face was so unexpected that it knocked Johnny half off the bed. Slowly he pushed himself back up to a sitting position. "Please, Mac," he whispered. "I'm sorry."

"Yeah? Yeah?" Mac grabbed him by both shoulders. "Don't look at me like that, you bastard, you idiot, you—"

"Mac?" Johnny tried to escape from the vise-like grip, but Mac dragged him back and hit him several more times across the face, knocking his glasses off. Johnny was crying now, making no effort to defend himself.

"I saw you talking to that bastard. Who is he?" Each word was punctuated by a slap.

"Just Simon."

"Who is he?"

"Just a guy, Mac. Just somebody I talk to. He hangs around, like me." Johnny tried to grab Mac's hand. "Please don't hit me again. I didn't do anything wrong. I never said a word I shouldn't. Don't be mad."

"How do you know what you said?" Mac formed a fist and it collided with Johnny's gut. Johnny bent over with a retching gasp. "You're so stupid you don't even know what you're saying half the time." He hit Johnny again.

"Mac, I'm sorry, I'm sorry, so sorry, please don't be mad at me." Blood gushed from his nose and ran down into his mouth.

"You want to get us killed or busted?"

Johnny shook his head. "No, no," he moaned helplessly, blood and tears mingling on his face.

"Or maybe the guy is some kind of freako; did you ever think about that?"

"I don't understand."

"No? Don't you? Jesus, how can anybody be so damned stupid? How come I put up with you all these years? He could be some kind of sex creep. Maybe he wants to fuck you. Would you like that?" Mac stopped, breathing heavily. Something terrible passed through his eyes, something that Johnny couldn't understand. "Or maybe he already has. What have you been doing, creep? Huh?" He hit Johnny across the face again.

"No, please, no, Mac. . . ." Johnny felt an utter black terror filling him, a fear so overwhelming that it even obliterated the physical pain of the attack. He trembled uncontrollably, reaching out with both hands, trying desperately to grab onto Mac. He wasn't trying to escape from the beating; he only wanted to hold onto Mac and make this nightmare end. "Oh, please," he said in a hoarse whisper. "Oh, please."

Suddenly, Mac froze. His face lost all its color as he stared down at Johnny's huddled, bloody body. *"Ohchrist,"* he said. "Oh sweet Jesus." He crouched down and again his hand reached toward Johnny's face. This time, he only touched one cheek, a fleeting caress. Then he stood and left the room, slamming the door as he went.

Johnny crawled across the floor toward the door. "Mac," he whispered brokenly. "Mac, please, don't go . . . I'm sorry . . . Mac . . ." But the door stayed closed. Johnny leaned against it, crying silently.

It was nearly dawn before Johnny finally dragged himself up from the floor. Moving like an automaton, he changed from his bloodied clothes, putting on a pale blue T-shirt that was too big, meaning it must have been Mac's, and some clean Levis. He washed his face and combed his hair, then grabbed his jacket and left the room.

He noted dully that the car was gone.

Mac was gone.

Johnny had no plan, no idea beyond that of finding Mac, of making him know how sorry he was for being bad, of having Mac come back. He had to come back, of course. There was no other way.

He walked for hours, all day, not stopping to eat or drink or rest his aching legs, covering the area, looking anywhere he thought Mac might be.

It was almost dark when he finally started back toward the motel. A block away, he nearly bumped into Simon.

Simon stared at him, a strange light flickering through his eyes. "What the hell happened to you?"

Johnny realized for the first time that his face was swollen and sore. "Nothing," he mumbled, trying to step around Simon.

Simon grabbed his arm, then released it immediately when

Johnny flinched in a new spasm of fear. "Johnny, who hit you? Was it Mac?"

Johnny forgot that Simon wasn't supposed to know, couldn't possibly know about Mac. He just shook his head. "I can't talk to you. Go away and don't come around me anymore. Please." He spoke desperately. "Please." He started to walk again. "Just leave me alone so I can find Mac."

"He can't do that to you," Simon yelled after him. "You shouldn't let that son of a bitch treat you this way."

Johnny ignored him. The blue car was parked in its usual spot and he stopped by it, resting a hand on the hood, and drawing several deep breaths.

The door was unlocked and Johnny walked in.

Mac, shirtless and barefooted, was sitting on the bed. He raised his head slowly, looking at Johnny with reddened eyes. Neither of them spoke for a long moment. Johnny took a hesitant step toward him. "I'm sorry, Mac," he said softly.

Mac shook his head. "Don't," he said. "You didn't do anything. It was me. I know you never said a word to that guy about the business. I know nothing else happened." He lowered his gaze and stared at his hands; both palms turned upwards helplessly. "All you did was talk to him. It doesn't matter."

Johnny sat down next to him. "You ran out on me. I was scared."

Mac sighed. "I won't do it again."

"But I was scared."

After a moment, Mac lifted one arm and pulled Johnny into a loose embrace. "I'm so goddamned sorry, babe. It won't happen again, I swear."

Johnny nodded, accepting that. "Thank you."

Still holding him, Mac lay back on the bed. "God, I'm tired," he said heavily.

"Me, too." Johnny was quiet for a time. "Mac?" he said finally. "Hmm?"

"Nobody ever did . . . what you were talking about."

"I know."

"Why did you say it, then?"

"Oh, shit, Johnny. I was mad. When I get mad and drunk, I don't know what the hell I'm saying." Now Mac was quiet, one hand rubbing across Johnny's back in long strokes. "Can I tell you something, kid?"

Johnny nodded.

"It's kinda weird." Mac seemed to think before speaking

again. "I was with this broad last night, you know, screwing her."

"Yeah?" Johnny's voice was soft.

"But then I looked at her and . . . it wasn't her I saw."

Johnny raised his head and looked down into Mac's face. "Who was it, Mac?"

Mac swallowed twice. "You."

"Me?" Johnny bit his lower lip. Then he shrugged and rested back on the bed again, his head on Mac's shoulder. "That's funny," he said.

Mac seemed to be waiting for him to say something else.

Johnny sighed. "Can we go to sleep now, Mac? I'm so tired."

"Sure, kid. Go to sleep."

Johnny smiled faintly and closed his eyes.

Mac stared at the ceiling, aware of Johnny's weight pressed against his side, trying not to look at the bruised and battered face. There was so much to think about and so much of it was scary. He wanted to forget what he'd done, forget his despair during the last hours sitting here waiting for the kid to come back. Wondering if he *would* come back. That was a dumb thing to worry about. Shit, he could beat Johnny regularly, and still the guy wouldn't leave.

Poor Johnny.

Poor me, he thought.

But there wasn't anything he could do for either one of them. So he reached one hand to turn off the lamp and then he fell asleep.

He stood outside the window, waiting until the light went off. Driving back to his motel, he stopped at a red light. When the hooker approached, Simon gestured her into the car. They parked in an alley. There was only one thing she could do in the front seat of a VW, so she did it and he paid her twenty bucks.

Then he went to his room and went to sleep.

Chapter 7

He made one more preliminary visit to Frost's apartment building, fixing it all firmly in his mind so that he could tell Johnny every detail. On the way back to the motel, he stopped and picked up a pizza for supper.

Johnny was watching a Randolph Scott movie on the television, but he sat up with a smile when Mac came in. "Hi."

"Hi, yourself," Mac replied, putting the pizza box down next to him. "Haven't you seen that before?"

"Yeah, but it's not too bad."

Mac took off his jacket and opened a couple of beers, then sat down with him. "You want to go see a movie after we eat?"

"Don't you have a game or someplace to go?"

"Nope, not tonight. We have to make an early start in the morning."

"Oh." Johnny was paying more attention to the food than to him.

Mac thrust a hand-drawn map in front of him. "You study this."

"Yeah, okay, soon as the movie's over."

He dropped the paper. They finished eating just as the news came on. Johnny had no interest in that, so he turned the volume all the way down, leaving just the flickering picture. "I don't want to go anywhere," he said. "Can we just stay here?"

Mac shrugged. "Sure, if you want."

Johnny leaned back against the wall, studying the map. Mac watched him, looking at the still-visible traces of the beating. He sighed wearily, and Johnny lifted his head. "What's wrong?"

"Nothing. I'm just tired."

"Why don't you go to bed?" Johnny always had a logical solution for every problem.

"It's not that kind of tired, kid." He leaned forward a little, trying to ease the tension in his neck. "I've got this worn-out feeling that goes all the way through me. Don't you ever get tired of this whole mess?"

"Mess?"

"This life we lead. If you can call it a life."

"Oh." Johnny seemed to consider the question briefly, then shook his head. "I don't mind very much, Mac."

Mac wanted, suddenly, to make him understand just how rotten it all was. "Johnny, I've screwed us up so good. There's no way out. We're trapped and there can't be any happy ending. Not for us."

Johnny set the map aside and folded his arms, like a man fighting off a chill. "Don't talk about things like that, please. It scares me."

"It should. You ought to be damned scared. And it's all my fault." He got up abruptly and walked over to the window.

"Christ, you should have put a bullet into *my* head years ago. We'd both be better off."

"I love you, Mac," Johnny said.

Mac was watching the cars go by out front and he only half-heard the soft words. "What?"

"I love you," Johnny said again.

This time the words reached him. Love? Mac wanted to laugh at the pathetic declaration. What the hell do you know about love, he thought. Shit, you're like a baby who can't tell where he begins and his mother leaves off. You don't know what love is. You only need me.

He turned around, wanting to say all that, and found himself staring into Johnny's face, into the absurdly blue eyes shining behind the glasses. But, he thought, if you don't love me, nobody does. All these years. He lifted his hand and ran two fingers through tousled blond hair. "I love you, too, kid," he said finally. "Very much."

"I know."

"Do you?" His fingers tightened in the soft strands. "Ahh, Johnny," he said. "I tried, you know? I wanted everything to be okay for us."

"It is okay, Mac, really."

Mac grimaced and turned toward the window again. "Why do you like to sleep with me, Johnny?" he asked quietly.

Johnny was a moment answering. "Because it feels good," he said.

Mac gave a bitter laugh. "Yeah, it does that," he agreed. "Sometimes it feels too damned good."

"I don't understand."

"Don't you?" Mac looked at him. "Let me tell you a secret, baby. I don't understand either."

"Does it matter a whole lot?"

Mac was surprised by the question; he thought about it, then shrugged. "Doesn't matter a goddamned bit," he said. "If it ever starts to matter, then we might have a problem." He rubbed the back of his neck. "Go to bed, kiddo. We have to get up early."

He watched as Johnny undressed and slid between the sheets, then he turned off the television and the lights. Sitting on the edge of the bed, Mac lit a cigarette. He sat there for a long time, smoking and watching Johnny sleep.

Chapter 8

He woke up slowly, knowing that he had to move, but putting it off until the last possible moment. Johnny was sprawled next to him, still sleeping soundly. At last, Mac slid from the bed and began to dress. He put on grey slacks, a green knit shirt, the familiar battered windbreaker, and tucked the .45 into his pocket. "Johnny," he said, as he stood in front of the mirror to comb his hair.

Johnny stirred, then sat up quickly. "Huh?"

"Rise and shine, kiddo."

"Oh, yeah, right."

As Johnny washed and dressed, Mac packed all their belongings, so they wouldn't have to come back afterwards. He was tired of this room, this city, and only wanted to leave it behind as quickly as possible. He lit a cigarette and leaned against the door as Johnny donned the holster and pulled his jacket on.

Johnny turned with a smile. "I'm ready."

Mac nodded. They each carried a suitcase to the car. "You want to get some breakfast?"

Johnny thought about it, then shook his head. "After, I guess. Could use a Coke."

Mac drove through the parking lot, stopping at the office to pay their bill. On the way back to the car, he got a Coke from the soda machine.

"Thanks," Johnny said, taking the can from him. He slumped in the seat, his legs propped against the dash, and drank thoughtfully.

"You okay?" Mac asked.

"Uh-huh."

"Want to go to Vegas after?"

"Fine. Whatever you want."

"Well, I thought we might. I figured if we could double the money from this job, we could go to Mexico. Nobody would bother us there. You could swim, whatever. How does that sound?"

"Okay. Whatever you want."

Mac sighed. "What do *you* want, kid? Why does it always have to be my decision? Don't you have an opinion?"

Johnny glanced at him. "Sure, I have an opinion."

"Terrific. What is it?"

"I want to do whatever you want. That's my opinion."

Mac looked at him for an instant before turning his eyes back to the road. "Johnny, you're crazy."

"Yeah, I guess I am."

The car turned and went into the alley behind the apartment building. Mac stopped and shifted in the seat so that he was looking at Johnny. "I was kidding," he said. "You're not crazy."

Johnny shrugged. "I don't guess it matters very much one way or the other, does it?"

Mac reached out a hand and touched Johnny's arm. "You mad at me?"

A brilliant smile crossed Johnny's face. "Of course not. I never get mad at you."

"I don't know why the hell not."

He shrugged again. "Because."

Mac snorted. "A great reason."

"Maybe it's because I'm crazy."

It took him a moment to realize that Johnny was kidding. "Shit," he said. "Get your ass out of here. Be careful."

"Sure." Johnny got out of the car and walked up the path. It took him a little longer than usual to open the door, but then he gave the familiar V-for-Victory sign and disappeared inside.

It was exactly one minute later by the clock on the dash that Mac heard the shots. For one frozen, terrible instant, he sat still. It was the first time he'd ever heard the sound of gunfire at one of their jobs, and the echoing roars paralyzed him.

At last he moved, throwing his body out of the car and running toward the building, pulling the gun from his pocket as he ran. "Johnny!" His cry rang through the quiet morning air.

He burst into the hall and ran around the corner. The door to Frost's apartment was marked by several bullet holes. He had time to notice only that one fact before the door was flung open. Frost stood there, a small machine gun in his hands. Bullets began to spray the hallway.

Mac felt the lumps of hot metal crash against his body. He fell to his knees, dropping the gun. "Johnny?" he said again, this time in a whisper.

From behind him, someone fired a single shot, and Frost crashed to the floor.

Mac tried to crawl, but his body wouldn't do what he wanted it to. "Johnny?" he said through pain-filled gasps. "Babe, where are you?" He couldn't move.

A face appeared above him, vaguely familiar. It was the man he'd seen Johnny talking to in the bar. Simon. They looked at one another for a long moment. Mac kept watching as Simon picked up his fallen gun and left another in its place. "Hey," he managed to say, feeling the blood trail from his mouth. "Johnny?"

"Yeah," the guy said. "I know. He'll be okay."

Mac tried to shake his head. This guy didn't understand. Johnny needed him. But before he could try to explain all of that, he felt a sudden absence of pain, and a grey curtain began to descend slowly over his consciousness. I'm dying, he thought, surprised to realize that the knowledge saddened him. "I'm sorry, baby," he said in a loud, clear voice. Oh, damnit, he thought. This is so fucking stupid.

Simon closed McCarthy's eyes gently. He sat there numbly, only half aware of the screams coming from inside another apartment. His plan, such as it had been, went no further, and he didn't know what to do next.

The door to the garage suddenly jerked open with a crash. A primeval roar of naked pain filled the hall. Johnny, blood streaming from the cut on his head where Simon had hit him minutes before, half-crawled and half-ran to the body. "Mac?"

He threw himself across the bloody form. "Mac? Mac? Don't be dead, please, I'm sorry, I'm sorry, it's all my fault. Please, open your eyes, Mac. I love you, please don't be dead, please, Mac, pleaseplease. . . ." His words dwindled off, becoming soft, unintelligible moans, as his hands kept up their frantic stroking of the dead man's face.

Simon could hear the squeal of sirens in the distance. "Come on, Johnny," he said urgently. "We have to go. Come on." He took Johnny's arm with one hand, while his other reached in and took the wallet from Mac's pocket. He pulled on Johnny, but the crying man didn't move. Simon got impatient. "Come on," he said, jerking Johnny away, dragging him across the floor toward the garage.

"Mac? Mac?" Johnny kept up the whimpering pleas all the way to the car. Simon opened the passenger door and shoved him in. He ran around to the driver's side and jumped behind the wheel. They pulled out of the garage and drove around the corner just ahead of the first squad car.

He didn't relax until they were well away, heading toward the freeway, then he eased up on the accelerator. Johnny sat huddled against the door, still crying. He cried like a child, in long helpless sobs, making no effort to wipe the tears or his running nose. "It's okay," Simon muttered. "You don't have to be scared anymore. It's all over now, Johnny."

Johnny didn't say anything.

After another couple of minutes, Simon pulled the car over to the shoulder and stopped. He reached into the glove compartment for some tissues. "Here," he said.

The only response was a blank stare from red, tear-filled eyes.

Simon used the tissues to wipe Johnny's eyes and nose. "Now stop it," he said sharply, as if to a misbehaving child. "This isn't going to help. He's dead. That's all. Now stop it."

He didn't even know if Johnny heard him. The tissues went into a wadded heap on the floor and Simon started the car again.

They drove for a long time, stopping only once for gas and food. Johnny wouldn't eat, just stared at the hamburger until Simon, angry and frustrated, tore the sandwich into small pieces and fed them to him one by one. "Say something, Johnny, willya? You don't have to be afraid anymore."

He suddenly remembered something the cop in New York had told him, about Johnny's mute act the time he got busted. Well, Mac wasn't going to show up this time, so Johnny would just have to snap out of it on his own.

Simon squeezed Johnny's shoulder and shook him a little. "I did it for you," he said. "Don't you understand?"

Johnny only looked at him.

After vaguely heading south, Simon finally stopped at a motel very near the Mexican border. Johnny sat in the car while he registered, paying in advance with some of the cash from Mc-Carthy's wallet.

The room was small and not too clean, but it didn't matter. Johnny sat on one of the beds, both hands folded in his lap, his face blank. Simon sat on the other bed, watching him. "We'll go to Mexico," he said finally. "Stay there a while, just in case anybody's on our tail. I don't think they are, though." He waited a moment, but there was no response, so he stood. "I'll go get some food. You wait here. Understand, Johnny? Stay here."

He paused long enough to turn on the television. An old rerun of "I Love Lucy" was on, and Simon saw that Johnny's eyes shifted to the screen, although his face remained blank.

* * *

The rest of the day and evening passed slowly. They ate in the room and watched television, all in silence, except for Simon's occasional remarks. The late news came on, and Johnny sat impassively through the lead story of the double-murder in L.A. Even when an old army photo of Alexander McCarthy was flashed on the screen, Johnny did not react.

Simon walked over and turned the TV off. "We better get some sleep."

Johnny stood and began pulling off his bloody clothes.

Simon waited until the blond was between the sheets before undressing and crawling into the other bed. Once there, he rather surprised himself by falling asleep.

He didn't know how long he'd slept or exactly what woke him, but he was jerked into complete wakefulness immediately. Moonlight streamed into the room through the window. Johnny was standing in the middle of the room, his face still empty of emotion, his gun pointed at Simon's head. Simon felt his gut tighten, but his voice was cool when he spoke. "What the fuck are you doing, Johnny?" he asked mildly. There was no answer and the gun never wavered. "You're going to kill me, is that it? Gonna blow my head off, boy? Well, you just go right ahead. What the hell; my life ain't worth shit anyway. Not anymore." He stared into the pools of blue vagueness shining in the white moonglow. "But, Johnny," he went on tenderly, "if you kill me, what happens next? You'll be all by yourself. Do you want to be all alone, Johnny? Mac is dead. If you blow my head off, who's gonna take care of you? Being with me is better than being alone, right?"

It was two full minutes before the gun slowly lowered and then dropped to the floor. Johnny stood there, hands at his sides helplessly. Another minute passed before he spoke, the faint whisper so soft that Simon could barely hear him, even in the middle-of-the-night quiet. "We didn't bring my clothes," he said. "You'll have to buy me new clothes, because those are all dirty and I can't wear them anymore."

"In the morning, Johnny."

"Blue is my favorite color."

"Okay."

Johnny took a deep breath. "Can I get into bed with you?"

Simon stared at him. "What?"

"I don't like to sleep by myself." His voice shook a little and he stopped, rubbing his eyes with the heel of one hand. "Mac always let me."

After a moment, Simon nodded. "Okay," he said. He scooted over as far as he could in the narrow bed.

Johnny stretched out, not touching him, and they both stayed very still for a long time.

"Johnny?"

He turned his head and looked at Simon, but didn't say anything.

"Were you and Mac getting it on?"

"I don't understand," Johnny murmured vaguely.

Simon opened his mouth to explain, then only shrugged. "Never mind, kid. It doesn't matter."

Johnny turned over, so that his back was to Simon. In only a few minutes, his breathing had taken on the even rhythm of sleep. Simon reached across him for cigarettes and matches. Lighting one, he lay back and stared at the ceiling.

He was tired.

Epilogue

The Mexican sun was hot.

Simon lifted the can of beer and took a long drink. "I could maybe get a job with a security firm or something," he said thoughtfully. "What do you think?"

There was no answer from Johnny. Tanned and burnished gold from their long days on the beach, he was busy reading an old copy of *TV Guide* that some previous American tourist had left in the hotel room. He didn't even look up when Simon spoke.

Another gulp of beer. "We just have to decide where we want to go. East somewheres, I guess, huh?"

Loneliness, Simon had decided during the past three weeks, was sitting in a hotel room with John Griffith.

It was getting hotter as the sun moved toward its midday peak. Simon finished the beer in a gulp. "We better go in for awhile," he said. "I don't especially feel like getting heatstroke."

Obediently, Johnny closed the magazine and got to his feet. He carefully brushed the sand from his blue jeans.

"Chicago, maybe," Simon continued. "Let's think about Chicago, huh?" When Johnny didn't even look at him, Simon felt his fingers clench into a tight fist. "Goddamnit," he said suddenly, "goddamnit, Johnny. Can't you ease up just a little? Everybody else is gone. My partner. My wife and kid. They're all gone. Mac is gone. We can't bring any of them back, kid. It's just you and me now. Doesn't that make us even?" He kept both hands at his sides, wanting to reach out and grab Johnny and shake him until there was some kind of a response. He sighed. "There aren't any good guys in this story, Johnny. There's just one dumb Jew ex-cop and one spaced-out TV junkie." He almost wanted to laugh; it was so fucking stupid.

Johnny glanced at him. "Can I get an orange juice?" he asked.

Simon flexed his fingers. "Yeah, kid, sure."

"Thank you," Johnny replied politely.

Simon kicked at the sand. "Sure." He shoved both hands into the pockets of his khaki slacks and started toward the hotel. Johnny followed, humming some private melody. Simon thought that if this damned lonely feeling inside his gut didn't disappear he would lose his mind. He stopped walking. "Hey, Johnny, you want to see what's on at the movie tonight?" The hotel ran English language films once a week for the tourists. "How's that sound? We'll eat dinner someplace, then go to the movie. Maybe it'll be a western. What about it?"

"Okay, Simon," Johnny said. "Whatever you want." He ducked his head, watching as his feet moved through the sand.

Simon tilted his head back, staring up into the flawless blue sky. He knew exactly what the rest of the day would bring. They'd go into the hotel bar. Johnny would get a large orange juice and punch up that damned Nat King Cole song on the jukebox. He always played the same song, time after time, until Simon sometimes woke up humming "Mona Lisa." He'd spend the whole afternoon there with Johnny, drinking lousy cheap beer and waiting. He wasn't even sure what it was he kept waiting for. Maybe it was just for real life to begin again.

He sighed once more and started walking again, following Johnny across the beach.

The Luckiest Man in the World

by Rex Miller

Rex Miller writes about a 500-pound serial killer named Chaingang. For starters, that is. Miller's landscape fuses grand opera and traditional film noir *. . . Thomas Harris as filmed by Francis Ford Coppola. What gets overlooked in all the clamor is how good Rex is at everyday emotions and fears. He's a real writer.*

First published in 1989.

"Zulu Six, Zulu Six." He could imagine the PRC crackling, the bored tone of somebody's RTO going, "Dragon says he's got movement about fifty meters to his Sierra Whisky, do you read me? Over." And the spit of intercom garble. Guy in the C & C bird keying a handset, saying whatever he says. Fucking lifer somewhere up there generations removed from the bad bush. Yeah, I copy you, Lumpy Charlie, Lima Charlie, Lumpy Chicken. Whatever he says. Bird coming down. Charlie moving at the edge of the woods. Thua Thien Province. Northern Whore Corps. The beast killing for peace, back then. Dirty-Dozened out of the slammer by military puppeteers. Set in place by the spooks. Very real, however.

"Chaingang" his nickname. The fattest killer in the Nam. Thriving on blast-furnace heat like some fucking plant. He was the beast. He had killed more than any other living being. Over four hundred humans, he thought. A waddling death machine. "Gangbang" they would call him out of earshot. "Hippo." He had heard them. Other names he ignored. These arrogant children who knew nothing about death.

He flashed on the woods, so similar to these, and to a pleasant memory from long ago. He was about two miles from the house.

"There goes Bobby Ray," the woman called to her husband, who was bringing logs in, and watched a truck throw gravel.

"Nnn," he grunted in the manner of someone who had been married a long time.

"He's another one don't have anything to do but run the road all day."

The husband said nothing, loading kindling.

"Drive up and down, up and down, drive a daggone pickup like he was a millionaire." She had a shrewish, sharp voice that grated on a man, he thought. He put a large log down in the hot stove.

"Now you gonna' run to town to pick up that daggone tractor thing an' you coulda' got it yesterday when you was in there at Harold's, but *noooooo.*" She was a pain in the ass. *"You* couldn't be bothered." She was working herself up the way she always liked to do, he thought. He knew the old bitch like a damn book. "You waste a fortune on gas for that truck and—"

He spoke for the first time in hours. "Go get the boy."

"Then you expect us to get by with the crop money bad as it was last year and—" She just went on like he hadn't said anything. He looked over at her with those hard, flat eyes. She shut her mouth for a second, then said, "I don't know where he's at. He'll be back in a minute. Anyway, you don't seem to realize . . ." And she was droning on about how he always thought he could write it off on the tax and that. Christ on a *crutch,* if he hadn't heard that a thousand blamed times, he hadn't heard it once!

Wasn't that the way of a woman? Worry you to damn death about some little piddling thing all the time! He sat down at the kitchen table and pulled out his beat-up wallet, opened it. She had the food money. He had the gin check and the check ol' Lathrop had given him, what—three weeks back?—and he better cash that dude if it was any good anyhow. He'd dump the woman and the boy and he'd go cash the checks and make the deposit and there'd be enough left over to get some suds. He could taste the first one right now. Sharp bite of the shot and then that nice cool taste of the foam off the head of the beer.

She was running that mouth all the time, man couldn't even count his money. Going on about Bobby Ray Crawford but he knew it was her way of goading him. He'd get her in the truck and that would do it. She always shut up when they went some-place. He was getting warm in the kitchen with the hot fire going, but *damn* he couldn't stand to listen to that shrill hen anymore, and he got up and pulled his coat off the peg and stomped back outside to find the boy.

The boy had just come out of the woods on the south of the house. Thick woods maybe ten meters from the edge of the fields in back of the house, and he and the dog had been kicking around in there looking for squirrel sign and what not. Shit, the boy thought to himself, fuckin' Aders done killed off all the fuckin' squirrel. Otis and Bucky Aders had hunted all this ground to damn death for ten years. You didn't hardly see no sign at all no more. Once in a while where they cut but shit, they was plumb hunted out.

The dog was what the beast had heard as he entered the woods from the south side; just a faint, yapping bark that had penetrated one of his kill fantasies as he walked down the path-way that obviously led to a treeline. (Hearing the faint noise on another level of awareness and tucking it away in his data stor-age system for later retrieval.)

Life for the beast had been largely lived that way, in fantasy, daydreaming half the time, living out the fantasies the other time. Imagined flights to lift him first from his hellish childhood of torture and degradation, and mind games to alleviate the pain of suffering. Then, later, the thoughts to vaporize that claustrophobic ennui of long institutionalization. So it was not in the least unusual for the hulking beast to be fantasizing as he cautiously made his way through the woods.

For a time he had daydreamed about killing—the preoccupa-tion that was his ever-present companion, the thing he liked the best, the destruction of the human beings—and the terrain had triggered pleasant memories. As he carefully negotiated the swampy area around a large pond, he imagined the vegetation-choked floor and green, canopied ceiling of a South Vietnamese jungle, and the shadows of tall trees and wait-a-minute vines, and the triggering of a daydream alerted him to the presence of possible danger.

There were always parallels to be found. This, for example, was rice country. Here in this flatland in between the old river levees you could easily imagine a field crisscrossed by paddy dykes. Where he would have been watching for traps, falls, mines, and the footprints of the little people, here he watched for hunters.

The beast loved to come upon armed hunters in the woods and he had been fantasizing about a dad and his son; shotguns he would later take; a dog. How easily he would do the man, then stun the boy and use him before he did him, too. The thought of the boy filled him with red-hot excitement that immediately tingled in his groin and plastered a wide, grotesque smile across his doughy countenance. His smile of joy was a fearsome thing.

How easy and enjoyable it would be to do the daddy first. Take the boy's shotgun away. *Lad*, he thought. Take the *lad's* shotgun, then bind and gag and hurt him. How easy and necessary it would become to cause the pain that would bring his relief. He had the killer's gifts—the survival talents—but he'd learned that it was in those times of biological need, when the scarlet tide washed through him, that he had to be particularly cautious. Sometimes when he did the bad things he became careless.

He was not an ignorant man and in some ways he was extremely intelligent. According to one of the men in the prison where the beast had been confined, a Dr. Norman, he was a sort-of genius. "A physical precognate," Dr. Norman had told him, "who transcended the normalcy of the human ones." He was grossly abnormal. He did not find this an unpleasant thought.

The beast saw himself as Death, as a living embodiment of it, and he had availed himself of all the death literature during long periods of incarceration, devouring anything from clinicians to Horacio Quiroga. And none of it touched him. Death was outside of these others. He thought perhaps Dr. Norman was right, in his rather bizarre theorizing. But it was of no consequence to him either way.

The beast knew nothing of presentient powers. It was simply a matter of experience; preparation; trusting the vibes and gut instincts; listening to the inner rumblings; staying in harmony with one's environment; riding with the tide; keeping the sensors out there.

He could not fantasize because of inner rumblings that had

intruded upon his pleasureful thoughts, but these were the demands for food. His appetites were all insatiable, and he was very hungry, had been for the entire morning.

Instinctively, he knew the small animals could be had. Their tiny heartbeats were nearby and he homed in on such vibrations with deadly and unerring accuracy, but this was not the time for game. He wanted real food and lots of it. He salivated at the thought of the cheese and the meat of the enchiladas he'd eaten the evening before. He was *HUNGRY*. It had been the last food he'd had in thirteen, maybe thirteen and a half hours, and his massive stomach growled in protest.

The beast was six feet seven inches tall, heavy with hard, rubbery fat across his chest, belly, and buttocks. Four hundred pounds of hatred and insanity. His human name was Daniel Edward Flowers Bunkowski-Zandt, although the Zandt part wasn't even on the official dossiers or the sophisticated computer printouts. They also had his age wrong by a year, but the fact that he had weighed fourteen pounds at birth was quite correct. His powerful fingers could penetrate a chest cavity. He had once become so enraged that he had squashed a *flashlight battery*—so strong was his grip.

It would be incorrect to say that the beast hated humans. In fact, he enjoyed them. Enjoyed hunting them just as sportsmen enjoy killing game; much the same. He differed only in that he liked to torture his game first, before he killed it. Cat-and-mouse games with his play pretties. Sex sometimes. But then when the heat and the bright-red waves were at their highest ebb, he would take their hearts. He would devour the hearts of his enemy—the human beings—and that was what he loved.

The beast whose human name was Danny-Boy wished that it were summer or at least that the pecan trees to the west had something for him. There would be nothing on the ground, either, he knew. *No sweet pecan nutmeats for Danny.* But that was all right. He'd be out of the woods soon, literally and figuratively. And with that he stepped daintily over a rotten log in his big 15-EEEEE bata-boos, and he *was* out of the woods, in plain view of houses and traffic. With surprising quickness the huge beast dropped back into the cover of the trees.

"Them fuckin' river rats done hunted *out* ever'thing awready. Pah-paw," the kid whined as he patted the hound absentmindedly. "Fuckin' Punk," he said without malice.

"Them fuckin' river rats enjoy life ten times more'n *you* ever will," his father told him. Let him chew on *that* a bit. "Let's go," he said, and got into the Ford pickup.

Bunkowski saw the woman leave the house from where he stood, frozen immobile behind a massive oak. Watching the far-away tableau from his vantage point. He saw the boy climb over the side and get into the bed of the truck, for some reason. The woman came out, did something and went back inside momentarily, came back out and got into the truck. The gate was lowered and the hound jumped into the truck; the beast saw it pull out slowly, go out of sight, then reappear to the east of the tar-papered home.

The beast looked up and the sky corroborated his inner clock, which ticked with a frightening machinelike precision at all times. He saw that it was after 9:30 A.M. (It *was* 9:32, at that second. He had not looked at a clock or watch for over thirteen hours.) In a second's camera-eye blink he saw that there was no corn in the field, saw the dangers of the road to his east and west, then turned and slogged through the woods toward the fence he'd seen.

Stepping over the rusting barbed wire he emerged cautiously from the safety of the woods, made his way in the direction of the house. He knew certain things and it was not part of his character to question how he knew there was a horse or horses pasturing close by, that traffic would be a light but continuous presence on the gravel road, that nobody else was in the house. He moved into the treeline that bifurcated the two fields and walked slowly toward the home, favoring his sore ankle a little.

There was a snow fence behind the barns, where a leaky-looking rowboat and an ancient privy rotted away, and he was behind the fence and sensed something, stopped, stood very still, slowing his vital signs to a crawl. Freezing motionless for no apparent reason.

"Oh, that's *real* great," the man was telling the woman in the truck, who whined.

"I'm sorry, I'd didn't *mean* to leave it, I didn't do it on purpose." She had left her grocery list and her money in the kitchen.

"If ya hadn't been runnin' your mouth," he started to say; but he just let it trail off and slammed the gearshift into reverse, backing out of the turn row. Just my luck, he thought.

"We goin' *back?*" the kid hollered at his dad, who ignored him, put it in drive and started back in the direction of their house. The man was disgusted.

The beast knew the people were returning. He felt it and then, a beat later, saw the pickup coming back up the gravel road. He was in a vile mood and his ankle was bothering him and he knew he would enjoy taking them all down. He was very hungry, too, so it would be easy for him to do very bad things to this family of humans.

"I'm goin' to the john," the man told his wife as they went back into the house. "You goin' to be ready to go?"

"I'll be ready," she said, and went into the kitchen. The kid was sitting on the tailgate as Bunkowski walked into the yard. The dog barked at him, the kid told it to shut up.

"Howdy," the huge man said.

"Where'd *you* come from?" the kid asked him. Chaingang thought how easily he could go over and twist the boy's head off. It would be like snapping a pencil in two.

"Over yonder," he said. "Your folks home?"

"Yeah," the kid said.

"Yes?" a woman said through the partly open back door.

"Ma'am. I was hitchin' a ride and this guy's car broke down and I been walkin', quite a way. I was wonderin' if you folks would mind if I rested in your yard for a while?" He could easily pull the door open and knock her out. Go in and chainsnap the man. Come back and get the boy. He was about to make a move, but she said,

"You just sit down and rest yourself. Make yourself to home." And she started asking him where the car had broken down and did he want a lift back to the car and did he want to call somebody, and he kind of got taken off his stride and so he went and sat on the steps.

"You from around here?" the boy asked. The beast only shook his head.

Inside the house he heard the man say something and she said ". . . broke down back over . . ." (something he couldn't make out) and the door opened behind him and the man said,

"You need a ride?"

"Well, I don't mind if it's no bother," Bunkowski said pleasantly, thinking he'd go ahead and make the move now.

"It's no trouble. You can ride into town with us. If you don't mind sittin' back there with the boy." The man said it without any undue emphasis.

"I'd be real grateful."

"No problem," the man said, stepping around the huge bulk that filled his back steps.

The last place where he'd come upon a family, he'd killed everybody in the house. Three people. Man and wife and a son —just like this. The kid, as if reading his mind, moved over out of the way, back into a far corner of the truck bed.

"Get over here, Punk," the boy said to the dog, who wagged and obeyed. "Don't worry," he sneered. "He don't bite."

"What's his name? Punk?" Chaingang sat on the cold steel. Shifted his weight slightly so as not to break the tailgate off, and the truck rocked like a safe had been dropped into it.

"Little Punk." The kid scratched the dog. "We found him starvin' over on the dump. Somebody dropped the fucker. He didn't look like nothin' but a punk." The dog licked the kid's face once and he pushed it away. "Fuckin' Punk."

"Looks like a good dog," the huge man said.

"He's awright."

"You ready?" the man said to nobody in general, and he and the wife got into the truck and they drove off down the road, Chaingang Bunkowski bouncing along in the back of the truck.

When the beast had been a child, a dog had been his only companion and friend. He loved animals. Watching the boy with the dog had calmed him down, but he wasn't sure what he would do yet. He might take them all down anyway.

When the pickup reached the crossroads of Double-J and the levee road, Chaingang banged on the window and asked the man to stop. He got out, walked around by the driver. There were no other vehicles in sight.

"Doncha wanna go on to town?" the man asked him. Bunkowski fingered the heavy yard of the tractor-strength safety chain in his jacket pocket. Three feet of killer snake were coiled in the special canvas pocket. He thought how easy it would be to take them, now.

"I guess not. This'll do." He nodded thanks to the driver, who shrugged and started off. Chaingang stood there and watched the luckiest man in the world drive away with his family.

The Party

by William F. Nolan

William F. Nolan has worked in virtually every medium telling virtually every kind of story. I prefer his crime and horror work. He is able to articulate fear better than most writers because he keeps most of his fear small and subtle. And when he's rolling, he's a fine and gifted stylist, right up there with anybody you care to name.

First published in 1967.

Ashland frowned, trying to concentrate in the warm emptiness of the thickly carpeted lobby. Obviously, he had pressed the elevator button, because he was alone here and the elevator was blinking its way down to him, summoned from an upper floor. It arrived with an efficient hiss, the bronze doors clicked open, and he stepped in, thinking *blackout. I had a mental blackout.*

First the double vision. Now this. It was getting worse. He had blanked out completely. Just where the hell was he? Must be a party, he told himself. Sure. Someone he'd met, whose name was missing along with the rest of it, had invited him to a party. He had an apartment number in his head: 9E. That much he retained. A number—nothing else.

On the way up, in the soundless cage of the elevator, David Ashland reviewed the day. The usual morning routine: work, then lunch with his new secretary. A swinger—but she liked her booze; put away three martinis to his two. Back to the office. More work. A drink in the afternoon with a writer. ("Beefeater. No rocks. Very dry.") Dinner at the new Italian joint on West

Forty-Eighth with Linda. Lovely Linda. Expensive girl. Lovely as hell, but expensive. More drinks, then—nothing. Blackout.

The doc had warned him about the hard stuff, but what else can you do in New York? The pressures get to you, so you drink. Everybody drinks. And every night, somewhere in town, there's a party, with contacts (and girls) to be made. . . .

The elevator stopped, opened its doors. Ashland stepped out, uncertainly, into the hall. The softly lit passageway was long, empty, silent. No, not silent. Ashland heard the familiar voice of a party: the shifting hive hum of cocktail conversation, dim, high laughter, the sharp chatter of ice against glass, a background wash of modern jazz. . . . All quite familiar. And always the same.

He walked to 9E. Featureless apartment door. White. Brass button housing. Gold numbers. No clues here. Sighing, he thumbed the buzzer and waited nervously.

A smiling fat man with bad teeth opened the door. He was holding a half-filled drink in one hand. Ashland didn't know him.

"C'mon in fella," he said. "Join the party."

Ashland squinted into blue-swirled tobacco smoke, adjusting his eyes to the dim interior. The rising-falling sea tide of voices seemed to envelop him.

"Grab a drink, fella," said the fat man. "Looks like you need one!"

Ashland aimed for the bar in one corner of the crowded apartment. He *did* need a drink. Maybe a drink would clear his head, let him get this all straight. Thus far, he had not recognized any of the faces in the smoke-hazed room.

At the self-service bar a thin, turkey-necked woman wearing paste jewelry was intently mixing a black Russian. "Got to be exceedingly careful with these," she said to Ashland, eyes still on the mixture. "Too much vodka craps them up."

Ashland nodded. "The host arrived?" *I'll know him, I'm sure.*

"Due later—or sooner. Sooner—or later. You know, I once spilled three black Russians on the same man over a thirty-day period. First on the man's sleeve, then on his back, then on his lap. Each time his suit was a sticky, gummy mess. My psychiatrist told me that I did it unconsciously, because of a neurotic hatred of this particular man. He looked like my father."

"The psychiatrist?"

"No, the man I spilled the black Russians on." She held up the tall drink, sipped at it. "Ahhh . . . still too weak."

Ashland probed the room for a face he knew, but these people were all strangers.

He turned to find the turkey-necked woman staring at him. "Nice apartment," he said mechanically.

"Stinks. I detest pseudo-Chinese decor in Manhattan brownstones." She moved off, not looking back at Ashland.

He mixed himself a straight Scotch, running his gaze around the apartment. The place *was* pretty wild—ivory tables with serpent legs; tall, figured screens with chain-mail warriors cavorting across them; heavy brocade drapes in stitched silver; lamps with jewel-eyed dragons looped at the base. And, at the far end of the room, an immense bronze gong suspended between a pair of demon-faced swordsmen. Ashland studied the gong. A thing to wake the dead, he thought. Great for hangovers in the morning.

"Just get here?" a girl asked him. She was red-haired, full-breasted, in her late twenties. Attractive. Damned attractive. Ashland smiled warmly at her.

"That's right," he said, "I just arrived." He tasted the Scotch; it was flat, watery. "Whose place is this?"

The girl peered at him above her cocktail glass. "Don't you know who invited you?"

Ashland was embarrassed. "Frankly, no. That's why I—"

"My name's Viv. For Vivian. I drink. What do you do? Besides drink?"

"I produce. I'm in television."

"Well, *I'm* in a dancing mood. Shall we?"

"Nobody's dancing," protested Ashland. "We'd look—foolish."

The jazz suddenly seemed louder. Overhead speakers were sending out a thudding drum solo behind muted strings. The girl's body rippled to the sounds.

"Never be afraid to do anything foolish," she told him. "That's the secret of survival." Her fingers beckoned him. "C'mon . . ."

"No, really—not right now. Maybe later."

"Then I'll dance alone."

She spun into the crowd, her long red dress whirling. The other partygoers ignored her. Ashland emptied the watery Scotch and fixed himself another. He loosened his tie, popping the collar button. *Damn!*

"I train worms."

Ashland turned to a florid-faced little man with bulging, feverish eyes. "I heard you say you were in TV," the little man said. "Ever use any trained worms on your show?"

"No . . . no, we don't."

"I breed 'em, train 'em. I teach a worm to run a maze. Then I grind him up and feed him to a dumb, untrained worm. Know what happens? The dumb worm can run the maze! But only for twenty-four hours. Then he forgets—unless I keep him on a trained-worm diet. I defy you to tell me that isn't fascinating!"

"It is, indeed." Ashland nodded and moved away from the bar. The feverish little man smiled after him, toasting his departure with a raised glass. Ashland found himself sweating.

Who was his host? Who had invited him? He knew most of the Village crowd, but had spotted none of them here. . . .

A dark, doll-like girl asked him for a light. He fumbled out some matches.

"Thanks," she said, exhaling blue smoke into blue smoke. "Saw that worm guy talking to you. What a lousy bore *he* is! My ex-husband had a pet snake named Baby and he fed it worms. That's all they're good for, unless you fish. Do you fish?"

"I've done some fishing up in Canada."

"My ex-husband hated all sports. Except the indoor variety." She giggled. "Did you hear the one about the indoor hen and the outdoor rooster?"

"Look, miss—"

"Talia. But you can call me Jenny. Get it?" She doubled over, laughing hysterically, then swayed, dropping her cigarette. "Ooops! I'm sick. I better go lie down. My tum-tum feels awful."

She staggered from the party as Ashland crushed out her smoldering cigarette with the heel of his shoe. *Stupid bitch!*

A sharp handclap startled him. In the middle of the room, a tall man in a green satin dinner jacket was demanding his attention. He clapped again. "You," he shouted to Ashland. "come here."

Ashland walked forward. The tall man asked him to remove his wristwatch. "I'll read your past from it," the man said. "I'm psychic. I'll tell you about yourself."

Reluctantly, Ashland removed his watch, handed it over. He didn't find any of this amusing. The party was annoying him, irritating him.

"I thank you most kindly, sir!" said the tall man, with elaborate stage courtesy. He placed the gold watch against his forehead and closed his eyes, breathing deeply. The crowd noise did not slacken; no one seemed to be paying any attention to the psychic.

"Ah. Your name is David. David Ashland. You are successful, a man of big business . . . a producer . . . and a bachelor. You are twenty-eight . . . very young for a successful producer. One has to be something of a bastard to climb that fast. What about that, Mr. Ashland, *are* you something of a bastard?"

Ashland flushed angrily.

"You like women," continued the tall man. "A lot. And you like to drink. A lot. Your doctor told you—"

"I don't have to listen to this," Ashland said tightly, reaching for his watch. The man in green satin handed it over, grinned amiably, and melted back into the shifting crowd.

I ought to get the hell out of here, Ashland told himself. Yet curiosity held him. When the host arrived, Ashland would piece this evening together; he'd know why he was there, at this particular party. He moved to a couch near the closed patio doors and sat down. He'd wait.

A soft-faced man sat down next to him. The man looked pained. "I shouldn't smoke these," he said, holding up a long cigar. "Do you smoke cigars?"

"No."

"I'm a salesman. Dover Insurance. Like the White Cliffs of, ya know. I've studied the problems involved in smoking. Can't quit, though. When I do, the nerves shrivel up, stomach goes sour. I worry a lot—but we all worry, don't we? I mean, my mother used to worry about the earth slowing down. She read somewhere that between 1680 and 1690 the earth lost twenty-seven hundredths of a second. She said that meant something."

Ashland sighed inwardly. What is it about cocktail parties that causes people you've never met to unleash their troubles?

"You meet a lotta fruitcakes in my dodge," said the pained-looking insurance salesman. "I sold a policy once to a guy who lived in the woodwork. Had a ratty little walk-up in the Bronx with a foldaway bed. Kind you push into the wall. He'd *stay* there—I mean, inside the wall—most of the time. His roommate would invite some friends in and if they made too much noise the guy inside the wall would pop out with his Thompson. BAM! The bed would come down and there he was with a Thompson submachine gun aimed at everybody. Real fruit-cake."

"I knew a fellow who was *twice* that crazy."

Ashland looked up into a long, cadaverous face. The nose had been broken and improperly reset; it canted noticeably to the left. He folded his long, sharp-boned frame onto the couch next to Ashland. "This fellow believed in falling grandmothers," he declared. "Lived in upper Michigan. 'Watch out for falling grandmothers,' he used to warn me. 'They come down pretty heavy in this area. Most of 'em carry umbrellas and big packages and they come flapping down out of the sky by the thousands!' This Michigan fellow swore he saw one hit a postman. 'An awful thing to watch,' he told me. 'Knocked the poor soul flat. Crushed his skull like an egg.' I recall he shuddered just telling me about it."

"Fruitcake," said the salesman. "Like the guy I once knew who wrote on all his walls and ceilings. A creative writer, he called himself. Said he couldn't write on paper, had to use a wall. Paper was too flimsy for him. He'd scrawl these long novels of his, a chapter in every room, with a big black crayon. Words all over the place. He'd fill up the house, then rent another one for his next book. I never read any of his houses, so I don't know if he was any good."

"Excuse me, gentlemen," said Ashland. "I need a fresh drink."

He hurriedly mixed another Scotch at the bar. Around him, the party rolled on inexorably, without any visible core. What time was it, anyway? His watch had stopped.

"Do you happen to know what time it is?" he asked a long-haired Oriental girl who was standing near the bar.

"I've no idea," she said. "None at all." The girl fixed him with her eyes. "I've been watching you, and you seem horribly *alone*. Aren't you?"

"Aren't I what?"

"Horribly alone?"

"I'm not with anyone, if that's what you mean."

The girl withdrew a jeweled holder from her bag and fitted a cigarette in place. Ashland lit it for her.

"I haven't been really alone since I was in Milwaukee," she told him. "I was about—God!—fifteen or something, and this creep wanted me to move in with him. My parents were both dead by then, so I was all alone."

"What did you do?"

"Moved in with the creep. What else? I couldn't make the being-alone scene. Later on, I killed him."

"You *what*?"

"Cut his throat." She smiled delicately. "In self-defense, of course. He got mean on the bottle one Friday night and tried to knife me. I had witnesses."

Ashland took a long draw on his Scotch. A scowling fellow in shirt-sleeves grabbed the girl's elbow and steered her roughly away.

"I used to know a girl who looked like that," said a voice to Ashland's right. The speaker was curly-haired clean-featured, in his late thirties. "Greek belly dancer with a Jersey accent. Dark, like her, and kind of mysterious. She used to quote that line of Hemingway's to Scott Fitzgerald—you know the one."

"Afraid not."

"One that goes, 'We're all bitched from the start.' Bitter. A bitter line."

He put out his hand. Ashland shook it.

"I'm Travers. I used to save America's ass every week on CBS."

"Beg pardon?"

"Terry Travers. The old 'Triple Trouble for Terry' series on channel nine. Back in the late fifties. Had to step on a lotta toes to get that series."

"I think I recall the show. It was—"

"Dung. That's what it was. Cow dung. Horse dung. The *worst*. Terry Travers is not my real name, natch. Real one's Abe Hockstatter. Can you imagine a guy named Abe Hockstatter saving America's ass every week on CBS?"

"You've got me there."

Hockstatter pulled a brown wallet from his coat, flipped it open. "There I am with one of my other rugs on," he said, jabbing at a photo. "Been stone bald since high school. Baldies don't make it in showbiz, so I have my rugs. Go ahead, tug at me."

Ashland blinked. The man inclined his head. *"Pull* at it. Go on —as a favor to me!"

Ashland tugged at the fringe of Abe Hockstatter's curly hairpiece.

"Tight, eh? Really *snug*. Stays on the old dome."

"Indeed it does."

"They cost a fortune. I've got a wind-blown one for outdoor scenes. A stiff wind'll lift a cheap one right off your scalp. Then I got a crew cut and a Western job with long sideburns. All kinds. Ten, twelve . . . all first-class."

"I'm certain I've seen you," said Ashland. "I just don't—"

"'S awright. Believe me. Lotta people don't know me since I

quit the 'Terry' thing. I booze like crazy now. You an' me, we're among the nation's six million alcoholics."

Ashland glared at the actor. "Where do you get off linking me with—"

"Cool it, cool it. So I spoke a little out of turn. Don't be so touchy, chum."

"To hell with you!" snapped Ashland.

The bald man with curly hair shrugged and drifted into the crowd.

Ashland took another long pull at his Scotch. All these neurotic conversations . . . He felt exhausted, wrung dry, and the Scotch was lousy. No kick to it. The skin along the back of his neck felt tight, hot. A headache was coming on; he could always tell.

A slim-figured, frosted blonde in black sequins sidled up to him. She exuded an aura of matrimonial wars fought and lost. Her orange lipstick was smeared, her cheeks alcohol-flushed behind flaking pancake make-up. "I have a theory about sleep," she said. "Would you like to hear it?"

Ashland did not reply.

"My theory is that the world goes insane every night. When we sleep, our subconscious takes charge and we become victims to whatever it conjures up. Our conscious, reasoning mind is totally blanked out. We lie there, helpless, while our subconscious flings us about. We fall off high buildings, or have to fight a giant ape, or we get buried in quicksand. . . . We have absolutely no control. The mind whirls madly in the skull. Isn't that an unsettling thing to consider?"

"Listen," said Ashland. "Where's the host?"

"He'll get here."

Ashland put down his glass and turned away from her. A mounting wave of depression swept him toward the door. The room seemed to be solid with bodies, all talking, drinking, gesturing in the milk-thick smoke haze.

"Potatoes have eyes," said a voice to his left. "I really *believe* that." The remark was punctuated by an ugly, frog-croaking laugh.

"Today is tomorrow's yesterday," someone else said.

A hot swarm of sound:

"You can't get prints off human skin."

"In China, the laborers make sixty-five dollars a year. How the hell can you live on sixty-five dollars a year?"

"So he took out his Luger and blew her head off."

"I knew a policewoman who loved to scrub down whores."

"Did you ever try to live with eight kids, two dogs, a three-legged cat and twelve goldfish?"

"Like I told him, those X rays destroyed his white cells."

"They found her in the tub. Strangled with a coat hanger."

"What I had, exactly, was a grade-two epidermoid carcinoma at the base of a seborrheic keratosis."

Ashland experienced a sudden, raw compulsion: somehow he had to stop these voices!

The Chinese gong flared gold at the corner of his eye. He pushed his way over to it, shouldering the partygoers aside. He would strike it—and the booming noise would stun the crowd; they'd have to stop their incessant, maddening chatter.

Ashland drew back his right fist, then drove it into the circle of bronze. He felt the impact, and the gong shuddered under his blow.

But there was no sound from it!

The conversation went on.

Ashland smashed his way back across the apartment.

"You can't stop the party," said the affable fat man at the door.

"I'm leaving!"

"So go ahead," grinned the fat man. "Leave."

Ashland clawed open the door and plunged into the hall, stumbling, almost falling. He reached the elevator, jabbed at the DOWN button.

Waiting, he found it impossible to swallow; his throat was dry. He could feel his heart hammering against the walls of his chest. His head ached.

The elevator arrived, opened. He stepped inside. The doors closed smoothly and the cage began its slow, automatic descent.

Abruptly, it stopped.

The doors parted to admit a solemn-looking man in a dark blue suit.

Ashland gasped "Freddie!"

The solemn face broke into a wide smile. "Dave! It's great to see you! Been—a long time."

"But—you can't be Fred Baker!"

"Why? Have I changed so much?"

"No, no, you look—exactly the same. But that car crash in Albany. I thought you were . . ." Ashland hesitated, left the word unspoke. He was pale, frightened. Very frightened. "Look, I'm—I'm late. Got somebody waiting for me at my place.

Have to rush . . ." He reached forward to push the LOBBY button.

There was none.

The lowest button read FLOOR 2.

"We use this elevator to get from one party to another," Freddie Baker said quietly, as the cage surged into motion. "That's all it's good for. You get so you need a change. They're all alike, though—the parties. But you learn to adjust, in time. We all have."

Ashland stared at his departed friend. The elevator stopped.

"Step out," said Freddie. "I'll introduce you around. You'll catch on, get used to things. No sex here. And the booze is watered. Can't get stoned. That's the dirty end of the stick."

Baker took Ashland's arm, propelled him gently forward.

Around him, pressing in, David Ashland could hear familiar sounds: nervous laughter, ice against glass, muted jazz—and the ceaseless hum of cocktail voices.

Freddie thumbed a buzzer. A door opened.

The smiling fat man said, "C'mon in fellas. Join the party."

Predators

Edward Bryant

Edward Bryant has lately been making the transition from award-winning science fiction writer to horror writer. Few writers are as good at capturing urban terrors. He has a real feeling for all the panic we take with us when we bolt ourselves into our apartments and hope that dawn comes soon. The story here is a particularly powerful one.

First published in 1987.

Her nostrils were choked with the stench of bus fumes and all the other myriad odors crushed down into the streets by the winter inversion layer. Another day of looking for work in the city . . . Still no luck.

Lisa Blackwell's first reaction to the person who'd moved in upstairs was bewilderment. She could smell the fresh Dymo label on #12's mailbox in the downstairs hall. It read "R. G. Cross." Evidently the moving in of furniture and whatever other personal belongings had taken place earlier in the day, while Lisa had been hitting the job agencies for interviews.

The afternoon hadn't gone well. Lisa didn't like the cold, cloudy October weather—it looked as if it was going to snow. Worse, she didn't think she had uncovered any good employment leads. It had been weeks now, and the money the missionaries had given her was running out. She didn't want to check the balance in her new checking account. It was so important to make it here . . . Lisa wanted her parents to be proud.

Her apartment had been restful, a quiet refuge, with no one living upstairs. But now she had a neighbor. The first thing she learned about him—Lisa assigned him a gender upon no particularly firm evidence—was his taste in music. It was raucous and simplistic. She felt the vibration as soon as she entered her own apartment and shut the door. Then he punched the volume up. The bass line predominated. From time to time, a buzzsaw treble would slice through the bass. Lisa thought she could see the ceiling vibrate. Her ears hurt.

She decided to endure it. Surely he would get tired, leave, go to sleep, choose a more interesting album. Lisa understood that what she was listening to second-hand was heavy metal. She had learned that she preferred jazz. She loved the intricate rhythms. If worst came to worst, Lisa knew she could call the building managers and complain. That privilege had been explained to her when she'd moved in.

The next thing she discovered about her neighbor was the fact of his sexual activity. At about seven o'clock, Lisa was taking a pound of ground beef out of the refrigerator. The heavy, sweet odor hung in the air. She felt—as well as heard—the stereo upstairs turned down. Then she heard heavy steps clump out onto the third-floor landing and descend. On the ground floor, the foyer door squeaked open. Two sets of footsteps ascended. She heard voices—a treble piping mixed with the bass rumble. The door to apartment 12 banged shut.

It wasn't, Lisa thought, as though she was truly eavesdropping. The building was about fifty years old; the construction, thin to begin with, was loosening up.

The music from above started again, though the volume wasn't as loud as it had been in the afternoon. At eleven, Lisa lay sleepless on her Salvation Army Thrift Store mattress. She needed her rest. Bags beneath her eyes at job interviews . . . no! She had just decided to throw on a robe and go upstairs to ask her new neighbor to turn the volume down when the stereo abruptly shut off. Lisa curled up in a warm ball.

The respite was brief. Sounds began again from upstairs. Since the apartment layouts were identical from floor to floor, her neighbor's bedroom was directly above Lisa's own. R. G. Cross's bedsprings were not subtle. She tried to ignore the rhythm, then pulled the ends of the pillow around her head when she heard private cries.

After a time, the squeaking stopped and the thumping began. In spite of herself, Lisa wondered what *that* noise meant: a steady, muffled *flump, flump*. Something that sounded liquid spattered on the floor above. How weird *was* R. G. Cross?

She didn't wonder long. The sounds stopped for good. Exhausted, homesick, a little lonely, wondering when she would ever get a job in this strange, new city, Lisa fell asleep.

She dreamed of a warm, lazy, savanna summer, and of lush sun-dappled foliage. It was all green and golden and smelled like life itself. She wanted to be again with everyone she'd left, Lisa thought fuzzily. Mama . . .

The next day was Saturday. Lisa had no interviews, but she did have a sheaf of application forms to fill out. She hadn't gotten up until noon. Between mild depression keeping her in bed, along with the simultaneous feeling of stolen luxury, she dozed away the morning.

When her eyes finally flickered open for good, her mind registered the time as 11:56. Digital clocks amazed her with their precision. Lisa rolled over on her back and remembered vaguely having been awakened earlier in the morning by angry voices from upstairs. She slowly and luxuriously stretched, then padded toward the bathroom.

Lisa brushed her hair and cleaned her teeth. Then she put on her gloves, terrycloth robe, and slippers, and went downstairs to collect her newspaper. The stairway was chilly, as though someone had left the outer door propped open.

She encountered a tall, blond stranger in the front hall. Lisa scented him before she actually saw him. He smelled of some sharp, citrus cologne.

"Hi, there," He shoved a large, tanned hand at her. "You're my downstairs neighbor, right? I'm Roger."

Lisa glanced at the mailbox and back at him. "R. G. Cross."

"That's me." He grinned widely. For a second, all Lisa could see was the array of flawless white teeth. "Mighty nice to meet you."

His hand overpowered hers. She withdrew her fingers, sensing he could have crushed down much harder. Roger leaned back against the wall and hooked his thumbs in his jeans pockets. He was more than a full head taller than she, though Lisa could stare level into the eyes of most of the men she'd met. He had an athlete's powerful physique. He probably works out every day, she thought. His jaw was strong. Roger's eyes were a bright, cold blue; his hair, tousled and light. His grin didn't seem to vary from second to second by a single millimeter.

Roger unhooked one thumb to gesture at the mailbox. "You must be L. P. Blackwell."

Lisa nodded politely and started to turn toward the steps with her paper.

"What's it stand for?"

"Lisa Penelope."

Roger stuck out one long leg so that his foot partially blocked her exit. "Oh yeah? Could stand for a lot of other things."

Unsure what to do now, Lisa paused at the foot of the stairs. She examined her options. The list was short.

Roger said, "Could stand for Long Playing . . ."

She stiffened, feeling a chill of apprehension.

"Like with a record album." He chuckled at his own joke. "Long playing, all right. Stereo too, probably." He smiled at her expression, then looked slowly and deliberately down the front of her to the floor, and then back up again.

"Excuse me, but I need to get upstairs." Lisa made her voice sound as decisive as she could.

"So what's the hurry?" His voice remained warm and friendly.

"I need to fix breakfast." She regretted saying anything the moment the words came out, but by then it was too late.

"I haven't had breakfast yet either," Roger said. "You like breakfast? I know I do. Best way to start the day."

Lisa looked straight ahead, up the stairwell. She sighed and said nothing. She didn't want this to mean trouble.

"We could do it together," said Roger. "Breakfast. What sort of meat do you like in the morning?"

"Please move your leg." He slowly, with great deliberation, evidently savoring the power of the moment, withdrew his foot from her path. "Thank you." Lisa resisted the impulse to bound up the steps two at a time.

He called after her, "Hey, don't mind me, L. P. I'm feeling good today. Great night, last night. Now I'm just high-spirited, you know?"

Lisa fumbled with her keys. She heard slow, steady steps ascending the staircase. She practically kicked the door open when the latch clicked. Once in the refuge of her apartment, she closed and locked the door. Then she turned the dead-bolt home. She did not want trouble. She had enough on her mind already.

"Damn it," she said under her breath. "Damn them. Why are they like that?"

Lisa spent Saturday afternoon filling out job application forms. Unfortunately she recognized her employability problems, not the least of which was her inability to type. After two hours of laborious and exquisitely neat printing, she took a break and made a pot of rich cambric. In rapid succession, she turned on a TV movie, switched it off, picked up a new paperback mystery she'd bought at Safeway, then put it down when she realized she wasn't concentrating on the plot.

Someone knocked at her front door.

Lisa hesitated.

Her building dated back to the late 'twenties or early 'thirties. Lisa's managers had told her that with some pride. This was a building that hadn't been razed to make room for a modern and characterless highrise. Some of the art deco touches still remained. About half the renovated apartments had glass spy-tubes in the front doors so that the tenants could scrutinize whatever callers stood on the other side. Lisa's door had something that antedated the tubes. She could open a little hinged metal door set at face height, and look out through a grill of highly stylized palm trees cast in some pewter-colored metal.

If she opened the little door. She hesitated.

There was a second, more insistent knock. She heard the floor-board creaking of someone shifting his weight. She could hear breathing on the other side of the door.

Lisa reached for the latch of the small door and pulled it open. She looked into the apparently eternally grinning face of Roger Cross.

"Oh, hi," he said nonchalantly.

"Hello." Lisa made the word utterly neutral.

"Hey, listen. I want to apologize for sort of coming off the wall before. You know, stepping out of line." Roger met her gaze directly. He reached up with one hand to scratch the back of his head boyishly, tousling the carefully styled blond hair. "I didn't mean to come across as such a turkey. Honest."

"It's all right," said Lisa. She wasn't sure what else to say. "Thanks for saying that."

"Say, could I come in?"

He must have seen something in her expression. Roger quickly added, "You know, just for a little while. I thought maybe we could sit down and talk. Get acquainted. You know, I really want to be a good neighbor." The grin became a sincere smile. "And friends."

Lisa said nothing for a few seconds, trying to get a handle on this. "Not—now, thanks, I'm not ready. I mean I wasn't expecting company and—"

"I don't mind a mess," Roger said. "You should see my place. A real sty."

She momentarily noted his vocabulary and wondered that he knew a word like "sty." He definitely didn't seem rural. But then, she thought, she knew she had never met anyone like this before. "No. Really. We—I can't."

He switched tracks. "Hey, L. P., you living on your own for the first time?"

Startled, Lisa said, "How'd you know that?"

"I thought so. You look pretty young. Going to college?"

She couldn't help responding. "No. I haven't had much formal schooling."

"Neat accent," he said. "I can't quite place it. From the South?"

She nodded. "A ways." *Dappled sunlight on the leaves.* Lisa felt a sudden stab of homesickness like an arrow piercing her side.

"Great winters here. You come north to live so you could ski?"

"No." It had never occurred to her to ski.

"That's why I came here. That and work. I've got a great job with an oil company. Marketing."

Floundering, Lisa said, "That must be . . ."

"Oh yeah, real interesting. Get to work with the public. Meet people." The sincere smile became more engaging. "Say, you come out here to get away from your family?"

"Uh, yes," she said. Lisa felt more pangs, equally painful. *Food, warmth, security, all provided. Her mother's satiny touch.* She suddenly and desperately wanted to see her parents again. She wanted so much to be on her own, but she also needed to be stroked and reassured. For the thousandth time she regretted leaving home.

"I know what it's like," said Roger earnestly. "I've been on my own for a long time. Never knew my father. Mother died when I was real young. Really I've got no family." His voice lowered. "I know it gets real lonely here in the city."

"Yes," said Lisa. "It does."

"Let me make things up," he said. "You want some hot coffee? I've got some great Colombian grind up in my place."

"I drink tea."

"Got all the Celestial Seasonings flavors. Or black, if you want it."

"No thanks," she said. "I just made a pot." Lisa turned her head and glanced across the living room at the pot of cambric slowly cooling beneath the quilted cat-print cozy. "It'll be getting cold, so I'd better go." She thought of the skim forming on the surface of the milk. Lisa turned toward him again. "Excuse me, please."

"Wait!" he said, seeming a little frantic now. "This is impor-tant—"

"Yes?"

"Listen, how's your laundry?"

"Beg your pardon?" What *was* he talking about?

"Don't you do your laundry on the weekend?"

"Well, yes." Lisa had lived in the apartment for little more than a month, but already discovered that she hated the laun-dry room. It was a dark, dank cell in the basement beneath the house next door. The laundry served both buildings, as the two were owned by the same company. The room contained two sets of coin-operated washers and dryers. All the machines were usually in use all the weekend daylight hours. It was a secluded and uncomfortable place at night.

The closest commercial laundromat was more than a mile away, and Lisa had no car.

"I'm gonna do a load sometime tonight," said Roger. "If I don't no socks and underwear for Monday morning. If you want to come along and do a load too—" He spread his hands. "I could escort you, make sure no freako jumps out and grabs you. We could get in some civilized conversation down there. Don't you need to wash some clothes?"

Of course she did. Lisa had been putting off the laundry room expedition. She really did need clean clothing for Mon-day. "Thanks anyway," she said. "I've got to stay in tonight and work. I've got a lot to do."

"I think you're lying," said Roger quietly.

"I really do have—"

"*Lying!*" Roger slammed the heel of his hand against the door. It jumped and rattled in its frame. Lisa involuntarily stepped backward.

"So what's wrong with me, you black bitch?" Roger shoved his face forward so that he blocked the entire opening. It occurred to Lisa that his was like looking out of a wild animal's cage—or into one. There was a fixedness to his eyes that she wondered might be madness. She had done nothing to bring this on her-self. *Nothing!*

"Listen, I'm sorry," she said, stepping forward and flipping the little metal door firmly shut. She heard him outside, now speaking to the closed door.

"These doors are old. Not stout at all. I could kick this one down in just two seconds. Just like the big bad wolf . . ."

"Please go 'way," said Lisa. "I'll call the manager."

"You think you're gold, don't you?" His voice was low and intense. She could hear him working into a frenzy. "You think *it's* gold."

"Go. Please."

"You know who I am, Lisa? I'm the boogey man. And I eat up little girls just like that."

Lisa decided that perhaps if she didn't answer him any more, he'd go away.

"So don't answer. I know you're there."

She still said nothing.

"You know who you are?" Roger's chuckle decayed to something horrible. "You're a puckered little prude. I think maybe you need to be loosened up."

Lisa tried to back away from the door quietly, hoping none of the boards in the hardwood floor would creak.

"*I hear you!* You know what else you are, L. P.? You're a real fruitcake."

She continued to step quietly away from the door.

Roger laughed, almost a giggle. He said, "You're *so* weird, girl. Right out of the sticks—or is it off the plantation? Who else would wear gloves with a terrycloth robe. You—"

He said a string of things she didn't want to hear, including a few she didn't understand. Finally he seemed to run out of obscenities. Roger evidently turned away from the door and his voice became muffled. His deliberate, slow steps clumped upstairs. She heard his door open and slam shut.

Even though he was gone, she still tried to move as quietly as she could toward the couch and the tea cozy. The pot was still warm, so she poured herself a cup of well-steeped cambric. The milky, soothing scent filled the living room.

Lisa Blackwell had never before encountered anyone like Roger Cross. She had heard of them—creatures like him. A danger to their kind. She said to herself softly, "What is wrong with him?" And was confounded by the inexplicable.

Later that evening, Lisa heard Roger go out. She listened to the sound of him descending the back stairs, past her kitchen door. Something trailed his footsteps with a series of soft impacts. It made her think of something large and dangerous, dragging its prey. Almost against her will, she went to the kitchen window and looked down as the building's rear door swung open. Roger emerged, dragging a laundry bag.

So he does have a load to wash, she thought. Not that it made any difference. The man was clearly disturbed, a defective individual. Roger rounded the corner of the adjacent house and was lost to sight.

Lisa went into the living room and looked at the number she'd written on the piece of paper taped beside the telephone. She called the managers, a married couple who lived in the house above the laundry room. She got it wrong on the first attempt and had to dial again.

Joanne, the female half of the managerial team, answered the phone and Lisa identified herself.

"Right," said Joanne. "You're in number ten. What can I do for you?"

Lisa hesitated, then gave the woman an abbreviated account of her encounters with Roger, leaving out most of the things he'd said that she didn't want to repeat. It was still enough to kindle concern in Joanne's voice.

"You might be interested in knowing," the manager said, "that you're the second complaint. I heard from the tenant in number two. Our studly friend gave her a come-on too. Nothing as jerk-off as his thing with you, but it was still scummy enough for her to mention it to me." She hesitated. "I only talked to the guy a little when he first came to look at the apartment. He seemed harmless enough then."

Lisa said nothing.

Joanne volunteered, "Listen, if you're really upset tonight, you're welcome to come over here. Joe and I have a couch you can use. You won't have to worry about that guy sneaking around your place."

Lisa considered it. "No," she finally said. "Thank you very much, but no. I'd have to go home sometime. Anyhow, I'm probably just overreacting. I'll go ahead and stay here tonight and keep my door double-locked."

"You're sure? Really, it's no problem if you want to come over."

"Thanks again, Joanne. I'm sure." No, she wasn't sure, but she wasn't going to admit it. If she were going to be on her own in the city, then she'd just have to learn to cope. Breaking free. That's what she had come here for. Roger G. Cross wasn't going to spoil it for her.

"I've got an idea," Joanne said. "The owners'll be back from vacation Monday. First thing Tuesday morning, I'll get hold of them and explain about you and the other tenant that jerk hassled. Maybe the owners can find grounds to evict the son of a bitch, okay?"

Lisa thanked her and then kept the phone pressed to her ear long after Joanne had set down the receiver. She listened to the indecipherable whispers of the dead line, then the click and dial tone. Finally she hung up and sat there, not moving and blindly staring at the knotted fiber wall-hanging her friends at home had given her.

She realized she was tired, very tired. Stress. She had read articles about it. It was not a condition she was accustomed to in her old home. It did not please her.

In bed, she felt the cold desolation of being alone and lonely in a strange place. The feeling hadn't changed in all these weeks. She reminded herself she would keep trying.

After a long time, and not until she heard the telltale sounds of Roger Cross returning from the laundry room and closing his door, Lisa fell asleep.

She dreamed of traps.

In the morning, she woke tense, the muscles in her shoulders tight and sore. She awoke listening, straining to hear sounds from the upstairs apartment. She heard nothing other than the occasional traffic outside and the slight hum of the clock by the bed.

Lisa lay awake for an hour before uncurling and getting out of bed. There was still nothing to hear from upstairs. Finally she put on her robe and gloves and went into the living room, hoping for sun-warmth from the east windows. It was another cloudy day.

She almost missed the scrap of paper that had been slipped beneath her front door. Lisa gingerly picked the thing up and examined it curiously. It was a heart cut from a doubled sheet of red construction paper. The heart bore the inscription in wide, ink-marker slashes: "R. C. + L. P." She set the thing down on the coffee table and stared at it a while. Then she crumpled the Valentine into a ball and dropped it into the kitchen trash sack.

Lisa returned to the front door, opened the spy panel and looked out. Nobody. She opened the door a crack. No one lurked outside on the landing. She quietly and quickly descended the flight to the foyer. No one confronted her when she claimed her Sunday paper from the skiff of snow sifted on the front step. Roger didn't ambush her when she returned to her own door. The building was still and quiet, just as it had been every other Sunday Lisa had lived there.

The telephone rang as she closed the door. Lisa picked up the receiver and heard Roger's voice say, "Listen, Lisa, please don't hang up yet, okay?"

This confused her. She hesitated.

"Did you get what I left you?"

"The heart?" she said, still feeling she was lagging.

"I know you must have found it—the Valentine. I didn't want to knock and wake you up."

She wasn't sure of an appropriate response. "Thank you."

"I'm really sorry about yesterday. Sometimes I get into moods, you know? I guess I was sort of on the rag." He chuckled.

Lisa didn't answer.

"Did you like the Valentine?"

"It's—early, isn't it?"

There was an odd tone in his voice. "You're worth anticipating, Lisa."

"I'm going to go now," she said.

"Don't you dare," he said quietly. "I need to talk to you. I want to see you."

This was more than enough. "Goodbye." She set the phone down.

Lisa fixed a light breakfast—her ordinarily healthy appetite was diminished—and read the newspaper while she ate. She discovered she was reading the same headline paragraph over and over. She flipped to the comics section.

The phone rang. This time she let it ring half a dozen times before answering.

Roger. His voice was coldly furious. "Don't you *ever* hang up on me, Lisa. I can't stand that."

"Listen to me," she said. "Don't bother—"

"Never do that!"

"—me again," she finished. "Just. Go. Away."

There was a long silence. Then it sounded like he was crying.

Lisa set the receiver down. She realized she was gripping the hand-piece as though it was a club. She willed her fingers to relax.

She paced the perimeter of the living room until she decided there were more productive outlets for her nervous energy. For part of the afternoon, she scrubbed out the kitchen and bathroom. By sundown, she'd begun to relax. Roger was apparently not home. Either he impossibly wasn't moving so much as an inch, or he'd gone out before she had awakened. The hardwood floor didn't squeak up there. No sounds filtered down from the bedroom. The stereo was mute.

When the telephone rang, Lisa stared at the set as though it were a curled viper. She allowed it to ring twenty times before answering. It could be an emergency. It could be Joanne or someone else. She picked up the receiver and said, "Hello?" Nothing. "Hello," she said again. Someone was there. She could hear him breathing. Then the other receiver clicked into its cradle. In a few seconds more, Lisa heard the hum of the dial tone.

Roger Cross was a new listing in directory assistance. Lisa dialed the number the computer voice intoned. When she held the receiver away from her ear, she could hear the telephone ring upstairs. No one answered.

By early evening, Lisa found she was ravenous. She fixed herself a splendid supper of very rare steak and ate every morsel. She wondered if Roger were in some suburban singles bar picking up easier prey. While washing the day's dishes, she began to contemplate the unpleasant possibility of having to move to another neighborhood. It wasn't fair. She wouldn't go. She *liked* this apartment.

The phone rang. Lisa ignored it. Ten minutes later, it rang again. And ten minutes after that. Finally, she picked up the receiver with a curt *"What."*

"Hey, don't bite my head off." It was Joanne. The manager hadn't seen Roger all day either. She was calling to check on Lisa. Lisa told her about Roger's harassment.

"You could try calling Mountain Bell."

"Maybe I will," said Lisa.

"Listen, the offer's still open if you want to stay over here."

Lisa felt stubborn. Territorial. "No," she said. "Thank you."

"Hang in there and I'll talk to the owners on Tuesday," said Joanne.

Lisa thanked her and hung up.

By eight o'clock, Lisa was again immersed in comfortable cleaning routines. She swept all the floors. Then she gave the shower curtain a scrub-down. She dusted the shelves in the walk-in closet and put down Contac paper. Finally she returned to the bathroom and considered running a hot bath. It occurred to her she was out of clean towels. In fact, she was out of *every-thing* clean.

It sank home that she didn't really have anything clean and neat to wear in the morning. Lisa knew it would be an error to appear at interviews in limp Western shirts and grubby blue-jeans. She had one good wash-and-wear outfit. Her first inter-view was at nine; that meant she would have to catch the bus before eight. Something had to be done about the laundry to-night. Since coming to the city, she'd been called *too* clean, *too* neat. She couldn't help it.

Lisa didn't relish the idea of taking her dirty clothes and soap and bleach into that very cold night and descending to the laun-dry room next door, but there seemed to be no alternatives. Lisa cocked her head and glanced at the ceiling. She still had not heard a sound from upstairs. Maybe Roger had got lucky at some bar and no longer concerned himself with her. Perhaps he had drunk too much and fallen in front of a speeding truck. That thought was not without a tinge of hope.

It wasn't getting any earlier. She would need a full night's sleep.

Lisa stuffed everything she would need into the plastic laun-dry basket and unlocked her rear door. The back staircase was dimly lit by exit signs on each landing. The light cast her shadow weakly in front of her on the yellowed walls.

She counted. Seven steps down to the landing. Turn a blind corner to the left. Seven more steps to the first floor. Before opening the outer door, she belatedly fumbled for her keys. They were in her hip pocket.

The night was just as cold as she had anticipated. She felt the goose flesh form. The fine hairs rose on the back of her neck. The cracked concrete slab sidewalk extended the length of the apartment building. Lisa walked toward the alley, her stride faltering for a moment when she noticed the door of the garage across the alley hanging open. She thought she saw something move within the deeper darkness of the interior. She heard nothing. Probably just imagination. Probably.

She followed a branching path to the right, around a pair of blighted and dying elms. Now she was at the rear of the house where her managers lived. The building was an elaborate Victo-rian which had been converted into apartments sometime in the 'fifties. The original brickwork was plastered over and painted green. All the windows in the rear of the house were dark.

The long, straight flight of cement steps led to the basement and the laundry room. One, two . . . She realized she was counting the steps under her breath . . . five, six . . . The temperature dropped perceptibly as she descended. . . . ten. A level space and then a door. The sign tacked on the outside read: LAUNDRY EQUIPMENT AND PIPES WILL FREEZE IF DOOR REMAINS OPEN.

Lisa pushed the door open. The wood had swelled and the bottom scraped the cement floor. The hall was not illuminated, but she could see light glowing from within the laundry room, ahead and to her left. The hallway was long and dusty. She scented the odor of must and mildew. Eventually the passage-way ended in darkness, where Lisa knew were locked storage rooms and a barricaded staircase leading up to the rest of the house.

Her steps echoed slightly as she hefted the basket and started toward the laundry room. She felt, rather than heard, the door swing shut behind her. She didn't turn and look. Don't get paranoid, she thought.

Inside the laundry room, she set the basket down beside the more reputable-looking of the washers. The place smelled of neglect and decay. Lisa had the exaggerated feeling that even clean clothes could get dirty instantly just by being brought into this room. The brick walls showed through the crumbling plas-ter. The ceiling was a maze of haphazard exposed piping and conduits, ribbed from above by skeletal strips of lath.

She had loaded the washer and was adding the bleach when she heard the outside door scrape open distantly. She smelled the citrus cologne.

Lisa heard footsteps advance down the corridor toward the doorway of the laundry room. There was no place she could go, so she set down the bottle of bleach and waited.

Roger filled the doorway, grinning as happily as ever. "Hi there, L. P.," he said. "I waited a long time for you. It's cold out here." He rubbed his hands briskly. "It gets lonely in the dark."

"What do you want?" Lisa said.

"To get to know you." His voice warmed like syrup heating on the kitchen range. "I like hair that dark and sleek. I love green eyes. Too bad you don't have more on top—" His gaze flickered to her chest. "—but no one can have everything."

She stood still, hands at her sides.

"Nice night for finishing chores." Roger glanced at the

washer. "You might want to take those clothes out of the machine."

"Why?" she said.

"Just spread 'em out on the floor. I think you'll be a lot more comfortable." He made fists of his hands, then unclenched them.

"I don't think so," Lisa said.

"Oh? Why not?" Roger's teeth shone dully in the forty-watt glow. They looked as yellowed as old ivory.

"My family taught us to fight if we were in a corner." The words came out quietly, calmly.

"Well, I think your family is stupid." Spreading his arms slightly, Roger started forward. He hesitated when Lisa didn't retreat into one of the corners. Then he edged off to her right. Lisa finally reacted, moving away, but still facing him, following the contour of the wall. She was slightly closer now to the door.

"Keep going," he said.

She looked back at him uncertainly.

"It's no accident you're by the door," he said. "I'm fast. Very fast. You won't make it to the stairs."

"I'm not going to run," said Lisa.

"Oh yeah? Why not?" Roger stared at her, apparently bewildered.

"All I wanted to do was live here peacefully," said Lisa. She sighed. "But you had to push." She held up her hands, palms out. Worn leather shone. "You think I'm weird. A fruitcake, right? Well, I am weird. But I'm not like you." She slowly began to peel off her gloves.

His eyes stayed fixed on hers. Lisa smiled sadly at him. She felt her muzzle unhinge slightly, the jaw sliding forward. Her gloves dropped to the floor, a sound as muffled as the snow that had fallen that morning. She knew he was looking at the teeth. He should have looked at her hands. Her claws.

When she returned to her apartment with her laundry, she bathed herself, and then went into the bathroom to stare at her own face in the mirror. *Sunlight through the leafy canopy dappled patterns on her flanks.* She examined the openings in her fingertips where the claws could fully extend. "Mama," she whispered. "I don't like it here."

But she would persevere. She knew that. She would make a life for herself.

Lisa listened to the distant sirens, the drone of an airplane, a sharp noise that might have been either a backfire or a gunshot.

The city disturbed her.

She wished she felt safe.

In the Fast Lane

by Thomas F. Monteleone

Thomas Monteleone's dark humor gives most of his stories a hardboiled authenticity. He is not especially enamored of the human animal, and he can't seem to keep that fact a secret. Like Ed Bryant, he started out in science fiction but found his true voice, I think, in horror. He is the dark bard of the horny urban male and is sensible enough to know that such a lifestyle carries its own doom.

First published in 1981.

Another one was coming up behind him—the one, he knew, to finally get him.

Looking in the rear-view mirror, John Sheridan watched the headlights of the car approach his position on the Interstate. There were no other cars in sight. Even though he was doing sixty-five—the most he dared in drizzling rain and ghost-tread tires which should have been replaced months ago —the lights were gaining on him. Homing in like a missile or a sparrow-hawk.

He white-knuckled the steering wheel with both hands as the dark, rain-flecked vehicle pulled abreast of him in the left lane. It seemed to hang motionless for a moment, keeping pace with John. Sensing its dark presence, he wanted to turn, to look at it, but could not. It was as though his neck had become paralyzed. He tensed for the killing blow. . . .

Now!

But suddenly the other car was moving off, punching a hole in the misty rain, marking its path with a smear of red taillight.

John sagged behind the wheel, and was suddenly aware of his pulse thudding behind his ears, his breath rasping in and out, between clenched teeth. The whole fear-fantasy of someone creeping up on you on the highway and blowing you away was not an isolated nightmare. John had mentioned it to strangers in bars over lonely beers, and many had admitted to the same crazy fear. A couple of the weirder-looking guys had even said they imagined themselves, at different times, as both victim and predator. John knew what they meant—he'd imagined it too. Even though sometimes he thought he might be going goddamned crazy.

A lot of road-time could make you like that.

The wispy rain appeared to be easing off, and he angrily cut off the windshield wipers as he remembered the gun. The panic had throttled him, choked off all clear thinking, and he had forgotten he now carried something for the predatory sedan if it ever caught up with him—and he had a praeternatural feeling that it would eventually catch up with him.

But there was no sense in punishing himself. He would simply be ready the next time. The highway ahead and behind him was empty and dark, like the flat and wetly shining hide of giant eel. John found it comforting. He licked his lips, reached for a cigarette, lighted it.

Once again, death had slipped up beside him, but had passed him by. He felt the terror slip away from him as he accelerated and pushed towards Woodbridge and home. It was past four a.m. and he was glad the road was clear, even if just for the moment. He sometimes wondered how long he could hang on, being on the road so much. All this driving was making him more than a little crazy.

But like they said: if you want to make a lot of money, and you can't be a doctor or a dentist, then be a salesman.

And John was a hell of a salesman, that was for certain. At thirty-six, he was easily the best pipe-hawker Bendler & Krauch Plumbing Supply ever had. John's territory comprised of Delaware, Maryland, and Virginia, and he'd posted more plumbing fixture accounts with more clients in that territory than any other sales-route in the country.

His secret was simple: stay on the road. The more you travelled and talked to possible clients, the more you sold. Of course the guys in the office with families just couldn't stay out on the road for two, three weeks at a time the way John did. But what did he care if he didn't see his tacky little apartment in Suburban Virginia? He had nobody in his life, parents both dead, and not even a pet to worry about. Besides, if he kept it up at his present pace, by the end of the year he would have earned more than a hundred and fifty grand. Not bad for a guy with a degree in Cultural Anthropology.

The thought of the annual income made him smile, despite his nervousness. He took a final drag off the Marlboro and pushed it out the window into the slipstream. In doing so, he glimpsed a flash of light in the side-view mirror.

Even though the roads were still slick-lethal, he pushed down on the accelerator and his Chrysler New Yorker surged forward. Despite this, the headlights grew larger and more distinct, filling the rear-view mirror. The oncoming vehicle slipped out into the left lane of the Interstate, getting ready to pull alongside.

His hands grew moist, his heartbeat jumped up towards the fibrillation end of the scale. The glare of the other car's lights filled the rear-view mirror, a white, cool explosion of light reflected into John's face.

This was the one. The marrow in his bones sang out with conviction.

The other car's tires were keening in the rain, whirling at high-speed, sucking up the wet asphalt, almost hydro-planing. It became a roar, a scream in his left ear as he heard it, pulling abreast of him. His New Yorker was starting to drift back and forth across the right lane, losing traction, and still he pushed his speed higher.

But the other car continued to accelerate, gaining, overtaking him in the night, wanting only to keep pace for a single, final instant.

No!

The single word bounced around in an empty room in his mind. The car was in the blind spot of his side-mirror. In another moment it would be next to him.

John Sheridan knew that he must turn his head to the left. Maybe then it would be all right . . . ?

The idea that looking at the other car, actually looking into its dark glass, might end the craziness was appealing to him. For months now, he had been too terrified to even think of it, but suddenly, it seemed like the only solution.

To look over and see a normal human being would be all the proof, all the cure, he would require.

And so, as the dark shape pulled abreast of him, seeming to hang motionless for an instant, he recalled how all the craziness had started. John turned to regard the vehicle in the fast lane. . . .

. . . He had been driving back from a 10-day selling spree through Western Maryland. The hour was late and the traffic on Interstate 270 heading south from Frederick was practically non existent. He had purchased the New Yorker, and despite his endless smoking the "new" smell of the interior had not yet worn away. The in-dash stereo was blowing some electronic music by a Japanese guy named Kitaro, and John was leaning back, enjoying the powerful, gliding ride of the big Chrysler as he cruised the fast lane.

As he cleared a slight rise in the highway he was abruptly aware of a vehicle ahead on his right in the slower lane. Squinting out into the night, he could see a big, heavy car—a shapeless hulk, slicing through the darkness. John pushed down on the accelerator, moved to slip past the other vehicle. But as he pulled alongside, the other driver jammed on his brakes, slipped back in behind him in a crazy, erratic piece of driving. John thought nothing of this as he returned his gaze to the road ahead. And then the other car was pulling out on the left, jumping onto the shoulder and moving abreast of him.

As this happened, John felt the eyes of something staring at him. The skin on the back of his neck seemed to ripple as a coldness entered him. It was a very bad feeling—the empty bore of unknown eyes looking at you, through you.

The other car was still there, pacing him along the shoulder like a predatory beast. Without thinking, John looked over and saw that the other car's window was down, and that out of the darkness within, there came a black cylinder, pointed at him.

In that instant, he recognized it as the business-end of a gun barrel. It seemed to grow larger in his mind's eye—until it was like staring down the mouth of a bottomless well.

He may have screamed at that point, he could not remember, but suddenly the New Yorker was swerving sharply to the left. His tires definitely screamed and the heavy sedan lurched dangerously close to the car on the left, which had also swerved to avoid him. As John fought with the wheel to gain control, the other car accelerated and raced ahead into the darkness.

He was left breathless as his body thumped with the shock of adrenaline which now ebbed out of his bloodstream. The crazy bastard had tried to *kill* him!

He couldn't believe it even as he watched the other car's taillights dwindle to tiny red specks on the horizon ahead. And yet it was true. John didn't know what to do first. Should he chase the guy down? Stop and call the police?

He realized that he hadn't caught a license number. In fact, had not even seen the guy's face—the end of the gun had seemed so big to obscure all else. The thought of pursuing the other car was not appealing. He didn't want to think about what he might do if he actually caught up with him. Better to just get it together, pull off at the next exit where there might be a phone, and report the incident to the State Police.

He drove on for another few minutes, gathering his thoughts and his composure. No other cars passed him. It was very late and few vehicles were still out on a weeknight. In the distance, on the shoulder of the Interstate, he could see the blood-red glow of taillights.

Cautiously, he eased off on the gas and approached the other car. As he drew closer, he could see from the configuration of the lights that this vehicle had not been the one which had attacked him. This car was sluiced off the road at a bad angle, had cleared the shoulder, and was tilted up onto a grassy bank.

An accident, maybe. He pulled in behind the other car and stopped, studying it for a moment in the wash of his headlights. He couldn't see anyone in the car, and he wondered if they had left the car to go for help. A crazy thing to do, especially if they had left all their lights on.

Leaving his own lights on, John left the car and walked slowly to the derelict. For some reason, he felt defenseless and naked in the cold play of his own headlights. With each step forward, he felt worse about the entire scene. Something was wrong here. The feeling hung over everything like a foul odor; you couldn't miss it. And as John approached the driver's side, he saw the bullet-hole in the side window, and the fear-thought not allowed now capered madly through his mind.

Through the fractured glass, he could see a body, a formless shape lying on the front seat. Fighting back the panic, he reached for the door handle and depressed the latch.

He didn't want to see what awaited him, but he had no choice. As the door swung open, he heard a woman's voice moaning in pain, trying to speak.

When he leaned in to pull her up into his arms, he saw that she was a young woman in her twenties. He could also see the blood on her cheeks, and the hole in her skull where her eye had been. (He would later learn from the doctors that the bullet had entered her left eye, and in one of those crazy, life-saving quirks of fate, had exited through the sinus cavity under her right eye without damaging the brain.) The visual effect was so unnerving, so unreal, she looked like she wore a cheap mask.

He carried the victim to his car, and drove her to the nearest hospital where they saved her life, but not her eye. Her description of her attacker was as vague and yet as similar as John's, and he knew that the bastard would not be found, would not be caught.

And that meant that he was still out there somewhere, running the highways, ready to try again. As time passed, the incident did not grow less vivid in his mind, but more so. When he could sleep, his dreams were filled with visions of the dark sedan. When awake, he could not get the single obsessive thought from mind—that the driver would eventually find him, and complete the job unfinished. . . .

. . . John Sheridan peered through the dark glass of the other car, and for an instant saw his own reflection, which masked the face of the driver. But that no longer mattered.

It was him, he could feel a reptilian chill in his certainty.

And this time, there would be no panic. This time John was prepared, and in a long-planned maneuver, he jammed on his brakes for an instant. The effect was startling as the car on the left seemed to hurtle forward.

Cutting the wheel hard, John slipped in behind the predator, tail-gating him crazily. The driver of the other car seemed confused with the sudden turn of events. John kept his New Yorker close behind the sedan as it weaved from side to side in the fast lane. Reaching beneath the driver's seat, John pulled out the .38 calibre special he had purchased in the sporting goods store in Springfield.

Now the sonofabitch would know what it felt like . . .

He cut the wheel to the left and slipped his heavy car onto the shoulder, to the left of the fast lane. His worn tires whistled and scritched as they purchased on the loose gravel, but he accelerated anyway. A touch of his finger lowered his right window and the howling dampness of the night leaped in.

Lurching crazily, the New Yorker raced along the shoulder, gaining on the dark sedan, pulling alongside with an inexorable movement. The other car could not escape now. Looking over, John picked up the gun and sighted along its short length. The car in the fast lane was drifting into view through the open passenger's window.

The night rushed by, the windstream ripping and tearing at him. His forward speed was close to ninety as he kept the pace, and suddenly he was abreast of the predator. Forgetting about the road ahead, he looked to the right, aimed the gun.

Through the dark glass, he could see the vague shape of a face in profile, looking straight ahead. As the two cars plunged into the night, side by side, he waited and watched until the face turned to look at him. He wanted the bastard to stare down the bottomless well of the gun barrel. And then, as if on cue, the other driver turned—

—and John Sheridan faced *himself*.

It was a single slice of time, a solitary instant which exploded like a photographic flash in his mind. Impossibly, John stared at his other self, his *doppleganger* in the other car. And in that strobe light of recognition, he felt the acid burn of *deja vu* as the other car swerved dangerously close to him.

Things happened quickly then. He grabbed the wheel tightly, crushed down the accelerator, and jumped back into the fast lane as he tore quickly away from the other car. He was confused now, but he kept thinking about how easy it would have been to have pulled the trigger.

He continued at high speed until he advanced upon another car in the right lane. It was a woman, alone, looking straight ahead. Slowing, he pulled alongside, raised the gun, and waited for her to turn her face . . . so he could look her in the eye.

The Perfect Crime

by Max Allan Collins

Max Allan Collins' Nate Heller novels get mentioned right after his work on the Dick Tracy comic strip. Should be the other way around, the Hellers being the definitive historical detective novels of my generation. But I'd like to say a few fond words for his other two series characters, Mallory and Quarry, both of whom have appeared in a number of short but powerful novels that display Collins' talent as a social critic and adventure writer. Look them up.

First published in 1988.

She was the first movie star I ever worked for, but I wasn't much impressed. If I were that easily impressed, I'd have been impressed by Hollywood itself. And having seen the way Hollywood portrayed my profession on the so-called silver screen, I wasn't much impressed with Hollywood.

On the other hand, Dolores Dodd was the most beautiful woman who ever wanted to hire my services, and that did impress me. Enough so that when she called me, that October, and asked me to drive out to her "sidewalk cafe" nestled under the Palisades in Montemar Vista, I went, wondering if she would be as pretty in the flesh as she was on celluloid.

I'd driven out Pacific Coast Highway that same morning, a clear cool morning with a blue sky lording it over a vast sparkling sea. Pelicans were playing tag with the breaking surf, flying just under the curl of the white-lipped waves. Yachts, like a child's toy boats, floated out there just between me and the horizon. I felt like I could reach out for one, pluck and examine

it, sniff it maybe, like King Kong checking out Fay Wray's lingerie.

"Dolores Dodd's Sidewalk Café," as a billboard on the hillside
behind it so labeled the place, was a sprawling two-story hacienda affair, as big as a beached luxury liner. Over its central,
largest-of-many archways, a third-story tower rose like a stubby
lighthouse. There weren't many cars here—it was approaching
ten a.m., too early for the luncheon crowd and even I didn't
drink cocktails this early in the day. Not and tell, anyway.

She was waiting in the otherwise unpopulated cocktail
lounge, where massive wooden beams in a traditional Spanish
mode fought the chromium-and-leather furnishings and the
chrome-and-glass-brick bar and came out a draw. She was a big
blonde woman with more curves than the highway out front
and just the right number of hills and valleys. Wearing a clingy
summery white dress, she was seated on one of the bar stools,
with her bare legs crossed; they weren't the best-looking legs on
the planet, necessarily. I just couldn't prove otherwise. That
good a detective I'm not.

"Peter Mallory?" she asked, and her smile dimpled her
cheeks in a manner that made her whole heart-shaped face
smile, and the world smile as well, including me. She didn't
move off the stool, just extended her hand in a manner that was
at once casual and regal.

I took the hand, not knowing whether to kiss it, shake it, or
press it into a book like a corsage I wanted to keep. I looked at
her feeling vaguely embarrassed; she was so pretty you didn't
know where to look next, and felt like there was maybe something wrong with looking anywhere. But I couldn't help myself.

She had pale, creamy skin and her hair was almost white
blonde. They called her the ice-cream blonde, in the press. I
could see why.

Then I got around to her eyes. They were blue of course,
cornflower blue; and big and sporting long lashes, the real Mc-
Coy, not your dimestore variety. But they were also the saddest
eyes I'd ever looked into. The smile froze on my face like I was
looking at Medusa, not a twenty-nine-year-old former sixth-
grade teacher from Massachusetts who won a talent search.

"Is something wrong?" she asked. Then she patted the stool
next to her.

I sat and said, "Nothing's wrong. I never had a movie star for
a client before."

"I see. You came recommended highly."

"Oh?"

Her voice had a low, throaty quality that wasn't forced or affected; she was what Mae West would've been if Mae West wasn't a parody. "A friend of mine in the D.A.'s office downtown. He said you got fired for being too honest."

"Actually, I like to think I quit. And I don't like to think I'm *too* honest."

"Oh?"

"Just honest enough."

She smiled at that, very broadly, showing off teeth whiter than cameras can record. "Might I get you a drink, Mr. Mallory?"

"It's a little early."

"I know it is. Might I get you a drink?"

"Sure."

"Anything special?"

"Anything that doesn't have a little paper umbrella in it is fine by me."

She fixed me up with a rye, and had the same herself. I liked that in a woman.

"Have you heard of Lucky Luciano?" she asked, returning to her bar stool.

"Heard of him," I said. "Haven't met him."

"What do you know about him?"

I shrugged. "Big-time gangster from back East. Runs casinos all over southern California. More every day."

She flicked the air with a long red fingernail, like she was shooing away a bug. "Well, perhaps you've noticed the tower above my restaurant."

"Sure."

"I live on the second floor, but the tower above is fairly spacious."

"Big enough for a casino, you mean."

"That's right," she said, nodding. "I was approached by Luciano, more than once. I turned him away, more than once. After all, with my location, and my clientele, a casino could make a killing."

"You're doing well enough legally. Why bother with ill?"

"I agree. And if I were to get into any legal problems, that would mean a scandal, and Hollywood doesn't need another scandal. Busby Berkley's trial is coming up soon, you know."

The noted director and choreographer, creator of so many frothy fantasies, was up on the drunk-driving homicide of three pedestrians, not far from this café.

"But now," she said, her bee-stung lips drawn nervously tight, "I've begun to receive threatening notes."

"From Luciano, specifically?"

"No. They're extortion notes, actually. Asking me to pay off Artie Lewis. You know, the bandleader?"

"Why him?"

"He's in Luciano's pocket. Gambling markers. And I used to go with Artie. He lives in San Francisco, now."

"I see. Well, have you talked to the cops?"

"No."

"Why not?"

"I don't want to get Artie in trouble."

"Have you talked to Artie?"

"Yes—he claims he knows nothing about this. He doesn't want my money. He doesn't even want me back—he's got a new girl."

I'd like to see the girl that could make you forget Dolores Dodd.

"So," I said, "you want me to investigate. Can I see the extortion notes?"

"No," she said, shaking her white blonde curls like the mop of the gods, "that's not it. I burned those notes. For Artie's sake."

"Well, for Pete's sake," I said, "where *do* I come in?"

"I think I'm being followed. I'd like a bodyguard."

I resisted looking her over wolfishly and making a wisecrack. She was a nice woman, and the fact that hers was the sort of a body a private eye would pay to guard didn't seem worth mentioning. My fee did.

"Twenty-five a day and expenses," I said.

"Fine," she said. "And you can have any meals you like right here at the Café. Drinks, too. Run a tab and I'll pick it up."

"Swell," I grinned. "I was wondering if I'd ever run into a fringe benefit in this racket."

"You can be my chauffeur."

"Well . . ."

"You have a problem with that, Mr. Mallory?"

"I have a private investigator's license, and a license to carry a gun. But I don't have a chauffeur's license."

"I think a driver's license will suffice." Her bee-stung lips were poised in a kiss of amusement. "What's the real problem, Mallory?"

"I'm not wearing a uniform. I'm strictly plainclothes."

She smiled tightly, wryly amused, saying, "All right, hang

onto your dignity . . . but you have to let me pay the freight on a couple of new suits for you. I'll throw 'em in on the deal."

"Fine," I said.

So for the next two months, she was my only client. I worked six days a week for her—Monday through Saturday. Sundays God, Mallory and Dodd rested. I drove her in her candy-apple red Packard convertible, a car designed for blondes with wind-blown hair and pearls. She sat in back, of course. Most days I took her to the Hal Roach Studio where she was making a musical with Laurel and Hardy. I'd wait in some dark pocket of the sound stage and watch her every move out in the brightness. In a black wig, lacy bodice, and clinging, gypsy skirt, Dolores was the kind of girl you took home to mother, and if mother didn't like her, to hell with mother.

Evenings she hit the club circuit, the Trocadero and the El Mocambo chiefly. I'd sit in the cocktail lounges and quietly drink and wait for her and her various dates to head home. Some of these guys were swishy types that she was doing the studio a favor by appearing in public with; a couple others spent the night.

I don't mean to tell tales out of school, but this tale can't be told at all unless I'm frank about that one thing: Dolores slept around. Later, when the gossip rags were spreading rumors about alcohol and drugs, that was all the bunk. But Dolores was a friendly girl. She had generous charms and she was generous with them.

"Mallory," she said, one night in early December when I was dropping her off, walking her up to the front door of the café like always, "I think I have a crush on you."

She was alone tonight, having played girlfriend to one of those Hollywood funny boys for the benefit of Louella Parsons and company. Alone but for me.

She slipped an arm around my waist. She had booze on her breath, but then so did I, and neither one of us was drunk. She was bathed gently in moonlight and Chanel Number Five.

She kissed me with those bee-stung lips, stinging so softly, so deeply.

I moved away. "No. I'm sorry."

She winced. "What's wrong?"

"I'm the hired help. You're just lonely tonight."

Her eyes, which I seldom looked into because of the depth of the sadness there, hardened. "Don't you ever get lonely, you bastard?"

I swallowed. "Never," I said.

She drew her hand back to slap me, but then she just touched my face, instead. Gentle as the ocean breeze, and it was gentle tonight, the breeze, so gentle.

"Goodnight, Mallory," she said.

And she slipped inside.

"Goodnight," I said, to nobody. Then to myself: "Goodnight, you goddamn sap."

I drove her Packard to the garage that was attached to the bungalow above the restaurant complex; to do that I had to take Montemar Vista Road to Seretto Way, turning right. The Mediterranean-style stucco bungalow on Cabrillo, like so many houses in Montemar Vista, climbed the side of the hill like a clinging vine. It was owned by Dolores Dodd's partner in the Café, movie director/producer Warren Eastman. Eastman had an apartment next to Dolores' above the restaurant, as well as the bungalow, and seemed to live back and forth between the two.

I wondered what the deal was, with Eastman and my client, but I never asked, not directly. Eastman was a thin, dapper man in his late forties, with a pointed chin and a small mustache and a widow's peak that his slick black hair was receding around, making his face look diamond-shaped. He often sat in the cocktail lounge with a Bloody Mary in one hand and a cigarette in a holder in the other. He was always talking deals with movie people.

"Mallory," he said, one night, motioning me over to the bar. He was seated on the very stool that Dolores had been, that first morning. "This is Nick DeCiro, the talent agent. Nick, this is the gumshoe Dolores hired to protect her from the big bad gambling syndicate."

DeCiro was another darkly handsome man, a bit older than Eastman, though he lacked both the mustache and receding hairline of the director. DeCiro wore a white suit with a dark sportshirt, open at the neck to reveal a wealth of black chest hair.

I shook DeCiro's hand. His grip was firm, moist, like a fistful of topsoil.

"Nicky here is your client's ex-husband," Eastman said, with a wag of his cigarette-in-holder, trying for an air of that effortless decadence that Hollywood works so hard at.

"Dolores and me are still pals," DeCiro said, lighting up a

foreign cig with a shiny silver lighter that he then clicked shut with a meaningless flourish. "We broke up amicably."

"I heard it was over extreme cruelty," I said.

DeCiro frowned, and Eastman cut in glibly, "Don't believe everything you read in the papers, Mallory. Besides, you have to get a divorce over something."

"But then you'd *know* that in your line of work," DeCiro said, an edge in his thin voice.

"I don't do divorce work," I said.

"Sure," DeCiro said.

"I don't. If you gents will excuse me . . ."

"Mallory, Mallory," Eastman said, touching my arm, "don't be so touchy."

I waited for him to remove his hand from my arm, then said, "Did you want something, Mr. Eastman? I'm not much for this Hollywood shit-chat."

"I don't like your manner," DeCiro said.

"Nobody does," I said. "But I don't get paid well enough for it to matter."

"Mallory," Eastman said, "I was just trying to convince Nicky here that my new film is perfect for a certain client of his. I'm doing a mystery. About the perfect crime. The perfect murder."

"No such animal," I said.

"Oh, really?" DeCiro said, lifting an eyebrow.

"Murder and crime are inexact sciences. All the planning in the world doesn't account for the human element."

"Then how do you explain," Eastman said archly, "the hundreds of murders that go unsolved in this country?"

"Policework is a more exact science than crime or murder," I admitted, "but we have a lot of corrupt cops in this world—and a lot of dumb ones."

"Then there *are* perfect crimes."

"No. Just unsolved ones. And imperfect detectives. Good evening, gentlemen."

That was the most extensive conversation I had with either Eastman or DeCiro during the time I was employed by Miss Dodd, though I said hello and they did the same, now and then, at the Café.

But Eastman was married to an actress named Miranda Diamond, a fiery Latin whose parents were from Mexico City, even if she'd been raised in the Bronx. She fancied herself as the next Lupe Velez, and she was a similarly voluptuous dame, though her handsome features were as hard as a gravestone.

She cornered me at the Café one night, in the cocktail lounge, where I was drinking on the job.

"You're a dick," she said.

We'd never spoken before.

"I hope you mean that in the nicest way," I said.

"You're bodyguarding that bitch," she said, sitting next to me on a leather-and-chrome couch. Her nostrils flared; if I'd been holding a red cape, I'd have dropped it and run for the stands.

"Miss Dodd is my client, yes, Miss Diamond."

She smiled. "You recognize me."

"Oh yes. And I also know enough to call you Mrs. Eastman, in certain company."

"My husband and I are separated."

"Ah."

"But I could use a little help in the divorce court."

"What kind of help?"

"Photographs of him and that bitch in the sack." She said "the" like "thee."

"That would help you."

"Yes. You see . . . my husband has similar pictures of me, with a gentleman, in a compromising position."

"Even missionaries get caught in that position, I understand." I offered her a cigarette, she took it, and I lit hers and mine. "And if you had similar photos, you could negotiate yourself a better settlement."

"Exactly. Interested?"

"I don't do divorce work. I don't sell clients out. It's a conflict of interests."

She smiled; she put her hand on my leg. "I could make it worth your while. Financially and . . . otherwise."

It wasn't even Christmas and already two screen goddesses wanted to hop in the sack with me. I must have really been something.

"No thanks, señorita. I sleep alone . . . just me and my conscience."

Then she suggested I do to myself what she'd just offered to do for me. She was full of ideas.

So was I. I was pretty sure Dolores and Eastman were indeed having an affair, but it was one of the on-again-off-again variety. One night they'd be affectionate, in that sickening Hollywood sweetie-baby way; the next night he would be cool to her; the next she would be cool to him. It was love, I recognized it, but the kind that sooner or later blows up like an overheated engine.

Ten days before Christmas, Dolores was honored by a famous British comedian, so famous I'd never the hell heard of him, with a dinner at the Troc. At a table for twelve upstairs, in the swanky cream-and-gold dining room, Dolores was being feted by her show-biz friends, while I sat downstairs in the oak-paneled Cellar Lounge with other people not famous enough to sit upstairs, nursing a rye at the polished copper bar. I didn't feel like a polished copper, that was for sure. I was just a chauffeur with a gun, and a beautiful client who didn't need me.

That much was clear to me: in the two months I'd worked for Dolores, I hadn't spotted anybody following her except a few fans, and I couldn't blame them. I think I was just a little bit in love with the ice-cream blonde myself. But she was a client, and she slept around, and neither of those things appealed to me in a girl.

About half an hour into the evening, I heard a scream upstairs. A woman's scream, a scream that might have belonged to Dolores.

I took the stairs four at a time and had my gun in my hand when I entered the fancy dining room. Normally when I enter fancy dining rooms with a gun in my hand, all eyes are on me. Not this time.

Dolores was clawing at her ex-husband, who was laughing at her. She was being held back by Patsy Peters, the dark-haired rubber-faced comedienne who was Dolores' partner in the two-reelers. DeCiro, in a white tux, had a starlet on his arm, a blonde about twenty with a neckline down to her shoes. The starlet looked frightened, but DeCiro was having a big laugh.

I put my gun away and took over for Patsy Peters.

"Miss Dodd," I said, gently, whispering into her ear, holding onto her arms from behind, "don't do this."

She went limp for a moment, then straightened and said, with stiff dignity, "I'm all right, Peter."

It was the only time she ever called me that.

I let go of her.

"What's the problem?" I asked. I was asking both Dolores Dodd and her ex-husband.

"He embarrassed me," she said, without any further explanation.

And without any further anything, I said to DeCiro, "Go."

DeCiro twitched a smile. "I was invited."

"I'm uninviting you. Go."

His face tightened and he thought about saying or doing something. But my eyes were on him like magnets on metal and instead he gathered his date and her décolletage and took a powder.

"Are you ready to go home?" I asked Dolores.

"No," she said, with a shy smile, and she squeezed my arm, and went back to the table of twelve where her party of Hollywood types awaited. She was the guest of honor, after all.

Two hours, and two drinks later, I was escorting her home. She sat in the back of the candy-apple red Packard in her mink coat and sheer mauve-and-silver evening gown and diamond necklace and told me what had happened, the wind whipping her ice-blonde hair.

"Nicky got himself invited," she said, almost shouting over the wind. "Without my knowledge. Asked the host to reserve a seat next to me at the table. Then he wandered in late, with a date, that little *starlet,* which you may have noticed rhymes with harlot, and sat at another table, leaving me sitting next to an empty seat at a party in *my* honor. He sat there necking with that little tramp and I got up and went over and gave him a piece of my mind. It . . . got a little out of hand. Thanks for stepping in, Mallory."

"It's what you pay me for."

She sat in silence for a while; only the wind spoke. It was a cold Saturday night, as cold as a chilled martini. I had asked her if she wanted the top up on the convertible, but she said no. She began to look behind us as we moved slowly down Sunset.

"Mallory," she said, "someone's following us."

"I don't think so."

"Somebody's following us, I tell you!"

"I'm keeping an eye on the rearview mirror. We're fine."

She leaned forward and clutched my shoulder. "Get moving! Do you want me to be kidnapped, or killed? It could be Luciano's gangsters, for God's sake!"

She was the boss. I hit the pedal. At speeds up to seventy miles per, we sailed west around the curves of Sunset; there was a service station at the junction of the boulevard and the coast highway, and I pulled in.

"What are you doing?" she demanded.

I turned and looked into the frightened blue eyes. "I'm going to get some gas, and keep watch. And see if anybody comes up on us, or anybody suspicious goes by. Don't you worry. I'm armed."

I looked close at every car that passed by the station. I saw no one and nothing suspicious. Then I paid the attendant and we headed north on the coast highway. Going nice and slow.

"I ought to fire you," she said, pouting back there.

"This is my last night, Miss Dodd," I said. "I like to work for my money. I feel I'm taking yours."

She leaned forward, clutched my shoulder again. "No, no, I tell you, I'm frightened."

"Why?"

"I . . . I just feel I still need you around. You give me a sense of security."

"Have you had any more threatening notes?"

"No." Her voice sounded very small, now.

"If you do, call me, or the cops. Or both."

It was two a.m. when I slid the big car in in front of the sprawling Sidewalk Café. I was shivering with cold; a sea breeze was blowing, Old Man Winter taking his revenge on California. I turned and looked at her again. I smiled.

"I'll walk you to the door, Miss Dodd."

She smiled at me, too, but this time the smile didn't light up her face, or the world, or me. This time the smile was as sad as her eyes. Sadder.

"That won't be necessary, Mallory."

"Are you sure?"

"Yes. Do me one favor. Work for me next week. Be my chauffeur one more week, while I decide whether or not to replace you with another bodyguard, or . . . what."

"Okay."

"Go home, Mallory. See you Monday."

"See you Monday," I said, and I watched her go in the front door of the Café. Then I drove the Packard up to the garage above, on the Palisades, and got in my dusty inelegant 1925 Marmon and headed back to my apartment at the Berglund in Hollywood. I had a hunch Dolores Dodd wouldn't be pulling down a wall bed in *her* apartment tonight.

My hunch was right, but for the wrong reason.

Monday morning, sunny but cool if no longer cold, I pulled into one of the parking places alongside the Sidewalk Café; it was around ten-thirty and mine was the only car. The big front door was locked. I knocked until the Spanish cleaning lady let me in.

She said she hadn't seen Miss Dodd yet this morning. I went up the private stairway off the kitchen that led up to the two apartments. The door at the top of the stairs was unlocked; beyond it were the two facing apartment doors. I knocked on hers.

"Miss Dodd?"

No answer.

I tried for a while, then went and found the cleaning woman again. "Maria, do you have any idea where Miss Dodd might be? She doesn't seem to be in her room."

"She might be stay up at Meester Eastmon's."

I nodded, started to walk away, then looked back and added as an afterthought, "Did you see her yesterday?"

"I no work Sunday."

I guess Maria, like God, Mallory and Dolores Dodd, rested on Sunday. Couldn't blame her.

I thought about taking the car up and around, then said to hell with it and began climbing the concrete steps beyond the pedestrian bridge that arched over the highway just past the Café. These steps, all two-hundred and eighty of them, straight up the steep hill, were the only direct access from the coast road to the bungalow on Cabrillo Street. Windblown sand had drifted over the steps and the galvanized handrail was as cold and wet as a liar's handshake.

I grunted my way to the top. I'd started out as a young man, had reached middle age by step one hundred and was now ready for the retirement home. I sat on the cold damp top step and poured sand out of my scuffed-up Florsheims, glad I hadn't bothered with a shine in the last few weeks. Then I stood and looked past the claustrophobic drop of the steps, to where the sun was reflecting off the sand and sea. The beach was blinding, the ocean dazzling. It was beautiful, but it hurt to look at. A seagull was flailing with awkward grace against the breeze like a fighter losing the last round.

Soon I was knocking on Eastman's front door. No answer. Went to check to see if my client's car was there, swinging up the black-studded blue garage door. The car was there, all right, the red Packard convertible, next to Eastman's Lincoln sedan.

My client was there, too.

She was slumped in front, sprawled across the steering wheel. She was still in the mink, the mauve-and-silver gown, and the diamond necklace she'd worn to the Troc Saturday night. But her clothes were rumpled, in disarray, like an unmade bed; and there was blood on the front of the gown, coagulated rubies beneath the diamonds. There was blood on her face, on her white, white face.

She'd always had pale creamy skin, but now it was as white as a wedding dress. There was no pulse in her throat. She was cold. She'd been dead a while.

I stood and looked at her and maybe I cried. That's my business, isn't it? Then I went out and up the side steps to the loft above the garage and roused the elderly fellow named Jones who lived there; he was the bookkeeper for the Sidewalk Café. I asked him if he had a phone, and he did, and I used it.

I had told my story to the uniformed men four times before the men from Central Homicide showed. The detective in charge was Lieutenant Rondell, a thin, somber, detached man in his mid-forties with smooth creamy gray hair and icy eyes. His brown gabardine suit wasn't expensive but it was well-pressed. His green pork-pie lightweight felt hat was in his hand, in deference to the deceased.

Out of deference to me, he listened to my story as I told it for the fifth time. He didn't seem to think much of it.

"You're telling me this woman was murdered," he said.

"I'm telling you the gambling syndicate boys were pressuring her, and she wasn't caving in."

"And you were her bodyguard," Rondell said.

"Some bodyguard," said the other man from Homicide, Rondell's brutish shadow, and cracked his knuckles and laughed. We were in the garage and the laughter made hollow echoes off the cement, like a basketball bouncing in an empty stadium.

"I was her bodyguard," I told Rondell tightly. "But I didn't work Sundays."

Rondell nodded. He walked over and looked at the corpse in the convertible. A photographer from Homicide was snapping photos; pops and flashes of light accompanied Rondell's trip around the car as if he were a star at a Hollywood opening.

I went outside. The smell of death is bad enough when it's impersonal; when somebody you know has died, it's like having asthma in a steamroom.

Rondell found me leaning against the side of the stucco garage, lighting up my second Camel.

"It looks like suicide," he said.

"Sure. It's supposed to."

He lifted an eyebrow and a shoulder. "The ignition switch is turned on. Carbon monoxide."

"Car wasn't running when I got here."

"Long since ran out of gas, most likely. If what you say is true, she's been there since Saturday night . . . that is, early Sunday morning."

I shrugged. "She's wearing the same clothes, at least."

"When we fix time of death, it'll all come clear."

"Oh, yeah? See what the coroner has to say about that."

Rondell's icy eyes froze further. "Why?"

"This cold snap we've had, last three days. It's warmer this morning, but Sunday night, Jesus. That sea breeze was murder —if you'll pardon the expression."

Rondell nodded. "Perhaps cold enough to retard decomposition, you mean."

"Perhaps."

He pushed the pork pie back on his head. "We need to talk to this bird Eastman."

"I'll say. He's probably at his studio. Paramount. When he's on a picture, they pick him up by limo every morning before dawn."

Rondell went to use the phone in old man Jones' loft flat. I smoked my cigarette.

Rondell's brutish sidekick exited the garage and slid his arm around the shoulder of a young uniformed cop, who seemed uneasy about the attention.

"Ice-cream blonde, huh?" the big flatfoot said. "I woulda liked a coupla scoops of that myself."

I tapped the brute on the shoulder and he turned to me and said, "Huh?" stupidly, and I coldcocked him. He went down like a building.

But not out, though. "You're gonna pay for that, you bastard," he said, sounding like the school-yard bully he was. He touched the blood in the corner of his mouth, hauled himself up off the cement. "You go to goddamn jail when you hit a goddamn cop."

"You'd need a witness, first," I said.

"I got one," he said, but when he turned to look, the young uniformed cop was gone.

I walked up to him and stood damn near belt buckle to belt buckle and smiled a smile that had nothing to do with smiling. "Any time you want to pay me back, man to man, I won't be hard to find."

He tasted blood and fluttered his eyes like a girl and said

something unintelligible and disappeared back inside the garage.

Rondell came clopping down the wooden steps and stood before me and smiled firmly. "I just spoke with Eastman. We'll interview him more formally, of course, but the preliminary interrogation indicates a possible explanation."

"Oh?"

He was nodding. "Yeah. Apparently Saturday night he bolted the stairwell door around midnight. It's a door that leads to both apartments above the Sidewalk Café. Said he thought Miss Dodd had mentioned she was going to sleep over at her mother's that night."

"You mean, she couldn't get in?"

"Right."

"Well, hell, man, she would've knocked."

"Eastman says if she did, he didn't hear her. He says there was high wind and pounding surf all night; he figures that drowned out all other sounds."

I smirked. "Does he, really? So what's your scenario?"

"Well, when Miss Dodd found she couldn't get into her apartment, she must've decided to climb the steps to the street above, walked to the garage and spent the rest of the night in her car. She must've gotten cold, and switched on the ignition to keep warm, and the fumes got her."

I sighed. "A minute ago you were talking suicide."

"That's still a possibility."

"What about the blood on her face and dress?"

He shrugged. "She may have fallen across the wheel and cut her mouth, when she fell unconscious."

"Look, if she wanted to get warm, why would she sit in her open convertible? That Lincoln sedan next to her is unlocked and has the keys in it."

"I can't answer that—yet."

I was shaking my head. Then I pointed at him. "Ask the elderly gent upstairs if he heard her opening the garage door, starting up the Packard's cold engine sometime between two a.m. and dawn. Ask him!"

"I did. He didn't. But it was a windy night, and . . ."

"Yeah, and the surf was crashing something fierce. Right. Let's take a look at her shoes."

"Huh?"

I pointed down to my scuffed-up Florsheims. "I just scaled

those two-hundred-and-eighty steps. This shoeshine boy's nightmare is the result. Let's *see* if she walked up those steps."

Rondell nodded and led me into the garage. The print boys hadn't been over the vehicle yet, so the Lieutenant didn't open the door on the rider's side, he just leaned carefully in.

Then he stood and contemplated what he'd seen. For a moment he seemed to have forgotten me, then he said, "Have a look yourself."

I had one last look at the beautiful woman who'd driven to nowhere in this immobile car.

She wore delicate silver dress heels; they were as pristine as Cinderella's glass slippers.

The coroner at the inquest agreed with me on one point: "The high winds and very low cold prevailing that weekend would have preserved the body beyond the usual time required for decomposition to set in."

The inquest was, otherwise, a bundle of contradictions, and about as inconclusive as the virgin birth. A few new, sinister facts emerged. She had bruises *inside* her throat. Had someone shoved a bottle down her throat? Her alcohol level was high—.13 percent—much higher than the three or four drinks she was seen to have had at the Troc. And there *was* gas left in the car, it turned out—several gallons; yet the ignition switch was turned on. . . .

But the coroner's final verdict was that Dolores died by carbon monoxide poisoning, "breathed accidentally." Nonetheless, the papers talked suicide, and the word on the streets of Hollywood was "hush-up." Nobody wanted another scandal. Not after Mary Astor's diaries and Busby Berkley's drunk-driving fatalities.

I wasn't buying the coroner's verdict, either.

I knew that three people, on the Monday I'd found Dolores, had come forward to the authorities and reported having seen her on *Sunday*, long after she had "officially" died.

Miranda Diamond, Eastman's now ex-wife (their divorce had gone through, finally, apparently fairly amicably), claimed to have seen Dolores, still dressed in her Trocadero fineries, behind the wheel of her distinctive Packard convertible at the corner of Sunset and Vine Sunday, mid-morning. She was, Miranda told the cops, in the company of a tall, swarthy, nattily dressed young man whom Miranda had never seen before.

Mrs. Wallace Ford, wife of the famed director, had received a brief phone call from Dolores around four Sunday afternoon. Dolores had called to say she would be attending the Fords' cocktail party, and was it all right if she brought along "a new, handsome friend?"

Finally, and best of all, there was Warren Eastman himself. Neighbors had reported to the police that they heard Eastman and Dolores quarreling bitterly, violently, at the bungalow above the restaurant, Sunday morning, around breakfast time. Eastman said he had thrown her out, and that she had screamed obscenities and beaten on the door for ten minutes (and police did find kick marks on the shrub-secluded, hacienda-style door).

"It was a lover's quarrel," Eastman told a reporter. "I heard she had a new boyfriend—some Latin fellow from San Francisco —and she denied it. But I knew she was lying."

Eastman also revealed, in the press, that Dolores didn't own any real investment in her Sidewalk Café; that she made no investment other than lending her name, for which she got fifty percent of the profits.

I called Rondell after the inquest and he told me the case was closed.

"We both know something smells," I said. "Aren't you going to do something?"

"Yes," he said.

"What?"

"I'm going to hang up."

And he did.

Rondell was a good cop in a bad town, an honest man in a system so corrupt the Borgias would've felt moral outrage. But he couldn't do much about movie-mogul pressure by way of City Hall; Los Angeles had one big business and the film industry was it. And I was just a private detective with a dead client.

On the other hand, she'd paid me to protect her, and ultimately I hadn't. I had accepted her money, and it seemed to me she ought to get something for it, even if it was posthumous.

I went out on a Monday morning—four weeks to the day since I'd found the ice-cream blonde melting in that garage— and at the Café, which still bore her name, sitting alone in the cocktail lounge, reading *Variety* and drinking a Bloody Mary, was Warren Eastman. He was between pictures and just two stools down from where she had sat when she first hired me. He was wearing a blue blazer, a cream silk cravat, and white pants.

He lowered the paper and looked at me; he was surprised to

420   THE PERFECT CRIME

see me, but it was not a pleasant surprise, even though he affected a toothy smile under the twitchy little mustache.

"What brings you around, Mallory? I don't need a bodyguard."

"Don't be so sure," I said genially, sitting next to him.

He looked down his nose at me through slitted eyes; his diamond-shaped face seemed handsome to some, I supposed, but to me it was a harshly angular thing, a hunting knife with hair.

"What exactly," he said, "do you mean by that?"

"I mean I know you murdered Dolores," I said.

He laughed and returned to his newspaper. "Go away, Mallory. Find some schoolgirl who frightens easily if you want to scare somebody."

"I want to scare somebody all right. I just have one question . . . did your ex-wife help you with the murder itself, or was she just a supporting player?"

He put the paper down. He sipped the Bloody Mary. His face was wooden but his eyes were animated.

I laughed gutturally. "You and your convoluted murder mysteries. You were so clever you almost schemed your way into the gas chamber, didn't you? With your masquerades and charades."

"What in the hell are you talking about?"

"You were smart enough to figure out that the cold weather would confuse the time of death. But you thought you could make the coroner think Dolores met her fate the *next* day— Sunday evening, perhaps. You didn't have an alibi for the early a.m. hours of Sunday. And that's when you killed her."

"Is it, really? Mallory, I saw her Sunday morning, breakfast. I argued with her, the neighbors heard . . ."

"Exactly. They *heard*—but they didn't *see* a thing. That was something you staged, either with your ex-wife's help, or whoever your current starlet is. Some actress, the same actress who later called Mrs. Ford up to accept the cocktail party invite and further spread the rumor of the new lover from San Francisco. Nice touch, that. Pulls in the rumors of gangsters from San Francisco who threatened her; was the 'swarthy man' Miranda saw a torpedo posing as a lover? A gigolo with a gun? A member of Artie Lewis' dance band, maybe? Let the cops and the papers wonder. Well, it won't wash with me; I was with her for her last two months. She had no new serious love in her life, from San Francisco or elsewhere. Your 'swarthy man' is the little Latin lover who wasn't there."

"Miranda *saw* him with her, Mallory . . ."

"No. Miranda didn't see anything. She told the story you wanted her to tell; she went along with you, and you treated her right in the divorce settlement. You can afford to. You're sole owner of Dolores Dodd's Sidewalk Café, now. Lock, stock and barrel, with no messy interference from the star on the marquee. And now you're free to accept Lucky Luciano's offer, aren't you?"

That rocked him, like a physical blow. "What?"

"That's why you killed Dolores. She was standing in your way. You wanted to put a casino in upstairs; it would mean big money, very big money."

"I have money."

"Yes, and you spend it. You live very lavishly. I've been checking up on you. I know you intimately already, and I'm going to know you even better."

His eyes quivered in the diamond mask of his face. "What are you talking about?"

"You tried to scare her at first—extortion notes, having her followed; maybe you did this with Luciano's help, maybe you did it on your own. I don't know. But then she hired me, and you scurried off into the darkness to think up something new."

He sneered and gestured archly with his cigarette holder, the cigarette in which he was about to light up. "I'm breathlessly awaiting just what evil thing it was I conjured up next."

"You decided to commit the perfect crime. Just like in the movies. You would kill Dolores one cold night, knocking her out, shoving booze down her, leaving her to die in that garage with the car running. Then you would set out to make it seem that she was still alive—during a day when you were very handsomely, unquestionably alibied."

"You're not making any sense. The verdict at the inquest was accidental death . . ."

"Yes. But the time of death is assumed to have been the night *before* you said you saw her last. Your melodrama was too involved for the simple-minded authorities, who only wanted to hush things up. They went with the more basic, obvious, tidy solution that Dolores died an accidental death early Saturday morning." I laughed, once. "You were so cute in pursuit of the 'perfect crime' you tripped yourself, Eastman."

"Did I really," he said dryly. It wasn't a question.

"Your scenario needed one more rewrite. First you told the cops you slept at the apartment over the café Saturday night, bolting the door around midnight, accidentally locking Dolores out. But later you admitted seeing Dolores the next morning, around breakfast time—at the *bungalow*."

His smile quivered. "Perhaps I slept at the apartment, and went up for breakfast at the bungalow."

"I don't think so. I think you killed her."

"No charges have been brought against me. And none will."

I looked at him hard, like a hanging judge passing sentence. "I'm bringing a charge against you now. I'm charging you with murder in the first degree."

His smile was crinkly; he stared into the redness of his drink. Smoke from his cigarette-in-holder curled upward like a wreath. "Ha. A citizen's arrest, is it?"

"No. Mallory's law. I'm going to kill you myself."

He looked at me sharply. "What? Are you mad . . ."

"Yes, I'm mad. In the sense of being angry, that is. Sometime, within the next year, or two, I'm going to kill you. Just how, I'm not sure. Just when, well . . . perhaps tomorrow. Perhaps a month from tomorrow. Maybe next Christmas. I haven't decided yet."

"You can't be serious . . ."

"I'm deadly serious. I'll be seeing you."

And I left him there at the bar, the glass of Bloody Mary mixing itself in his hand.

Here's what I did to Warren Eastman: I spent two weeks shadowing him. Letting him see me. Letting him know I was watching his every move. Making him jump at the shadow that was me, and all the other shadows, too.

Then I stopped. I slept with my gun under my pillow for a while, in case he got ambitious. But I didn't bother him any further.

The word in Hollywood was that Eastman was somehow—no one knew exactly how, but somehow—dirty in the Dodd murder. And nobody in town thought it was anything but a murder. Eastman never got another picture. He went from one of the hottest directors in town, to the coldest. As cold as the weekend Dolores Dodd died.

The Sidewalk Café stopped drawing a monied, celebrity crowd, but it did all right from regular-folks curiosity seekers. Eastman made some dough there, all right; but the casino never happened. A combination of the wrong kind of publicity, and the drifting away of the high-class clientele, must have changed Lucky Luciano's mind.

Within a year of Dolores Dodd's death, Eastman was committed to a rest home, which is a polite way of saying insane asylum or madhouse. He was in and out of such places for the next four years, and then, one very cold, windy night, he died of a heart attack.

Did I keep my promise? Did I kill him?

I like to think I did, indirectly. I like to think that Dolores Dodd got her money's worth from her chauffeur/bodyguard, who had not been there when she took that last long drive, on the night her sad blue eyes closed forever.

I like to think, in my imperfect way, that I committed the perfect crime.

Paint the Town Green

Robert Colby

Robert Colby was a staple of the Gold Medal fifties and produced one of its best novels, The Captain Must Die. *He has not stopped writing and, as this story demonstrates, not stopped competing well against the generation that came after him. This is a small masterpiece.*

First published in 1977.

W hen the plane set down at L.A. International, Brock rented a car and drove to the Beverly Hills Hotel, a rambling cloistered structure in the lush money-green suburbs. By 9 o'clock he was checked into one of the private bungalows on the grounds, and within an hour he was placing an ad in the *Los Angeles Times:*

LARGE CASH SUMS OFFERED FOR QUICK, SURE PROFITS
Out-of-state speculator with heavy capital reserve considering unique, exciting ventures with instant profit potential. No fast-buck deal too adventurous. Calls accepted daily between noon and 2 P.M. only. Ask for Mr. T. C. Brock.

At the bottom of the ad he wrote the phone number and paid for a one-week run. Then he checked into another hotel, a towering structure in the heart of L.A. He took a splendid room overlooking the city on the floor just below the top of the building, which was occupied by a skyview restaurant. To this room he brought the fine custom suitcase containing his clothing and other belongings, having left a cheap overnighter and an attaché case, both weighted with old magazines, at the bungalow. Long experience had taught him that when trouble developed, as it often did, it was best to conduct business in one place and sleep in another.

The next day at noon Brock was in the bungalow screening calls from the hustlers who had read his ad in the paper. Most of the shell-game propositions to take the rich dude from out of town were obvious frauds. There were offers of ready-to-soar mining stocks—gold, diamond, or uranium, take your choice. Land that was fairly bubbling with oil could be leased for a bargain price. The scoop on a fixed horse race was for sale, and there was a matchless opportunity to back a self-proclaimed card shark in a game of high-stakes poker. A map guaranteed to pinpoint the location of buried treasure on an island in the South Pacific was a steal at fifty grand.

Brock wasted no time on these: They were small-time cons with nothing that suited his purpose. He needed the perfect combination.

In the first three days he took only two calls that were intriguing enough to arouse his interest. The first call was from a man with just a hint of Spanish accent. He spoke softly and with soothing charm, in the formal, nearly stilted manner of one who has learned his English in the old country.

"My name is Carlos," he said. "The last name is difficult and of no importance. The only importance, sir, is the extent of your interest to purchase a quantity of, uh, not so legal items that can be instantly exchanged for a profit ratio in the near vicinity of eight and one-half to one."

"Are you going to tell me what you're talking about, or do you want me to guess?"

"On the phone, Mr. Brock, it is not possible to be so very much definite. But let me say further that the items I will exhibit to you for your approval are green in color and of a size to fit the wallet. They are of a quality not to be believed. In fact, without a tiresome study, they cannot be told from the genuine article. Yes?"

"Yes. I'll take a look and decide for myself. Meet me here at my bungalow on the hotel grounds—number fourteen. If you're not here within the hour, I'll be gone."

"I am not far removed," said Carlos. "Half an hour will be sufficient."

The second offer that seemed worthy of at least a look came just a few minutes later. The woman had a cultured, weary way of speaking, as if she had done it all and had it all long ago. Her name was Mila—they rarely gave last names—and she was forced to part with a fabulous diamond ring worth six hundred thousand for a paltry four hundred grand. The ring had been a gift from her husband and she had told him that she had lost it. Though he was an extremely rich man he refused to give her more than a meager amount of money to spend, and this was her way of getting the cash she needed to cover some pressing personal debts.

The story was probably a fabrication, but diamonds never lie to people who understand them and, telling the lady to stop by with the gem in exactly two hours, he put down the phone and began a regal lunch, delivered complete with a frosty martini, by room service.

A wiry man of medium height, Brock seemed always a bit wide-eyed, his expression slightly startled, as if he were a visitor in an alien land which he found full of curious and entertaining surprises. His manner of dress, though somewhat excessive, was grand. Against the background of a midnight-blue suit, he wore a pearl-gray tie that was fastened with an emerald-studded pin. His gold wristwatch was embellished by a dial of ruby chips, and his outsize diamond ring had the wink of superb quality.

Carlos arrived just as a waiter was removing the debris of Brock's lunch. A small neat man with a small neat moustache, he had jet-dark hair, mild coffee-colored eyes, and an apologetic smile. He was impeccable in a beige gabardine suit with stitched lapels and leather-trimmed pockets. He said he came from Bogotá, and there was about him the quiet, well-mannered air of Latin aristocracy. Chatting easily, in no apparent haste to transact his business, he told Brock he had once been in partnership with his father, an exporter of coffee to the United States and other countries.

"For a long time," said Carlos with one of his apologetic smiles, "my father's business of exporting the coffee was truly magnificent. Then it became very bad, you see. And my father, he began to export in secret a few drugs—the heavy stuff—you know? He was soon caught and sent to prison where, sadly I must tell you, he died."

Carlos smiled in a way that was appropriately sad. "I was not used to poverty, could not abide with it," he continued. "So now I make my living where you find the much greener pastures, on the other side of the fence." With a twinkle he lowered his head in a mock attitude of shame.

Probably, thought Brock, the superfluous charm and small talk concealed as wily a rascal as could be found anywhere. "All right," he said, "let's see what you're selling."

"Pardon?"

"Did you bring it with you—the funny money?"

"Funny money?" Carlos presented a face of round-eyed innocence.

"Carlos, don't waste my time with games."

"Very well. But how do I know you are not the police?"

"Counterfeiting comes under the jurisdiction of the Secret Service. And the boys of the SS don't usually advertise to catch criminals."

Carlos nodded. "Yes, I suppose not. In any case, I have brought nothing with me to sell, only samples."

He removed three bills from an envelope he took from his pocket and handed them over. There was a twenty, a fifty, and a hundred. The texture of the paper was excellent. It was aged just enough to give it the authentic feel of usage. More, the color of the ink was exact, and with the naked eye Brock could not find the least imperfection in the engraving of the bills. Only after he examined them minutely with a pocket magnifying glass under a strong light did he spot the single flaw—the absence of red and blue fibers in the paper.

"Well, what do you think?" said Carlos. "Are they not beautiful?"

"They appear to be quite good," Brock said carefully, though he had never seen better and doubtless they would be accepted by anyone but an expert who had been forewarned. "Where did you get them?"

Carlos shrugged. "The details, no. But I will tell you this much: The bills were shipped from my country where we have some of the world's finest papers and inks—and a retired engraver who fashioned plates for the U.S. government before he entered our service."

"A former U.S. engraver, huh?" Brock snorted. "And how much can you deliver?"

"At once, three hundred thousand. More in a week or two."

"Mmm. And what is your price?"

"Fifteen percent of face value. Forty-five thousand for the three hundred grand."

It was a good price. Fakes of that quality were so rare that

Carlos could ask and get twenty percent. But to test him, Brock shook his head. "Too much. Ten percent—thirty thousand for three hundred of the bogus."

Carlos looked wounded. "But surely, Mr. Brock, you will not haggle with me over bills of such perfection. They will pass anywhere, even in the banks. No, fifteen percent is entirely fair and I will stand firm."

"You're right," said Brock. "I shouldn't haggle with you, and I won't."

Carlos beamed.

"So I'll just say once more—thirty thousand. That's my final offer." He stood and fastened Carlos with the unblinking gaze of relentless decision.

Carlos went through the motions. He groaned, sighed, pursed his lips, and made a pretense of calculation with his fingers. Then, clucking, his face agonized, he slowly nodded and said, "You are a hard man, sir. You leave me just the small margin of profit. But yes, because I have many obligations at this time, I will deal with you on your terms. Thirty thousand it is."

Brock shook his hand and said, "Bring the phonies here to-night at nine. If they're identical to these samples, we'll make the exchange."

"What you ask is impossible, sir," Carlos said, plucking the samples from Brock's fingers, and tucking them into his pocket. "Even when we are most sure, as with a man of your distinction, we never take chances. No, you will come to us, and if we are certain you are entirely alone the transaction will be completed."

"Well, I have little time for such nonsense, but the bills seem good enough to warrant some inconvenience."

Carlos handed him a typewritten slip of paper. "At nine to-night, then."

Brock glanced at the address and nodded. "At nine."

"And the thirty thousand in U.S. legal? You will have it with you?"

"Naturally."

With a fine show of teeth Carlos stepped to the door, flipped a salute, and went out.

Brock ordered another martini from room service. Sipping it as he waited for "Mila," the lady with the diamond, he reflected on his dialogue with Carlos. Since the bills were incredibly good imitations, he would never let them go for ten percent of face value. Therefore, he must be working some sort of flimflam. Well, each to his own game. And his own reward.

Mila was on time. Her knock had the sound of delicate intrigue. A slender young woman with a dainty kind of elegance, she had tawny hair parted in the middle and gathered to one side. Her sleepy eyes and dreamy smile made him wonder if she might be flying on something with narcotic wings. She wore an expensively tailored gray suit that seemed incongruously severe.

"Are you Mr. Brock? My name is Mila." Her speech was over-polished, as if by years of exposure to people of quality and education.

"Come in," he said, and she entered a bit wearily, or timidly—she wasn't an easy person to read. She floated across the room to a chair, her delicate shoulders curved in a languid slouch.

"Would you like something—a cocktail?"

"No, thank you, I don't drink."

"Well, for some people that's wise, I think." He sat facing her.

She toyed with the clasp of her gunmetal leather purse. "I don't usually answer ads of any sort, Mr. Brock. But yours was irresistible. And quite providential under the circumstances."

"I imagine."

Her drowsy eyes wandered over him. "What sort of business are you in?"

"Various investments, speculations."

"I gathered that from your ad. Would you care to be more specific?"

"No."

"I see. Well, I mean, if you're serious about buying the—"

"Mila—if I wanted seriously to buy a costly ring at Tiffany's, what would they require of me?"

She smiled. "Maybe they would extend credit."

"Will you?"

She shook her head. "Naturally, I must have cash."

"Then it's that simple. You want to sell and I have the cash."

Nodding, she opened her purse and handed him a black velvet box. He lifted the lid and removed the ring, a large pear-shaped stone of fiery brilliance and exquisite cut. Fingering it, finding it cool to the touch, he carried it to the window and drew it across the pane, leaving a sharp clear line where the stone cut the glass. As he studied the impression the diamond had left, he caught sight of two young men who were standing together in front of the opposite bungalow. Dressed in sportcoats and slacks, they seemed merely guests making idle conversation. But Brock's nearly infallible instinct told him they were stationed there as guards to be sure he didn't try to grab the ring, and that likely they were carrying weapons.

Now, with his own diamond, Brock tried to scratch Mila's stone. It was impossible. Inserting a piece of white notepaper beneath the gem, he peered into its center with a magnifying glass, checking color and purity. Then, as he held the ring in the palm of his hand feeling the weight of it and discounting the setting, he decided that the stone was probably worth the four hundred thousand she was asking, and a good deal more. Certainly it was the most beautiful diamond he had ever examined at close range, and there had been many.

"Of course, I don't have enough magnification to be certain," he said as he sank back into his chair and gazed appreciatively at the ring, "but it seems a nearly flawless blue brilliant. Very nice."

"My husband bought it in Europe," she said. "It should be worth more in this country. It weighs nearly fifty carats."

"Well, I don't have the instruments to check it, so I would have to get it appraised."

She looked dismayed.

"Really, you wouldn't expect me to invest that kind of money without an appraisal," he said.

She nodded. "But I can't possibly let the ring out of my sight."

"No, that would be foolish." He considered. "There's a jeweler right here in the hotel. Why don't we take a little walk and see if he can give us an evaluation."

She thought about it, anxious-eyed, biting her lip. "Well, all right—yes, we could do that."

He stood and gave her the ring. "Shall we go then?"

They left the bungalow. The two young men in sportjackets, lean-bodied, hard-faced, were now head to head, studying what seemed a racing form. As they gestured and made comments, one of them darted a glance at him. He wondered if they were hired guards or accomplices. In any case, they were sure to follow.

Mila walked beside him in silence, her tension almost palpable. They entered the hotel. He sensed the watchdogs behind him but did not turn. They went down a flight of stairs to the arcade, following it past assorted shops to the jewelry store.

Mila spoke to the clerk and handed over the ring. For a few seconds he gave it a cursory examination through his loupe.

When he removed the eyepiece, his expression was one of contained awe. He flicked a calculating glance at Mila as if trying to match the royal quality of the diamond with the woman who owned it. But then his face became bland and he said, "I'm not prepared to give you a formal appraisal, just an estimate."

Mila looked at Brock, who nodded and said, "For now that would do."

The jeweler removed the stone from its setting and inspected it at length under intense light. He measured it with calipers and weighed it on a scale, jotting figures on a scrap of paper. After pondering over his notations, he returned the gem to its setting and came back with the ring.

"It's a beauty," he said with an approving shake of his head. "I'd say somewhere between six and seven hundred thousand. Call it six-fifty, roughly."

As she carefully tucked the ring back into the velvet box, Mila looked at Brock with an I-told-you-so expression.

Back outside, he spotted her protectors. Not far removed, they stood gazing into a shop window, faking an enthusiastic discussion of the items on display.

"You've got a deal," Brock said. "It's only a matter of price."

"You don't like the price!" She looked indignant. "Mr. Brock, didn't you hear the man say—"

"I heard him, yes."

"Well, then—isn't it an absolute *steal* at four hundred thousand?"

"A steal, yes. No doubt. Then why do you come to me? Why don't you sell it to a commercial buyer of diamonds at four hundred, or even better?"

Her face sagged. "You know very well that I can't. They ask questions. For a ring worth more than half a million, they want proof of ownership. And only my husband could give them that."

"Exactly."

"So you're ready to take advantage."

"I'm in business to take advantage."

She sighed. "How much, then?"

"Let me think about it. Phone me here at nine in the morning. That will give me time to make arrangements with the bank."

Her lips tightened. "Well, I won't come down much, I'll tell you that. And it must be cash, no checks of any kind."

"Cash, of course."

"Very well, I'll phone you at nine sharp."

"If you don't mind, I won't see you out. I want to stop off at the barbershop."

"Good-bye, Mr. Brock."

Her dreamy expression gone a bit sour, she turned and walked off, clipping past the bodyguards. As Brock went into the barbershop and sneaked a look, they lost interest in the window display and sauntered after her.

He lingered a minute and followed, heading for the lobby. It was a lucky guess. They were there, the three of them huddled in a corner, conversing. Anticipating their departure, he ducked out a side door, found his car in the parking area, and drove it up near the exit. Folded down behind the wheel, two cars in front screening him, he saw them come out, separately— Mila first, her boys behind. The boys went off in a white Ford sedan, she left in a taxi.

He tailed the cab cautiously to the estates of Bel-Air and hung well back as it climbed a road embowered by huge old trees hemming the houses of the rich and the mansions of the very rich. He could see Mila through the back window of the cab. She didn't turn once to look back, though probably in the unfamiliar car and wearing his sunglasses she wouldn't have recognized him.

Soon the taxi wheeled left into a private driveway, and he braked to wait. When the cab returned, he drove on, taking a look at the house as he passed. It was a great library of a place, barely visible from the road. High and square and formal, it sat atop a knoll, neatly combed grounds spilling green around it.

Just beyond, he maneuvered about and parked. As he sat thinking what to do next, a gardening truck slid out of the drive that had swallowed the cab and came toward him. He got out and flagged it down. The driver was an old guy with a craggy, pleasant face. Brock asked him if he worked for the people in the library-type mansion. He said yes, but only once a week. He was an itinerant gardener with other customers in the neighborhood. He had a crew and a couple of his men were on a job down the road. He was on his way to pick them up. Yes, he knew all about the people up there on the knoll, but he was in a hurry. Brock asked him if twenty bucks would buy about ten minutes. He grinned and cut the motor, then motioned for Brock to sit on the seat beside him.

The lady who owned the place was a Mrs. Alberta Wilmont. Before he died, her husband ran a shipping company—freighters. He left her millions. No, the young woman who just arrived in a taxi was not Mrs. Wilmont, she was Marian Ainsworth, a kind of secretary-companion who was distantly related to Alberta Wilmont.

"Did Mrs. Wilmont ever own a diamond ring that was stolen?"

"You bet she did! The ring was worth a fortune. About a month ago, while everyone was away from the house, burglars broke in. How they did it without tripping the alarm system nobody can figure. The thieves drilled the safe, swiped the ring and some less valuable jewelry, and a few hundred in cash. It was front-page stuff in the paper."

Brock asked a few more questions, gave the gardener the twenty, and twenty more to keep his mouth shut. Then he hustled away to the newspaper office and combed back issues until he found the account of the burglary. This done, he made a number of calls and finally hit what could be the jackpot.

Shortly before 9:00 that evening, with just a few magazines locked in his attaché case, he drove toward the address Carlos had given him. It was an apartment house in an old section of Hollywood on a narrow street above Franklin. The building was large and might once have been magnificent, but now its crusty facade cried neglect and despair, most of the windows dark, the entrance bleakly lighted.

He found an alley that led to a subterranean garage below the apartment house and drove down the ramp. He was in a gloomy dungeon of pillared space, empty but for a pair of junkyard heaps in a corner, squatting beside a late-model black Cadillac. Parking next to the Cadillac he climbed out cautiously with the attaché case. Clutching the grip of a holstered .38 revolver, one of several weapons he had collected from a long string of bad boys, he stood motionless, listening. The silence was so dense within the cavernous garage he could hear a distant murmur of traffic, the bleating of a horn.

Peering inside the Cadillac he circled quietly to the front and reached under it to test the radiator. It was warm, almost hot. Someone had arrived not long before.

On rubber-soled shoes he crossed the garage and came to the mouth of a dim corridor. Pausing again to listen, he moved on —past the doorways of a shadowy boiler room and a gutted laundry to an elevator. The car was somewhere above, but there was no indicator to show its location.

He pressed the button and heard the creak and whine of the

elevator's descent. In the wan light the scabby, cement walls displayed a nearly endless scrawl of graffiti. Cobwebs nestled in corners, a light fixture dangled, the rank odor of urine invaded the torpid air.

When the approaching mutter of the car told him it was near, he stepped aside, out of range. But when it opened, the elevator was empty. Brock thumbed the 7 button, though Carlos's slip of paper designated apartment 8E.

The elevator rattled slowly up to the seventh floor and stopped. He was greeted by a dark, fetid corridor of doors flung wide open upon vacant apartments. Gaping in wonder, he crossed the threadbare remnant of a carpet, found the stairway, and mounted soundlessly to the eighth. Here he cracked the door and peeked out.

Under the subdued light from overhead fixtures, the eighth and top floor seemed clean and tidy enough, the carpet in good repair, the brown doors to the apartments sealed. Puzzling it, Brock concluded that the rest of the building was probably abandoned. As he stopped to consider his strategy, he saw Carlos hurry around a bend in the corridor and come to stand, head inclined, at the elevator.

He looked so foolishly ineffectual and unfrightening that Brock wanted to laugh out loud. Instead he moved quietly up behind him and dropped a heavy hand on his shoulder.

Carlos snapped around, wild-eyed, his jaw dropping in terror.

"Looking for me Carlos?" Brock grinned.

Carlos groaned. "What the hell you doing, man! I thought you were—"

"An undercover agent of the SS. Right, Carlos?"

He nodded. "Yeah, something like that. I am looking to see why you don't show," he said.

"I couldn't find 8E," Brock said. "I must've been going the wrong way."

"Ah, well—no problem," Carlos answered. "Come—" He had been staring with fascination at Brock's case and as they moved down the hallway he asked nervously, "You have brought the money?"

Brock gave the case an affectionate pat. "Thirty big ones. And you have the queers?"

"The queers?" His expression flickered, brightened. "The phonies, ah yes, of course!" He gave a dental exhibition. "They are in the apartment, where we shall make the exchange."

He led Brock to the rear of the building and turned into a narrow passage. It terminated at the point where the doors to apartments 8E and 8F faced each other across a faded strip of carpet. The hall, lit by a single naked bulb, was dim. The air had a musty smell, tainted with something indefinable, like molding garbage.

They were at the door to 8E, Carlos bringing out a set of keys, Brock telling himself that he would not go into the apartment unless he entered with an arm locked about Carlos's neck, the .38 visibly pressing his head, when he sensed a movement and turned swiftly. Behind him, the door to 8F had been opened and an enormous Latin towered above him, grimacing fiercely as he hoisted a baseball bat and slammed it down.

Brock had begun to duck out of range or the blow would have crushed his skull. Instead, it glanced thunderously off the back of his head, dropping him to the floor.

Vaguely focused, his eyes opened upon a hazy scene. He was floating above a shimmering landscape. There was a blur of twinkling buildings and streets while below, dim and far away, a pool of white circled and tilted. It appeared to grow toward him, then recede, as if seen through binoculars that would not adjust. And he could feel the hard thrust of something against his chest.

In the background voices drifted to him, as from a radio badly tuned. Carlos was pleading with someone called Mario, saying it wasn't necessary to kill the man, just take his money and run. But Mario said no, it was too risky. "No, Carlos, this mama is gonna commit suicide. He's gonna fly down from that window and—squash!—you got a bird who sings no songs!"

Brock got the message. And fear jabbing him to life, he brought it all into focus. He was draped over a windowsill, gazing down a perpendicular wall to a moon-washed court eight stories below. The tilting, spinning face of the court, composed of unrelenting cement, winked at him.

But even as this understanding jolted and sickened him, Mario reached down and scooped him up with ridiculous ease. Poising himself, aiming Brock at the open mouth of the window, he did not notice that while one of Brock's hands dangled limply the other was under his jacket, bending the barrel of the .38 toward the great mass of his chest.

Brock squeezed the trigger—once, twice, and again, knowing that while the big ones may fall harder, they do not always fall faster. No doubt the first bullet was an incredible surprise, for Mario simply stood rooted, as if considering the impossibility of it, his eyes dilating with astonishment. The second shot caused him to stumble backward, and the third buckled him slowly to the floor. Only then, with a mortal sigh, did he liberate Brock from the clutch of his arms.

Carlos tried to run, but Brock caught him at the door and ordered him at gun point to empty Mario's pockets and bring him the contents. The dead man was carrying $6,700 in hundred-dollar bills that proved, after close examination, to be genuine U.S. green. Carlos, on the other hand, was in possession of only ninety dollars.

"Carlos," Brock said sternly as he pocketed the bills, "I've been thinking seriously of killing you, and this doesn't help your cause."

Seated on the floor, hands laced behind his neck, Carlos had been watching with resignation, as one who hopes for nothing but to survive. His face flashing alarm, he said tremulously, "I have little money because in the organization of the counterfeiting I am only a passer of the bills. Mario was in charge of the passers and the money in his wallet was to pay us our humble percentage."

Brock made a clucking sound. "How sad." Gingerly, he felt the lump on the back of his head. "You may lower your hands now, Carlos, and you may smoke. A condemned man is always entitled to a last cigarette."

Carlos gave him a look of such gaping horror that Brock decided to ease off a bit. "However," he added, "if you can find some way to repay me for this night of treachery, I might be persuaded to change my mind."

"Anything—anything at all that you wish," Carlos said feverishly.

"What did you do with my case, Carlos?"

He pointed. "Over there in the closet. It is locked and we could not open it."

"And where is the three hundred thousand in bogus?"

Carlos hesitated and Brock leveled the .38. "Hurry, Carlos, I'm aching to kill you!"

"No, no! The bills are down in the trunk of Mario's Cadillac. He was supposed to distribute them to the passers later tonight."

Brock reached for a set of keys resting on the floor with the assorted items Carlos had taken from Mario. "You'd better not be lying," he warned. "Let's go and see."

Toting his attaché case, he descended with Carlos to the garage. One of Mario's keys opened the trunk of the Cadillac, and when the lid was raised there was indeed a carton holding three hundred grand in bogus bills. Brock ordered Carlos to transfer the carton to the trunk of his rented sedan. When this was done he locked the attaché case in with the counterfeits and gave Carlos the keys to the Cadillac.

"Because you tried to prevent Mario from killing me," he told Carlos, "I'll make you a present of his car. You're a pussycat in a jungle and I'd advise you to get out of this racket and into plumbing, or something equally suited to your talents. At heart, Carlos, you're not a bad little fellow, and in fact I've become rather fond of you."

"You are fond of me? Truly?"

"Truly." Brock nodded solemnly. He opened the door of his rental, climbed in, and wound the motor.

"You are a strange man," said Carlos. "Most remarkable. But really, who are you, sir?"

"There's a tax on evil, and I'm the devil's own collector," Brock answered with a wisp of a smile. He backed and drove off.

Marian Ainsworth, alias Mila, phoned him the next morning on the dot of nine. "Three hundred thousand," he said.

"No."

"In cash."

"Well—"

"It'll take time for the bank to get that much money together. Be here at four this afternoon."

"I can't make it until eight this evening."

"At eight sharp, then." He cut the connection.

She was a few minutes early. When he opened the door and she stepped in, he spied her accomplices lingering in the shadows. A hundred to one they were the burglars who stole the ring —with her blueprint of the alarm system, and at a time when she told them the mansion would be empty.

She was wearing a black lace cocktail dress. She looked stunning. Was there to be a little party to celebrate the split of a hundred grand apiece?

She stood fidgeting at the center of the room, her eyes screaming her haste.

Enjoying it, he said, "A little drink? To toast our transaction?"

"I told you, I don't drink!" she snapped.

"Ah, that's right. Too bad."

"Have you got the cash?"

"Have you got the ring?"

She dipped into her black-beaded evening bag and passed him the velvet box. It was the same diamond, he determined that immediately, but pretending to suspect otherwise he tested and inspected it with even more care than he had the first time.

"The money is in that overnighter," he told her finally, pointing to the chair where he had left it. "You may keep the bag—I'll toss it in as a bonus."

Counting the cash, she was intensely concentrated, her face taking on a feral quality. Before she began, she selected several bills from random stacks and examined them closely. But, apparently satisfied, she went on to count the bills with furious speed, then nodded and said with a hectic smile, "Well, it seems to be all here!"

She picked up the bag and all but bolted for the door, where she turned and said, "Now you own a diamond valued at more than half a million dollars, Mr. Brock. All you have to do is find someone to buy it. Mmm?"

She went out.

She was right, of course. It would be difficult to find anyone who would buy the ring at full price, no questions asked. But then, he had never intended to sell it. He hunted his rental in the parking area, found it, backed, and turned to drive away.

Just then Marian Ainsworth's accomplices loomed up out of the darkness. One at each side of the car, they aimed pistols at him. "OK, buddy, let's have the ring!" barked the one at his window.

"Don't get nervous, boys," he soothed. "I've got it right here in my pocket."

It was suicide to reach for his gun, so he brought the box out and started to hand it over. But then, with a trembling hand, he faked dropping the box to the floor. Bending to recover it, he rammed the pedal and gunned off blindly. They both fired at him, almost together. But they were too late.

He sat up just in time. The car was veering off toward a tree as it raced down the drive to the street. He straightened the wheel, braked a bit, and glanced into the rearview mirror. They were jockeying the white Ford out of a parking slot, coming after him.

He cut north into a cloistered residential section of fine old houses, squealing around a series of corners.

It was no use. They were trailing him through every turn, hardly a block behind. He thought of braking suddenly and leaping out with his gun to fire at them, but changed his mind when, losing them for a moment as he wheeled around a tight curve, he spotted the tip of a driveway that vanished between a gateway of tall hedges. He swung into it at reckless speed, yawing dangerously, correcting, erasing his lights, slowing as he climbed and swept around to the house, a pillared old colonial.

There was a garage with its door open and a vacant space inside. He slid into it, cut the motor, and listened. Nothing. He had lost them. But now, from a window somewhere above, came the shrill voice of a woman calling, "Is that you, Walter?"

He was seated at a partitioned booth in a secluded corner of the restaurant atop the hotel where he had his getaway room. He had told the hostess that a Mr. Arnold Bevis would be looking for him shortly, and now he was sipping a Manhattan, winding down, feeling good.

He had just ordered another when a plump little man with a Vandyke beard bustled over at the heels of the hostess. "I'm Arnold Bevis," he said and flashed a smile. They shook hands and Bevis squeezed in across the table, setting a briefcase on the cushion beside him. The waitress delivered Brock's second Manhattan and he asked, "Will you have one with me, Mr. Bevis?"

Bevis shook his head. "No, thanks. I have an appointment with Alberta Wilmont and there isn't time."

The waitress departed and Brock said, "You told Mrs. Wilmont you've recovered the ring?"

"I told her we *thought* we had recovered it. And now, if you will, Mr. Brock, let's see if we have."

Brock produced the velvet box, opened it, and slid it across to Bevis, who brought implements from his briefcase and, after testing to be sure the diamond was genuine, removed it from its setting, weighed, and measured it. "Did you know, Mr. Brock," he said, "that like fingerprints no two diamonds are alike? When we insure a diamond, we chart all of its individual characteristics. That way, there can be no mistake about its identity."

He wrote figures in a notebook, fixed a loupe to his eye, and, studying the diamond in the light from the table lamp, continued to make notes. Finally, he took an insurance appraisal form from his case and compared it with his notations.

Nodding, he said, "Yes, this is our baby all right." He returned the stone to its setting, put his tools away, and stared curiously at Brock. "I looked up your ad in the *Times* and I can see how it would attract those two who stole the ring. But how did you get it away from them without giving them the money?"

"That's a trade secret, Mr. Bevis. But I'll say this much—I had to do some fast shuffling to escape them. And if I didn't have the devil's own luck, I wouldn't be sitting here waiting for you to bless me with the reward."

Bevis took a check from his case and passed it to Brock with a release form. "Fifty thousand is a very large sum. We seldom pay rewards in excess of five percent and I had a tough time getting approval from my company—especially since you were in a hurry."

Brock looked at the check and signed the release. "I'm always in a hurry, Mr. Bevis. The coals are hot and I have to jump fast."

"And so do I. I'm running late." Sealing the ring and the release in his briefcase, Bevis eased himself from the booth. "You know, I never will understand how the burglars were able to silence a complex alarm system and break in at the precise time when everyone was out. It makes me wonder if somebody was feeding them information."

"That's possible," said Brock.

"You'll give a description of those hoods to the police, won't you?"

"Of course," Brock lied.

Bevis shook his hand and disappeared.

Brock sipped his Manhattan and gazed out through the wall of glass at the gaudy splash of the night city. Let the cops uncover Marian Ainsworth if they could. She was a crook and her choice of playmates was atrocious. But she was a beauty with plenty of style. Under other circumstances . . .

He shook his head. In the morning he would fly to Alaska. As the foreman of a welding crew working the pipeline, he would be on leave in Fairbanks with great wads of accumulated pay to spend. The hustlers of that amoral outpost in the wilderness would be lurking there, just waiting for a sucker like him. And his rewards would be extravagant.

Jody and Annie on TV

by John Shirley

John Shirley is, to a fault some would say, his own man. He wrote some of the best science fiction and horror of the eighties and has now moved to Los Angeles where he is writing film scripts. All by himself, he's redefining noir *as I understand it. As he does here.*

First published in 1992.

First time he has the feeling, he's doing 75 on the 134. Sun glaring the color off the cars, smog filming the North Hollywood hills. Just past the place where the 134 snakes into the Ventura freeway, he's driving Annie's dad's fucked-up '78 Buick Skylark convertible, one hand on the wheel the other on the radio dial, trying to find a tune, and nothing sounds good. But *nothing*. Everything sounds stupid, even metal. You think it's the music but it's not, you know? It's you.

Usually, it's just a weird mood. But this time it shifts a gear. He looks up from the radio and realizes: You're not driving this car. It's automatic in traffic like this: only moderately heavy traffic, moving fluidly, sweeping around the curves like they're all part of one long thing. Most of your mind is thinking about what's on TV tonight and if you could stand working at that telephone sales place again . . .

It hits him that he is two people, the programmed-Jody who drives and fiddles with the radio and the real Jody who thinks about getting work. . . . Makes him feel funny, detached.

The feeling closes in on him like a jar coming down over a

wasp. Glassy like that. He's pressed between the back window and the windshield, the two sheets of glass coming together, compressing him like something under one of those biology-class microscope slides. Everything goes two-dimensional. The cars look like the ones in that Roadmaster videogame, animated cars made out of pixels.

A buzz of panic, a roaring, and then someone laughs as he jams the Buick's steering wheel over hard to the right, jumps into the VW Bug's lane, forcing it out; the Bug reacts, jerks away from him, sudden and scared, like it's going, "Shit!" Cutting off a Toyota four-by-four with tractor-sized tires, lot of good those big fucking tires do the Toyota, because it spins out and smacks sideways into the grill of a rusty old semitruck pulling an open trailer full of palm trees. . . .

They get all tangled up back there. He glances back and thinks, *I did that.* He's grinning and shaking his head and laughing. He's not sorry and he likes the fact that he's not sorry. *I did that.* It's so amazing, so totally rad.

Jody has to pull off at the next exit. His heart is banging like a fire alarm as he pulls into a Texaco. Goes to get a Coke.

It comes to him on the way to the Coke machine that he's stoked. He feels connected and in control and pumped up. The gas fumes smell good; the asphalt under the thin rubber of his sneakers feels good. *Huh.* The Coke tastes good. He thinks he can taste the cola berries. He should call Annie. She should be in the car, next to him.

He goes back to the car, heads down the boulevard a mile past the accident, swings onto the freeway, gets up to speed—which is only about thirty miles an hour because the accident's crammed everyone into the left three lanes. Sipping Coca-Cola, he looks the accident over. Highway cops aren't there yet, just the Toyota four-by-four, the rusty semi with its hood wired down, and a Yugo. The VW got away, but the little caramel-colored Yugo is like an accordion against the back of the truck. The Toyota is bent into a short boomerang shape around the snout of the semi, which is jackknifed onto the road shoulder. The Mexican driver is nowhere around. Probably didn't have a green card, ducked out before the cops show up. The palm trees kinked up in the back of the semi are whole, grown-up palm trees, with the roots and some soil tied up in big plastic bags, going to some rebuilt place in Bel Air. One of the palm trees droops almost completely off the back of the trailer.

Jody checks out the dude sitting on the Toyota's hood. The

guy's sitting there, rocking with pain, waiting. A kind of ski mask of blood on his face.

I did that, three of 'em, bingo, just like that. Maybe it'll get on TV news.

Jody cruised on by and went to find Annie.

It's on TV because of the palm trees. Jody and Annie, at home, drink Coronas, watch the crane lifting the palm trees off the freeway. The TV anchordude is saying someone is in stable condition, nobody killed; so that's why, Jody figures, it is, like, okay for the newsmen to joke about the palm trees on the freeway. Annie has the little Toshiba portable with the 12″ screen, on three long extension cords, up in the kitchen window so they can see it on the back porch, because it is too hot to watch it in the living room. If Jody leans forward a little he can see the sun between the houses off to the west. In the smog the sun is a smooth red ball just easing to the horizon; you can look right at it.

Jody glances at Annie, wondering if he made a mistake, telling her what he did.

He can feel her watching him as he opens the third Corona. Pretty soon she'll say, "You going to drink more than three you better pay for the next round." Something she'd never say if he had a job, even if she'd paid for it then too. It's a way to get at the job thing.

She's looking at him, but she doesn't say anything. Maybe it's the wreck on TV. "Guy's not dead," he says, "too fucking bad." Making a macho thing about it.

"You're an asshole." But the tone of her voice says something else. What, exactly? Not admiration. Enjoyment, maybe.

Annie has her hair teased out; the red parts of her hair look redder in this light; the blond parts look almost real. Her eyes are the glassy greenblue the waves get to be in the afternoon up at Point Mugu, with the light coming through the water. Deep tan, white lipstick. He'd never liked that white lipstick look, white eyeliner and the pale-pink fingernail polish that went with it, but he never told her. "Girls who wear that shit are usually airheads," he'd have to say. And she wouldn't believe him when he told her he didn't mean her. She's sitting on the edge of her rickety kitchen chair in that old white shirt of his she wears for a shorty dress, leaning forward so he can see her cleavage, the arcs of her tan lines, her small feet flat on the stucco backporch,

her feet planted wide apart but with her knees together, like the
feet are saying one thing and the knees another.

His segment is gone from TV but he gets that *right there* feeling again as he takes her by the wrist and she says, "*Guy,* Jody,
what do you think I *am?*" But joking.

He leads her to the bedroom and, standing beside the bed,
puts his hand between her legs and he can feel he doesn't have
to get her readier, he can get right to the good part. Everything
just sort of slips right into place. She locks her legs around his
back and they're still standing up, but it's like she hardly weighs
anything at all. She tilts her head back, opens her mouth; he can
see her broken front tooth, a guillotine shape.

They're doing 45 on the 101. It's a hot, windy night. They're
listening to *Motley Crue* on the Sony ghetto blaster that stands on
end between Annie's feet. The music makes him feel good but it
hurts too because now he's thinking about *Iron Dream.* The band
kicking him out because he couldn't get the solo parts to go fast
enough. And because he missed some rehearsals. They should
have let him play rhythm and sing backup, but the fuckers
kicked him out. That's something he and Annie have. Both
feeling like they were shoved out of line somewhere. Annie
wants to be an actress, but she can't get a part, except once she
was an extra for a TV show with a bogus rock club scene. Didn't
even get her Guild card from that.

Annie is going on about something, always talking, it's like she
can't stand the air to be empty. He doesn't really mind it. She's
saying, "So I go, 'I'm *sure* I'm gonna fill in for that bitch when
she accuses me of stealing her tips.' And he goes, 'Oh you know
how Felicia is, she doesn't mean anything.' I mean—*guy*—he's
always saying poor Felicia, you know how Felicia is, cutting her
slack, but he, like, *never* cuts me any slack, and I've got two more
tables to wait, so I'm all, 'Oh right poor Felicia—' and he
goes—" Jody nods every so often, and even listens closely for a
minute when she talks about the customers who treat her like a
waitress. "I mean, what do they think, I'll always be a waitress?
I'm *sure* I'm, like, totally a Felicia who's always, you know, going
to be a *wait*-ress—" He knows what she means. You're pumping
gas and people treat you like you're a born pump jockey and
you'll never do anything else. He feels like he's really *with* her,
then. It's things like that, and things they don't say; it's like
they're looking out the same window together all the time. She
sees things the way he does: how people don't understand.

Maybe he'll write a song about it. Record it, hit big, *Iron Dream*'ll shit their pants. Wouldn't they, though?

"My Dad wants this car back, for his girlfriend," Annie says.

"Oh fuck her," Jody says. "She's too fucking drunk to drive, *any*time."

Almost eleven-thirty but she isn't saying anything about having to work tomorrow, she's jacked up same as he is. They haven't taken anything, but they both feel like they have. Maybe it's the Santa Anas blowing weird shit into the valley.

"This car's a piece of junk anyway," Annie says. "It knocks, radiator boils over. Linkage is going out."

"It's better than no car."

"You had it together, you wouldn't have to settle for this car."

She means getting a job, but he still feels like she's saying, "If you were a better guitar player . . ." Someone's taking a turn on a big fucking screw that goes through his chest. That's the second time the feeling comes. Everything going all flat again, and he can't tell his hands from the steering wheel.

There is a rush of panic, almost like when Annie's dad took him up in the Piper to go skydiving; like the moment when he pulled the cord and nothing happened. He had to pull it twice. Before the parachute opened he was spinning around like a dust mote. What difference would it make if he *did* hit the ground?

It's like that now, he's just hurtling along, sitting back and watching himself, that weird detachment thing . . . Not sure he is in control of the car. What difference would it make if he *wasn't* in control?

And then he pulls off the freeway, and picks up a wrench from the backseat.

"You're really good at getting it on TV," she says. "It's a talent, like being a director." They are indoors this time, sitting up in bed, watching it in the bedroom, with the fan on. It was too risky talking out on the back porch.

"Maybe I should be a director. Make *Nightmare On Elm Street* better than that last one. That last one sucked."

They are watching the news coverage for the third time on the VCR. You could get these hot VCRs for like sixty bucks from a guy on Hollywood Boulevard, if you saw him walking around at the right time. They'd gotten a couple of discount tapes at Federated and they'd recorded the newscast.

". . . we're not sure it's a gang-related incident," the detective on TV was saying. "The use of a wrench—throwing a wrench from the car at someone—uh, that's not the usual gang methodology."

"Methodology," Jody says. "Christ."

There's a clumsy camera zoom on a puddle of blood on the ground. Not very good color on this TV, Jody thinks; the blood is more purple than red.

The camera lingers on the blood as the cop says, "They usually use guns. Uzis, weapons along those lines. Of course, the victim was killed just the same. At those speeds a wrench thrown from a car is a deadly weapon. We have no definite leads. . . ."

" 'They usually use guns,' " Jody says. "I'll use a gun on your balls, shit-head."

Annie snorts happily, and playfully kicks him in the side with her bare foot. "You're such an asshole. You're gonna get in trouble. Shouldn't be using my dad's car, for one thing." But saying it teasingly, chewing her lip to keep from smiling too much.

"You fucking love it," he says, rolling onto her.

"Wait." She wriggles free, rewinds the tape, starts it over. It plays in the background. "Come here, asshole."

Jody's brother Cal says, "What's going on with you, huh? How come everything I say pisses you off? It's like, *anything*. I mean, you're only two years younger than me but you act like you're fourteen sometimes."

"Oh hey Cal," Jody says, snorting, "you're, like, Mr. Mature."

They're in the parking lot of the mall, way off in the corner. Cal in his Pasadena School of Art & Design t-shirt, his yuppie haircut, yellow-tinted John Lennon sunglasses. They're standing by Cal's '81 Subaru, that Mom bought him "because he went to school." They're blinking in the metallic sunlight, at the corner of the parking lot by the boulevard. The only place there's any parking. A couple of acres of cars between them and the main structure of the mall. They're supposed to have lunch with Mom, who keeps busy with her gift shop in the mall, with coffee grinders and dried eucalyptus and silk flowers. But Jody's decided he doesn't want to go.

"I just don't want you to say anymore of this shit to me, Cal," Jody says. "Telling me about *being* somebody." Jody's slouching against the car, his hand slashing the air like a karate move as he talks. He keeps his face down, half hidden by his long, purple streaked hair, because he's too mad at Cal to look right at him:

Cal hassled and wheedled him into coming here. Jody is kicking
Cal's tires with the back of a lizardskin boot and every so often
he kicks the hubcap, trying to dent it. "I don't need the same
from you I get from Mom."

"Just because she's a bitch doesn't mean she's wrong all the
time," Cal says. "Anyway what's the big deal? You used to go
along peacefully and listen to Mom's one-way heart-to-hearts
and say what she expects and—" He shrugs.

Jody knows what he means: The forty bucks or so she'd hand
him afterward "to get him started."

"It's not worth it anymore," Jody says.

"You don't have any other source of money but Annie and she
won't put up with it much longer. It's time to get real, Jody, to
get a job and—"

"Don't tell me I need a job to get real." Jody slashes the air
with the edge of his hand. "Real is where your ass is when you
shit," he adds savagely. "Now fucking shut up about it."

Jody looks at the mall, trying to picture meeting Mom in
there. It makes him feel heavy and tired. Except for the fiber-
glass letters—*Northridge Galleria*—styled to imitate handwriting
across its offwhite, pebbly surface, the outside of the mall could
be a military building, an enormous bunker. Just a great win-
dowless . . . *block.* "I hate that place, Cal. That mall and that
busywork shop. Dad gave her the shop to keep her off valium.
Fuck. Like fingerpainting for retards."

He stares at the mall, thinking: That cutesy sign, I hate that.
Cutesy handwriting but the sign is big enough to crush you
dead if it fell on you. *Northridge Galleria.* You could almost hear
a radio ad voice saying it over and over again, "Northridge
Galleria! . . . Northridge   Galleria! . . . Northridge   Galleria! . . ."

To their right is a Jack-in-the-Box order-taking intercom.
Jody smells the hot plastic of the sun-baked clown-face and the
dogfoody hamburger smell of the drive-through mixed in. To
their left is a Pioneer Chicken with its cartoon covered-wagon
sign.

Cal sees him looking at it. Maybe trying to pry Jody loose
from obsessing about Mom, Cal says, "You know how many
Pioneer Chicken places there are in L.A.? You think you're driving in circles because every few blocks one comes up. . . . It's
like the ugliest fucking wallpaper pattern in the world."

"Shut up about that shit too."

"What put you in this mood? You break up with Annie?"

"No. We're fine. I just don't want to have lunch with Mom."

"Well goddamn, Jody, you shouldn't have said you would, then."

Jody shrugs. He's trapped in the reflective oven of the parking lot, sun blazing from countless windshields and shiny metal-flake hoods and from the plastic clownface. Eyes burning from the lancing reflections. Never forget your sunglasses. But no way is he going in.

Cal says, "Look, Jody, I'm dehydrating out here. I mean, fuck this parking lot. There's a couple of palm trees around the edges but look at this place—it's the surface of the moon."

"Stop being so fucking arty," Jody says. "You're going to art and design school, oh wow awesome I'm impressed."

"I'm just—" Cal shakes his head. "How come you're mad at Mom?"

"She wants me to come over, it's just so she can tell me her latest scam for getting me to do some shit, go to community college, study haircutting or something. Like she's really on top of my life. Fuck, I was a teenager I told her I was going to hitchhike to New York she didn't even look up from her card game."

"What'd you expect her to do?"

"I don't know."

"Hey that was when she was on her Self-Dependence kick. She was into Lifespring and Est and Amway and all that. They keep telling her she's not responsible for other people, not responsible, not responsible—"

"She went for it like a fucking fish to water, man." He gives Cal a look that means, *no bullshit.* "What is it she wants *now?*"

"Um—I think she wants you to go to some vocational school."

Jody makes a snorting sound up in his sinuses. "Fuck that. Open up your car, Cal, I ain't going."

"Look, she's just trying to help. What the hell's wrong with having a skill? It doesn't mean you can't do something else too—"

"Cal. She gave you the Subaru, it ain't mine. But you're gonna open the fucking thing up." He hopes Cal knows how serious he is. Because that two-dimensional feeling might come on him, if he doesn't get out of here. Words just spill out of him. "Cal, look at this fucking place. Look at this place and tell me about vocational skills. It's shit, Cal. There's two things in the world, dude. There's making it like *Bon Jovi,* like Eddie Murphy —that's one thing. You're on a screen, you're on videos and

CDs. Or there's *shit*. That's the other thing. There's *no fucking thing in between*. There's being *Huge*—and there's being nothing." His voice breaking. "We're shit, Cal. Open up the fucking car or I'll kick your headlights in."

Cal stares at him. Then he unlocks the car, his movements short and angry. Jody gets in, looking at a sign on the other side of the parking lot, one of those electronic signs with the lights spelling things out with moving words. The sign says, *You want it, we got it . . . you want it, we got it . . . you want it, we got it . . .*

He wanted a Luger. They look rad in war movies. Jody said it was James Coburn, Annie said it was Lee Marvin, but whoever it was, he was using a Luger in that Peckinpah movie *Iron Cross.*

But what Jody ends up with is a Smith-Wesson .32, the magazine carrying eight rounds. It's smaller than he'd thought it would be, a scratched gray-metal weight in his palm. They buy four boxes of bullets, drive out to the country, out past Topanga Canyon. They find a fire road of rutted salmon-colored dirt, lined with pine trees on one side; the other side has a margin of grass that looks like soggy Shredded Wheat, and a barbed wire fence edging an empty horse pasture.

They take turns with the gun, Annie and Jody, shooting Bud-Light bottles from a splintery gray fence post. A lot of the time they miss the bottles. Jody said, "This piece's pulling to the left." He isn't sure if it really is, but Annie seems to like when he talks as if he knows about it.

It's nice out there, he likes the scent of gunsmoke mixed with the pine tree smell. Birds were singing for awhile, too, but they stopped after the shooting, scared off. His hand hurts from the gun's recoil, but he doesn't say anything about that to Annie.

"What we got to do," she says, taking a pot-shot at a squirrel, "is try shooting from the car."

He shakes his head. "You think you'll aim better from in a car?"

"I mean from a *moving* car, stupid." She gives him a look of exasperation. "To get used to it."

"Hey yeah."

They get the old Buick bouncing down the rutted fire road, about thirty feet from the fence post when they pass it, and Annie fires twice, and misses. "The stupid car bounces too much on this road," she says.

"Let me try it."

"No wait—make it more like a city street, drive in the grass off the road. No ruts."

"Uh . . . Okay." So he backs up, they try it again from the grass verge. She misses again, but they keep on because she insists, and about the fourth time she starts hitting the post, and the sixth time she hits the bottle.

"Well why *not?*" she asks again.

Jody doesn't like backing off from this in front of Annie, but it feels like it is too soon or something. "Because now we're just gone and nobody knows who it is. If we hold up a store it'll take time, they might have silent alarms, we might get caught." They are driving with the top up, to give them some cover in case they decide to try the gun here, but the windows are rolled down because the old Buick's air conditioning is busted.

"Oh right I'm *sure* some *7-11* store is going to have a silent alarm."

"Just wait, that's all. Let's do this first. We got to get more used to the gun."

"And get another one. So we can both have one."

For some reason that scares him. But he says: "Yeah. Okay."

It is late afternoon. They are doing 60 on the 405. Jody not wanting to get stopped by the CHP when he has a gun in his car. Besides, they are a little drunk because shooting out at Topanga Canyon in the sun made them thirsty, and this hippie on this gnarly old *tractor* had come along, some pot farmer maybe, telling them to get off his land, and that pissed them off. So they drank too much beer.

They get off the 405 at Burbank Boulevard, looking at the other cars, the people on the sidewalk, trying to pick someone out. Some asshole.

But no one looks right. Or maybe it doesn't feel right. He doesn't have that feeling on him.

"Let's wait," he suggests.

"Why?"

"Because it just seems like we oughta, that's why."

She makes a clucking sound but doesn't say anything else for awhile. They drive past a patch of adult bookstores and a video arcade and a liquor store. They come to a park. The trash cans in the park have overflowed; wasps are haunting some melon rinds on the ground. In the basketball court four Chicanos are playing two-on-two, wearing those shiny, pointy black shoes they wear. "You ever notice how Mexican guys, they play bas-

ketball and football in dress shoes?" Jody asks. "It's like they
never heard of sneakers—"

He hears a *crack* and a thudding echo and a greasy chill goes
through him as he realizes that she's fired the gun. He glimpses
a Chicano falling, shouting in pain, the others flattening on the
tennis court, looking around for the shooter as he stomps the
accelerator, lays rubber, squealing through a red light, cars
bitching their horns at him, his heart going in time with the
pistons, fear vising his stomach. He's weaving through the cars,
looking for the freeway entrance. Listening for sirens.

They are on the freeway, before he can talk. The rush hour
traffic only doing about 45, but he feels better here. Hidden.

"What the *fuck* you doing?!" he yells at her.

She gives him a look accusing him of something. He isn't sure
what. Betrayal maybe. Betraying the thing they had made between them.

"Look—" he says, softer, "it was a *red light*. People almost hit
me coming down the cross street. You know? You got to think a
little first. And don't do it when I don't *know*."

She looks at him like she is going to spit. Then she laughs, and
he has to laugh too. She says, "Did you see those dweebs *dive?*"

Mouths dry, palms damp, they watch the five o'clock news and
the six o'clock news. Nothing. Not a word about it. They sit up
in the bed, drinking Coronas. Not believing it. "I mean, what
kind of fucking society *is* this?" Jody says. Like something Cal
would say. "When you shoot somebody and they don't even say
a damn word about it on TV?"

"It's sick," Annie says.

They try to make love but it just isn't there. It's like trying to
start a gas stove when the pilot light is out.

So they watch "Hunter" on TV. Hunter is after a psychokiller. The psycho guy is a real creep. Set a house on fire with some
kids in it, they almost got burnt up, except Hunter gets there in
time. Finally Hunter corners the psychokiller and shoots him.
Annie says, "I like TV better than movies because you know
how it's gonna turn out. But in movies it might have a happy
ending or it might not."

"It usually does," Jody points out.

"Oh yeah? Did you see *Terms of Endearment?* And they got
Bambi out again now. When I was a kid I cried for two days
when his Mom got shot. They should always have happy endings in a little kidlet movie."

452   JODY AND ANNIE ON TV

"That part, that wasn't the end of that movie. It was happy in the end."

"It was still a sad movie."

Finally at eleven o'clock they're on. About thirty seconds worth. A man "shot in the leg on Burbank Boulevard today in a drive-by shooting believed to be gang related." On to the next story. No pictures, nothing. That was it.

What a rip off. "It's racist, is what it is," he says. "Just because they were Mexicans no one gives a shit."

"You know what it is, it's because of all the gang stuff. Gang drive-bys happen every day, everybody's used to it."

He nods. She's right. She has a real feel for these things. He puts his arm around her; she nestles against him. "Okay. We're gonna do it right, so they really pay attention."

"What if we get caught?"

Something in him freezes when she says that. She isn't supposed to talk like that. Because of the *thing* they have together. It isn't something they ever talk about, but they know its rules.

When he withdraws a little, she says, "But we'll never get caught because we just *do it* and cruise before anyone gets together."

He relaxes, and pulls her closer. It feels good just to lay there and hug her.

The next day he's in line for his unemployment insurance check. They have stopped his checks, temporarily, and he'd had to hassle them. They said he could pick this one up. He had maybe two more coming.

Thinking about that, he feels a bad mood coming on him. There's no air conditioning in this place and the fat guy in front of him smells like he's fermenting and the room's so hot and close Jody can hardly breathe.

He looks around and can almost *see* the feeling—like an effect of a camera lens, a zoom or maybe a fish eye lens: Things going two dimensional, flattening out. Annie says something and he just shrugs. She doesn't say anything else till after he's got his check and he's practically running for the door.

"Where you going?"

He shakes his head, standing outside, looking around. It's not much better outside. It's overcast but still hot. "Sucks in there."

"Yeah," she says. "For sure. Oh shit."

"What?"

She points at the car. Someone has slashed the canvas top of the Buick. "My dad is going to kill us."

He looks at the canvas and can't believe it. "Muther-*fuck!*-er!"

"Fucking assholes," she says, nodding gravely. "I mean, you know how much that costs to fix? You wouldn't believe it."

"Maybe we can find him."

"How?"

"I don't know."

He still feels bad but there's a hum of anticipation too. They get in the car, he tears out of the parking lot, making gravel spray, whips onto the street.

They drive around the block, just checking people out, the feeling in him spiraling up and up. Then he sees a guy in front of a Carl's Jr., the guy grinning at him, nudging his friend. Couple of jock college students, looks like, in tank tops. Maybe the guy who did the roof of the car, maybe not.

They pull around the corner, coming back around for another look. Jody can feel the good part of the feeling coming on now but there's something bothering him too: the jocks in tank tops looked right at him.

"You see those two guys?" he hears himself ask, as he pulls around the corner, cruises up next to the Carl's Jr. "The ones—"

"Those jock guys, I know, I picked them out too."

He glances at her, feeling close to her then. They are one person in two parts. The right and the left hand. It feels like music.

He makes sure there's a green light ahead of him, then says, "Get 'em both," he hears himself say. "Don't miss or—"

By then she's aiming the .32, both hands wrapped around it. The jock guys, one of them with a huge coke and the other with a milkshake, are standing by the driveway to the restaurant's parking lot, talking, one of them playing with his car keys. Laughing. The bigger one with the dark hair looks up and sees Annie and the laughing fades from his face. Seeing that, Jody feels better than he ever felt before. *Crack, crack.* She fires twice, the guys go down. *Crack, crack, crack.* Three times more, making sure it gets on the news: shooting into the windows of the Carl's Jr., webs instantly snapping into the window glass, some fat lady goes spinning, her tray of burgers tilting, flying. Jody's already laying rubber, fishtailing around the corner, heading for the freeway.

*   *   *

They don't make it home, they're so excited. She tells him to stop at a gas station on the other side of the hills, in Hollywood. The Men's is unlocked, he feels really right *there* as she looks around then leads him into the bathroom, locks the door from the inside. Bathroom's an almost clean one, he notices, as she hikes up her skirt and he undoes his pants, both of them with shaking fingers, in a real hurry, and she pulls him into her with no preliminaries, right there with her sitting on the edge of the sink. There's no mirror but he sees a cloudy reflection in the shiny chrome side of the towel dispenser; the two of them blurred into one thing sort of pulsing . . .

He looks straight at her, then; she's staring past him, not at anything in particular, just at the sensation, the good sensation they are grinding out between them, like it's something she can see on the dust-streaked wall. He can almost see it in her eyes. And in the way she traps the end of her tongue between her front teeth. Now he can see it himself, in his mind's eye, the sensation flashing like sun in a mirror; ringing like a power chord through a fuzz box. . . .

When he comes he doesn't hold anything back, he can't, and it escapes from him with a sob. She holds him tight and he says, "Wow you are just so awesome you make me feel so *good* . . ."

He's never said anything like that to her before, and they know they've arrived somewhere special. "I love you, Jody," she says.

"I love you."

"It's just us, Jody. Just us. Just us."

He knows what she means. And they feel like little kids cuddling together, even though they're fucking standing up in a *Union 76* Men's restroom, in the smell of pee and disinfectant.

Afterwards they're really hungry so they go to a Jack-in-the-Box, get drive-through food, ordering a whole big shitload. They eat it on the way home, Jody trying not to speed, trying to be careful again about being stopped, but hurrying in case they have a special news flash on TV about the Carl's Jr. Not wanting to miss it.

The Fajita Pita from Jack-in-the-Box tastes really great.

While he's eating, Jody scribbles some song lyrics into his song notebook with one hand. "The Ballad of Jody and Annie."

They came smokin' down the road
like a bat out of hell
they hardly even slowed
or they'd choke from the smell

Chorus:
Holdin' hands in the Valley of Death
(repeat 3X)

Jody and Annie bustin' out of bullshit
Bustin' onto TV
better hope you aren't the one hit
killed disonnerably

Nobody understands em
nobody ever will
but Jody knows she loves 'im
They never get their fill

They will love forever
in history
and they'll live together
in femmy

Holdin' hands in the Valley of Death

He runs out of inspiration there. He hints heavily to Annie about the lyrics and pretends he doesn't want her to read them, makes her ask three times. With tears in her eyes, she asks, as she reads the lyrics, "What's a femmy?"

"You know, like 'Living In femmy.' "

"Oh, infamy. It's so beautiful. . . . You got guacamole on it, you asshole." She's crying with happiness and using a napkin to reverently wipe the guacamole from the notebook paper.

There's no special news flash but since three people died and two are in intensive care, they are the top story on the five o'clock news. And at seven o'clock they get mentioned on CNN, which is *national*. Another one, and they'll be on the "NBC Nightly News," Jody says.

"I'd rather be on 'World News Tonight,' " Annie says. "I like that Peter Jennings dude. He's cute."

About ten, they watch the videotapes of the news stories

again. Jody guesses he should be bothered that the cops have descriptions of them but somehow it just makes him feel more psyched, and he gets down with Annie again. They almost never do it twice in one day, but this makes three times. "I'm getting sore," she says, when he enters her. But she gets off.

They're just finishing, he's coming, vaguely aware he sees lights flashing at the windows, when he hears Cal's voice coming out of the walls. He thinks he's gone schizophrenic or something, he's hearing voices, booming like the voice of God. *"Jody, come on outside and talk to us. This is Cal, you guys. Come on out."*

Then Jody understands, when Cal says, *"They want you to throw the gun out first."*

Jody pulls out of her, puts his hand over her mouth, and shakes his head. He pulls his pants on, then goes into the front room, looks through a corner of the window. There's Cal, and a lot of cops.

Cal's standing behind the police barrier, the cruiser lights flashing around him; beside him is a heavyset Chicano cop who's watching the S.W.A.T. team gearing up behind the big gray van. They're scary-looking in all that armor and with those helmets and shotguns and sniper rifles.

Jody spots Annie's Dad. He's tubby, with a droopy mustache, long hair going bald at the crown, some old hippie, sitting in the back of a cruiser. Jody figures someone got their license number. He can picture the whole thing: The cops had the license number, took them awhile to locate Annie's Dad. He wasn't home at first. They waited till he came home, since he owns the car, and after they talked to him they decided it was his daughter and her boyfriend they were looking for. Got the address from him. Drag Cal over here to talk to Jody because Mom wouldn't come. Yeah.

Cal speaks into the bullhorn again, same crap, sounding like someone else echoing off the houses. Jody sees people looking out their windows. Some being evacuated from the nearest houses. Now an *Action News* truck pulls up, cameramen pile out, set up incredibly fast, get right to work with the newscaster. Lots of activity just for Jody and Annie. Jody has to grin, seeing the news cameras, the guy he recognizes from TV waiting for his cue. He feels high, looking at all this. Cal says something else, but Jody isn't listening. He goes to get the gun.

*   *   *

"It's just us, Jody," Annie says, her face flushed, her eyes dilated as she helps him push the sofa in front of the door. "We can do anything together."

She is there, not scared at all, her voice all around him soft and warm. "It's just us," she says again, as he runs to get another piece of furniture.

He is running around like a speedfreak, pushing the desk, leaning bookshelves to block off the tear gas. Leaving enough room for him to shoot through. He sees the guys start to come up the walk with the tear gas and the shotguns. Guys in helmets and some kind of bulky bulletproof shit. But maybe he can hit their necks, or their knees. He aims carefully and fires again. Someone stumbles and the others carry the wounded dude back behind the cars.

Five minutes after Jody starts shooting, he notices that Annie isn't there. At almost the same moment a couple of rifle rounds knock the bookshelves down, and something smashes through a window. In the middle of the floor, white mist gushes out of a teargas shell.

Jody runs from the tear gas, into the kitchen, coughing. "Annie!" His voice sounding like a kid's.

He looks through the kitchen window. Has she gone outside, turned traitor?

But then she appears at his elbow, like somebody switched on a screen and Annie is what's on it.

"Hey," she says, her eyes really bright and beautiful. "Guess what." She has the little TV by the handle; it's plugged in on the extension cord. In the next room, someone is breaking through the front door.

"I give up," he says, eyes tearing. "What?"

She sets the TV on the counter for him to see. "We're on TV. Right now. We're on TV. . . ."

Snow Angels

Loren D. Estleman

Loren D. Estleman's Amos Walker novels are some of the best private detective books of the past two decades. Estleman is also the best western writer of his generation. And his crime trilogy about Detroit was praised by mainstream and genre critics alike. The amazing thing is that Loren accomplished all this before turning forty.

First published in 1991.

They were the unlikeliest visitors I'd had in my office since the time a priest came in looking for the antiquarian bookshop on the next floor.

She was a comfortably overstuffed sixty in a plain wool dress and a cloth coat with a monkey collar, gray hair pinned up under a hat with artificial flowers planted around the crown. He was a long skinny length of fencewire two or three years older with a horse face and sixteen hairs stretched across his scalp like violin strings, wearing a forty-dollar suit over a white shirt buttoned to the neck, no tie, and holding his hat. They sat facing my desk in the chairs I'd brought out for them as if posing for a picture back when a photograph was serious business. Their name was Cuttle.

I grinned. "Ma and Pa?"

"Jeremy and Judy," the woman said seriously. "Ed Snilly gave us your name. The lawyer?"

I excused myself and got up to consult the file cabinet. Snilly had hired me over the telephone three years ago to check the credit rating on a client, a half-hour job. He'd paid promptly.

"Good man," I said, resuming my seat. "What's he recommending me for?"

Judy said, "He's a neighbor. He sat in when we closed on the old Stage Stop. He said you might be able to help us."

"Stage Stop?"

"It's a tavern out on Old US-23, a roadhouse. Jeremy and me used to go there Saturday night when all our friends were alive. It's been closed a long time. When the developers gave us a hundred thousand for our farm—we bought it for ten back in '53—I said to Jeremy, 'We're always talking about buying the old Stage Stop and fixing it up and running it the way they used to, here's our chance.' And we did; buy it, that is, only—"

"Dream turned into a nightmare, right?"

"Good Lord, yes! You must know something about it. Building codes, sanitation, insurance, the liquor commission—I swear, if farming wasn't the most heartbreaking life a couple could choose, we'd never have had the sand for this. When the inspector told us we'd be better off tearing down and rebuilding—"

"Tell him about Simon," Jeremy snapped. I'd begun to wonder if he had vocal cords.

"Solomon," she corrected. "The Children of Solomon. Have you heard of it, Mr. Walker?"

"Some kind of Bible camp. I thought the state closed them down. Something about the discipline getting out of hand."

"A boy died in their camp up north, a runaway. But they claimed he came to them in that condition and nobody could prove different, so the charges were dropped. But they lost their lease on the land. They were negotiating a contract on the Stage Stop property when we paid cash for it. Solomon sued the previous owner, but nothing was signed between them and the judge threw it out. They tried to buy us off at a profit, but we said no."

"Took a shot at me," Jeremy said.

I sat up. "Who did?"

"Well, someone," Judy said. "We don't know it was them."

"Put a hole in my hat." Jeremy thrust it across the desk.

I took it and looked it over. It was stiff brown felt with a silk band. Something that might have been a bullet had torn a gash near the dimple on the right side of the crown. I gave it back. "Where'd it happen?"

"Jeremy was in front of the building yesterday morning, doing some measuring. I wasn't with him. He said his hat came off just like somebody grabbed it. Then he heard the shot. He ducked in through the doorway. He waited an hour before going back out, but there wasn't any more shots and he couldn't tell where that one had come from."

"Maybe it was a careless hunter."

"Wasn't no hunter."

Judy said, "We called Ollie Springer at the sheriff's substation and he came out and pried a bullet out of the doorframe. He said it came from a rifle, a .30-30. Nobody hunts with a high-powered rifle in this part of the state, Mr. Walker. It's illegal."

"Did this Springer talk to the Solomon people?"

She nodded. "They denied knowing anything about it, and there it sits. Ollie said he didn't have enough to get a warrant and search for the rifle."

I said he was probably right.

"Oh, we know he was," she said. "Jeremy and me know Ollie since he was three. Where we come from folks don't move far from home. You'll see why when you get there."

I hadn't said I was going yet, but I let it sail. "Can you think of anyone else who might want to take a shot at you?"

She answered for Jeremy. "Good Lord, no! It's a friendly place. Nobody's killed anybody around there since 1867, and that was between outsiders passing through. Besides, I don't think anybody wants to hurt either one of us. They're just trying to scare us into selling. Well, we're not scared. That's what we want you to tell those Solomon people."

"Why not tell them yourself?"

"Ed Snilly said it would mean more coming from a detective." She folded her hands on her purse in her lap, ending that discussion.

"Want me to scare *them?*"

"Yes." Something nudged the comfortable look out of her face. "Yes, we'd like that a whole lot."

I scratched my ear with the pencil I used to take notes. "I usually get a three-day retainer, but this doesn't sound like it'll take more than half a day. Make it two-fifty."

Jeremy pulled an old black wallet from his hip pocket and counted three one hundred-dollar bills onto the desk from a compartment stuffed full of them. "Gimme fifty back," he said. "And I want a receipt."

I gave him two twenties and a ten from my own wallet, re-placed them with the bills he'd given me, and wrote out the transaction, handing him a copy. "Do you always come to town with that much cash on you?" I asked.

"First time we been to Detroit since '59."

"Oh, that's not true," Judy said. "We were here in '61 to see the new Studebakers."

I got some more information from them, said I'd attend to their case that afternoon, and stood to see them out.

"Don't you wear a coat?" I asked Jeremy. Outside the window the snow was falling in sheets.

"When it gets cold."

I accompanied them through the outer office into the hall-way, where I shook Jeremy Cuttle's corded old hand and we said goodbye. I resisted the urge to follow them out to their car. If they drove away in anything but a 1961 Studebaker I might not have been able to handle the disappointment.

I killed an hour in the microfilm reading room at the library catching up on the Children of Solomon.

It was a fundamentalist religious group founded in the 1970s by a party named Bertram Comfort on the grounds that the New Testament and Christian thought were upstarts and that the way to salvation led through a belief in a vengeful God, tempered with the wisdom of King Solomon. Although a number of complaints had been filed against the sect's youth camp in the north woods, mostly for breach of the peace, the outstate press remained unaware of the order's existence until a four-teen-year-old boy died in one of the cabins, his body bearing the unmistakable signs of a severe beating.

The camp was closed by injunction and an investigation was launched, but no evidence surfaced to disprove Comfort's testi-mony that the boy died in their care after receiving rough treat-ment Solomon only knew where. The Children themselves were unpaid volunteers working in the light of their faith and the people who sent their children to the camp were members and patrons of the church, which was not recognized as such by the state.

There was nothing to indicate that Comfort and his disciples would shoot at an old man in order to acquire real estate in Southeastern Michigan, but before heading out the Cuttles' way I went back to the office and strapped on the Smith & Wesson. Any place that hadn't had a murder in more than 120 years was past due.

An hour west of Detroit the snow stopped falling and the sun came out, glaring hard off a field of white that blended pave-ment with countryside; even the overpasses looked like the ruins of Atlantis rearing out of a salt sea. The farther I got from town the more the scenery resembled a Perry Como Christmas special, rolling away to the horizon with frosted trees and here and there a homeowner in Eskimo dress shoveling his driveway. The mall builders and fast-food chains had left droppings there just like everywhere else, but on days like that you remembered that kids still sledded down hills too steep for them and set out to build the world's tallest snowman and lay on their backs in the snow fanning their arms and legs to make angels.

Judy had told me she and Jeremy were living in a trailer behind the old Stage Stop, which stood on a hill overlooking Old US-23 near the exit from the younger expressway. At the end of the ramp, an aging barn she had also told me about provided more directions in the form of a painted advertisement flaking off the end wall. I turned that way, straddling a hump of snow left in the middle of the road by a county plow. Over a hill, and then the gray frame saltbox she had described thrust itself between me and a bright sky.

As it turned out, I wouldn't have needed either the sign or the directions. The rotating beacon of a county sheriff's car bounced red and blue light off the front of the building.

I parked among a collection of civilian cars and pickup trucks and followed footsteps in the snow past the county unit, left unattended with its flashers on and the two-way radio hawking and spitting at top volume, toward a fourteen-foot house trailer parked behind the empty tavern. A crowd was breaking up there, helped along by a gangling young deputy in uniform who was shooing them like chickens. He moved in front of me as I stepped toward the trailer.

"We got business here, mister. Please help us by minding yours."

I showed him the license, which might have been in cuneiform for all the reaction it got. "I'm working for the Cuttles. Who's in charge?"

"Sergeant Springer. Until the detectives show up from the county seat, anyway. You're not one of them."

I held out a card. "Please tell him the Cuttles hired me this morning."

He looked past me, saw the first of the civilian vehicles pulling out, and took the card. "Wait." He circled behind the trailer. After a few minutes he came back and beckoned me from the end.

The sergeant was a hard-looking stump about my age with

silver splinters in the black hair at his temples and flat tired eyes under a fur cap. The muscles in his jaw were bunched like grapeshot. He was standing ankle-deep in snow fifty feet from the trailer with his back to it on the edge of a five-acre field that ended in a line of firs on the other side. A few yards beyond him, a man and woman lay spreadeagled side by side on their faces in the snow. The backs of the man's suitcoat and the woman's overcoat were smeared red. More red stained the snow around them in a bright fan. They were dressed exactly as I had last seen Judy and Jeremy Cuttle.

"Figure the son of a bitch gave them a running start," the sergeant said as I joined him. "Maybe he told them if they made it to the trees they were home free."

"Who found them?" I asked.

"Paper boy came to collect. When they didn't answer his knock he went looking."

"Anybody hear the shots?"

"It's rabbit season. Day goes by without a couple of shotgun blasts . . ." He let it dangle. "Your name's Walker? Ollie Springer. I command the substation here." I could feel the wire strength in his grip through the leather glove. "What'd they hire you for?"

"To hooraw the Children of Solomon. Jeremy thought they were the ones who took a shot at him yesterday. Who identified them?"

"It's them all right. I started running errands for the Cuttles when I was six and my parents knew them before that. If Comfort's bunch did this I'll nail every damn one of them to a cross." His jaw muscles worked.

"Any sign of a struggle?"

"Trailer's neat as a button. Judy was the last of the great homemakers. Bastard must've got the drop on them. Jeremy didn't talk much, but he was a fighter. You don't want to mess with these old farmers. But you can't fight a jinx."

"What kind of jinx?"

"The Stage Stop. Everybody who ever had anything to do with the place came to no good. Last guy who ran it went bankrupt. One before that tried to torch the place for the insurance and died in prison. I took a run at it myself once—nest egg for my retirement—and then my wife walked out on me. I guess I should've tried to talk them out of it, not that they'd have listened."

"Mind if I take a look inside the trailer?"

"Why, didn't they pay you?"

"Excuse me, Sergeant," I said, "but go to hell."

There was a door on that side of the trailer, but the deputy and I went around to the side facing the Stage Stop. Gordy should have set up his post closer to the road; the path to the door had been trampled all over by curious citizens, obliterating the killer's footprints and those of any herd of Clydesdales that might have happened by. Inside, Judy Cuttle had done what she could to turn a mobile home into an Edwardian farmhouse, complete with antimacassars and rusty photos in bamboo frames of geezers in waistcoats and glum women in cameoes. A .20-gauge Remington pump shotgun, still a fixture in Michigan country houses, leaned in a corner of the tiny parlor. Without touching it I bent over to sniff the muzzle. It hadn't been fired recently.

"Jeremy's, Ollie says," the deputy reported. "He used to shoot pheasants till he slowed down."

The door we had entered through had a window with a clear view to the tavern and the road beyond. The purse Judy had carried into my office lay on a lamp table near the door. The quality of the housekeeping said she hadn't intended it to stay there for long. I wondered if they'd even had a chance to take off their hats before receiving their last visitor.

An unmarked Dodge was parked next to the patrol car when we came out. On the other side we found a plainclothesman in conversation with Sergeant Springer while his partner examined the bodies. Their business with me didn't take any longer than Springer's. I thanked the sergeant for talking to me and left.

So far the whole thing stank; and in snow, yet.

Judy Cuttle's directions were still working. A houseboy or something in a turtleneck and whipcord trousers answered the door of a gray stone house on the edge of the nearby town and showed me into a room paneled in fruitwood with potted plants on the built-in shelves. I was alone for only a few seconds when Bertram Comfort joined me.

He was a well-upholstered fifty in a brown suit off the rack, with fading red hair brushed gently back from a bulging forehead and no visible neck. His hands were pink and plump and hairless, and grasping one was like shaking hands with a baby. He waved me into a padded chair and sat down himself behind a desk anchored by a chrome doodad on one end and a King James Bible the size of a handtruck on the other.

"Is it Reverend Comfort?" I asked.

"Mister will do." His voice had the enveloping quality of a maiden aunt's sofa. "I'm merely a lay reader. Are you with the prosecutor's office up north? I thought that tragic business was settled."

"I'm working for Judy and Jeremy Cuttle. I'm a private investigator."

He looked as if he were going to cry. "I told the officer none of the Children were near the property yesterday. I wish these people could lay aside the suspicions of the secular world long enough to understand it is not we but Solomon who sits in judgment."

"I notice you refer to it as *the* property, not *their* property. Do you still hope to obtain it for your camp?"

"Not *my* camp. Solomon's. All the legal avenues have not yet been traveled."

"It's the illegal ones I'm interested in. Maybe you've got a rebel in the fold. It happens in the best of families, even the God-fearing ones."

"The Children love God; we don't fear Him. And everyone is accounted for at the time of yesterday's unfortunate incident."

"Yesterday's yesterday. I'm here about today."

"Today?"

"Somebody shotgunned the Cuttles behind their trailer about an hour ago. Give or take."

"Great glory!" He glanced at the Bible. "Are they—"

"Gone to God. Knocking on the pearly. Purgatory bound. Dead as a mackerel."

"I find your mockery abhorrent under the circumstances. Do the police think the Children are involved?"

"The police think what the police think. I'm not the police. Yesterday somebody potted at Jeremy Cuttle, or maybe just at his hat as a warning. Today he and his wife engaged me to investigate. Now they're not in a position to engage anything but six feet of God's good earth. I'm a detective. I see a connection." I looked at my watch. "It's three o'clock. Do you know where the Children are?"

Again his eyes strayed to the Bible. Then he placed his pudgy hands on the desk, jacked himself to his feet, and hiked up his belt, the way fat men do. "I have Solomon's work to attend to.

'Go thou from the presence of a foolish man when thou perceivest not in him the lips of knowledge.' "

" 'Sticks and stones may break my bones,' " I said, rising, "but any parakeet can memorize sentences." I went me from his presence.

Ed Snilly, the lawyer who had recommended me to the Cuttles, lived in an Edwardian farmhouse on eighty acres with a five-year-old Fleetwood parked in the driveway sporting a bumper sticker reading HAVE YOU HUGGED YOUR HOGS TODAY? His wife, fifty-odd years of pork and potatoes stuffed into stretch jeans, directed me to the large yellow barn behind the house, where I found him tossing ears of dried corn from a bucket into a row of stalls occupied by chugging, snuffling pigs.

"One of my neighbors called me with the news," he said after he'd set down the bucket and shaken my hand. He was a wiry old scarecrow in his seventies with a spotty bald head and false teeth in a jaw too narrow for them. "Terrible thing. I've known Judy and Jeremy since the Depression. I'd gladly help out the prosecution on this one gratis. Do you suspect Comfort?"

"I'd like to. Did you represent the Cuttles when they bought the Stage Stop?"

"Yes. It was an estate sale, very complicated. Old Man Herndon's heirs wanted to liquidate quickly and wouldn't carry any paper. Jeremy negotiated to the last penny. I also stood up with them at the hearing with the State Liquor Control Commission. A license transfer can be pretty thorny without chicanery. I'm not sure we'd have swung it if Ollie Springer hadn't appeared to vouch for them."

"I'm surprised he spoke up. He told me the place was jinxed."

"I can see why he'd feel that way. Old Man Herndon was Ollie's father-in-law. The Stage Stop was going to be a belated wedding present, but that ended when Herndon's daughter ran out on Ollie. The rumor was she ditched him for some third rate rock singer who came through here a couple of years back. I think that's what killed the old man."

"So far this place is getting to be almost as interesting as Detroit."

"Scandals happen everywhere, but in the main we country folk look out for one another. That's why Ollie helped Judy and Jeremy in spite of his personal tragedy. To be honest, I thought they were getting in over their heads too, especially later when they talked about digging a wine cellar and adding a room for pool. They were looking far beyond your usual mom-and-pop operation."

"Is gaming that big hereabouts?"

"Son, people around here will go to a christening and bet on when the baby's first tooth will come in. Phil Costa's made a fortune off the pool tables in the basement of his bowling alley out on M-52. Lord knows I've represented enough of his clientele at their arraignments every time Ollie's raided the place."

"Little Phil? Last I heard he was doing something like seven to twelve in Jackson for fixing the races at Hazel Park."

"He's out two years now, and smarter than when he went in. These rural county commissioners stay fixed longer than the city kind. Phil never seems to be around when the deputies bust in."

"So if the Cuttles went ahead and put in their poolroom, Little Phil might have lost business."

"It's a thought." Snilly picked up his bucket and resumed scattering ears of corn in the stalls. "A thought is what it is."

The Paul Bunyan Bowl-A-Rama, an aluminum hangar with a two-story neon lumberjack bowling on its roof, looked abashed at mid-afternoon, like a nude dancer caught under a conventional electric bulb. A young thick-shouldered bouncer who hadn't bothered to change out of his overalls on his way in from the back forty conferred with the office and came back to escort me past the lanes.

Little Phil Costa crowded four-foot ten in his two-inch elevators, a sour-faced baldy in his middle years with pointed features like a chihuahua's. Small men are usually neat, but his tie was loose, his sleeves rolled up unevenly, and an archaeologist could have reconstructed his last five meals from the stains on his unbuttoned vest. He didn't look up from the adding-machine tapes he was sorting through on a folding card table when I entered. "Tell Lorraine the support check's in the mail. I ain't about to bust my parole over the brat."

"I'm not from your ex. I'm working for the Cuttles."

"What the hell's a Cuttle?"

I told him. He scowled, but it was at a wrong sum on one of the tapes. He corrected it with a pencil stub. "I heard about it. I hope you got your bread up front."

"Talk is Judy and Jeremy were going to add a pool room to the Stage Stop."

"How about that. What's six times twelve?"

"Think of it in terms of years in stir." I laid a hand on top of the tape. "A few years back, two guys who were operating their handbook in one of your neighborhoods were shotgunned behind the New Hellas Cafe in Hamtramck. The cops never did pin it to you, but nobody's tried to cut in on you since. Until the Cuttles."

The farmboy-bouncer took a step forward, but Costa stopped him with a hand. "Get the bottle."

It was a pinch bottle filled with amber liquid. Costa took it without looking away from me and broke the seal. "You a drinking man, Walker?"

"In the right company. This isn't it."

"I wasn't offering. This stuff's twenty-four years old, flown in special for me from Aberdeen. Seventy-five bucks a fifth." He upended it over his metal wastebasket. When it gurgled empty he tossed in the bottle. "On their best night, that's what the Cuttles' room might cost me. Still think I iced them?"

"I'm way past that," I said. "Now I'm wondering who takes out your trash."

"You trade in information, I'll treat you. Check out a guy named Chuckie Noyes. He's a Child of Solomon, squats in the cemetery behind the Stage Stop property, the old caretaker's hut. I knew him in Jackson before he got religion. He did eleven years for killing a druggie in Detroit. Used a shotgun."

"Why so generous?"

He tipped a hand toward the adding-machine tapes. "I got a good thing here, closest I ever been to legit in my life. Last thing I need's some sticky snoop coming back and back, drawing attention. Time was I'd just have Horace here adjust your spine, but if there's one thing I learned on the block it's diplomacy. Dangle, now. I open at dusk."

"Seventy-two," I said.

"What?"

"Six times twelve."

"Hey, thanks." He wrote it down. "Come back some night when you're not working and bowl a couple of lines. On the house."

For the second time that day, police strobes had beaten me to my destination. They lanced the shadows gathering among the leaning headstones in what might have been a churchyard before the central building had burned down sometime around

Appomattox. Near its charred foundation stood a galvanized steel shed with a slanted roof and a door cut in one side. As I was getting out of the car, two uniformed attendants wheeled a body bag on a stretcher out through the door and into the back of an ambulance that was almost as big as the shed. Sergeant Springer came out behind them, deep in conversation with a man six inches taller in a snapbrim hat and a coat with a fur collar. The two were enveloped in the vapor of their own spent breath.

"I'll want it on my desk in the morning," said the big man, pausing to shake Springer's hand before pulling on his gloves.

"Will do, Lieutenant."

The lieutenant touched his shoulder. "Bad day all around, Ollie. Get some rest before you talk to the shooting team." He boarded an unmarked Dodge with a magnetic flasher on the roof. The motor turned over sluggishly and caught.

"Chuckie Noyes?" I asked Springer.

He looked up at me, then down at his fur cap. "Yeah." He put it on.

"Who shot him, you?"

"Uh-huh."

"He do the Cuttles?"

"Looks like."

"You're not the only one having a bad day, Sergeant."

"Guess you're right." He fastened the snaps on his jacket. "I came here to ask Noyes some questions, thought he might have seen or heard something living so close. He had an antique pin on his chest of drawers by his bed. Judy wore that pin to church every Sunday. Don't know how I missed not seeing it in the trailer. Noyes saw it same time I did. He tried for my gun."

"Were you alone?"

"What?" He lamped me hard.

"Nothing. You folks in the country do things differently."

"I don't expect to lose sleep over squashing a germ like that, but it doesn't mean I wanted to. Now we'll never know if he was working for Comfort or if he slipped the rest of the way over the edge and acted solo. He had a record for violence."

"So Little Phil said."

"That germ. Guess you'll talk to just about anybody."

"It's a job."

"A stinking job."

"Everything about this one stinks," I agreed. "Sleep tight, Sergeant."

* * *

I'd always heard God-fearing people went to bed with the chickens. Another myth gone.

At 11:45 P.M. I was still parked down the road from Bertram Comfort's gray stone house, where I'd been for over an hour, warming my calcifying marrow with judicious transfusions of hot coffee from a Thermos and waiting for the lights to go out downstairs. A couple of minutes later they did. I was tempted to go in then but sat tight. Just after midnight the single lighted window on the second story went black. Then I moved.

I'd brought my pocket burglar kit, but just for the hell of it I tried the knob on the front door. Comfort had the old churchman's prejudice against locks. I let myself in.

I also had my pencil flash, but I didn't use that either. There was a moon, and the glow reflecting off the snow shone bright as my best hopes through the windows. I found my way to the study without tripping over anything.

I didn't waste time going through the desk or looking behind the religious paintings for a wall safe. During my interview with Comfort his eyes had strayed to the big Bible on the desk one too many times for even the devoutest of reasons.

The book was genuine enough. There were no hollowed-out pages and an elaborate red-and-gold bookplate pasted to the flyleaf read To MR. BERTRAM EZEKIEL COMFORT, FATHER OF THE FAITH, FROM THE CHILDREN OF SOLOMON, flanked by Adam and Eve in figleaves. A dozen strips of microfilm spilled out of a pocket in the spine when I tilted the book.

I carried the strips over to the window and held them up to the moonlight. They were photographed documents bearing the identification of the records departments of various police organizations. The farthest came from Los Angeles. The closest belonged to Detroit. I read that one. Then I put it in my inside breast pocket, returned the others to the Bible and the Bible to its place on the desk, and left, my sabbatical completed on the bones of another Commandment.

The next day was clear and twenty degrees. The sky had no ceiling and the sun on the snow was a sea of cold white fire. Breathing was like inhaling needles.

The air was colder inside the empty Stage Stop building with the raw damp of enclosed winter. The old floorboards rang like iron when I stepped on them and my breath steamed around the gaunt timbers that held up the roof. Owls nested in the rafters. The new yellow two-by-fours stacked along the walls were bright with the anticipation of a dead couple's exploded vision.

"Jesus, it's cold in here," said Ollie Springer, pushing aside the front door, which hung on a single scabbed hinge. "Is the cold locker closed at Pete's Meats?"

"It's a hall. The Cuttles might have appreciated the choice. Thanks for coming, Sergeant."

"You made it sound important over the phone. It better be. The lieutenant's waiting for my report on Chuckie Noyes."

"I've got something you might want to add." I handed him the microfilm slip I'd taken from Comfort's Bible.

"What is it?"

"Noye's arrest report on a homicide squeal he went down for in Detroit a dozen years ago. Since you mentioned his record yesterday I thought you'd like to see the name of the arresting officer."

He was holding it up to a shaft of sunlight coming in through an empty window, but he wasn't reading.

"The city cops are jealous of their reputations," I said. "When they take a killer into custody they sometimes forget to release the name of the rural cop who actually busted him during his flight to freedom; but a report's a report. Just a deputy then, weren't you?"

"This doesn't mean anything." He crumpled the strip into a ball and threw it behind the stack of lumber.

"Detroit has the original. Bertram Comfort maintains the loyalty of the more recalcitrant members of his flock by keeping tabs on their past indiscretions; that's where I got the copy. I figure when you found out Noyes was back in circulation and hanging around your jurisdiction, you either hired him to kill Judy and Jeremy or more likely threatened to bust him on some parole beef if he didn't cooperate. Then you offed him to keep him from talking and planted Judy's pin in the caretaker's hut where he was living. The simple plans are always the best. As a Child of Solomon he'd be blamed for trying to help secure the Stage Stop property for Comfort's new camp.

"I guess I'm responsible for accelerating their deaths," I went on. "Someone—you, probably—made a last ditch attempt to scare them off the other day by taking a potshot at Jeremy. When he and Judy hired me instead to investigate, you switched to Plan B before I could get a foothold. You're one impulsive cop, Sergeant."

"Why would I want to kill the Cuttles? They're like my second parents." He rested his hand on his sidearm, a nickel-plated .38 with a black knurled grip.

"It bothered me too, especially when I found out you spoke up for them at the hearing before the State Liquor Control Commission. But that didn't jibe with what you told me about thinking this place had a hoodoo. I should have guessed the truth when Ed Snilly said they decided later to expand the Stage Stop. At first I thought it was their plans for a pool room and the competition it would create for Phil Costa, but that was chump change to him, not worth killing over. It was the wine cellar."

"What wine cellar?"

"There isn't one now, but there was going to be. You were right in there cheering them on, in spite of your own bad luck with the place and the wife you said left you, until you found out they were going to dig a hole." I paced as I spoke, circling a soft spot in the floor where the old boards had rotted and sunk into a depression eight feet across. He was watching me, trying to keep from staring at my feet. His fingers curled around the grip of the revolver. I said, "I made some calls this morning from my motel room in town, got the name of that rock singer everyone says your wife ran off with. I called eight booking agents before I found one who used to work with him. He didn't skip with anyone's wife. He died of a drug overdose in Cincinnati a couple of months after he played here. Nobody was with him or had been for some time."

"If you stayed at the motel you know she spent a night with him there," Springer said. "It was all over the county next day. They were both gone by then."

"Your wife didn't go as far as he did. No more than six feet from where we're standing, and all of it straight down. Those rotten boards lift right out. I checked before you got here."

"Plenty of room under there for two." He drew his gun.

"Drop it, Ollie!"

He pivoted, snapping off a shot. The bullet knocked a splinter off the big timber the sheriff's lieutenant had been hiding behind. The big man returned fire. Springer shouted, fell down, and grasped his thigh.

"Drop it, I said."

The sergeant looked down at the gun he was still holding as if he'd forgotten about it. He opened his hand and let it fall.

"Thanks, Lieutenant." I took the Smith & Wesson out of my coat pocket and lowered the hammer gently. "Sorry about the cold wait."

He holstered his own gun under his fur-lined coat. "Ollie was right about this place." He shook loose a pair of handcuffs.

I left while he was reading Springer his Miranda and went out into the cold sunshine of the country.

The Memorial Hour

Wade Miller

The name Wade Miller appeared on some of the most acclaimed suspense fiction of the forties, fifties, and sixties. Bob Wade and Bill Miller made up the team and their work appeared everywhere, from Playboy *to the movie screen, Orson Welles'* Touch of Evil *being based on their novel. Bob Wade carries on alone after the death of his partner. HarperCollins is reissuing many of the famous Max Thursday titles and Wade is working on a new one. He's a fine writer.*

First published in 1960.

Jackie, to my annoyance, made his first appearance in my office at three o'clock on a Thursday afternoon.

For the past year I had kept that particular time open for meditation since it was the hour that my wife Helen met her death in the automobile accident. Not even my receptionist knew that these weekly periods were memorial in nature; I let her believe I was taking a mental coffee break.

Nor was this a deception, for a psychiatrist can only absorb so much of other people's problems before he feels the need to clear his mind. And in the year since Helen died, I had been working very hard—burying my sorrow in my practice so to speak.

Consequently, I was disturbed to see a new patient usurping the hour that I considered my own private affair. Though I had no choice but to make the best of it, I intended to reprimand Linda, my receptionist, for her thoughtlessness with the appointment book. As it turned out, I became so caught up in the abnormality of the case that I never did correct her.

My new patient, a virile young man, acted as if he realized his presence was unwelcome. He slouched in the big leather chair opposite me, fixed his eyes on the wall above my head, and read aloud my credentials in a mocking voice. " 'Know all men by these presents that John Kermit Conover, having completed the studies prescribed by law . . .' Oh, surely that must give you godlike powers, Dr. Conover."

"Not at all." No need to take offense; many frayed personalities react defensively to the analyst at first. "The diplomas merely demonstrate that I've had some seven years of certain special training. I'm only another man, like yourself."

"No," he said quickly. He was strangely anxious. "No, we can't be anything alike." In appearance, at least, he was right. He had the smooth athletic grace of youth, the good looks of health and eagerness, and he seemed expensively well-dressed, while I . . . well, I am now fifty-three, as conservative and quiet and gray as my office walls.

"Suppose we begin with your name," I suggested.

He relaxed into his former arrogance. "Jackie Newman?" he asked with a smile. I had no doubt that it was fictitious, not that this would be especially unusual. "You call me Jackie. I'm afraid we're going to see a lot of each other."

"All right, Jackie. I hope I may be able to help you. However—"

"Look, you've got it framed there on the wall that you're a psychiatrist. You solve people's problems, don't you?"

"Not exactly. Everyone must solve his own problems. My job is to help you uncover and understand what your problem really is. Then you supply the therapy."

"Oh, nice setup," Jackie snorted. "You get the fee while I do the work."

"It's significant that you look at it that way. Do you often have feelings of being cheated?" He stared at me angrily but didn't answer. "You see, as a detached observer, I'm frequently able to detect what the patient is too emotionally bound up in to see for himself. Then I'm able to help."

Jackie dropped his head. "You can't help me," he muttered. "Nobody can. I already know what is wrong with me."

"Then let's talk about it."

"I'm afraid," he said simply. His face, free of the taut lines of arrogance, turned soft and childlike. "Unless something stops me, I know I'm going to do something bad."

"How do you mean—bad?"

"You know," His right hand twitched in a small clawing gesture. "Something violent—hurt somebody."

I reassured him that the urge to violence is imbedded in us all. It is better that the patient not think himself wholly unnatural. "Now, have you ever done anything violent, Jackie?"

"No. Not yet. But lately—well, I've been taking things, stealing . . ."

"What sort of things?"

He folded his arms, as if hugging something tightly against his chest. "Oh, things." He kept his eyes on the upright desk pen in front of me. "Nothing I actually need. But I wanted to—I get this wanting feeling inside that makes me keep taking them, more all the time."

I tried to probe deeper but with no results. What were his emotions at the time of the act? How did he feel about it afterward? I knew that the nature of the stolen objects would provide a key to his compulsion, but Jackie kept sliding away from the subject. "I'm not worried about the stealing!" he finally burst out petulantly. "It's the other thing—what I told you before."

"You believe that theft is the stepping stone to something worse, is that it?"

"Well, I keep getting urges, like I was foaming inside. Like just taking things isn't enough. Like there's something even better I could do."

"Can you give me an example?"

All he gave me was a knowing smile. Nor would he admit to any dreaming, when I took that tack. Psychiatry is the only branch of medicine where the patient will conceal his symptoms, hide them even from himself. But the outstanding fact that Jackie had come to me at all was encouraging, so I said, "Let's go about it another way. Tell me about yourself."

He related his history with some pride. It was a rambling discourse and the more I heard, the more dead certain I became that he was making it up as he went along. Although totally alone in the world now, he claimed to have come from a wealthy family upstate, to have served with distinction in the army—"I got the Purple Heart twice"—and, following this, to have pursued several vocations, among them automobile racing and uranium prospecting. In view of his youth, his story sounded somewhat incredible.

He must have sensed my disbelief because he broke off abruptly. "How do you like it so far?" he demanded. "Are you jealous?"

"Let's say that you've raised certain questions in my mind."

"Well, they'll have to wait," he said bruskly, and rose. "Either I'll see you next week or I won't. I'm like that."

Not until after Jackie was gone did it occur to me that I'd failed to tell him that this particular appointment hour was inconvenient. Then, examining my own reactions, I decided that my omission was intentional: I wanted Jackie to return. He displayed, bad manners and all, possibilities that gripped my interest beyond the cloudy merits of his case.

My receptionist came in. "Doctor, Mrs. Greer has canceled out on her four o'clock. Some unexpected company. She hoped you wouldn't mind."

"It suits me fine," I told her. "That last patient gave me a splitting headache."

"I'll get you some aspirin," she said, instantly solicitous. I often wondered what prompted Linda to choose to work for a psychiatrist; she is such a completely uncomplicated personality. A pretty brunette, her buxom femininity and animal vitality sometimes struck me as incongruous amid the neuroses and psychoses of my practice, as if she were moving cheerily among the dead. Yet she was efficient enough and though not a graduate nurse, she fulfilled many of a nurse's functions. "By the way, Doctor, I was wondering—since we don't have anybody else coming in today—if I could get away a little early. It's our anniversary and Ed and I were planning to have dinner in town and maybe go to a show."

"Anniversary? Has it been a year already?"

"No, just six months." Linda giggled. "It probably sounds silly to you—but we're still so darn thrilled about being married . . ."

"Don't apologize for being happy," I said. "So few people are."

I thought about Jackie quite a bit during the next week, though I was by no means sure I would ever see him again. However, he appeared on schedule the following Thursday. This time he was sullen and less communicative, except to admit that he was still stealing "things."

In his depressed state he had either forgotten or discarded his previous account of his life; what little he would tell of his background varied greatly from before but sounded to me more probable. The one solid nugget of information I uncovered was that Jackie had briefly attended the same university as I, but I was unable to exploit this common experience to establish the rapport I desired.

He had quit school out of boredom, and he mumbled something about the girls there that I didn't catch and he wouldn't repeat. It included the phrase "sweaters and bare legs," and I surmised privately that his trouble was sex-centered but he wouldn't respond to that line of questioning either. Nor would he speak at all of the seven-year period following college, muttering, "Why talk about it? It's all over." Or—his favorite form of dismissal—"It isn't important."

The consultation left me somewhat despondent, partly the gloomy contagion of his own mood but mostly because I felt I was getting nowhere.

Yet the following week Jackie surprised me by bringing with him in a shopping bag the articles he had stolen. They bore out my first theory as to the center of his trouble. The "things" turned out to be brassieres—most of them fancy with lace or bright in color—and he was compulsively explicit as to when and where he had taken each one. Some had come from clotheslines in various parts of the city, but many of them were new with price tags still attached.

"Why are you telling me this today when you wouldn't before?" I asked.

"Because I'm finished." Jackie was jubilant, pacing back and forth excitedly, refusing to settle in the patient's chair. "I'm not going to steal any more of them. It's just a matter of deciding to exercise self-control."

"Have you ever considered—despite this theft aberration, which is minor—that you might be under too complete control? That you might be hiding from yourself something of real importance?"

He turned to me with a hurt expression. "You don't think I am cured."

"You may be. But it's seldom that easy, Jackie."

"You'll see," he promised, earnest as a five-year-old. "I brought this stuff up here so you could give it back to the people I took it from."

I agreed, though I knew it was an impossible task. To return all that stolen lingerie to its rightful owners would provoke questions that I wouldn't be able to answer. So I simply pressed the shopping bag into the bottom drawer of one of the filing cabinets that stood in the anteroom to my office, intending to dispose of its contents at a more convenient time.

Linda discovered Jackie's loot before I remembered to do so, however. When I entered my office one morning, she was standing in the anteroom, peering astonished into the shopping bag. "Doctor, what on earth are these things?"

I explained, telling her a little about the patient but without mentioning his name of course. She laughed. "Isn't that ridiculous? Stealing stuff like this!"

"To you, perhaps," I said, a trifle annoyed. "But I can assure you it's deadly serious to him. Somewhere there is a deep and terrible rift in his personality."

Jackie never mentioned the brassieres again and as far as I could tell his thefts had stopped. He proudly gave the credit to his new-found "self-control" but it seemed to me that his interests had merely passed on to other, and possibly more sinister, areas. Whereas he still refused to fill in the seven-year gap in his life, he suddenly began talking at great length about women he knew, or had known. All of them, according to him, fell over themselves with eagerness to win his favors.

Finally, as both his loquacity and the affairs became repetitious, I suggested that he might be indulging in fantasy.

Jackie laughed heartily. "I told you that you were jealous of me, didn't I? Just because I've got what it takes. Here you're supposed to treat me and you don't even see how stodgy you yourself are."

I said gently, "You may not believe it, but I was young once myself."

"Not really, I'll bet. I'll bet you always had your nose buried in some book. I'm different. Why, before I quit college . . ." And he was off again, describing with relish an erotic and possibly fictitious escapade. On the other hand, it was also conceivable that he was telling the truth; he was both handsome and aggressive enough. There was always that nagging doubt in my mind as I tried to pin down which was the real Jackie.

Interspersed with his amorous reminiscences was an infrequent moment of insight into Jackie's present activities. I learned that he had bought a pair of binoculars and was spending much of his time in the big park near my office. He was watching people—he called it "studying" them.

"Nothing wrong with that," he said when I questioned him about it. "I'm expanding myself. Have to share the world with my fellow human beings, so I might as well get acquainted with them." He gave me a quick crooked grin. "The other day I watched your Linda, sitting on the grass, eating lunch out of a paper sack. I guess she was tanning her legs. Pretty jazzy for you, having something built like that around the office all day."

It was poor clinical practice but I had to become stern with him at that point. "Linda's an extremely nice girl and happily married. You'd better forget about Linda."

Jackie only smirked. In his exhilarated moods he enjoyed trying to put me on the defensive, to reverse momentarily our relationship. But he was indignant when I suggested he give me the binoculars. He flatly refused. Yet, although I didn't press the point, at the conclusion of the session I discovered that he had left them behind on my desk. I stored them away with the stolen lingerie in the filing cabinet.

During the next few weeks the collection grew steadily. Detailed drawings and floor plans of buildings, maps and written schemes for various adventures upon which he had decided to embark. Most of these were juvenile fancies but I was concerned with the recurring motif of aggression. And no matter how fanciful, all these plans represented sex substitutes—as did his actions at this time—and I was faced with the increasingly difficult job of separating what Jackie actually did from what he claimed he had done.

First, he mentioned smashing a few windows here and there. Then he recounted entering some empty houses under construction in a new tract. From this he passed on to breaking into occupied dwellings, mostly apartments in the downtown section where women lived alone. These illegal entries were accomplished in the early morning hours and he would, he claimed, creep into the bedroom and watch the sleeping woman for a while and then stealthily depart without awakening her.

"Aren't you afraid of being caught?" I asked him.

"I'm not afraid of anything," he boasted. Most of the time he was openly scornful of his fellow human beings, particularly those in authority, such as the police—or me, whom he also equated with authority. Yet Jackie occasionally underwent periods when he seemed genuinely ashamed of his behavior and he would draw up solemn "commandments" for virtuous living which he soon broke or evaded.

I began watching the newspapers to see if any of his presumed exploits were mentioned. They were not, but this didn't necessarily prove anything one way or the other. Breaking windows —or even knocking down a little girl on a lonely street, as he claimed to have done once—was probably too minor to make the papers.

Then one day I saw an item that sent a chill through me. A divorcee, returning home late one evening, surprised a prowler in her bedroom. They scuffled, and she was wounded in the shoulder, apparently with an ice pick. Her assailant had fled.

I felt an icy certainty that Jackie was the attacker. As he had feared from the first, he was progressing steadily from small aberrations to larger horrors. And it troubled me constantly that I could find no way to get inside him and discover the truth about him.

Sure enough, Jackie described the attack at our next Thursday afternoon consultation. He was pale and frightened of what he had done. His hand shook as he turned over to me the ice pick that he said was the weapon. Then I was faced with a terrible dilemma, undoubtedly the most tortured problem of my career. On one hand, it seemed plain that Jackie Newman was dangerous to society and it was my duty to turn his case over to the police. On the other hand, before me sat a patient in agony whom police methods could neither help nor cure. While over all, like a fog, lay the vast complication that Jackie might just as easily have read the same news story as I and fitted it neatly into his own life picture. So wherever the truth lay hidden, there also was my duty.

Linda noticed my extreme depression. "Doctor, you've been working much too hard. Why don't you get away for a while? A vacation would do you good."

"I'd like to, Linda, but I'm afraid this is no time for it. I'd be afraid I was running away. There's a case I have to see through."

"Oh, surely it could spare you for a week."

"Not this patient. I'm hoping I can pin it down to hysterical fantasy—that the patient's sustained emotional conflict is causing him to retreat from his real self. But so far I can't get through to the *actual* patient, as it were."

I had made my decision. Jackie was my responsibility. I was

aware that I must avoid the professional trap of becoming too absorbed in my patient, lest I identify with him rather than remaining in detachment. Already, I felt, I was showing an unwarranted fatherly concern.

I found hints of other dangers too, both to myself and to others. Jackie was evidencing classic symptoms of megalomania of which the ultimate expression, of course, is murder. He now talked about going armed "because my life is in danger"— though, as far as I could tell, he did nothing about this. He finally admitted to nightly dreaming—dreams of himself as the master criminal, of manipulating vast conspiracies, of running rampant in a big black car.

His periods of contrition were less frequent and he became more openly suspicious of me and my methods, ironically at precisely the time when he needed me more than ever. When I suggested the use of pentothal to aid us in getting at the roots of his psychosis, Jackie flatly refused.

He scowled when I asked his reasons. "You know why."

"Not when it might help. Pentothal merely relaxes the mind's subconscious defenses. That's why it's sometimes called the truth serum." I explained the value of confession in insight therapy. "Almost all of us practice some form of confession as a natural safety valve. A child uses his mother, a husband his wife or vice versa . . . why, before my wife died, I often made her my confessor to get rid of whatever repressions I might have."

Once again Jackie's refuge lay in trying to turn my words against me. "People confess because they're afraid, right?"

"That's a very rough generalization."

"Why don't you admit that you had to make a full report every night to your wife because you were afraid of her?"

"Because it wouldn't be true."

"There's the mind's subconscious defenses speaking," Jackie scoffed. "You're the one who needs the truth serum, Doctor. Maybe you'd find out things. Like maybe these meditation periods that I've been butting into are really celebrations that your wife is dead, and now you're free."

"Free to do what?" I inquired wearily. My headaches were beginning earlier these days.

"Free to hire that bosomy brunette, for one thing. Your wife wouldn't have let you play games like that in her day, would she?" It struck me that even Jackie's grins and grimaces were becoming more depraved as time went by. "I study people, too, Doctor. I know what goes on."

Linda. Jackie's thoughts revolved more and more about Linda these days. His growing interest in my young receptionist seemed to me like an ominous line on a fever chart, climbing steadily upward.

At first, there had been only veiled remarks which led to more open discussion, no matter how I attempted to discourage the subject. Then began the letters—long pencil-scrawled communications addressed to her, warped forms of ordinary love letters that were born in indecency and grew into obscenity. But none of them was mailed or delivered to her; each was handed over to me first and was added to Jackie's dossier, which by now was rather extensive. Furthermore, Jackie made no effort to approach Linda personally, perhaps because I warned him severely against any such attempt.

I also warned Linda, but more obliquely. I mentioned that there seemed to be a rash of prowlers molesting women these days, adding lightly, "But I don't imagine your Ed leaves you by yourself very much, Linda."

She laughed. "I'll say not. Ed's home every evening. I keep telling him I didn't get married to be alone."

I was relieved. With her husband to protect her at home and with me to keep a sharp eye on her during office hours, I didn't believe that Linda was in any particular danger even if Jackie should prove to be a violent case. I was still convinced that he was an hysterical fantast, a half personality living in a dream world of juvenile aspirations and compulsive lies.

Then, for a time, we seemed to make real progress. Jackie reverted to his earlier desire to be helped. Although he sat puzzled and uncommunicative, he listened attentively to me. He continued to make his sweeping resolutions for better behavior but now he apparently kept most of them. He confessed to prowling aimlessly through the city streets at night but without the accompanying acts of petty vandalism. He admitted that he still experienced the same wild urges but now he took a morose pride in standing up to them. Most significant of all, he didn't speak of Linda as frequently, and he wrote no more erotic letters.

For the first time I began to believe that the battle had turned, that Jackie was going to come home to himself.

One Thursday afternoon he appeared in a highly agitated state. For a full half hour he sat fidgeting in the big leather chair, saying nothing, not looking at me. All at once he blurted,

"Worthless little tramp—she deserves anything that happens to her!"

I knew instinctively whom he meant but I had to be sure. "Linda?"

"Oh, I see things. Last night, through her window, she and that stupid ape she's married to. Kissing and hugging and fooling around—not even decent enough to pull down the blinds."

"Jackie, you promised—"

"It makes you sick." His hands were clenched together in fury. "Her trotting around in just her slip and that moron grinning at her while all the time it should have been me in there." He added incongruously, "They had steak for dinner, too."

I listened despondently as Jackie raged on, describing in painful detail the actions of Linda and her husband. He had spent the entire evening crouched on the fire escape outside their apartment, watching and listening. Finally I interrupted him.

He didn't act as if he heard me. "Her slip, it had a lace heart over the left breast. The prettiest thing you ever saw—so pretty it made you want to tear it."

"Jackie, listen to me! This has got to stop!"

He looked sly. "I didn't do anything. Why are you getting so excited?"

I said angrily, "What you did do was bad enough!" I had to make an effort to calm myself. "You're intelligent, Jackie—you know yourself where this sort of behavior is leading you. I've believed that, between the two of us, we could solve your problems. But any future actions of this sort and I'll be forced to get outside help."

He rose and came to stand over me, eyeing me oddly. "But, I don't think you really want to cure me, Doctor. I think you rather enjoy me."

Then he left.

I spent the rest of his consultation hour staring at the telephone, wondering again if I should call the police and put an end to the whole business. But I couldn't bring myself to lift the receiver. One more conference, I decided; then I'll know for sure. And I was absolutely certain, without reason, that Jackie would return.

He came back on schedule the following Thursday, his manner serenely confident. I was concealing my own nervousness. I said, "Jackie, have you been thinking about our previous conversation?"

He smiled as he walked around my desk to stand over me again. "Oh, yes."

"Then I gather that you've come to some decision."

"Yes, I've finally made up my mind. I'm going to reform—right afterward."

"Afterward?" It hurt my neck to look up at him. "After what?"

"After I take care of Linda. That's what I've needed all along to get the evil out of my system. Then I'll be able to be good forever and ever." His voice rang with relief and boyish exuberance. "It's such a simple cure."

I could scarcely believe I'd heard his fantastic suggestion. "Jackie," I whispered, "this is all wrong. How can you even think of—"

"Just this one last bad thing," he announced. A trace of saliva gleamed at one corner of his mouth. "Then everything will be finished. You know I *have* to do it, Doctor. So you call her in here and let me get it over with." He began to unbutton his shirt.

"No!" I said. "This has gone far enough! Sit down and make yourself think how impossible this is!"

"But it'll be so easy. I'm stronger than you are. And we're all alone here."

That much was true. At this moment Jackie was the master. But I made a last plea. "Jackie, at least think what you're doing to yourself! Think of the consequences! Think what they'll do to you!"

"I've got to find peace," he said solemnly. "They'll understand that when I tell them. Now let's see—where did we put that ice pick?"

I found myself unable to move. Through a faint haze I watched him pull open the filing cabinet drawer and rummage for the ice pick. I understood exactly what he intended to do, but I was powerless to interfere. As in a nightmare, I seemed to have no conscious will of my own. Jackie dominated everything. I saw him push the buzzer to summon Linda and I waited for the terrible act that was to come.

The door opened and she appeared, a smiling healthy picture of normality in her white uniform. "Yes, Doctor?"

"Come all the way in," Jackie said huskily. "I've been waiting a long time."

She took a step forward, then her eyes widened incredulously as Jackie prowled toward her. "What's the matter?" she asked, backing away. "What are you doing with that ice pick?"

She screamed as Jackie sprang at her, hugged her close, then began tearing at the open throat of her uniform. She was stronger than Jackie had expected—she was fighting for her life. She got hold of his right wrist and with both hands held the sharp spike away from her breast while Jackie's free hand pounded her face and clawed at her dress. And through it all I remained paralyzed with horror, watching the brutal assault.

Linda, writhing to escape, slipped and sprawled to the floor at Jackie's feet. Jackie bared his teeth in a wild outburst of triumph. He raised the ice pick for the final blow. Linda shrieked for mercy, calling his name.

But it was not Jackie's name she called. It was my name.

"Doctor Conover!" she screamed. "For God's sake, don't kill me!"

Abruptly the piercing headache clamped down on me again and I was no longer a spectator to attempted murder. I was the attacker. I stared down in horror at the ice pick in my hand, at Linda huddled at my feet. Not Jackie Newman but Dr. John Kermit Conover.

I was Jackie.

No wonder that I had been so completely absorbed in his "case," since it was my own. Linda, screaming my name, had broken through the barrier of my lifelong repressions and I could see the terrible significance of the identity I had invented, the "new man" I longed to be.

Jackie—everything I never was. Now I could look back on my empty life—the vise of early marriage at college, the seven years of medical training under the spur of Helen's ambition. Not even Jackie, the amoral dream figure of myself, had been willing to speak of those seven years. "He" had not been afraid of the truth. I hated Helen. I was glad she was dead. But she died too late for me to change my life and enjoy my new freedom.

Standing there, shaking with the pain of revelation, I wasn't aware that Linda had scrambled away. She came back quickly with half a dozen men from the surrounding offices. They approached me cautiously but they had nothing to fear. I dropped the ice pick and fell to my knees before them.

And now I sit here in a strange locked room, awaiting the tenth—or is it the hundredth?—visit by a trio of men who will question me about the rift in my personality. I know all the words. Hysterical fantasy . . . self-suggestion . . . sustained emotional conflict . . . It doesn't matter. Jackie will never return.

And neither will I.

Pretty Boy

by Billie Sue Mosiman

Billie Sue Mosiman is one of dark suspense's new lights. Her work is fierce, unique, and powerful as you will see here.

First published in 1991.

I knew I never should have gotten involved with a pretty boy. Grandma married a pretty boy much to her distress. He was vain, she said years after his death. So vain about his clothes and his tortoise shell comb set, so *vain,* she said in her creaky old woman's voice, that when he came down with pneumonia he wouldn't let her call a doctor for it was improper anyone should see him disheveled and incontinent in the cherry four-poster bed. Being pretty, Grandma concluded, had killed my grandfather before his time.

But I didn't think about these admonitions when I met Bobby Tremain. There are some experiences in life that defy common sense and the validity of good advice.

It was the winter of 1967 and I had come to Louisville by way of Atlanta where no one wanted to hire a nineteen-year-old college dropout. They didn't much want to hire me in Louisville either so I took a job selling candy behind the counter at Stewart's Department Store. The boyfriend who had come to Atlanta to drive me to Louisville, where he attended television repair school, worked in the mail room of Stewart's. I figured he could stand it, I could stand it.

It was Christmas season and he was busy wrapping gifts and mailing them worldwide. I was busy eating all the chocolates I could stuff into my mouth when the other sales girls weren't looking. Swiping candy kept my appetite abated and stretched my paycheck considerably.

I was content with my job until Christmas Eve. Customers flocked to the counters ordering last minute gifts of filberts, pounds of pistachios wrapped in red foil, boxes of fancy mints and divinity and bridge mix chocolates. I hadn't a moment to filch a lemon drop, my feet hurt, it had begun to snow hard and my walk home to an apartment on Chestnut Street promised to be a miserable cold one. As if all this were not punishment enough for my sins of minor theft, Jerry, the boyfriend working in the mail room, wandered up to the counter during this mad rush and handed me a small black felt ring box.

"Marry me," he said.

Just that. No preamble, no romance, just "marry me."

"I'm busy, Jerry. Please."

"Open it. This isn't a joke, I promise."

"Miss, could you wait on me? I'd like two pounds of walnut fudge and a pound and a half of the pecan. Could you wrap it?"

I gave the fudge-hog in the mink a look insuring she wait another minute. Beyond that and I'd hear from her was the look she returned. After all it was Christmas and her time was more valuable than mine.

"I can't accept it. You know that, Jerry." I pushed the little box back across the shiny glass counter top. "I'm busy, I have to go."

While weighing and wrapping the fudge I glanced twice at where Jerry stood with his hands hanging at his sides staring at the jewel box. I hadn't meant to be so cold about it, but what did he expect? He knew I didn't love him; I didn't love anyone. Besides, he was a year younger than me and his parents would kill him if he got married. Just because I let him drive me from Atlanta to Louisville didn't mean we should spend our lives together. What was wrong with his head?

The day after Christmas I began looking for another job. Stewart's was too far to walk and too close to Jerry. Across the street from my apartment house stood Louisville General Hospital. The building was a solid piece of craftsmanship, the best looking architecture within four blocks. My apartment house, a sleaze bag resort for the poor and semi-stupid nineteen-year-old like myself, was a red brick dwarf compared to the soaring many-storied structure of Louisville General. If I found a job at the hospital I could come home for lunch, save a dollar or two. That was my main interest, saving money. I had big plans Jerry knew nothing about. I was headed for the golden West, for San Francisco and the famed Haight-Ashbury district where flower children danced through one long carnival night. But I could never get there if I didn't save traveling money and a stake to sustain me when I arrived.

My first interview with the personnel director of Louisville General went poorly.

"How old are you?" he asked, looking over the rims of his glasses. He had to be forty if he was a day. I could usually charm old farts.

"Nineteen."

"Where are your parents, your family?"

"They live in upstate New York."

"Why don't *you* live in upstate New York then?"

"Why should I? I'm nineteen."

"Hmmm." He pondered this winsome bit of logic a moment. "Aren't you afraid to live on your own?"

"No."

"Where do you live?"

"Across the street. I have an apartment. I could be here anytime you needed me. It's quite convenient."

He pushed the glasses up his nose and sniffed as if he could actually smell the stained linoleum covering of the apartment lobby floor, the dust coating the plastic plants, the mustiness of the worn red diamond-patterned hall runners. "Don't you think that's a dangerous place for a young girl to live alone?"

"It's fine. It's cheap. No one bothers me. I play gin rummy with a couple down the hall."

"Umm hmmm. And what do you know about hospital work?"

I sat forward and put forth my most earnest face. "I don't know anything, but I'm willing to learn. I thought I'd do well in the admitting department. I can type and file and do anything I'm trained to do. I know I don't have work experience, but I'm quick; I catch on fast." I paused when I saw a ghost of a smile creeping onto his lips. He was not taking me seriously and that was unfair. "Best of all," I concluded, "I live right across the street and I can come work anytime you need me."

I thought I'd convinced him despite the smug little smile, but finally he shook his head and said, "You shouldn't be in this city alone, a girl as young as you. You've no experience . . ."

I stood, realizing I had been dismissed. But I had not given up. I knew what I wanted—out of the candy department and away from Jerry's lovesick gaze—and I was determined to have this job. The director was vastly underestimating my ability to suffer patronizing attitudes. I could take it until the cows came home if that's what he wanted. He had not seen the last of me.

I waited two days. In preparation I quit my job at Stewart's much to Jerry's chagrin. ("What are you doing? How can you leave me this way?") I camped in the secretary's office until she let me see the personnel director a second time.

"You again."

"Oh yes. I'm free now. I quit my job and I can start here anytime you like."

He sighed, propped his glasses higher on the bridge of his nose. "Young lady . . ."

"I know I don't have any qualifications, but you won't find a more eager and able learner. I've had two years of college; I know how to learn."

"We really don't . . ."

"I'll take the scummiest job you have open. If you want, I'll make beds, scrub floors, clean toilets, anything. You have to give me a chance. And I live right across the street, I can . . ."

"Come anytime we call. Yes, you've mentioned that."

I smiled. I was earnest and young and winning. How could I miss? Still it took two more trips into the director's office to convince him he couldn't do without my services in Louisville General. I imagine I simply wore the man down, but that is youth's prerogative. Older people cannot fly in the face of unabashed enthusiasm and energy. It tires them.

I had not been working in the admitting department two weeks before I met the pretty boy. The admitting supervisor had me going into the wards to verify insurance information. Most of the patients had no insurance to verify. Seven out of every eight hour stint I spent interviewing welfare mothers with new babies. I don't know why the hospital thought these women had changed their ways, succumbed to middle-class values, and carried hospitalization now when most of them had been in these wards delivering babies only the year before. But I was not to question procedure. I was to ask my silly questions about income and insurance and write down the answers.

In my second week on the job I entered the men's ward for the first time. A patient had come in the night before through emergency and I was to verify the insurance on him. My papers said he was twenty years old and he had been shot in the leg.

Shot? Now wasn't that an interesting injury? It beat gallstones and the maternity ward all to hell.

I wandered through the big open ward blushing at the

whistles and hoots coming from the beds. Men of all ages sat up on their pillows, swiveled their bodies at my passing, and generally had a good time making me uncomfortable. "Bobby Tremain?" I called out above the din. "Where is Bobby Tremain?"

"I'm right here," came a deep male voice behind me. "I'm Bobby."

I turned and was at once awestruck by his beauty. Blond, curly haired, features chiseled fine and noble as the face of Jesus in the Pieta I had seen in the New York World's Fair. From what I could see beneath the sheet he also possessed the physique of Michelangelo's David. I must have appeared dumbfounded because Bobby cocked his beautiful head and said, "Well? Did you want me?"

The way he said *want me* sent shivers running. Did I want him? Oh yes, absolutely, I wanted him clothed or unclothed, bedridden or healthy, in his hospital bed in full view of thirty men or alone on a deserted mountain top before the eyes of heaven. A terrible thing for him to ask, did I want him.

I managed to move to his bedside. "Hi . . . I'm supposed to . . . uh . . . ask you some questions . . ."

"Ask away." He punched the pillow behind his neck. Overhead pulleys held his right leg in traction, the massive cast covering it from groin to toe. He winced when he moved and even his grimace was an appealing sight. For the first time in my life the maternal instinct flared. I wanted to mother and protect, take a stranger into my arms and soothe away the pain. That emotion should have alerted me. You don't mix mothering with sexual attraction. Not if you have two years of college under your belt, something you'd think would make you immune to psychological transgression.

"Oh, this?" he asked, noticing my stare. He lightly slapped the blinding white cast on his thigh. "It looks like I'll have to wear this baby for months. I guess I'd better get used to it."

"Who shot you?" This was not on the questionnaire, but it was of the uppermost importance to me. I already felt my anger building at whoever committed the desecration of a perfectly Adonis-like creature.

"Cop. Cop did it."

"No."

"Yep. But I guess I deserved it. I was running away."

"Why?"

"I was scared."

I nodded my head. Of course he had been scared, poor baby, who wouldn't be scared of a cop? Everyone trembled when confronted with people who carried guns. "What had you done?"

He smiled, casting a silver net of shivers over me again. There was something menacing in his smile, enough menace to make it fascinating, mesmerizing. "I didn't do anything," he said. "I swear it was all a mistake."

To anyone else, to someone older and less naive, to someone more worldly wise and cynical, his words would have condemned him from the outset. Criminals always swear innocence. It's to be expected. But I was not fully mature or wise to the ways of the world. I was a girl on the lam from parental authority, heading for the hippie revolution that had bypassed middle America, and I believed when people spoke, they spoke the truth. What profit a lie? To a stranger? A girl come to verify insurance? What profit that?

"You see I was driving with an expired license. A cop car pulled up behind me with his lights on and I panicked. He said later I was speeding, but I don't think I was. I knew, though, I'd get in trouble about the license so I did something dumb. I tried to get away."

"You shouldn't have."

"Don't I know it! It was the dumbest move in my life. I got it into my head that I'd outrun him and get home. I turned down streets and took a wrong turn somewhere and got lost."

"You could have stopped."

"Not by then. You don't know cops. You run from the bastards and you're in deep shit. Well, this wrong turn led to a deadend. I did have to stop then. I was cut off. I got out of the car and in the glare of the headlights, I ran up a hill to a high fence. I was climbing over when he shot me." He shrugged as if to say that's life, you win a few, you lose a lot, big damn deal, it happens all the time.

My outrage boiled over. "Just for climbing on a fence? Didn't he say 'halt' first or anything?"

Bobby, having enlisted my sympathy, shook his head.

"He just started shooting without even warning you first?"

Bobby nodded, eyes shyly downcast.

"Oh, you should get a lawyer and put that cop in jail. He had no right to shoot like that. He might have killed you." The thought of Bobby Tremain dying, hanging from a fence in the dark with bullet holes in his back made me sick with fury. How dare a trigger happy cop shoot down such a pretty boy just because he panicked over an expired driver's license! It was obscene. It was the establishment bulldozing down the youth of America. You couldn't do anything you believed in, you couldn't change the system, you couldn't save yourself and the future from the bloodsuckers. It was a travesty.

It was also love. Now I had an inkling of what Jerry felt for me. I lived, breathed, dreamed Bobby Tremain. Every day at the hospital I used my ward-hopping privilege to look in on him. I brought him magazines and candy bars from the hospital gift shop. I plumped his pillows and held the water glass to his fine lips. I told him how I had never been farther west than Texas and how I yearned to see the Pacific ocean. How it was like a narcotic and I was a junkie, just had to make it out West before I died from the cold sweats and the hot tremors.

"How will you get there?" he asked.

"I'm saving my money. I have a hundred and twenty dollars saved so far."

"That's not a bad sum," he said. "That would buy gas."

"Oh, I'm going by bus. I want to see Salt Lake City and Reno. Besides, I don't have a car."

"I do," he said and my head went faint. Was this a proposal we travel together? If I supplied expenses would he take me in his car? I feared to hope. Bobby was too beautiful for me. Angels do not consort with fragile, flawed earthlings.

Bobby remained in Louisville General six weeks. He confided he must go to court and face charges the day he was to be released. "They're going to hang me," he said. "That cop'll make sure of it."

"What about your parents, didn't they hire a good attorney?"

He laughed and turned away his head. "I don't have parents. Not so you'd notice. I left home when I was fifteen. I haven't seen them since so I'm on my own in this deal. They'll railroad me into prison where I'll never see daylight again."

"You can't let that happen, Bobby."

He turned back to me, eyes brimming, the sky blue of the irises thunderhead dark and troubled. "I have a car," he said. "It was impounded, but a friend of mine got it out for me. I've always wanted to see the land west of the Mississippi."

I trembled in ecstasy at the thought of having Bobby all to myself even though I was not ready to abandon Louisville and my good job yet. What would Jerry say? What would my supervisor and the personnel director say? Then there was the fact I would be abetting a felon or something along those lines. All I knew about cops and the law came from television. I *did* know that what Bobby proposed meant flight from justice and without me and the money I had saved, he couldn't do it.

"I don't know, Bobby . . ."

He caught my hand where I stood next to him and drew me down toward the bed. In front of God and the whole men's ward he kissed me to the accompaniment of catcalls and shrill whistles. I was signed, sealed, stamped, and delivered. Just exactly what Bobby wanted.

"Meet me here at six in the morning," he whispered. "A court appointed officer is coming for me at ten. I have to get out before then. We'll have to be very quiet about it."

"But your hospital bill . . ."

"Let the state pay it. That's what they're good for."

You don't listen to pretty boys, that's what my grandmother told me. You don't listen to silky promises from the cunning lips of an angel in disguise. Even Lucifer was pretty. The prettiest. And look what he is responsible for, she said.

These thoughts plagued me all night while snow swirled down from a night sky onto Chestnut Street. The one window in my first floor efficiency apartment was barred and looked out on a narrow alley. On the other side of the alley stood a fence and on the other side of the fence reared an ancient structure that housed the Juvenile Detention Center. Cries and howls from my unfortunate neighbors often startled me awake in the night where I lay in the dark imagining the horrors taking place mere feet away from my window.

The snow had stopped by five in the morning. I sat on the ratty brown sofa with two suitcases parked next to me. This was a momentous decision, maybe more important than the decision to quit college or to take up Jerry on the offer of a ride to Louisville.

The apartment, bare and depressing before, now bore down my spirit with the full weight of its poverty. There was a long uneven rip in the linoleum starting at the bathroom door and zigzagging to the foot of the sagging double bed. Roaches marched in hordes across the white porcelain sink counters, unafraid of interference. Pine wood shelves, once painted black but now peeling, separated the dining alcove from the living-sleeping room. The shelves were barren of the odd decoration, the few books of poetry I owned, the bunch of dried flowers Jerry had brought to show he was a good sport when I landed the job at the hospital.

What was I giving up by leaving with Bobby? Nothing but an experiment in low living, Friday night gin rummy games with the out-of-work couple down the hall, Saturday night forays to the YWCA where we all sat around sipping tepid Cokes and listening to the latest bad folk singer strum and sing of the times they are a'changin.

I craved more excitement than Louisville offered. I wanted to taste the adult life, get myself into corners and out again, pay my own rent, buy my own navy blue pea coats for Kentucky winters, talk myself into better jobs. And I wanted Bobby. How I wanted Bobby.

It was in Reno that I left him. I knew I had to by the time we drove across the Utah line toward Salt Lake City. It wasn't just the pistol he'd secreted in the car pocket. That scared me, but I could have found a way to understand it. No, it wasn't just that. The angel was tarnished as greening brass. Outside the sterile hospital atmosphere, Bobby let down his guard and showed a cruel, hateful, manipulative side. On the outskirts of Reno he was complaining how his leg hurt and how my excited chatter got onto his nerves.

"Do you always blabber on this way?" Sarcasm dripped from his voice. It coated the air inside the car, turned it as frigid and disgusting as frozen vomit. I cringed against the door. "Don't you ever shut up? God, you'd think you had something to say."

Yes, I thought I had. It's possible I was wrong about that the way I'd been wrong about Bobby.

On a dim side street we took a room from a smirking hotel manager and fought in the rickety elevator about whose fault it was we stayed in fleabag hotels. The room, the only one in the city we could afford, overlooked a shadowed, windswept shaft cornered by the backsides of three smog-grayed buildings. Bobby had been too tired from the trip for making love, even once, and I thought perhaps the glorious event might occur in this tawdry room and make it a magical, special place. Something had to happen to save me from jumping into the shaft. But Bobby was ill-natured as a dog in pre-heat and continued to rag me about everything.

"Who needs to go to San Francisco," he bitched. "Anyplace will do. Why not L.A.? I should go to Hollywood."

"Hollywood's phony."

"And you think your pukey friends hiding out in Haight-Ashbury are for real?"

"Bobby don't." We had already been over this particular terrain before. Hippies to him meant acid heads, free love, and panhandling. He wanted nothing to do with riffraff. He was about enlightened as some of my southern redneck relatives.

"I'd have some kind of chance in Hollywood. I have the looks to get into the movies."

He was right about that, but at this point I could have told him he didn't have the personality. Hollywood might be shark-infested, but as far as I knew they hadn't yet found interest in mean-spirited gila monsters.

"Bobby, love me. Make love to me." I expected the logistics to be difficult considering the leg cast, but any sort of impossible maneuvering was preferable to listening to Bobby bitch. The more he opened his mouth, the more I loathed him, the more I wished I were back at Louisville General with my clipboard and my wards to wander.

"Is that what you want?" he asked. "Is that all you've ever wanted from me? One good fuck?"

I wilted under his gaze. "I only want you to love me, Bobby."

"Love!" He let go a splutter of breath, exasperated. "What do you know about love? What do you know about anything for that matter? You really bought that story I told you, didn't you?"

"Don't tease me."

"I won't tease you. I won't tell you what a fucking dunce you are. What a damn brainless dummy you are."

"Bobby, please."

"I won't tell you that cop shot me because I drew on him. I won't tell you if he hadn't shot me in the leg, I might have splattered his idiotic brains all over the sidewalk. No, I won't tell you anything truthful because you'll believe any lying bullshit I feel like making up."

"You wouldn't kill a cop."

He laughed and of course it was true, he would do it, he would kill if pressed to it, he would destroy like the avenging angel he was if he felt the slightest whim. He was right. I was a fucking dunce. I was the biggest fucking dunce ever came down the fucking pike.

"What are you doing?" he asked.

"I'm getting my suitcase."

"What for?"

"I'm leaving now, Bobby. I don't have to take this anymore."

"Hey, wait a minute. What is this bullshit?"

"It's goodbye shit, that's what it is." I was at the door. Bobby lay disadvantaged where he had fallen onto his back on the bed when we entered the room. He struggled to get the cast to the floor and lever himself onto his feet.

"Don't you dare walk out that door. It's my car. *My* car, you bitch!"

"And it's my money, Bobby. I worked months for it. It's my dream, this trip. It was your escape and I was stupid enough to provide it for you. But it's my dream. I've done all I mean to ever do for you." I had the door open and one foot in the hallway.

"I'll find you if you dump me here." He was onto his feet and tottering, reaching for the cane he used where it leaned against the arm of a busted-spring chair. It all pressed down then, swallowing the two of us in a murky cloud. The window facing the airshaft. The gloom, the faded rose bouquet wallpaper, the smell of urine spilled and soaked over a period of years, the old bad scent of dried semen, the stench of despair, of dreams trounced and smashed and lying without pity upon the floor.

"You mean you can try to find me. You won't, though. If I were you I'd be careful running red lights and skipping out on hotel bills. Which is what you'll have to do here because I'm not leaving you a penny, Bobby, not a penny."

"Aw, don't be that way. I was just kidding ya. My leg's hurting, that's all, I was outta my head, baby. I'm in a bad mood but I wanna apologize. You don't believe that crap I said, do you? I made it up, really, come here, baby, let me do to you what you want, let me make a little . . ."

"Goodbye, Bobby." I was into the hall. He approached the door, his face red and livid with splotches. He was not so pretty now. He was not at all pretty. How could I have been so blind as not to see? "By the way," I said, making for the elevator while he painfully followed, leaning against the aged wallpapered wall for support, the heavy cast clumping along the floor. "I threw away your goddamned pistol in Salt Lake. I found it and threw it in a garbage can at a service station."

"I'll . . ."

The elevator door slid shut before he reached me. The chugs and clangs of the cables rang in my ears as I descended to the lobby floor. "Goodbye, Bobby," I whispered. "I wish I could say it had been fun."

There weren't many pretty boys in Haight-Ashbury. It's hard to be pretty when you're stoned and vacant-eyed. LSD trips do not make for pretty. The ones I found there I left as pickings for other, weaker girls. Someone should have told them not to get involved. Pretty boys either die stubbornly of pneumonia or they do crime like crime wants to be done. Either way they aren't worth the bother to spit on.

Bobby found me two months later. I didn't think he could, but the street talked. That's what the street did best in Haight-Ashbury in 1967, talk and sell shit.

Someone told him I'd crashed with a girl everyone called "Petunia," Pet for short. She had a two-room dump on the ground floor of a dilapidated, condemned building just three blocks off the main drag. The only working toilet was on the second floor and the way it worked was we poured a bucket of water into it. Bathing, when it was done, came from the same bucket. But the pad was free, who was going to complain?

I was nearly bummed out with the hippie crowd. That's what you said then—bummed, crashed, talking shit in the pad. I thought hippiedom would be fun, the sex fantastic, the drugs more than adequate. The truth was the people in the midst of this revolution were crazy as hell, the sex, when you could get it, was listless and uninspiring, and the drugs gave me ultra-paranoid dreams where ten-foot tall cats tried to scratch out my eyeballs. So much for the Golden West and the counterculture movement. Just one more demonstration of bad taste.

Pet was a sweetheart, though, and even if she slept all day and hallucinated all night, she was good people. If the hippie heart was to be found, she had it cornered. I needed clothes, she went scavenging and brought back brocaded vests, silk pants, rich, colored scarves. I got hungry, she disappeared and returned loaded down with a feast extraordinaire, everything from pizza to chicken soup and sardines, to plums so purple and ripe they made your mouth run water just to look at them. I don't know how she did it, but she knew how to supply our two rooms with everything but electricity. And she was working on that.

Sweeping long dishwater blond hair from her sleepy, hooded, brown eyes she said, "Babe, I got connections. We'll have a free line into the power company by week's end."

Pet came from San Diego. "That pit of vipers. Sailor lech types and Chicano macho types. You can have it."

She was going nowhere. "This is the best place on earth. This is where God settled in."

I tentatively put forth the traitorous notion that we were floating through life and maybe should rejoin the establishment, get a job, get a *real* apartment, make some honest cash.

Pet gave me a pained look and took up her place on the three stacked mattresses that lay on the floor. "Get smart, babe. You don't want straight time. It's slow poison and you know it."

At that point I wasn't sure she was right. Poison, yeah, it was out there in three-piece suits and nappy haircuts, but wasn't there a middle ground somewhere? Couldn't you play the game and still win? Stealing from the electric company wasn't my idea of making remarkable social progress.

That was the day and the dying conversation we were having when Bobby showed up.

He loomed in the open doorway, grinning an evil, twisted smile. "Found you," he said quietly.

"Friend of yours?" Pet asked. "He's pretty."

So she thought so too. But she didn't know Bobby Tremain.

He wore faded jeans and a ripped black tee-shirt. The cast was gone, but he leaned a little sideways against the door as if the leg was still a problem.

"Hello, Bobby. Goodbye, Bobby."

"You won't get rid of me so easy this time. I came for my car."

"You come for revenge. I know you, Bobby."

"Hey now, cool out," Pet said, climbing off the mattresses and going to where Bobby leaned. "Whatchu wanna fight for, babe? How about a few tokes, get you mellowed out?"

"You get away from me, you pothead," he said.

Pet held up both hands. "Hey, fine. *Sae la vie*, man, and all that good shit, you know what I mean?"

"My car," he repeated, his gaze boring into me.

"I had to sell it, Bobby. So get another one." Saying this did not give me the satisfaction I thought it would.

He moved past Pet and limped across the room. He stood much too close and I could smell the danger coming off him like a cologne too heavily splashed on the skin. I couldn't look him in the eye. A trill of fear finger-walked up my spine. I didn't remember him being this big, this overwhelming. Maybe the cast had made him seem vulnerable. Without it, he was gargantuan, a nightmare, a reject from one of my last doped out visions of cats and bells and Pepsi cans that said things like, "Pardon me while I kiss the sky." He blocked the light from the grimy windows. I backed away, slowly, oh so carefully.

"Leave me alone, Bobby."

"I'm going to kill you."

I sucked in my breath because I knew this was the truth, the unvarnished, absolute truth. Grandma hadn't told me pretty boys might be homicidal. But then how would she know?

Pet laughed nervously. "Listen, man, that's a little stringent for somebody taking your car, don't you think? What if I see if I can get you another car? I might be able to do that if you're sweet."

Bobby turned faster than I thought he would be able to. "Sweet, my dimpled ass! Now you get outta my face, you understand? This ain't got nothing to do with you, but if you want, I'll just make this a twosome. Two for the price of one, are you getting my drift, little honey?"

Pet changed color. She was creamy California sun beige and turned white as cottage cheese. Her small mouth pinched down tight as a lid on a catsup bottle. Her eyes blazed with more formidable emotion than I'd ever seen from her before. I didn't know if she was impressing Bobby, but she sure as hell impressed me. This was warrior territory and Pet had on her paint.

"Out," she commanded, pointing to the door. "You get out."

Bobby threw me a dark glance before limping past her to the hall entry. "Later, baby."

When the front entrance door slammed, I was finally able to breathe, but not too easily.

"Hell, where'd that freakzoid come from? That the one you left in Reno?"

"That's him. He wanted to shoot a cop. I think we better believe his threats."

"And what? Decamp my place? Move in with some heads? Uh uh, he don't scare me *that* bad. I've run into bad and he ain't it."

"Pet, I don't think you understand. Bobby's the devil. He's after me and if you get in the way, he'll get us both. You heard him."

"I *heard* him, the sonofabitch, but he won't make me run." She drew her skinny self up and stalked to the mattresses. She reverently took up a dope pipe from the scratched bedside table and tapped crumpled fragrant leaves into it.

"Maybe you better go," she said after she had the pipe glowing, the smoke sucked into her lungs. She closed her eyes.

"If I leave and he comes looking, he'll hurt you, Pet. I swear he will."

"You let me worry about Pretty Boy. I got friends, you know, who'll watch out for me. But I think you oughta go. You been wanting to cut out anyway. This is the perfect time, babe."

She was right, of course. I had to get away. If I wasn't around maybe he would come for me, leave Pet alone. But what if he didn't? How would I live with that?

"I'll take off tomorrow," I said, sighing. I pushed aside the tie-dyed curtains over the stained sink. "Right now I'll make some tea. I can't stop shaking, he's so goddamned *big* . . ."

"Bucket's upstairs," Pet said dreamily. "Upstairs is the bucket. Right by the toilet, where it is, you know, that's where the water is, in the bucket, the fucking bucket's big as the fucking toilet bowl, holds plenty . . ."

"Yeah, Pet. I know. Go to sleep."

And she did. Sweetheart Petunia of the blond-brown hair, the heart of gold, the soul of a warrior, the friend in need, the space cadet who know how to live free . . . almost free.

Pet slept the rest of the day, as was her custom, and woke around ten p.m. to go tooling the street while I packed my meager belongings.

She returned at midnight babbling about electricity and how the current *flows,* man, how it surrounds you everywhere in a city. "It's in the wires," she said, her eyes darting around the peeling walls. "And there's wires everywhere."

I agreed as to how there were a lot of wires, yes, but it was nothing to get uptight about and what had she taken, exactly? It didn't seem to be sitting too well with her whatever it was.

"Oh," she waved a hand around the air, "just a little sumpthin special, sumpthin I think I'm gonna like . . . umm-mhmmm . . . like pretty fucking good . . .

"One of these days I'm gonna FLY, sweet honeychile mine!" She leapt into the air, transported into a jet-glide fantasy. It took me an hour to get her down and onto the mattress. She tossed and turned in the dark and made me hold her while she shook with cataclysmic episodes of sudden trembling.

So small. Only three years older than me, Pet seemed much younger, more innocent and trusting than I had ever been. Which was saying a great deal considering the mess I'd made of my heretofore young years.

I held onto her for dear life and thought about what would happen to her when I left on the morrow. Here I thought she'd been protecting me, providing me with a way to live, when all the while it was I who had been her pillar, her Gibraltar. This was not the first time I'd coached Pet through the throes of a drug-induced delirium. Before it was just something I did without thinking about it. It was what we all did for one another. But if I weren't here who was going to hold on to Pet and keep her from flying so high the clouds would forever claim her?

Well, I'd make her go with me, that's what I'd do. I'd kidnap her if I had to, get her out of this madhouse, away from the free-floating anxieties and the paranoid dream world. Away from the singing wires and the pills and the tabs of stuff and the smoke, away from the Bobby Tremains.

Pet stopped convulsing and snored peacefully, her mouth open and smelling of an apple she must have snatched from a food-vendor earlier. I drowsed, but held onto Pet's hand to give us both security in the black quiet hours before dawn. I didn't like those hours, especially on nights Pet needed watching.

At first I thought I was dreaming when I heard a door creaking on its un-oiled hinges. Bobby's silky voice ("I'm back.") brought me partially awake. I sat up in bed, trying to untangle the Indian woven spread from around my legs, fighting with the material, fighting off the deep sleep trance that had hold of my mind.

"What . . . ? Who's there? That you, Bobby?"

Pet slept on. I gripped her right arm and buried my nails in her tender flesh. She did not respond. Whatever she'd taken was enough to put her out for the longterm. *Oh Pet. Oh Pet, please wake up. Jesus, Pet, don't crap out on me now . . .*

"She can't help you."

I could see him as deeper shadow sneaking across the room, hunched, lurching sideways, something in his hands, something with a long handle, a baseball bat, an axe, something bad, real bad.

"Bobby . . ."

"You took my fucking car."

Halfway across the room.

"Bobby, I'll pay you back."

"You dumped me in fucking Reno."

Three-fourths of the way across the room.

"Bobby, c'mon, you gotta listen to me, I was crazy about you, don't you know that, don't you know how you treated me?"

Halted.

What was the handled thing? How bad was it? If I threw up my arms, could I stop the damage?

"You break my fucking heart," he said.

"Bobby, you don't want to do this. You're just mad, I admit you've got reason to be mad," I lied breathlessly. "But didn't I get you out of the hospital, out of Louisville? Didn't I help you escape prison? Didn't I? Doesn't that count?"

"It took me two months to track you down," he said. His voice was just all wrong, all wrong. I'd never heard him sound so calm, so utterly insanely calm. Tundra would double freeze from this voice.

I shook Pet violently. She groaned and turned onto her back. *Oh Pet, oh Pet, why did you get drugged out tonight?*

"I'm sorry, Bobby, honest I am. If I had it to do over again, I'd never take your car."

"And leave me stranded. Had to sneak out of that goddamned room. Had to *panhandle* like some fucking hippie buddy of yours to get coffee money. Had to *hitchhike* outta Reno. Had to *walk* in the fucking rain and wind in Sacramento. You want to make up for that?"

"Yeah, Bobby, I do. I mean I will, just tell me what I can do, okay? We don't have to be enemies. We don't, we just don't."

At the foot of the mattresses.

Baseball bat. That's what it was. He was going to bash my head in, that's what he was going to do. Fuck *me*, Bobby Tremain was Death and grimmer by far than the Reaper could ever hope to be.

"Bobby . . ."

"Get outta the bed."

"Sure, sure, right away." I scrambled from beneath the covers and judged my chances of getting around him and to the open door. They weren't good. They were so bad to be nearly nonexistent. Bobby was just too big, he took up too much room, his arms were too long, the bat too heavy, the world too goddamned unfair. I was going to die for paying back in kind? I was going to end up a bloody mass of brain and teeth in a Haight-Ashbury condemned apartment house? While Pet slept oblivious and woke to find her drug dreams have invaded the real world? In Bobby's inelegant parlance, what kind of shit was this?

It's hard to believe it when you're about to die. You try to think of anything, but that. You do little calculations of your chances and weigh them in your favor. You pray, I don't care if God left you high and dry when you were in the cradle. You think up great excuses, beautifully exaggerated lies, and make yourself believe they're working. Because if they aren't, the alternative isn't even thinkable.

Bobby came toward me and I squeezed shut my eyes against

him. He was Raw Hide and Bloody Bones from my Alabama childhood, he was the Swamp Thing, he was Frankenstein's monster and the faceless intruder who came to people asleep in their safe homes. He was a force of Nature against which there is no recompense.

"No, Bobby, please."

He gently moved me aside so he could stand next to the side of the bed I'd just vacated. His touch made me jangle and jump like a rabbit in a cage. "Bobby . . . don't . . ."

"I won't," he said softly and then lifted the long spear of dark in both hands and crushed Pet's skull with one fast heavy downward stroke.

"JESUSJESUSOHMYGODNONONONO!"

I was behind him and I had his arms and he was off balance and toppling, we were both falling and the floor came up, smacked us hard, and I screamed in his ear, screamed and screamed in his filthy, horrible, inhuman ear. We rolled, I scratched at his face, at his eyes, his nose, his mouth, his neck, his chest, his arms. I screamed and he screamed and the night bloomed napalm lights as he struck me and I struck back hard as I could, hard as I knew how, hard as my frenzy allowed. The bat skittered under the bed, the bloody weapon was lost, and Bobby was scooting for it, frantic to have possession again, so he could bash me, so he could do to me what he'd done to a poor, sleeping, totally innocent dreamer. His legs flailed to free himself from the lock I had on his body, and I heard it *-crack-* the way you hear thunder erupting on the edge of a blast of ozone from a bank of storm clouds. His leg, broken again, shattered I hoped, splintered to a million pieces, like . . . like . . . Pet . . . like . . . Pet . . . shattered, splintered, broken.

Smashed. Beyond redemption.

Hit him, hit him, that's all I could think, hit him until he stops, until he vanishes, until he's gone, until he's dead, dead, dead and gone.

Three street loungers, guys hopped up on something or other, stumbled into the foyer led on by our screaming. They tottered into the melee, only sober enough to take Bobby from my fury and hold him while the police came for him and the ambulance came for what was left of Pet.

"Man," one of my rescuers kept saying. "Man, this is shit-for-brains, this is bad, dude, this is sick and revolting, you sonofa-bitch, how'd you think you could do this, don't cry, you fucking whiner, we don't care if your leg hurts, we *hope* it hurts, by God, we hope it fucking *kills you,* man!" Then he kicked him. And kicked him some more before the cops showed.

Well, it didn't kill him. Left him further maimed, but it was the state who killed pretty Bobby Tremain. Not literally. He died in a prison riot, shot right through his gorgeous heart, was the report. Sometimes, like really, there's a little justice out there in the lousy establishment, you know what I'm telling you?

I heard in later years Jerry married a jockey and set up his own television repair shop in Cairo, Illinois.

I drove through Louisville recently to show my teenage girls where I had lived and worked on Chestnut Street. The hospital had been razed to the ground. Only the cement steps remained leading up to a flat grassy expanse open to the sky. The sleazy apartment house was gone too and in its place stood a one story modern office building. Even the detention center was gone. It was as if none of it had ever been, as if 1967 had been but a fantasy. But lots of people from that year feel that way. You ask them, find out.

"I met a boy in that hospital," I told my daughters as we drove slowly past what had been and was no more. "He was the prettiest thing, but . . ."

"Boys aren't pretty, Mom. Boys are handsome or good-looking or cute. *Girls* are pretty."

They have a lot to learn, my young feisty children. But I doubt if warnings will do a bit of good. At least that has been me and my grandmother's educated experience.

You can't persuade a girl to stay away from a pretty boy. You can't tell a woman there aren't any heavensent angels walking this mean earth.

Secrets

by Gary Lovisi

Gary Lovisi is a new writer who has worked for years publishing Paperback Parade, *which is the one of the crime field's best historical publications . . . giving readers an in-depth look at the evolution of the paperback novel down through the decades. Now Gary plans to start writing some books of his own. This story is a very good start.*

First published in 1993.

Some things are never meant to be seen, never meant to be understood. When Stacey, our precocious five-year-old daughter came in the house from playing outside in the backyard and told me what had happened to Tommy Bracken's parents across the fence, I didn't know what to think.

"They're dead, Daddy. Tommy told me he killed them," Stacey said, with a kind of grim determination you never see in a child.

The police came soon afterwards and there was the usual investigation and reporters. The bodies of Tommy's mother and father were carried out in bags. A scene I'll never forget. I can only imagine the horror Stacey was feeling at the time.

Tommy Bracken was taken away by the Social Service people. He was so . . . unconcerned. It was incredible. Tommy had always been a good kid, a little wild, but no real problem and certainly not capable of anything like killing his parents. He was only six years old! There could be no reason for it. How could he have done it? He was Stacey's best friend. They played together every day. They shared secrets.

Stacey was unnaturally quiet for days afterwards. We expected something of the sort and hoped she'd pull out of it on her own. Naturally the police had asked her a lot of questions about Tommy, what he and Stacey had talked about that fateful day in the back yard. All Stacey would say was that Tommy had admitted to killing his parents. He said he'd used a butcher knife from the kitchen, done it while they were sleeping. The police verified the murder weapon. Then Stacey shut up tighter than a clam. She wouldn't say anything else about what happened that day or anything about Tommy Bracken. We all tried to get her to talk about it, we thought it would be good for her to get it out, but she wasn't going to say another word. I figured it best not to press her, she'd talk when she was ready. She was only 5 years old for heaven's sake! To be exposed to so much at that young age was a lot even for the most precocious of children to handle. Stacey was Tommy's best friend. Now they had a secret she couldn't talk about. I didn't like that.

One day she told me she had words she couldn't say buried way down deep inside her. They were a secret she could never say. If she told, the secret would come to life and the words would cease to be mere words and become something real and very bad.

The shrink didn't help much. Stacey refused to talk to him about Tommy and their secret.

The dreams began about two weeks later. She didn't cry out. She was a brave little girl. She just lay in bed whimpering, shaking, alone and so small in the sheets, hardly moving at all. Fearful to move, to breathe. When Gail and I went into her room she was as pale as a ghost, her flesh cold and clammy. She hadn't been getting much sleep lately, obviously none that particular night. There were big, dark rings around her eyes. She hadn't eaten well the last few days. She was losing weight. Gail and I were so scared. We didn't know what was happening but we knew we had to do something to save our little girl.

The next day we made an appointment with Dr. Torrence, a shrink friend who specialized in children's problems. Stacey wouldn't talk to him either. He tried a lot of ploys and strategies but none of them worked.

"I have to keep quiet about it, Daddy," she whispered to me on the drive home from the doctor that afternoon. "Tommy explained it all to me. You know, Tommy didn't *really* kill his mommy and daddy. Tommy was a good boy. Something else did it, something very bad, and if I mention it it will come to life and kill again. Then someone else will have to take the blame for it like Tommy did. That's what Tommy told me. That's the way it works. I can't talk about it. If I say the word it will happen again, more people will die, someone else will be blamed. You understand, Daddy?"

Well, I told this all to Dr. Torrence. The next day Gail and I brought Stacey to see him again. They talked for a long time.

Finally Dr. Torrence called Gail and me into his office. We told Stacey to sit in the waiting room for a few minutes.

"You see," Dr. Torrence said in his usual confident voice, "Stacey has received a terrible trauma. Not only the violence, which was so close to her, a very real part of her world and very scary to a small child, but her best friend was involved. And the crime, so terrible . . . She feels somewhat to blame. She's weaving herself into Tommy's problems. Trying to help him in her own way."

I said, "Is she creating this story to prove Tommy is really innocent? The way she makes it sound, it's as if Tommy was actually trying to protect us all from something very bad. Something we don't understand. It all seems so twisted."

"Of course. In Stacey's mind she wants things to be the way they were before this tragedy happened. Kids are like that, they don't understand finality. So she makes up this bogeyman responsible for the killings. It is a natural enough reaction for a child after all she's been through."

"I think I understand, Doctor," Gail asked quickly, "but what can we do to help her?"

"The most important thing is to break open this secret, enter this secret world of hers and get her talking about it so she can realize that it is just a fantasy, a natural reaction to a terrible tragedy that a child can not understand, and nothing more."

It was a difficult session. Dr. Torrence, Gail, and myself trying to get Stacey to talk about the secret she and Tommy shared. We followed the instructions Dr. Torrence gave us and after a grueling hour of explanation, pleading, and hugs by each one of us Stacey finally seemed resigned to talking. Eventually. Though she tried to put it off as long as she could. She was obviously under tremendous pressure, full of fear, and finally she broke down in a stream of tears. Perhaps finally accepting the fact of Tommy's horrible deed for the first time now. Gail jumped up to console her, in tears herself at the suffering of our only child. I tried to play the big strong male. It wasn't easy. It tore me apart to see her so upset but by facing the problem I hoped we'd finally get this settled so we could go on with our lives.

Stacey moved out and away from Gail's loving embrace, to stand alone in the center of the room.

"I'll tell Tommy's secret, but I'll only tell Daddy," she said, and she looked at me so serious and added, "you must promise *never* to tell anyone."

I smiled, "Sure, Pumpkin. Come over here and whisper it in my ear."

Stacey came up close, that serious look on her small delicate face, climbing upon me, placing her mouth close to my right ear.

"Go ahead, Princess. Tell me what was such an important secret between you and Tommy."

"Daddy?" she whispered so carefully.

"Yes," I replied quietly, Gail and Dr. Torrence watching us intently.

"I love you, Daddy."

"I know, Pumpkin," I said smiling and giving her a little squeeze, "Mommy and I love you too."

"I won't tell Mommy. It's better if I only tell you. You're a man. You're strong. Tommy told me it would happen quick for them, but you'll have to live with it for a long time. Like me. Like Tommy. It's not easy, Tommy said if I ever had to tell anyone, you should be the one. Sometimes secrets can be so hard to keep. Tommy said I should tell you. You would understand."

"That's fine, Stacey, now tell me all about this secret of yours."

Her lips brushed my ear. So slightly. She whispered a word, so lightly. I wasn't sure I'd even heard it. I don't know what it meant. It didn't make any sense, but somehow deep within me I knew that it didn't have to make any sense. No sense at all.

I looked at Stacey and she seemed so sad now.

I said, "What did you say, Pumpkin?"

She came up close again, and in a barely perceptible tone said something that sounded like "La-La." It made no sense. I couldn't figure it. Maybe that's not the word she said. I don't really know now. She said, "La-La, Daddy. Tommy told me La-La."

I don't know why the silly, meaningless words disturbed me so much. Why I grew so immediately fearful. I got goose bumps all up and down my arms. Chills surging through my body.

Gail looked at me so strangely, saying, "Ben? Are you alright?"

Dr. Torrence said, "Mr. Combs? Mr. Combs? Can you hear me?"

Stacey said, "Daddy? Remember, we have a secret now. Don't tell anyone."

Dr. Torrence, Gail and Stacey were found dead a few hours later by the doctor's next appointment. I waited patiently for the police to arrive. I never said a word. I couldn't even open my eyes until I was placed in the cell downtown. Later, when it was time for my trial, I pleaded guilty. Nothing much mattered by then anyway. I was convicted and thrown in a prison where they throw away the key. I didn't care. I never talk about it now. I can never tell the truth about what happened. My wife, my daughter, one of the city's most noteworthy doctors. All dead. And now I have a secret with Stacey, one that I'll never reveal.

I've thought a lot about it these long years. I don't know what it could mean. How such a thing could be. I don't know what really happened, how it could happen, I can't explain it, but I was innocent of the murders. I never killed Stacey, Gail or Dr. Torrence, but of course no one would ever believe that. Some things are not meant to be seen, some are never to be understood. One of them is what happens when you whisper a certain word into someone's ear.

The reporter comes every day now. At first I thought he was ok, some yuppie liberal hotshot out to do some good, but he's become a real pain-in-the-ass. He's certainly determined, I'll give him credit for that if nothing else.

He says, "Mr. Combs, I know there's a lot you've never told about the murders. I know you're holding back, keeping a secret maybe. I want to know what it is you're hiding."

I tell him to shut up and leave me alone. I tell him if he only knew the truth he'd never be able to handle it. It would crush him. Wipe that permanent-press arrogance right off his face forever.

That really got him. He must have smelled a story. He wouldn't leave me alone after that. He'd come and visit me every day, badgering me, laying the guilt trip on me about Gail and Stacey. Like I didn't feel bad enough about what had happened. But I kept telling him I did not kill them and Dr. Torrence. It was not I who did it.

He laughed. I think he was trying to get at me. Goad me. Well, he was doing a good job at it.

"I'm *really* innocent!" I protested, telling him, one man to the another. It was all off the record. I'd never admit it publicly. I couldn't. It was still a secret I shared with Stacey. It was our only connection now.

He smiled, condescendingly, patronizingly, "Sure you are. Now why don't you tell me all about it?"

"No! I really am innocent! I didn't kill them! I would never do such a terrible thing!"

"Then who did, Mr. Combs?"

That was it. I was silent.

He nodded. Smiled that hateful smile of his.

"I can't tell you." I said quietly.

"Of course you can't. That's all very convenient. Why don't you just admit it, like you did during the trial. You're backpeddling now. Why don't you give me the details. The public wants to read about this stuff. How you did it? Why you did it? What was going through your mind as you were killing your wife and daughter?"

Bastard! I was about to plow his head right into the bricks when I changed my mind. He thought I was some vintage crazy who heard voices, saw things, got secret messages from somedamnplace! I'd show him.

He took my inaction as a sign of weakness. I figured this sick parasite might just deserve to know my secret after all.

And God help me, I broke my promise to Stacey. I moved close to the reporter and whispered a word in his ear.

The reporter moved back from me. Slowly. Carefully. Visibly scared now with a strange look on his face. He called out loudly, "Guards! Guards! Get me the hell out of here!"

I relaxed. It would be all over soon. The look in his eyes gave it all away. I knew by the time the guards came I would be long dead and free from this horror my life had become. It would finally end for me. For him it would just be beginning. Too bad, but he'd be blamed for my murder, there could be no other rational explanation. I smiled as he came at me. This would really put a crimp into his journalistic career. He'd gotten the best story there ever was, but he'd never be able to write one word about it.

Some things are not meant to be seen, others too terrible to understand.